VISIONS

VISIONS

JUSTIN JAMES

This book is a work of fiction. Any references to real people, names, places, characters, incidents or events are entirely coincidental and pure fiction.

Published by Webmad
200 N. Service Road #211
Oakville, Ontario
Canada L6M 2Y1
First Digital Edition May 2021
First Paperback Edition May 2021

Copyright © 2021 by Justin James

Made in the U.S.A.

ISBN 978-0-9881006-4-0

To the pursuit of love

Dramatis Personae

Known Mystics and their Primals

DRAKE   Mystic soulbind of PYROS, Primal of Fire.

TALIA BLAINE   Mystic soulbind of EREIKOS, Primal of Lightning.

DESMOND WELLS   Mystic soulbind of ORION, Astral Primal. Deceased.

AVALON   Mystic soulbind of ARCHEON, Supreme Primal. God-king of Haven.

"HADRONOX" (AXEL HART)   Mystic soulbind of HADRONOX, Primal of Darkness. Affiliated with Haven.

"IKO" (FLYNN DARKE)   Mystic soulbind of IKO, Primal of Shadows. Former Crimson Hand. Affiliated with Haven.

"PRISM"   Mystic soulbind of PRISM, Spatial Primal. One of Hadronox's Broken. Former names and titles unknown. Affiliated with Haven.

"SILAS"   Mystic soulbind of SILAS, Serpent Primal. Affiliated with Haven.

"RAMSI"   Mystic soulbind of RAMSI, Plant Primal. Affiliated with Haven.

KIKA CALLAWAY   Mystic soulbind of HYDRAXIA, Primal of Oceans. Pirate Queen and Captain of the *Redemption.*

ERIS CALLAWAY   Mystic soulbind of VENTUS, Primal of Wind. Pirate Princess and Captain of the *Icebreaker.* Daughter of Alessia Callaway.

EAMON CALLAWAY   Mystic soulbind of HAYLIAN, Primal of Ice. Former Captain of the *Icebreaker* and founder of the First Pirate Federation. Father to Kika and Alessia Callaway. Deceased.

LORD BRANDON VAYNE   Mystic soulbind of VARRUS, Primal of the Void. Famed duelist. Former Cormack captain known as Vayne the Red.

VIRGIL   Mystic soulbind of LOGIOS, Primal of Knowledge. High Teacher overseeing The Library on El Aria.

New Phoenix Expedition and Earthlings

ALLEN LEE   Biologist. Former starfish researcher at Pladaw industries.

SAM SAMSON   Sergeant. Leader of CHARLIE, spec-ops squad.

CHIP HAMAL   Hydrologist. Former rocket scientist.

ANNIE CHU   Electrical engineer. Former geologist.

AJAX SYKES   Private. Soldier in ALPHA, spec-ops squad. Conscript.

CHRIS JONES   First lieutenant. Helicopter pilot in ECHO, spec-ops squad.

CHARLES SKENDER   Senior scientist, genetic engineering. Deceased.

ALAINA LEE   Homemaker. Former sous-chef. Allen's wife. Earth-side.

LYN LEE   Allen's daughter. Earth-side.

DANNY LEE   Private. FLR Freedom Army. Allen's brother. Earth-side.

The Library on El Aria

CATO   Adept at The Library on El Aria.

FELIX   Adept at The Library on El Aria.

MEGHANA AYUR   Apprentice at The Library on El Aria.

MANALI AYUR   Apprentice at The Library on El Aria. Meghana's sister.

KARIM AL'JAFFAR   Apprentice at The Library on El Aria.

SHEIKH AMIR DOHARI   Sheikh of El Aria. Patron of The Library.

House Godwin and Citizens of Deuzos

KING GAIUS GODWIN   King of Deuzos.

QUEEN ALESSANDRA GODWIN   Queen of Deuzos.

PRINCE ELLIOTT GODWIN   Eldest son of Gaius. Disgraced author.

PRINCESS ASHE GODWIN   Secondborn to Gaius.

PRINCE CAIN GODWIN   Thirdborn to Gaius.

PRINCE ALPHONSE (AL) GODWIN   Youngest son of Gaius.

GERHART GODWIN   Youngest son of King Alarak Godwin (Deceased). Brother of Gaius. Lord of Linz. Commander of Fort Gerhart.

BASTIAN GODWIN   Son of Gerhart. Sixth in line of succession.

BLAZE MUSTANG   The Golden Knight. Pride of the King's Rangers.

House Tallawyn and Citizens of Tallamar

KING ARTHUR TALLAWYN   King of Tallamar.

QUEEN MARIA TALLAWYN   Queen of Tallamar.

PRINCE ALWIN TALLAWYN   Firstborn of Arthur.

PRINCE GEORG TALLAWYN   Secondborn of Arthur.

AMMA (AMMALIE) BLAINE   Talia's grandmother. Lyon resident. Deceased.

LYDIA DARKE   Flynn's wife. Barrington resident.

LUCIAN DARKE   Flynn's firstborn son. Barrington resident.

CASSIUS DARKE   Flynn's youngest son. Barrington resident.

Unaffiliated

HATCH HICKS   Itinerant merchant and aspiring entrepreneur.

MERCER MACLEOD   Leader of Mercer's Mercs. Informal leader of Arillia.

LONG FAN   Leader of the Long Corps mercenaries.

GILES DUFLEUR   Mercenary. Loosely affiliated with Long Corps.

LUC DUFLEUR   Mercenary. Loosely affiliated with Long Corps.

CLAYTON CALLAWAY   Kika's husband. Former Captain of *Vae Victus*. Deceased.

ALESSIA CALLAWAY   Kika's sister. Former Captain of the *Dawnchaser*. Deceased.

THERESA WINTER   Chieftain of Obersteier. Daughter of Alexey Steinfaust.

Unaffiliated

HATCH HICKS   Itinerant merchant and aspiring entrepreneur.

MERCER MACLEOD   Leader of Mercer's Mercs. Informal leader of Arillia.

LONG FAN   Leader of the Long Corps mercenaries.

GILES DUFLEUR   Mercenary. Loosely affiliated with Long Corps.

LUC DUFLEUR   Mercenary. Loosely affiliated with Long Corps.

CLAYTON CALLAWAY   Kika's husband. Former Captain of *Vae Victus.* Deceased.

ALESSIA CALLAWAY   Kika's sister. Former Captain of the *Dawnchaser.* Deceased.

THERESA WINTER   Chieftain of Obersteier. Daughter of Alexey Steinfaust.

I. Fire In The Snow

Drake

Damn it!"

A hail of sweat bombarded the soft springtime snow. Drake sucked air into his depleted lungs, staring at his singed palm in disbelief. As the chilling wind whipped flurries across the glade, capricious snowflakes drifted onto his exposed hand, sizzling and melting upon contact. "Why can't I get this?"

You lack strength. And patience, Pyros rebuked in a dull roar that reverberated through Drake's skull.

"Yeah?" Drake doubled over, panting as he battled to catch his breath. A bitter blast of cold accompanied each gulp of air, needling through his chest like shrapnel of ice. Scoffing, he righted his chest and tried to ignore the stitch forming in his side. "Got any advice I can use, or just condescending remarks?"

Pyros was quiet for a contemplative moment, save for the omnipresent crackling of his embers. An inextinguishable fireplace in Drake's chest. *Mostly condescending remarks,* the Primal admitted.

Stubbornness triumphed over fatigue, and Drake squared off against his nemesis: the stalwart spruce that stood ten feet in front of him. He extended his right arm parallel to the ground, palm facing upward. "This time, I'll do it," he vowed.

That's what you said last time, Pyros rumbled helpfully.

Ignoring the taunt, Drake focused intently on his blistered hand. A familiar heat swelled in his chest as he invited Pyros to flow through him and out into the mortal world. His blood ran hot, carrying the flicker of intent from his mind to his hand. A fledgling ember leaped to life, dancing mischievously in his palm. The devilish spark grew as it flickered and twirled, maturing into a rapidly spinning orb. At last, the chaotic flame balanced obediently in his hand, maintaining a manageable size in its spherical rotation.

"That's it!" Drake exclaimed, dizzy with unexpected satisfaction.

I can make it bigger, Pyros boasted eagerly.

"No!" Drake answered sharply. The sphere momentarily lost its shape, scattering wisps of flame away from the orb and into the snowy air. Sweating as if the frozen forest were a sun-beat desert, he centered himself, reining the fire back into order. "This is about control, Pyros. There will come a day that calls for precision. The goal isn't always to conjure the biggest inferno you can."

You lack the balance to control my ire. The stamina to wield my wrath.

"Stop telling me what I can't do—tell me how to do it!" Irritation shot through him as the rebellious flames broke rank, dispersing into a fiery column that scorched the evergreen branches above him.

A high-pitched yelp followed. Drake glanced up to see a fuzzy brown blur flailing its paws through the air. It fell into the snow, leaving a deep print where it landed in the fresh powder. The squirrel surfaced from its hole, then chittered a pointed rebuke at Drake before scurrying deeper into the woods.

In time. Your body and spirit will grow. You will one day become a worthy conduit.

"I've been training all day," Drake complained, holding his arms above his head in an effort to relieve the stitch in his side. "I'm still not getting it."

Battle is training. We were merely playing in the snow, mocked Pyros.

Bristling, Drake reignited his palm with renewed purpose. "You said I needed to build strength and balance—that's what I'm doing. After all, not like practice can make it any worse."

Pyros rumbled in consideration. *I suppose practice cannot hurt. You may proceed.*

Feeling all but spent after numerous failed attempts, Drake poured the dregs of his concentration into spinning the volatile ball of fire in his hand. The sphere dutifully held its shape, whirling expectantly in his palm.

"Now!" Drake bellowed. Flipping his palm to face the opposing tree, he lunged forward and willed the orb to fly from his hand. The fireball hissed through the air and slammed into the center of the trunk. Smoke billowed from the impact zone, disappearing into the wintry air. A swirled, charred mark of his successful attempt was left behind in the wood.

"Finally," he panted, feeling a rush of heat fill his head. From the past several days of training, he had learned to recognize his limit. Body aflame, hands scorched from misfires, vision blurring, he knew any further attempts at manifesting Pyros' strength would cause him to collapse in the snow.

Such a small fire, Pyros crackled in disappointment. *I hunger still. Feed me. Or cede control, that I may feed myself.*

"You're exhausting, Pyros," sighed Drake.

Your hunger subsides. You feel sated. We'll change that in time, promised the Primal.

"Scared the pants off of that squirrel, didn't 'cha?" a playful voice jested from behind.

Drake felt the fire inside him quiet as he turned to face Talia. The street urchin from Lyon stood between two snow-dusted trees, grinning brightly. She looked at peace here, rosy cheeks and specks of snow seasoning her hair. The stubborn notch in her eyebrow served as a reminder of the girl's scrappy upbringing, but her buoyant spirit never stayed down for long.

"Shouldn't you be helping Chieftain Winter?" Drake said, attempting to hide how out of breath he was. Pyros exited his headspace entirely, leaving behind smoldering embers in his chest. Once rested, he could stoke the coals to resummon the Primal.

"All done. Food's packed, flasks are filled, and Theresa assigned a guide to see us to the southwest border. All that's left is a month's trek through mountains and blizzards," Talia reported sunnily.

"Who's the guide?"

"Bask Noressen of Obersteier. Theresa said he's supposed to take the Aofstieg next year, and this is some kind of navigation training for him."

"Aofstieg? Does that mean our guide's some fourteen-year-old kid?" balked Drake.

"Firstly, fourteen isn't a kid anymore," Talia interjected defensively. "But... Yeah. It's better than us going it alone. Besides, he's probably studied maps of Nordos for his test, right? He'll know what he's doing."

He nodded reluctantly. "Yeah... You might be right. I don't like relying on some random kid, but these northerners are built different."

Drake reflected on the few and fierce Nordos customs he knew. From their brutal Aofstieg ritual to become *Citiza,* to their Vokoz-Dinye death

3

matches that ordered society, to the bare-knuckled sparring between children in Bjornheim, the shared culture of the clans was strength and lethality alone. Almost all Nords were practiced killers, with many men and women having drawn blood by the age of fifteen from friends and comrades they grew up with. If not for their deadly training and rituals, Nordos' population would be more than double its current number.

Despite the incongruity with his own worldview, he understood the rule of this harsh, northern world: only the strong survive. The weak would likely die in battle for their nation regardless, but their weakness in war could cause the deaths of comrades as well. By culling the weak and hardening every heart in Nordos, chieftains and commanders knew their soldiers wouldn't hesitate to carry out their duties to the highest degree possible. Even a fourteen-year-old understood this; even this *Bask Noressen* boy would have a killer's instinct.

"Well, when you're done terrorizing the local wildlife, want to head back to Obersteier?" invited Talia.

Drake fought back the smile creeping to his lips. "Let's go," he agreed, stepping forward. His eyes defocused suddenly, throwing him off-balance. He crashed forward into the knee-deep snow.

"Drake!" Talia cried out, rushing to his side.

His vision swam, flushing him with a wave of acute nausea. Shutting his eyes, he dragged his knees underneath him and pressed his hands into the snow to stabilize his balance.

"Are you okay?" Talia asked, placing a hand on his back.

"I'm fine," Drake lied, staggering clumsily to his feet. His vision was still black.

"Then stop walking like a drunken moose," Talia suggested, slipping under his arm to support him as he continued stumbling forward.

Drake accepted her help for the next few steps as he regained his coordination. Once confident that he wouldn't tip over again, he disengaged her assistance and quickened his pace to lead. Still battling insipid nausea. "So, this Bask will take us to the border. I'm assuming that's where his watch ends?"

"I guess so," shrugged Talia. "I think once we're back in Tallamar, we're on our own. Do you know how to get to the Cradle?"

Scratching his head, Drake stared up at the gray, cloudy sky. "Depends on where we exit Nordos. We'll probably want to get on the highways heading to the east-central border in the Haiglands. We can't cross the Scar in the north, and I'd rather avoid Arillia if we can."

"Arillia?" inquired Talia.

"Yeah—the last lawless corner of civilization," Drake noted without any particular respect. "Freecity, Arillia: home of mercenaries, smugglers, outlaws, and business magnates. It's no place for children."

"If it's so bad, why don't they just send in soldiers to fix it?" Talia wondered.

"It's between Tallamar and Deuzos—so in a way, it's both kingdoms' problem and neither kingdom's problem," Drake said in non-answer. "Would you waste men and resources trying to wipe out a hive of well-armed murderers who are probably hurting your enemy?"

"Probably not?" guessed Talia.

"Tallawyn and Godwin both have their crown-jewel fortress less than a day's walk from Arillia. They'll contain the anarchy, but neither wants to spend the lives of their men trying to dislodge the cesspool completely. In turn, the mercenaries try to keep a low profile with the neighbors and offer their services to any interested party without prejudice. Long story short—no Arillia if we can help it," summarized Drake.

"And after the Haiglands checkpoint?"

"We go to the Cradle," shirked Drake.

"Which is where?" Talia pressed.

"In Deuzos," Drake answered vaguely.

She sighed. "I'm guessing that's a *cross-that-bridge-when-we-get-there* problem?"

"Correct," Drake said with finality. Talia made a poor effort of hiding a chuckle. "What?" he demanded, scrunching his nose.

"Oh, nothing," Talia answered with a sly grin. She gasped suddenly and turned to him. "I just remembered one other thing Theresa said."

"And that would be..."

"She said if she's not back tonight, I should remind you of your pact—four favors she can call in for anything, at any time. She said you'll be playing a part in making her Highlord," relayed Talia.

"Hmm."

"That whole Vokoz-Dinye thing she was going on about? Killing her birthfather, Alexey Steinfaust, and taking his seat as ruler of Nordos?"

"I remember all that," Drake curtailed her. "I'm wondering what part she wants me to play in making her Highlord."

He considered the desperate pact he had made to find Eamon upon first arriving in Obersteier—the debt had already escaped his mind, though he knew his blood-oath was not a bargain to be taken lightly. The Nords' blood-oaths were bargains of fable, whispered and rumored across the southern kingdoms; he could recall several outrageous examples of dark deeds paid on favors owed, overshadowed by the unspeakably gruesome fates of fools who carelessly reneged. When the time came to pay back Theresa, he would honor his obligation in full—though he hoped he'd meet the end of his own path long before then.

"Well," Talia mused stoically. "Guess only time will tell."

II. The Library On El Aria

Allen Lee

"Ajax, you look a little green."

"Feeling green, sir," the dark-eyed soldier from Alpha called back to Samson. Ajax Sykes' skin took on a pallid hue as the veins across his bald head bulged like maggots beneath the surface. A permanent scowl of dissatisfaction stained his face. Folding his arms across his chest, the gunner quietly comforted himself without openly displaying weakness.

Rare for his kind to get motion sickness, Allen thought as the cabin persevered through the stomach-churning descent of the helicopter together.

At last, the bird touched down on solid ground. The blades and motors whirred to a dormant state, and the restraints released automatically. The hatch flew open to reveal a hostile landscape. In the distant low ground, dust and sand reigned. Refraction distorted the desert air outside, reminding Allen of his favorite hot spring.

"Takes you back, doesn't it, sir?" commented Frank Sykes—unrelated to Ajax, Allen had clarified.

"I've seen enough sand for one lifetime. Hell, at least there's a bit of grass up here," Samson said after a short pause. His seat had a different viewing angle to the world outside, ostensibly to a more promising terrain.

"Gentlemen, welcome to The Library on El Aria," Virgil announced grandly, rising to his feet. He led the way out of the cargo hold, Cato in tow.

"Hold your horses, Swanson," Samson called after Virgil.

"Me, sir?" asked Roy Swanson.

"Not you," Samson answered his squad-mate irritably. "Shaggy," he clarified in reference to Virgil's unkempt black hair.

"Come, Sam Samson. I will show you your new home," invited Virgil.

"Now wait just a minute—we still need to have a conversation about what we're doing here. Now's the time for tactical thinking," insisted Samson.

"Very well," abided Virgil, turning on the ramp to address the group of ten foreigners. "If you allow me, I will lead you on a tour of the campus. The Library on El Aria consists of two barracks, one senate forum, and one great library. You will see the bustling metropolis of El Aria down below, governed by Sheikh Dohari. The sheikh graciously commissions our research, providing security, materials, and a steady stream of eager scholars from the world's finest university. Our partnership with El Aria, nearing a millennium in friendship, has allowed us to assimilate all of human knowledge in one centralized place. Nowhere in Kyros can one find such expansive troves of information as exist here. This cumulative effort of ten thousand souls, many lifetimes dedicated to researching and sharing the fundamental truths of our world, has delivered agricultural revolutions, medical breakthroughs, and quantum leaps in our scientific capabilities."

"Dandy. How are you fixing the portal?" interjected Samson, visibly annoying Cato.

"Of course. The portal," mused Virgil. "My understanding is that none of you currently possesses the capabilities to repair the portal, thus I will need to personally see to the task. I will partner each of you with one of my disciples to gather any pertinent knowledge you may have—for instance, I believe Annie Chu's knowledge of electricity may be of some use. Beyond this, I will dedicate a full day from each week to engineering a solution."

"One day a week's not going to cut it! We've been locked in the dark for months. Lord only knows what's happening on the other side right now," Samson objected.

Cato scoffed, taking exception to the sergeant's offensive tone. "You baffling imbecile! Show some respect to Master—"

Virgil raised a hand to interrupt his disciple. "The portable library device Allen provided will assist me greatly. I intend to transfer the entirety of this information to our archives, but I suspect the knowledge component alone will not be the bottleneck of this project. My greatest challenge will be gathering the requisite resources and constructing the necessary technologies that will enable the completion of our end goal.

"You may notice, for instance, that the library's structure is wooden—I, of course, know how to construct a house from stone and glass and metal. However, we lack both an abundance of these materials and a robust logistics network to deliver them to us on a whim. Inertia and nostalgia also play a hand in the library's design, but I digress. I anticipate I will discover the theoretical blueprint for long-distance spatial relocation within one day of dedicated work. I can then place work orders for the various materials we will need to progress our primitive technologies in preparation for the portal's construction, but we will ultimately be at the mercy of El Aria's supply chain. I therefore urge you, Sam Samson, be patient. Through cooperation, we will reach our objectives."

"Bah," Samson acquiesced. "I'd hate to say you're dragging your feet on this, but I'll leave the thought hanging like a fart in a warm shed."

Cato balked at Samson's unrelenting brashness. "Master Virgil is one of the most sought-after men in the world. Students come from far and wide to learn at his feet, travelling thousands of miles to take his exams in hopes they may learn among the erudite chosen to advance society's collective knowledge. Even his hand-selected disciples—the apprentices and the adepts—may only hope for hours of his invaluable time over the course of a year. To be given one full day each week is an unparalleled blessing!"

"Gesundheit," blurted Samson, unmoved. "Anyway—for now, our mission is stuck like a high-school wedding ring on a pastry chef's fourth finger. My men's first priority will continue to be repairing the portal—however, in light of the material constraints, I will defer in part to your discretion of how to fill any spare time, so long as they're staying in fighting shape."

"I was hoping you would come to that conclusion," Virgil accepted brightly. "I'll have my disciples feed your soldiers three meals a day. In return, your soldiers may join the security force to guard The Library from vandals. Thieves and their ilk. Given your equipment, I expect this should be a simple task. From time to time, I may also request your assistance in transporting materials, including those for the portal, from the town below. I anticipate few of your warriors will add distinctive contributions to our vault of knowledge, but I may take on any diamonds in the rough as disciples if warranted."

"Eat food, shoot thieves, carry wood... after we get in three hours of conditioning every morning from five to eight. Doable, boys?"

"Sir!" the soldiers responded in unison.

"Allen Lee has already proven to be an asset in knowledge discovery— he will join me as a full-time novice to support the research of one of my apprentices. In time, as he comes to understand the process, he will author his own books and conduct his own experiments. I wish to speak with Chip Hamal and Annie Chu further, individually, to discover their aptitudes. Now, may I proceed with the tour?" concluded Virgil.

"As you will," humored Samson.

Allen fell in line with the soldiers departing from the helicopter. He peered over the side of the mountain and saw El Aria—a jewel of civilization nestled in the infinite dunes of swirling golden sands. Although too far to identify any individual people, he admired the grandeur of the city, decorated with fabrics of many colors stretched between the sandstone roofs. Outside the walls topped with silver ramparts, disorganized rows of tents huddled in the city's shadow, their cloth notably more decrepit than the canvased patches inside. The vast city appeared to grow richer toward the center, culminating in a walled inner city that boasted elegant ivory towers. One imposing palace rose above the rest, buffered by orderly columns of greenery and water features—an unmistakable marker of the sheikh's great wealth in a desolate land.

Turning his head away from the entrancing city in the sands, he fixed his attention on the plateau of sparse green on top of the mountain. He saw the four distinct buildings spread out before him and marveled at their size.

"The senate," began Virgil, indicating the circular building to their right. The dome featured stained-glass windows at regular intervals up its sides and curved roof, every pane depicting a scene Allen could not see clearly from his position. Despite its beauty, the structure wore perceptible signs of age. Its walls appeared to be a similar sandstone material as the city used below. The stone walkway through the rectangular entrance, guarded by two simple albeit thoughtfully trimmed pillars, was visibly downtrodden in the center. The sides of the once-even flooring rose nearly a foot above the frequented middle.

"Here," continued Virgil, "is a house of discourse. Scholars travel from afar to take my entry examinations in this venerable hall. When not actively testing prospective students, the senate is host to both lectures and debates. Although some lessons I must teach my disciples directly, I encourage the mental sparring of adepts, eager to prove and improve their own philosophies. I often passively moderate such enlightened discussions, as one learns more from discovery than instruction. Unfortunately, this chamber, like the library, is available only to my students. I thank you in advance for your understanding."

"I didn't even go to class when I was a student; no reason to start now," granted Samson.

"Excellent. Allen, I think you'll quite enjoy the senate. I'll instruct your mentor to bring you to the next plenum—you'll find that Cato quite enjoys the sport, as well," Virgil said as an aside.

"Sounds interesting," Allen smiled cheerfully.

Virgil nodded. "The building ahead of us is the great library—again, only available to my students. The El Arians provide guards to mind the various access points; Samson, you and your men will receive schedules to supplement their numbers."

"Why so many guards in the first place?" Samson asked, suspicious. "Was there some battle of the books I should know about?"

Allen looked up ahead and noted the sixteen guards stationed outside the library's entrance, all clad in off-white robes and dark-red moccasins. Each carried a weapon resembling a scimitar on his right hip. Although their faces were largely obscured by covers of white cloth that reached from ear to ear, Allen sensed their unfriendly gaze upon the newcomers.

"These brutes are primarily a deterrent against would-be thieves; the mere presence of guards is typically enough to dissuade undesirable behavior. Sheikh Dohari is also quite protective of the secrets within these walls—detailed maps of every land, multifaceted histories of conquerors and the conquered, and schematics of powerful weaponry are among the collection. If rivals from other sheikhdoms were to pillage The Library, they would uncover much that could be wielded with malice."

"Why does this Dohari let you run this kind of operation at all, if his secrets are lying around in open books?" questioned Samson.

"We have an understanding. My purpose is to gather all that's known and discover all that yet remains a mystery. This destiny I inherited from Logios himself, whose long line of hosts have been employed in the timeless pursuit. Dohari's predecessors have similarly passed down the time-honored partnership ever since the first Sheikh of El Aria, who founded his kingdom several centuries into our unending quest. As friends, El Aria benefits greatly from our discoveries, and through commissions, can influence progress and innovation to meet their needs. However, they may never censor or attempt to censor our work, else we would cease to bestow our gift unto them."

"Sounds like a shaky alliance to me," Samson said skeptically.

"Nonetheless, it endures," smiled Virgil. "It helps that the El Arians may not enter the library. Once they join the academy, they are my students first before they are El Arians; the guards and army are only permitted outside. Plus, the library itself is so vast that it would take years for the El Arians to discover the full extent of knowledge I have pieced together on their domain."

And vast it was. Even from the outside, Allen regarded the building with unreserved amazement. In addition to the sixteen guards at the foot of the impressive front steps, groups of four patrolled dutifully around the perimeter. Weaving between the soldiers were men and women in white togas similar to Cato's who carried scrolls and books with an air of purpose. Framed with low hedges and flowers, the wooden structure looked more like a palace than a simple library. Allen was unsure how high the broad building towered, but he estimated it to be over fifteen stories tall.

"Cato, would you kindly show these good people to their quarters and have our chefs prepare a special dinner? Surely, they are hungry after their travels," bid Virgil.

"This way," instructed Cato, leading the soldiers toward the two squat lodges that knelt in the shadow of the great library.

"Go on ahead. I'm going to catch my own dinner," Samson decided standoffishly.

Cato furrowed his brow. "There is very limited flora and fauna in the vicinity. Why would you prefer to hunt rabbit and cacti when I can offer you fine beef and fruit from our kitchen?"

"I'd hate to be an inconvenience," returned Samson with a frown. "But speaking of beef—Shaggy, you owe me a grill!"

Allen saw a ghost of a smile touch Virgil's face. "I did promise I would support your research into the perfect burger. Very well—Cato will add the grill to his list. Now please, be civil and join your comrades for supper."

"Nah," declined Samson. "Now I'm in the mood for rabbit and cactus. You kids have fun, though."

"We'll regroup after dinner, sir," said Frank, following Cato.

"I'd kill for a cigarette... and a little booze," lamented Ajax, bringing up the rear.

"Allen, I want to show you something," Virgil pulled him aside as the others departed.

Allen followed Virgil past the guards and up the wide stone steps. Within one of the two grandiose wooden doors marking the entry, a smaller, more functional person-sized door was carved out. Allen followed Virgil inside but stopped past the doorway, frozen in wonderment at the great library.

The doors spilled out onto a wooden platform that overlooked a vast foyer complete with vaulted ceilings, one hundred feet from floor to ceiling. The soaring bookshelves lining the room reached just as high, laden with myriad scrolls, pictures, and books. White-togaed students of various shapes and sizes buzzed around the library, scaling ladders and reading leather- and cloth-bound tomes of new and old. The only sunlight into the library came through carefully constructed slits near the roof that filtered beams onto faded murals. Allen assumed the design was intended to protect the ancient books from aging. In lieu of natural light, crystal chandeliers hung above the rectangular hall to shed illumination below. The students also carried paper lanterns with them. Allen felt great anxiety just thinking about the fire hazard.

"This is the first floor, containing over twenty million books and encyclopedias. The first nine thousand blue-backed books you see on the wall to our right serve as a directory for the higher floors, sorted by topic. Please ask any page you see walking around, denoted by their black robes, to retrieve documents from the higher floors. They also have a strong sense of the library's layout and can help you find what you're looking for on this floor. I plan to incorporate your search technology for our next remodeling in ten years, but these ardent stewards are a workable solution for the present."

"What should I be doing?" asked Allen, overwhelmed by the sea of information before him.

"For now, enjoy. Explore all our humble collection has to offer. I will send word to your mentor to contact you—though you skipped the training role of the pageship, you must still perform the duties of a novice. Your assigned mentor will guide you on their experiments and research, and you will assist them as you continue to learn more about The Library and our mission. I hope you discover a passion to lead your own studies on topics that interest you."

Allen caught himself gawping and closed his mouth. "Thank you, Virgil. This place is incredible."

Virgil smiled kindly and patted an avuncular hand on Allen's back, inadvertently threatening his balance. The excitement of the library has briefly distracted Allen from his stump leg, although his precarious balance was an omnipresent factor that grounded him back in reality. Still, his excitement won out, silencing his self-pity and grief.

He could hardly fathom the trillions of words scattered across the neatly bound pages surrounding him. His single regret was that he had only one life to explore it all. Even if he spent every day reading from now until his end, he wouldn't make a dent in the collection.

"If you grow hungry or inspired, a page will take you to the appropriate room. I will see you soon, Allen Lee. Welcome to The Library on El Aria."

III. The History of Everything

Allen Lee

It was like a theme park.

In fact, it was like the best darn theme park Allen had ever visited.

As he strolled through the labyrinth of book-laden shelves that towered over him like skyscrapers, he couldn't help but feel a sense of unadulterated awe. He had lost himself in the ground-floor grid within minutes. Wooden signs jutted out at seemingly random intervals, likely to indicate the contents of each section.

Allen switched on his glasses' communicator function, pausing as he focused on the screen overlay appearing before his eyes. The glasses followed his eye movements with retinal tracking, seamlessly opening the translation application downloaded into the frame. He scrolled to his plug-in languages and selected the custom Deuxian script developed with Virgil's assistance.

The blue loading bar flashed briefly across his vision, soon replaced by his augmented field of view. The hieroglyphic signs were replaced by more familiar characters.

Smiling to himself, Allen reflected on his own good planning. Although his favorite pair of glasses—the ones Alaina had bought for their ten-year anniversary—had been shattered in the lab breakout, Allen always kept a spare pair in a hardened case in his pack, along with a deck of cards, a pen and pad, and a roll of floss. Some had questioned the glasses, many had disparaged the floss, but he had his reasons.

Perusing the aisles with newly translated signs, he considered sampling the assortment. Pausing below a sign that read *Flora & Fauna of Taoxos*, he picked up a green-backed book titled *Red-eyed Tree Bears: Volume One*. Leafing to a random page in the first half of the book, Allen read about the Taoxian bear:

The Red-eyed Tree Bear, having no relation to the Red-eyed Lemur of the southern continent, is a nocturnal animal. Electing to hunt in packs rather than face the unpredictable beasts of the Taoxian jungle alone, these deadly predators subsist on a diet of rats, mice, and boonjoo leaves. Although generally averse to encounters with man, these bears will fiercely protect their dens. Beware this mid-sized bear's sharp claws, piercing bite, and noxious odor...

"Huh," Allen remarked to no one in particular. He didn't exactly know where Taoxos was, nor what a boonjoo leaf might taste like, but he found the excerpt interesting. Curious how someone could fill an entire book with notes on this one animal, he cursorily flipped through its pages, skimming the titles of subsections. He identified passages relating to evolution history, bone structure, and a surprisingly lengthy appendix on Red-eyed Tree Bear mating habits.

He put the book back on the shelf. An annoyed "Humph!" sounded from a short, black-clad page behind him. Glowering at Allen, the irritated young man drew the green-backed book, slid over two hard-covers in the same row, and returned the tome to its rightful place on the shelf.

"Sorry," Allen muttered self-consciously as the page disappeared into another row. He tilted his head back to stare at the tall stacks. "I wonder what else they have..."

Crossing over several rows and delving deeper into the library, Allen found himself in the modern history section. He paused below a brown sign marked *Modern History of the Kingdoms of Kyros* and selected a brown-backed book inscribed *Godwin's Deuzos: Power and Politics*. Thumbing a page with the title *Family: Overview*, Allen read on:

Gaius Godwin, first of his name, son of King Alarak Godwin and elder brother to Gordon Godwin (deceased) and Gerhart Godwin (Lord of Linz in the Lowlands), celebrated his first birthday at the turn of the century. An accomplished strategist and peerless conqueror, Gaius is best known for the unification of Deuzos and annexation of the Forlorn Steppes, rectifying his father's alienation of the kingdom's primary metals depot and high-security prison—the Rock (located immediately south of the Burning Gorge). Though not formally credited due to the political nature of the Cormack-Tallawyn campaign known as the 'Red War', Gaius' only recorded defeat as Commander in Chief of the Godwin army was at the infamous Freedom's Last Stand, which ended the proxy war in the Thornlands. As the Blind King's army was crushed in the hinterlands surrounding Aurelle, the routed Godwin-backed forces were snuffed out on their retreat to Tyranos. Although never formally recognized as a participant in the war, multiple intercepted communications between the Godwins and Cormacks confirm the involvement of the golden army in the historic battle that defined Tallamar in the modern age.

"Godwin," murmured Allen, testing the name on his tongue. Although he had no further context on this king or any other in Kyros, he was surprised by the clear tone of admiration the author had taken in the biography. Allen continued reading about the Godwins, skipping ahead to the bolded subtitles for each family member:

Prince Elliott Godwin: firstborn of Gaius and Alessandra, Prince Elliott was born ten years to the day of the outbreak of the Red War. Despite tutelage under the most accomplished generals and tacticians in Godwin's kingdom, Prince Elliott never adapted to life on the battlefield. In two particularly memorable occasions of the royal court, Prince Elliott flouted his inheritance as the future king, referencing his idol (the renowned poet, Ilya Astaire) in his personal ambitions for the future. Despite his professed passions for poetry and the arts, Prince Elliott has yet to author a work worthy of critical acclaim. His first attempt at publication, 'Kiss Me in the Moonlight, You Saucy Vixen', was subjected to great ridicule and mockery from the general public. Only six hundred copies were printed—five hundred and ninety-seven of which were hastily recovered by the King's Rangers a day after their release. According to official press channels, the novel was a tasteless subversion of the royal name created by a clandestine clan of malicious writers. Publisher Ralph Heins was summarily hanged as a result of this fiasco.

"I wonder..." Allen said to himself, closing the book but keeping his place marked with a finger. He spotted a black-clad page passing behind him. "Excuse me, sir?"

A youthful woman turned to face him with a cocked eyebrow. He had mistaken her by the short haircut, but he immediately recognized his mistake as he mirrored her confused face.

"Oh, uh... I meant, um... Pardon me, misses lady—madam... Um..." he stumbled awkwardly, hoping she hadn't taken offense.

"Yes?" she interrupted in a nasally voice, sparing him from further embarrassment.

"I was just wondering if you had a book here?" Allen inquired vaguely.

"We have many books here. It's a library," she answered dryly.

"Ah, of course," stammered Allen.

The young page stared at him blankly, unamused.

"Yes, I was wondering if you had a book called... Uh..." Allen lowered his voice and dared to request, "*Kiss Me in the Moonlight, You Saucy Vixen?*"

Impossibly, the page's eyebrows shot up higher. "I'll check and get back to you," she said, disappearing into the books with impressive speed.

Allen cleared his throat self-consciously. Nodding as he replayed the interaction, he suddenly remembered the book in his hand. He reopened it.

Princess Ashe Godwin, secondborn of Gaius and Alessandra, inherited her father's battle acumen. Despite her political marriage to Lord Gresham Pyke of the Forlorn Steppes, Ashe continues to reside in the capital with her family, often visited by the Lord of the Rock. Although the full extent of her involvement with the golden army is unclear, Ashe reportedly oversees field drills with some regularity...

Prince Cain Godwin, thirdborn of Gaius and Alessandra, has led men into battle during several small-scale conflicts, most notably the failed Kilkenny Revolt. Known for brutality and bloodlust, Cain is the most capable swordsman of the family and can often be found in the vanguard of his battalion. Cain regularly acts as Gaius' second on the battlefront, although the title of second-in-command remains to be appointed, leaving some to speculate about a quiet rivalry between Cain and Ashe. No woman has ever formally commanded the golden army, aside from the interim rule of Queen Anna the Second after the death of her husband, King Raymund Godwin.

Youngest son Prince Alphonse (Al) Godwin continues to study under the king's hand-selected tutors, most notably including the reluctant and grossly overqualified Honorable Nephew Tacchus Godwin. Prince Al shows neither the strategic prowess of Ashe nor the combat confidence of Cain, which may either be a factor in or result of the comparatively limited time Gaius spends with Alphonse.

Renown for her unmatched beauty, Queen Alessandra Godwin...

Allen's breath caught. He closed the book heavily and tapped the frame of his glasses. Scrolling to the *Photos* application with his eyes, he rifled through his chronologically ordered photos. He stopped on his favorite—the family portrait with him, his beautiful wife Alaina, and his wide-eyed daughter Lyn in front of a blue studio background.

He missed them. He missed them a lot.

His mind drifted across the universe to them. He wondered what they were doing. How they were. He prayed that life continued in his absence—that Lyn ate her sugary cereal and Alaina kept their plants alive. He prayed that they were happy and safe from their frightening world. And yet, some guilty part of him hoped that they missed him. That they felt his absence.

He thought of Danny and hoped his brother was still alive—that they had miraculously ended the war without further casualties. Reality gripped his fantastical thoughts, planting an unshakable anxiety for his loved ones. He recalled the lifeless face of his best friend Charles—uplifting and silly and full-of-life Charles who died wearing his goofy suspenders. If such good could be snuffed out without cause or warning, he couldn't help but imagine the worst for others in the line of peril.

"Is this what you were looking for?" a nasally voice ripped him from his thoughts.

Allen caught himself wiping a tear from his eye as he turned to face the page. He observed the red book in her hand—*Kiss Me in the Moonlight, You Saucy Vixen (By Elliott Godwin)*—complete with a scandalous graphic of a buxom woman draped over a lithe man with long, blond hair, covered only by a beam of silver moonlight.

Red in the face, Allen hurriedly abandoned the request: "I think I must have mistaken the title. Sorry about that!"

"Right," said the page, voice grinding with disapproval. "Guess I'll put this back, then." She and her eyebrows disappeared into the maze of books.

Allen scuttled into an adjacent section, bashful of the fact that his fellow disciples might have witnessed the exchange. He stopped under a sign that read *Principles of Mathematics*. Inspecting a book titled *Basic Trigonometry*, Allen discovered that some things never change:

The three interior angles of a triangle will always sum to one hundred eighty degrees. If one is a right angle of ninety degrees, then the remaining two angles must sum to ninety degrees and are therefore acute angles.

"Yep," Allen returned the book to its proper place on the shelf, quickly bored of its simple and familiar contents. He pressed onward, electing to be pickier about the books he sampled. He walked past *Heroes and Villains of*

Kyros, Known Primals and their Pasts, and *Tried-And-Edible Recipes* before arriving at a section called *Origins of Creation.*

Scanning the titles on the shelf in front of him, he took an interest in *The Beginning: Makers of Creation, Destruction, and Balance,* along with *Birth of the Primals* and *Val'Helios.* His hand hovered above the second title as his eyes continued to scan the shelf.

"Allen?" asked a cheerful voice behind him.

He spun and met the stunning green eyes of a tawny woman with a golden circlet in her neatly fixed hair. She had a depth in her gaze that told him she didn't just see the world—she understood it. Hers was a dizzying aura of kindness and intellectual curiosity. The same that had drawn him to his wife.

Caught off-guard, Allen awkwardly sputtered: "Y-ello?" Discreetly clearing his throat, he discombobulated his words: "Yes! Hello! I'm Allen Lee." He extended a sweaty hand toward the woman in white.

"Meghana Ayur," she returned a humored smile, grasping his forearm. "Nice to meet you, Allen Lee. I'm told you're Master Virgil's newest disciple?"

Allen nodded. "Yes. Sort of. I think we might be friends."

"Wow," she said with mock amazement. "Impressive for a novice. I hope you'll still be up for assisting my apprenticeship work?"

"Oh, I see! You must be my apprentice—I mean, my mentor," Allen corrected, subtly wiping his damp palms on his pants. He wasn't sure why he was so anxious. He decided it was likely a remnant reaction from the shock of Elliott Godwin's novella.

"Yes. I am sure we will learn from and teach one another. I suspect you are interested in knowing the subject of our work?" probed Meghana, earning an eager nod from Allen. "Excellent. I am currently working on the development of a cure for the blood plague afflicting the Lowlands in Deuzos. I've completed the background and transmission sections for archiving—the plague originated from rats aboard ships arriving from the southern continent—and am beginning the trial phase for a cure. I've formed several hypotheses for the remedy, but the high death rate and relatively agile mutations of the disease makes it difficult to find living subjects. Naturally, time is an important factor for us—as the plague spreads, more will die. We must discover and disseminate a cure as soon as possible."

"Impressive work," Allen nodded thoughtfully. "I actually might have relevant knowledge that could help—a primitive solution, but I once created a drug from scratch to battle a bacterial infection as part of an entry-level science elective. Creating a particular kind of mold is the key."

"One of my three hypotheses—a more deliberate evolution of the moldy-bread technique used by the early tribes of Ayrabos to survive the sand plague. Additionally, we should test some herbs that grow in the Blackwater and dart frog toxin from the tribes of the southern continent. I recommend reading the abstract I've written on the subject, and we can go from there," she suggested in a friendly tone.

"Of course. What will my tasks be?"

"You'll see my proposed procedure in the abstract, but since you seem to know about mold cultures, I may let you lead some of that hypothesis testing with just a little supervision. I can continue sourcing volunteers for our trial phase—you will undoubtedly need to gather materials that come into town for me, as well as prepare the mold-based treatment. I may also ask you to summarize your notes in written form as needed. We'll work hard, but I want this to be an enjoyable experience for you too. Think of us as partners—friends, even. I'll teach you everything I know about life at The Library, and in time, I'm sure you'll make a great apprentice as well," proposed Meghana.

"Fantastic! I'm excited to get started."

"Since we're in a bit of a bottleneck while we wait for the subjects and frog toxin to arrive, you should keep exploring The Library over the next few days. We'll also set up time to eat, chat, and learn about each other throughout the week. For tonight, I'll have my notes delivered to your bed in the barracks. Let's meet up again tomorrow to talk over any initial questions you have?"

"Absolutely. Sounds like you've got this all planned out," commended Allen, impressed by her organization.

"That's because I do," she answered smartly. "By the way, you should take this book with you if you haven't read it already," Meghana suggested, producing a copy of *Modern Heroes in the Land of Gods*. "The writing jumps around a bit, but there are some truly great stories in there. I think you'll like the characters."

"Will I have enough time outside of work for a casual read?" Allen hefted the book in his hand uncertainly.

"Of course," Meghana answered with an enchanting smile. "Research is important, but we must remember we are still only human. Our meaningful work may be our duty, but we must not forget to truly live and enjoy the world we've created."

IV. The Homestead

Drake

I misspoke when I said I was hungry. I'm starving."

"What exactly am I supposed to do about that?" Drake inquired with a sigh. He was hungry too.

Their aloof and impersonal guide, Bask Noressen, had parted ways two days ago at the border dividing Nordos and Tallamar, taking his share of the food with him. They had crossed the frozen tundra and reached dried patches of yellow and gray grass—evidence of the rain's prolonged neglect.

Although certainly frigid, the air was no longer freezing. Drake hoped that their off-road wandering through the grasslands would soon bring them across wild animals or a roadside inn. At the very least, they needed to find a stream soon; they had no more than half a day's water between them. He knew that starvation was painful, but dehydration could kill much faster.

"I just thought I should inform you before I resort to eating my own foot to survive," Talia bemoaned dramatically.

"I think all those nuts and roots spoiled you," Drake snorted. The tradeoff they made bringing nonperishable food on their journey was certainly flavor. They hadn't enjoyed a proper meal since they left Obersteier.

Tapping the purse tucked under his shirt, Drake considered his precarious financial situation. They had blown through most of the money gifted by Lady Kika and were running dangerously low on reserves. Based on the half-hearted jingle of the pouch, he doubted they had enough kroner to stay overnight at an inn. He would need to consider the most expedient means to replenish the funds.

"Hey, Drake? Is that a house?" Talia pointed ahead into the distance.

Drake squinted at the horizon. Only grass and gently sloping hills. "I don't see anything."

They marched toward the phantom homestead, dragging their feet through untraveled grass. Drake lifted a hand to block out the late-morning sun, scanning for movement or any other signs of life. He knew the rural types tended to be protective of their land and were typically hostile to strangers who appeared unannounced on their doorstep.

He looked at Talia and saw the girl dutifully trudging forward despite the unmistakable discomfort on her face. He recognized that, as miserably tired and hungry as he was, the kid must have been suffering even worse. To her credit, she had kept her complaints to herself for the most part, unquestioningly plowing ahead alongside him.

If there was a farm at the other side of this seemingly infinite field, he wouldn't be leaving without food.

"See it now?" Talia asked quietly, as if the distant house might hear.

Drake scrunched his eyes. He could make out a small, decrepit home standing alone in the prairie. Although the tin roof was impacted toward the corners, matching the peeling paint on the outer walls and wild grass growing around the property, the structure was undoubtedly somebody's home.

"I see it," Drake mumbled, focusing his vision on the house while watching for movement in his peripherals.

"Think anyone's home? Maybe we can ask them for food," suggested Talia hopefully.

"Not sure," Drake considered carefully. "We don't know what kind of people live here, if anyone still does."

Drake spotted a brick well in the grass, stationed approximately fifty yards from the house. He drew the waterskin from his bag, took a long sip, and handed it to Talia. "See that well over there?"

"Fill the waters?"

"You got it. Keep your head down while I check out the house."

"You're not going to do anything crazy, right? They're just farmers, Drake," Talia said warily.

"Not if it can be helped," he answered noncommittally. "Stay out of sight until I'm back."

"Okay," Talia accepted, uncertain but obedient.

Drake skulked forward through the knee-high grass, moving swiftly from a crouched position. His Nord falchion hung accessible at his hip; his knife stayed in its sheath, fastened to his right calf. Passing the well, he observed the homestead: a dusty front porch, cracked windows, and canvas sacks piled next to the back door.

He deftly drew his knife without breaking stride, deciding the shorter blade would be best for close quarters. Kneeling in front of the canvas sacks, he ran the tip of his blade through one. Oats spilled onto the ground.

With a cursory look over his shoulder, Drake immediately detected a small tuft of brown hair floating through the grass toward the well. He made a mental note to practice stealth with Talia when time permitted.

Returning his focus to the task at hand, Drake placed a hand on the doorknob and slowly turned it until he heard the bolt disengage. He swung the door open slowly but steadily, cringing when the hinge creaked at the end of his movement. No dogs or other rabid defenders rushed to meet him. He paused in the doorway, straining to hear whether the noise had alerted any unseen occupants.

Cautiously satisfied that he remained undetected, Drake slipped inside. It took a moment for his eyes to adjust to the dim interior, illuminated by only indirect sunlight through the door and kitchen window. He surveyed the room, taking in its chipped countertops, sparse cabinets, and blandly personalized decor. Four chairs were crammed around a wooden table in the corner of the small kitchen. The candle in the center had burned down.

A steaming-hot pie rested on the windowsill. The smoky aroma of burned wood sweetened the room; red coals in the fireplace confirmed the recent baking. Someone was still living here.

Battling the hunger that tempted him to try the pie, he crept through the kitchen, determined to secure his surroundings before lowering his guard.

Drake spotted a closed door in the opposite corner of the kitchen, on the wall perpendicular to the neighboring, doorless hallway. He stalked along the lefthand wall toward the door, minding his step on the old wooden floors. The hair on his neck stood suddenly, alerting him to danger ahead. He froze, hearing a pair of light footsteps approaching from around the corner.

He swiftly prowled forward another two steps, crouching half a yard back from the doorway. Gripping his knife tight in his right hand, he waited in the shadows, listening carefully to the even footfalls.

The toe of a black boot poked into the room, and Drake leaped into action. He sprang forward around the corner and thrust his knife into the oncoming occupant.

A gargled scream escaped the woman as Drake's knife opened her throat. Too slowly, he clamped a hand over her mouth, muffling her scream as he ripped the knife across her neck. The unsuspecting victim's eyes widened as she crumpled to the floor. Blood splashed onto dusty hardwood.

"Shit."

Adrenaline quickened his breath as he stood over the corpse. Her face was twisted in surprise and pain. Frozen in horror. Strands of gray mingled with her black hair. A dark red stream flowed onto her blue gown, staining it purple.

"Maureen?" a concerned voice called from behind him. Drake turned as the kitchen's second door swung open, revealing an aging man built like a strong bull. He carried a butcher's hatchet in his right hand, freshly covered with blood. Matching stains darkened his gloves and apron. Black eyes bulged with shock and anger as they narrowed on Drake.

"You!'" the butcher snarled. "What have you done!?"

Drake retreated a step and stumbled, tripping over the lifeless limbs that cluttered the narrow hallway. He pushed off the wall to regain his balance, squaring off against the hysterical widower.

The butcher roared in anger, flexing his broad chest and knotted shoulders as he charged. He hacked diagonally at Drake, who deftly retreated from the hatchet's range. The butcher swung a mighty backhanded blow, lodging his blade several inches into the wooden wall.

As he attempted to unstick his hatchet, Drake leaped forward and drove the knife into his chest. The enraged homeowner bellowed a guttural cry. Releasing his grip on the hatchet, he crashed his arms down inside Drake's shoulders. Grabbing by the neck, the big man slammed him into the wall.

Desperate to keep his feet on the ground, Drake kicked him in the A-frame. Although his restricted movement weakened the kick, the blow was enough for Drake to secure his grip on the knife, pull it from the man's chest, and plunge it into his left eye.

The butcher shrieked in pain as Drake twisted the blade. Falling free from the man's grip, Drake pressed the attack, hammering the hilt of knife with his left hand. Three punches later, the full length of the blade was buried in the man's skull. Finally, the hulking defender dropped to his knees. Drake yanked the bloody knife free, and the man fell sideways, crashing awkwardly against the wall opposite the buried hatchet.

Panting heavily, Drake attempted to slow his breathing as he listened for any additional defenders hidden in the wings. Hearing none, he crouched and patted down the pockets of the fallen, hoping to find some coin they'd no longer need. Disappointed by his search, he peered down the hallway, then back into the kitchen. He decided to finish searching the ground floor before moving on to the upstairs of the couple's homestead.

Rifling through the cabinets, Drake found a meager assortment of vegetables and a loaf of old bread. He slid the acquisitions into his bag, then decided to investigate the back room from which the butcher had emerged.

A sickening odor emanated from the dark room, striking him at the threshold like a battering ram. The windowless gloom was disturbed only by a lone lantern on the floor. He lifted the light, holding it above his head and behind his field of view as his vision acclimated to the low light.

At the edge of the lantern's glow, four shelves built into the wall on his right snagged his attention. He cautiously edged closer, letting the dim light spill over the miscellaneous contents ordered on the wooden planks. The top shelf held worn farmer boots, wire-frame glasses, a simple pearl necklace, muddy brown pants, and a scruffy teddy bear with a red bowtie. The other shelves were similarly adorned with mismatching clothing and keepsakes.

Hung on the wall beside the shelf was a ledger. Drake held the lantern closer to the parchment and read the latest entry:

3-13: 2 men's boots, worn. 1 silver watch. 1 linen tunic, torn. 1 wedding band, fake gold. ~160.

Frowning at the cryptic journal, Drake faced into the darkness once more. He advanced slowly, carefully, holding his knife at the ready and listening for any sign of unrest hiding in the darkness with him.

The floorboards creaked with every step, playing a haunting melody beneath his feet. The lantern's glow seemed to die as he moved forward, casting its glow nearer and nearer his feet.

A shallow splash accompanied his last step. He glanced down and lifted his boot to find a thin layer of dark liquid on the floor. Staring at the unidentified substance, Drake realized the lantern's glow was disappearing into a black curtain hanging inches in front of his nose.

He steeled himself, gripping the curtain with his knife hand. A deep breath. Muscles twitching with anticipation.

With a sudden yank, he threw the curtain aside, putting himself face to bloody face with an inverted cadaver. Drake recoiled in horror of the exposed corpse, skinned and hung from its feet by meat hooks. A deep gash ran down the body's midsection. Two wooden buckets were positioned underneath—one full of gizzards and organs that recently belonged to this butchered person, the other ineffectively catching the blood dripping from the man's head and hands.

Drake backed away from the grizzly sight, unsuccessfully battling back the overwhelming urge to vomit. He retched, expelling his empty stomach onto the blood-stained floor. Hot with nausea, Drake stumbled out of the room and slammed the door shut behind him.

He grabbed the pitcher of water from the kitchen counter and washed out his mouth, spitting the foul taste of bile onto the floor. He took a second sip of the warm water and swallowed, unpleasantly rough on his irritated throat.

Looking up, Drake registered the hot pie cooling on the windowsill. He apprehensively reached his knife in front of him, slicing through the crust in a horrorstruck attempt to determine what kind of fruit was used.

No fruit hid under the crust of the homemade pie—only red and brown clumps of ground meat.

He doubled over, emptying out his stomach onto the kitchen floor.

His retching ceased at last, and he staggered to the counter. Fruitlessly, he tried to rinse out his mouth with the last of the water. The foul taste remained, and his throat burned, drier than before.

Standing shakily, he ventured back into the hallway, determined to clear through the upstairs before calling off his search. There had to be something salvageable. None of those tattered, orphaned belongings in the butchery. He stepped over the deplorable slaughterers, regarding their slain forms with contempt.

Down the hall, Drake passed through an open living room with a single large chair. He climbed up the narrow stairs, pausing as he reached the landing. Looking between the two closed doors, he realized either one could contain additional armed defenders.

He flung open the left door, holding his stained knife ready in front of him. A cursory scan of the simple room revealed two beds and a closet full of simple, raggedy clothing. Men's.

Empty.

He returned to door number two and kicked it down, well past the time for stealth. The unoccupied room featured a broad dresser, a made bed, and two barren nightstands. As Drake entered the room, he nearly tripped over an uneven plank. Kneeling to inspect the loose floorboard, Drake inserted his knife into the crack adjacent to the suspicious plank. Forcing the hilt down, he easily pried the concealing wood from its place, revealing a poorly hidden stash.

Two canvas bags were nestled under the boards. He extracted both, planting the weighty pouches on the floor before untying their strings.

The first was filled to the brim with kroner, albeit mostly copper. He transferred the money to his purse, upending the sack to ensure he had drained the last of it into his possession. Satisfied, he wiped his bloodied blade off on the cloth, returned it to its sheath, and tossed the empty bag back into its hole.

The second bag contained an assortment of jewelry, widely ranging in value from knockoffs to generation-old family heirlooms. He lifted one silver, heart-shaped locket, and pressed the button on top to reveal the inscription locked inside:

Dearest Nia, my love for you will never die. —*Tommy*

Drake closed the locket and turned the silver piece over in his hand. He was certain he could find a buyer to fence the jewelry, but something felt off about vending these ill-gotten prizes. Possibly only because he was still shaken by his face-to-face encounter with the cannibalistic couple's latest prey, he considered the locket's past. Every bracelet, wedding band, and necklace in the stash shared a similar, personal story. Each piece belonged to someone now dead, from or for someone they loved. Infinite sentimentality was imbued in each forlorn item, haunted by their late owners' spirits.

He wondered if their counterparts were still alive, left to imagine the fates of the memorabilia and their intended owners. Never knowing for certain. Never finding closure. The collection might have also included a few matching wedding bands.

Rapping his knuckles on the floor in thought, Drake momentarily left the open bag sitting on the floorboards, uncommitted to taking or leaving the trinkets. Their circumstances were undeniably sad, but money was money. After all, it wasn't like their previous owners had any further use for them.

Standing to take in the rest of the room as he waffled on the decision, Drake noticed a framed family portrait resting on the dresser. He walked over and held it in his hand. A slightly younger-looking version of the slain husband

and wife sat unsmiling in the center of the photo. On either side of them stood a grown man who shared his mother's stark forehead and his father's stature.

Drake dropped the frame, shattering the portrait's glass casing. A cold shiver ran down his spine.

There were two more.

A loud shriek pierced his ears, originating from outside.

"Talia!" Drake cried out. He flew out of the room and down the stairs like a bat out of hell. His feet couldn't move fast enough; he sprinted through the hallway and out the kitchen door in a blur that felt like an eternity. His eyes took a moment to readjust to the blinding sunlight, but then he saw it.

"Drake!" screeched Talia, struggling for her life against one of the sons come alive from the family portrait.

The wide-foreheaded man straddled her in the long grass, delirious with power. He brandished a dagger in his right hand, angling the blade toward her scalp. She was trapped under him, squirming futilely against his weight. She pushed against his wrist with both hands as hard as she could. His slobbering grin revealed that he was enjoying the struggle.

"Pyros!" Drake channeled his fury into force.

An orb of flames manifested in his right hand, stealing the attention of her assailant. Drake thrust his arm forward, launching the fireball through the air. The flames slammed into the man's stunned face.

Talia recovered her attacker's knife as he flailed in pain. She drove the blade into his leg, then his side, then anywhere she could strike from her disadvantaged position. The burning man fell off her, writhing in the dry grass as he attempted to quell the flames. Talia pushed herself free from him, rolling away as Drake charged forward.

The grass beneath Drake's feet ignited as he dashed across the plains with inhuman speed. He reached through the rising flames that engulfed the stranger and planted his palm on the man's head. A rush of heat flowed through his arm, stoking the flames into a dense inferno that devoured his opponent, leaving nothing but ash and cinders in his place.

The fire crawling down Drake's sleeves extinguished itself, though the grassland continued to burn. Flames danced at the edge of his vision as he caught his breath. He felt inextinguishably alive. His blood ran hot, offering a short and ready fuse should his pyromaniac inclinations return.

Excellent... Excellent! Pyros roared inside his head. *But I hunger for more. I shall consume that ramshackle kindling next!*

Drake ignored his Primal, searching for Talia. She sat huddled on the grass, holding her knees tight to her chest. Sobbing silently. Her pack and two water flasks lay in the grass beside her.

"You all right?" Drake kneeled to talk to her at eye-level.

She avoided his gaze for a long moment, staring blankly at the flames accumulating behind him. Eventually, she sniffled and gave a curt nod. "I'll be okay," she said shakily.

"Good," Drake helped Talia to her feet. He tucked the water skins into his bag and slung her pack over her shoulders. "We've got to move before this fire gets out of control."

Over his shoulder, Drake witnessed the destruction he left behind. Fire spread outward from the ground he crossed, like a sea of flames parted by his unholy wake. Already, the fields of grass between the well and the house blazed with fury. The fire reached the tin-roofed house and ravaged the timber walls, consuming the homestead with unrestrained gluttony.

Through the rising flames, Drake imagined a face staring back at him. Whether real or an aberration of the cursed souls slain here today, Drake could not tell, but the phantom's visage of ire burned into Drake's memory long after the rising flames obscured its view.

They jogged away from the homestead, slower than Drake would have alone, but the encroaching wall of flames appeared to scorch the earth behind them only as fast as they traveled. Sweat-soaked and soot-dusted, they reached a narrow dirt road that ran perpendicular to their path. Westward.

The scene behind him had since deteriorated into an unmitigated hellfire, razing the fields and blackening the skies as far as the eye could see. Somewhere deep within him, he felt satisfaction at the pyre. Just a little deeper, he felt a dangerous hunger for more.

Talia lifted her head for the first time as rolling thunder echoed across the plains. In the distance ahead, the dark and turbulent sky was not that of smoky destruction, but a combative thunderstorm heading their way—and Drake stood in the middle. The hellfire that was; the storm still to come. Caught between the wall of heat behind him and the cold, pressurized front ahead, he witnessed the terrible authority of nature's fiercest battlefields.

Only he wasn't between two great powers—somehow, he himself had become one of the battlegrounds.

V. Unfavorable Odds

Drake

Kites soared through the skies over Dunloy.

As Drake approached the front gates of the bustling walled town, he spotted two sets of banners proudly framing the entry: the wolf-sporting, white-and-blue cloth that claimed the town for Tallawyn's domain, and a red boar on yellow background that marked the Badlands province.

The swine symbol of the former Cormack kingdom had somehow survived the Red War, despite the many other cultural shifts introduced by the Tallawyns. Gone was the hooded-cobra flag of Tyranos. Both the Haiglands and Badden Roggos regions were unkindly renamed, now respectively the Badlands and the Blasted lands. Yet this one porcine vestige of Cormack identity persevered through the administrative rework, likely in hopes that some might see Tallawyn rule as a union rather than an occupation.

A third, diminutive flag hung between the two stately pairs of banners, as if the tailor had discovered in surprise that only a quarter sheet of fabric remained. Drake identified the ensign as Dunloy's only due to its uniquely outrageous design. On an expedition to the southern continent, one of the chieftains of Clan Dunloy once encountered a river horse—a hippopotamus, as some called it. Eschewing their clan's history as the Green Hawks, the chieftain redesigned his house colors to prominently feature the majestic animal. A hundred years later, Drake now stared at the round faces of three purple hippos, grinning from their place of honor on the white fabric.

Attempting to mentally reconstruct maps he had glimpsed long ago, Drake placed himself somewhere west of the mines but still east of the Scar. Given the harvestable fields they had traversed to reach this town, he assumed they were on the outskirts of the Badlands. It would be wisest to head south to the migrant city of Midpoint, where they would be able to continue west to the eastern checkpoint. As the only safe pass through the Scar and into Deuzos, the No Man's Road beyond the checkpoint was the obvious path forward.

Buzzing trumpets and thundering drums brought Drake back to his senses. He saw the hawk kites in greater detail now, their motley colors soaring on the breeze. They danced freely to the festive music, as did the hundreds of revelers streaming through the front gates of Dunloy.

"What's going on?" Talia looked to Drake for an explanation. "Are they having a party?"

"Sounds like it," Drake answered as they continued to the gate.

Approaching the town, he spotted two guards stationed off to either side of the yawning jaws of the metal gate. Weapons sheathed, they waved the merchants and rural visitors inside.

"Let's go," encouraged one in a thick Cormack accent.

"Keep it moving," called the other in a tired, colorless tone.

The music grew louder as Drake entered the city. Navigating through the cluster of indecisive people mulling around the gate, he began to remember why he preferred the countryside. He continued down the thoroughfare with Talia in tow, briefly pausing behind a crowd of dancing and clapping attendees. They stood facing a makeshift, wooden stage erected outside a drugstore. Ten drummers and eight horn players enchanted the audience with regal melodies. A hanging wooden arm loomed behind them, alerting Drake to the fact that the stage also doubled as the gallows.

"They're so good," Talia grinned at Drake, her enchanted voice hard to hear over the roaring instruments and din of the crowd.

"That's good," Drake folded his arms, reflecting just how much Talia had been through lately. He was glad that they had stumbled across the town during a festival; the kid deserved some time to relax and have a taste of fun. They could explore Dunloy today and continue their journey tomorrow.

"Rumble in the Ring begins in five minutes!" squawked a shrill voiced to Drake's left. A frail, short-haired boy wore wooden boards on his chest and back advertising the event. *Five kroner, five fights—only at the arena!*

"Come and see this afternoon's matinee challenges! Seamus the Blind takes on Igor the Giant; Declan the Swift versus Aoife the Grotesque; Don the Defeated against five tusked and testy boars! Who will win? Who will die? Will there be a sale on pork chops after the tournament? Only one way to find out!"

"What's *matinee* mean?" Talia asked Drake.

"I think it's the first show of the day. Usually, those are just warmup fights for the professional gladiators. Want to go see them?"

"Not really," Talia said reluctantly. "I think I've seen you fight enough people that it wouldn't be worth paying to see others get whacked. You know?"

"Ah," Drake accepted disappointedly, momentarily considering how he might not have been the best influence on the kid. Called out in plain terms, the spectacle of the arena was agreeably brutish. "Well, there's plenty of other things we can do around here."

They walked farther down the street, passing several restaurants, inns, and stores. The crowd thinned out the deeper they explored, apparently a sign that most travelers were happy to settle for the first tavern they came across. Still, the buzzing crowd was thick enough that passersby continually jolted him with their elbows.

"What about the bath house?" Drake pointed out the marble building on their right. His favorite were the refreshingly cold pools, although he would sit in the boiling water for a few minutes beforehand to create a starker contrast.

"It rained last night," dismissed Talia. "I feel plenty clean from that."

"All right," Drake acknowledged, looking around for other options. He spotted a wooden sign that featured a pair of dice and stopped immediately. An excited grin split his face. "I've got a great idea."

"Breaded chicken cubes?" Talia sized up a stall on their left.

"No," Drake sighed before considering her idea. On second thought, he whistled at the chef behind the food stand and held up two fingers.

The chef nudged the chubby boy next to him. The kid grabbed two skewers and crossed the gap between the stand and its prospective customers, dodging oblivious traffic on his way to Drake.

"Eight copper, please," the boy held out a greasy palm.

"Eight?" Drake challenged, suspicious. He reached a hand into the newly acquired stash of kroner hidden under his shirt.

The chunky boy shrugged. "It is a festival," he said, testing Drake on his generosity.

Drake paid the boy, then raised a hand in thanks to the shopkeeper, who matched the wave and added a smile. He handed one skewer to Talia and bit into his own. The pleasant texture of the chicken was a surprise—the chef had done a good job of keeping the moisture in the meat. He hated it when negligent cooks allowed their chicken to get stringy and dry.

"Good, right?" Talia asked between happy bites.

"Good," Drake grunted, primitively tearing another cube off the stick with his teeth.

"You were saying something?" Talia reminded him.

"Right," Drake said, chewing. "Ever been to a gaming house?"

"Of course," Talia's tone dripped with sarcasm. "I'm a professional gambler. I just do the whole *homeless-fourteen-year-old* bit as a side hustle."

"You're hilarious," Drake said dryly.

"And single, too," Talia added, winking mischievously at the confused boy behind the chicken stand.

"Come on," Drake nudged, piloting them toward the gaming house.

"I can't go in there," Talia frowned. "I'm fourteen."

"You're sixteen," Drake corrected her, raising an eyebrow.

"Some might say you're a bad influence on this young, impressionable kid," Talia floated the thought innocently.

"Some could also stay out here and make small talk with the chicken boy while I play inside," Drake retorted, leaving the decision up to her.

Talia shrugged to herself. "I always thought I was mature for my age." She pushed the door open and preceded Drake inside.

The gaming hall was smaller than any he could remember, but it had all the staples. Six separate games of dice were playing out around the matted floor, each with two to six players and a dealer huddled around wooden baskets. The nearby group of young men were exuberantly supporting their friend as he pressed a winning streak, while a fuming, purple-shirted gentleman and his embarrassed wife were shocked by another stroke of misfortune in the opposite corner of the room.

Two card tables were stationed against the wall to either side of the door, both at full occupation for the moment. On the far end, a frightening woman clothed in many feathers told the fortune of a portly woman with laboriously styled hair. The busy bar was a short distance away from the fortune teller, perhaps an intentional design owing to her penchant for grim predictions.

"'Scuse me," a rough Cormack voice addressed Drake from the right. "Is she old enough to be in here?" The sturdy bouncer scratched his thick, hairy neck as he pointed to Talia with his free hand.

"I'm sixteen," Talia answered coolly.

"Any proof of that?" the doorman challenged skeptically.

Drake pulled the purse out of his shirt and jiggled the money in the bag. "Sounds like she's sixteen."

The bouncer performed a cursory scan of the establishment, likely to check that no city guards were present. "Good enough for me," he decided indifferently, returning his rump to its well-acquainted stool.

"Cool," Talia whispered to Drake as they walked the perimeter of the room around the matted floor.

"You ever played dice before?" asked Drake.

"Didn't I tell you I'm a professional?" she jested quietly.

"These diced are fixed! They're fixed, I tell you!" bellowed the purple-shirted man, stamping his feet on the mat.

"Oh, Pete," his wife lamented beside him.

"I ain't never seen three snake-eyes in a row! I ain't never!" Pete cried out, red in the face and shaking his fists in the air.

"We're out of money, Pete," the woman bleated sheepishly.

"Just one more roll—I know my luck's changing! It's coming around the corner!" Pete insisted, reaching for the dice in the dealer's fist.

Jubilant whoops erupted from the young crowd at the opposite side of the hall, causing purple-shirted Pete to tremble with rage.

"I said one more roll, damn it!" he demanded of the dealer.

"What would you like to wager?" the mustachioed dealer humored him, depositing the last of Pete's lost money into a pouch at his side.

"Give me another roll; I just paid your salary for the year!" Pete implored the dealer.

"Unfortunately, sir, we only accept cash wagers," the dealer declined.

Pete leaned closer to the dealer and asked in a hushed voice, almost inaudibly: "Can I wager Timmy?"

"Pete!" his wife exclaimed, aghast. "For the third time, you cannot wager our son in a game of dice!"

"Don't listen to her!" Pete urged the dealer.

"Unfortunately, sir, we only accept cash wagers," repeated the dealer, nodding to the bouncer. The big doorman waddled over, footsteps crashing mightily on the mat.

"Time for you to go get some sunlight, Pete. We look forward to your next visit."

Pete straightened his shirt, bristling with indignation. "This place is a den of thieves! Criminals! Gangsters!" the gambler announced to the room.

A few visitors looked up from their games to watch the spectacle, but all the regulars played on without pause.

"You'll never see me in this shoddy establishment again!" Pete vowed as he stomped off toward the door. "Come on, Emma!"

"Oh, Pete," sighed his wife, trailing in his footsteps. "Maybe your sister can lend us a bit of money for supper..."

Drake clapped a hand on Talia's shoulder. "Looks like a spot just opened up," he said brightly.

They sat in front of the suited man with the carefully waxed mustache, who nodded to them upon their arrival. "Good afternoon, sir. Good day, madam. Will you be playing together or separately?"

"Together," Drake pulled ten copper kroner out of his pouch.

"Very good, sir," the man acknowledged, twiddling his mustache. He produced a cup containing two dice, placed the ten kroner bet on one side of a box, and matched the sum with another ten on the other side of the divider. "I assume you are familiar with the game of Sevens?"

"I am," Drake took the cup. "But why don't you explain it for her?"

"Very good, sir." After clearing his throat, the man turned his neutral gaze to Talia and explained: "Sevens is a simple game played with two dice. The shooter—he or she who throws the dice—uses this cup to roll two dice into this bowl," he said, tapping the flat-bottomed wooden bowl on the ground in front of him. "Before the shooter rolls, all bettors will call *high* or *low*. If you call *high* and the sum of the two dice is greater than seven, you win. If you call *high* and the sum is seven or below, you lose—and vice versa. If you roll two ones or two sixes, the wager is doubled—so, if you are correct in direction, you win twice as much, and if you are incorrect, you lose twice as much."

"I'm no math genius, but it sounds like you're pissing away your money more often than you're making it back," Talia remarked to Drake.

"But in this game of luck and skill, surely the best will find riches?" mused the dealer, twiddling his waxed mustache with greater intensity.

"Let's see it," Talia motioned to Drake, unconvinced.

"High or low?" prompted the dealer.

"High," Drake answered, rattling the dice in the cup. He upended the dice into the bowl:

Two-five.

"Unlucky, sir. Would you like to wager again? You may also *double or nothing* your loss."

"Double or nothing," Drake declared with conviction.

After extracting his ten kroner, the dealer rotated the box for Drake to fill its empty side. Drake fished another ten copper pieces from his pouch and placed the bet in the box.

"High or low?" asked the dealer.

"High!" persisted Drake, reloading the cup. He vigorously shook the vessel, then dumped the dice into the bowl.

Three-Three.

"Damn!" Drake growled, slapping a hand to his face as the dealer drained his funds from the box. "I was going to say low, too."

"Drake?" said Talia.

"Yeah?"

"This game kind of sucks."

"It's... fun when you win," Drake sighed, down twenty copper kroner. "You try one."

"This is stupid," insisted Talia, fishing in his pouch for coin. She drew a silver piece.

"One silver, high," she said, tossing it into the box and taking the dice.

"That's a confident first bet," Drake sighed. He reflected that the heavy bag of copper kroner he had acquired wasn't actually worth all that much; after Talia lost the silver piece, he'd be down an equivalent of forty copper on the afternoon—before accounting for the chicken skewers.

Talia rattled the dice and dumped them into the bowl.

Six-six.

"Congratulations, madam! You're a natural," praised the dealer. "Would you like to double or nothing?"

"Now, Talia—" Drake leaned forward to disclose his learned strategy. "Keep in mind there's no real advantage to taking the double or nothing when you're up. You're basically just betting three silver as a new bet. I'd take the money and make another one-silver bet, so you don't risk it all."

"You had your chance to play," Talia dismissed, nodding at the dealer. "Double or nothing, low," she ventured, collecting the dice.

"I don't think that's a good idea," Drake cautioned as she rolled.

One-one.

"Oh, madam—congratulations! With your great luck, you should try the lottery next door," the dealer squealed with forced delight, handing Talia nine silver kroner.

Talia raised knowing eyebrows at Drake yet managed to restrain herself from voicing any further taunts.

"All right," Drake grumbled as he fished forty copper coins from his pouch, severely depleting the mass of his purse. "Forty copper, low."

"You have nothing to prove," Talia assured him smartly.

"Quiet," muttered Drake, picking up the dice.

The dealer efficiently placed two silver on the opposite side of the betting box.

Drake shot the dice into the bowl, encouraging luck with a shout of: "Come on!"

Six-six.

"Oh—so sorry, sir. That will be an additional forty copper," the dealer informed him with manufactured regret.

Drake lowered his head darkly. "These dice are rigged," he mumbled in indignation. Pete might have been onto something.

"You can borrow some of mine, but we're done playing this game," Talia chastised him before settling the balance owed.

"Thank you, madam," the dealer nodded with a twinkle in his eye and a shine on his glistening mustache. "I hope to see you return soon!"

"Come on," Talia helped an inconsolable Drake to his feet.

"What a stupid game," Drake bristled.

"I want to check out the tarot cards," said Talia.

"There's another game we could play—Elements," Drake suggested, pointing to the card tables.

"I think you've had enough gambling for today," Talia passed him half of her remaining winnings to put in his purse.

Drake sighed dejectedly. "You may be right," he accepted, pocketing the four silver.

The fortune teller locked eyes with them long before they approached, staring uncomfortably from beneath her hat of assorted feathers. "I knew you would come today," she claimed aloofly as Talia took the seat opposite her. Drake occupied the adjacent seat off to the side of the table, folding his arms as the seer clumsily shuffled her deck of cards.

"How much to read my fortune?" asked Talia.

"For ten copper, I will peel back the veil of mystery that shrouds your future," whispered the seer, staring vacuously into the space in front of her.

"I, too, see a vision," mumbled Drake peering into the kitschy crystal ball. "You will waste ten kroner on a con artist."

"Don't mind Drake," Talia reassured the seer. "I'm sure he wouldn't have lost eighty kroner at the mats if he had visited you first."

"The mats," scoffed Drake, amazed at the hubris to begin nicknaming parts of the gaming house after only two rolls of the dice.

"Yes!" agreed the seer, moving her hands oddly in front of her nose. "I foresaw his financial misfortune in the tea leaves this morning."

Drake groaned in disbelief.

"He'll take a fortune reading too," Talia decided, sliding a silver kroner to the woman.

"Would you like a tarot reading, or would you prefer I peer into the flames of the crystal ball?" asked the seer, eagerly accepting the payment.

"Ball," Drake rolled his eyes at the eccentric charade.

"I'll take the tarot cards," Talia said with more abiding excitement.

"First—Drake" the seer said his name slowly and shakily, as if the fact that she caught his name in conversation just moments ago should impress him.

Talia raised her eyebrows at him in anticipation, as if to emphasize how impressive the mystic before them was.

The fortune-teller swirled her hands around the crystal ball, and the flame flickered slightly inside. "I see... a dark past... and a darker future. You are one who does not believe in the mystic arts of scrying but will one day become a believer of seers. You are not from this place. I see... blood. Lots of blood—on your shirt," she said, suddenly pointing at a faded stain on Drake's chest, "but, also, on your hands... Maybe some not on your hands..."

"Okay," frowned Drake, unimpressed. "Anything else?"

"I see... love! But not love—tragedy. Love like the flame in this crystal ball—burning brightly, but destined to burn out, never to be reignited. I see a struggle for your life—against beasts, men, and powers beyond. I see Deus, and he does not look happy... Finally, I see fire..." the seer trailed off mysteriously.

"I hope you don't see me leaving a tip," Drake snorted scornfully.

"I do not," the woman cackled to herself. "Now, girl," she shuffled the tarot cards, staring intently at Talia.

The woman flipped over six cards—the ace of swords, the two of winds, the two of stone, the jack of hearts, the eleven of swords, and the four of flames. She started moving the cards around the table. "Oh, no!" she gasped in horror, rearranging the cards until they had all returned to their original positions.

"What do you see?" asked Talia, leaning across the table.

"This is a very grave fortune, young lady. A grave fortune, indeed," she lamented, pointing to the first card. "The ace of swords is the executioner. You will witness an execution in the near future—whether stoning, hanging, or guillotine, the execution will be seared into your memory for the rest of your life. You will have many questions, about justice and innocence and goodness... but you will have no answers."

"Given that executions are a cornerstone of Tallawyn's justice system, I'd call that a safe hedge," Drake commented.

"The two of winds is the card of the wanderer—you will never find a home, and you shall always be on the move. Property ownership is not in your future."

"Probably right about that one," Talia accepted with a considerate nod.

"But this is where it gets interesting—the two of stone—the rock. You will find your home and build a deep, unbreakable relationship with someone who brings you joy in this life... be it family or friend... You will support each other like rocks, unyielding and without compromise, for better and for worse."

"Well now, sounds like you have no home and you've got a home—all the bases are covered," Drake mused.

The seer carried on. "Next, the jack of hearts—juvenile love—you will find a boy you might have loved, but it is not to be. Your romance will be short-lived, and your heartbreak great. This love will never be rekindled."

"Bummer," Talia snapped her fingers.

"The eleven of swords—the massacre. You will stand at the center of untold death and destruction... and there will be blood—so much blood. That blood may even be on your hands!" gasped the seer, eyeing Talia as if she had committed murder in front of her.

"That's... dark..." managed Talia unsmilingly, apparently having much less fun with the fortune teller now.

"Last, the four of flames—the card of the burning grave. I foresee your untimely death—in a hot, fiery place. Fire... Fire! Fire..." the woman frowned at Drake suspiciously. "This is your future, girl. I wish I could change it."

"Can't you just shuffle the deck and give her six new cards?" Drake asked incredulously.

"I wish I could... but that is not the way of the seer," the feathered woman lamented helplessly.

"All right, well that's ten minutes of my life I'll never get back. Ready to go, Talia?" Drake stood from the table.

"Yeah, sure," Talia agreed shakily.

They left the gaming hall and returned to the street outside, heading toward the inns near the front gate.

"What if it's true?" asked Talia, her voice breaking with concern.

"If her fortune telling was worth a damn, she wouldn't be flipping cards for ten copper apiece in the back of some third-rate gambler's den. Forget about it," Drake dismissed.

They continued down the main road, stopping before a large crowd gathered at the drugstore stage. The horns and drums no longer played. Drake peered over the masses to see a black-hooded man with an ax standing next to the long arm of the gallows. A dark-haired man stood on the block, center-stage, with a noose coiled around his neck.

"Drake?" Talia squeaked, standing on her toes to see the stage.

"It's nothing, Talia. Towns like this have an execution every week. It's just some criminal who did something wrong and got caught."

An unapologetic announcer took to the stage and unfurled a scroll containing the list of charges brought against the wriggling, bug-eyed man on the box. "Declan Mulligan: you are charged with the crimes of arson, burning crops of the state, three counts of murder, one count of disfiguring the dead, one count of perjury, and resisting arrest. For your crimes, you have been sentenced to hang from the neck until dead. Do you have any final words before we send you to Deus for judgement?"

The accused's brow wrinkled in sorrow, sweat glistening from his red face as he squealed like a swine at the butcher's table. "Please—I didn't do it!" the man gulped, shouting above the clamor of the crowd. "I was with my mistress last night—that's why I lied to the investigators! I don't know anything about no arson!" sobbed the man.

"I suppose you'd say the farmstead burned itself? We will hear no more of your lies, Declan. Say your final prayers."

"Farmstead?" Talia questioned Drake. "Drake, I think that was…" Talia stopped short of confessing to arson with a crowd of witnesses gathered around them. "That man's innocent, isn't he?"

Drake observed the stranger onstage with hard eyes, knowing the man had been charged with another's crimes. "There are no innocent men—just criminals and the wicked who haven't been caught."

"Deus have mercy on your soul," prayed the lawman, a bitter tone spoiling hopeful words.

The executioner kicked the box out from under the accused, leaving him flailing in the air, suspended by his neck. As the color drained from the man's face, the executioner swung an ax into his midriff, expelling his innards onto the stage to the collective cheers and groans of disgust from the crowd.

Talia's eyes remained glued to the stage, her mouth agape in horror. "Drake! We should have…"

"There was nothing for us to do," Drake stopped. "His crimes are his own. He was punished accordingly. They wouldn't condemn someone to death without hard proof he was guilty," he lied knowingly.

Talia let him guide her through the crowd, but her eyes lingered on the gory spectacle. "This is like the execution the seer was telling us about."

"I told you, executions happen all the time around here. You were bound to see one sooner or later," he deflected uncomfortably.

Talia tore her eyes from the stage to look at Drake. "Are we going to end up on that stage one day?"

"Of course not," he answered sharply, looking back at Talia. "I can promise that we'll never wind up like that—we're not those kinds of people."

Drake turned his eyes to the path ahead and pushed his way through the enthralled audience. He wasn't sure how Talia took his words, but he knew he was right—he would never let them be captured and dragged onto a stage for mindless, half-drunk revelers to watch their execution.

VI. Checkpoint

Drake

Not that I'm asking..."

Talia paused to make sure he had registered her preface. She had been quite patient as they marched down the unending road. "But if I were asking, I might ask: how long until we're there?"

Drake grunted in a mixed expression of a scoff and a laugh. "I don't know. Not like I've been here before either."

It was hot in the Haiglands.

Upon a ridge they had traversed shortly after leaving Dunloy, Drake spotted the famous red rocks of the Badlands. Eschewing the westward path through miles of hostile terrain to Fort Eerie, they followed the winding road south to Midpoint, passing vast beds of dry shortgrass instead. Still, whether an objective precursor to the scorching summers in the Badlands or just a shade of contrast with the cold of Nordos, the air was already much hotter than he liked.

"Okay," said Talia, pressing the subject. "But if you had to guess, how far would you say we are from Midpoint?"

"I don't know," repeated Drake. "We passed a sign yesterday that said it was two hundred eighty-three miles away. We've probably walked about forty since then. Maybe another six, seven days? At some point, we still need to head west through the Badlands to reach the Scar."

Talia sighed. "I guess I shouldn't have asked."

"Got somewhere to be all of a sudden?" challenged Drake.

"No," Talia drew out the word in aggravation. "I've got nowhere to be."

He looked sidelong at his coffee-eyed companion. "Have you thought about what you want to do when this is all over?"

"What do you mean?" she tilted her head with a puzzled expression.

"After we get to the Cradle and settle up with Avalon—do you know where you want to go, what you want to do?" Drake rephrased.

Talia puffed out her cheeks, exhaling a long, pensive breath as she studied the thin clouds for inspiration. "Is it okay to say I haven't thought that far ahead?" They continued in silence while Talia mulled over the future in her mind. "I guess it doesn't really matter, as long as we're together. Right?"

We.

Of course, part of Drake had expected life to return to normal after he took vengeance for Avalon's obscure crimes and reached his journey's end— although he still did not know what *normal* was. Whatever the past held, life had changed for him. Talia was irrevocably part of his world now. He could not imagine a life without her. He was grateful that she considered him part of her future world as well.

"Sure," he said simply, burying the swell of sentiment.

A pair of blurry strangers appeared farther on up the road, heading their way. From afar, Drake could see both wore swords at their waists, along with matching sets of baggy beige pants and sturdy brown boots. The taller, shaggy-haired one wore a leather cuirass that allowed him to show off his bulky arms. The smaller, hairless one wore an unremarkable brown tunic. Dust and faded sunburns mocked their faces. Evidence that the road was their home.

Drake fluidly crossed in front of Talia, positioning himself on the inside of the path with her on the outside. The approaching strangers mirrored the movement. As they neared each other, he stared straight ahead, looking past the taller man's shoulder. The stranger did the same, but in his peripheral vision, Drake caught the younger boy beside him staring.

Drake took two strides past the man when both halted their footsteps.

"You there," addressed the man in an authoritative tone. Drake saw from the corner of his eye that the stranger had not turned to speak to him. Both Drake and the blond man beside him stood with one hand on the hilt of their sword. "Are you travelling from Dunloy?"

"Aye," Drake affirmed curtly.

"Did you encounter a man named Derek O'Conor?" asked the man.

"Never heard of him," Drake returned flatly, concluding their business.

"Thanks," nodded the man shortly. The footfall resumed, and he and the teenage boy continued their way north.

Drake and Talia continued south without sparing them a second look.

After the pair had disappeared far behind them, Talia stared over her shoulder at the known horizon. "Wonder what they're after."

"I'm guessing they're bounty hunters," provided Drake. The shorter one looked too young to be an experienced hunter, but he guessed the older brother was making efforts to teach him.

"Bounty hunters?" repeated Talia.

"Yeah. They basically hunt people for money," clarified Drake.

"How's that allowed?"

"Well, usually it's the governor or king or whoever issuing the bounty. Some criminal did something bad to piss them off, and the Tallawyns of the world are willing to pay people to bring those criminals in. Dead or alive."

"Can't they just send soldiers or police after them?"

"I guess the fugitives don't typically stay inside their towns, so it's hard for governors to track them down. Plus, if they're really dangerous, it probably saves a lot of hassle to send a bunch of bounty hunters after them and only pay whoever gets the job done," reasoned Drake.

"In other words, better a bunch of amateurs kill themselves chasing dangerous criminals than risk the lives of actual soldiers?" paraphrased Talia.

"Some are pretty much professionals. But... yeah. You get the idea."

"That's dark," deemed Talia.

"I wouldn't dwell on it too much," advised Drake. "A lot of things in this world are dark if you look too close."

Talia blew air out of her mouth in astonishment. "Crazy. You said usually it's the governor or king, right? Who else writes up bounties?"

Drake nodded. "It's big money down in Arillia since the place is damn near lawless. You get rich businessmen from Deuzos or Tallamar—or wherever, really—who open contracts worth more than any from the government. Might be a business interest or just a grudge to settle, but I'd wager that most murders you hear about are connected to black-market bounty hunters."

"And that doesn't scare you?" Talia asked in disbelief. "Just a bit?"

"If it makes you feel any better, chances are the Tallawyns already put out a bounty on us after Lyon. Hasn't stopped us yet, has it?"

"You're really bad at this whole *reassurance* thing, you know that?"

Drake grunted in place of an answer.

As they walked farther south, more and more dirt-path tributaries fed travelers into the main road. They passed traders, naturists, bounty hunters, ramblers, and artists on their walks. Drake noticed a small squad of trainees by the riverbank, likely sons of noble families enrolled in a private academy with hopes of becoming knights. The infantry in every lord's army was respected; the cavalry was revered. Almost as if the simple act of holding a weapon atop a horse made one a hero.

Their charm wasn't universal. Drake had always viewed the mounted knights as stuffy and arrogant. Special operatives, on the other hand—Godwin's King's Rangers or the shadowy guild known as Tallawyn's Crimson Hand—were the well-rounded killers he held innate respect for.

"I used to be good at drawing, you know," Talia commented as they passed a lanky painter hunched over an easel on the grass.

"Yeah?" humored Drake.

"I was never great at drawing people, but I liked to draw landscapes and scenery," she expanded.

"None of that abstract stuff?"

"Nah. I always thought that was a load of crap. I mean, why does an orange circle have to represent *the togetherness of humanity*? Looks like a circle to me," Talia ranted pointedly.

"You should draw me something sometime," encouraged Drake.

"Sure," agreed Talia. "I guess once all this is over and we have time..."

"We'll buy you some art stuff when we get to Midpoint. I'm sure you'd have time while I'm putting dinner together at night," proposed Drake.

"That'd be fun. Thanks," she smiled, surprised by his thoughtfulness.

Drake spotted a fork in the road up ahead, but his attention was immediately gripped by the unruly cluster of people assembled a little down the path on the right.

"What's going on?" inquired Talia.

Drake didn't like mixing in with big crowds. Too often, large groups turned into mobs or riots—and whoever was on the other side of that crowd was typically motivated to quell the uprising with speed and prejudice.

He read the wooden signs nailed to a post on the left of the forking road. Two planks pointed straight ahead, reading:

Tyranos: 102mi, S
Frontier: 172mi, SW

One sign pointed past the gathering mass of uproarious travelers:

Midpoint: 148mi, W

"That doesn't look good," Drake said in a low voice. He overheard the group of three traders grumbling beneath the signposts.

"It's absolutely outrageous!" complained one.

"Who do these Tallawyns think they are, anyway?" cried out another.

"Drake?" Talia asked, seeking an explanation.

"Let's see what all this excitement's about," he said calmly, disguising the blending apprehension and frustration rising within him.

They approached the assembly on the westward road to Midpoint, stopping at the back of the crowd of thirty or forty people.

"Please disperse in a calm and orderly fashion!" a voice shouted from the front of the group.

Drake peered over the assembly and saw a blockade guarded by eight soldiers—junior men, likely stationed symbolically or to provide information. Not a force intended to stop determined travelers.

"I'll take my chances! Let us through!" yelled a voice from the front of the mob.

Some of the crowd drifted back to the highway as newcomers from the road joined Drake at the back.

"What's going on?" Drake asked a broad, balding man in front of him.

"Road to Deuzos is closed," the man grumbled in reply. "I don't see how they can do this all of a sudden—I've got a big shipment coming in from Blackrock I'm supposed to pick up from the Grotto. My customers are going to be furious!"

"What are you hiding?" demanded a voice hidden in the crowd.

"People," addressed one of the soldiers in a placating tone. "I will say again—Midpoint is closed for your safety and for the safety of Tallamar. Due to recent conflict on the western border, we have closed all travel to Deuzos. It is not safe for you to continue west at this time."

"I've got family in Deuzos—I'm not worried about Godwin's soldiers!" shouted a fiery woman near the front. The mob echoed her sentiment.

"What if we just go around you?" threatened a haughty man.

"Our highway checkpoint has been established here for your benefit only," explained the soldier, reverting to his scripted instructions. "In addition to the dangerous skirmishes on the border near Dun Kilmough, the pass from Midpoint through the Scar has been blocked by earthquake debris. There is no land-based passage to Deuzos at this time, particularly through Midpoint. You can pass us, but you would just be walking two hundred miles to be told the same by our garrison at Midpoint."

"What about Arillia?" challenged the balding man in front of Drake.

Drake watched two soldiers exchange a look of uncertainty between themselves. "As always, Freecity, Arillia remains open," answered one.

A second soldier took a slightly different tone: "You may still leave to Freecity, Arillia, but know you risk becoming stranded. The Frontier is on equally high alert and heightened screening is in place for all travelers. Additionally, Fort Banning is expected to increase security measures—if you go to Arillia, you do so with the possibility of being denied reentry to either Tallamar or Deuzos indefinitely."

The revelation sent a ripple of distressed murmurs through the crowd.

"Stuck in Arillia for Deus knows how long? That's even worse for business!" the man in front of Drake scoffed, turning to make his way back to the road.

"We thank you for your understanding!" cheerfully added a younger-looking guard, earning a sigh from one of his comrades.

"Well?" Talia looked to Drake for their newly revised plan.

Drake perceived that she knew their next and only option to continue forward but had allowed him to make the final decision. The words disagreed with his tongue, but it was the right call. He failed to swallow the contempt in his answer. "I guess we're going to Arillia."

VII. Curing The Blood Plague

Allen Lee

Miraculous.

His left knee bent and unbent as he tensed his quadriceps. It was a strange sensation and would take time to get used to, but the metallic upgrade was certainly preferable to his wooden prosthetic. He felt more like a cyborg and less like a pirate.

"You can remove the pin here to unscrew your leg at night; just clip it back when you want to reattach it," instructed Virgil, rising from his knee.

"I can't thank you enough, Virgil. Really," Allen bowed gratefully.

Virgil waved a dismissive hand. "You're part of our El Arian family now, Allen. I want your life here to be as enjoyable as possible. Have you been making use of our modest library?"

"Certainly. I sometimes feel I'm reading more than I'm contributing," Allen admitted guiltily.

"As it should be," approved Virgil. "One cannot contribute to the collective knowledge without first studying what has been written. I myself often look to my pupils for inspiration—even for subjects as simple as apples and horses," smiled the philosopher, reminding Allen how quickly he had mastered a new language from a digital dictionary.

"You'll be glad to hear that Meghana's research is going well."

"Oh?" invited Virgil.

"We're waiting on the frog toxin to come in to test another hypothesis, but she's already discovered how to reliably grow Penicillium mold. We believe that this could cure the subjects afflicted by the blood plague."

"Wonderful. I'll prepare fermenters to enable your production. We'll have Meghana board a ship to Tidestone tomorrow."

"You... already knew how to cure the blood plague?" Allen asked, stupefied.

"I read about your discovery of antibiotics and agree they should work against bacterial plagues—I just haven't had the time to write it down and begin production." Virgil explained.

"Isn't the plague extremely deadly?"

Virgil smiled patiently. "We cannot lambast ourselves for the good we have not done—or could not do as swiftly as we would have liked. The plague afflicting the Lowlands is grave, indeed, but there are a great many injustices to confront in our world. Death and pain are unfortunate prerequisites of our human condition; when we focus our attention on one corner of the world, we must often forsake another. Parenthetically, philanthropically curing plagues is a poor revenue model for long-term ambitions. Resources are not free, and the sick rarely have means to reimburse us. Thus, we focus our efforts on what enables our sustained operation when we must, always striving to do the good we can."

Allen nodded slowly, though he continued to struggle with the clinical concept. Logically, he understood time and resources were not free—but it still felt wrong. It pained him to know they had a solution to the Lowlands' suffering but were unable to administer it.

"So, Meghana and I will be heading out tomorrow?"

"Just Meghana," clarified Virgil. "I have full confidence in her ability to conduct and catalog the cure on her own. Additionally, I anticipate crossing the Basket could be rather dangerous at present. I would prefer if you remained here, so that I am not risking the lives of two skilled disciples."

"If it's dangerous, I should go with her," Allen protested instinctively.

Another patient smile. "Allen, do you truly believe you would be an asset—rather than a liability—in your state? I will send an escort from Ayrabos to lend her protection, of course. I suspect their chances of survival would be higher if you chose to remain behind."

Allen leaned on his mechanical foot, then marched in place for a few steps. He had not yet mastered the awkward motion. Although undoubtedly better than the wooden limb he had begun to view as a permanent fixture, it was no replacement for flesh and bone. He would have an uncomfortable gait for a long time, and running would be a lifelong challenge.

Beyond his impaired mobility, Allen knew he didn't have it in him to raise a sword against another person. If Meghana was attacked, the Ayrabos guards would be her best line of defense—he would only get in the way.

"I'll let her know when I see her today," Allen offered reluctantly.

"I'll send a page to invite her to my study tonight. I'd like to thank her for the great work she's been leading and provide some guidance for her journey to the Lowlands. Please, do let her know you're both invited to today's midday gathering in the senate—I suspect it will be a contentious one, and I look forward to the arguments presented by both sides."

"I'll let her know. Thanks again for the leg, Virgil," Allen tapped his prosthetic as he walked with Virgil to the door.

"Enjoy the day, dear Allen," Virgil closed the door with a final nod, leaving Allen in the hall.

While most of the library was designed for function, fitting as many books into orderly shelves as possible, this corridor was inarguably extravagant. Beautiful murals and detailed paintings adorned the walls on either side, while a heavenly fresco spanned the ceiling. Beams of light entered through carefully planned slits in the western wall, illuminating the hall without directly exposing the artwork to harsh rays.

A lanky, black-clad page appeared suddenly behind him. "Shall I guide you to the ground floor?" the page offered, startling him.

"My goodness gracious," Allen mumbled, retreating a step from the uncomfortably close guide. "Yes, please. Just... don't sneak up on me like that."

The man led him to an oddly realistic painting of a squirrel sitting in a green armchair across from a grandfather clock wound one minute to midnight. The squirrel was enthralled by a black-covered book entitled *New markets in the age of production.* The page leaned into the wall next to the painting, which turned inward to reveal a concealed staircase.

Allen followed the page into the dark stairwell, illuminated only by the lanky guide's lantern. The man pulled a cord, and the section of wall containing the squirrel painting rotated back into place. After descending several flights of stairs, Allen emerged from the end of a bookshelf into the ground floor.

Abandoned by the page, Allen proceeded toward the exit. On his way, he paused, craning his neck to get a better view of a familiar face.

"Hamal!" called Allen, striding over to the hydrologist.

"Lee!" Chip returned, bookmarking his page with a finger. He turned his attention to his comrade. "Haven't seen you in a minute. How's it going?"

"It's going!" exclaimed Allen cheerfully. "And you?"

"Can't complain," shrugged Chip. "Well, I could, but who'd listen?"

Allen laughed at the hydrologist's banter. They hadn't spent a lot of time together and weren't particularly close, but Hamal was one of those people who could effortlessly get along with anybody.

Chip glanced over his shoulder to ensure no one was within earshot, then whispered: "I think Samson's been wanting to talk to you. We've been a little worried lately."

"Worried? About what?" Allen whispered back.

Chip neurotically peeked over his shoulder again, absentmindedly flicking the book cover with his free hand. "It started with Frank. You know how he got sick, and the doctor here said it was allergies to the local pollen?"

Allen nodded slowly, not fully up to speed on the diagnosis. He vaguely remembered hearing something along those lines several weeks ago but spent most of his time in the library. The soldiers outside had rarely crossed his mind, aside from his regular brooding on the portal's reconstruction.

"He passed away. Then, one by one, the same happened to the rest of Charlie. Except for Sam. Jones and Annie Chu are both laid up sick in bed now, too. I went to see her in the infirmary. She said she was doing better, but she didn't shipshape to me. You, me, Sam, Roy, and Ajax are the only healthy ones left. We still can't reach Echo, and if Jones dies..."

"Then we have nobody who can fly the helicopter," finished Allen.

Hamal leaned in closer. "Right. Do you get the feeling Virgil is trying to help us fix the portal, or...?"

"I think so," Allen answered faithfully. "It seems he has spent some time thinking about it. I know he's a busy man—lots of people need his help. I've been helping him on some work to cure a plague in Deuzos."

"I like to play the hero as much as anybody, Allen, but don't get distracted. I know you want to help these people, but our first priority—" Hamal hacked suddenly, then turned his head to finish the cough into his elbow.

Allen cringed as he felt wet droplets land on his cheek.

"Sorry," the hydrologist mumbled, pulling out his handkerchief and dabbing off Allen's face. "It's the stuffy air in here. All I was saying: our priority has to be helping our own people."

"I know—of course," Allen agreed despite himself, reflexively raising a hand to wipe his cheek. While he felt a humanitarian urge to aid all those he could, he acutely felt Alaina's absence. Every night he went to sleep, he felt the emptiness lying beside him. A piece of him was missing, stranded across space. His heart also ached for his daughter, Lyn. He would have given anything to rewind time to Pladaw—every day, home by five o'clock to his perfect family.

A world-shattering notion weighed deep in his stomach, lurking on the edge of his thoughts. Although he refused to confront his feelings directly, part of him knew the world he had left behind was vastly different from what it must now be. The death of his lifelong best friend, Charles, was sobering evidence that memories of the past could not endure against the precariousness of today. He had lost track of the days, but he knew he had been absent for well over a year. They had been faring poorly in the war, and Danny's odds of survival on the frontline weren't encouraging. Chances were the invasion of his homeland was long finished. If Alaina had somehow survived, she had likely accepted his death—and perhaps even moved on.

He regretted his last, incendiary phone call with his brother. He wished he had spent more time with Lyn, his baby girl, and although he could not regret his time at work, he would have spent fewer hours watching sports. If he had another chance, he'd have told Charles his suspenders were fashionable. Told his wife he loved her—even though he said it every day, and he was certain she knew, he would have told her again, and again, and again.

"Allen?" Chip interrupted his brooding. "Sam and I are worried that Virgil played us... that he's been killing us off slowly and has no intention of building the portal."

The thought made Allen light-headed. He unsuccessfully attempted to focus on his breathing, struggling to form words to express himself. "That doesn't make sense," he managed. "Virgil's been so good to us. He's feeding us and giving us a place to stay, and we don't have any other option to get back."

"Perhaps he has been good to you. I've seen him once since we arrived at El Aria—I get the feeling we're not anywhere close to being top of mind. Sam thinks we might need to take some form of escalated action."

Allen shook his head. "I'm sure this is all just a misunderstanding. I'll talk to Virgil and ask him to give us a progress update; I have to imagine this is a hard technology for any one man to construct—even him. Of course, he won't be able to do it overnight, but I know he has a good heart. Think about it— when your people's settlers first went west, they brought all sorts of diseases with them, deadly because their environment was different than the natives'. It's possible the local environment has uncommon viruses infecting our people."

Chip spread his hands, unconvinced. "Just thought you should know our thinking. Perhaps it is just a misunderstanding—another stroke of bad luck. All I know is that he'd have to have a heart of gold not to hold a grudge after being our prisoner for years."

"I'm late for lunch, but I'm sure everything will work out. Things can only go up from here."

"Be seeing you, Allen," Chip bid in farewell, reopening his book.

Allen exited the library and immediately spotted the radiant smile of his assigned mentor. Her green eyes reached him from across the grassy field, and she raised a hand in greeting. Her white robes flowed gracefully with her hair in the hilltop breeze.

Allen crossed over to her, uncontrollably mirroring her warm smile.

"You seem in a good mood," Meghana remarked.

Allen helplessly felt his grin widen. "Got a new leg today."

"Oh yeah?" she tapped his left leg. "Sturdy stuff. It's nice."

"Virgil thinks I can eventually start running on it. He also said we're invited to his lecture at noon," Allen passed along informatively.

"That's great," Meghana beamed. "We'll have to have a quick lunch, then. I figured we could eat overlooking the city?"

"That's a great idea," Allen approved. He pointed to the basket on her arm. "What've you got there?"

"Just sandwiches," she answered, walking toward the city. "I had one of the pages prepare them for us, along with a flask of wine."

"Works for me," Allen's stomach rumbled. Wine with lunch was a strange tradition Meghana had introduced him to, but he had grown to enjoy it. He initially feared that Virgil would not approve, but it was unconcernedly written off as 'sometimes, people like to add a shine to their day'.

They sat on a gentle slope overlooking El Aria. Allen easily spotted the soaring towers below that marked the homes of Ayrabos' wealthiest citizens. Somewhere down there, Sheikh Dohari was overseeing his vibrant metropolis. Allen hoped to one day visit the city and explore its local culture and cuisine.

"Oh—Virgil also mentioned he plans to send you on a boat to the Lowlands tomorrow."

"Tomorrow? But I haven't finished producing the cures, and we're still waiting on the frog toxin."

"He's arranging fermenters to help you produce medicine on the ship."

Meghana shot him a suspicious look. "And how did he know so much about the progress of my work?"

"I just told him you were doing a great job and had it pretty much solved. He came up with the fermenters idea and said I should stay back while you do fieldwork. He's sending a page later to bring you by his office to chat."

Meghana's expression softened a little. "You told him I was doing well? You didn't describe our work as your experiment?"

"Of course not!" Allen dismissed emphatically. "You're the one who's been leading this amazing work; I've just been assisting. You're going to cure the blood plague—the credit's all yours."

"And Virgil seemed happy?" she asked hopefully.

"Yeah—he said you're exceptionally capable and he looks forward to your finished work. I don't think I've done enough to earn a spot in fieldwork, but hopefully, I'll start a project of my own soon and can work my way up."

Her gentle smile returned. "Sorry if I got a little defensive—it's just, it can be hard being one of the few women here, you know?"

"Say more?" he encouraged, regarding her intently as he took another bite of the sandwich.

"Well, for example: on my last study, I was working alongside Felix Demasus—as equals. I spent months developing a salve for cut wounds that stopped infections, while Felix prioritized another project, creating a more durable, lighter alloy for swords. In hindsight, I should have erased his name from our report and handed it in immediately. Instead, he suggested we coauthor each other's works to increase both of our total publications. I agreed.

"I lent him my completed dissertation to review so that he would be able to answer any of Virgil's questions, since we would have defended the manuscript together. In exchange, he lent me his. Only after I finished reading his work, I saw Virgil's signature on the inside of the back cover—he had already presented his findings on the alloy and gotten Virgil's approval. When I confronted him about it the next day, he returned my dissertation to me, and guess what I see?"

"Oh no," Allen predicted empathetically.

"Not only is Felix's name on the cover of the manuscript instead of mine, but I turn to the last page and see Virgil's signoff. He stole ten months of my best work and passed it off as his own! On top of that, he starts strutting around, showing off his two newly acclaimed publications; meanwhile, people are staring at me like I've done nothing but sit on my hands for the past year—and when I try to tell people it was my work, they think *I'm* trying to take credit for *his* work!" Meghana clenched her fists tightly, battling to keep tears out of her eyes as her voice cracked.

"That's awful! How can he get away with that? Did you talk to Virgil?"

"Virgil's impossible to get an appointment with. I talked to him about it a month later and he didn't even care—he said, 'It doesn't matter whose name is on a book, so long as we've expanded the sum of our collective knowledge'... but it matters to me! I worked so damn hard on that book" she explained with a pained, pleading look in her bright eyes.

"I'm so sorry that happened to you. It just isn't right," commiserated Allen, unsure what else he could say. He couldn't imagine working so hard on something only for someone else to swoop in and steal his credit. This Felix character was clearly a despicable man with no shame.

"It's obviously not your fault," sighed Meghana. "I just really hope karma keeps him on her list."

"What goes around comes around," promised Allen supportively. "I know it doesn't make up for Felix, but know that Virgil sees you're doing great work on the blood plague cure. This study is all you—you don't even need to put my name in the footnotes."

She searched his eyes for any signs of derision or sarcasm. She smiled when she realized he was being goofily sincere. "Of course I'll put your name in the footnotes. Sharing success with others doesn't diminish my own—just don't be surprised if I don't lend you my finished draft overnight."

"I can live with that," Allen accepted warmly.

"You're a good listener, you know that?" Meghana stroked his neck.

"Oh. Thank you," Allen mumbled awkwardly.

She leaned in and pressed her lips against his. Allen instinctively tensed up and recoiled, dropping his half-eaten sandwich all over himself.

"Sorry—" Meghana apologized quickly, covering her mouth in shock. "That was stupid of me—I'm sorry. I... ugh," she grimaced.

"It's okay, sorry," Allen joined in the apologies. "You just surprised me is all. I'm sorry. You're a beautiful woman, but I can't," he gestured to the ring on his left hand. "It's not you; it's me."

"I'm so stupid," Meghana buried her head in her hands and groaned.

"Sorry! Really, if I wasn't married—I mean, you're smart, and beautiful, and kind," he bumbled in assurance, feeling heat rising to his cheeks.

"The good ones are always taken," lamented Meghana, reaching for the flask of wine. She swallowed a bitter sip. "What's her name?"

"Alaina," Her name felt heavy on his tongue. He wondered if she had cosmically sensed his betrayal. He guiltily hoped she would never have to find out. He certainly hadn't intended to kiss his mentor.

"Kids?" asked Meghana.

"One: a beautiful baby girl. Her name is Lyn."

"Do you miss them?"

"Of course," he laughed at the absurdity of the question, then said more somberly: "Every day. They're always on my mind, but I'm worried. I'm worried that I'll never get to see them again."

"If The Library's the only thing stopping you from seeing them, you could always leave. You probably won't be invited to return, but I imagine seeing your family might be worth it."

"I think The Library is my only hope of seeing them again," amended Allen. "They're far, far away. Virgil is the only one who can help me go the distance."

"Like, Taoxos far?"

"Farther. Much farther."

Meghana frowned. "Well, I hope you get to see them again one day. Alaina's lucky to have you."

"You know... I've been thinking about that a lot lately. I'm not doing much for her right now—if she would have chosen another man, maybe she'd have someone who could protect her."

"Again—you should leave The Library if your heart's somewhere else! Go be with her if you feel she needs your protection."

"It's not that simple... and I'm also not the best at protecting. I would do anything for her, but I'm just not a tough guy."

"Women don't always need a tough guy. Most women do want one who sticks around, though," advised Meghana.

"There was one time we went out for food, Alaina and I. This was less than a year after we got married. We were walking a few blocks back to our apartment, when this guy comes out of an alley and pushes me to the ground. He starts kicking me... and I just lie there. Curled up in a ball. Then he hits Alaina and knocks her to the ground. Threatens us with a knife and takes our money and her jewelry, and then he's gone. I'm battered and aching and probably bleeding, but I crawl over to Alaina to help her up."

Allen paused, seeing his wife's face in his thoughts. He reached out a hand through the air in front of him. "And I see her face, and she's got this big bruise under her eye. I couldn't help myself—I started crying. Then, she's trying to console me and tell me everything's okay, that we're okay... but all I could think was that I failed her. I wasn't man enough to protect her. I was useless."

Meghana stared at him with empathetic eyes. "That's not your fault, Allen. You were attacked and unarmed—the jerk that mugged you is to blame."

"We never really spoke of the incident after that night, but it's something I'll never forget. I can't forgive myself for being so weak, and yet it's not like I've gotten any stronger since. If it happened again today, nothing would be different."

"She loves you, Allen—and you clearly still love her. There's always going to be some stronger thug on the streets, but just because he can hurt others doesn't make him a good husband. Doesn't mean he can give love. You're a good man, Allen."

He forced a smile, unconvinced but appreciative of her kind words. "What about you—no kids, I take it?"

"Fortunately not," Meghana smiled softly. "I prefer my research to rearing little ankle-biters. I do have a little sister, though. She used to work here—I guess I can relate to what you said about failing to protect someone you love. She failed her apprenticeship and ruined an important experiment commissioned by the sheikh himself. Her shame must have been unbearable, seeing as she left The Library without even a parting word to me."

"That's sad to hear. Were you close?"

"Not necessarily best friends, but we were family. We were close enough that I feel I at least deserved a goodbye."

"Maybe she just needed a little time to herself? I'm sure she didn't disappear intentionally to hurt you."

"I know she didn't mean it to offend me. She's just always been like this, you know? A flighty little bird, living in her own world. I just want to know that she's okay."

"I'm sure she'll reach out to you when she's ready," assured Allen.

"Yeah. I guess you're right," Meghana took another swig from the flask, emptying the wine. "Well, that was a surprisingly heavy lunch. I think Virgil's lecture will be starting in the senate soon; shall we go?"

"Let's," agreed Allen.

VIII. Et Al

Allen Lee

The senate's interior was spectacular.

A concentric seating arrangement of increasingly elevated rings around the lowered senate floor ensured that all spectators had a clear view of the stage. Robed men and women stood in the stone walkways separating the long marble slabs of seating, exchanging ideas and speculating about the coming event.

"There isn't a doubt in my mind: Cato will wipe the floor with him," posited an older, balding scholar.

"Cato has been away for too long. Felix has won three in a row—last week's match wasn't even close," rebutted another.

"I dare say there are no losers—only winners, for having made the intellectual exchange and challenging our own assumptions," asserted a third.

The second laughed. "You would say that. You got your philosophical hiney handed to you by Felix last week."

"Sticks and stones," shrugged the third.

"I would postulate that Felix's words did, in fact, hurt you. At the very least, sticks and stones could never do the same to your reputation..." the balding scholar interjected.

"Perhaps words do hurt," the third smarted wistfully.

A hush rippled over the crowd. They took their seats as Virgil strode to the center of the room.

"Welcome, students—to the greatest arena known to mankind. A battleground where facts and rhetoric are our soldiers, and truth emerges as the battered victor," Virgil presented regally.

The audience clapped respectfully, demonstrating their enthusiasm and support without resorting to any manner of crass hollering.

"Today, we gather to grapple with a challenging question of justice and societal morality. Cato will present his case that, in the case of capital crimes, the death penalty is not only morally permissible, but ethically obligatory."

A short round of clapping ensued—whether in support of Cato or his thesis, Allen was unsure.

"As always, a debate must have two sides, each plausible to emerge victorious. Today, Felix will seek to persuade you that the death penalty is intrinsically morally impermissible."

Another round of applause followed for Felix.

Allen noticed that Meghana chose not to clap. He folded his hands across his chest, silently siding with her against the contender.

Virgil held up a hand, quieting the room. "Cato, Felix: please come to the senate floor. I trust you will conduct yourselves with the utmost decorum and acuity, but I will interject if I feel the debate drifts too far to sea. Cato, you may begin when ready."

To an excited chorus of applause, Virgil took a seat in the front row, opposite the entryway. A black-clad page dashed around the ring to present with him a cup of water.

Cato and a man Allen presumed to be Felix entered the senate. Cato scowled, commanding an air of gravity as he stormed into the room. His muscles rippled imposingly beneath his toga. Allen thought he'd be equally suited for a wrestling or gladiatorial match.

Felix smiled at the crowd, issuing short waves to his supporters. His blond, careless hair scored the first point against Cato's glinting scalp. Although smaller than his opponent in both height and mass, Felix looked at ease on the senate floor. Despite scores of eyeballs trained on him from around the room.

Allen admonished himself for admiring the man's confidence. Instead, he chose to view his demeanor as arrogance. Although he would likely have sided with Felix's position on the topic, he hoped that Cato would wipe the floor with him. Intellectually speaking.

Cato addressed the room. "The premise of my argument is simple, friends. Although I suspect we may not all agree that killing is wrong, I am

confident we would all concur that murdering innocent citizens is immoral. Take, for instance, a baby born to farmers. The child's destiny is simply to grow old tending crops and helping his neighbors. A wicked man comes to the farm, burns the crops, and kills the child and mother. If we can agree that this man's act is immoral, and we know he could be legally punished under capital crimes, then we agree on a prime candidate to consider for capital punishment. Will you concede this preface, Felix?"

"I accept that this is one caricature of a man who would normally be handed the death penalty," Felix allowed.

"Then I will proceed with my argument. First, there is the tenet of divine retribution—that all guilty people deserve to be punished proportionally to the severity of their crimes. That the sanctity of life should not be violated by another is a widely accepted principle within religion and society. If a man takes another's life, is his own not justly added to the scales?"

"Divinity belongs in churches, not the senate," quipped Felix. "Your argument buckles under its own weight. First, we must consider the soldiers— men who routinely kill in the name of civil society. Of course, if we considered our own society to be unjust, then we would be compelled to change. However, once we've established that we live in a just society, we gain the means to look outward and judge others. We would, perhaps, understand other ways of life while retaining the moral superiority of our own. Whether we would be compelled to intervene against their morally inferior execution of justice is a separate matter, but suppose they chose to attack us.

"Now, our soldiers kill and die in defense of our land and our morally superior society. We may understandably regard them as heroes, brave enough to sacrifice what we are unwilling to. However, the foreign combatants likely command a similar respect from their own societies, fighting under the auspices of justice. Could it not be said that both soldiers are murdering plausibly innocent people? Are we morally compelled to kill the surviving soldiers who return from war?"

"I do not recall the part of the allegory in which the farmer's boy was conscripted," Cato countered, earning quiet laughter from his support base.

"Then let us discuss the farmer's boy. His murderer is now morally condemnable because he acted to steal life from the boy; can we agree, Cato?"

"Continue," Cato invited.

"So, if the act of taking a life is condemnable, then certainly killing the murderer would be as well. When the felon is marched on stage to be hung, does the hangman not become a killer himself? Should we proceed to hang the hangman?"

Cato opened his mouth to object, but Felix raised a finger to indicate he had not yet finished his point. "Of course, I could argue that only acts are morally permissible or impermissible and that people, as the perpetrators of acts, are dynamically fluid enough to enact both good and evil into the world. Perhaps the murderer of your farmer's boy was forced to take the boy's life; perhaps, an even wickeder man had credibly threatened his family and coerced him to perform the murder—some who advance theories of care ethics would say the man's obligation is first to his own family's wellbeing. Let's say, then, for the rest of the killer's life, he would seek to contribute immeasurable good to the world—perhaps he would operate an orphanage, feed the hungry, and work diligently on the farmer's land to atone for his sins. To kill him now would be to leave society worse off—all the good he intended to do would go undone. So, Cato, tell me: is divine retribution justification for the death penalty, or simply an uglier vein of vengeance masquerading as moral?"

"Your argument is somehow even frailer than you, Felix," attacked Cato. "To kill a killer as a vigilante may invite further questions of vengeance, but we choose to govern ourselves under a collective societal agreement that manifests in laws. We create and obey rules."

"The necessity of rules seems to indicate a rather primitive evolution of moral reasoning," jabbed Felix.

"Precisely the kind required for your killer," retorted Cato. "Now, in this society where we have declared that none shall kill another, there must be punishment for disobeying our collective understanding. The execution you have described does not make the hangman a killer, because the execution is divine retribution. The hangman is merely an instrument of society or Deus himself; he does not become a killer, for the murderer on trial already placed his life on the scales of society when he broke the code. By killing the innocent child, he has killed himself—the weapon used in his suicide was therefore the judicial system of his society."

"Society is an interesting limb to trust your weight upon, Cato. I'm confident we can all agree that, whatever the philosophical premise of justice is or should be in society, the execution rarely meets the bar of righteousness. Given that our states are ruled by men, we cannot absolve men from their immoral roles in its execution under some guise of divine justice. In practice, I would further posit that the wealthy and powerful members of our society are granted inequitable power over the poor—even in the creation of laws, beyond their upholding.

"I suspect an upcoming argument of yours would be deterrence: you believe the death penalty, as a spine behind your rules, would prevent crimes. However, I know you have no factual evidence to support this. So your death penalty fails to deter crime and instead presents itself as a weapon for the state's elite to wield against the poor. Moreover, innocent people are trialed and executed out of prejudice and convenience. Say that the murderer was not found at the scene of the crime, rather, only the farmer. The local magistrate does not like the farmer, thus has him executed under the guise of justice to close the case. This is not a theoretical occurrence—this happens in our world, in our time. Therefore, capital punishment is a sloppy machination for the state to inequitably exert its *divine retribution* under the cloak of justice."

"Dear Felix, I believe you have misunderstood our topic discussion!" laughed Cato. "You seem to be arguing against either corruption in statehood or the propensity for man to seek out power for deplorable and inequitable doings. Our discussion is on the theory of capital punishment—the malign or moronic execution on the part of individuals has no place in our exploration of morality. And so, I believe you are running out of arguments. Perhaps you would argue that civilized society has no place for this cruel form of justice, but I could laugh such an emotional argument out of the senate. Certainly, any rule must have teeth to be effective in governing society—it is unethical to murder, and it is insensible to suggest murderers need not face punishment. Would you argue a lifetime in prison is more just? Folly. One of three things is true. The extended sentence is crueler than the crime itself, the loss of freedom does not equate to the value of a life, or you believe a system built upon the principles of *rehabilitation* has a function to serve in the afterlife. You may also object that capital punishment is a waste of resources, but like the matter of erroneously administered punishments, your argument relies on tactical execution rather than philosophy.

"And thus, after wanton outbursts and parading, we return to the sole *philosophical* tenet of your argument: that an innate respect for life ethically precludes society from killing human beings, regardless of their crimes. This, I'm afraid, is little more than a childish escape from your moral duty. To obey the societal contract that allows our civilized existence, we must uphold justice. Perhaps the murderer finds rehabilitation in their sentence—having forfeited their life, they have no further reason to carry on their evil ways and may repent ahead of their eternal judgement. Regardless, the undeniable advantage is this: the executed killer will never commit murder again. There is no chance for them to break out of prison, kill another inmate, or lend weight to threats made against survivors. Their injustice is concluded, and the balance of morality may continue in dignified society. I'll concede that the death penalty should not be celebrated as a spectacle, for there is no moral reason to view the loss of life as entertainment; however, I return to the core of my argument and assert: the guilty deserve to be punished in accordance with their crimes."

"I believe you have made your point, Cato," moderated Virgil. "Felix, would you care for the final word?"

Felix addressed the audience with a sweeping motion of his hand. "I believe I have articulated my points clearly. Cato insists we can only debate in an esoteric world of hypotheticals and refuses to engage me in a more realistic world, such as that in which we live. My conclusion is this: philosophy should serve to better our world through practical means; any philosophy that cannot be executed intact is little more than hot air."

"A well-defined position, Felix. You may both take your seats," invited Virgil, taking the floor. "Although some may undoubtedly leave this senate discussing whether Cato or Felix won the debate, I must remind you all that neither won—rather, learning was the victor. Both sides of the matter challenged and attempted to defend their reasoning, and I believe we are all wiser for that."

An appropriate surge of clapping supported Virgil's reaffirmation of their intellectual pursuit.

"Cato obliterated him. All I see left of Felix are the smoldering remains of his toga," Allen overheard the balding scholar whisper to his neighbors.

"What? You're crazy, Cornelius! He had to make up a theoretical world to get around Felix's argument," objected another.

"You may wonder why I chose a topic of policy for today's discussion," Virgil clasped his hands behind his back, waiting for the room to quiet.

"Because we may one day advise kings on this very consideration!"

"So that we may educate the world by our own school of philosophy!"

"Perhaps," Virgil nodded. His eyes roved the audience. "But consider this: perhaps the answer does not matter. As you conduct your own discourse on this topic, I hope you listen for underlying values. Beliefs and assumptions. In this, you may find richer conversation: what is death? How freely may we transact life, and does our answer change if we believe each life has meaning? Does death matter, or only life? Why?"

Virgil hung his head. He chuckled as something he said resonated with him. "I'll leave you two alms of advice," he held up two fingers. "First: never accept an argument without first considering the other side. Even if you remain convinced of your initial hypothesis, your defense will be stronger for having considered an opposing perspective. Second: always ask *why.* You cannot win an argument without first understanding the set of facts and considerations behind your position; similarly, and perhaps more importantly, you cannot win over hearts without understanding the emotional factors driving your adversary's position."

Virgil abruptly exited the senate, leaving his sagely advice hanging in the air behind him. After a respectful moment of contemplation, an exodus of philosophers followed in his path. Their lively discourse over the winner of the performance may have overshadowed the debate itself.

"It's invigorating to just stop and think about these things, isn't it?" Meghana said in Allen's ear.

"I can honestly say I've never seen anything like that," he agreed.

"This was my first one, too. Thanks for getting me invited." Meghana hung her head for a few steps. "I hope to be on the floor someday."

"Really?"

"Well, minus the whole 'fifty-people-staring-at-you' thing. It'd be awesome to embarrass Felix in front of everyone, though."

"What side were you on?"

"Obviously Cato's," she raised her eyebrows meaningfully. "But even beyond their discussion—it makes you think about the morality concerning life. If the farmer was a vigilante and came after the murderer, would he be ethically excused? Is his pain sufficient justification for his vengeance, or only enough to allow understanding?"

"Killing's always wrong," Allen shrugged uneasily. "I could never do it. Life is just too valuable."

Meghana chuckled to herself. "But why?"

XI. A Tenuous Alliance

Iko

*D*eath eats up the land like a hell-hearted stallion, but Iko holds the reins.

He wiped his bloody daggers on the slain soldier's cloak and returned the twin blades to their sheaths. His unused sword hung at his hip, a haunting relic from his nobler years as a captain in the north. Although necessary, the bloodshed enacted this day did not deserve the steel skin of such an honorable blade. The ignoble tools of an assassin were a more suitable fit.

At his will, a mass of swirling black shadows rose from under the three bodies that formerly guarded the eastern watchtower. They vanished through the darkness, one by one, on a course to join the others.

Prepared for his primary obligation of the day, he straightened his back and breathed in the musty air that clung to the stone.

Inhale.

Hold.

Exhale.

It was a matter of poise that he should not rush back to Avalon the second the task was done. A matter of dignity. Lackeys run from directive to directive, eager for the comfort of a command. Title or no title, his was noble blood. He was no servant; he was the right hand of a god-king. A finely tuned instrument of order and reorder. Soon he would return, calm and composed, ready to lead their shared machinations to reality. As soon as he had taken a moment to honor his peerless work. As soon as the winds fled his presence and the rocks recorded his name, witnesses that he engineered fate in this land.

Somewhere farther east, under the same watchful sun, a queen was unknowingly eating her last supper. Drinking her final sip of wine.

Ignorance is a pity.

With that grim acknowledgement, Iko submersed himself in a pool of shadows. The cold, ephemeral darkness whisked him away from the garrison, shepherding him to more familiar, bloodless stonework.

"Good. You have arrived."

The greeting was neither warm nor hostile but simply confirmatory. Avalon spoke as if the world's fate had already been written, coauthored by himself. Every event's unfolding was merely recitation of the script destiny had carefully composed—of course Iko arrived on time, just as he was instructed; Avalon had already declared it so.

"Will Hadronox be joining?" asked Iko.

"No need." Avalon's hard, golden eyes stared across the courtyard to the ostentatious, shimmering keep. "He is preoccupied, and I would prefer to keep a card unrevealed to our temporary allies."

"But Prism and I were requisite to your plans?" Iko clarified, glancing at the black-robed figure next to Avalon. Beneath the shadows of her hood, a faint purple and black haze rose from her eyes. No strings threaded her limbs, but she remained one of Hadronox's broken marionettes all the same. The light inside had been smothered—one among hundreds of dead men walking.

"Prism is my transportation; you are here to demonstrate that I lead an organization beyond myself," Avalon answered patiently. As always, he wore a neutral expression, his face a mask of unreadable or nonexistent emotion. The highs and lows of human passion were beneath him.

"I'm curious why you would bother with showmanship at all. I imagine you could just as easily decimate half the city to demonstrate your power. Moreover, I'd posit you could travel to every city with Prism and wipe them all off the map," mused Iko.

"Trust that I have considered these options, Iko. If I appear to act alone, then the kingdom would foolishly turn their thoughts to overcoming me. Although they would never succeed, they would spend their every resource opposing me. Opposing our future. I loathe to sit at the table with vipers, but optics are a necessary evil; with an army of gods behind me, they can have no hope for resistance or disobedience. The king and his people will bow to my will and serve our purpose.

"In my reflections, I have discerned that my deliverance of their cities and souls would be insufficient. Not only do we risk culling our own kind in the crossfire, but we would ultimately be unsuccessful in our extermination. Cities make for convenient targets, but like cockroaches, humanity would survive even if every dot on every map were erased. I could expend all my days and stretch out my hand, but pockets of civilization here or afar would endure. Hamlets. Forgotten villages. Backwoods farmers and cave-dwelling bandits. They would all survive, unscathed. Given time, I foresee a future in which those on the fringe of human society, long forgotten by us, join against a common enemy and destroy our Haven... Instead, I see a more satisfactory fate: unleash human nature against itself. When the world plunges into eternal conflict, these kings will cull one another on our behalf with prejudice that seeps down into the overlooked cracks of society. The greatest era of peace we can hope for is one of unending war."

Iko gazed into Avalon's golden orbs of hatred, searching for hints of madness or brilliance. The unyielding vengeance that surreptitiously fueled the god-king failed to stir Iko one way or the other, but his voracious ambition was contagious. Part of Iko wondered whether the Primals' safe haven was truly the engine of Avalon's drive, or whether vindictive retribution fueled him instead. The distinction was unimportant, in practicality, as their desires were aligned. The world had proven itself irredeemably cruel, and only a sanctuary secured by the most powerful forces on Kyros could offer hope for a better future.

"I suppose Kyros is perpetually on course for the next war—let us begin the final crusade," invited Iko, aware that Avalon had invested several minutes to sate his lieutenant's curiosity.

"Prism," commanded Avalon, returning his gaze to Godwin's castle. "The throne room."

Iko's stomach lurched as air and matter bent around him. Momentarily disoriented from the blink, he felt carpet replace the grass beneath his boots. At once, the air was stuffier and cooler, insulated by stonework within the great hall. Despite his accustomed familiarity with Prism's relocation abilities, the transition still made him nauseous; he much preferred the cool corridors of his shadows.

"Gaius," Avalon's voice filled the room, instantly silencing every other conversation. The absence of Godwin's title, *King*, was intentional—whether meant as provocation or a reminder of the king's place among betters, Iko was unsure.

Iko released a ripple of shadows along the ground, emanating outward from his position. He felt the interruptions in their paths to the walls, instantly allowing him to focus on the others present in the throne room. First, as was his custom, he noticed the armed soldiers. Five feet behind their entry point, two standard-bearing pikemen and two swordsmen flanked either side of the needlessly large double doors. He knew their weapons featured the golden emblem of Godwin's kingdom—a double-headed eagle above even scales—which matched those displayed on the standards.

Spaced roughly ten feet apart, crossbowmen lined the sides of the hall. All except one diagonally to his right were stunned by their sudden appearance and had yet to react. Without turning to look, Iko imperceptibly motioned his finger, urging the shadows cast by the torches behind the responsive bowman into action. Dark tendrils coiled around the soldier's neck, suffocating him as if suddenly corporeal. He dropped his crossbow, clawing at the untouchable noose in vain. Iko mercifully returned breath to the man, dismissing the reach of his living shadows.

Finally, he studied the group on the red carpet ahead of him. Before the stairs up to the stage, a lowly serf kneeled on the floor. Likely pleading for lower taxation or some other manner of assistance in sustaining his simple livelihood. On the stage, six knights in golden suits of armor flanked the central throne. One missing. Godwin's Rangers carried whatever weapons they were most proficient with, gold in color from hilt to blade.

Of course, the gold veneer was only for show. A sturdier alloy was used for the functional construction of each hammer, trident, and spear on stage. Only one of these knights' faces was visible—the largest in stature of the six, both wide and tall, had an impressively waxed mustache and single strand of matching blond hair that bravely interrupted his barren head. His blue eyes matched Iko's, though the man's rugged, almost rectangular face was much bulkier. He held his shoulders back and chin high. Honorable. Loyal. Proud.

Despite their matching sapphire eyes, the mustachioed stranger was irreconcilably colored into a different mural. Iko knew that even without their inexplicable, unworldly entrance, the peach-skinned soldiers in the room would have regarded him with trepidation. By virtue of his Val'Kyran ancestry, he was an outsider here, as he had been all his life. Today, their familiar fear of unfamiliarity inadvertently served his needs.

More accurately, they served Avalon's needs.

The king these Rangers were sworn to protect sat in a velvet-maroon throne, center-stage. Gaius Godwin, gaudily dressed in his royal court attire, regarded the newcomers unsmilingly. Streaks of gray invaded his black beard, as was likely the case for the hair beneath his crown. His tired eyes carried the weight of a long and illustrious career in warfare and politics. Death would one day secure his legacy, but he could not relinquish the reins yet. The peril with legacies is the next generation's ability to uphold them.

On either side behind him sat a likewise pompously dressed royal. The young man on the right was immediately recognizable by his scowl. The clean-shaven prince's sword rested in its scabbard against the throne, matching the austerity of his golden breastplate and greaves. His mussy, dirty-blonde hair betrayed an aura of otherwise unshakable control. His nose looked as if it had been broken twice before, and faint wrinkles on his forehead bore witness to the ever-present frown on his face. Cain Godwin was a warrior first, though his silk cloak served as a reminder that he had much more promised in his future.

The third royal was likely Princess Ashe. Her face was surprisingly plain. Small lips and a diminutive nose. Perceptive eyes. Her glowing blond hair, at least, was one aspect of beauty she inherited from Queen Alessandra. Of the three Godwins, she looked most surprised to see the unexpected guests appear in their throne room.

"Avalon. What a surprise... though I wouldn't go so far as to call it a pleasant one," Gaius greeted flatly. He nodded almost imperceptibly, signaling his attentive Rangers to clear the room.

The broad, helmetless knight addressed the room in a strong voice that suited his stature. "Dearest swords of Godwin: I ask you wait outside until this business is concluded. You may also leave, farmer."

"But King Godwin—about my stock..." pleaded the serf, his plight unresolved.

"I thank you for your understanding and cooperation!" firmly bid the thunderous golden knight, somehow appearing to flex through his heavy armor.

"Yes... Yes, of course," the serf mumbled as he slunk out into the hallway, escorted by the black-and-gold-shirted soldiers.

Once the doors had closed, separating Godwin's inner circle from the common folk, the father addressed his children: "Cain, Ashe—please go to your chambers. The rest of you, too. I need only Blaze for this."

Both younger Godwins hesitated but reluctantly followed their father's orders. Five of the golden Rangers left with them through the side door, leaving only the broadest behind—Blaze Mustang, the Golden Knight.

Despite the nationwide circulation of propaganda extolling the war hero, Iko knew Mustang's story was largely fabrication. In public parades and battle against lesser men, the Golden Knight moonlit as a Mystic—one protected by the indomitable Primal of Might. While surely demoralizing enemies and inspiring his own men, the farce would not long hold up against a true Mystic, particularly one molded by battle. Blaze Mustang was an impressive soldier— one of the best, even—but he was only a man.

Still, there was little to gain in exposing the Golden Knight's façade. In some cities and many towns throughout Deuzos, Mystics were still revered as descendants of gods. Of course, these old traditions of worship only survived because the public believed the Godwin family was the lineage of Deus himself. While many believed the storied history of the Mystics, a growing few felt worse than fear and distrust toward them.

The most prominent threat to Mystics in the Westerlands came from the cultists—the Brotherhood of Ardent Faith. Through their increasingly widespread efforts, public sentiment seemed to have shifted in recent decades toward suspicion and contempt. In some communities, distinctions were drawn between benevolent heroes like Blaze Mustang the Golden Knight and villains like Vayne the Red. In others, primarily in Tallamar but even within Godwin's realm, hatred manifested in bloodier form. Iko suspected the fanatics had been responsible for the recent death of another Mystic, Rogar, in Koln.

After the door had shut leaving only five in the vast throne room, Gaius addressed his visitors: "Why have you come?"

Avalon slowly ascended the steps to the stage, erasing the artificial height difference between them. Now looking down on the king who sat in his throne, Avalon answered: "When last we spoke, I was under the impression we had reached an agreement."

"Ha!" Gaius barked mirthlessly. "Agreement is a choice word for *ultimatum*. Yes, you made your demands clear."

"So you understood our deal, and yet you failed to uphold your end," accused Avalon.

"If you have something to say, say it," Gaius invited unceremoniously.

"A Mystic was killed in your streets of Koln, hung like a swine for all to see. Your duty was to gather every Mystic in Deuzos on my behalf—you are now already one short of the bargain," summarized Avalon.

"This is the first I'm hearing of it," Gaius answered evenly.

"Which finds you no favor with me. Your incompetence is not my concern. The price for your kingdom's continued existence is your hand in gathering my Mystics."

Blaze bristled at the uninvited guest's tone but wisely refrained from speaking. Gaius studied Avalon and the two silent Mystics for a long moment, attempting to regain some semblance of control. Finally, he said: "I am the rightful King of Deuzos. Seventh in my name. I will not bow, Avalon, and I will not be cowed by your threats. I'd sooner see the world burn than serve you."

Iko sensed Avalon was nearing the extent of his patience. They may have misjudged Gaius. Seeing an opportunity, he stepped in with a suggestion: "What if you did not serve us, but, rather, we kept a cooperative partnership?"

"What kind of partnership?" Gaius cocked an eyebrow.

Avalon nodded to Iko, inviting him to continue his proposal.

"We have been candid with you about our desires—we wish to take the Mystics away from here and relocate them to our safe haven. This advantages you as well, as several potentially powerful enemies will be removed from play. As a token of our goodwill, we will also aid you in your battle against Tallawyn."

"There is no battle against Tallawyn," Gaius countered. "Only border tensions which will likely resolve themselves within a few months."

"Ah—then I take it you haven't heard the news," Iko dangled airily.

"Tell me," demanded Gaius Godwin.

"The Tallawyns slaughtered Fort Banning this morning."

"Impossible," Godwin dismissed with a snort. "Fort Banning is one of the most secure strongholds in the east. The whole Tallawyn army couldn't break though our lines there."

"I suspect you'll hear from your own in short order," Iko sighed his regret. "Regardless, I'd advise you to reconsider your response—just in case."

Gaius leaned back in his throne, sizing up the Val'Kyran. Distrustful eyes had read his skin countless times before. Measuring. Doubting. Judging. Iko suppressed a knowing grin as he watched the king struggle to heed this warning from a nameless Val'Kyran.

"We would not join your frontlines," Avalon interrupted, outlining the boundary of their partnership. "But we will make efforts to support your victory in the coming war, and you can be assured that no Mystics will oppose you. We will intervene swiftly if Tallawyn brings any to the front."

Gaius considered his visitors in silence. Iko suspected the king knew he was being strongarmed. Humiliated. His earlier outrage had been an expected reaction, but perhaps the king was thinking quicker than he let on. Perhaps this farce of a negotiation was now part of an elaborate political dance, a feint of cowed surrender covering his simmering resentment. Concealing patient anger. Or perhaps he was only what he seemed.

The king spoke. "If, inexplicably, Tallawyn truly invaded Fort Banning, then there will be war, and we would be starting on the back foot. Your terms, if I understand them, are that we would remain uninvolved in each other's affairs to the extent possible—Deuzos gathers every Mystic we can for you, and you prevent any from joining the Tallawyns. One fewer variable on my board."

"Correct. I expect you believe your golden army is capable of defeating the Tallawyns without us, but we'll offer you contingent insurance nonetheless— if their armies ever reach the walls of your capital, you can rely on my people to remove them," offered Avalon.

"And the dead Mystic in Koln?" raised Gaius, bringing the explosive matter back into discussion.

"We'll forgive this troubling lapse of your duty, but it will not be tolerated to happen again," warned Avalon.

Iko added his diplomatic voice to the mix: "We believe a group of religious fanatics committed the act—a group called the Brotherhood of Ardent Faith. I suspect they are subverting your kingdom in other ways, or at least recruiting your citizens into their cult. See what you can do to eliminate them."

King Gaius exhaled slowly, shifting his gaze between the Val'Kyran and Avalon. "Blaze," he decreed. "When you renew the contracts at month's end, see to it that every mercenary guild in Deuzos has an active bounty on this cult. We'll quell these zealots as a show of good faith for our... allies."

"It will be done, Your Majesty," Blaze rumbled dutifully.

"Then our business is concluded," decided Avalon. "We will return on the eighth of every month to relieve you of our Mystics. We'll be watching the warfront from afar—I wish you good fortune in your coming campaign."

Prism blinked the three outsiders out of Godwin's courtroom and into the familiar halls of Avalon's keep above Val'Kyros.

Iko overcame the custom dizziness and nausea by focusing on the ill-maintained stonework of their home until his vision stabilized. "A success, I would call it."

"Indeed," acknowledged Avalon.

"Allow me to ask—why did we seek to remain uninvolved in the war? Is this about protecting our people?"

Avalon read the Val'Kyran with cold eyes, as if unsure whether Iko was attempting a joke. "A benefit, certainly, but it was Godwin who wanted us to remain uninvolved. His only concern is to hold onto his infirm rule—straw in a hurricane. So long as pride blinds him from fearing defeat, he would neither bow to us nor see us fighting alongside his men in the fields."

"Would a show of our joint power not be in his interest? Surely, the world would see him as a strong king with powerful allies," wondered Iko.

"They would see powerful allies," Avalon corrected thoughtfully. "Our deal works because Godwin retains the illusion of power. If Mystics battled against him, his enemies would quickly find the golden army is breakable. If we battled alongside him, his subjects would know that we hold the power—not their king. Even if we had no interest in orchestrating a coup ourselves, his reliance on allied Mystics would expose him for the weak despot he is."

Iko was impressed that Avalon had gleaned so much about the Godwin king. Given his disposition toward humanity, it was surprising he had subdued his disgust long enough to listen. Perhaps he still underestimated Avalon. Nevertheless, he did not regret having lent his silver tongue to the negotiations.

"Hmm. Well, no time like the present to instigate a war. I will return shortly thereafter," Iko bid adieu, slipping into darkness.

He felt the cool rush of shadows transport him to the dingy cells below Fort Banning. He emerged in the underground prison, drawing a deep breath as he prepared himself for his duty. No matter the kingdom, the air was musty.

A warden yelled something at one of the prisoners locked behind bars, but Iko did not hear. He strolled across the cool cobblestone floor toward the torchlight of the Godwin soldier, moving in no particular hurry. He drew two knives from the sheaths resting on his ribs, twirling the blades as he focused on the impossible task ahead. One only he could accomplish.

Prism warped in next to him, dropping two lifeless Tallawyn bodies on the floor of the Godwin prison. Above ground, the well-fortified stronghold and surrounding encampments were still blissfully unaware of their presence. That would soon change.

"Hey—you there!" the warden accosted him as Prism warped away. "Identify yourself!"

Torchlight revealed the man's face. Wrinkled with age and scarred from a violent life of handling the inmates below Godwin's most renowned fortress. The warden looked angry to see him—not surprised or terrified that the Val'Kyran had somehow bypassed the regiment defending the checkpoint.

Iko closed his eyes and fell forward, plunging into the pool of darkness on the floor. He tightened his grip on the daggers as he traveled through the cold, otherworldly pathway.

For a moment, he felt his Primal's will at the edge of his consciousness. A bow between two better halves before they initiated their shadowy dance. The feeling passed, and then they were one once again.

Iko emerged from a cloud of shadows behind the warden. He deftly reached around the Godwin's neck and pressed a knife to his pink throat. Then, Iko answered his question: "Today, I am Tallawyn."

X. Blood Oath

Drake

A well-trodden path parted the sea of scorched earth.

On their southwesterly pilgrimage to the Frontier, they had passed many remarkable travelers along that red dirt road. Among them were sizeable contingents of traders, tourists, bounty hunters, and vagabonds. The occasional ramshackle inn enjoyed great business along the highway, though Drake found it peculiar that pairs and triads of competing inns popped up together after long stretches of barren road. As they left one such establishment behind them to begin the morning's trek, he noticed someone was following in his shadow.

"Keep walking," instructed a woman's voice with an untraceable accent.

"I don't take too kindly to orders," Drake warned, continuing forward.

"How do you feel about oaths?" answered the woman.

Drake exchanged a sidelong glance with Talia but said nothing. They walked until they achieved a small pocket of space around them, outpacing the travelers behind without overtaking those ahead.

"Left," instructed the woman.

"What do you mean, *left?*" Drake demanded, turning his head to the vast nothingness in that direction.

The woman veered off the path. He followed. They left the civilized highway behind, venturing into the morning sun, away from Arillia.

Finally, once the road had faded from view, the woman addressed him: "I come on behalf of Chieftain Theresa Winter," she announced importantly.

"I figured as much. What's she want?"

"First, I am to remind you of your oath. We Nords take our pacts—"

"Get to the point," Drake interrupted irritably. "What's she want?"

"Frostfang," the agent answered succinctly. "Centuries ago, Highlord Demos inherited this legendary sword crafted by the originators themselves. The sword was passed down from highlord to highlord until Miroslav the Iron Mountain lost it, along with his life, in a duel shortly after the Kirscheis action. The victor was whispered to be the famed Cormack duelist, Brandon Vayne. Highlord Steinfaust has made no discernible effort to reclaim the artifact, and Chieftain Winter believes it is her destiny to ascend wielding the greatsword. You will acquire it from Vayne and deliver it to me; I will await you at the inn."

"I think I've heard of Brandon Vayne," Talia chimed in.

"I think anyone who's lifted a sword has heard of Brandon Vayne," asserted Drake.

"Didn't he have something to do with the Dark Age of Heroes?" Talia made the connection.

"Sure. They say he traveled the world challenging anyone who called himself a legendary swordsman. Never lost a fight, either. For a while, you stopped hearing stories about famous warriors—just the strategists. Nobody wanted to get on his list."

"His castle is less than an hour's travel west from here. I don't care how you get your hands on the sword—steal, fight, beg—but you will bring it to me today," instructed the Nord expectantly.

Drake let out a breath of air. "Well, if we're lucky, we'll avoid a fight... but we'll manage whatever goes down. You'll get your sword today."

You have a powerful weapon his past opponents did not, encouraged Pyros from within.

"Keep going dead ahead—you can't miss it," the Nord directed, turning back toward the highway.

As they set off against the blinding sun, Talia apparently felt the turn of events warranted further discussion. "You don't think we're getting in over our heads on this, right?" she asked for reassurance.

"Who knows," Drake shrugged. "All things considered, it ain't so bad."

"Didn't you say this guy's the best duelist in the world?"

"*Was* the best duelist... but that was a long time ago. As far as I know, his name's just an urban legend now. Who knows if he's even still alive?"

"What'll we do then? Sounds like you owe that sword to Theresa."

"We'll ask his kid for it," Drake said simply. "Or whoever's left in the castle—they must know where to find it. Can't imagine anyone would pawn it."

"And even if he's old—you sure we could beat him?"

Pyros' spectral form flashed above Drake, his bullish horns aflame with indignation. *I will not be made to cower before any mortal!*

"Alright. Crack on then, Pyros," Talia grinned despite her worry.

"We've been through worse, kid," Drake added as a final note of assurance. "We're gonna be just fine."

"What about the Nord?" Talia asked.

"What about her?" Drake returned.

"How did she know where to find us?"

Drake considered this for a moment, squinting against the sun. "Well, they knew we were heading to Deuzos. Guess that road was probably the best way of getting there."

"So you don't really know?"

"Does it matter?"

Talia scrunched up her mouth. "I guess not," she relented, returning them to silence.

The castle came into view before long. It was unlike any Drake had ever seen.

Some elements were familiar; the ornate limestone masonry rivaled even Tallawyn's preeminent architecture, as did the vaulting towers of the keep. A magnificent arched entryway marked the center of the structure, large enough for a horse-drawn carriage to pass through if needed. The stone path leading to this entryway began suddenly amid the red dirt, somehow as spotless as the milky walls.

Drake might have called the castle a thing of beauty if not for the bizarre state of its right side. An uneven diagonal cut ran through the pristine stonework; to the right of this line, the limestone was missing. It did not look unfinished, nor did it appear to have been damaged by projectiles or the elements—there was no rubble, only the uncanny failure of the structure's continuity. It was as if part of the castle had disappeared, vanished into thin air.

The castle grounds were eerily quiet to match. No servants scurried around to carry out their duties; no grass or flowers penetrated the red dirt. The one possibility Drake did not account for was for the castle to be abandoned entirely. Forsaken and forgotten, left to erode alone. If the sword wasn't here at all, they would have a problem on their hands.

"That's crazy," Talia marveled under her breath. "What do you think happened?"

"No idea. Storm or something?" he said, disbelieving his own words.

"Maybe," Talia allowed, unconvinced.

His thoughts were disrupted by a lone *cluck*. Off to the left of the castle, a lone, black-feathered chicken observed him. Head cocked sideways, it clucked again, then strolled in an aimless circle, occasionally stopping to peck the ground.

"Is that a chicken?" Talia checked.

Drake blinked. "That... yeah. That's a chicken."

"Hey—isn't that the guy from the Twins?" Talia pointed at the archway.

Drake raised a hand to shield his eyes from the sun. He spotted two black-clad figures emerging from the castle: one a familiar Val'Kyran man and the other an olive-skinned, brown-haired woman. The man held a palm over his face, rubbing his weary eyes. They were too far away for Drake to see the woman's expression clearly.

"Looks like we may end up fighting today after all," mused Drake, advancing toward the pair. He had a score to settle with both of them—the Val'Kyran, Iko, for thrashing him outside Lyon, and the woman, Prism, for stabbing him through the back at the Twins. He counted Prism a second time for calling a horde of Tallawyn soldiers to their position, ultimately leading to Desmond's death.

"Be careful," advised Talia.

"I've got it," Drake answered confidently, feeling the heat of Pyros' fury swell in his chest. He raised his voice to bellow across the plain of red earth: "Looking for me?"

Iko raised his head curiously and pointed forward. The air around him and the woman warped, then he reappeared closer, just ten yards in front of Drake. "Oh, the ironic whims of fate."

Drake met his blue eyes unflinchingly. The Val'Kyran's mouth slowly turned up into a smile. His carefully manicured moustache twitched as he spoke. "They say when one door closes, another one opens. I hope you've had a chance to reconsider my offer, now that you have learned a costly lesson at the expense of young Orion's life."

"I suggest you clear off before this gets ugly," Drake drew his sword.

Iko calmly drew his knives, letting his arms rest at his side. "I see you remember me, girl. Before I'm inclined to teach your belligerent guardian a lesson he should have heeded the first time, I'll offer you a chance to join us. No more running around—just a nice home where you'll always be safe. Where you will be protected and cared for. All you have to do is say, *yes.*"

"*No,*" emphasized Talia, folding her arms defiantly.

"We done talking?" Drake frowned, itching to unleash Pyros.

Iko flicked a dagger into the air above him and balanced its landing skillfully on the edge of his other blade. He bounced the knife back into the air and caught it with an underhand grip. "When last we met, I hoped to educate the boy. I hoped he would see through your pernicious lies and understand that you could not protect him. Today, I intend only to remind you of your place. A nail that brazenly sticks out its head is sure to be hammered."

Iko dashed forward, and Drake followed suit. Their blades clashed in a shower of sparks, colliding head-on. Iko retreated a step, inviting Drake to swing across his body. The sword tip brushed the Val'Kyran's beard. Instead of recoiling at the near-miss, Iko pressed his advantage following Drake's delayed recovery, stepping outside his guard and beating the blade to prevent a back-handed stroke.

As Drake turned to spin, Iko's knuckles slammed painfully into his ribs. He disengaged, taking a moment to recover. Talia stood a few yards back, out of harm's immediate way.

"I would have assumed that some newfound abilities accompanied your impudent bravado. Have you nothing to show me?" challenged Iko.

Drake snorted angrily and yelled: "Pyros!"

Flames ignited along the length of his sword, flickering hungrily in the dry air. Drake held the sword out toward the Val'Kyran in challenge.

Smiling, Iko held his fists together in concentration. A black shadow briefly flickered behind him. A moment later, a wide, circular pool of darkness bubbled through the red dirt, replacing the ground beneath Drake's feet. "I regret to inform you that your little party trick does not make you a contender against Iko. Pyros has slept far too long to be of any true consideration."

"You're about getting on my last nerve," Drake growled, lashing out with his sword. As Iko predictably dodged backward, he willed flames to fly forward from his blade. The fire cut through the air, narrowly missing Iko as the Val'Kyran slipped into the shadowy pool beneath them.

Drake anticipated Iko appearing behind him, spun his sword, and met Iko's reactive guard. Embers showered from Drake's halted blade, singeing

Iko's exposed cheek as he ducked his head. Iko knelt, disappearing back into the pool of shadows.

The coalescing tendrils of shadows rose, a dark miasma reaching up to Drake's hip. He stood on alert for a long moment, unsure where Iko would emerge next.

"Behind you!" Talia warned futilely.

A fist crashed into the back of Drake's head before he could react. He spun to face his assailant, but Iko had already dispersed into an airborne cloud of shadows. The barrage continued a moment later as Iko reappeared and disappeared, striking at his vulnerabilities and vanishing before any chance of reprisal.

A cloud of smoke appeared in front of Drake's eyes. Iko emerged and jabbed above Drake's lowered guard, catching him on the chin and sending him crashing to the ground. From his back, Drake slashed through the air, sending a wave of flames through the empty space recently occupied by Iko.

You're making us look bad! accused Pyros angrily.

"Do something, then!" Drake snarled as Iko materialized three yards in front of him. Drake scrambled to his feet, bruised but not beaten. He felt Pyros vying for control of his limbs and decided to let the Primal guide him without relinquishing control entirely.

"How many times do I need to teach you this lesson?" Iko spat in disapproval. The shadowy pool beneath their feet rippled, and he disappeared into the darkness once again.

With Pyros' fury coursing through him, Drake leaped into the air and unleashed a blast wave from his body. The flames exploded outward from him, erasing the pool of shadows with their fierce illumination, scorching the blasted soil underfoot.

When the last of the shadows dissipated in the blast, Iko tumbled out backward. He grimaced as he rose to his knees. "Impressive. I truly cannot see a way for us to continue sparring without one of us meeting an early demise. However, I suspect your flames would be outclassed by Prism."

The black-robed woman appeared at Iko's side, freezing Drake with a chilling expression. Now that she was near, he could clearly see her features. A thin black haze rose from her glassy almond eyes. She had a small upper lip and thin eyebrows, contrasted by her pronounced cheekbones. Freckles ran down the bridge of her olive nose. It was easy to imagine her smiling, laughing, but she did not. Like the muggy air around them, she stood uncannily still, vacantly gazing through him.

Despite the inexcusable pain she had inflicted when last they met—for Drake assumed this was the same *Prism* he had fought west of the Twins—he couldn't help but take a second to stare. Of all the women he had encountered on his worldly travels, many far more elegant or sensuous, she was undoubtedly the most beautiful he'd ever known.

Her eyes briefly glowed purple as she held out her hand, conjuring a familiar rapier from midair. Drake steeled himself for combat, unwilling to become distracted. He had faced her once before and knew her agility was nearly uncontestable. To protect himself and Talia, he would need to predict her attacks which seemed apathetic to the ostensible distance between them.

"Remind him of his place," ordered Iko.

Prism suddenly appeared in front of Drake, thrusting her thin sword toward his stomach.

He defensively brought the falchion across his body, somehow passing through her sword without hitting it. The rapier dug into the flesh above his hip, sending a needle of pain through his abdomen.

Pyros exerted his influence. Before she had a chance to withdraw her blade, Drake opened his mouth and spewed fire into her face. The flames inexplicably stopped in front of her nose, leaving her perfectly unharmed, but continued through the air behind her.

He leaped backward, dislodging the rapier from his midriff. Aware that his own blade was unlikely to help him, he sheathed the falchion, focusing solely on his connection with Pyros.

Four balls of flame released in quick succession from his left hand. Each fireball disappeared before hitting Prism, then flared against the ground some distance behind her.

He willed a wall of flames to charge across the ground toward her. She effortlessly vanished, reappearing beside him to carve several cuts into his arm before blinking away. She materialized above the scorched ground, hovering in midair. Despite her peerless attacks and evasion, she seemed completely unbothered by the exertion, remaining ominously still. While Drake scowled in pain, panting heavily from his failed attempts, she waited patiently, eyes glowing purple as she levitated.

"You can't hit her, Drake!" Talia shouted some sage advice.

"Whaddya mean, *I can't hit her?*" Drake glowered, feeling challenged.

"Her Primal's like an invisible shield," Talia expounded unhelpfully.

"Talia, unless you've got something helpful to say, stop distracting me!"

"Prism is much more than an invisible shield," Iko commented, sounding rather amused.

The woman disappeared from the air, then appeared on all four sides of Drake at once. The mirages lashed out, drawing blood from his back, chest, and arms with the tips of their swords. The clone behind him swept out his legs, sending him crashing onto his back.

"Excellent. Now, give him a nice little scar," instructed Iko, absently touching his right cheek. "Give him a permanent reminder of what happens when you act out of turn."

The four copies of Prism merged into one standing above him. Drake coughed as he lay on his back, disarmed and powerless even despite Pyros' added strength. He felt the Primal's will within him, urging him to continue fighting, but he was done. His energy was rapidly flagging, and he had no delusions that this woman was unbeatable. If she could control space and freely bend the unassailable laws of nature, foundational principles of existence he could not even imagine altering, then he and his dwindling flames would be no match.

She raised her sword, preparing to etch a hard lesson into his face. He stared into her glassy, emotionless eyes, wondering what could be running through her mind. She appeared to be an indomitable force, capable of forging any destiny she chose—and yet, both Iko and the Cormack they called Hadronox seemed to wield her as a mere pawn in their bidding. For a fleeting moment, and only because the agonizing carving of his flesh had not yet begun, he felt a deep sadness for her.

The empathetic feeling vanished as she lowered her arm, sending the tip toward his cheek. He braced for the searing pain, baring his teeth but managing to keep his eyes open. Instead, to his surprise, the cold, bloodied tip of the steel blade merely rested against his cheek.

"Prism? Was my order unclear?" stammered Iko, in shock himself.

"Rapscallions! Clear off my land!" a hoarse voice cried from the castle.

Blueish black fissures ruptured the air around them erratically. Drake immediately identified that these were different from the pools conjured by Iko—rather than wayward shadows skirting across the ground, these fissures were perfectly round rings and spheres detonating without warning.

"We're departing!" Iko shouted to Prism.

She removed her boot from Drake's chest and warped away, taking Iko with her.

One wayward fissure landed on the ground alarmingly close to Drake's ear. A moment later, a large gap of soil was missing, leaving a sizeable crater in the red courtyard. Drake scrambled to his feet, beleaguered but aware this new threat was likely deadlier than the peril from which he had miraculously emerged unscathed—or at least without irreparable disfigurement.

In the archway of the damaged castle stood an old man, huffing and puffing as he rested his hands on his knees. Several sunspots marked his bald head. He wore a red and white officer's uniform, perhaps a more dignified combination than the red and yellow that signified Cormack infantry. Drake assumed he must have been a captain or noble, as evidenced by the numerous medals that clung to his chest.

The old man addressed the remaining trespassers: "I... Rap... Who are you, again?"

XI. Lord Vayne

Drake

T alia exchanged a puzzled look with Drake.

"Lord Vayne?" she inquired.

"Yes?" the bewildered man returned.

"My name's Talia. That's Drake," she pointed. "My dad was also a Cormack—in the army. We were hoping you could help us find something."

"Oh," murmured the old man. He smacked his gob in thought, licking his lips with a narrow tongue. "An army man, you say? Yes, I do suppose we have an army... Yes, yes. Do come in!"

The aging lord turned and ambled through the castle archway with the assistance of a scepter.

Talia crossed over to Drake, gingerly stepping around the deep crater. "He looks like he's seen better days," she commented.

"Hope he still has the sword," Drake added.

They crossed the red dirt and walked down the white entryway, staining the immaculate stones with each step. Through the archway, they followed their meandering host down the hall to the left. Lord Vayne's red coattails swished behind him as he ascended the three steps leading into the dining hall.

The hall featured a long table with a total of fourteen plush seats. The standard golden plates and silver cutlery expected of nobles were present, as were countless paintings and battle trophies adorning the walls on all sides. Most impressive was a wide mural that appeared to depict a map of the world.

Red tallies marked the various continents and provinces. Drake's eyes scanned the vastness of the world, from the southern continent of Baltos, to the white castle that marked his present location on Destos, all the way to the unfamiliar landmass he guessed to be Taoxos. Glancing west of the white castle, he charted a path in his mind past Arillia, through the Foothills, and ultimately into the undetailed Riverlands. He knew somewhere in the dense hinterlands, the Oracle awaited him in the Cradle of Life. He could not tell the best path forward but recognized he would travel through one of three provinces: the Basket, the Lowlands, or the Highlands.

Lord Vayne stooped and picked up a tome resting in front of the map. "Did you say your father was in the army?" he asked, opening the book.

"Yes, but that would've been like fifteen, twenty years ago," said Talia.

"I see," he lifted a trembling hand to turn the page. "Are you here because I killed him?"

"No!" Talia reassured him swiftly. "I only mentioned him since you're both Cormacks. I thought, as a captain, you might have known him..."

"Name?" Vayne frowned thoughtfully.

"Blaine," Talia blurted, a little too excited. She paused to recompose herself. "Patrick Blaine."

Lord Vayne scratched his chin thoughtfully. "Varrus, do we know a Blaine?"

A rumble of distorted echoes rang through Drake's head, as if he had two conch shells pressed against his ears. Over Lord Vayne's shoulder, a ghostly, gray form phased in and out of existence. A spectral green flame surrounded the small, wingless imp with long, grotesque ears and horns. A shrill voice answered its master: "Never heard of him. Sorry, kid."

"It's okay," Talia said with an unmissable note of disappointment in her tone. "We're actually here to ask for your help with something else."

"Oh? What's that?" the once-fearsome duelist wet his lips once more.

"Do you have a sword called Frostfang?" interjected Drake.

"Frostfang," repeated the lord in contemplation. "If you could just answer one question for me..."

"Of course," allowed Drake.

"Who... are you?" Vayne inquired, looking around the room as if shocked they had somehow broken into his home.

"I'm Talia; he's Drake," she answered.

"I see," muttered Vayne. "And what can I do for you..."

"Talia," she provided.

"Hmm?" he asked, growing more confused.

Talia clasped her hands patiently. "My name is Talia. Can you please give us a sword called Frostfang?"

"Frostfang?" repeated the man in puzzlement.

Growing increasingly frustrated, Drake started scanning the prized swords hanging around the room. Most carried a small placard underneath listing the sword's name, past owner, and region of origin. There were weapons from Highwind, Tyranos, and Talos—some even as far as Ayrabos. None of these blades were the Frostfang from Nordos he needed.

"You know how you're a duelist?" Talia attempted.

Vayne scoffed. "I'm the greatest of all time. I cannot be beaten."

"Right," Talia allowed, moving the conversation forward. "You beat a Nord a long time ago—Highlord Miroslav. What did you do with his sword?"

The man's lips trembled as a smile slowly crept onto his face. "I... I remember him. He was a great... bah! The person with the sword who... who does the attacking and the..."

"He was a great fighter?" Talia offered with a pained expression.

Lord Vayne shook his finger, indicating that she had identified the right word. "A great fighter... Yes. I keep a list of all my victories in this..." Vayne trailed off, holding the red tome.

"May I see the book?" Talia asked politely.

The lord nodded and slowly extended his withered hand, allowing her to take the book. She leafed through the pages, skimming the titles.

"Where'd you learn to read?" asked Drake.

"Amma," she answered without looking up.

A surprised look dawned on the lord's face. He pointed a gnarled finger at Drake and asked: "Are you... Amma?"

Drake sighed impatiently. He could hardly imagine how this old geezer had survived on his own for as long as he had; it was unthinkable that he had ever been the world's most feared duelist.

"Highlord Miroslav the Iron Mountain, defeated in honorable combat on the thirteenth of September, in the eighth year of his reign. His sword, Frostfang, added as a worthy treasure to the collection of Lord Vayne and Varrus of the Void."

Enlightened, Lord Vayne snapped his fingers. "I just realized! There's an animal named *fly*, but no creature bears the name *walk* or *swim*."

The imp reappeared on Vayne's shoulder. "He's been getting worse. It's partly my fault—so you can imagine how I feel about it! The only time he's really himself is when he's got a sword in his hand. Hey, buddy!" the imp rapped his little knuckles on the side of Lord Vayne's head. "It's just about lunch time. You hungry?"

"Please! What's on the menu, Varrus?"

"Whatever I'm making!"

Drake felt a rumble from his chest. He allowed Pyros into his thoughts. *We'll need to duel them to get the sword.*

Drake nodded in agreement. He didn't take pride in thrashing a dotty old man, but Varrus made it sound like the Cormack was only lucid in duels. Perhaps it was a familiar rush of adrenaline.

I sense displeasure within you, diagnosed the Primal.

All the stories told about this guy, all the men he's killed in battle—and now this is the pathetic shell of a man left behind, Drake conveyed in thought.

He felt the quiet crackling of Pyros' flames within him. *Do you worry you will end up the same? That your failing memory was just the beginning, and that I will make you a senile husk?*

Drake didn't bother to convey a reply. He knew the Primal could feel his thoughts as soon as he experienced them himself. Although his memory seemed to be healing—mundane details gradually returned, and he hadn't forgotten anything since escaping that cult's prison—key fragments of his past continued to evade him.

"Can we join you for lunch?" Talia imposed.

"Why yes, of course. Please, have a..." the lord gestured at the chairs.

I won't end up like him, Drake reassured both Pyros and himself.

Pulling out a chair to join Talia at the table, he decided recovering his past self was simultaneously the most and least important objective on his mind. Whatever fragments of his memory were missing could wait until they reached the Cradle. With or without recollections of his hometown or past life, he was who he was. But beyond inertia, Avalon tipped the scales in continuing west; Drake needed to understand the inexorable hate he harbored toward the golden-eyed stranger. That one hidden detail robbed him of many nights' sleep.

Lord Vayne sat across from Drake. He took the folded napkin from the table and formed a bib. Varrus appeared on his shoulder and announced: "Three birds, coming right up!"

An oblong, blue-and-black portal appeared in the doorway, from which a bizarre, spectral being emerged. Its blackish purple body had sporadic markings of blue, giving it the appearance of a celestial sky. Its muscular upper half ended in a hunchback that rose a foot above its far-forward head. Two golden manacles bound the creature's wrists, and although no chain connected them, Drake suspected the being was not acting of its own free will. A black trail of shadows swirled behind it as it swept across the floor, carrying three platters of food to the table.

The creature lowered a tray in front of Lord Vayne, then circled around the table to deposit a matching meal in front of Talia and Drake. As the being neared Drake, he heard an uncomfortable dissonance sounding like mad whispers inside his head. A low, rumbling voice stood out among them: "I hate this place."

"The hell is that thing?" Drake demanded as the creature slithered back through the portal, departing from their presence.

"Just a voidling, Amma. No cause for alarm," Lord Vayne resolved as he sawed through his broiled chicken with an expensive-looking knife.

Drake stabbed a piece of okra with his fork, then scooped a clump of mashed potatoes and shoveled the payload into his mouth.

"Drake!" Talia admonished between bites. "Don't just lump it all together—that's disgusting!"

"All goes to the same place," he justified stoically. Admittedly, his table manners left room for improvement. Most of his meals had been consumed without cutlery, often with him hunching over a campfire or sitting on a stump. Regardless, the food was delicious, and he was hungry. Unless the lord of the house took great offense, he'd eat however he liked.

"Some water? Wine?" offered Varrus.

The portal reopened, and the voidling returned with two pitchers. He poured red liquid into a chalice for the lord, then paused in front of Talia.

"Two waters, please," she requested, pointing to her and Drake's cups.

The voidling obeyed. Drake heard another wave of whispers as his cup was filled: "Your fate will be the same."

"Deus," Drake exclaimed, taken aback. "Are they always so creepy?"

Their host hadn't paid the comment any attention. Instead, Vayne sat back from his half-eaten food and stared at the wall behind Drake. "If you race against yourself, do you finish first or last?"

Drake looked at Talia, who shrugged between bites of okra.

"If only my wife were here to enjoy this sumptuous meal," lamented Lord Vayne.

Varrus folded his arms and scampered to his lord's other shoulder, where he perched like a gargoyle. "Brandon, you don't have a wife."

"I don't?" the Cormack's lip quivered sadly. "Oh. Well, I think I should have liked one."

"You're a duelist. Not a poet," remarked Varrus.

"Oh. Well do I still do... with the sword, do I..."

"You don't fight anymore, Brandon," Varrus explained in a tired, pitying tone that suggested this was not their first time having this conversation.

"What do I do?" asked the lord.

"Eat your food, Brandon," encouraged the imp.

As Drake finished his meal, Lord Vayne took another bite of potatoes and chewed for an inordinate amount of time. He stared at his guests while he chewed, eyes studying Drake for a few seconds, then switching to Talia, then back to Drake, and so on.

Their host swallowed and remarked: "My, aren't you a pretty young lady!" He smiled avuncularly, looked at Drake, then back to Talia. "Hello. Who are you?"

"I'm a duelist. I'm here to fight you for a sword," challenged Drake, throwing his soiled napkin onto his tray.

"Drake," Talia dissuaded diplomatically.

"A duelist? Splendid! Please, please," Lord Vayne rose from his seat and began hobbling to the doorway.

Drake rose from his chair, rounding the table to follow in the elderly captain's wake.

"Heavens, ho!" Vayne exclaimed, pointing at the wall. A section of bricks glowed blue and then disappeared, leaving a gaping hole behind as a circumstantial reminder they had ever existed at all. "That was close! I saw a..."

"Spider," supplied Varrus.

"Right—that's right. I saw a... Hmm..."

"You saw a spider!" Varrus groaned, momentarily losing his temper.

"I did? Where?" Lord Vayne spun and opened another rift to the void, sending the corner of his table into the ether.

"Outside," directed Varrus. "We have a challenger to beat."

The captain stepped through the vanished section of wall leading to the courtyard. Drake followed into the sunlight and was momentarily impressed by the interior courtyard. Green grass covered the space from wall to wall. A small fountain inexplicably trickled in from the corner, providing fresh water to the estate. Two grand sliding doors on the opposite end of the rectangle marked the intended entryway.

"Very well. Challenger, name your terms," Lord Vayne stopped in the center of the courtyard.

"Swords," declared Drake. "Leave Varrus out of it, and I'll leave Pyros out of it. We fight until one yields. If I win, you give me the Frostfang."

"And if I win, I'll claim your sword—what do you call it?"

Drake unsheathed his Nord falchion and hefted it in his hand. "This?" In truth, it had no name. It was merely a tool to serve him in battle. After he had lost his cutlass to Eamon, Theresa had provided the blade. There was nothing particularly special about it. "I call it Winter's Edge."

"Very well. We'll wager Frostfang against Winter's Edge, and our Primals will remain passive observers." Brandon held both hands outstretched. A heavy claymore appeared in his grasp. He studied the magnificent greatsword and nodded to himself upon confirming its identity.

The crossguard's design featured a white bear head, complete with emerald eyes that glowed blue. Drake couldn't read the Nordish inscription that ran down the blade but felt certain the sword lived up to its fabled name.

A voidling emerged from the wall and accepted the Frostfang. It floated off to the side, obediently holding the prize in escrow until the match was complete.

"May I offer you a duelist's rapier?"

"I'm good," Drake hefted his sword over his shoulder.

"Good. Then let us begin," initiated Lord Vayne, holding out his arm.

Drake raised his guard, ready for the rapier to appear in his opponent's hand. Instead, Vayne suddenly held the long neck of a startled-looking chicken.

"Bruce! You're not supposed to be here," admonished Brandon, gently tossing the chicken to the side.

The agitated bird flapped its wings to control its descent onto the grass, then strutted off through the hole into the kitchen.

Lord Vayne held his hand out once more, conjuring an intricate rapier from thin air. "Allez!"

He leaped forward with surprising agility, eyes glowing gray as Varrus lent him strength. Drake batted the thrust away, then hacked across his body as

Vayne searched for a follow-up. The Cormack easily retreated a step and fluidly turned defense to offense, rocking forward with a fast riposte.

Drake was ready for intricate swordsmanship but woefully unprepared for his opponent's deft footwork. Vayne hovered on the edge of his reach, dictating the tempo of their clash as he danced in and out. Drake was keenly aware that a careless strike would leave him open against this expert fencer—but waiting on his heels for Vayne to slip up would likely yield no better results.

He drove forward, slicing overhand and attempting to close the gap between them. He knew if he could crowd the lord and stand inside his guard, he stood a chance at overpowering the man with brute force. Still, he had to be careful to avoid getting caught by the sharp, unfailing point that separated them.

Lord Vayne sidestepped the strike, thrusting at Drake's exposed shoulder. Drake lurched back, arcing his sword defensively and buying a fleeting pocket of space.

Any way you can help here? Drake entreated Pyros.

I could light him on fire, Pyros offered as Drake clumsily parried a lunge.

We either have to cheat without getting caught, or we have to kill him and the voidling together, declined Drake.

That one won't burn, Pyros warned as Drake shuffled several yards away from his opponent.

Drake worried the voidling would disappear with the sword if its master was killed dishonorably. As the old man advanced toward him, he searched for another avenue to victory.

You're getting tired, observed Pyros.

"Asshole!" Drake shouted at his Primal, clashing swords twice before withdrawing once more.

"That language falls short of gallant!" huffed Lord Vayne indignantly.

He's old. He must also be fatiguing, even with Varrus.

Drake realized what his Primal was trying to tell him. He didn't need to win the fight; he just had to draw it out long enough for his opponent to flag.

"You fought admirably, but our battle ends here," declared Vayne.

Coattails flashing behind him, the lord lunged forward. Drake jumped backward, narrowly avoiding the tip of the rapier. Without pause, the captain continued his assault, thrusting at Drake's chest. He parried to the outside of his body, but Vayne slipped his tip underneath, leaning forward as his sword flew unfettered toward Drake's heart.

Blood slowly dripped onto the grass between their feet.

Drake hollered in pain. The piercing metal stung inside his flesh.

He tightened his grip on the falchion, sensing the narrow window of opportunity. The rapier's tip remained lodged in the palm of his left hand; he pushed his hand deeper against the blade, firmly grasping the tip to prevent its recovery. Drake swung his blade at Lord Vayne's extended sword arm, roaring as he attacked the vulnerability.

Vayne released his grip on the rapier and dodged backward, allowing his sword's hilt to clatter to the ground. He held out his arm and conjured a new weapon. He stared at Drake for a long moment as he attempted to control his breathing. "Yield to me."

Drake pulled the rapier out of his hand, inviting a rush of blood to trickle down his forearm. He plunged the tip of his falchion into the ground, then held his free fingers against the bleeding palm. Grimacing, he cauterized the wound with a burst of fire, sealing the puncture with a nasty scar.

Gripping the hilt of his falchion with his good hand, Drake steeled himself to resume combat. "Tired already?"

Lord Vayne gave a short bark of laughter. "Tired? My boy, I haven't felt so alive in years." His eyes looked clearer. Sharper. It was as if the fog of old age had been lifted once he resumed his rightful place in battle.

"Yeah? How's your body keeping up?" Drake bantered, buying a moment to recover himself.

"Fit as a fiddle!" Lord Vayne pounded his chest proudly. The captain took a step forward, leaning slightly off kilter. Although he battled to maintain a confident smile, the discomfort on his face was plainly discernable as he raised a hand to his lower back. Through his victorious veneer, he offered Drake quarter once more: "The next hit I score may be fatal. Yield now."

"Can't do it—I need that sword." Drake said evenly.

Lord Vayne lowered his weapon. "What, that old claymore? I have no use for it. Its owner was weak—hardly worth remembering. Moreover, I'm growing too old to wield such heavy steel... If it means something to you, go ahead and take it."

"Even if I yield?" clarified Drake.

"No other way. I'll be forced to kill you if you don't yield, and then you would get no use out of that sword, would you?" mused Vayne.

Drake lowered his sword in return. His hand stung from the wound. He'd been through enough for one day. In all honesty, he wasn't confident he could beat the Cormack duelist, even in his aged form. He suspected the lord was having similar thoughts—that he had conceded this opportunity to Drake because he, too, feared he might lose. Feared that Brandon Vayne's perfect record would be besmirched in the eleventh hour.

Although good sense alone should have compelled him to take the compromise, Drake hesitated. He had a chance to beat the world's most famed duelist and claim his prize in one fell swoop. Alternatively, he could get what he came for and leave without further injury—all he had to sacrifice was his pride.

"Drake," Talia exhorted, standing alongside Bruce the chicken.

Scowling, Drake returned his eyes to the meek old man who had battled him into submission. He begrudgingly dropped his sword to the ground and knelt. "I yield."

"Crivens!" exclaimed Lord Vayne, slouching forward and pressing on his knees for support. He swatted the air, swapping his blade for a scepter. His words tumbled out in a thick Haiglands accent that demanded Drake's full attention to comprehend. "My wee bones were about to give out. Ah dinnae know if ah could go another round."

"Are you all right?" Talia asked, stepping closer to triage head trauma.

"You sound different," observed Drake.

"Aye, thanks, lassie," Brandon stepped forward, forcing himself to remain upright but occasionally leaning on the scepter for support. "Ahm pure done in but feel like a man again—feel like Vayne again."

Varrus appeared on his shoulder. "Like I said—he's only himself with a sword in hand. Before he was Lord Vayne, he was Brandon the Backwater. Spent most his life aspiring to act like a noble; he wanted Brandon Vayne's story to live forever."

"Aye. It's a funny thing. Ye spend yer life becoming the master of something, and ye finally do. One day, ye wake up and know yer the best; ye know you'll ne'er lose a fight to no one... and yer proud. Ye've won. But then what? Ye know ye cannae die, and now ye cannae really live. There's nobody left who can give ye a real fight like when ye was young. When the world was new. Then ye got nothin' left to strive for; ye got no purpose!"

Lord Vayne took a few slow steps forward. In the indirect sunlight, Drake could see the withered state of the aged captain. Deep crow's feet and frown lines were etched in his skin like valleys. His bushy eyebrows added a sense of earned gravity to his visage, though the bulging bags under his eyes betrayed his exhaustion.

"And one day," Vayne continued in his practiced, educated voice, "you get old. Once you've earned your castle, once your name is known throughout the world, you stop to look around. And you realize none of it really mattered. You have no one with whom to share the success you worked so hard to attain. Even the fans who cheered your name can hardly wait for someone to finally defeat you. They don't want the old Vayne anymore; they want the *next* Vayne. They're tired of your story. Even your body fails you, siding with your younger opponents—hoping you'll lose so it may finally rest."

Brandon Vayne pointed at the fallen falchion at Drake's side. A moment later, the sword vanished into the void. The man held up a finger as Drake began to protest: "We did wager that the winner keeps Winter's Edge. I'll treasure it as the prize of my final battle. Now, the last treasure I have left in both this life and the next is my story. The legend of the undefeated Lord Brandon Vayne must transcend. Once you leave here today, I will ensure none may challenge my title again. For your part, I hope you will continue to spread my tale on your travels so that I may live forever."

"Lord Vayne, the swordsman only time could beat," revered Drake.

The voidling floated over to them. It extended both arms, presenting the Frostfang to Drake. As he grasped the hilt of the heavy claymore, the voidling's whispers echoed in his head: "Send me back, lesser creature."

"Thank you, Lord Vayne," Talia bowed graciously. "If you don't mind me asking—do you still need all the swords in there?"

"Talia," admonished Drake.

"What? You're going to need a new one," she remarked, pointing to his empty sheath.

"Truth be told, I never needed any of those trophies. I lived for the battle, not the spoils of victory. Take what you'd like."

Talia tilted her head, encouraging Drake to take action before Vayne changed his mind. Drake nodded his appreciation to their host. "Thanks," he said shortly, stepping through the vanished wall into the dining hall.

He cursorily scanned the weapons hanging on the walls, both behind and without glass cases. He knew Vayne was somewhat erratic, so he resolved to make a quick selection before the lord's mood swung the other way.

He scanned a few placards, strolling along the length of an unbroken wall with Talia in his wake. An elegant poniard with a shiny glass spiral in place of its hilt belonged to Ciara the Cunning, a Cormack assassin active before the Red War. An intricate, handmade battleax with a long wooden hilt was once wielded by an Eastwind sailor named Arne the Gilled. A double-headed eagle regarded Drake solemnly from its golden shield, having failed in its duty to its former owner, Gordon Godwin.

His eyes glossed over the warhammers, maces, and halberds, fixating on a rather simple arming sword. He opened the glass case and lifted the knight's blade. The placard said it was crafted for Hoggar Tallawyn, deceased uncle of King Arthur Tallawyn. Two ancient words were inscribed on the hilt of the well-balanced blade: Deus Chaeri—*Deus greets you.*

Drake abandoned his tattered sheath and fastened the pristine fabric laid at the bottom of the display case around his hip. Once the deadly artifact was secured, he made his way down the hall, toward the exit.

As he emerged from the archway into the sunlight, Drake heard Varrus' shrill voice call out to them. "Wait!"

"Hold," Brandon raised a hand to them. Another hole in the wall had appeared behind him recently. "Varrus said he had a word for you."

The imp crouched on Lord Vayne's head, perching like a gargoyle. "The others that were here—they're part of something big. My advice? Either join them or stay the hell out of their way."

"Noted," Drake acknowledged, turning to leave. He managed only five steps before Lord Vayne called out to him again.

"Wait!"

"What?" demanded Drake.

The taken-aback Cormack captain held out a finger. He licked his lips, frowned, and asked: "Who are you?"

XII. A Long Day

Drake

The Nord was resting on the porch outside the inn.

She stood as Drake approached, eyeing the claymore strung across his back. An imperceptible nod, then she strolled around the side of the building, leading him off the main thoroughfare. He followed her to the back, Talia in step beside him.

"I'm impressed," she remarked, turning to face him. "Retrieving the Frostfang was no small accomplishment. How is Lord Vayne?"

"Here's your sword," Drake said curtly, slinging the heavy blade off his shoulder. He took a final look at the careful craftsmanship of the bear forged into the crosspiece—an intricate flourish that lent credence to the cold slab of metal worthy of a name. He extended the hilt to her. "We done here?"

Her arm dipped as she accepted the blade, underestimating its weight. "Consider one favor to Chieftain Winter repaid. I will send word and return north with the sword."

"All right then." Drake turned to leave. Glancing up at the afternoon sun, he estimated about two hours before sunset and dithered. He could write the day off, spend the night at the inn, and start fresh the next morning. He was hungry and liked the idea of someone else cooking. Alternatively, he could risk the road, close a little more of the gap to Arillia, and leave it to chance. Fifty-fifty whether they encountered another inn or had to make do with nature's bed for the night.

"A word of advice," the Nord interrupted his thoughts. "I heard there was an incident at Fort Banning last night and darker tidings from this side of the Scar; if your destination lies west of Arillia, you may want to make haste."

"What do you mean, *incident?*" Drake narrowed his eyes.

"So long," the Nord bid, beginning her long journey north.

"I didn't like the sound of that," commented Talia.

"We'd better get a move on."

They resumed their westward march, stopping only once to pull a handful of dry rations from their bags. Their pace was sustainable, though the Nord's cryptic warning spurred them to walk faster than the usual flow of traffic on the highway. They passed caravans big and small, all seemingly oblivious to any *incidents.*

A surprising number of wagons cluttered the road. Some carts bore the sigil of Tallawyn's courier network, likely sent to deliver food and supplies to the Frontier. The two cohorts of travelers conspicuously absent from the road were nobles and vacationers; every man, woman and child on the highway had a gritty appearance reflective of the harsh, red environment they traveled across.

By the time the sun finally fell behind the horizon, casting a hellish glow across the grassless plains, exhaustion had long settled into Drake's bones. It had been an unusually long day, and his two skirmishes at the castle had left him feeling sluggish the rest of the afternoon. The sun was no less oppressive than usual, but a gentle breeze had done its best to assuage his discomfort. Now, the cool wind called him to sleep.

"How far are we, do you think?" asked Talia.

"From the Frontier? Don't know. Doesn't look like we're getting there tonight," Drake assessed.

Six tents were clustered off the right shoulder of the road ahead. As he walked nearer, Drake saw several men and a couple women settling in for the night. Sitting around the campfire. Tending to horses. Fussing with their cargo.

One of the portlier men by the fire raised a hand in greeting. He did not smile, but rather eyed the travelers calculatingly. With learned suspicion. "Evening," he called out flatly.

"Evening," returned Drake. "Know how far to Frontier?"

"Hour, hour and a half," answered the merchant. "They close the gate at sundown; you won't be making it through tonight."

"Thanks," acknowledged Drake, continuing farther down the road.

Once the campsite's glow had faded from view and the dim red skies fell to black, Drake veered off the road, traveling a few minutes north of the beaten path. Their fire would be visible to any late travelers with sharp eyes, but he was too tired to care. They were close enough to the Tallawyn garrison that he doubted they'd encounter bandits, and they were far enough from the road that any passing scouts on horseback wouldn't wake them. As far as he was concerned, the day was long over.

He dropped his pack in the dusty red dirt and unfurled his bedroll. "Give me a hand?"

Talia pulled a log out of his pack and laid it in the dirt. She wrapped a couple sausages in foil, ready to lay them on the coals once Drake completed his responsibilities.

He took a knee next to the log and held his palm out, facing the wood; a long second passed, and nothing happened. "Pyros?" he requested haggardly. "You dozing off?"

The living furnace inside his chest heated up as his connection with the Primal strengthened. A puff of flames leaped from his right hand, catching on the wooden log. Drake lowered his hand to the edge of the log, scorching the wood and producing a small deposit of hot ash and embers.

His palm stung as he withdrew it from the flames. He inspected the skin and found it blistered and red. "What the hell, Pyros?"

I... the furnace in him cooled as the Primal fell silent. *We must rest,* his deep voice conveyed in an uncharacteristically humble admission.

"What'd you do to your other hand?" demanded Talia. She knelt next to him and grabbed it for a closer inspection.

"Nothing," he pulled away instinctively.

Talia dug through her pack and produced a roll of bandages. "Let me wrap those at least—you don't want them reopening and getting infected."

He was too tired to argue. He dully allowed her to wrap his injured hands, both singed and one pierced by a sword. All things considered, it had been a rough day.

"That looked like it hurt," she commented, indicating his stab wound.

"It did," he confirmed.

"Did it hurt a lot?" Talia pulled the bandage over his thumb one way, then reversed her decision.

"I'll give you one bit of advice from today—don't let people stab you."

"There," she presented, tying off the wrapping on his right hand. "I'll take care of dinner. You should drink some water," she suggested, laying the sausages onto the hot ash adjacent to the fire.

"Fine," he accepted the flask and drank deeply. Now that they had stopped, he wanted nothing more than to sleep. He wasn't particularly hungry, but he knew a little food tonight would give him strength in the morning.

With the sun down, the temperature had dropped sharply. Their small fire was a noble guardian, staving off the chilling night air. While an inn would have been preferable, they had certainly faced harsher conditions before, and he was in no mood to gripe about his modest privileges.

"One or two?" Talia asked.

"What?"

"Sausages."

"Oh," understood Drake. "One's fine."

"Okay. I'll have two," Talia shared informatively.

Drake grunted his distracted acknowledgement, staring now into the low flames. For a brief moment, he thought he saw images dancing in the fire. He took another sip of water to quell the hallucinations.

"So," Talia sat cross-legged by the fire. "Crazy day, huh?"

"Sure," Drake allowed dryly, lying on his side and propping himself up with his elbow.

"That Brandon Vayne guy seemed... off. What do you think was wrong with him?"

"I don't know." Feeling her curious eyes boring into him as she awaited further comment, he added: "Something with his memory. It sounded like Varrus might have done something to his brain."

"Scary," reflected Talia. "You don't think... You don't think something like that could happen to us, do you?"

Drake glowered in silence. Though his spotty memory had been failing him for a while, he had yet to make the attribution to Pyros. He supposed it was possible the gaps in his identity had been burned away by the Primal, but he suspected the cult that held him prisoner on Baltos was the likelier cause. At least his mental acuity seemed to have stabilized. He hadn't forgotten anything since his escape—or rather, he didn't think he had.

"Sorry!" Talia realized. "I know that's a touchy subject for you. I didn't mean it in a bad way. I was just worried I'd end up... you know."

"Like me," Drake finished.

Talia rolled her eyes. "Not *like you*, per se, but the whole 'gaps-in-your-memory' thing... That scares me."

Drake felt the corner of his lip twitch. "You're not going to end up like me, Talia. This wasn't Pyros' fault. Besides, the Oracle's going to fix it when we get there."

"Right," agreed Talia. "Of course. You don't think that's just a part of getting old, do you?"

"Getting old sucks, but no. You can count on stiffer joints, a few more wrinkles, and worse hangovers, but most people's minds don't break like that. Hell, most people aren't even lucky enough to live that long."

"What's a hangover like?" Talia wondered.

Drake eyed her suspiciously, unsure whether she was pulling his leg. "How old are you now?"

"I don't know," she whistled, searching the starry sky as she attempted to divine an answer. "Fifteen, maybe? What month's it, even?"

"Most respectable establishments won't serve you under sixteen," mused Drake. "Gotta work on your story, there."

"Is drinking fun?" she asked.

"For a little while, when you're young," Drake considered. "Kind of just becomes an expensive habit when you're older. Probably more reasons not to, but it takes the edge off for some."

"Edge off of what?"

Drake made a vague circular motion with his bandaged left hand but found no additional words to add.

"Not hearing a lot in the *pros* column for getting old," noted Talia.

"It's part of life," he said stoically. "You find the good in the bad and live with it."

"I suppose wrinkles and hangovers don't sound too daunting."

"You're going to be fine, kid," Drake promised.

"Yeah. I'm sure you're right. It's just scary something like that could happen to someone like him. I mean, he's famous; he's unbeatable."

"Life has a way of beating us all. If it makes you feel better, everyone gets their own lumps. Same shit, different pile."

"Kind of does, in a weird way," reflected Talia. "Thanks, Drake."

"Pig's probably done," he changed the subject, pulling his knife free from the sheath on his calf. He handed the hilt to Talia.

She speared the three wrapped sausages and dropped one in front of Drake, careful not to touch the hot metal before it had a chance to cool. She gingerly peeled open the foil of her first sausage with the tip of the knife, revealing dark-seared skin.

"Looks ready," Drake held his hand out for the knife. Talia returned the blade to him, and he returned it to its sheath. "Let it sit for a minute before you eat—gives it a chance to cool off a little. Tastes better."

"Okay," Talia folded her arms to restrain her hungry impulse.

Drake saw her mind whirring through her eyes, processing a new line of thought. He readied himself for the inevitable questioning.

"No offense," Talia prefaced tactfully, "but wasn't it weird how that woman didn't scar you? I thought for sure she was going to cut up your face."

"Just because you put *no offense* before a sentence doesn't make it any less rude," admonished Drake.

"But wasn't it weird?" insisted Talia.

"Can't I just be glad she didn't?" The same thought had surfaced in his mind several times throughout the day, but he wasn't keen on voicing that he *should* have been stabbed. Part of him was frustrated with how badly he had been outclassed; despite proving a match for the Val'Kyran who had thrashed him outside of Lyon, he still didn't stand a chance against the woman—Prism. Even Pyros had been stumped, sheepishly explaining away his part in the undignified loss with: *I can't be expected to do everything.*

"Sure, I mean, I'm happy she didn't disfigure you into a hideous freak... but didn't it look like she wanted to? And didn't it sound like that Iko guy wanted her to? I wonder why she didn't."

Drake recalled the moment with crystal clarity: winded and on his back, he had looked up into soulless eyes shadowed by black and purple haze. For just a second—a fleeting moment he thought he had imagined—two deep brown eyes pierced through the veil to reach his. Almost recognizing something in what they found. The cool rapier's tip *was* destined to wound him, but it had been capriciously halted by a benign whim.

"Sorry the show disappointed you," Drake snorted sardonically. He took a bite of sausage to emphasize his point, accidentally scalding his tongue and the roof of his mouth with the sizzling juices inside. He hastily followed it with a swig of water, but the damage was done; against his own advice, he had rushed to eat and would no longer be able to enjoy the flavorful meat.

"Not true," moaned Talia, evidently exasperated by his sarcasm. "By the way, are those ready?"

"I'd give it another minute," Drake advised, taking another sip of water.

"I did feel bad today—when she was kicking your ass," Talia continued. "Touching."

"But seriously, I feel like I'm always just standing on the sidelines while you're fighting for both of us. I feel like dead weight, but I want to help."

"We had this conversation before, Talia. You don't need a weapon."

"But if I had a—" she rebutted, making a stabbing gesture.

"You know I don't want you running around with swords or knives. It's a false sense of security—remember last time?"

She huffed in frustration, then took a deep breath to reset, not ready to let the subject go. "You said if I find a bow, I can keep it."

"I don't remember saying that at all," disputed Drake.

"I already kind of know how to shoot—my daddy taught me," reasoned Talia. "If I find a bow, I promise I'll mainly use it for hunting. I'd only use it for defense if there was a group of bad guys after us and you couldn't handle them all by yourself. Think about it—remember how good Nadya was with a bow? I could totally do that."

"You forgetting how that ended? The bow didn't exactly do much to help her," rebuked Drake.

Talia swallowed her rebuttal, deliberately and painstakingly avoiding a confrontational tone. "You will still be in charge, and I'll always listen to what you say. I'll only use it as a last resort. I won't shoot at anyone anywhere near you, and if I ever get in a bad way, I'll drop the bow and take off running. Please? Just say: if I find myself a bow, you'll let me keep it."

"Fine," acquiesced Drake, beleaguered and inexplicably swayed by her argument. Perhaps owed to his repeated losses and near-death encounters, part of him recognized he couldn't protect her forever. Before her astonishment shifted to celebration, he held up a finger to name his conditions: "But weapons aren't toys, Talia. I mean it. If you find a bow—and I sure as hell ain't buying you one—you don't aim it at people unless your life depends on it, and you never aim it anywhere near me. You're gonna take care of your own gear, but you're not ever going to risk your life for a wooden stick. Now, I'm serious—if it ever gets bad, you run fast as you can."

"Yes! I can do that," Talia assured hurriedly, clearly worried he would change his mind and revoke the agreement.

"We'll see," Drake took another bite of sausage. It had cooled down enough to eat, but his sense of taste was still fried.

"Maybe I'll find one in Arillia," hoped Talia.

"Arillia's really not the kind of place we want to overstay our welcome," cautioned Drake.

"You've been before? What's it like?"

"I might have been... I'm not sure. It feels familiar. Anyway—I know enough about it. It's where the pond scum of the world and all the headhunters mingle from both Tallamar and Deuzos; it's not a place for kids. You're not leaving my sight for a second while we're there."

"Whatever you say. You're the boss," deferred Talia, taking the first bite of her dinner. She had evidently decided one momentous victory was enough for the night.

"Get some sleep," Drake advised, settling into his bed. "If we make good time tomorrow, we'll hopefully get through there by sundown."

"Are we normal, Drake?" Talia asked out of the blue.

"What kind of question is that?" he answered with his eyes closed.

"Is this what life's supposed to be like? I mean, will I ever be a normal girl, doing normal girl things, living a normal girl life?" she wondered.

"Does it matter?" Drake muttered.

"No," Talia groaned, used to that answer.

"Being normal is overrated," Drake said through a yawn. "Boring people with boring lives. Everyone's got problems—the taxman, the king, those merchants back there. They all moan about little things that don't really matter. Look for the good in the bad, and you'll be happy with your lot in life; at least it's not boring."

"Same shit, different pile," echoed Talia.

"Exactly," approved Drake, oddly proud his lessons were sticking.

A long pause hung in the air—a silent night, save for the crackling fire. Although sleep called him to its lulling embrace, he clung to consciousness for a spell longer, sensing one more question lurking on her the tip of her tongue.

"Drake?" Talia probed, checking if he was still awake.

"Hmm?" he grunted.

"Do you think Deus is real?"

"Goodnight, Talia."

XIII. Freecity, Arillia

Drake

The first rays of dawn's early light stirred him from a dreamless sleep.

Although the warmth of his bedroll tempted him to close his eyes for just one more minute of shelter from the cold morning, Drake groaned and kicked himself out into the open air, rolling to his knees. Lethargy and gravity pulled him back to the ground, but his discipline won out. On his feet, he wiped his groggy eyes and stretched, momentarily blinded by his sudden ascent.

When his vision returned, he saw Talia sit up and stretch her arms, yawning like a lion. "What's all the commotion about?"

Drake pushed through his torpor and packed his bedroll. "Come on. Time to get moving."

"It's early," Talia protested, lying back down with hands over her eyes.

"Early bird gets the worm," he shared wisely.

"Second mouse gets the cheese," she retorted.

"I'm leaving you behind," he threatened, collecting his equipment and starting toward Arillia.

"You would never!" she challenged groggily.

"Just head keep heading west. I'll meet you there," Drake called over his shoulder.

Talia groaned mightily, prying herself from her bed. "Wait up!" she shouted, scrambling to get her pack in order.

"Early bird," Drake reminded her, continuing on without pause.

Thirty seconds later, he heard hurried footsteps approaching from behind. Talia came up alongside him, panting as she slowed to a walking pace.

"You're a bully," she grumbled.

"I've been called worse," he shrugged.

"Were you actually going to leave me behind?"

"Early bird," Drake whispered unabashedly, looking her in the eye.

They were among the first travelers back on the road as the sky turned from reddish orange to blue. The frigid air soon gave way to a familiar and pleasant warmth, not yet risen to the smothering heat of a Haiglands afternoon. The companionable breeze returned, carrying a new saltiness on its breath.

The Frontier saw them before they saw the Frontier. Pairs of armed Tallawyn riders scouted the road, not bothering to stop their patrol for the likes of Drake and Talia. They were faceless vagabonds, two among hundreds of wanderers passing between civilized land and the Freecity that sprouted in its shadow. Even the immaculate white horses paid them no mind, snorting in derision as if to protest that they had to share the same roads with commoners.

The garrison was well defended. A border wall spanned the visible horizon, stretching as far north and south as the eye could see. Watchtowers punctuated the wall at consistent intervals, manned by a skeleton crew of blue-and-white tabards. The bowmen beneath the soaring wolf banner were likely a fresh shift, chatting with their comrades and strolling across the ramparts.

The road passed through a yawning gate, tall and wide enough to fit three large wagons at a time. One such vehicle was currently undergoing inspection as its four owners stood patiently to the side. An apple was levied from the cargo, then the wagon was free to continue on its way.

One of the six sentinels motioned Drake and Talia closer. Two were positioned on the near side of the gate, an additional two on the far side, and two reserves sat on a crate in the shade.

The sentry took another bite of his green apple and held up a hand to signal that Drake should wait for him to finish chewing. After many deliberate crunches, the soldier swallowed and asked: "What business brings you through the Frontier?"

"Mercenaries looking for work in Arillia," Drake answered shortly.

The guard took another unhurried bite of the apple, shifting his eyes back and forth between them. "Mercenaries," he repeated flatly. "What kind of work do you do?"

"Whatever pays," Drake provided uninspiringly.

"I feel that," munched the sentry. "Not bounty hunters, I'd assume?"

"Dock work, trader caravans, ranches," Drake listed dispassionately.

"Fair enough," shrugged the Tallawyn. He pointed at Talia. "Family?"

"Yes," Drake said succinctly.

"Makes sense. Arillia's not much a place for kids, mind."

"I'm not a kid," Talia protested touchily.

"Oh yeah? How old are you?"

"Fift—sixteen," she lowered her pitch convincingly.

"Right," the sentinel said with a deadpan expression. He took another slow crunch of his apple, either to satiate his voracious appetite or to emphasize his disbelief. "You'll want to work on that before you hit the taverns, mind."

Drake placed a hand on Talia's shoulder, dissuading her from further discourse. "All clear?" he asked.

The man tilted his head side to side. "Got anything to pay the toll?"

"The toll?" Drake repeated, unamused.

"You've been using roads maintained by Tallawyn. This is a Tallawyn checkpoint. Do you have something to pay the toll?"

"We're looking for work out west. Couldn't find any money here," Drake answered evenly.

"In the bags?" the sentinel gestured with his apple core.

"A bit of wood, tattered old clothes," listed Drake.

The sentinel looked Talia up and down, then sized up Drake again. His eyes momentarily paused on the sheath at Drake's side but continued their holistic assessment shortly after. Judging their grubby appearances, the sentry decided they had little of value to offer him.

"Go on, then," he decided, stepping sideways to allow them passage. "Just remember it was Don McGinn who gave you free passage; next time you're through these parts, it'd be nice if you had something to show thanks."

"Your service is appreciated," Drake praised emptily.

Past the checkpoint, Drake felt a sudden surge of freedom. He looked back and saw the imposing stone wall framed with two massive blue-and-white banners. With those colors ended Tallawyn's sphere of influence. He was past the westernmost point of the kingdom, walking now in a wild land governed by no lord. This road ran through the independent den of rogues named Arillia. While he would be foolish to let his guard down now, he felt a weight lifted off his shoulders knowing that the king's law could no longer reach him.

The bounties in Lyon and bloodshed in Dunloy were consigned to the past, but the scars inflicted at the Twins yet remained.

No distance would ever be enough to escape the festering guilt over Desmond's death; regardless of what flags flew above him, Drake would carry on knowing he had failed to protect the boy who trusted him with his life.

He placed a paternal hand on Talia's shoulder, vowing to himself that he would not fail twice.

"What's got you all serious?" Her eyebrow arched in palpable surprise.

"We've officially left Tallamar. You've never been this far, have you?"

"No. But, to be honest, it still feels a lot like the other side of the wall," Talia confessed, gesturing at the red dirt all around them. She stopped walking and turned to face the bypassed garrison, holding up a hand to shield her eyes from the blinding sun. "Huh. Is that a hawk?"

Drake followed her gaze and saw a large brown bird descend onto one of the watchtowers. Seconds later, the bells echoed across the towers.

The iron teeth of the gate slammed shut.

"Whoa. What do you think's going on?" Talia wondered.

"As long as it doesn't become our problem," Drake dismissed.

"Guess that Nord woman was onto something," she reflected.

"This is why we don't sleep in," he reaffirmed, recognizing an extra ten minutes of rest might have locked them in on the other side of the wall.

"Was that the early bird you were talking about?" she said of the hawk.

Within the next three hours, he spotted a blue sparkle on the southern horizon. As they caught up to the horse-drawn cart they had seen at the border, passing a few soon-to-be-disappointed travelers heading toward Tallamar, he recognized the sparkle belonged to a shimmering ocean. Rocky cliffs dropped off to churning waters below—a violent boundary dividing free land and the indomitable sea.

He smelled them before he saw them.

A sprawling tent city fanned out to the north of the road, acting as a marketplace with more-and-less permanent housing. Drake spotted a herd of twenty cows fenced in a large pen between tents, destined either for the auction block or to enter the local food chain—processed by the butcher and sent to the taverns for cooking.

The pavilions of tents buzzed with activity. Shoppers weaved between makeshift lodging and transient shops. A pillar of smoke rose from a portable forge near the front of the tent line, identifying the blacksmith to buyers in need of his services while inadvertently suffocating his neighbors.

As he observed the fray, Drake watched shoppers repeatedly intrude into one unfortunate denizen's tent. Still slumbering from the night before, the man would groggily shake a fist at the opened flap of his tent. Seconds later, another wayward vagrant would pull back the canvas again.

"Look at it!" marveled Talia, nearly colliding with traffic going the opposite way.

Drake steered her to an unobstructed path. "I see it. Arillia must be farther ahead."

"This isn't Arillia?" asked Talia, shocked. "It's bigger than most cities."

"It's a migrant camp. Guess it's part of Arillia. These folks live between worlds—didn't want to live under any king. I know Arillia has a port, but I don't see any ships here. Must mean we've got more road to go."

Talia gave him a disappointed look. "You don't want to check this place out at all?"

A withered man stumbled out from behind a tent and into the road. Worn rags spilled from his frail body, much too large for him. One arm ended in a stump; the nails on his good hand were yellow and warped, matching his few remaining teeth. Beady eyes stared at Drake's chest from under drooping, discolored eyelids. The man scratched his ear violently as he spoke to Drake through ragged breaths: "I need some more. Please! Just a little more..."

He reached out his gnarled hand for a resupply. Drake swatted the arm away and used his left hand to topple the stranger into the nearest tent.

"Drake!" Talia objected in shock.

"No," Drake pointed at the addled man, guiding Talia forward with his left hand.

The collapsed junkie spaced out, staring into the sun with glassy eyes.

"Little harsh, no?" she questioned once they had distanced themselves from the incident.

"Their kind of people can turn violent real fast. Plus, you don't know if they're carrying diseases or trying to lure you into some kind of trap. Nothing good ever comes out of helping strangers."

"I don't know if I agree with that."

"You don't have to agree with it. My word goes," Drake reminded her.

"What if we get into trouble sometime and need a stranger's help?"

"Only time we'd ever be in that position is if we got into trouble because of strangers—see point *A*," Drake concluded.

"I was a stranger when you helped me," Talia countered quietly.

"That's different," he delineated without directly noting that Desmond had been responsible for his decision.

"How's it different?" she pushed.

"Because I said so."

Talia rolled her eyes and stared straight ahead. "Well if *you said so*."

"You understand I'm just trying to keep you safe, right? Maybe the guy with twice as many years of life experience knows what he's talking about?"

"Maybe," she considered, folding her arms. "Even though you can't remember most of it," she muttered as an afterthought.

"Now that was both rude and uncalled for. Didn't your daddy ever teach you manners?"

"I guess he died before he could give me that lesson."

Drake offered no response. They walked on in silence.

"Sorry," she mumbled finally.

"What's that?" he asked innocuously.

"Sorry!" she groaned in exasperation. Sighing through her frustration, she composed herself. "I know you're just trying to protect me. I don't know; just feels like you go a little overboard sometimes."

"It's overcautious until the one time it's not. Now, I know you know this: we don't get to make mistakes in this world. I know your life hasn't exactly been easy, but you don't know half of how bad people can get. There are a lot of dark, twisted creeps out there, and there's a whole lot more normal people who do bad things. My job is to make sure you don't have to find out about any of that the hard way—your job is to trust me. Okay?"

"I know," Talia relented unequivocally. "I appreciate it. I do. I guess part of me just wants to believe the world isn't so bad, you know?"

"I get it, kid," Drake acknowledged gruffly, "but the world ain't always what we wish it was. Gotta make the best of what we got."

"Heard," registered Talia.

"Anyone ever tell you what happened to Tyranos after the Red War?"

"Nope," she said shortly, possibly taking the knowledge gap as a slight.

"After the war, a lot of the Cormacks who survived the front lines came home feeling none too happy about how it all ended. Many felt the generals who signed the peace treaty had sold out their king. Many also felt betrayed by the Godwins, who took the Blasted Lands west of the Scar as their own. The war was over, but a lot of fighting-aged men still saw enemies on all sides."

"When Tallawyn merchants started coming down to Tyranos, the Cormacks wouldn't let them into the city. Even though it was under Tallawyn occupation. They were understandably pissed. Hell, your dad might even have been one of the resistors before he moved up to Lyon."

Talia's attention perked up with this last comment. "Well, it's all Tallawyn land now; what happened?"

Drake nodded. "So, the Tallawyns had a problem: they could send armed escorts to bring their merchants into the city, but most of the Cormacks still wouldn't do business with them. They kept buying from their own. One day, the general occupying Tyranos, Gabriel Snively, had an idea. He ordered a dozen wagons of poppies from the Great Plains and put a big tariff on alcohol coming into the city. Snively paid a few of the locals to peddle the cheap opium in the streets, and a couple weeks later, half the city's hooked on the stuff.

"The Cormack men stopped showing up to work, Tallawyn merchants took over trade, but now they had a new problem: no Tallawyn citizens wanted to move to a poor, drugged-out city. So Snively made opium illegal. Started off by killing Cormacks in the streets who looked like they were laced—that led to riots, so eventually they just started rounding them up and exiling them west of the new border. Those Cormacks started flowing west to their cousin cities in Deuzos, like the Grotto, but the Godwins didn't want them bringing their opium problem with them. So they also built a wall stretching from the Scar to the sea. Now, you've got all these Cormacks stuck between two kingdoms that don't want them."

"Dang. That's messed up," Talia winced.

"Yep. Eventually, the exiles made Arillia. All the world's rejects kept ending up here, and it turned into the Freecity. Today, it's a big trade port—sometimes the only way for Tallamar to get goods from Deuzos and vice versa. Plus, you've got a ton of mercenaries who'll take undesirable work anywhere. Dangerous bounty hunting, protection for merchants, seasonal labor... it's better than it was, but Arillia still has a big drug problem. Among other things."

"What happened to the people left behind in Tyranos?"

"The Cormacks?" Drake clarified. "Most of the men were killed or chased off. Then a bunch of Tallawyn soldiers stepped in to marry the widows. Decade or two later, I guess it's pretty much like every other city in Tallamar."

"Yikes. Okay, you win—the world's a bad place," Talia accepted darkly.

"That's the spirit," commended Drake.

"And you didn't make that up?"

"Nope. All true."

"Pretty solid memory there, all of a sudden," Talia noted suspiciously.

Drake spread his hands. "I don't know what it is. I can remember facts and figures just fine. My memory only gets fuzzy on the personal stuff."

"Weird," Talia remarked. "Do you know where you heard that story?"

"Nope," admitted Drake. "I know someone told it to me. Wouldn't have learned it from a book. But I can't remember who."

"Bizarre," said Talia. "It's almost like there's a part of your brain that remembers general stuff, and a different part that remembers personal stuff."

"Looking for some kind of doctor certification?" he teased.

"I'm just saying, man. I think I might be onto something," she shrugged indifferently.

On the southwestern horizon, the port of Arillia finally came into view. The docks were bustling like a dozen Freeports. Sailors swarmed like ants, carrying cargo between warehouses. Glimpsing between shops and halls, the permanent and much more impressive cousins to those of the tent city, he saw a line of wagons extending in front of a formidable stone building that cast its shadow over half of the pier.

On the north side of the main road, a concentric cluster of taverns, inns, bars, and pubs made up a small village. Despite the fact that the day had barely reached noon, a flock of rowdy carousers roamed the village, hopping thirstily from one roof to the next, passing out on the patios, and pissing in the alleys between establishments.

Drake made a mental note to confine his business to the south side of Arillia.

Turning off the road and toward the pier, they stepped into a wide, rectangular forum that connected the shops to the east, the docks in the south, and the hill farther west. Little traffic seemed to flow to and from the hill, but the Freecity looked like a vibrant capital of commerce in all other directions.

"So, what's the plan?" Talia asked.

"Well," Drake considered, "We're running low on food, so we'll want to top off while we're here. I'll admit I'm a little curious about the merc hubs, but I don't know if we want to go rubbing elbows with their kind in the halls."

"Would be fun," Talia shrugged. "Up to you."

They crossed the bustling forum, passing free people of all shapes and sizes. He saw Val'Kyrans walking alongside packs of Nords, heard Cormack and Eastwind accents haggling over fees, and smelled the restaurants selling exotic delicacies from Taoxos and Ayrabos. Some a little too exotic. Among the scents rose one particularly pungent odor of cumin, onions, and garlic. He wouldn't be found within an ass's roar of that eatery.

To his left, stumbling out on the porch of an eatery marked by both foreign and common lettering, two drunken soldiers in blue-and-white Tallawyn uniforms were causing a scene.

"I'll cut your head off, you big chicken! I'll piss in your mouth, and then I'll cut your head off!" the Tallawyn threatened, pointing an accusatory finger behind him. His other hand was draped around the neck of his comrade, who struggled to keep the drunkard on his feet.

"Run home, pup," spat an armored man in a gold-and-black tabard, emerging from the restaurant after them.

"Bawk! Bawk!" squawked the Tallawyn soldier, attempting to free himself from his friend's support. He succeeded and began to strut around, precariously close to the edge of the porch, flapping his arms like a chicken. "Bawk! You're a... a chicken!"

"Bad dog!" the Godwin soldier shoved the drunk Tallawyn, sending him tumbling down four steps and onto the grass.

The Tallawyn struggled to regain his footing. "I'll kill ya, you... bawk..." he cradled his head in his hands, presumably attempting to stop the world from spinning around him in a desperate attempt not to vomit.

The standing Tallawyn took issue with the Godwin's attack and swung a sucker punch reprisal that caught him unawares. The Godwin barely flinched. He grabbed the Tallawyn with one hand on his neck, one hand on his shirt, and grappled him to the floor. The pair rolled down the stairwell after the first, knocking over one oblivious bystander in the process.

A short, honey-toned man emerged from the shop wearing a flowing white robe and headdress. A much larger man, perhaps seven feet tall and twenty stone heavy, emerged behind him. Long dreadlocks spilled over his rippling arms—folded to add a credible threat behind the proprietors' warning.

"Hey!" the white-robed man pointed a stern finger at the tussling men below. "You no do that here! Go to Ring. Or wet district. No fight in my store!"

The combatants disentangled themselves, continuing to exchange taunts as they distanced from each other.

"Want to take this to The Ring?" challenged the less-drunk Tallawyn as he scraped his friend off the ground.

"Come find me—I'll kick your teeth in," taunted the Godwin, puffing out his chest as he walked away to the north.

"Begone!" the mountainous Val'Kyran roared from the porch.

Both the Godwin and the Tallawyns hastily vanished into the crowd.

"What the hell's the wet district?" Talia laughed to Drake.

A neighboring bystander overheard the comment and contributed: "He means the Slippery Slope—or the sloppy slope, depending what time of day you go. It's the drinking district across the road."

"Thanks," Talia said appreciatively. "What's The Ring?"

"Not from around here, I take it?" the lanky stranger grinned. "That's the hill up there—the one battleground of true lawlessness. MacLeod set some rules for the Freecity, but anything goes up there. No reason for most folk to head that way unless you've got a grudge to settle. Or you're looking for private bounties."

"Private bounties?" Drake repeated, passively interested.

"Sure. Most of the public bounties are posted in the guild halls—whenever the Godwins have problems with criminals in their land, or the Tallawyns in theirs. Private bounties can go on anyone, guilty or innocent, as long as the money's real. Gets a little messy when Tallawyns open contracts on Godwins and vice versa, but there had to be a market for it somewhere. The bounty hunters who take those tend to be a bit more competitive, though—I wouldn't go looking for trouble up there unless you're trying to kill somebody."

"Good to know," said Drake. "Thanks."

"Cooper," the man mistook Drake's acknowledgement as an invitation to introduce himself. "Gordon Cooper."

"You take care now, Cooper," Drake dismissed, steering Talia toward the pier.

"Seemed like a nice guy," Talia remarked cheerfully.

"This whole city's a dump," decided Drake.

They passed in front of a particularly crowded building, outside of which an animated crier rang a small, handheld bell. "Postings of the hour are on the boards! Make up to thirty silver for a mostly-honest day's work!"

"That's the merc hall, then?" Talia asked.

Drake pointed at the worn sign above the building. By the imprint in the weathered paint, he could tell the label used to say, 'Guild Hall'. Instead, it was now the 'Gild Hall'.

"Guess there's no *you* in *guild,* huh?" Talia cracked.

Drake let out a long puff of air through his nose. He was frustrated by the joke, but he was more annoyed that he hadn't thought of it sooner.

They continued south toward the pier, parallel now to the long line of transport vehicles. Talia abruptly stopped and pointed at the harbor. "Hey!"

"What?" Drake halted, following her finger.

"Look at that ship!" she indicated an impressive galleon that towered above its neighbors, visible even overtop the logistics warehouse. "Do you see that flag? Does it mean what I think it means?"

Drake saw the black flag flying from the ship and grinned. "That's a pirate ship."

Talia's mouth hung open as she stared at him in disbelief. "Just out in the open like that? Didn't Tallawyn destroy them all? Aren't they worried the royal navy will come for them?"

Drake's grin grew into a knowing smile despite his attempt to compose himself. "How about it? You want to meet a pirate today?"

Talia raised an eyebrow, sensing a trap. "Aren't you the one who's always going on about how careful we need to be? Now you're saying you want me to go meet bloodthirsty, murderous pirates?"

"I'd probably ease up on the name calling when we see them, but otherwise, sounds like an idea."

Talia shook her head, incredulous. "What other words would you even use to describe pirates?"

Drake tilted his head in thought as he walked. "I think they prefer *Masters of the High Seas.*"

"Oh, come on," Talia objected doubtfully. "Now you're just being ridiculous."

"This way," Drake called to her.

"Hang on, are you serious? We're actually going down there to meet pirates? I mean, the food shops are literally right here," Talia pointed behind the Gild Hall.

"This might come as a surprise, but before I met you, I happened to be a pirate," stated Drake.

"Seriously? Like, actual-factual?" Talia probed with a smirk.

"It's true," he confirmed. "How much do you want to bet we get down there and that ship's called the *Redemption*?"

"I'm not betting anything," Talia declined, holding up her hands.

"Smart girl. I was worried Dunloy had ruined you."

"Professional gamblers know when to walk away from the table—you'll learn your lesson one of these days," she patronized, much to his chagrin.

Down on the busy docks, Drake navigated to the pirate ship moored at the pier. As he wound his way through laboring sailors passing by with barrels and cargo and handcarts, he felt the refreshing sea air reawaken something within him. Part of him wanted to throw himself into the calm turquoise waters, which were protected by the natural windward peninsula, but he managed to keep himself in check.

They reached the jetty extending alongside the imposing galleon. Gesturing to the rear section of the boat, Drake identified the familiar word etched into weathered wood: *Redemption.*

"No way," Talia laughed incredulously. "I'm being hustled. This can't be real."

"Oi!"

Drake heard the scowling voice and immediately recognized he was among friends. He turned to face a familiar, portly man in pinstriped trousers. "Cutlass. Two, two-and-a-half feet."

"Hagan!" Drake recalled. He extended a hand to the armorer. "Good to see you're alive and well."

"Likewise, laddie," Hagan rumbled shortly. "Ho, ye! Barnacle brains! Dinnae spill that!"

"Aye, just lost me feet. Mind that dodgy plank," another pirate warned from Drake's right. The familiar man peered over the cumbersome barrel he was lugging to shore. "Gawblimey!"

The pirate nearly dropped his barrel upon spotting Drake. He shifted the load in his hands to view him more clearly. "Bloomin' heck. Drake, innit? You all right?"

"I am. Sorry, I can't place the name."

"Aye, no worries. It's Bartholomew. I must look diff'rint with the beard, eh?"

"That's it," Drake affirmed pleasantly. "Is Kika around?"

"Aye, I finks she's gone for a cheeky pint on the hill. Nills n'em should be there 'swell."

"Thanks, Bartholomew. This is Talia, by the way."

"Ah! Cheers, Talia," Bartholomew said, resuming his duties.

"Awrite," Hagan nodded amicably before wandering off to extend another crew member some colorful encouragement.

"Let's head up to the hill," Drake suggested, retracing their steps along the docks.

"That was so cool," gushed Talia. "I mean, they're total rebels, right? And they looked just as cool as I thought they would... smelled a little on the strong side, but who ever said don't meet your heroes?"

"You always had a thing for pirates?" Drake laughed.

"Sort of," explained Talia. "I remember when I was young, my daddy used to tell me stories before bed. My favorite was about the Cormack captain, Arthur McCallaway. He used to be a normal seafaring captain, but then he became a pirate outlaw and single-handedly robbed Tallawyn's prized ships. He even defeated the royal navy and sacked Port Eastwind."

"Oh yeah?" Drake frowned. "Sounds like a violent story before bed."

"Pretty strong anti-Tallawyn messaging, now that I think about it," reflected Talia. "Still, I liked the ideas behind it: never let anyone tell you what to do, fight to stay free, don't pay taxes... Actually, that sounds a bit like your life lessons, doesn't it?"

"Then you can see why I had a brief career in piracy," Drake smiled. "What was that name again? Arthur McCallaway?"

"That's right," Talia confirmed.

"You not seeing it?" Drake asked.

"Seeing what?" Talia blinked.

"You're really not seeing it?"

"Tell me!"

"Arthur McCallaway... Eamon Callaway..."

"But he wasn't a..." Talia drifted off in contemplation.

Drake paused at the top of the pier and scanned the docks for a familiar vessel. "Yes, he was." He pointed out an elongated pirate ship on the opposite side of the harbor. "That was his ship—the *Icebreaker*. He was a real pirate, just a different name."

Talia wasn't sure how to feel about the revelation. "I mean, on the one hand, he looked pretty unimpressive when we first met him... but that's gotta be long after his prime, right? He was cool back in the day—like Brandon Vayne?"

"I think he'd live up to most of the tales," Drake evaluated respectfully.

"Cool. Then, yeah. Today's been a cool day," Talia nodded, content.

"Wait till you meet Eris and Kika. I think you're really going to like them," promised Drake.

"I'm excited!" bubbled Talia. "Tell me about them?"

"Kika's basically the Pirate Queen. She's the captain in charge of all the other pirates. I think Eris is her kid niece or something. She also has a ship."

"What? Their *captain's* a woman? She must be badass."

"They're also both Mystics, which probably doesn't hurt."

"I'm already sold, man," Talia tittered. As they began ascending the western hill, distancing themselves from the throngs below, Talia's smile slowly faded into a line of apprehension. "Hold on. Wasn't this hill the place those guys were calling The Ring? Didn't they warn us not to come up here?"

"Kika's a friend," Drake assured her. "If she's up here, I'm sure we'll be fine."

At the top of the slope, the hill leveled out to a ring of flat ground with a small crater in the center. Inside the crater, a wide wooden signboard held several wanted posters with hand-drawn faces and descriptions. Beyond the board, two sizeable but lonely buildings rested atop the hill. The building on the left seemed dormant, but the tavern to the right was very much alive. Jovial music escaped through open windows, both the stringed and brass varieties.

Drake looked out to sea and saw a great view of the harbor. He easily identified the *Redemption* but marveled at the surprising number and variety of crafts moored at the docks. A little farther out to sea, Drake spotted a small fortress on an island. Inside the four stone walls, a luxurious manor rested atop a bed of well-maintained flowers and grass.

Returning his attention to the path in front of him, he stopped short of the gateway to the flat hilltop. The ceremonial entryway spanned six yards across, matching the full width of the ascending path. On either side of the gateway, two tall poles jutted out from the ground, together suspending a banner that warned in red-painted lettering: *Entering The Ring.*

To punctuate the boundary, a thick red line was painted across the ground from pole to pole. Drake noticed this arbitrary line was repeated in front of the buildings on the opposite side. Judging by the bloodstains mixed in with red dust in the space between the banner and the tavern, he interpreted that the zone between red lines was the lawless battleground Cooper had warned him about.

Two armed swordsmen stood on the near side of the red line—in the safe zone. The shirtless sentinels flexed threateningly as Drake approached.

"Hey, greenie," spat one of the men. "You don't want to be here unless you got a death wish. This is The Ring, got it? Run along and play farmer at the hall down there."

"Hmm," Drake voiced, unconvinced. "I see a tavern I'd like to visit on that side of the hill, and I don't see any reason I should stay thirsty over here."

The men exchanged incredulous glances, then burst into laughter. "You deaf or something? A little stupid, huh?" the shorter, more sunburned one on the left tapped his head meaningfully.

The uglier one on the right chortled. "You step across that line, we'll put a knife in you. This bar's for respected mercs only."

One such respected merc emerged from the tavern that very second. He casually strolled over, weapons visible but sheathed on his person.

"Like I said," Drake cracked his neck, resting his hand on the hilt of his sword. "I'm mighty thirsty. Sounds to me like I just need to put you two in the ground, then I can enjoy a drink. That right?"

"Do you know who we are?" scoffed the taller man, revealing hideous, sharklike teeth.

"We're *MacLeod's Mercs*, moron. The best of the best. Go ahead, cross the line. See what happens," taunted the shorter one.

"Yo! Dumb and dumber," the respected merc called from behind them. He stopped ten feet away from the red line, clearly in no hurry to cross to safety. "He's with Lady Kika. Put a sock in it and enjoy your sunbathing."

The shorter swordsman scowled, turning to address the newcomer. "Who the hell's that, and why would I care? I'm with *MacLeod*—that's a name you should remember."

The newcomer pushed a strand of long brown hair out of his eye and rested a hand on his hip. Now that Drake could see him clearly, he recognized the pirate. He had a deceptively boyish appearance, but Drake knew he was around his own age and a well-respected archer on Kika's crew.

"I'm warning you," Hervey tried diplomatically. His tone suggested that he didn't truly care whether they heeded his advice. "Lady Kika's bad side is not a side you want to be on."

The taller gatekeeper scoffed in derision. "I never heard of no Kika. That name don't mean a lick to me, boy!"

Drake heard a pack of footsteps come to a halt shortly behind him. Near his right ear, a familiar voice addressed the mercenaries. Her soft yet powerful tone caused the hair on his neck to stand at attention.

"My name is Lady Kika. If you have any unresolved affairs to settle in this life, I suggest you remember the name."

XIV. Grand Ambitions

Drake

*D*amn, she's hot!"

"Talia!" Drake scolded out of the corner of his mouth.

"Well, I mean, come on!" she fawned quietly as Kika strutted up to the red line. "Don't you think so? How can I look like that?"

In truth, he was thinking along the same lines. She looked as beautiful as ever in her black boots and blazing-red cutoff jacket that matched her flowing hair. She seemed healthier, too. Her shoulders were set back in a familiar posture of nonchalance, but he sensed an air of newfound purpose about her. Like the wind had returned to her sails.

"Close your mouth," Drake chided Talia. "It's rude to stare."

"Don't tell me your names—I don't care," Kika said as she stopped one pace short of the red line. "I will now walk into The Ring. I will count to three, and you rats can either scurry off or test my patience. I expect you'll have the courtesy to refrain from wasting a lady's time with limp words."

Lady Kika crossed the red line and took three paces forward. She turned to face Drake with a bored expression and counted: "One... Two..."

The pair of MacLeod's Mercs exchanged affronted looks, then drew their swords. Cockily, they strutted toward Kika.

"Three."

In one swift motion, she drew both of her twin blades simultaneously and swung them to either side. On her left, she calmly deflected an overhand blow aimed at her head. On her right, she slashed through the exposed throat of the slower, shorter sentinel. Blood spurted a surprising distance as the vein was severed; before the spatter reached the ground, Kika swung her left sword around in an upward stroke. The mercenary flinched, holding his sword in front of his face. Her blade sliced under his armpit, rending the artery and immediately spilling a fountain of blood.

The mercenary cried out in agony and dropped his sword, collapsing to the ground and cradling himself in a fruitless attempt to stop the bleeding.

Kika calmly returned her swords to their places on her hip, then started toward the board in the crater of The Ring.

Drake looked to his side and found Talia beaming.

"I want to be her when I grow up," she fantasized, enthralled by the Pirate Queen.

"Get in line," a young girl said from behind them.

Drake turned to see a small pack of pirates gathered around a girl as jaunty as the breeze. Standing a head-and-a-half shorter than him, she matched Kika's ensemble from her black boots and pants down to the two knives on her right hip. Instead of a trimmed jacket Kika like sported, the girl completed her outfit with a green corset that matched her bandana. Just a hint of vibrant flair.

"You've gotten taller, Eris," Drake greeted truthfully. He thought back to the little girl he rescued from the prison on Baltos and marveled at how she had grown. She was at least a head taller than when last they met, and her face was beginning to take on more of an oval shape like her aunt's. He might not have recognized her at all, if not for the added context of Kika's presence.

Eris casually folded her arms behind her head. "I've been drinking a lot of milk," she disclosed proudly.

"Talia'," the older girl introduced herself, peering around Drake.

"Eris," replied the girl in green. "I'm gonna be the next Pirate Queen."

"That's awesome," Talia smiled supportively. "It's nice to meet you."

"Ditto. How do you fit into all this?"

"I'm with Drake," Talia explained shortly.

Eris scrunched her mouth. "Ventus, tell me something I don't know."

The faint outline of a jade vortex appeared behind Eris, complete with claws and haunting ephemeral eyes. Drake heard the Primal's voice ring in his head: "I sense both Pyros and Ereikos; we are joined by flame and skyfire."

"Lightning," Talia corrected cagily. "I'd like to think I'm more than a birthmark, though."

"I can respect that," Eris nodded coolly. "Looks like you've finally got your stuff together, Drake."

"I'm getting there," he replied in good humor. "You always had this big of an attitude?"

"What can I say? I've been drinking a lot of milk," she reminded him. "Nills says I'm incorrigible."

"Aye," one of the pirates stepped forward with a puckish smirk, "but I've thought worse."

"Oh, Nills," Eris bantered, flipping her brown hair over her shoulder. "That's why we keep you around."

"Good te see ye among the living, Drake," Nills said with a handshake.

"All right, Drake?" said another. He might have been named Gunner.

Drake didn't recognize the other two. The Val'Kyran stepped forward and thumped his chest. "I am Obina Kakowana. You may call me Obi."

"Obi it is," Drake folded his arms.

The last pirate meekly raised a hand where he stood. "Creighton."

"Sure," Drake acknowledged.

"Shall we?" suggested Eris.

"Should we do anything about him?" Talia gestured to the gatekeeper who was still writhing on the ground. His movements had slowed, and the color fled his skin.

"No need," Nills said, crossing the line. "He'll be dead in a minute."

The gaggle of pirates followed Nills into The Ring, with Obi bringing up the rear. Obi took a moment to kneel beside the dying man and offer a few unheard words. He made a prayer sign with his hand, pulled out a knife, and mercifully slit the mercenary's throat. Then, he jogged to catch up to the pack.

"So those are pirates," marveled Talia.

"Those are pirates," echoed Drake.

"Enter The Ring?" Talia tilted her head.

Drake stepped forward, crossing the red line into the combat zone. Despite the fact that he was among friends, he felt uneasy knowing the land had been earmarked for lawless killing. Of course, little would prevent someone from committing murder on the "safe" side of the line, but there was at least a small degree of comfort in knowing it was frowned upon.

Eris and the pirates walked into the bar while Kika stood in the crater, reading the board of wanted posters. Drake joined her in the pit, examining the bounty board himself.

"These bounties offer limitless wealth for anyone ambitious enough to read them," Kika mused. "All you have to do is end a few lives and hope yours will last long enough to enjoy the reward."

"Not my preferred stream of income," decided Drake.

"No," agreed Kika. "You're a true philanthropist; you'll do it for free."

"Never was much of a businessman," he shrugged.

A ghost of a smile touched Kika's lips as she turned to face him. "It's good to see you, Drake. I imagine we have much to discuss."

"I reckon I have time for a beer with an old friend," Drake concurred.

Kika tilted her head toward the posters. "See anyone you recognize?"

The board featured over a hundred bounties, each offering ludicrous sums of money for the unlucky model in the portrait. His eyes skimmed over bankers, bandit leaders, lords, generals, and more. Eventually, he spotted a remarkably accurate sketch with the description:

> *Kika Callaway, Pirate Queen and Scourge of the Free Waters*
> *—500 gold, wanted dead or alive*
> *Return proof to Lord Fiore of Dominion for payment*

Another poster was nailed on the board directly below the first, this one for eight times the reward:

> *Kika, Pirate Mystic — 4,000 gold, alive.*

The signature at the bottom of the latter was one Mercer MacLeod. Drake spotted a few other rich contracts by Mercer, including one blanket offer to pay the same handsome reward for any living Mystic.

"Huh. Still sixteen thousand for the four of us," calculated Drake.

"The more things change," laughed Kika.

"You're rather calm considering you've already done the trouble of delivering yourself to Arillia," he observed.

"Everyone who's anyone in this town is on that board," downplayed Kika. "Two thousand for Mercer, fifteen hundred for Long Fan—even Nills has two hundred from Tallawyn."

"Why don't you just take yours down?"

"I worked hard to get up there," smiled the Pirate Queen. "Besides, it's a tighter community that ventures up the hill. Normally, if you bagged someone from the tavern, someone else would be ready to bag you right after. There's one exception, though."

"Mercer," guessed Drake.

Kika nodded. "The swine hides on his island in the bay. He's been hunting Mystics for a few years now. That cult of yours might have bankrolled whatever happened to you and Eris, but he made it happen. Looks like he's making out for himself better than he deserves. I wonder if he'll have the stones to come up the hill and face me; I don't imagine he could miss my ship."

"Sounds like you're fixing to settle a score."

"I am," admitted Kika, "but Mercer's just another name on my list. I have bigger plans in the works. Let's grab a drink."

Kika led him and Talia up the steps in front of the tavern. She swung the door open, inviting Drake into a raucous melee of chaotic debauchery, the likes of which he'd never seen. Booths, tables, and barstools were packed despite the minimal traffic to and from the tavern. A stage by the door supported seven musicians playing an electric. A little rough around the edges themselves, they danced and interacted with daring mercenaries who threw themselves on stage. One fat, shirtless man climbed onto the elevated platform and stole one musician's tuba, giving it a long blow before he grew light-headed and tipped over onto the singer playing tambourine. She crawled out from beneath the weighty drunkard, continuing her performance without pause.

Despite the slatted skylights and swinging chandeliers, the room was dim and brewed a strong odor of sweat and alcohol. No one looked up as he walked in, engrossed in their own conversations and shenanigans. Revelers in various stages of undress stood on tables, swigged from flasks and bottles, and sang their favorite tunes, apparently indifferent to what the band chose to play.

Kika discreetly held up two fingers, then weaved her way through the overcrowded assembly of bodies. The back of the tavern was still unpleasantly noisy but fortunately less tightly packed than the front. Kika approached a round table in the corner occupied by two bull-necked beefcakes. Menacing brawlers with more tattoos than teeth. The pair immediately stood and exited the area, leaving the table free.

Kika pulled out a chair and sat with her back to the wall. Drake sat adjacent to her, likewise choosing a seat with a vantage of the crowded tavern. Talia sat with her back to the fracas.

A short moment later, a mug of mead landed in front of Drake. Another appeared in front of Kika. Eris took up a chair next to Kika, delicately lowering her own flagon of milk onto the sticky table. The remaining gang of pirates hovered nearby, leaning against the wall or adding an additional physical buffer between the Pirate Queen and the rest of the floor.

Drake took a draft from his stein, which proved surprisingly flavorful. He leaned closer to Talia and half said, half shouted: "We still need to get food for the road."

Kika nodded to Eris, who held her hands in a diamond in front of her. Ventus glowed behind. A moment later, the cacophonous tavern was muted.

"Whoa," Talia exclaimed, taken by surprise.

"I prefer not to shout," Kika explained, quite audibly. "Eris is bending the airflow to muffle sounds entering and leaving our table. We can speak freely here."

"I was just telling Talia, we still need to resupply," said Drake.

Kika nodded. "Why don't we take care of that now? Nills, you and the men take Talia into town. See that she gets what she needs."

"Aye, Lady Kika," Nills obliged.

"Can I go too?" Eris asked hopefully.

"You're staying with me," Kika declined with a swig from her glass.

"You going to be all right?" Gunner asked.

"I was going to ask you the same," Drake said evenly, uncomfortable with letting Talia out of his sight.

"Don't worry; they'll take care of her. Isn't that right, Nills?"

"Aye, milady. She couldn't be safer in a strongbox," he promised.

"I'll be back soon, Drake. We'll be safe," Talia assured him.

"Fine," he leaned back in his chair. "Don't do anything I wouldn't do."

"Honestly, Drake," she frowned. "You need to set tighter boundaries. That leaves me way too much room to get into trouble."

Drake smiled to himself as she departed with the pirates.

"I don't recall you mentioning kids. How did this one enter the fold?" Kika asked, leaning forward.

"Long story," Drake's eyebrow twitched as he swallowed another gulp of his drink. "She had nowhere else to go. Joined me on the road to Laval, stuck around after."

"Part of the family, now?"

"I'd say she is the family—whatever that means."

"I don't know how I feel about her," Eris wrinkled her nose in distrust.

"Hmm?" Kika invited. "And why's that?"

Eris crossed her arms in thought. "She seems fine, but Ventus says I should watch out for Ereikos. He sounds nasty."

"So you like Talia, but you don't like her Primal," Kika rephrased.

"Well, yes," conceded Eris, still on the fence. "But her Primal is part of her, right? So I should watch out for her, too, right?"

"It's true; our Primals are part of us." The gentle smile returned to Kika's lips. "But they don't have to define us. You can like Talia without liking her Primal; I suspect she harbors similar feelings."

"I don't want to get lightninged," Eris explained cautiously.

"That's why you have Ventus. You're not *scared* of Talia, are you?"

"'Course not!" Eris denied vehemently. "I'm the one-and-only Pirate Princess! Nobody's better than me; I am the greatest!"

"So?" Kika prompted her verdict.

"Okay!" Eris acquiesced, raising a resolute fist. "Me and Talia are going to be friends, but I'm going to beat the bleeding heck out of Ereikos if he gives me any lip!"

"Language," Kika chided half-heartedly.

"'Scuse me," Eris apologized. "Don't blame Bartholomew—he isn't teaching me new words again. I just hear him say it sometimes."

"Mhm," Kika filed the nugget away for later review. She returned her attention to Drake, who was processing another sip of the bitter drink. "And you? I sense you've succeeded in awakening Pyros."

A surge of warmth bubbled inside him. He allowed the Primal passage, summoning the avatar of fire above him for a fleeting second. "We're getting along. For the most part," he said shortly.

We get along best when you obey my commands, speculated Pyros.

"I take it you found him, then," Kika buried her muzzle in the tankard for a long draft, unmistakably hanging onto his next words despite her practiced indifference.

"Yes," Drake said, fumbling for the right words. He felt that, given the number of occasions he had to deliver bad news to relatives of the deceased, he ought to have been better at it by now. "He's no longer among the living, but you were in his thoughts until the end. He wishes you well."

Kika nodded sullenly. "Been a long time coming." She swirled the contents of her drink, clearly experiencing an influx of emotions. Finally, she found solace in quoting scripture from the First Codex: "Weep not for the men who die, for they live on in the infinite cycle. From ashes to ashes, some earn their seat at the eternal feast; others live on in eternal memory. Blessed are they, for the departed no longer suffer trials on Kyros. Their strife was short; their peace is unending. Weep not for the men who die."

Drake lifted his stein in a toast to her fallen father and completed the verse: "Weep for the living, for they alone bear the loss, and they bear the loss alone. Weep for the living, for their peace was a fleeting encounter, their sorrow a lifelong companion. Child, weep not for the men who die; weep for the living, for their burden is to survive."

Kika poured half her brown ale out onto the wooden floorboards and gulped down the rest to pay her respects to the fallen. When she returned the drained stein to the table, Drake could read the unanswered questions in her eyes—but she did not ask them, and he did not answer.

"At least everything worked out for you. Right, Drake?" Eris interjected in a childish attempt to lighten the mood. Despite her inherited status as a demigod, she was still just a kid. Like most younglings, she seemed to have a strong aversion to silence.

Uniquely mature, Talia was the one apparent exception to that rule.

Drake considered the question. Despite his longstanding precept not to waste time or energy grieving the dead, he had failed Desmond in a way that continued to harrow him. The First Codex verse spoke true; grief was a tax on the living that made no difference to the deceased. His dull or acute regrets mattered not to the fallen star child; and yet, with every intrusive thought that besieged his brain, Drake remembered details he had overlooked in their time together. He thought of the boy's lopsided smile, always bright despite missing a few teeth. He recalled how, even on the faded plains beset by Hadronox's darkness, Desmond's light shone through. The boy had no grand ambitions or visions of conquest; he only aspired to live. To once again experience a sunrise surrounded by the love of his small-town family.

And now he was lost.

Lost—another feeling Drake could not escape no matter how far he traveled. Although he was stronger than he had ever been, he felt no closer to uncovering his purpose. No closer to knowing himself. His obscured raison d'être was buried somewhere in those haunting golden eyes. Supposedly, he'd find Avalon in the Golden City—Highwind, capital of Godwin's Kingdom of Deuzos. But instead of pursuing his enemy north into the Highlands, he drifted west after a fickle hope that the Oracle might heal his broken memory. Chasing shadows across the four corners of the known world. Even Kika's forsaken father couldn't escape his destructive whirlwind.

Had everything worked out for him?

"Yep," Drake said emptily. He glanced around the bar, searching for any other familiar faces. Remembering the deck of cards at the bottom of his pack, he realized there was another pirate he hadn't seen. "Is Beckett around?"

Kika raised her empty drink in the direction of the bar, signaling for a replacement. She stared at Drake in thought, resting a fist in front of her mouth and an index finger on her temple. She nodded without looking at the server as two filled mugs replaced the empty steins. "No," she answered shortly.

"Ah," Drake frowned. "Not at all, then?"

"Not at all," Kika clarified somberly. "Kojo's death was hard on him. They were close, the two of them... Damn shame."

"You always expect to lose a few in battle," Eris said softly, resting her chin on her glass of milk. "It's the ones you lose after that surprise you. I miss them. They were nice men."

"For the living," Kika raised her mug.

Drake mirrored her toast and had a hefty swig. He was surprised by the strength of the mead; if he drank to every unfortunate soul to have fallen since last he sat with Kika, he wouldn't be able to rise from his chair.

Lowering her stein, Kika pulled a small, rectangular package out from an interior jacket pocket. She slid the brown box open, revealing a tray holding two fat cigars. Based on the impressions, Drake assumed it had once held five.

"Smoking is a terrible habit, Eris," Kika lectured as she pulled one out.

"Then why are you lighting a cigar?" Eris cocked a smart eyebrow.

Kika tucked her box and its last remaining cigar into her jacket, then held up the chosen smoke under her nose. She closed her eyes and smelled the old tobacco roll. From where Drake sat, it looked a little soft.

"Tradition is but a remnant of love," she said with a reminiscent smile.

"Tradition for what?" asked Eris.

"Clayton Callaway," Kika started, regarding Drake as she answered the question. "I don't believe most of the crew knew, but we were married. For his vows, he presented me this box of cigars. He said no matter what comes, no matter how violent the storm around us, the cigars would be a reminder that life goes on. That as I burn the tobacco to remember the end of one chapter, I can count on the cigars that remain to guide me through the rest of my story. His foresight of our world was something I didn't appreciate until he was gone...

that these moments we think define us should be savored while they're here, then let go of when we're gone. As long as I can look forward to blowing one more memory into the wind, one more taste of burning ash on my tongue—my purpose here is not yet ended."

"So, one to go?" Drake observed, furrowing his brow.

"The first was for my first failure as a captain; it was my second prize. The *Redemption* is now my third ship. My first ship was called the *Boundless*—we were stalking a merchant heading inland, west of the Basket. I had my men sail through the night to make up lost ground, but the hull caught on rocky shoals hidden in high tide. Three hours later, we were taking on water and had to abandon ship. The merchant got away, of course, and I never salvaged the bones of that rotten tub. Under the eyes of the forty salty crewmates my father had assigned to my ship, I pulled out my first cigar and went down to the beach to smoke. I remember how my hands trembled—the fear, knowing I was a green captain and a sixteen-year-old girl who had just marooned a seasoned crew with little loyalty to her."

"What happened next?" Eris leaned forward, apparently also hearing the story for the first time.

"Nills walked over to give me a light, and Clayton's cigar helped steady my nerves. This was before I had Hydraxia to counsel me. There was talk of mutiny among the crew, naturally. Our quartermaster, John Blackburne, was the lead instigator. He had two particularly influential crew members backing him—Billy Moody and Nathaniel Searle. I suspect they harbored the intention long before I wrecked us on the inland coast of Deuzos, but they were certainly emboldened by my blunder.

"I remember saying to Nills as I burned the cigar: 'Is this all fate had in store for Captain Kika?' To my surprise, fully aware that he would have had an unchallenged majority of the crew's support if he threw his hat in with the mutineers, he said: 'Your tale doesn't end here; it ends when you surpass your father's name. Your work is finished when every ship and every port fears the name *Callaway*.' Blackburne rallied the crew and called for my removal, but Nills somehow convinced exactly half plus one to side with me. Blackburne and his men deserted, and the rest of us made the best of what we had."

"How'd you get out of that one?" Drake looked at the captain with newfound admiration.

"Long story short, headed south along the river, raided a storehouse, and stole a merchant ship from the harbor. As we sailed back to the Federation islands, we lucked into crossing paths with Clayton. He and Alessia had both set off to find me after my return was a week late. We met my sister again back in the waters near the islands, but that's a different story. That's when I almost lit this one," Kika concluded, raising her cigar.

Drake realized Kika was likely referring to the icy scene Eamon had drawn in the caves, but he decided not to speculate. The subject seemed rather touchy for her, particularly given the fresh confirmation of Eamon's death.

"What about the other two?" Eris asked with burning curiosity.

"The second was to get me through Clayton's death. It sounded absurd when he told me to save it for that day. I didn't even want to consider it to be a possibility. But, like I said, I didn't appreciate his foresight. The third was for if I should ever outlive a child of ours."

"But you don't have any kids," objected Eris.

Kika forced a smile. "No. But I have you. And as long as I'm around, no harm will call your name."

"Which will be forever, hopefully," Eris wished.

"Nothing here is forever, my dear."

"So, number four is for Eamon. What occasion are you saving the last for?" Drake leaned back in his chair.

"I can't yet see the day—it's no time soon. I'll spend the fifth before the battle I know will be my last. But until then, I still have much to accomplish." Kika extended Eamon's cigar toward Drake. "Have a light?"

Drake invoked Pyros as he held his finger to the tip of the cigar. A steady flame flickered from his fingertip, slowly burning the brown paper around the tip of the roll. Kika brought the cigar to her mouth and took a long breath, then exhaled a cloud of white smoke into the dingy tavern air.

"Watch out!" a voice screamed from Drake's left, piercing Ventus' protective veil. A bald, hawk-nosed man appeared at their table. The sweaty intruder hoisted a chair off the ground and thrusted out its legs in an effort to keep Drake at bay in the corner.

"The hell?" Drake stood as one of the flailing legs spilled his stein onto his lap.

"Careful, girl! This man's a monster!" warned the concerned bystander.

"It's cool," Eris deescalated innocently. She puffed out her cheeks and blew a gust of pressurized air at the man, launching him and the stool against the wall. As he scrambled to his feet, confused and horrified by the experience, she smiled. "I'm a monster too."

"Wah!?" The man's eyes widened. He scrambled backward away from the table, crashing over another chair in the process. He picked himself up and held a trembling finger out toward the unholy table but couldn't find words.

"You idiot!" lambasted a voice behind him.

"Huh?" he turned his head.

An open-palmed hand cracked across his face, sending the hawk-nosed man reeling. He flailed his arms as he fell for a third time, inadvertently swiping Eris' milk off the table and hurling its creamy contents into Drake's beard.

"Deus damn you!" Drake growled indignantly, perilously close to having Pyros incinerate the man.

Kika handed him two square napkins that would do little to ameliorate the situation.

"He's obviously with Kika, you shameful excuse for a sellsword," the newcomer chastised him.

"But he summoned fire from his hand!" cried the hawk-nosed man.

"Now all of Arillia knows you're a sook!" The newcomer gripped him by the back of the shirt and the waistline of his pants, spun, and hurled him an impressive distance through the air. The hawk-nosed man landed on another table, spilling more drinks and frustrating a pair of burlier, perhaps less-forgiving patrons.

The new arrival turned to face them. "I humbly apologize, friend Kika. He has brought great dishonor to the Long Corps name." He bowed low to show his sincerity.

Drake got a good look at the man when he resurfaced. To his surprise, the man was one of the rare Taoxians who voyaged across the Great Sea. A refined professionalism was evident in his tidy hair and thin mustache. He did not look weak, but his body had little excess, matching thin lips and eyebrows and pronounced, red cheekbones. He was a little shorter than Drake but easily a head taller than the Taoxian who ran the restaurant at the bottom of the hill. He wore a gray tunic the style of which Drake had never seen; its collar was permanently raised, and several golden latches seemed to hold the cloth's modesty together. Unpresuming black slippers completed his ensemble. Drake would have written the man off as rather plain-looking if not for the two curved swords on his right hip—one thin and long, the other short and fat.

"All is forgiven. Right, Drake?" Kika cleared the air.

"Sure," Drake grumbled, ineffectively patting himself with the napkins.

"Thank you, friend Kika. I came seeking you as soon as I learned your presence graced our town once again," said the Taoxian.

"Please, join us." Kika lifted her tankard, wordlessly summoning three fresh drinks. "Drake, this is Long Fan. He's an old friend of mine and a recent business partner of my fleet."

Long Fan leaned forward a few degrees before taking Talia's empty seat. "A pleasure to meet you, Drake..."

"Just Drake," he nodded.

"Ah. Well met, Just Drake," the Taoxian smiled. "Friend Kika, I fear you have come at a most inauspicious time. The air is tense in Arillia, and war looms on the horizon. I fear that nationalistic loyalties will divide our Freecity, and our independence may be lost."

"If I've learned anything from our histories, Long Fan, it's that war is as much an opportunity as a headwind. I was hoping to find you today—I have a vision for Arillia, and you, my old friend, are in it," Kika tempted nebulously.

"I would have great interest in hearing your vision," invited Long Fan, sipping lightly from his cup.

"As you know, I have cause for bad blood with MacLeod," Kika started. Long Fan made a sound for her to continue. "While I'm grateful that you agreed to fence our goods procured at sea, I can't help but feel uneasy that MacLeod controls this town, and thereby, to some extent, my livelihood."

"Arillia is a Freecity with no kings; however, freedom is a vacuum, and power is the crown. Mercer has over six hundred men loyal to his name and the favor of all the guilds. If you mean him further animosity, your concern is valid," diagnosed Long Fan.

"I certainly mean him further animosity," Kika clarified with a wicked grin. "You remember the other project your men have been working on for me—in your warehouse on Red Island?"

"Yes," Long Fan smiled toothily. "I do not know how you obtained imperial technology, but discovering the manual was great fortune. I imagine the technology would provide great defense for a fort, or even act as a powerful siege weapon for conquering armies. I have nearly completed your contract for thirty cannons and plan to produce my own after. I hope you do not mind, but I have transcribed the manual for my own future operations."

"Naturally, I expected you to find profit in a dusty old tome. I'll gladly permit the copy for future use, but I would ask that you hold off on selling the weapon to others for a few years."

"We are friends, Kika, but you are asking me to sacrifice much wealth. Tell me: why should I do this for you?" Long Fan leaned forward, steepling his hands.

"Because it's in your interest, of course," Kika said with a wry smile. "I plan to outfit my ships with your cannons. Then, I'm coming after MacLeod. I'm going to level his island before I gut that pig. When he's dead, you'll be the natural replacement. Arillia will be yours."

Long Fan's eyes widened with surprise. "I admit, I have my doubts that these cannons will be effective aboard ships, but I trust you to know the seas. Your vision intrigues me, though I fear it may not transpire how you imagine."

"Go on," invited Kika.

"If the guilds see your flags attacking Arillia, you become persona non grata in the Freecity—for life. Even MacLeod cannot commune sentences to exile, nor could I in his place. If you strike at MacLeod, our business in Arillia would be concluded."

"Would our personal business be concluded?" tested Kika.

"Not personally, but professionally, I am afraid so. I could not risk others seeing you dock at Red Island; it is more important that I avoid the appearance of impropriety, rather than impropriety itself," he said regretfully.

"Fortunately, my vision does not require welcome in Arillia. You would come pick up cargo from me."

"I am afraid I do not understand," Long Fan held up a hand. "You do not have an island, nor would the risk be palatable for us to establish a personal shipping lane for the goods you liberate. I mean no disrespect, but your hauls are... inconsistent."

"Rest easy, Long Fan. The shipping lane will be more profitable than all your other operations put together, and the risk more than palatable. With our exclusive partnership, I'll have the only cannons on the seas. No ship or port will stand a chance; eventually, I expect resistance to our black flags may stop altogether. We'll be as much tax collectors as we are pirates—and you'll have a ship in the fleet dedicated to maintaining our trade route. Tell me: does that not sound profitable?"

Long Fan frowned thoughtfully. "It sounds well-conceived, friend Kika, but I struggle to understand the economics. Even with both of your ships earning a more reliable source of tribute, how can you match the profits I would gain by selling these cannons to the ports to ward you off?"

Kika laughed. "Long Fan, you misunderstand me. I'm not planning this operation with two ships—I'm founding the Second Pirate Federation. I will amass an armada of one hundred ships, each outfitted to the teeth. No one will stand in my way—not the ports, not the Golden Fleet, not even Dominion. I would own the oceans—no ship passing Arillia would clear my sea lanes without paying tariff. So, you can either make life harder for me and suffer taxes on all your merchants' shipping, or you can benefit in a monopolistic league with the Federation. How do those economics sound?"

Long Fan folded his arms and stroked his lip gravely. "Your vision is inspiring, friend Kika. I respect your offer of both carrot and stick. I will own no part in your disgrace should you fail, but I will profit greatly if the tapestry of time is stitched how you envision it this day. Know your ambitions have my full support, although I shall never announce it publicly."

"Then we have a deal," Kika clinked her glass to his, sealing the pact.

"And you, Just Drake? Are you part of Kika's crew—a loyal lackey who will nurture this vision to life?" Long Fan inquired.

"Actually, it's just: Drake," he corrected the Taoxian.

"Apologies, Just... Drake," Long Fan reattempted, leaning deeper into Drake's accent.

Drake opened his mouth to correct the mercenary but decided to let it go. Amazingly, Kika and Eris maintained neutral expressions.

"No," he answered. "I'm just a friend of Kika's. I'm headed out west."

"By land or by sea?" Long Fan asked.

"Guess I assumed land, but that's a fair point," Drake considered.

"Where you headed now?" Eris inquired.

Drake hesitated, unsure how much he was willing to say in front of the stranger. Eventually, he disclosed: "To the Riverlands."

"Won't be traveling by sea, then. All ports in The Basket are closed indefinitely," reported Kika.

"What?" Despite looming threats of war, he was shocked. The Basket was a major exporter of grain both throughout Deuzos and abroad. Especially in summer, it was inconceivable that the entire coastline would shut down.

"We intercepted a merchant ship returning to Tidestone after a long journey from Ayrabos. The captain said they were stranded at sea; the ports rebuffed them without rations. Said the port was a ghost town—nobody walking the streets except soldiers enforcing the strict lockdown. They didn't say why the Basket was quarantined, but if it holds that way, I don't know how Godwin's going to stock the Golden Fleet to defend against the Tallwayns," Kika recalled.

"Damn. Guess sea's off the table again," summarized Drake.

Long Fan added his wisdom to the conversation. "If you are traveling to the Riverlands by land, the Basket is usually the wisest approach, but I fear the quarantine may impede your way. The Golden Road past the Highlands, through Styria, is another option, but the journey is long. It could be winter before you reach the Riverlands—assuming you make it that far."

"Assuming I make it that far?" Drake repeated skeptically. He wasn't sure if it was just a byproduct of the few drinks he had consumed, but he took offense to the comment.

"A great army descends from Highwind—led by Prince Cain himself. I suspect other forces will be rallied to join the frontlines, firstly to secure the fallen garrison at Fort Banning. Like friend Kika's carrot and stick, Godwin has been gathering Mystics in the capital by open palms and iron fists. If his forces uncover your identity, your journey will surely be derailed. Furthermore, the Foothills are home to many religious zealots. Some also seek Mystics, though I believe for different purposes. It is irony that, in the land of the gods, so many are hostile to those bearing marks of the Primals."

"Okay," Drake accepted, unsure how his ego should respond. "So, Lowlands?"

"Yes, your only remaining path is through the Lowlands. The swamps are inhospitable, and many of the locals, worse. However, I do have two mercenaries loyal to me working on a hunting contract at the Crossroads. Perhaps, if your coin is kind, these ferrymen will provide you further guidance on your way," suggested Long Fan.

"How will I find them?" Drake asked, unsure whether he would seek help from mercenaries even if he happened to run into them.

"They are brothers: Luc and Giles Dufleur," answered Long Fan.

"Tallawyns? That sounds like a Thornlands name," Drake surmised.

"The father was a Tallawyn exile who served in my Corps; the mother was a Val'Kyran. They met and died in Arillia, and now the boys earn a living as mercenaries."

"How old are they?"

"I would guess the eldest is twenty-four. The youngest, sixteen. They both resemble their mother; I'm sure you would have no trouble finding them in a place like the Crossroads. Such backwater towns are less vibrant than our Freecity," Long Fan noted meaningfully.

"Got it." Drake had never been to the Riverlands; while his instinct told him he'd be fine without Long Fan's mercenaries, he was at least willing to tuck the nugget away to make the decision later.

"We're home!" Talia announced, sauntering up to the table with a new bow on her back.

"Your belongings," Obi dropped two heavy sacks onto Drake's lap.

"I see you found your bow," Drake noted suspiciously, relocating one of the bags to the floor. He used his foot to slide it toward Talia.

"Courtesy of Dunloy's gaming house," Talia bragged as she unslung it from her shoulder.

"You know it's not good for the bow to remain strung when you aren't using it," Drake faulted her.

Talia handed the bow to Gunner, who proceeded to unstring it while she pulled her pack onto her back. She turned around, allowing Gunner to tie the wooden frame to the back of her bag.

"I hope you know how to restring it yourself," grumbled Drake.

"The good news is, even if I break it, I can afford another one," Talia replied smugly. "Things all set in here?"

"I think so," Drake took a deep breath, then nodded politely to Kika and Long Fan. He didn't know when, if ever, he'd be back in Arillia. Based on Kika's own plans, it seemed unlikely fate would permit them to meet again. Still, he knew it was a small world. Perhaps destiny's crossroads would reunite them once more. "Sounds like we can't rest until we're past Fort Banning. Guess your first drink will have to wait for another night."

XV. Horse Trading

Drake

Ready?"

"As I'll ever be."

Drake absentmindedly rubbed the suede sleeve of his new, tan jacket. While typically averse to impulsive fashion purchases, he recognized his torn and bloodied attire failed to provide adequate cover against the elements and drew unnecessary attention to his presence. A humble merchant on the edge of town had the jacket displayed on a shaded rack, labeled at a surprisingly reasonable price. Spared the effort of haggling, Drake had even picked up a gray shirt to wear underneath. He was shocked by the comfort and quality of the vendor's clothing. It was hard to believe a craftsman who made such a solid product was stuck hawking his goods out of a tent on the outskirts of town. Absolutely shocking.

Drake felt a squish under his left boot. He lifted his foot and inspected the underside, finding a much greener shade of brown than he was expecting.

"You damn horse! What kind of a maniac lets their animal shit in the middle of the road?" Drake fumed, dragging his foot across the red dirt to peel off the dung.

"That was a pretty big pile," Talia remarked pitilessly. "Thought you would've seen it."

"Have I ever scolded you for giving me a warning?" he grumbled.

"I feel like you have," Talia shrugged, unable to cite a specific example. "I'll point out whenever I think you're about to do something stupid next time, but remember you asked for it."

"Please do."

He had been distracted—not just by his thrifty purchase, but also the task ahead. It would've been easy to stay overnight in the seedy Freecity, but he was anxious to get to the other side of the border. From what he could gather from the rumors, Fort Banning was uncharacteristically vulnerable now. With the Godwin army heading south from the capital and the Tallawyn army amassing at the Frontier, Arillia was the last place he wanted to be.

He imagined one of two scenarios would unfold. The first: Godwin's army would reinforce their garrison in time, dig in, and turn the land between the two borders into a warzone. The second: Tallawyn's men would rally first, cross the border into Deuzos, and begin their march on Highwind. Whatever campaign strategy and military tactics followed was above his paygrade—all he knew for certain was that Fort Banning stood directly in the warpath.

Fortunately, they still had several hours of daylight ahead of them. The oppressive afternoon sun was slowly soaring toward its evening retirement, unobscured by even a single cloud. In the twenty-or-so short minutes since leaving the tavern, his black hair had heated up halfway enough to cook an egg. He wiped a pooling bead of sweat off the bridge of his nose before readjusting the balance of his pack.

"I like that group," Talia resurrected the conversation that had been derailed by Drake's shopping spree.

"Knew you would," Drake said with a soft smile.

"Hey—after the oracle fixes your memory and we settle things with that Avalon guy, how about we join up with Lady Kika for a while? It'd be fun to go sailing with pirates!"

"It's not as glamorous as you'd think, kiddo. The way the boat lurches makes you sick. You're close quarters with a bunch of smelly men all day and night. The food's nothing to write home about."

"You didn't like it?"

"I didn't say that," waffled Drake. "It was an experience, for sure. Then again, plenty of things to experience on land as well."

"Especially with you," Talia noted. "It's funny; I never thought I'd leave Lyon, much less Tallamar. Now we're heading to the other side of the world."

"Technically, I think Taoxos would be the other side of the world."

"Four countries," Talia continued, unfazed. "I'll have traveled to four *different* countries. That's pretty crazy."

"What's the fourth?" Drake asked, perplexed.

"Deuzos," Talia answered blankly.

"No," Drake rolled his eyes. "I know Tallamar, Nordos, Deuzos—what's the fourth country?"

"Arillia," Talia declared matter-of-factly. "It's not owned by Godwin or Tallawyn, so it counts as its own."

"I guess." Drake was unconvinced a Freecity held the same status as a country or kingdom. "Still, I got you beat."

"What? But I've been with you the whole time! When'd you get to a fifth country?"

"I had a life before you, you know," Drake reminded her. "And the fifth was Baltos."

"With the pirates?" Talia pressed excitedly.

"No," Drake laughed. "Actually, kind of. That's where I met Kika."

"I wonder how many countries she's seen," Talia wondered reverently.

"At least seven," Drake guessed.

"Seven! Which ones?"

"Well, let's see." Drake held up his fingers as he counted. "We know she's been to the same five as me."

"Nordos?" interrupted Talia.

"Yes," Drake confirmed, recalling the sad clue provided by Theresa Winter. Damn shame she went all that way and never saw Eamon. "So, that's five. I think she's also done Eastwind and Val'Kyros, so that'd be seven."

"Whoa. She's been everywhere."

"Pretty cool," agreed Drake.

"Has she been to Ayrabos?"

"I don't know. You'll have to ask her next time we see her."

Talia groaned in frustration. "Who knows when that'll be?"

"You got a long life ahead of you, kid. Plenty of time to do it all," Drake reassured her.

"Think I found your culprit," Talia pointed to the right of the road.

Two dark-brown horses were corralled in a shoddy pen built just up to knee-height. The unsecured equines would have no trouble jumping over the fence if they were so inclined. For now, they munched happily from two large sacks of oats. In front of the pen, a man stood under a rickety billboard.

"Wait a minute... I know him," Drake identified, reading the yellow-lettered sign.

Hatch's Highland Horse for Hire!

"How do you know him? Thought this was your first time in Arillia."

"It is," confirmed Drake. "I ran into him in Lyon—about ten minutes before you ran into me."

"On the record, I did apologize for that," Talia clarified defensively.

"Noted. You also more than paid it back in Dunloy," Drake said to dispel any lingering shame or embarrassment she might still be carrying.

"Oh yeah! Cool. So, who's this guy? A horse trader?"

"Looks like it. I think he used to sell hooch."

"Hooch?" laughed Talia.

"Booze. Alcohol. It wasn't any good."

"I love that word," Talia giggled to herself. "Hooch. That's great."

Hatch's slumped shoulders straightened as they approached. Putting on his best salesman face, he leaped to life. "Welcome—to *Hatch's Highland Horses for Hire!*" presented the merchant, grandly splaying his fingers for emphasis. "Here at *Hatch's Highland Horses for Hire*, or huh-huh-huh-huh for short, we offer long-term horse rentals with zero down. That's right! Ride out of here today without spending a copper on your brand-new Highlander! Just sign a slip agreeing to thirty easy payments of thirty silver, and you're on your way!"

"I see you added a *huh*," remarked Drake.

"Huh?" sounded Hatch, puzzled.

Resisting the urge to add two additional *huhs,* Drake explained: "We met once in Lyon. You sold hooch back then. What brings you out here?"

"Oh," Hatch's shoulders slumped as he sheepishly wrung his hands. "Well, you see, the hooch business wasn't going so hot. I slightly overestimated the market for uniquely flavored hooch, and production turned out to be a minor disaster... So, one morning, I woke up, and I looked in the mirror, and I said, 'Hatch! Today's the day! You're down but not out. Every successful entrepreneur has pivoted sometime in their life. Today's the day you pony up and buy some horses!' And then I bought three great Highlanders."

Drake frowned, studying the two horses in the pen. The smaller one returned a moony stare, flicking its ears as it munched on oats. A mangy tail swatted its brown legs and hide in sporadic efforts to ward off bugs. Although Drake didn't know much about horses, he was fairly confident these lean equines were not Highlanders. Conspicuously absent from their hooves were the white boot-looking patches of fur the Deuzos warhorses were famous for.

These looked more like the common thoroughbreds of Tallamar.

"Did they charge you for three Highlanders?" Drake inquired.

"Yes!" wailed Hatch, knowing he had been found out. "That's exactly what my wife said! Then my mother-in-law piled on. 'Hatch, you deluded lout! Those aren't Highlanders. Have you never seen a Highlander before? Why would you spend so much money on something you know nothing about? You've pissed away my daughter's inheritance! You were set for life; all you had to do was *not* squander it on some idiotic business venture!'—But you know what? I say, a man can have dreams! And a man should follow those dreams!"

"I'm guessing your wife left you, your mother-in-law kicked you out on the street, and you had to flee creditors in Lyon?" Drake surmised darkly.

"Yes!" Hatch's eyes filled with water. He looked at Talia for pity, lip trembling violently enough to start a temblor. Tears rolling down his cheek, he squeaked, "I miss her."

"Oh," Talia sounded in an ineffective attempt to soothe him. Hatch burst into tears, falling back into his shabby chair. Talia awkwardly patted the grown man's hunched shoulder. "There... there?"

The discredited businessman blew his nose into the sleeve of his shirt, then picked up a dusty cup beside his chair. He grabbed the ladle protruding from the clay pot to his right and served himself a dark liquid. "Why is coffee always so hot? It's hot enough outside! I don't want hot coffee," he whimpered, sipping noisily from the cup.

"Well... You sold one, right? That's a start!" Talia noted optimistically.

Drake shook his head in subtle disapproval of her encouragement.

"Yes. That's right," Hatch sniffled, attempting to compose himself. "I did sell one yesterday—have the contract right here!" He produced a few loose pages from his shirt. Leafing through the disorganized sheets, he eventually singled one out and proudly displayed the inked contract in his right hand.

The smaller horse leaned over the railing and nibbled the paper, maintaining unblinking eye contact with Drake as he slobbered on the contract.

"Hey!" Hatch swatted the horse's nose with the stack of papers in his free hand. "Stop it! How do you think I'm paying for your oats?"

The horse tore off a corner of the page and slowly backed away from the fence, continuing to stare at Drake as it masticated.

"Mister Tall, Dark, and Handsome, no! That was the delivery address for payment! Now how will the customer know where to send his installments?"

"Hay, girl," Talia pointed an accusatory finger at the horse. "This is no time for horsing around, all right? I know it was a spur of the moment type deal, but you've got to behave better if you want to be the mane event."

"Did you say that was the payment address?" blinked Drake.

"Yes, which loosely describes directions to this pen, here. I named this stretch of road after my shop," bragged Hatch.

"But the buyer had a copy of the contract too, right?" Drake assumed.

Hatch stared at Drake, mirroring the horse's blank expression. He abruptly clutched his head in his hands and roared in shame. "Oh, Hatch! You knuckleheaded ignoramus! How's he gonna know where to send payments?"

"What a nightmare," Talia pitied out of the corner of her mouth as he continued to self-deprecate.

"Well, hate to be a neigh-sayer," Drake started, exchanging a sidelong look with Talia. "Tell you what, Hatch. Zero down? I'll take one of these *Highlanders* off your hands."

"You will?" the merchant wiped away a tear.

"Heck, we could take both," shrugged Talia.

Hatch scratched his nose uncertainly. "I think I'd better keep one. I've got to keep heading west to find some more horses. I thought I'd resupply in Arillia, but apparently Lord Barrio Hughes of the Grotto and Lord Gresham Pyke of the Rock are buying every horse they can find for their caravans and cavalry. The wealth those Godwins have! If I could get even a sliver..."

"Heading to the capital, then?" Drake inquired.

"I think so," ventured Hatch. "Sounds like I won't find many horses up in the Highlands either, though. I wanted to head to the Basket to try rounding up some wild mustangs, but I don't think they're letting people in. Poor folks—hope the bread shortage doesn't lead to starvation. Lord Rheinholm's cavalry school is quarantined with the rest of the province, but I bet he'll be snatching up all the local horses when they reopen. I thought about crossing the Aollean Forest to sell bear repellent, but Duskwood scares me. My only option's north through the Foothills—I'll make a name for myself in the Golden City!"

"Renting horses?" checked Drake.

Hatch shook his head. "To be honest, friend, I don't think I'm cut out for the horse rental industry. I'll do this as a side business until I can establish myself in Highwind—and then, circus!"

"With... all of your animals," Drake peered behind him, searching as if he might have missed the elephants and lions in the small pen.

"It'll start with just a horse, but that's how we'll grow scrappily—without wasted overhead! I'll add one animal at a time, real people-pleasers."

"Circus," Talia repeated slowly. "You sure?"

"It was between that or rounding up Mystics for Godwin. I hear he's upped the offer to five thousand gold kroner for every live one you bring in—that's twenty-five percent higher than Arillia's bounty!" Hatch placed a hand over his chest, surprising himself by stating the vast sum of money aloud.

"You? Mystic hunting?" Drake's eyebrows shot up in disbelief.

"I think we've seen one before," contributed Talia. "Kinda scary-looking, if you ask me."

"Oh, I know!" Hatch sighed dejectedly. "As much as I'd love to cash in on even one of them, I know I can't wrangle one of those monsters all the way to Highwind. I'll have to make my fortune the old-fashioned way."

"By buying dangerous—if not deadly—animals and trying to convince them to do tricks in funny hats," translated Talia.

"It's early days, but I think the circus has its merits," Hatch evaluated optimistically.

"Sounds like the man knows what he's doing," Drake waved his hand, writing the merchant off as a past, present and future failure. "You said you had a contract you wanted me to sign?"

"Sure do!" Hatch produced a paper from his vest, checking over his shoulder to ensure no muzzles were looming behind him.

The horses watched bemusedly from behind their bags of oats. The short one whinnied in appraisal of its owner's business acumen.

"I'd like the one that's not called Mister Tall, Dark, and Handsome."

"Shelby? She'll cost an extra two silver per month," upsold Hatch.

"I'm okay with that," Drake accepted the paper, causing Talia to raise her eyebrows in disbelief. He tilted his head slightly to signal he knew what he was doing. "Where do I sign?"

"Right here," indicated Hatch. He hurriedly produced a second copy. "Sign this, too—that way we'll both have a contract with the payment address."

"Smart," Drake praised approvingly, scribbling his name on the line.

"Great! You'll be fully satisfied with your purchase, I assure you. Come on over, Shelby!"

The larger horse didn't lift its head from the oat bag. Mister Tall, Dark, and Handsome neighed in protest, presumably slighted at being overlooked.

"Shelby!" Hatch called, leaning on the fence. The railing toppled inward, briefly threatening his balance. He marched across the pen to the larger horse, steering clear of several recently transmuted piles of oats. He tied a small bag of feed to the saddle, then led Shelby over to Drake.

"By the way," Drake secured his pack and Talia's bow to the side of the saddle. "How do you enforce the contracts?"

"Well, under Tallawyn law, any contract or business disputes can be processed through the Talos Business Bureau for remediation. There are also private collectors that could be hired, I suppose."

Mounting the horse, Drake decided against pointing out that they were no longer in Tallamar, and that the TBB likely didn't have jurisdiction out west. He held out a hand to help Talia onto the saddle. "You keep a good eye on that contract, Hatch," advised Drake.

"Foal me once," Talia added sagaciously.

"Thank you for your patronage!" bubbled Hatch, clearly believing he had made the deal of a lifetime.

"Bye now," Drake waved back, crumpling the contract into his pocket.

As they rode past the last tents on the west side of Arillia, Talia leaned into Drake's shoulder and asked: "Do you feel bad we ripped him off?"

"I'm gonna pay him," Drake lied.

Talia fixed him with an accusatory stare from her right eye, her left cheek still pressed against his back.

"Look, kid. Here's the truth: someone ripped him off yesterday, and someone else would've taken advantage of him tomorrow if we hadn't. Long-term horse rentals, no money down? In Arillia of all places? There's no world where that's a good idea. If it makes you feel better, you probably saved his life today. That guy hunting Mystics would've gotten ugly. Fast."

"You're right," relented Talia. "At least this way we got a horse. Better us than someone else."

"Exactly," approved Drake. "It's an ugly truth, but you're starting to get it. That'll serve you well in life. Once you realize everyone's in it for themselves, you learn to look out for your own interests a whole lot better. There's the way things are and the way we wish they would be—don't ever get the two confused."

"Motivational as always, Drake," Talia lauded flatly.

"I know I keep harping on this, and I don't like sounding like the bad guy here—it's just 'cause I care about you. I don't want you to have to learn these lessons the hard way like most people do."

"Even though you're probably right, it's hard not to feel like there are at least a few good people out there," Talia wavered.

"I know... and there might be. Thing is, it's not our job to look after them. That's what Deus is for."

XVI. Homeland Security

Drake

Deus," Talia mumbled hollowly, stunned at the carnage in front of them.

"What a mess," muttered Drake.

As Shelby trotted toward the gates of Fort Banning, Drake observed the eerie fortifications. Although no bodies littered the blockades and walls, evidence of a bloodbath remained. On the outer fortifications, tattered clothing and splotches of blood stained the shadowed wooden crates and netting. The Godwin banners that previously flew on either side of the gate were in scraps, carelessly scattered by the wind.

A grim, gray fortress extended above the wall. Two dismantled ballistae and several broken catapults littered the ramparts—a once-imposing stronghold few would dare challenge now fallen into shambles. The stonework seemed to be the sole survivor of the renowned Fort Banning.

"What do you think happened here?" wondered Talia.

"Nothing good," assessed Drake. "Makes our job easier, at least."

"Sure. Any idea how we get past the wall?"

"Through the gate?"

"Great—any idea how we get through the gate?" Talia leaned over his shoulder and pointed straight ahead.

Although the large, wooden outer doors were swung open, an iron portcullis awaited them in the shadow of the archway. Searching the wall for an alternative point of entry, Drake frowned. He suspected he could stack enough crates to get on top of the wall if needed but didn't see a way to get the horse through. He wasn't keen on abandoning their hard-earned rental.

"Well, it's not completely abandoned," observed Talia.

Drake squinted at the shadowy portcullis and saw two Godwin archers on the other side. He spurred the horse forward, heading toward the guards.

"Stop there," yelled one of the archers through the iron bars as he neared the gate.

Drake pretended not to hear him.

"I said stop!" the bowman repeated tersely, raising a crossbow to the slits in the barrier.

Drake pulled back on the reins, bringing Shelby to a standstill. He slid off the horse and handed the reins to Talia.

"Turn back immediately," commanded the sentry. "Fort Banning is closed until further notice."

"I'm returning to Highwind," Drake invented craftily.

"No, you are not. The border will remain closed for the foreseeable future," the man answered firmly.

Pyros? Drake called inside.

The Primal smoldered in his chest as their connection strengthened. *Shall we immolate these insolent pups?*

It's the gate—looks like iron. Can we burn through that?

Hmm, rumbled Pyros. *Perhaps.*

Perhaps? Drake questioned.

Will not know unless we try, answered Pyros.

Drake noted the absence of his Primal's usual bluster and decided that 'perhaps' wasn't enough to rely on. He continued to the gate and addressed the guards: "I understand King Godwin's offering five thousand gold for any Mystic who travels to Highwind. I come of my own will."

The guards exchanged uncertain glances. The rightmost one sneered, "You're no Mystic. Beat it, before I put an arrow in your skull."

Stopping just outside the archway, Drake glanced down at his right hand. Still wrapped in the bandages Talia had applied. He pressed his fingers against his palm, feeling the blisters under the wrapping. Knowing he would be scolded for ruining the bandages if he reinjured himself, he decided to leave the burn covered. Instead, he leaned back his head and sucked in a deep breath. Pyros appear behind him, concentrating his energy. Then, he exhaled sharply, spewing a puff of flames ten feet in the air.

"Good gods, man!" one of the archers dropped his crossbow.

The other held his finger on the trigger, visibly on edge.

Drake attempted diplomacy.

"Like I said, mine is the Primal of Fire. I answer the king's summons in Highwind. I'd love to do this peacefully. Otherwise, I'll burn down the gate and leave a big hole in the wall for the Tallawyn army to follow through tomorrow."

A mix of anger and fear formed on the jumpy soldier's face. "This wall has stood for decades. This is a solid iron gate—you can't just burn your way through that. Metal doesn't melt."

"How do you think they make swords?" Drake challenged, advancing closer to the gate. "I'm sure I could melt down your gate in no time, but I'll let you in on another secret: see those big holes in front of you? If your bows can reach me, my flames can reach you."

The soldier tightened his grip on the crossbow.

Drake temporarily halted his advance. He addressed them in a calm, deep voice. "I don't want to cremate the two of you alive. I'd rather not burn down the gate and leave the kingdom open to Tallawyn's forces, who amass at the Frontier as we speak. But, one way or another, I'm going to Highwind, where *our* king has summoned me."

"Just let him through, Rick. King Godwin did decree that all Mystics be brought to the capital," reasoned the rightmost guard.

Drake could tell he hadn't yet convinced the other Godwin. He saw the indignation in his eyes that refused to be talked down to—that considered pulling the trigger and killing the demigod who threatened his pride. Pyros whispered a cunning suggestion to him, which he repeated aloud: "I'm guessing you've never seen a Mystic before, Rick. You want to shoot me with that toy. Do you know what happens when a Mystic dies?"

"Don't do it, Rick," cowered the guard on the right.

For the first time, Drake saw fear flash in the prideful soldier's eyes. He channeled Pyros' ghostly form behind him and heard the Primal's wicked laughter fill the air. "If I die, the monster goes free. When your organs wither and hot ash packs your tongue, you'll find sticks and stones couldn't save you from its wrath."

The crossbow twanged, firing a bolt above Drake and through the apparition of Pyros. The useless arrow landed in the dirt behind him.

Pyros roared in fury, causing Rick to retreat a step and his comrade to trip over himself outright.

Such insolence cannot be tolerated! I have entertained this farce long enough. Consume him—NOW!

Drake felt the furnace inside him overheat. He instinctively knew he couldn't stop Pyros' rage now—he raised his right hand, pointing his palm at the hubristic soldier.

"Die!" Pyros bellowed through Drake, unleashing a pillar of flames through the portcullis. Rick hollered in agony as the stream of fire charred his ashy skin black. Drake's screams merged with Rick's as the fire spread across the bandages on his own hand, creeping down his wrist. He yanked back his hand to stop the salvo, tucking it inside his jacket to hide the blistering.

"Open the gate," Drake barked at the survivor, taking one last look at Rick. The soldier's garments continued to burn, though he was unmistakably dead. His face was horrendously disfigured, and his dried skin had compressed against his bones like jerky. "And get him out of my sight."

"Y-yes, sir," trembled the mortified Godwin.

Drake knew the horrors the man had witnessed would scar him for life. Rumors of the unholy power of the Mystics would likely ripple through the entire Godwin army by month's end. He hoped those rumors would serve to dissuade future conflict, though he recognized the opposite was a possibility.

The survivor patted down the low flames on the corpse's raiment with his iron gauntlets. He grabbed Rick's collar and dragged him out to the other side of the wall, quivering terribly as he went.

Drake turned away to inspect his right hand. The burn had worsened, blistering his palm and turning half his forearm pink. He recognized leaving the wound exposed to the elements for too long could cause a serious infection.

That's not happening again, he condemned Pyros.

The Primal rumbled back, *Feeble human. Your burns will heal. Your diplomacy failed, and I could abide his insolence no longer.*

You disobeyed me, Drake suspected.

I did what had to be done. She may be your child to protect, but you are mine.

Drake grimaced in pain as he walked back to the sunlight. The horse looked spooked, stamping its hooves in place. Talia gingerly held the reins in both hands, unsure how to direct the panicked animal.

Why did you burn my hand?

Your hand was burned because your connection faltered. You knew I would incinerate that whelp, yet you hesitated to sate my ire. Your pathetic bandages also blocked my path, lambasted Pyros.

An uneasy knot formed in his stomach. *You're dismissed,* he thought sternly, focusing on severing their connection. The furnace within went cold, sending a shiver down his spine.

He thought he had struck a harmonious balance with his Primal, but he was forced to reconsider their tenuous agreement. He recalled the panic he felt upon realizing that Pyros had circumvented him, priming a burst of fire he could not stop. Again, the Primal's fury had backfired on him, exacerbating his injuries. Pyros had acted impetuously, risking even Drake's own safety to satisfy his bloodlust.

As he walked over to calm the frightened horse with his bandaged left hand, Drake reflected that he had blindly ceded more trust to Pyros than he was comfortable with. Especially with Talia around, the Primal couldn't be given a channel to act so recklessly. He recognized he couldn't disavow Pyros entirely—too powerful a weapon to remove from his arsenal. Still, he resolved to be more prudent in the future. At the very least, he would allow his hands to fully recover before risking them again.

"That didn't sound good," remarked Talia.

"Just some trouble at the gate. They're opening it now," he explained as she shifted back in the saddle. He put a foot in the stirrups, planted his left hand on the pommel, and swung onto the horse's back.

"Your arm!" Talia gasped.

"I'm fine," he lied, spurring the horse forward. They stopped in the shade before the portcullis. A strong smell hit Drake's nose, emanating from the ashes smoldering behind the barrier. Fortunately, the body was no longer in the tunnel, and Talia was spared the disturbing sight.

"It'll take them a second to lift the gate," Talia reasoned, digging through her bag. "Let me at least start to wrap it."

"I said I'm fine," Drake declined.

"I'm not asking," Talia poured water on a clean white cloth, then gently patted the back of his right hand. He recoiled in pain, swearing colorfully. Unfazed, she grabbed his arm and continued dabbing the skin. She slid the rag back into her bag, trading it for a roll of bandages. Finally, she wrapped his wrist, then the rest of his hand, binding his fingers together in a mitt.

"You can steer just fine with your left hand," she advised, cutting off any potential objections.

"Where is this guy," Drake grumbled testily.

The portcullis slowly shuddered up from the ground with a discordant screech as the pulleys labored within the stonework. Once it had cleared three-quarters of the way, Drake spurred the horse forward, crossing into Deuzos.

On the other side of the wall, two unfamiliar soldiers knelt next to a smoking body laid before a heap of bloody remains. He had wondered about the bodies of the slaughtered garrison; now he had an answer. Evidently, the four Godwin scouts were temporarily holding the fort while a larger force was assembled from the nearby cities. Though the day's events were somewhat regrettable, their timing was a stroke of fortune. Although crossing westward would doubtlessly have been easier any time in the past, he realized in a short matter of days, it would become nearly impossible.

The Godwin he had encountered at the gate descended from the ramparts to join his comrades beside the fallen. Still trembling. The other two managed only distant stares at Drake—neither angry nor fearful, but resigned to whatever fate had in store.

"May we never meet again," Drake said shortly.

The oldest of the three nodded solemnly, recognizing the imminent danger was likely behind them.

Drake spurred Shelby into motion, cantering west down the road. After thirty minutes of maintaining the pace, the horse's steady breathing turned hot and heavy, and the road swung to the north. With the fort behind them and no sign of pursuers, he allowed the horse to recover in a trot.

"Lot of bodies back there. How do you think they all died?" Talia wondered aloud.

"Who knows? Could be defectors, mercenaries, a disease of some sort," Drake speculated, ruling out the latter on account of all the bloodstains.

"Those three survivors must be pretty lonely now," considered Talia.

"They weren't part of the fort's garrison. Whatever happened, it didn't look like anyone survived. Those three were just there to clean up and keep people out."

"I'm guessing one was too good at his job?" Talia ventured darkly.

"All those men are dead already," Drake deflected. "They just don't know it yet."

"Does Tallawyn have that big an army?"

"I don't know how big their armies are, but Tallawyn's is knocking at the door already. Godwin's is still on the road. Hopefully, we won't bump into either of them."

Within the hour, they encountered a Godwin banner. A lone soldier stood at a crossroads, likely to direct traffic away from the border.

"Signposts," Talia pointed behind him.

The horse slowed into the intersection, coming to a stop a few yards away from the unaccompanied Godwin.

"Hail!" greeted the man, waving a gauntlet. His oversized helmet tilted forward as he nodded, forcing him to readjust the armor. "The eastern border is closed... but you seem to be coming from that direction," he said, perplexed.

"We were just bringing some fish down to the garrison. Support the troops," invented Drake.

"I see," the Godwin placed his hands on his hips, unconvinced. "I've been here all morning and don't recall seeing you."

"We traveled along the coast," Drake answered curtly.

"Huh," the sentry folded his arms. "I've never heard of fishermen going out of their way to give soldiers their catch."

Sighing, Talia peered over Drake's shoulder. "Look, man. Sun's out, you're alive—for now—isn't that enough?"

"I... Well... Who?" the sentry stammered, dumbfounded.

"Save it for the Tallawyns," she advised benevolently. "We're just passing through."

"Well... All right. Just watch your speed," he warned in a token effort to impose his authority.

"Will do, Officer," Drake mumbled in an equally token effort to respect the soldier.

"Do you mind?" Talia made a shooing motion with her hand. "You're kind of in the way."

"Ah!" exclaimed the man, picking up his banner and trotting several paces to the left. "So I am. Ha."

Drake studied the revealed signboard. There were a few smaller towns he didn't recognize, but he discerned that the Grotto and Highwind were both down the road to the north. To the west, the Aollean Forest and Tidestone were separated by a nearby town called Daheim. His eyes rested on the name for a moment. A sharp pain suddenly erupted in his temple, forcing him to drop the reins behind the pommel and bring his left hand to his head.

"Can we help you?" Talia snapped.

Drake gritted his teeth and suffered through the abrupt spike of pain. When it passed, he glanced to his left and noticed the guard had been staring.

"Nope! Just here to help you if you need directions," smiled the Godwin. "Ah, look! A lilac," he excused himself, stooping to inspect a flower.

"Border patrol," Talia snorted derisively.

"Everyone's gotta make a living," Drake mumbled philosophically.

"Figured it out?" she asked.

"North," he answered, glancing up at the red sun. "Looks like we've got a little daylight left. Next town up is Ogsden—forty-nine miles. Doubt we'll make it there today, but I wouldn't mind finding an inn in that direction."

"Sounds like a plan, Stan," Talia approved.

"Stan?" Drake looked around in confusion. "That guy?"

"What a pretty lilac!" fawned 'Stan'.

"Just a joke," Talia dismissed, spurring Shelby into motion. "Not really a joke, actually. More of a... well, a rhyme, I suppose."

"A man named Stan," considered Drake. "Now that does rhyme. Man, Stan, can..."

"Plan?" Talia rolled her eyes.

"Plan," Drake approved. "S... Slan? Hmm, no. Ham. Ham for sure."

"Ham doesn't rhyme with plan."

"I'm rhyming with Stan."

"I don't think ham rhymes with Stan, either."

"It's called a slant rhyme, Talia. It's a poetry thing."

"All right," she accepted, deciding it wasn't a hill worth dying on.

"Slan-t. That's where I was going with that. *Slant* is a slant rhyme with Stan. Now *that's* poetry."

"Is it?" Talia pressed. "Is it really? I wouldn't know, of course—never read that stuff."

"It is," insisted Drake. "One day, you'll be cultured like me."

"If you say so," she relented.

"I say so," he affirmed.

Several slant rhymes later, the sun was disappearing over the horizon, casting the world into long shadows. A lone tavern appeared in the twilight, off to the side of the road. A few horses were hitched to posts in front of the pub. The more fortunate steeds ate from shallow sacks of oats.

Drake steered Shelby over to a free hitching post and dismounted. He began to tie a knot but decided to leave the reins loose over the hitch. It would be enough to convince the rented horse she was fixed in place. Realistically, any horse thief would be undeterred by a simple knot.

A neighboring stallion nickered its greetings. Talia slid off the far side and petted the friendly stranger, whispering words of affirmation. Drake pulled his pack off Shelby and strapped it over his back. "Get your bag," he instructed Talia, crossing to the front of his horse. He leaned over and pulled the sack of grain away from the neighboring horse to allow Shelby access. After confirming she had water in the trough, he stepped onto the porch, waiting for Talia to sling her bag over her shoulder.

"Can't we leave these on the horse?" she protested.

"We'll splurge on a room tonight. I saved a fortune getting a great deal on a horse," Drake boasted with a devilish smile.

He stepped through the swinging doors into the cantina, pausing in the doorway. The tavern was surprisingly packed. Every seat at the bar was taken, as were most of the tables on the floor. Scuff marks on the floor confirmed the tables and chairs were sometimes pushed to the side while a singer or band took the small stage in the back.

"Welcome to Aiden's!" a mousy, energetic woman popped up in front of Drake and waved a friendly hand in greeting. "Care to join us for dinner?"

"Yes ma'am," Drake attempted a smile. "We'll be looking for a room tonight, as well."

"We're unfortunately sold out of rooms, but there's plenty of food to go around. Right this way," she beckoned, leading them down an aisle near the right wall. She stopped in front of a vacant booth, four in from the door.

Drake frowned as Talia sidled up to the far side of the booth. He didn't like that the seating was right in the middle of the tavern. He also didn't like that Talia had chosen the seat facing the door, but he saw no opportunity to request a switch now. "Thanks," he said tersely to the waitress, putting his bag on the bench and sliding into the booth.

"Some menus?" the waitress asked with a smile.

Drake buried his head in his hand and rubbed his eyes.

"Some kind of meat and vegetables. Rice or noodles if you got it. For two," Talia ordered.

The waitress nodded, surprised by the young girl's commands but gradually accepting the order as Drake kept his head in his hand. "You got it!"

"Long day, huh?" Talia stretched her back, then drummed her fingers on the table.

"Water and beer," Drake grumbled, lifting his head. "Those are the two things missing from your order."

"And oats for Shelby," recommended Talia.

"Shelby has oats," he said slyly.

The waitress returned to deposit two plates of food on the table.

"That was fast," Talia raised an eyebrow at Drake.

"Is there anything else we can do for you tonight?" offered the waitress.

"Two beers, two waters," Drake ordered.

"Hmm," the waitress put her hands on her hips. "You said two beers?"

"What's the damage?" he reached into his purse.

The waitress counted on her fingers, lost her place, and counted again. "Thirty-eight?"

"Keep the change," Drake planted two silver kroner on the table.

"Weird," Talia remarked after the waitress left.

"What?" he sampled a bite of lukewarm food. The meals were likely prepared in mass batches and sat in the back until ordered.

"We're in Deuzos now, right? Why do they use Tallawyn currency?"

"Kroner? It's a Cormack currency, actually," shrugged Drake. "First standard currency. The Cormack kings came up with it back in the day, then the Godwins and Tallawyns took it up. Made things easy."

The waitress came by with a tray. She left four glasses on the table and disappeared without additional comment.

"Huh," Talia remarked, satisfied. "I see you ordered two beers, there."

Drake slid one tankard across the table, sipping deeply from the other. As he drank, he overheard a zealous rant from one of the tables to his left: "The people are his power! If we join the rebellion, we can stop the war before it begins. You want another hundred years of this shite? What, is *Cain* going to be our next king?"

"Pipe down, moron!" Drake watched one of the drunkard's tablemates deliver him a swift backhand.

"Blech!" Talia pushed the tankard back across the table. "Why's it so... bitter? Is that how they all taste?"

"More or less," Drake took another swig of his drink. Pretty good.

"Why do you like that stuff?"

"It's an acquired taste," he explained, accepting the second mug on his side of the table.

"I'm pretty sure that means you just keep drinking the stuff until you trick yourself to like it," she charged.

"You're not wrong," he admitted, enjoying another sip.

"Damn it, woman!" Drake heard a fist slam on the table behind him. Talia flinched. Frowning, he listened in as he continued to eat his greens. The voice continued, rising in volume and anger: "You always do this—and you do it to me on purpose, don't you? Don't you!?"

"I'm sorry, Tom!" apologized the shaky voice of the woman sitting directly behind him. "I didn't mean to!"

"Like hell you didn't!" Tom shouted back. "You conniving bitch. I said order two dinners, keep it under forty kroner. I was gone five minutes, and you order the most expensive thing on the whole damn menu! You know I don't make that kind of money, and you just had to rub it in my face, didn't you? Huh? I guess it's not enough that I'm out in the field all day while you kick your feet up at home, sat around like the useless hog you are?"

"I said I'm sorry, Tom! You know I never learned to read."

"You're a worthless sack of flesh, you know that? All that free time you have doing nothing all day, and you're still fat. You don't even have the decency to drop a few pounds while I'm hard at work! I had my pick of the lot, you know. I could've had your smoking hot sister, but I chose your sorry ass, Jean. And boy, have I regretted it ever since. You don't put half the work into this marriage as I do, Jean—and it's always the same excuse! You're anxious; you're depressed—well you know what? I'm depressed too! I'm depressed I married the one bitch in all of Deuzos who can't give me a son."

"Is that why you were over there womanizing with that whore at the bar?" Jean accused through embittered tears.

"What did you say?" Tom lowered his voice dangerously. Vindictively. "You sack of human garbage. Tell me, what did you say?"

"I only meant that—"

"Shut the hell up! I never did nothing to you. I'm a better man than you deserve. Who put these crazy thoughts in your head? You talking to your batty mother again? She's sick, Jean. The old widow's gonna die real soon."

Drake heard the woman yelp in pain. "Stop it Tom, you're hurting me! Let go of my arm!"

"Do something!" Talia implored him, leaning across the table.

Noticing her tight grip on her fork, Drake leaned forward to whisper: "Not our pig; not our farm. Ignore them."

"That's just like you," spat Tom. "Always have to make a big scene out of nothing."

"I said I'm sorry, Tom!"

"I said shut the hell up!"

Drake heard the distinctive crack of a hand slapping across a face. He felt the booth rock and heard the woman's quivering sobs.

"Just wait till we get home—then you'll be sorry," threatened Tom.

Talia clenched her fists and looked at Drake entreatingly. "Let's leave. I don't want to stay here anymore. Please."

Drake straightened his back, took one last mouthful of vegetables, and nodded his head. "Let's go," he said softly. "Don't forget your pack."

Drake slipped out of the booth and picked up his bag. He waited for Talia to stand, then turned toward the door.

As he walked past the violent booth on the way to the exit, he caught a glimpse of Tom out of the corner of his eye. The man had a thin head of gray hair that scarcely made up for his hairless lip. Despite his alleged work in the fields, he was remarkably fat. Some manner of sauce stained one of his several chins. He scowled at Jean, who in turn bowed her head and cried quietly.

Drake walked past the pair. Two hatted farmers were in the next booth over, evidently several drinks into the evening.

A bloodcurdling shriek erupted from the booth behind him, followed by a thump and the smashing of glass.

"Shit!" Talia yelped.

Hearing her voice, Drake spun around immediately. He looked from her to the booth, trying to make sense of what had happened.

Blood seeped onto the brown table, overflowing from the plate of half-eaten steak. Tom lay slumped over his dish, one arm dangling by his side, the other next to toppled glassware. Protruding from his ear, the crystal-handled poniard was wet with the man's rapidly draining blood.

Drake recognized the knife from Lord Vayne's collection and finally registered what had happened.

Talia yanked the knife out of the man's skull, hastening the rush of fluids escaping from his head. "Shit," she repeated, panting heavily. "I'm sorry," she apologized to the blanching woman across the.

For just a moment, Drake stared into the widow's fearful eyes. She had a young, plain face, but her spindly fingers looked worn and old. Beneath her uneven brown hair, she had a distinctive pink-and-red splotch marking the skin around her left eye—likely the remnant of a terrible burn suffered long ago.

"Move," Drake guided Talia by the shoulder.

"Murderer!" one of the men at the neighboring table yelled after them.

"Go!" Drake urged, pushing the stunned Talia toward the door.

"Stop them!" yelled another.

A hand grabbed Drake's jacket as he hurried past the neighboring booth. Drake turned and saw a burly man winding up a fist. With no time to think, he called on Pyros.

A sadistic satisfaction coursed through Drake as Pyros willingly lent his power. The heat rose from his stomach and erupted from his mouth in a cone of fire. The burly man staggered backward, releasing his grip on Drake as he swatted at the flames ravaging his body. His friend tried to douse the fire with beer as others rapidly rose to confront Drake.

The piercing gaze of a bald, white-robed man reached Drake from the bar. The zealot pointed a finger at him and yelled, "Mystic! Gold and glory to the man who captures this monster! Stop him!"

Talia looked back, swaying dizzily in the doorway. Her pack rested on the floor by her feet.

Drake barreled forward before the crowd could engulf him, picking the bag up with his left hand and propelling Talia through the swinging doors with his right. Pain racked his hands, but he had no time to consider it. "Run!"

XVII. Worlds Away

Allen Lee

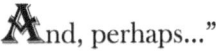nd, perhaps..."

Virgil looked around the senate at the scores of scholars hanging on to his final words. "That's all that happiness is—or at least, all we can expect it to be. Ergo, duty need not oppose happiness even when difficult or displeasing."

"Genius," the graying man beside Allen mumbled appreciatively into his beard. "Sheer genius."

Virgil smiled, adding: "I hope you'll take solace in my words as you conscientiously continue your research."

Good-natured and scholarly laughter vindicated his esoteric joke.

"I suspect none of you have forgotten," he walked the floor with his hands clasped behind his back, stopping before the entryway, "but I'll remind you that our semi-annual symposium will take place in one month's time. Our adepts' latest, most groundbreaking publications will be unveiled to our special family on El Aria. Perhaps equally exciting, you will have an opportunity to share your hard work with the broader world. This year, I have invited Sheikh Dohari to attend personally. In addition to renewing his contribution to our humble library, the sheikh intends to discover new curriculum to introduce in print at his university. I trust you all feel the same privilege I do—that we may continue to understand and shape the world, ever contributing our small part to the vast sum of human knowledge."

Cato stood from the front row. "It is an honor as always, teacher. We are fortunate beyond measure to live at this place and time."

Not to be outdone, Felix rose to his feet farther down the bench, clapping slowly. "How lucky we are to call The Library our home—a bastion of human achievement that has stood for a millennium. No school or city dares approximate the wealth of knowledge curated by thousands in these halls; countless lifetimes well spent to enrich these hallowed grounds, thrusting us centuries ahead of the rest of the world."

Virgil nodded politely, slowly backing toward the exit.

"Had I more than one measly life to give!" lamented Felix.

The man next to him, a hawk-nosed elder with one remarkably bushy eyebrow, placed a soothing hand on his shoulder while Virgil made his escape. "Weep not, noble Felix; your dedication to the advancement of our medical sciences is unparalleled. Your heroic deeds will be recorded in the timeless annals of history."

"I'm just... one... man!" Felix raised a regretful fist to underscore his mortality. *Was this a senate or an amphitheater?*

"Right," the paunchy observer beside Allen smacked his jiggling belly with both hands as he rose. "What's for lunch?"

The stream of white togas flowed out of the senate. Allen stayed on the marble bench, waiting for the congestion to pass.

The sun flitted through a stained-glass window, spilling a rose-colored ray onto the empty seat beside him. Lifting his head, Allen adjusted his loose spectacles and stared sulkily into space.

He missed Meghana.

A lot.

Reflecting on the thought saddened him immensely. Guilt burdened his conscience. He shamefully fidgeted with the platinum ring on his left hand—an accusatory reminder that his grief should have been solely centered around his wife and child. Perhaps he could also long to be reunited with his brother, Danny, but Meghana's absence was the most consistent catalyst to return him to his sullen mood. She was the only light inside this nightmare he was living.

Of course, he missed his family too.

He had lost count of how many times he had checked his dead phone. For all the technological advancements his world boasted over Kyros, they had never bothered producing a solar-powered phone. Now, the irreplaceable piece of technology rested uselessly in his pocket, as if he might one day find a way to recharge it.

More than anything, he wished he could recover one of the thousands of photos he had of Alaina and Lyn. Even the photo library on his smart glasses thwarted him, closing itself every time he tried to open the app. Some days, he was so focused on work that he forgot to remember them at all. This morning, however, began with a few transitory seconds of recalling his dream about them. He glimpsed his wife's silky black hair and Lyn's little pink raincoat, but he couldn't picture their faces. A minute later, he remembered only remembering.

His anchor was a family photo taken over the holidays just before Lyn's third birthday. He mentally reconstructed the photo and saw Alaina's thin lips. Her high cheekbones. Carefully manicured eyebrows. Then Lyn's button nose. Tiny hands and wide eyes. They were his world, but the details evaded him. *Did her chin have a scar? What color were Danny's eyes? How tall was Lyn?*

His little girl would keep growing without him. He'd been gone a long time. Regretting that he hadn't kept track of the days, Allen guessed she'd be four or five by now. He wondered if she was enjoying her first year of school. Wondered if Alaina had enrolled her in violin lessons like they had planned.

Wondered if they had already forgotten him.

They must have been worried out of their minds the first night he didn't make it back from work—the first bedtime he failed to kiss Lyn and her teddy bear goodnight. Sometime after the portal collapsed, once they realized there was no way to reactivate it from their side, the military would have sent word to his family. Alaina would've been heartbroken; Lyn probably wouldn't have understood why daddy couldn't come home.

He couldn't imagine what came after. Allen knew he was alive, so he held out hope he might one day make it back to them. But they had no idea. After missing for two years, could he believe that Alaina had clung to hope that he'd return? He deluded himself into believing he'd easily recognize Lyn when he saw her again, but would she remember him as she grew older?

He realized the perfect image he had selfishly held onto all this time, the pristine picture of him one day knocking on the door of his suburban home and seeing his family shed tears of relief, was a fantasy as far removed from reality as could be. It was unrealistic to think their world would wait for him. More likely, after she cried and mourned and grieved for him—a thought that weighed heavily on his heart—she would have had to move on.

His heart couldn't balance the scales. On the one hand, he loved her too much to imagine her suffering over him. He wanted her to be happy. He didn't want her to live a life of pain. And yet, it pained him to imagine that she could adjust to a life without him. It hurt his heart to wonder if she had sold their family home and moved back with her parents, or if she had remarried and Lyn grew up none-the-wiser, comfortably calling some stranger *Dad*.

His tormented jealousy reverted to grief as his thoughts darkened a shade further. There was a grim probability that his home had been destroyed in the invasion, and that Danny had met the same end as Charles. Maybe there was nothing to return to at all. Maybe, even if he could go back, he'd only find desolation. Time moved on. The world he knew was lost forever.

Enter Meghana.

His assigned mentor was his only friend in this place. The other adepts were as insufferable as they were factionalized. Cato and Felix were often at the center of the spectacles and had large cohorts of followers and admiring peers, but others had made names for themselves as well. Archedontus was full of himself, Estaphotes had a violent and bombastic temper, and Song Ta rarely spared a word for anyone. The former dean of Ayrabos University, Khalifa Kornuchak, was the best of the lot, but even he had callously dismissed Allen as a half man. In reference to his leg, Kornuchak had offhandedly informed Allen that *people like him* would have been put down in the city.

Whenever Virgil was busy attending to other matters, Meghana had been the one person who made Allen feel like he belonged. She had tried to introduce him to other colleagues, but they were often lukewarm interactions. Karim had indulgently eaten lunch with them on a few occasions, though he always seemed to be short on time whenever Meghana wasn't around. Alevi had been nice to him in the two minutes they chatted outside the senate, but he hadn't seen her around The Library since then.

It was the little things he missed most. The transient passages of time they used to spend together had kept his spirits up. Short walks between the bookshelves as they took a break from work. Exchanging his favorite movie plots for Meghana's ramblings about her favorite heroes of legend. Moonlit snacks on the hill and deep chats about life only they could understand—these were the moments that made every day worth living.

Without her, the campus felt a lot bigger, and he felt a lot smaller. He was happy for her, undoubtedly. She had worked long and hard to develop a cure for the blood plague and was making a difference in the lives of those poor people in the Lowlands. It sounded like Virgil had given her the high accolades she strove for. She deserved every bit of recognition coming her way and more.

But he was lonely.

The days stretched on, stealing ever more of his resolve as they ticked by. After learning that starfish ostensibly didn't exist on Kyros and his niche expertise was rather useless, he had taken to reading book after book in the vast library as he awaited her return. Time with Virgil was few and far between, and he couldn't find it in himself to dive into research on a new, unfamiliar topic.

He thought about the kiss. It had made their goodbye a little more awkward than it should have been. He hoped things would go back to normal between them by the time she returned from her journey to Deuzos. She was too good a friend to lose over something small like that.

Oddly, in her absence, that surprise had endeared her to him. At least it was a sign of validation that she liked him as well—even if in a slightly different way. In another world, if he hadn't committed himself to Alaina, perhaps he would have felt differently too. Maybe even in this world, if he were certain he'd never make it back home...

Lifting his head, Allen realized he was now alone in the spacious auditorium. Slowly pushing to his feet, he scolded himself for sinking back into sadness. If there was any hope of getting back, no matter how small, he had to try. He owed it to them. Of subsequent importance, he owed it to himself.

Till death do us part.

In another life, he could have dedicated himself to his studies as one of Virgil's scholars. But if he wanted to make an earnest effort to return home, he had to be more deliberate about his needs now. His research would be solely focused on finding a way back. He didn't want to believe Hamal, but if he was right about Virgil throttling their efforts to leave, even unintentionally, Allen had to step up and demand the help they needed.

Politely, of course.

He descended the stairs to the center of the auditorium, listening to his footsteps reverberate throughout the chamber as he went.

Tightness abruptly gripped his lungs. Too slowly, Allen raised an arm to his mouth and hacked a violent cough.

He opened his eyes and saw the splatter of blood in the crook of his elbow. On the white wall behind, specks of his bodily fluid stained the hallowed stones. Red-faced, he wiped the stones with his palm, managing to rub off most of the stain and smudging what remained. He inspected the splatter on his elbow, unsure what to do about it, absent a handkerchief. He regretfully lifted the bottom of his toga and used the inside to clean himself off.

Sorrowfully, he brooded how his body also seemed to be reacting to Meghana's absence. Days after she left, this hacking cough had started to ail him, racking his body and stealing small doses of blood. He had consulted one of the scholars who helped run the infirmary but was told it was just seasonal allergies. No cause for concern. A second, unsolicited opinion suggested that he might've caught the blood plague from discussing it too openly. Needless to say, Allen hoped the first disciple was correct. Otherwise, he had low confidence the primitive infirmary would be of much help to him.

Exiting into the hot sun, he shielded his eyes from direct light as they adjusted to the ambient brightness.

"Hey! Glasses! That you?"

Allen looked up to see a familiar face in a camouflage uniform. The soldier was smoking a cigarette, an assault rifle slung casually over his shoulder in a way Allen suspected went against the military's safety protocol.

"Nice toga," Ajax Sykes eyed him up and down. His dark, unsmiling eyes drilled into Allen with a disapproving look.

"Thanks," Allen tried not to take offense.

"That leg of yours crap out yet?" Ajax blew out a puff of smoke.

"It's hanging in there," Allen answered with a polite smile.

"Yeah? Ah, well. Give it time," Ajax murmured indifferently.

"Things well with you?" Allen returned respectfully.

"Can't complain," grunted Ajax. "Well, I could, but who'd listen?"

"Not me," Allen half-joked with a playful swing of the arm.

"That right?" Ajax muttered with a deadpan expression.

"Say, where'd you pick up those cigarettes, anyhow?"

"What, this?" Ajax pulled the cigarette out of his mouth for inspection. "Had some kickin' around from back when. Don't worry about it."

"I see," Allen said, not seeing at all. He supposed it was possible Ajax had a case of them squirreled away somewhere on the helicopter. "I don't smoke, myself."

"Shocker." Ajax looked Allen's toga up and down once more.

"How's Sam and the others?" Allen clasped his hands in front of him.

"Haven't seen Samson in a couple days," Ajax raised his eyes, as if searching the clouds for answers. "He's hiding out around here, somewhere.

Went and got all paranoid after Swanson went AWOL. Refuses to eat or sleep near anyone else."

"Roy went missing?"

"Deserted, probably," speculated Ajax. "Can't say I blame him. Guess that makes me the last man standing... Well, and you, I guess."

"What about Chip Hamal? Or Jones?"

"Jones is dead. Forgot about Chip. Hamal's in the infirmary, probably with that disease that's going around."

"I better go visit him," Allen decided, concern bubbling within him. He wondered if he had contracted the disease himself but tried not to think it into existence. It was just seasonal allergies. The medic said no cause for concern.

"You deaf? I just said he's got that disease. Don't you doctors know you're supposed to stay away from sick people?"

"You're really the only other one left?" Allen said, feeling his world shrink even more.

"If you got something to say, come out and say it," challenged Ajax.

"Nothing. Just shocked to hear we lost everyone," Allen said non-confrontationally. In truth, he was sad to hear the news. It was just like life to take away the nice people and leave the jerks behind.

"Thought so. Look on the bright side, Glasses: at least they got *rest in peace* instead of *rest in pieces*. Not the worst way to go."

"It's been nice catching up, Ajax. I've got to run. I'm going to see if I can help Virgil get the transporter fixed."

"What for?" scoffed the soldier, blowing another ring of smoke. "It's over. Done. We failed. Big Red was only days away from stomping our boys back home—and that was years ago, when we had at least a snowflake's chance in hell of getting out of this dump. There's nothing to go back to."

"We have to try. Our families are waiting for us."

Ajax laughed darkly. "I ain't got nothing but a few last-call bargirls waiting for me, and they're probably a smoldering pile by now. Just like your family. Just like everyone else. Time for you to wake up and smell the ashes."

"How could you say such a thing?" gasped Allen.

Ajax took a long puff from his cigarette, then blew a heavy stream of smoke in Allen's face before flicking the butt at his toga. "Look, pal. I'm the reality check you needed: this is your life now. There's no *going back*, all right? Now run along and play schoolgirl with the other skirts here."

Allen balled his fists, indignant at the soldier's brazen neglect of duty. He couldn't believe a uniform would so easily abandon his countrymen and give up on his homeland. All this time they had traveled together, Allen never knew Ajax was such a coward. A defector, if not a traitor.

"Really, princess?" chuckled Ajax. "You want to hit me, don't ya? Go ahead. Right here," Ajax tapped his chin goadingly with his free hand.

Allen wisely refrained from escalating to a physical altercation. Instead, he pointed a censuring finger. "You're nothing but a spineless, slimy mollusk!"

Ajax squinted at him. "A slimy what now?"

"A mollusk," Allen spat venomously.

"A mollusk... Like one of those snail things?" clarified Ajax.

"Yeah. A mollusk," Allen held firm.

"Really? Sure you don't want a second go at that one?" offered Ajax.

"You're a reprehensible, spineless, slimy slug—and that's the last word I'll have for you," Allen steamed.

"Come on, princess. No need to get your dress in a bunch. I'm just shooting the breeze," disarmed Ajax.

Allen stormed off as fast as he could hobble toward the library. He'd find Virgil inside, and the guards at the door would keep Ajax out. He didn't care if it was a joke or not; it was mean-spirited, and he didn't like that.

"Come on," Ajax groaned over his shoulder. "At least leave on a good insult. Here, I'll show you: *Glasses, get your buy-one-get-none leg and matching dull-as-rocks personality back here so I can whoop your candy-ass.*"

Allen presented an unfriendly finger above his head. He heard cackles of laughter behind him but didn't look back.

It hurt. In many ways, it reminded him of his time long ago at the new high school. He would not have expected a grown man to have the capacity for such petulant, nasty behavior. He also would've expected himself to have grown a thicker skin by now, but he had been wounded by the exchange, nevertheless.

Personal insults aside, Ajax had mocked his belief in returning to his family as unrealistic. The thought comingled with his own doubts and fears, and his shoulders sunk lower than they otherwise would have. Fleeing the hostile world outside, he crossed into the unspoiled sanctuary of the library.

It was hard to maintain his emotional resilience alone. He would have settled for even Sam's company at this point, but he had no clue where to find the sergeant. Not inside, obviously—the soldiers weren't allowed past the doors.

In a precautious effort to avoid Ajax, he planned to spend the night in the library again. There was nothing for him outside anyway.

If only he had Meghana's company. She would know exactly what to say to make him feel better. It was one of her many talents.

Hobbling through the maze of bookshelves, Allen crossed paths with several pages as he stumbled through the science and alchemy sections but decided against asking for directions. He suspected visitors were normally admitted only if summoned. Better to ask forgiveness than permission in securing an audience with Virgil. He could find his own way.

Allen reached the intersection where the library expanded, both wider and deeper. The soaring bookshelves touched the distant ceiling, illuminated by lanterns precariously hung from strings between shelves or carried by the black-clad pages who roamed the aisles. One of these bookcases concealed a staircase to Virgil's office. Unlike the main stairwell to the library's upper floors, this hidden passage was rarely traveled by the authorized pages.

The only problem with the secretive path was that the path was a secret to him, too. Despite all the time he had spent in the library, he hardly even knew it. There was so much to explore, and the irregular layout of long and short towers made the grid difficult to navigate comprehensively. He wandered with a loose sense of direction, aware he was most likely going the wrong way.

Four steps into the aisle on the right, Allen was certain he had made a wrong turn somewhere. The shelves here abandoned the grid design, scattered in tightly clustered columns instead. He stuck his head around the corner and was surprised to see a short three-by-one-yard block of shelves without a second access way. The lawless, chaotic arrangement of this section created an unnavigable labyrinth. He suspected Lyn would have loved it for hide-and-seek, somehow managing to hide herself in the least-obvious corner of this maze.

Returning to the previous aisle, Allen scanned the bookshelves, curious what section he had discovered. No signs hung from the shelves, and many of the hardcovers were unmarked or bore only numerals in place of titles.

A page rounded the corner at the end of the aisle, then walked toward Allen. As if under pressure to have a purpose in this section, Allen picked up a nameless tome with a sky-blue cover and flipped it open to a random chapter. He adjusted his glasses and read the hand-written words under the dim light.

Lest the world's seeds grow to strangle the forest, in the name of earthly balance and mortal inferiority, give in to the one called Faith. Your birth was preordained, but your death, a mercurial tiger stalking in tall grass. A primitive beast chases you. Fiercely. Fervently. Ferociously. To endure, you must seek Life's blessing. To endure, you must be Anonymous. Adamant. Ardent.

You are also a tiger stalking in the tall grass. Your spring fangs cannot possibly endure the forest alone. But look, cubs! Hope! Abide in the purest vine born from the seed. Come, cubs; let us frolic together and give in to Faith. Now, we hunt joyfully, pursuing our pursuer. Cubs, naïve cubs, in our pack, you are safe. But cubs, killer cubs, you mewl and romp under my guidance, and I, under Faith's. May she command us unto Life. Life is life; Life is death.

Allen removed his glasses and wiped the lenses with his toga. Either they had a smudge on them, or he was reading the scribblings of a madman.

An orange glow spilled onto the pages.

Allen looked up and saw the black-clad page had stopped in front of him to offer a lantern. The man's square chin protruded from underneath the black hood, although his eyes remained hidden.

Gingerly accepting the lantern, Allen muttered thanks and pretended to return his attention to the blue book. Once the page had left, likely in search of a new lantern, Allen closed the book and slid it back into place on the shelf.

Thankful for the added light to guide him but feeling decidedly less sneaky, Allen pressed on deeper into the labyrinth, curiosity triumphing over the fear of getting lost. He wondered if anyone had ever mapped it all.

Quickly rounding several corners in a row, Allen stopped to let the dizziness pass. Quiet voices reached him from down the aisle to his left. He reflexively shrunk, retreating a row and pressing himself against the corner of the bookshelf. He knew there were no rules governing where he could go on the ground floor, but even so, his first instinct was to conceal his presence.

The whispers grew a little louder, and Allen heard footsteps working their way down the aisle he had just left. Noticing his exposed lantern's glow on the floor, he pulled a thick tome from the shelf and swapped it with the lantern, then replaced the book sideways to cover the gap. Returned to shadows, he closed his eyes and held his breath, desperate to remain hidden.

As the voices neared, Allen strained to make out what they were saying. He recognized Felix's voice first, tiredly answering his colleague.

"It will be ready. We have all the evidence we need."

"But the symposium is less than a month away! You haven't even begun writing..." it was a woman's voice. Allen thought it sounded familiar.

"No, Alevi. I have not begun writing. However, I have done just about everything else. So if you want your name on the publication, you have two weeks to put something coherent on paper."

Felix's weary voice passed through the short section adjacent to the row that concealed Allen. The voices grew fainter as they continued down the aisle to the right. Allen thought he heard Alevi say something about sample size, but it didn't register.

He lowered the heavy tome and saw a thin wisp of gray smoke emerge. With great alarm, he pulled the lantern from the bookshelf and knelt to inspect the damage. A concentric black mark had burned into the hazel wood, but luckily nothing had ignited. Anxiously, he returned the tome to the bookshelf, holding the lantern away from his body like a live hand grenade.

Allen stepped into the next row, staring down the deserted path Felix and Alevi had taken. Part of him was interested in hearing more about Felix potentially underperforming at the symposium. On behalf of Meghana, he hoped the snobbish scholar did fail in front of Virgil and the sheikh. It was just unfortunate that Alevi would likely be thrown under the bus as the junior researcher.

With lingering trepidation about accidentally torching the life's work of some poor researcher, Allen proceeded down the row at an unhurried pace, hopeful he would find a page to relieve him of his fiery responsibility. He took the branching path to the left, then followed the shelves as they forced him into another two right turns. He slowed as he approached an unlit offshoot guarded by a deterring sign written in several translatable and untranslatable languages:

Stop! Restricted Area!

He paused at the entryway, glancing around to see if any wandering eyes would accost him for crossing the line. Technically, it didn't say for whom the restriction applied. Perhaps it only meant pages weren't allowed, or that the section contained proprietary research that shouldn't be shared with outsiders.

Rereading the sign as if it might offer additional guidance, Allen felt curiosity tug him forward. Under normal circumstances, he might've doubled back to ask for express permission. Today, however, he longed for something to distract him. This well-hidden passageway of secret knowledge was exactly the medicine he needed.

Plus, he rationalized to himself, Felix and Alevi had likely ventured down this section as well, and they wouldn't go anywhere out-of-bounds for disciples. At worst, though he could hardly stomach the thought, he could always lie and say he was trying to catch up to them to lend an extra hand on Felix's publication. Restricted or not, Allen was sure any offer of free labor to advance the adept's career would be a trump card to keep him out of trouble.

Besides, it was just a library. What secrets could these books hold that the thousands of other shelves didn't know?

To test that very thought, he picked up a red-covered book with the numeral XIII written on the front. Flipping open to a random page with his left hand, he held the lantern above the book and squinted his eyes. To his dismay, the whole text seemed to consist of nothing but illegible squiggles and symbols. He tilted the page back and forth in an effort to activate his translator, but the foreign text remained indecipherable.

"Darn," Allen whispered, returning the mysterious book to the shelf.

He hurried down the dim aisle, belatedly realizing it would be poor form to get caught six feet away from the sign that marked the restricted section. Halfway down the row, an offshoot interrupted the shelves on his right. Allen hesitated, foot off the ground as he considered walking past the offshoot. Impulsively, he rotated his leg and planted his foot on the divergent path, then strolled all the way to the dead end some ten yards later.

Raising his lantern to eye-level, he scanned the spines of the books for something written in a language he could read. One black-covered book with white text stood out to him. The serif lettering simply read:

PAIN. M.A.

"Huh," Allen pulled the tome from the shelf with his left hand. "A restricted book on muscular atrophy?"

He attempted to smoothly flip the book open to a random page but fumbled the motion. The tome slipped through his fingers and landed on the carpet with an audible thud. Wincing, he glanced behind him as if expecting a security force of burly Ayrabos guards to have been conjured by his clumsiness.

With rising anxiety, he knelt to recover the book, resting the lantern on the ground next to him. He reached for the black tome with both hands out of respect for the author, careful to ensure he did not drop it a second time. As he scooped the book off the floor, his hand swiped a loose thread on the carpet.

Allen inspected the dark-green strand of yarn. Although his eyesight was dubious at best, the string appeared to be a different shade than the dark-blue carpet. Tucking the forbidden book under his left arm, he slowly tugged the unsecured fiber. Once the yarn was taut, he heard a muted squeak as the floorboards shifted in place.

Perplexed, he put aside the black book and gripped the loose string with both hands. He adjusted his position to a squat, then lifted with his legs, pulling the string away from the floor.

A section of the carpet separated, squeaking as it swung upward on two worn hinges. Allen peered into the space below the trapdoor. A gray staircase descending into darkness.

An anxious glance over the shoulder confirmed he hadn't been caught in the act. Not yet. He picked up the lantern and ventured a nervous step into the stone stairwell. Almost surprised that he didn't immediately trigger a series of alarms, he ventured another step inside, then a third.

To conceal his trespass, he reached up to the string hanging from the underside of the raised trapdoor and pulled it shut behind him. Instantly, the air felt ten degrees cooler, causing the thin hairs on his arm to stand.

He slowly descended the stairwell, a surprisingly deep shaft of at least forty steps. Every rasp of his metal leg made him wince. He was unsure what the punishment would be if he got caught in the restricted section, but he was certain he'd rather not find out.

With no idea what might be hidden down here, so far under the earth, his imagination ran wild. At first, he guessed the section was some manner of bomb shelter, panic bunker, or escape tunnel built in case The Library ever fell under attack. However, he doubted that Virgil would allow its innumerable books collected over many lifetimes to fall into the hands of aggressors. More likely, this sealed-off section hid a collection of top-secret scrolls and tomes. Perhaps they included national secrets that had to remain shielded from even their Ayrabos benefactors. An even more exciting possibility, the concealed bunker housed a museum—a collection of the world's finest art and historical artifacts gathered here, protected against the elements and would-be trophy hunters. Or, maybe, Virgil had simply decoded the secrets of the universe and left them on a chalkboard. The possibilities were endless.

Allen noticed the speed of his descent had accelerated. His pulse raced from a dizzying concoction of excitement and nervousness. He stopped before the wooden door at the end of the stairwell, placing a hand on the knob.

His hand froze. A chill ran down his spine. Heartbeat hammering, he strained his ears, listening for an echo of the haunting shriek he thought he had heard. A banshee's wail, cried from the belly of the mountain itself.

A long, breathless moment later, he placed the lantern on the stone step behind him. No other eerie cries leaked through the wooden door, and he ascribed the imagined scream to his jumpy nerves.

Allen slowly turned the knob and pushed the door open. A wide, well-lit corridor greeted him. Stone walls—excavated, not built.

He stepped into the hallway, forgetting the lantern on the steps behind him. To his left, two doors mirrored one another on opposite walls of the corridor, about fifteen feet away. Beyond these, the passageway opened into a wider chamber with white pillars spaced evenly between the walls and the arched double doors at the far end.

To his right, the long shadow of a man writing furiously at his desk loomed into the hall through an open doorway.

With a violent bang, the door slammed shut behind Allen.

He nearly jumped out of his skin, heart pumping in his ears as he spun around. Naturally fearing the worst, he was half-expecting to see the three-headed dog of Hades staring back at him.

But there was no one there.

The door was either weighted to close on its own or got caught in a cross-breeze. Allen turned his attention to the long shadow. It didn't stir from its place, hunched over its quill.

Hurrying away from his present location, Allen slunk off to the left, half running on the tips of his toes as he traversed the exposed section of stone. He slowed his pace as he neared the two closed doors, cautious about alerting any scholars on the other side. Miraculously, he passed by without incident.

He peered around the corner and found the pillared chamber empty. Despite the humility and austerity that were cornerstones of The Library, this space appeared to be primarily decorative. Two functional doors guarded the end of the hallway, but the rest of the expansive room simply existed to exist. Crown molding adorned the walls. Carved, geometric patterns embellished the floor. Silver sconces cast the room in flickering candlelight. Allen estimated the area to be perhaps sixty feet by forty feet. The pillar formation ran six deep down the length of the hall and four across, totaling twenty-four evenly spaced towers. Each was uniquely sculpted with intricate detail, the cumulative effort of which must have demanded thousands of labor hours.

Allen walked toward the double doors, taking a second to admire the artwork in the stone. Delicate tapestries of animals, men, and glyphs covered the pillars, elegant without pretentious depictions of tragedy or divine prophecy.

The door at the far end of the hall cracked open.

Allen ducked behind the nearest pillar as the door swung inward. Pressing himself against the stone, he sucked in a breath and held perfectly still. Two pairs of agitated footsteps tapped across the floor. The door shut behind them. Allen could hear concern in the familiar voice as it spoke.

"The inconvenient truth, pupil, is that brilliance alone cannot save this place. Virgil would never openly admit it, but he recognizes the fate of his great library is in our hands. We, in turn, are beholden to the financial whims of the uneducated elite below. Our duty is to deliver."

Cato.

"I understand, Cato. Of course I understand!" hissed a frustrated voice, bringing the footsteps to a halt. "But you mustn't forget our founding purpose—his guiding vision! We do what we must in the name of human advancement. To build the sum repository of all that's known. Knowledge is truth, Cato. Truth is duty. We cannot publish sham results to the world for a few coins."

"Bah!" growled Cato. "A few coins, Cornelius. Really! You know Dohari is balancing his treasury as the drums of war play in his parlor. If he should pull his endowment, the oasis of our resources will shrivel up like a sun-dried prune. Experimentation could not possibly continue, fueled by will and polite discourse alone. Our noble purpose cannot be held hostage by banal material necessities such as food, parchment, and supplies. I will not allow it."

"But Cato, your experiment failed. To present your solution as proven science would be a danger to the world. What if the El Arians actually use it?"

"Hah! A danger to the world. What nonsense you speak, Cornelius. The Library on El Aria *is* the world. You worry about a few Ayrabos halfwits, the same simpletons who pass their time pissing in their hands and brandishing rocks against one another, all for the proud ownership of a few acres of sand. They're lower lifeforms, pupil, and should be regarded as such when weighing decisions. In the same way we disregard ants as inconsequential inhabitants in our world, and with the same dispassion Deus surely pays us mortal men who blindly wander his universe, we must discard any consideration wasted on those lowly men of state and church."

"Had you a heart, friend, I would implore it to consider those lowly men as providers of our privileged lifestyle. Instead, I'll implore you to respect the scientific method. I will have no part in publishing meritless lies," Cornelius vowed stingingly.

"You will transcribe my notes as instructed, Cornelius. I spent years on this research; despite what your baseless reports from the prairies suggest, I am confident in both my solution and its remedy. The experiment worked exactly as intended. It was merely the ill advice of Virgil's pet that set this unfortunate mutation into motion. If your heart weighs so heavily, send an anonymous note to your underlings—fire is an effective intervention against the bacteria."

"Who is left to light those fires?" pitied Cornelius.

"Had I a heart, I might attempt to console your misguided empathy," Cato commiserated flatly. "Instead, I will remind you that the report remains unwritten, yet the clock keeps ticking. I'll entertain no more of this nonsense until the endowment has been secured. Go, pupil, and help me save this singularly holy sanctum."

"You are a wicked man, Cato," aspersed Cornelius, his voice heavy with defeat. "I will nonetheless do as you ask. What's done is done, and I have committed myself to his transcendent vision. Once I finish this report, I'll send a note to every household in Deuzos—I swear it."

"You cannot get out of your own way, Cornelius. So much wasted potential. You might as well send a live flame with every letter, as if you could make a difference. Death is preordained, pupil. Their clocks were merely set to an untimely hour."

Allen felt a cough rising in his lungs and attempted to suppress it, holding his hand over his clenched mouth. The weighty sensation overpowered him, first exiting through his nose, then bursting from his mouth. He ripped a throaty cough, wetting both his hand and the white pillar behind it with blood.

"You there! Come out of hiding!" demanded Cornelius.

Allen closed his eyes, paralyzed in disbelief at his rotten luck. He silently prayed that another fugitive would appear from behind a pillar to offer himself up instead. Allen would leave the secret staircase behind. Venturing into the restricted section had not been worth the risk.

"Come out," Cato repeated with a growl.

Allen slowly rounded the pillar with his hands raised.

Up close in the orange torchlight, Cato looked even brawnier than usual. He folded his bulging arms. A deadly scowl darkened his face.

"I might have stumbled into the wrong section," stammered Allen.

"So Virgil's pet appears. What do you think you overheard, outsider?" triaged Cato.

"Nothing! I swear," Allen said quickly, shrinking away from the bigger—much bigger—man. "I was just looking for the staircase to Virgil's office. I wanted to see him."

"Is that so?" He took an involuntary step back as Cato loomed over him, staring unsmilingly through him as if already visualizing the messy streak on the floor he would leave in Allen's place. "Well then. Let's go see Virgil."

Dragging his feet back toward the entryway, Allen looked over his shoulder, trying to gauge whether Cato meant any harm. The adept gave him a strong, unbalancing nudge forward, confirming they were not on friendly terms.

He gulped, unsure how he should be feeling. He had imagined the worst when he initially got caught. The fact that Cato hadn't yet ground him into a pulp was encouraging. The fact that he was still breathing suggested his darkest fears were overworked. Maybe it wasn't as bad as it seemed.

Admittedly, he expected Virgil would protect him. The shaggy-haired sage would raise his avuncular voice in his defense, and no real harm would come to pass. He might just receive an embarrassing scolding. Even though the section was restricted, he couldn't imagine any extreme consequences would be enforced. Virgil wouldn't kick him out of The Library.

Would he?

Allen reached the stairwell up to the main floor of the library, spotting his lantern on the steps where he had left it. With a grunt, he scooped up the lantern and began the arduous ascent.

"Fascinating," Cato commented flatly behind him.

"Hmm?" Allen looked back.

As he stared into the cold, dangerous eyes of the senior disciple, it dawned on him that he wasn't yet safely under Virgil's protection. He was in an isolated stairwell forty feet below ground. Alone with a sly brute whom he had ostensibly caught doing something shady—something that even Cornelius, one of his most loyal followers, had declared reprehensible.

As Allen mounted the fourth step, he reimagined the chilling scream he had sensed there earlier. A cold bead of sweat ran down his neck.

Cato smiled.

"You don't look half as worried as you should be."

XVIII. Relentless

Drake

I'm sorry."

He lost count of how many times Talia had choked out those words. She had stopped crying hours ago, submitting to a shattered state of shock and exhaustion. She sniffled, burying her head deeper into his back.

The horn sounded again.

That damned horn.

Drake looked over his shoulder and saw the silhouette of two riders trailing at a safe distance behind him. They were hidden on the shadowy road, cloaked by spiteful clouds that subverted the dying crescent moon. Still, Drake could picture their faces from the tavern. The wiry, horn-blowing figure was the bald zealot. The bulkier man was the first patron outside after Drake had fled the scene. Drake understood the zealot's motivation, but he was surprised the other man hadn't given up the chase like the rest of the pursuers.

Twice had Drake wheeled his horse around to confront them. Twice had they fled in the opposite direction until he gave up pursuit. He had also tried spitting a fireball in their direction, but the winds scattered his attack long before it landed. Despite Pyros' incessant urging, he decided against unleashing an inferno from his bandaged hands. With the adrenaline rush long passed, he feared his mounting weariness would make him sloppy.

He couldn't risk a backdraft hurting Talia.

"Come on," Drake whispered under his breath, digging his heels into the horse's flank.

Shelby obediently picked up the pace, resuming a loping canter. Drake could tell by her ragged breaths and rocky gait that she was flagging. Despite going the full day without sleep, the horse had resiliently kept up with his demands. He knew he couldn't ride her much harder but hoped this would be the last sprint. If he could lose their pursuers, he might be able to take her off-road and secure a campsite for her and Talia to rest. Then, he could double back and ambush the zealot, assuming the fanatic would follow their tracks when light returned. Drake estimated he had an hour until then and wanted to widen the gap as much as possible.

As if sensing his ambitions, the clouds maliciously parted, allowing the moon to cast its spectral spotlight on him. He looked back and saw two dark horses accelerating to match his pace.

Swearing colorfully, Drake leaned into the wind as Shelby flew forward. Their pursuers had the advantage; not only were their horses less tired from the prior day's travel, but they also carried a lighter load. *Presumably*—the one rider did look like a small mountain. He might've equaled the combined weight of Drake, Talia, and their belongings.

By the time a yellow glow painted the road, Shelby was huffing and puffing, swinging her head with every uneven step. Drake eased in the reins, returning the horse to a walk, and patted her mane to commend the effort. Knowing his last chance to slip away under the cover of darkness had failed, his tired eyes turned to the pursuers. Matching his new speed, they slowed their steeds to a trot, keeping their distance of just over a hundred yards.

Drake wiped his dusty eyes on an equally dusty sleeve. If only the road had cut through the hills to the west, they would've made it. He had considered braving the off-road but ultimately chose to stay the course under the belief that Shelby would fare better. He didn't want to lose the horse to entanglements in the wilds or a dead-end cliff; they had a lot farther to go, and the walk would be languishing on foot.

Squinting miserably against the rising sun, he recognized they would have to stop sooner rather than later. Losing the horse to exhaustion would be an equally unacceptable option.

The horn rumbled across the sky in its low, trembling tone. Drake briefly fantasized about jamming the instrument down the zealot's throat until he choked on it—or bludgeoning both of them over the head with it, pausing for short, improvisational solos. Maybe then they'd understand the insufferable aggravation that damn instrument had caused him.

Catching his mind wandering, he considered pulling off to the side of the road. Even in plain view, as long as he stayed awake, they wouldn't try to approach him. The cowards would keep their distance, and he could rest. Maybe even cook up some warm food. He wasn't particularly hungry, but the thought of wafting the savory smell of smoked meat downwind was enticing. Why wouldn't that be a good idea?

The horn sounded again. A boundless roar across the grassland.

That's why, Drake thought grimly. Although the horn had failed to rouse any additional pursuers thus far, he had no clue how many fanatics were burrowed around these parts. There was the separate issue of the southbound army. Although he wasn't sure how Godwin felt about Mystics these days, he assumed two witnesses to murder could likely stir up some problems for him.

"I'm sorry," Talia croaked glumly.

Drake heard the dryness in her throat and leaned over to pull his waterskin from the saddlebag. He held it over his shoulder for a long moment, then turned in his saddle and prodded her. "Hey," he said gently, pushing the flask under her nose. "Drink."

He watched her sullenly obey, holding the container with a shaky hand and unsuccessfully fiddling with the cap. Tweaking a muscle in his back as he turned, he took the flask, opened the cap, and returned the drink to her hands. "Drink," he encouraged softly.

She complied, pressing her lips to the flask and managing two small gulps before returning it to him. He took a swig for himself and replaced the cap, then slid the drink back into the bag.

"I'm sorry," she mumbled again, half-asleep.

"Listen to me, Talia," Drake reached back to comfortingly stroke her hair. "Everything's fine. All right? You're going to be okay. You're just tired."

As the horn blared through the dawn sky once again, Drake made his decision. He tugged the reins to the left, steering his horse off the road and onto the flat beds of green grass before the rolling hills.

"We're stopping here," Drake announced. He slid out of the saddle, landing heavily on his feet. His boots felt like stones, anchoring him to the earth. His inner legs were sore from the long ride in the saddle, and his lower back felt cramped. Still, now was not his time to rest. He reached up his hands to help Talia down.

She leaned into him, wrapping her arms around his neck as she tilted sideways off the horse.

His biceps strained as he slowed her descent. Seeing her puffy cheeks and red eyes, he pulled her in for a hug. Unsure what he should say or do, he tentatively patted her back.

"I'm..." Talia started weakly.

"You're okay," Drake whispered gently. "You're just tired. Lie down. Have a nap."

"But..." she protested hollowly, dropping to her knees and then curling onto her side.

Drake took a stake from the saddlebag and thrust it into the ground, then stomped on it once for good measure. He tethered the horse, which stood in place with drooping eyelids. Petting Shelby's forehead, he whispered, "Sorry, girl. We'll get that saddle off soon. Just hang in there."

"I thought it would be easy," Talia mumbled with closed eyes.

Drake knelt beside her. "What's that?"

"You always made it look so easy... I thought it'd be easy," Talia yawned, succumbing to exhaustion.

Drake shed his brown jacket and folded it into a rectangle. He gently raised her head to slide the makeshift pillow underneath. With the horse and girl taken care of, Drake stood and eyed their relentless pursuers.

The two men stared back from atop their horses, maintaining their safe distance. Drake waved a hand to let them know he'd be staying up with them.

The horn played its singular tune again, oblivious to the fact that its audience had heard its unskilled performance before.

Drake stretched his back and shook out his sore legs. He couldn't quite see the watchers' faces, though that had more to do with the limitations of his eyesight than the ambient lighting. Sizing them up, he weighed his options.

He couldn't confront them directly; they'd only ride away, or worse, they'd circle around to reach Talia. He wanted to sleep, if only just for a little while. Perhaps Pyros could awaken him if need be. New dangers had arrived with daylight. Travelers returning to the highway. Reinforcements arriving from the south. The army descending from the north. If he didn't sleep now, he suspected he wouldn't have another chance until nightfall. Even a few minutes of rest would suffice.

But he couldn't do it.

He knew if he lay down, he'd close his eyes, and within moments, he'd fall asleep. He wouldn't mean to, of course, but his guard would be down, and fatigue would win. If Pyros did not awaken him...

Drake looked over to Talia, who slept in the shade of the horse's tall body. In stark contrast to the trembling hands and shaking voice that plagued her since the incident, she drew long, steady breaths. He wanted to protect her peace as long as possible, though he knew the precariousness of their situation.

Turning to his rented horse, he fished around in the saddlebags until his fingers found the fancy one-handed fire striker. He took out the lighter and tossed it into the grass at his feet, then rummaged for some wood. A small chunk of timber joined the lighter in the dewy grass. A minute later, Drake located the final three ingredients and lowered his water flask, coffee grounds, and a small iron pot onto the ground.

Attempting to maintain a cool-and-collected appearance as he fumbled with his gear, Drake drew his knife and stabbed the center of the wooden log. He hammered his bandaged palm onto the hilt, driving the knife in deeper and splitting the wood. He wrangled the blade up and down, eventually cracking the timber enough for him to cleave it in two.

He arranged the two wooden pieces in a long 'V' shape, then balanced the iron pot on top. Careful not to spill, he filled the small vessel halfway, then took a sip of the temperate water before replacing the cap, awkwardly holding the flask against his body with his right arm as he wrestled the top on. Next, the bag of coffee grounds. Just a few shakes into the pot.

Finally, he stared at the two dry logs and awkwardly grasped the lighter with his thumb and middle finger. He had done it before with his right hand but never had a reason to practice the motion with his weaker side. Under his thumb, the striker ineffectively dragged across the face of the flint. He could feel Pyros ready inside him, lurking on the far side of their spiritual bridge. He resisted the Primal's presence, choosing instead to continue flicking the tool in his left hand.

Finally, a spark jumped from the lighter. "Got it!" The spark fell onto the wooden fuel, then died almost immediately after. "Damn!" Drake furiously repeated the motion, failing to conjure any additional sparks.

He felt Pyros' eager presence swirling inside him. Over his shoulder, Drake spotted Talia in the shadow of the recuperating horse. Still sound asleep. Back to the fire, he struck the flint again and again. Reluctantly, he invited

Pyros to assist. The spark leaped from the striker to the logs, instantly catching and traveling down the length of the wood under the pot.

You need not imprison me to keep her safe; only I can protect her, rebuked Pyros before voluntarily withdrawing from their conscious link.

Aggravated without a clear direction to lash out, Drake returned the grounds, water, and lighter to the saddlebag while the coffee began to boil. He stood with hands on his hips, scowling at the patient pursuers. With each sound of the horn, his thoughts toward the zealot and his beefy companion turned darker. At the very least, he was committed to ending their lives by day's end.

He scanned the horizon in all directions, assessing for any indication of trouble along his potential avenues of escape. To the west, the rolling hills rose higher and higher into the distance. A faded dirt path ran through them, starting slightly north of his current position.

On their right, the main highway ran north-south. Already, merchants and vagabonds traveled under the morning sun. Some stopped to exchange words with the vigilantes from the tavern, but the few who did all continued on their way shortly after. Whether they went to find help or had no interest in confronting a Mystic at someone else's behest, Drake neither knew nor cared.

To the east, across the road, the green grass flirted with the red rocks of the Blasted Lands. He had little desire to head back toward the Scar and away from his ultimate destination. A direct route north was preferred, but a detour southwest through the Aollean Forest would be acceptable. For now, if trouble came, he planned to either continue along the road north or flee to the western hills, then trust the topography to lead him to safety.

Approaching a sense of complacency through his own exhaustion, he stooped next to the simmering pot and breathed in its earthy scent of coffee. The smell alone was enough to reinvigorate his spirits. Lifting and shifting, he transferred the hot vessel to the grass, suffering a biting heat on his bandaged hands. Flapping them through the air, he tried to invoke a cooling breeze to mitigate the onset of pain his impulsive actions had caused him.

Drake kicked over the logs and stomped out the flames. After rubbing the charred ends against each other to remove some of the ash, he blew on the wood in an attempt to cool the surface, instead instigating a flight of embers. Begrudgingly, he set the hot logs down onto the damp grass. He'd return the fuel to his pack soon but thought it prudent to give them time to cool off first.

Imprudently, he lifted the hot pot of coffee to his lips and took a small sip. Tongue burned, roof of his mouth burned, he cursed the iron receptacle and bitterly slammed it on the ground. He patted the grass around him in search of his water flask, then ruefully realized he had already put it away.

The horn sounded jarringly—a mocking commentary on how he had managed himself.

Wiping the sweat from his brow, he glared at the steadfast observers. The timing must have been coincidental; they couldn't possibly have seen him scald his tongue on the coffee. Still, he vengefully imagined holding the zealot's face to the fire and pouring the bubbling pot over his stupid, glinting baldness.

Having already lost his sense of taste, he lifted the hot, excessively bitter liquid to his lips and swallowed some coffee along with his simmering rage.

Fifty minutes later, his heart rate had quickened, but he didn't feel any more alert. He had been reflecting on their predicament for some time. Caught in the doldrums. He was no longer worried about conflict; at this point, he welcomed it openly. Despite his increasingly grave wounds, he would gladly enter a skirmish against the resolute duo to end this stalemate. It was the unrelenting anticipation, the knife's edge he waited on, that kept his body wired and prevented him from resting—a dire affliction on his mental state.

He had also reflected on her last words before dozing off. *You made it look so easy.*

Drake struggled to come to terms with how he felt about the statement. Those words contained her respect and admiration for him. They also revealed her fractured trust. Betrayed by the worldview she had learned from him.

He didn't know what he could or should say, but he knew they would need to talk about it. He wouldn't force the conversation until she was ready. In a similar vein, brooding on it now wouldn't help him better navigate her young thoughts and emotions later. He had only just surfaced these feelings of hers, and he wanted to better understand what was going through her mind.

Countless faces he had cut down in battle flashed before his mind's eye, but he couldn't recall the first time he killed a man. He suspected he had also struggled with some strong feelings at the time. Perhaps even regret or sadness. Sometimes, he forgot not everyone had evolved the same hardened carapace of a kill-or-be-killed nomad. There were regular folk too—farmers, city socialites, children. Even some soldiers had never been put in a position that demanded they end another's life. He doubted most of those regular folk could bring themselves to do it.

In that respect, Drake grimly acknowledged Talia was right. It had become easy for him—almost stoically so. The cycle of conflict and violence was inseparable from him. Whoever he was before—whatever pity or hesitation he might have reserved in his banal role as a grim reaper of fate—had long since died. Now, there was only his world and the world out there; there was only his world and those who sought to steal it from him.

Doubling down on himself, he accepted his role in the gray. Death was a part of life. Its ubiquity preexisted him, and its longevity would easily outlast him. One day, it would claim even him in its wake. Some people knew farming and growing as a core component of life; others spent their days chasing love, and a select few lived to collect and count taxes. Death just seemed to be a bigger part of his—an overly extroverted neighbor, always knocking on his door.

Talia's breathing had grown rapid and uneven in the last few minutes, and he considered waking her up in case it was a nightmare. Ultimately, he decided the sleep would be good for her even if it was a little fitful. He risked another glance at the northern horizon, beyond his sleeping charge.

No riders appeared, but he couldn't shake the feeling that something ominous was approaching. Shelby had woken up some ten minutes prior and seemed uneasy. Perhaps it was just the drop in air temperature that had them both keyed up. Maybe it was the rumble of the dark clouds up ahead. Either way, he had learned to trust animals' instincts in times like these and was on the lookout for danger—man or otherwise.

The northern sky flashed brilliantly. A few seconds later, a long roar of thunder sang in harmony with the exhausted horn.

The horse's ears bolted up. Its body shook with an apprehensive neigh.

"Easy, girl," Drake petted the horse soothingly.

The horn sounded again, this time a few notes higher in tune.

Drake turned his attention back to the duo. He watched the zealot raise the instrument to his lips and answer in a long, low call.

It took a beat longer than it should have for the information to click in his head.

Finally, he recognized his time was up.

A lone rider descended from the north, signaling his presence with a squeaky blast of his horn. Traveling in a long arc around Drake, the vigilant duo raced to meet this new arrival.

A thunderclap shook the plains, heralding the violent storm to come.

"No!" Talia moaned.

Drake turned to find her squirming on the ground. She tossed her head from side to side, a pained expression contorting her face. Her ragged breaths mixed with whimpers of anguish.

"Talia," Drake said softly, tapping her shin in an effort to rouse her.

"No!" she panted, sweating as her breathing quickened.

"Hey! Talia!" Drake shook her leg.

Talia bolted upright, gasping with wide eyes as she lifted her hands in front of her. A blue jolt of electricity jumped from the third finger on her left hand to the fourth as she flexed them. Heavy breaths jerked her chest as she looked between her hands, apparently shocked to see them. "What...?" she managed, clearly disoriented as she slowly acclimated to the waking world.

"I'm here," Drake reassured her, resting a calm hand on her shoulder. "You were just having a bad dream. I'm here, and you're safe now."

Talia nodded, looking from her hands to him then back to her hands again. She was still dazed as Drake grabbed her arm and pulled her to her feet.

"We've got to get moving. Ready?" Drake bent to remove the stake that tethered Shelby. He slid the spike into the saddlebag, then checked that the packs were secure.

Talia languidly picked his crumpled coat off the ground and offered it to him.

"Why don't you keep that for now—looks like we're about to get rain," Drake suggested.

Talia obeyed, unfolding the soft suede jacket and slipping her arms through the oversized sleeves. She pulled the jacket up onto her shoulders and stared past Drake at the trio assembling in the road. "Who are... oh no."

"Talia?" Drake held up a hand to placate her.

"It was real," she retreated a step, cupping her hands over her mouth. "I... Did I..."

"Listen to me," Drake urged, taking two long strides to embrace her in a one-sided hug. He felt her shoulders trembling as she awakened to a reality that tormented her far worse than the nightmares. "It's over now, okay? What's done is done. We gotta move on. Keep pushing forward."

"I killed him," Talia sobbed, tears starting again from her puffy eyes. She leaned her head against Drake's sternum and slammed her palms into his chest with surprising force. "It was *me*. I *wanted* to kill him, and then I..."

"Don't overthink it," Drake pulled her in tighter. "He was pond scum and the world's a better place without him. That doesn't make you a bad person, all right? You're still good. You're not like..."

"I thought it would make me feel good," Talia cried. "I thought he was an evil, awful man and I could help her. Why did it feel like that, Drake? He looked so surprised..."

Another horn. Drake looked to the south and spotted a pair of bald riders in white robes. He understood Talia was in a delicate state, but he also acknowledged their circumstances would only get worse the longer they stayed here.

Struggling to find the right words, he settled for the wrong ones: "You do get used to it. When wicked people like that are alive, they're bastards late for their reservations in hell. The second you put a knife in 'em, they're just... dead. Then it's over, and when you're standing there after, you realize how weak they were. Then, you start to get in your head and doubt yourself. You start thinking maybe you went a bridge too far. *Maybe there was another way. It didn't have to end like this.* That's when you've got to remind yourself why you did it in the first place."

"I just wanted to help her..." She wept without restraint.

Drake held her at arm's length and fixed her with a steadying gaze. "There are no heroes, Talia. Only good liars and storytellers. Stick to keeping yourself and the people you love safe, and you'll never have to wonder whether you did the right thing."

"Did I?" sniffled Talia, searching his eyes for an answer. A bandage for her bleeding soul.

He took a breath. His first instinct was to lecture her. To help Talia protect herself in the future by pointing out the whole situation could have been avoided if she had just stayed out of business that wasn't her own. Wisely, he recognized he only had one shot to help her move on from this. "Everyone has their own sense of justice, Talia. Nobody's the villain in their own story... but for what it's worth, I would've done it if you hadn't."

Sniffling, she wiped the tears from her eyes. "You... would've?"

"Sure," he lied.

"But... you were already at the door. I was..."

"Talia, I swear," he gritted his teeth as he swallowed. He didn't know why this lie was so hard to tell, but he forced himself to carry it through.

Anything to lighten her burden. "I wanted to get you outside to the horse first. I would've gone back and finished it once you were safe; you just beat me to it."

She swallowed thickly, nodding as her eyes darted from his face to his scarred hands, then back to his face.

"Now, you just let me worry about all this heavy business, all right? It's my job to keep us safe, and I'm gonna work as hard as I can to do just that. Besides, I've got a real chance at *Employee of the Month*, so..."

A flicker of a smile broke through, accompanied by an emotional burst of mixed laughter and sobs. "That's so stupid," she managed.

The horn sounded again, reminding them that they were not alone. Drake glanced at the riders on the road and saw one of the recent arrivals was continuing north away from the others.

"I think our next job is to hop on the horse and get the hell out of here. Before we do, I want to make sure—you all good?"

Talia forced a nod, battling a trembling lip as she fought to maintain her composure.

"Let me hear from the horse's mouth," he insisted. "Not you, Shelby."

Talia smiled at his clumsy attempt to console her. "I'll be fine," she promised him bravely.

"Atta girl," he grunted, stretching his back as he returned to business as usual. Placing a boot in the stirrup, he swung his leg over and landed deftly atop the horse. He reached down a hand to help Talia climb on. The horse paced nervously as the approaching storm rumbled louder.

"Ready?" Drake asked over his shoulder, tugging the reins to angle them westward.

"Ready," Talia wrapped her arms around his chest.

He spurred the horse into motion, starting their flight into the rolling green hills. A chorus of three horns blared behind him, now registering as more of a mere nuisance than a threat. He was confident in his lead, and he expected he could lose them in the valleys and flats between knolls if they maintained their cautious distance. An extra two zealots didn't faze him in the slightest.

As they raced up the first gently sloping hill, which lazily crested some eighty feet above the flatland where they started, Drake glanced behind to confirm his lead. The pursuers were closer than expected, but they had not yet begun ascending the hill. Drake estimated he had at least a minute on them. If he chose his path carefully, he could grow that gap.

Just as he was about to face forward, a distant horn sounded from the north. He squinted, raising a hand against the high sun, which was presently still unencumbered by the amassing storm clouds. He spotted the fast-moving zealot on horseback, leading a column of at least ten black warhorses.

"Looks like they found some friends. Best we don't stick around for introductions."

"Over there!" Talia pointed left of the column.

"What?" Drake saw little except dark clouds and what appeared to be a torrential downpour on the distant road below.

"It's Godwin. That's the golden army."

Drake strained his eyes staring into the storm, searching for the army Talia had ostensibly spotted. His eyesight burned a few seconds more than they could afford. Finally, he saw the glinting gold through the black downpour.

His stomach dropped. The blurry streaks he had mistakenly identified as flooding were really thousands of soldiers armored for war. Their numbers were uncountable, their legions unlike anything Drake had ever seen.

"Should we get going?" Talia suggested apprehensively.

Drake refocused his eyes on the column of black horses behind the zealot. Especially in his injured state, he had no interest in provoking Godwin's army or fighting the elite suits of black armor heading his way. The leading rider disturbed him most—a knight so confident in himself that he openly wore a gold-plated suit of armor into battle. It was an arrogant, boastful target that dared anyone to try and take it from him.

Having forfeited much of his lead, Drake kicked his heels against the horse's flanks and shot forward, beginning the descent into the neighboring valley. The first drops of cool rain reached him, a gentle precursor heralding the wrathful storm to come. Explosions detonated in the encroaching clouds, howling warnings of their fury to him.

Part of him wondered if the sky-shattering ire was a standard drumbeat in nature's ever-cycling repertoire.

Part of him wondered if it was Talia.

XIX. Sanctuary In The Storm

Drake

Every successive hill they climbed was a little taller than the last.

The rolling foothills seemed to go on forever. To the north, a bleak horizon of conquered humps. To the west, kneeling knolls punctuated by a lone, domineering spire that towered above them all. The silhouette of the rocky crag leaped to life in the weeping sky as the storm hurled a lightning bolt at a smaller hill behind it.

A grim knot wound in Drake's stomach as he rode toward the spire. Lightning shattered the sky once more, and the image of the Twins flashed in his mind. First, the aftermath: a lone peak in an empty sky. A smoking mound where its companion once stood. Then, the ascent: an arduous, painful climb that taxed every muscle in his body.

And finally, the consequence.

Thunder freed him from the memory. As the horse's hooves slapped the muddy grass in the shadow of the thirteenth hill, Drake risked a glance over his shoulder. His eyes found Talia, still clinging tightly to him.

He would not fail twice. He would keep her safe.

Rounding the bend about fifty yards behind him, the tireless horn and its mounted companions continued their chase. The burly man from the tavern was not part of the current pack; his horse had bucked him after a roaring crash of thunder, temporarily setting back the three zealots behind him. They had made up ground since, but they weren't much of a concern.

Drake hadn't seen the real concern since starting his winding course through the valleys. The golden knight and his band of Godwin riders were likely still in pursuit, but there was cause for hope as conditions continued to deteriorate. The howling storm would drown out the signal horn, and his unpredictable path, a mystery to even himself, would throw them off his trail. As water flooded the valleys and loosened the soil, the horses would face greater danger of a misstep. There would come a point most reasonable riders would turn back to the roads, having lost the trail of their unplanned manhunt.

The fanatics would undoubtedly continue their chase until the bitter end. If both of his hands weren't blistered and bound by soggy bandages, he'd be looking forward to it. Instead, he resentfully weighed his odds. Normally, he'd have the confidence in himself to go three against one, particularly if they were merely untrained zealots swinging around pocketknives. The rain was the factor throwing him off. Not only would his footing be less reliable, but he suspected the elements would mute Pyros' usefulness if he got into a pinch.

Drake placed his right hand on the saddle's pommel to test himself. As he wrapped his fingers around it, grasping as if it were the hilt of his sword, pain shot through his palm. He was forced to abandon the attempt immediately.

Damn his luck. He had almost gotten away with it. Past the border, safely in Godwin's territory with nobody after them. For all of three hours, they were just two nameless wanderers on a peaceful journey west. They just had to kick the hornet's nest in a second kingdom.

Even if they escaped today, he wondered how fast news would travel. A Mystic and a murderous mite, they made a gossip-worthy pair of fugitives. The fact that he hadn't yet been forced to kill royal soldiers was the only mitigating detail he could name.

As the slope in front of him began angling upward, he was faced with a decision. Unwilling to risk exposure on the hill, he pulled the reins to the right, guiding Shelby down the northern fork of the valley.

A black horse emerged from around the knoll to the right, charging forward at full speed. The golden knight looked Drake's way and pulled up on the reins, slowing his charge. As the knight changed course to collapse on his prey, the column of knights rounded the bend behind him, fanning out as wide as the valley allowed. Water sprayed in the careering horses' powerful wake, a stampeding reflection of the storming black clouds above.

Abandoning his break to the north, Drake doubled back and shot down the southwestern trail. Some of the horses behind the golden knight continued westward down a parallel path in a bid to cut him off.

Exhausted and staring down death as a beleaguered shell of himself, Drake gazed upon the undaunted spire. The rock beckoned to him as his lone refuge in a sea of tumult. Hot on his tail, the energized Godwin riders erased any chance he had of slipping into the hills undetected. His odds of emerging victorious in an even battle were slim to none. The stony bastion of his last hope invited him closer, calling his name between cracks of lightning.

He heeded the spire's call, spurring the horse forward as fast as it would go. If he was lucky, he'd slip into a cranny halfway up and either wait out their search or sneak away after they passed. If he got caught, there could still be a way to talk themselves out of it. He wasn't as clever a thinker as some, but he was more confident in his tongue than his sword at this point.

Staring at the ominous cousin of the Twins, Drake reflected that he couldn't predict how the confrontation with the Godwins would unfold. If worst came to worst, this would be the hill he died on. He was determined to ensure that Talia wouldn't have to say the same.

Beyond the next hill, a small detachment of riders had set a course to intercept him, while another group continued westward in parallel. Glancing at the diverging path to his left, Drake doubled down and urged the horse straight ahead, charging up the rolling slope toward the spire. The iron-lunged zealots rode between the armored knights in a bizarre union of the king's chosen men and ardent heretics.

The slope steepened for the last ten yards, then leveled out, A flatter section supported the base of the spire. The rocky needle was wider than it had first appeared, perhaps a couple hundred feet in diameter at the base. A sloping path wound around the crag in a corkscrew, offering an obvious path of ascent. Without hesitation, Drake directed the horse to follow the path upward, sealing them to whatever fate the spire had in store.

The pursuers were almost upon him, less than a stone's throw away. A thunderous chorus of hooves pounded the ground behind him.

Drake wondered if he would even make it up the mountain. Would he be rewarded with a dignified death, high above the realms of men? Or would cold steel soon enter his back instead?

The coffee was making him jumpy. In his peripheral vision, he briefly imagined a face in the rocks to his left. Specter in the stone—a pale, eyeless face watching him pass. Risking a glance, Drake saw he was mistaken; it was just a peculiar formation in the rock face.

Lightning illuminated the sky as a sizeable rock came loose from the path above, crashing to the ground between Drake and his hunters. The leading zealot's mount reared in fright, bucking its rider underfoot of a warhorse. The knights shouted some unkind words at the zealots, but their voices were muted by the storm.

As the pursuers attempted to straighten out their ranks, Drake pressed his luck and continued up the spire, rounding the corner. Shortly after, another turn put him on a steep, eastward length. Not going fast enough. High above the surrounding hilltops, he peered over the edge as the treacherous track bent northward. Although the dark sky and sheets of rain obscured his vision, the sky-splitting flashes of light revealed that the rest of the knights had reached the base of the spire. Some appeared to be stationed at the bottom, patiently standing watch in case he managed to find an evasive path around the vanguard.

Rounding the corner westward, he encountered a squat figure holding out a quarterstaff to bar his way. Drake's first instinct was to run him down—let the horse trample the interloper and continue upward.

"Come! We help. Come!" the man shouted above the storm.

Drake looked back, worried the knights had suddenly materialized in his shadow. He regarded the stranger, whose stick was now peacefully slung across his back. The stranger clearly wasn't in league with the knights, but his hairless head gave Drake pause.

"No time! Hurry!" he urged, reaching out a hand to calm the horse.

Drake didn't exactly trust the man, but he was short on options and just about at the end of his rope. Connecting the miracle of the falling boulder with the pale stranger, he decided to go with his instinct. If the stranger wasn't sided with his enemies below, he was a friend for now.

"Grab your gear," Drake instructed Talia as he swung off the horse. He freed his bag from the saddle and threw it over his shoulders. Talia followed his lead, ensuring her bow was secure before appearing at his side. He dithered over whether to bring the third bag, cooking amenities and spare changes of clothes, but ultimately decided to leave it with the horse.

The stranger yelled something incomprehensible at the stone wall to Drake's left. A small, gray-robed boy appeared from against the rock formation. Gray pigment covered his face and bald head, helping him blend in with the background. They had a short exchange that Drake didn't understand, then the boy grabbed Talia's hand and started leading her toward the wall.

"Now wait a minute," Drake called after the boy, stepping forward to intervene.

The staff-wielding stranger placed a calming hand on Drake's shoulder and took the horse's reins with his free hand. "Natsuo help you. Go!"

Drake reluctantly followed Talia and the painted boy to the wall. Upon closer inspection, he noticed a gray-painted basket among the rocks, measuring four feet by six feet. Thin poles rose from each of the four corners, meeting high above the center in an impractical handle. The closest wall of the box lay flat against the ground like an open drawbridge. On the floor of the wicker vessel rested a pile of stones.

"Iwa o hiro," the boy shouted over the rain, pointing to the rocks. He lifted a small one and tossed it out of the basket, then repeated the odd phrase.

"I think he wants us to move the rocks?" Talia interpreted, stooping to move one of the heavier stones. She struggled under its weight but managed to dump it outside the basket. Changing up her technique for the next stone, she pushed it with the bottom of her foot out onto the open front flap of the box.

"Iwa o hiro," the boy pointed at Drake.

"Fine. Iwa oh hero," Drake snapped back, certain he was losing his mind. He felt dizzy, but he forced himself to support Talia's frenzied effort of clearing the basket, removing the stones she had piled up to clear additional landing space.

"Help me with this one," Talia groaned, struggling with the last rock at the bottom.

Drake stepped into the basket beside her and bent his knees, yelling in pain and exertion as he flipped the heavy stone once onto the basket's open wall, and another time onto the ground beyond it.

"Naibu," the boy gently shoved Drake back into the basket and stole a nervous glance down the narrow mountain road. No sign of trouble yet.

"I think he wants us to hide in here," Talia said, crouching in the tight space they had freed up.

Drake lifted the fourth wall, which tentatively snapped into place. As long as the wind didn't blow open the front of the box, it would have to do.

"Yousuke help. Satoshi help," the man with the staff shouted from atop the horse. Shelby met Drake's eyes and neighed, as if to say she wasn't sure about this whole idea, either. Her new rider angled her to the west and added:

"I make woo-yoo woo-yoo," he waved his hands willy-nilly to communicate the point, then clicked his heels, setting the horse into motion.

"He'll distract them," Talia thankfully translated.

It was dark and rainy enough that the riders likely wouldn't pause to inspect the well-disguised cover among the rocks. Especially if they saw the shadow of a horse up ahead, they wouldn't think twice about who was riding it.

"Appu!" Natsuo held the last syllable of the nonsensical note.

Drake unwisely lifted his head to peek over the side of the box, attempting to interpret what the kid was yelling about.

The boy was holding a thin cord that snaked up the side of the wall to the level high above. Natsuo swung both his hands away from the wall and yanked the cord over his shoulder, then abruptly leaped back into his alcove under the rock face.

Looking up, Drake registered a black cord looping around a wheel attached to the basket's handle. A surge of impending dread overtook him. The box rocketed off the ground, shooting skyward like an arrow.

The cable violently hissed as it yanked them higher and higher. What felt like both an instant and an eternity into the ride of terror, Drake saw the blur of a boulder pass next to them, hurtling to the ground like a meteor. He dully noted their fate was tied to that stone—a matching black coil rapidly chased the counterweight as they continued to fly upward.

He became distantly aware of Talia's screaming. She sat in the back corner of the basket, knees wrapped tightly to her chest. The sudden lurch had knocked him on his backside, and now he braced himself against the side and back walls as he held on for dear life. Every muscle in his body tensed as the wind howled past them.

The basket abruptly ceased its ascent, throwing Drake off the floor. He caught his balance on the back of the swinging box, landing on his feet as Talia stumbled forward and put her hands on the front wall. The hatch disengaged, swinging open to the howling sky.

Talia lurched with the falling wall, shrieking as her momentum carried her forward. Her foot left the ground, then her head passed the threshold of the box, followed by her shoulders, gravitating into the free fall.

Drake grabbed her bag and yanked her back into the basket, rocking the haphazard container as she landed against the back wall.

Talia continued screaming. Tears welled up in her eyes as she heaved deep breaths into her chest.

Drake scanned over his shoulder and was surprised to find another bald, gray-painted boy curiously staring at him over the rim of the basket.

"Kuru," he said sheepishly, pointing to the ground at his feet.

Lifting his hands over his eyes, Drake took a second for himself. He had been all but certain this slipshod catapult was going to be the end of him. Heart pounding like a drum, he glanced over the edge. He couldn't see the lower level through the darkness, and he assumed that meant they couldn't see him either. Somehow, he was miraculously still alive.

He realized Talia was still howling, ostensibly even more traumatized by the near-death drop. She was backed into the corner, staying as far away from the open wall as she could get.

With one shaking hand supporting him against the mountain-facing side of the box, Drake reached the other down to her. "Come on, Talia. We're alive. Time to get off this deathtrap before it craps out on us."

"I died!" Talia wailed between frantic breaths. "I literally died! I am now deceased!"

"Talia, I don't mean to alarm you, but there's a fifty-fifty chance that statement's about to be true if we don't get off this thing. I'm going to step off first, then you're going to make your way to this side. We're both going to be back on solid ground. Okay?"

Her wailing intensified, signaling to Drake that she had heard him.

He turned to see the boy standing beside the box with a confused expression. He must have been about seven.

"Piss off, will you?" Drake shooed him.

The drenched boy took a step back and stuck a finger up his nose.

"Rotten little shits," Drake swore, attempting to lift his leg over the wall. He failed the first time, finding his foot preferred to remain on the basket floor. On his second attempt, he managed to swing a leg over to the other side. "Bunch of booger-eating, ankle-biting, terror-inducing monsters, you kids. Where the hell are your parents?"

Drake fell forward out of the basket. His breath caught in his chest as he cleared the one-foot gap between the box and solid ground. "Damn you, you filthy little gremlins," he doubled over, resting his hands on his knees. Deep breaths. Deep Breaths. He held a hand in front of his nose and found it shaking uncontrollably. "See this? Do you see this?" He huffed, realizing the boy probably understood none of his tirade.

Talia's fevered cries reached him above the howling storm, reminding him he wasn't safe yet. Drake walked to the side of the basket and pulled it closer to shrink the gap. "Come on," he instructed Talia. "Just crawl along the back side to me. You'll be fine. Lots of solid ground up here."

"I can't," Talia shook her head.

"Honestly," Drake thought aloud, running low on ideas to compel her to action. "That's not a half-bad hiding place. I might just let you camp out here for a while. I'll come back for you when the coast is clear."

"You can't just leave me here!" bawled Talia.

"Two options, kiddo. Crawl over to me and get out of that rickety box, or cry a little quieter so they don't find you when they get up here."

Her tears intensified, but she forced herself into motion. Scooching her bum over one slide at a time, she kept against the back wall, eyes fixated on the exposed edge as if it might try to creep closer to her. She reached the near corner, then resumed her huddled position.

"Good. You made it. Now just stand up, and I'll get you out of there," instructed Drake.

"I can't," Talia repeated. She placed her hands on the back wall but couldn't find the strength to rise.

"Grab hold of me. I'll do the rest, but I need you to at least stand so I can pull you out of there. You can do it slow as you like, but you gotta do it."

"You're going to drop me," Talia accused worriedly.

"I'm not going to drop you," Drake assured her. "On three. Ready?"

"No," she answered.

"One," he started.

"I can't," she protested.

"Two," he placed a hand on hers.

"If you drop me, I'll kill you."

"Three."

Talia lurched to her feet and grabbed at Drake's jacket. He reached his bandaged hands under her arms, ignoring the searing pain as he pulled her over the side. She screamed in his ear, wrapping her arms around his neck.

"I've got you," he said in as calm a voice as he could muster, turning and lowering her to his side away from the cliff.

Talia stumbled forward and collapsed to the ground, curling into a ball.

"We made it," Drake announced, still shaken up himself.

The little boy tilted his head, confused by the spectacle. "Kuru?"

"Lay an egg!" Drake said testily as he sat himself on the wet ground.

The boy walked over to the wall. He gestured to an identical basket, complete with its front hatch hanging ajar.

"Not a snowflake's chance in hell," Drake waved his hands in a negative.

The boy did an impressive impersonation of a neighing horse, then swung an invisible sword through the air, saying: "Shing, shing!" He pointed at the basket again. "Kuru."

"Translator, tell him I'll take the stairs," Drake grunted as he stood.

"Okay," Talia agreed, still catching her breath. She turned to the boy. "Hey, kid—piss off!"

"Don't think he knows that one," Drake speculated, helping Talia to her feet. She took a few shaky paces with wobbly knees but managed to keep her footing.

"We're never doing that again," Talia asserted decisively. "Next time, we're turning ourselves in and living the rest of our lives in a dungeon. This is not happening twice."

"I'm pretty sure they'd hang us," Drake corrected her flatly.

"I'll tie the noose," conceded Talia.

"Think it'd be fair to do one each," he muttered darkly.

"Kuru," the boy neighed again, pointing at the basket.

"Nuh-uh," Talia declined.

"We're done with the baskets, kid. We'll take a hike," opted Drake.

The kid waved his hands frantically, then placed a thoughtful finger to his forehead. He pointed at the basket again. "Hide. Kuru. Hide."

Drake put his hands on his hips. "He might have a point. The horses will catch us if we're out in the open. If he's only saying that we should hide in the box, that might be our best move."

"I don't know, Drake. I don't trust it."

"Hide," repeated the boy, pointing to the box. "Kuru."

Drake walked over to the boy. A single stone rested on the floor of the basket, holding it down in the storm. "Just *kuru*," he confirmed, jabbing a finger out at the boy's chest.

"Kuru," nodded the boy, pointing at the basket. "Iwa o hiro."

"No," Drake shook his finger and puffed up his chest. "No, I don't like that one. None of that. No *oh hero*, no *apoo*. Okay? Just Kuru. No apoo."

"No Appu," the boy nodded emphatically.

"You sure, Drake?" Talia asked, walking up to him. She wrung out the bottom of her shirt, depositing a small flood of water onto the mountainside.

"He said no apoo," shrugged Drake.

"Forgive me if I lack confidence in your foreign language abilities," Talia muttered unapologetically.

"No apoo," Drake pointed at the boy with finality.

A toothy grin spread over the boy's face, assuring Drake that he was making a mistake here.

Drake stepped into the basket, eyeing the handle with suspicion. Sure enough, a rope was tethered to the top of the cross-section. He laughed nervously, suspecting he was being set up but not wanting to plant any new ideas in the young boy's head.

"I'm trusting you," Talia said weightily, stepping into the box.

"On the record, I want to say I think this is a bad idea. It's just the only idea we've got," Drake hedged.

The boy stepped into the box and reached for the stone.

"No! No," Drake swatted his hand away. "This stays here," he pushed the rock into the corner of the basket. "Right here."

The boy looked at him with surprised eyes but permitted him his wish, stepping away from the box. He lifted the hatch to secure the bin, then walked back into the shadows of the wall.

"How long do you think we'll need to wait here?" Talia asked, gradually starting to recover as she sat in her usual corner.

"Until they head back down, I guess," Drake answered. "They'll probably spend some time searching the summit. These guys have a war to get on with, though. I doubt they'll tear apart the mountain to find us."

"What's up with these mountain people, anyway? And where'd that kid go?" Talia asked.

"I've got no idea what's going on around here," Drake shook his head.

"Appu?" a faint voice called from the rocks.

"What? No, damn it!" Drake stood to yell over the side. "No ap—!"

A scream escaped his throat as the basket lurched into motion, flying up the side of the cliff. The second time, he at least knew what to expect from the ending. He bent his knees and gritted his teeth, readying himself for the sudden stop at the top.

The basket came to a violent halt, bouncing and swinging and churning his stomach. His feet left the ground, and for a moment he was perilously suspended above the guardrails. He came back down, catching his foot on the sliding rock. Balance lost, he lurched backward against the panel of the basket.

He heard a crack in the wooden frame.

The rear wall fell outward, carrying him backward with it.

"Drake!" Talia screamed.

For a moment, he felt weightless. Time slowed as he fell out of the basket. The sky flashed, and thunder roared a dramatic lament.

He hit the ground a second later, landing on his backpack with a thud.

Frowning, an orange-robed monk looked down at him. "Did Yousuke not advise you to remain seated?"

Breathing deeply, Drake tried to make sense of the world around him. He stared at the monk, then tilted his head to look at Talia.

"You okay?" she extended a hand and pulled him to his feet.

Under him, the collapsed hatch rested on solid ground—at least, as long as the wind didn't separate the basket from the cliff. He urgently picked himself up and dove onto solid land.

Talia crossed the gap with considerable ease next to him. Then, she and the orange-robed monk stared down at him together.

"I told him, damn it," Drake pushed himself off the ground, breathing heavily. "I told him I didn't want any appu, and he did it anyway."

"You must find it in your heart to forgive him," pardoned the monk. "Yousuke has not yet learned your language. He knows only Taoxian."

After the world stopped spinning, Drake focused on the monk's face. Serenity appeared to live inside that round head. Despite the storm, he looked like he had fewer worries than hairs on his bald head. With the monk's latest clue, the strange language, walnut eyes, warm beige skin, and unapologetic subversion of the Godwins finally made sense. "You're all from Taoxos?"

"We arrived many moons ago in the exodus. The storied explorer, Captain Callaway of the Westerlands, once visited our temple in Tsim Suna and told us of a free land beyond the reach of the emperor. We did not find his promised land, but destiny drew us onto these shores, and like you, onto this sacred and holy mountain."

"Any idea what the hell destiny wants with me now?" Drake quipped, unsure how his dry humor would translate across cultures.

"I am no seer. Perhaps Master Ichiro could read the Bakunnan leaves this dreary evening and interpret their will. For now, I suspect destiny would like you to follow me to the summit. Karu—come with me—to the monastery."

XX. The Monastery

Drake

P lease, take care in crossing over."

"Over what? I can't see a damn thing," Drake muttered as he followed Satoshi's silhouette.

A flash filled the sky, followed at once by the crash of thunder. For an unbelievable moment, Drake imagined the monk was levitating in midair over a chasm. As the afterimage burned in his eyes, he realized the man was crossing a thin plank, less than a foot wide, which spanned the three-yard gap to reach a slightly elevated plane.

"No," Drake balked. "Surely, you're joking."

"I am Satoshi," the monk corrected over his shoulder. "My brothers often recognize my sunny humor, but this I speak unsmilingly, like the weary rain returning to earthly captivity. This natural defense will be your shield, though you must accept its burdensome weight to wield it."

"You seriously don't have a ladder or something?" negotiated Drake.

"What's going on?" Talia asked behind him.

Drake considered his words carefully. "The path gets a bit narrow up ahead here. It's a short bridge; you'll be over it in ten steps."

"Bridge? Hang on—"

"Don't worry. It's not a *bridge* bridge. It'll be over as soon as you start it—ten steps. That's only five left-rights. You want to go first?"

"Where is it?" Talia tentatively stepped alongside him.

He knelt and patted his hand along the ground, eventually connecting with the end of the wooden beam. "Here, give me your hand." As she knelt beside him, he took her hand and guided it to the plank. "If you stay low, you might just be able to waddle across it without any trouble. It's really not far at all. You got this?"

"I guess," Talia answered uncertainly.

"That's the spirit. I'll be right behind you," encouraged Drake.

He heard her take two squeaky steps forward, then saw the blur of her image blend in with the darkness. Keeping one hand on the beam to hold it steady, he felt each gradual pace she took as a gentle dip in the wood. After twelve dips, the plank remained stationary. He thought he heard her voice call to him, but it was lost in the wind.

"Guess it's my turn," he said to himself, working up the nerve to cross. He felt the plank once more, spanning his fingers so his thumb and his pinkie gripped the sides.

It wasn't even a foot wide.

Swallowing his trepidation, he reminded himself Talia had already made the effort to cross. Now, she was counting on him to do the same.

One boot on the beam. He swung his left foot in front, trying his first step over the chasm. Taking a deep breath to steady himself, he tried to ignore the howling wind and rain buffeting him from his right side.

He took another dutiful step forward, keeping his center of gravity low. Then a fourth, a fifth, moving one foot meticulously in front of the other.

The sky lit up as he reached the halfway point, forcing him to reckon with his precarious mortality. A sudden onset of vertigo made his head spin, threatening to steal his balance and throw him to the rocky depths below.

"Drake!" Talia's screech reached him through the elements.

Teetering to the left, he threw up his right arm in a failing attempt to center himself. Drake rushed forward another step, hoping the momentum would rebalance him. Finding himself leaning farther to the side, he desperately bounded forward, hammering the center of the plank with his left foot, then sensing the instep of his right foot fall over the side.

He loaded his weight and sprung forward, feeling the plank slip backward in countermovement. His left foot hit solid ground, then his right. Momentum carried him forward, causing him to stumble into Talia before he regained his balance.

"Did I imagine hearing a wooden beam fall down the mountainside?" pondered Satoshi.

"That's my bad," Drake excused himself. "Guess we ain't going back the way we came."

"Full disclosure: I totally thought you were dead," Talia admitted.

"Thanks," Drake said flatly.

"For what it's worth, I wouldn't have gone over if I'd known what I was getting into. These guys need to put in a staircase," suggested Talia.

"It warms my soul to hear you enjoy stairs. Our final obstacle lies around this corner—a short ascent up Songzhou's Stairway, and we will be at the summit. Take solace, for the earth now protects you, and harm shall not call your name here."

"Guess he's not mad about the plank," Drake muttered to Talia as they fell into step behind the monk.

"What?" she called back.

"Guess he's not mad about the plank," Drake repeated, louder.

"Why do you have to break things whenever we go places? This is why we can't go places," she admonished him.

"We're going places right now," he challenged.

"Yes, because my sparkling personality opens many doors."

"What?" Drake called back, pretending not to hear.

"My sparking personality opens many doors!"

"Can't hear you," he fibbed.

"You're a lousy gambler and tend to snore," Talia shouted back.

"Hey now," Drake wagged a disciplinary finger at her. "I might say that was uncalled for."

"Thought you couldn't hear me." It was hard to tell in the darkness, but she might have rolled her eyes at him.

"Gambling is the son of avarice and the father of despair. It is a sure way to get nothing from something," mused Satoshi.

"Yeah, yeah. I've heard it all before. *Nine gamblers couldn't feed a rooster. Young gamblers, old beggars.* Got any wisdom about having fun and enjoying life?" Drake ribbed.

"Do you?" Talia quipped with a sidelong glance.

"To suffer is to live well; fun and enjoyment are breadcrumbs down the wanton trail of impiety."

"Ah. I get it. You're one of *those* Taoxians," Drake labeled derisively.

"Yes. We are the lucky souls incarnated to follow Sato's noble path."

They rounded the corner, then paused behind Satoshi. Unmoving, he stood facing away from them.

"We uh... We here?" Drake asked.

"We are at the base of Songzhou's Stairway. I wait for the sky to reveal the path once more so that ascension is possible."

"I don't love where this is going," Talia commented with good sense.

A bolt of lightning fried a neighboring hill. Drake marveled how the skies had chosen its low mark instead of the towering spire beside it. He wondered if there was a reason, or if it was just one of nature's strange ways.

"I ascend," announced Satoshi, leaving them behind.

"Whoa. That actually looks kind of fun," Talia laughed.

"What? I missed it," Drake returned his attention to the mountainside.

"There's like, six or seven pegs in the ground, each taller than the last. I'm going to try it!"

"Be careful!" Drake said nervously.

He saw Talia's figure step onto the first wooden pole in front of them, about two feet tall. She leaped forward, miraculously landing on the next spire. She leaped again.

"Whoa!" Talia cried out.

"Talia!"

He heard her land on the ground. She was quick to assure him, "I'm fine! Just lost my balance on the fourth one. Little bit of a drop."

"How the hell am I supposed to get up there?" Drake called back.

"It's not that bad! Each pole is like a foot higher than the one before it, and they're all the same distance apart. They're just a bit thin, is all. Try it!"

Drake groped through the air in front of him and eventually stubbed his toe on the first wooden pole. He discovered the foothold was thin enough to encircle between two hands. "What's wrong with these people," he groaned to himself.

The only silver lining was that his pursuers had no chance of catching him up here. Especially with that plank fallen to the bottom of the mountain, there was no way anyone could cross after him or beat him to the summit.

"Try it!" Talia encouraged again, approaching from a little to his right.

"Fine," he yelled back, planting his right foot on the first pole.

Drake balanced himself precariously, sweeping his left foot out in front of him in an unsuccessful effort to find his next step.

"You're not going to find it like that. You have to jump," advised Talia.

"I can't see where I'm jumping," he called back.

"Try harder?" she suggested.

Drake squinted into the darkness and groaned. Vaguely detecting the outline of an object in front of him, he readied himself, shifting the uneven load on his back. He leaped forward, extending his left foot toward the next pillar.

Aw, hell.

He had misjudged the jump, angling too low. His toe hit the side of the pole, then his shin slammed into the upper part as he toppled forward. A short drop through the dark, and his stomach landed on the wet ground. Pain and frustration conducted the staggering symphony of swears directed at the poorly constructed entrance.

Another burst of lightning fired through the sky. Drake looked up at the nine-foot wall beyond the seven wooden poles. Satoshi sat on the edge amid a stream of runoff from the storm. He waved emphatically, trying to draw their attention to the rope ladder he had let down next to him.

"You okay?" Talia crouched to help him up.

"I'm fine," Drake growled, grimacing at the sting of his bruised shin.

"Can you hold my bag? I want to try it again," requested Talia.

"He put a ladder down for us," noted Drake.

"I know. You can go ahead and take it! I just want to see if I can do it on a second try," she insisted.

"Talia," Drake began warily, shaking his head. "There's no reason for that. Last thing we want is you getting hurt up here."

"But—"

"Let's both just take the ladder. Please."

"Okay," she obeyed reluctantly.

"Thank you," he added obligatorily to reinforce her good behavior.

He followed her to the wall and found the ladder to be a much easier path of ascension. Although the unfixed planks turned in his hand and the ladder swung in the breeze, presenting a surprising challenge for his upper body, he was relieved to have mounted the final obstacle without further injury.

"Right—so where's this shrine of yours?" Drake asked upon rejoining Satoshi and Talia.

Satoshi bent to retrieve the ladder and stored it behind a boulder. "The monastery lies at the top of Songzhou's Stairway," the monk answered patiently.

"Okay," said Drake, not fully understanding.

"Ah!" Talia voiced her discovery. "This is the stairway."

"Yes. You are perceptive. Let us ascend—we are not far now."

"For Deus' sake," grumbled Drake, following closely behind Talia.

Their column of three ascended the stairway—a series of large, uneven, and slippery steps carved into the mountainside. Some were almost hip high, while others stood less than a foot higher than the previous. The irregularity forced him to work his way up in a combination of hands and knees.

Halfway up the stairs, his thighs and calves were burning. His back was ready to give out. He saw a faint glow far above him and, for a moment, thought he was ascending to the next world. As he gradually climbed nearer, he realized the lights were not a sign of his impending demise, but rather two lanterns affixed to either side of a wooden archway.

He frowned, surprised that such a light source could survive this storm. Curiosity gave him the last injection of energy he needed to reach the peak.

An orange, wooden gateway met him at the top, dulled and eroded by the elements. Unlike the typical rounded archways of Tallamar, this feat of architecture bore two straight, horizontal beams perpendicular to two strong, vertical pillars. The top beam curved slightly upward, like an elegant longbow.

Fixed in place on either end of the lower crossbeam, extending beyond the frame of the gateway, glass balls harbored floating candles. Water cascaded down the sides of these suspended orbs and drizzled from their open bottoms. A wide, hat-like shade rested on top of each orb, directing light to the entryway.

"They're so pretty!" The glow reflected in Talia's smiling eyes.

"These lights, like those in the proving grounds, are remnants of a forgotten home. They are neither items of beauty nor material possessions to impress others. These lanterns provide light where needed and help guide the wandering souls through a dark and cloudy night," Satoshi explained.

"I still think they're pretty," Talia maintained unapologetically.

Drake detected a grin on Satoshi's face as he paused under the glow of the lantern. "Then you would undoubtedly enjoy the lights of Sha Tong. The painted paper lanterns, golden puppets, and fiery dancers are an unforgettable spectacle... for the sinful masses who enjoy those types of things, of course."

"That sounds amazing," Talia listened earnestly. "Drake, can we go one day?"

"What, to Sha Tong? That's one hell of a hike from here, kiddo."

"Not right now, obviously," Talia snorted. "But like, in the future. We all need something to look forward to, right?"

"And yours is Sha Tong because they have pretty lanterns?"

"And golden puppets. And dancers," Talia noted. "Plus, you still owe me guitar and line dancing lessons. Don't think I've forgotten about those."

"You still owe me a drawing," countered Drake. "And I thought we agreed you were letting me off the hook for dancing."

"Nope," Talia stated factually. "It's in my book. I wrote it down. You promised."

"I want a second opinion," objected Drake.

"Please, this way," Satoshi interrupted, guiding them through the gateway and into the monastery compound.

Three clusters of lanterns illuminated different areas in the monastery grounds. Although hard to discern, the farthest group, to his left, hung from pillars surrounded by some strange aerial network of poles and ropes. He saw shadows dancing in the sky, weaving through the ropes and across precarious beams with apparent ease.

The cluster directly ahead of him hung from a similar, larger gateway that overlooked a flat, rectangular area. He saw the movements of dozens of bald, robed men of all sizes. They looked like copies of Satoshi, matching him down to the uncomfortably high socks their pant legs were tucked into.

The exhibition on display was mesmerizing. The monks were arranged in a military formation, each standing a set space apart in their diagonal grid, completing their movements with an inhuman degree of synchronicity and perfection. Despite the pouring rain and roaring thunder, he could not help but stop and stare as the troupe performed their routine, oblivious or indifferent to his presence.

The monks practiced with some manner of staff, similar in length and flexibility to the one wielded by the Taoxian at the base of the mountain. Each moved fiercely like lightning, while flowing fluidly like the rain coursing down the mountainside. They shouted over the storm as they kicked high above their heads, turned, thrusted their palms through the air, then performed an aerial spin, slamming their staves against the ground. The monks stood, spun around their weapons, then flipped, thrashing through the air in precise whirlwinds of planned chaos.

Planting one end of their staves on the ground, they leaped sideways onto the sticks and impossibly suspended themselves in midair, defying gravity as they balanced perpendicular to the ground. Drake exchanged awestruck glances with Talia, but his eyes were pulled right back to the spectacle. They twirled their weapons and rolled with uninterrupted grace. At the end of each fascinating sequence, they stopped abruptly to emphasize each movement as deliberate. Always within balance and control.

"What are they doing out here?" Talia asked Satoshi.

"Training," he answered shortly. "We are fortunate for the worldly challenges we may face today. In one week's time, we expect a blood moon. Master Ichiro will lead a twelve-hour demonstration ritual in honor of Sato's passing. So they will practice until the storm subsides, finding harmony in the raging elements. I will join them shortly. Please, this way."

"Wild," remarked Talia, mesmerized by the martial performance.

"Why aren't you with them right now?" Drake inquired, following him toward the third cluster of lights to their right.

"Master Ichiro bid I guide you to him. Tom Giang, my father, arrived late to meditation this morning. Natsuo, Yousuke and I joined him in his disciplining, so we must perform humble chores for the monastery before we may rejoin our brothers studying the Kon'chai—the flow of the universe."

"Kind of messed up they punish you for your dad's mistake," Talia commented.

"Although Master Sing urges us to behave as individuals, the Tom family still shamefully clings to the old ways of the empire. We feel a strong sense of duty to family, which can make some passages of Sato's teaching hard to internalize. Only Tom Giang was selected for discipline, but the Tom family acts as one," explained Satoshi.

"Huh," Talia said quietly, expressing Drake's thoughts as well.

They paused before a rectangular wooden temple. Drake thought it was a miracle the structure had never been struck by lightning—constructing the building way up here must have been a nightmare. If it ever caught fire and burned down, he imagined it would take over a year to rebuild. Come to think of it, he wondered how the monks managed to get enough food for themselves up here. Perhaps there was a mountaintop garden somewhere he hadn't seen.

"I would ask you remove your shoes before entering," said Satoshi.

Drake looked down and realized the man had been walking around the mountain barefoot. "Do I have to?"

The monk faltered uncomfortably. The shoes matter was evidently an important rule for him, but he hesitated to enforce it on a stranger.

"I'll do it if you have a fire inside," bartered Talia.

"We do not have a fire inside our wooden temple," Satoshi answered in a tone far less sarcastic than his words.

Grinning at Talia's proposition, Drake nudged her and joked, "That's all right. I can make one."

A tingle rose in his throat. He turned his head away from the temple and coughed, releasing a puff of fire into the air.

Damn it, Pyros! The hell was that? Drake frowned.

The soulbind before you was Taoxian. Wu Kai. One of few names that live on in my memory. These Ordonists honor the flame.

"Could it be?" gasped Satoshi.

"Guess the cat's out of the bag," Talia raised her eyebrows at Drake's indiscretion, then folded her arms and sized up the monk. "He's a Mystic."

The monk dropped to his knees and laid his hands and head on the wet steps outside the temple. "O' suffering one, Master Ichiro was wise to come to your aide. I humbly revere your journey to Val'Helios. May your crossing be swift and well-deserved."

"Whoa now, let's take a step back," Drake held up defusing hands. "I just don't want to take my boots off, is all."

"Of course! One of your stature would prefer to bear the soggy linens clinging to your feet. Though if I may beg of you, Mystic, please do not tread on the mat or the seven virtues. Both are sacred and quite challenging to clean."

"Easy, Satoshi—I won't go traipsing around on carpet just to make a mess of the place. Now, how do we open this door?"

Placing two hands against the door, Satoshi slid it sideways to reveal a well-lit interior. Rainwater accompanied Drake inside. An equally soggy Talia entered next, followed by Satoshi, who closed the door behind him. Indoors was more pleasant, though wind and rain pummeled the thin roof, giving Drake an uneasy feeling that the structure was seconds away from collapsing.

Inside was a simple room, dominated by a mat that ran all the way to the back wall. Several wooden pillars supported the structure, while light shone through paper walls around the perimeter. A thin passageway most likely ran between the wooden exterior and the paper walls, allowing for this lighting trick. Seven arcane glyphs were scrawled in a white slab of stone immediately in front of the mat—presumably the seven virtues Satoshi had warned not to tread on.

"I thought you said Ichiro was in here?"

Satoshi bristled at the unintended disrespect but managed to maintain a neutral face. "Resting. I will inform Master Ichiro that you are here. If you are able, I would appreciate your best effort to respect our monastery's way of life."

"Sure," Drake acquiesced.

"Hold on a second," Talia halted Satoshi, who patiently turned back to listen. "What kind of monastery is this? Like, what exactly is going on here?"

Satoshi nodded dutifully. "We are Ordonists. After Tsim Suna was lost, the monks and villagers came by merchant vessel to build this monastery. In this new sanctuary, we study the ways of Sato Tadori and follow his path through the infinite cycle."

"Who's Sato? And what's this about an infinite cycle?" pressed Talia.

"The infinite cycle... Isn't that when a Mystic dies and their Primal finds a new host? Pretty universal folklore," Drake interpreted.

"That is but one part of the cycle," corrected Satoshi. "It would take many moons to explain our ways of life and how they came to be, but I will offer a brief summary. At the core of Ordonist philosophy, we recognize that life is suffering, and that suffering both arises from and threatens balance. When you make peace with your worldly struggle, one small current among the great tides of life, you enter a state of existence we call *Joa Tonku*—harmonious suffering. Because suffering is a *Yeog'him*—an inverse, counterbalancing force—we understand the trials faced in life exist to counterbalance the unknowable ecstasy of the afterlife. Conversely, the pleasures that litter this world ensure none will be found in the after. To find *Joa Tonku* in this world allows us to follow in Sato's famed path to Val'Helios in the next."

This guy making sense to you? Drake asked Pyros.

Ordos is the Primal of Balance. My harmony is burning things.

Then here's your slice of suffering: we're not torching this monastery, Drake conveyed.

Not much of a monastery. Good tinder. Potential for great harmony.

"That sounds like an empty promise of *life sucks, and the harder it sucks, Deus might make up for when you die,*" Talia decoded.

"Deus is the force of creation. His *Yeog'him* is Karax. Ordos, the Thirdborn, is balance. Ordonism recognizes that balance is the true flow of the world. Neither creation, nor destruction. Unlike the Triumvirists, who claim the Makers are rulers and shapers of the world acting through the emperor, we recognize a created world in motion—always balanced, never better or worse."

"Okay. So I stand corrected. Continue?" invited Talia.

"The infinite cycle is not merely Primals cycling through hosts. It is the movement of souls—the spiritual migration of all living things. Every soul begins as a leaf on the Bakunnan tree, just as each fallen leaf marks a soul's graduation from this world to the final. From each Bakunnan leaf, a human is born into the warrior caste to learn discipline and the weight of life. Although these new souls may wander, they must learn to refuse the path of violence and reject the temptation to pursue worldly ambitions before they die. Success or failure to achieve this, through the infinite cycle, determines if one is reborn to a higher or lower caste of harmonious suffering. A soul's journey to spiritual mastery in *Joa Tonku* follows three ascending steps from the warrior's beginning: life as a common man, such as a farmer, life as a monk, and life as a Mystic.

"Each caste, spiritually higher than the last, rewards the hardened soul with greater trials of suffering. Like a legendary sword, the ascending souls are shaped and strengthened by the hot flames of fate's furnace, while the weak become brittle and crack. Failing to find spiritual master in any lifetime will cause one's soul to fall a caste—down from the humble warrior, the hedonistic souls may descend to merchants, nobles, and least of all, animals. This cycle of life on Kyros may last many lifetimes before one reaches the eternal afterlife, which is why we call it the infinite cycle."

"Hang on—so you're telling me kings and cows are the two worst things someone could be?" Drake checked.

"Life as a happy king is the straightest road to eternal damnation. Their souls are so weak, they fail to tolerate even the smallest trials of suffering. The disease of hedonism clouds their lives, and most become animals, choosing their lowly forms. A cow is a noble who has sinned shamefully, but one who wishes to change their ways. Should they die peacefully of old age, they will return as nobles with a chance to do better. The predators of the animal world, vultures and spiders and wolves, are too far gone. Even renounced of their curse of ambition, these animals still cling to bloodlust and violence. In the end, their souls become eternal kindling for the great hearth of Val'Helios."

"That end sounds brutal. What's supposed to happen when you're a Mystic? You get the 'biggest suffering' award and that's a win?" Talia asked.

"Mystics are the highest earthly caste in the infinite cycle because their suffering is legendary. That is why we monks seek to live plain, unmaterialistic lives. That is why we push our bodies to their limits and meditate many hours each day—to prepare our souls for the final burden of a Primal. Only Mystics can ascend from this world to the Eternal Palace of Val'Helios, where they can enjoy the eternal feast in the halls of the infinite, forever tethered to their Primal's soul. Kindred spirits from across the ages find peace unending in that hallowed palace beyond space and time."

"Works for me," Talia commented.

"No kidding," Drake agreed.

"How's this Sato guy fit in?" Talia asked, fascinated by the Ordonists.

"Nine hundred years ago, Emperor Sato Tadori, second of his name, ruled over Taoxos. He is the only man who ever traversed the full breadth of the infinite cycle. His great-grandfather, a former army general and founder of Taoxos' third imperial dynasty, the Sato Dynasty, was a wicked man. Sato the Elder subjugated and plundered neighboring provinces for wealth, brutalizing any who spoke against him. He fell prey to every vice man knows too well.

"His grandson, Sato Tadori, was an emperor like no other. When he took the throne, he dismantled the imperial military despite great furor from his generals. A year later, he journeyed to the mountains of Tsim Suna and meditated for seven days and seven nights. When he returned, he renounced his title and possessions, claiming to be reborn. The infinite cycle had offered him a chance to heal his soul. He invited the commoners to join him in raising a temple in Tsim Suna, then told them of his great journey's true beginning.

"Sato Tadori told his followers about his prophetic vision—that he was the reincarnation of Sato the Elder. After his corrupt soul had passed on, murdered by his only son, Sato Siji, he had chosen to be reincarnated as a great sea turtle so that none may pierce his unarmored back again. When he hatched on sandy shores, he recognized both nobles he had betrayed and lords he had elevated to power, circling as buzzards overhead. Wrathful, they swooped down and consumed the other hatchlings around him. Escaping the beach, Sato the Turtle was separated from his family and set off alone to find food. He found a jellyfish, but, as he swam nearer to eat it, he was halted by a great blue whale. Ordos, in mammalian form, cautioned him against eating the jellyfish. The whale told him of the infinite cycle and what terrible fate awaited him at the end of his destructive path. Taking his words to heart, Sato the Turtle lived seventy long years consuming only seagrass and algae.

"Sato Tadori named his enlightened following *Ordonism* in honor of the great blue whale that saved his soul. He spent the rest of his life teaching meditation and preaching the journey to salvation, traveling to villages across Taoxos to spread his philosophy. Of course, many believed he was merely an erratic, confused emperor who had thrown everything away. When he passed on one fateful autumn's day, his followers dispersed, gone back to their simple lives of farmers and shepherds and retirees. But the story does not end here.

"Fifteen years after Sato Tadori's passing, a powerful noble's youngest boy, Po Han, was invited along with his family to a gala hosted by Sato Hiroto, Tadori's younger brother and heir to the empire. Po Han's father, battling a terrible disease on his deathbed, sent his three sons to honor the Satos with a speech meant to recognize the great commercial progress of the empire. Po Han's eldest brothers read their dutiful statements, but as the youngest Po took the stage to address the crowd, he ripped up his speech and proclaimed that he was Sato Tadori's reincarnation. He decried the distasteful gathering and the suffocating avarice nursed by Hiroto's new laws, baffling Taoxos' richest and most celebrated aristocrats as he lectured them on frugality and sharing their wealth—and as he spoke of the infinite cycle.

"The emperor was furious. He ordered the boy be flogged in the courtyard and left to rot in a sunlit cage suspended above the square—to shrivel up and waste away in the heat. Despite his great torment, Po Han spoke only of the infinite cycle and his journey to salvation. Larger and larger crowds gathered to hear his words, and Sato's first followers returned to the temples to read his forgotten texts.

"Enraged by the attention the boy received, the emperor commuted Po Han's demonstrative punishment, instead sentencing him to be burned at the stake. The flames nipped at his clothes and seared his legs, but he did not scream. Nor did he cry. He reassured the crowd that his bodily pain was temporary, and that he had found the secret to peace. He had found *Joa Tonku*. As the flames scorched his body, his final words were a promise to his followers. He would return, reborn as a merchant, to guide them to salvation.

"Despite a period of persecution, Sato Tadori's legacy of Ordonism thrived following Sato Han's promise. A merchant, Mu Suk, was Sato's next reincarnation many years later. He was later reborn as Hoshi Takamaru—the famed gentle warrior who developed the non-lethal 'Art of the Flowing Staff' we practice still today. After Sato Takamaru came Sato Ren—the people's farmer, Grandmaster Sato Saito—the wandering monk, and finally, Sora the Starcaller.

"Sato Sora's final act was to put an end to the bloody civil war that ravaged Taoxos for a decade. Before a pitched battle could commence, Sato Sora rose above the grasslands and turned into a bright star. From the heavens, he called a beam of light to destroy the battlefield, leaving a giant crater in his stead, dividing the two armies. His light rained down on them in a shower of stardust, bringing the warring people below to their senses. The final emperor of the Sato Dynasty, Sato Shino, abdicated his throne to the leader of the rebel militia, signing an armistice that would lead to many years of great prosperity. The infinite cycle was made complete, and Sato's legacy eternalized."

"That's an incredible story," complimented Talia, a little teary-eyed.

Drake suspected Sora's sacrifice with Orion had stirred unhealed feelings within her. Even he felt moved by the Taoxian's tale, having never known so much about their ostensibly cultish following.

"Quite the story," Drake echoed finally. "But why tell us all this?"

"Aside from the fact that the young lady asked," Satoshi began with a half-bow, "I wanted to share Sato Sora's tale so that you may continue to reflect. Meditate on your destiny. Although Sato ascended to Val'Helios, our history is rife with sad accounts of Mystics who forgot their enlightened path and traded noble suffering for dishonorable conquest and pride. I pray Ordos' voice calls you. May your soul find its way to a less destructive future."

Drake wasn't sure how the comment was intended, but he received it uneasily. He wrinkled his nose, unsure how he should react now.

"Tom Satoshi, you forget yourself," a steady voice admonished from behind the far wall.

"Master Ichiro!" Satoshi bowed apologetically to the canvas.

The wall panel slid open, revealing a wrinkled man in orange robes that matched the style of the other monks. The sandaled man unhurriedly walked the room's perimeter, avoiding the sacred mat. He paused in front of Drake, then bowed slowly. "I greet you, honored Mystic. I am Master Harihara Ichiro. I watch over this monastery and the followers of Sato under my care."

"Nice to meet you, Mas-ter Ichiro," Drake nodded his head stiffly, uncomfortable with formalities.

"Satoshi," said the Master, "I believe it is sundown behind the storm. Gather the Toms and rejoin the others. I will see to our visitors."

"Master Ichiro," Satoshi bowed in acknowledgement.

"Oh, Satoshi?" Master Ichiro paused, having another thought.

"Yes, Master?" the monk bowed again.

"Please prepare the flying crane. I anticipate our guests will have need of peaceful recovery."

"Yes, Master Ichiro," Satoshi bowed to him once more, then again to Drake. He added a forgetful half-bow for Talia before returning to the storm.

"How'd you know we were coming?" Drake asked, curious why the Tom family had been stationed along the mountainside for him.

Master Ichiro clasped his hands behind his back. "As I meditated looking out over the hills from Songzhou's Stairway, I heard horns in the wind and saw an unusual gathering of clouds on the northern horizon. After many years, I have grown sensitive to the grand approaches of fate. With my single worldly possession, a spyglass gifted to us by the merchant who gave us safe passage from Taoxos, I saw your flight from the Brotherhood fanatics and the Godwin army. Under ordinary circumstances, they would loathe to cooperate. I then knew you and your suffering must be extraordinary."

"Solid guess," Talia commended, blowing air out of puffed cheeks.

"I studied the Bakunnan leaves as the storm approached. While I would experience great fulfillment from teaching you our ways and guiding you to meditate on what destiny has in store for you, I can see in your heavy eyes that you are weary and seek only a sanctuary for respite. Tom Hikaru will watch over you—in the shrine hidden in the wildwood. I suspect these warring men will fail to climb our skyward mountain but assure you they will find no trail of your departure to the shrine even if they succeed. You have my word."

"Thank you, Master Ichiro. Where exactly is this wildwood?" asked Drake. The supposed safety of the monastery invited his fatigue to catch up.

"Come, I will take you. It is but a short walk to the Bakunnan tree."

"Oh, before I forget..." Drake scratched his head.

"Yes?" invited Ichiro.

"We left behind a horse at the bottom of the mountain. Her name's Shelby," he started, waving his hand explanatorily.

"We will take good care of her. If possible, we will return her to you."

"I'd appreciate that," Drake thanked sincerely.

Returning out into the hostile elements, Drake followed Ichiro across the courtyard to a fourth set of lanterns. The odd-shaped tree they hung in was thick and curvy and branched out into cauliflower clusters of leaves. Some type of orange fruit dangled from its branches among the lights.

"I have a question," Talia broached. Ichiro considered her with a patient smile. Wrestling with how to tactfully ask, she finally opted for a direct approach. "Do you really believe in all that? Sato, Ordos, and all?"

Master Ichiro chuckled to himself. "It should seem I must, for here I am. Perhaps the stories happened on Kyros as tradition tells, or perhaps they are only myth. Yet if they were both history and myth, I suppose they would be very true indeed, for then we would see reality in its fullness: the concrete, which we can interpret by our senses, and the abstraction, which is the mystery that we do not presently understand. If now we see through a mirror dimly, then surely we will someday look upon the face of truth. Until that day, I will believe what little I have known. Perhaps one day, I shall know much more."

"Huh," Talia scrunched up her nose thoughtfully. "Guess I still have a lot of learning ahead, too. Thanks, Ichiro."

Master Ichiro gave Talia a gentle smile of encouragement, then turned to Drake. "I will not pry into your journey ahead, as I wish you to be at ease that no man harboring ill intent will pursue you as you go. However, I will strongly advise you against venturing through the Emerald Hills to the north. The Brotherhood, as they call themselves, claim to be pious monks, but their dark churches stand only for death and destruction. While we seek to help and eventually become Mystics on a path to ascension, these twisted harbingers would cull your kind with extreme prejudice. Even if your path lies in the capital, I urge you to avoid those houses of life in the slumbering, green hills. Travel west through the wildwoods, and you will go in peace."

"Won't hear an argument from me," Drake nodded. The leaves of the Bakunnan tree provided shelter against the rain, but the wind still whipped at his wet clothes. He stared into the dark sky ahead.

"Although the danger has passed, I sense you are in dire need of rest. May I deliver you to the shrine in the wildwoods?" offered Master Ichiro, respectfully lowering his bald head.

"Please," invited Drake.

"Hang on," Talia raised an apprehensive finger in protest.

"What?" Drake demanded, exhausted.

"I don't want to do another one of those flying box things," she placed her hands on her hips assertively.

Sighing, Drake turned to the short monk. "Please tell me you weren't about to put us on one of those flying box things?" he asked, siding with Talia.

Ichiro shook his head. "No. Those are only for going up. The way down is much more pleasant."

"See? More pleasant," Drake persuaded her. "Wait a second," he turned to face Ichiro. "How can going down be more pleasant? You're not talking about some big staircase we missed, are you?"

Ichiro picked up two bundles of rope from the base of the tree, then returned to Drake. "We shield the meek and the weary, and we seek to bring peace to those in conflict. Tom Hikaru will prepare you food and beds for as many days as you need to recover from your ordeal. Our compassion has no time limit. Please, trust my honor: the final step you must take is into this belt."

Drake shot Talia a questioning look.

"Let's just do it," she gave in, reaching out a hand to accept the bundle from Ichiro.

The monk lowered himself to one knee and opened the tangle of rope. "Please, place one leg in each loop."

"Okay?" Talia obeyed uncertainly.

Ichiro tightened the harness around her legs and waist, then moved to kneel at his feet. The Taoxian tugged twice on the readied rope, inviting Drake to put his leg in. Skeptically, he let Ichiro do whatever was being done.

"Good. You will now travel the flying crane. Please say hello to Tom Hikaru when you see her."

"What the hell's a flying crane?" Talia demanded, suspicion creeping into her voice.

"Not a box," promised Ichiro. "All you do is sit. Very safe. Without worry. Peaceful," he finished rattling off adjectives that held very little weight.

"Does it involve the word *appu*?" Drake asked.

"No appu," promised Ichiro.

"Fool me twice," Drake folded his arms warily. "I don't like appu, and I don't like no appu."

"Appu simply means *up*," Ichiro explained patiently. "No appu means *up, now.* I mean to say you will not go up from here. Now, would you be willing to role model the flying crane for your daughter? She looks as if she could use your reassurance."

"You heard him, *Dad*," teased Talia. "You first."

"I'll do it," Drake held up a finger to indicate he wasn't finished. "But Ichiro, I want to be clear: if I end up flying across the sky in a box, I'm going to burn a temple to the ground."

"No boxes," promised Ichiro. "Come this way, please."

On the far side of the tree, where only the outermost glow of the lanterns reached, the Taoxian lifted a three-legged stool from its side and stationed it on the grass. He patted it twice, indicating that Drake should sit.

"Here?" Drake asked needlessly, earning a nod from Ichiro.

Drake sat, looking back at Talia uncertainly. She shrugged.

Ichiro placed a wet foot on Drake's thigh, grabbed the loop of rope fixed to his waist, and leaped upward, swatting a hand into the leaves of the tree. The monk landed lightly on Drake's leg. A few fast movements fumbling with the rope, then he dropped back down onto the grass.

"Hey, what's that all about?" Drake demanded.

"Comfortable?" Ichiro inquired, walking behind him.

"Enough?" Drake answered suspiciously, turning his head to watch the monk. He felt a pulling tension on his body from where Ichiro had affixed his harness to the tree.

"Good. Spread your wings, flying crane," instructed Ichiro.

A flash of light filled the sky, revealing to Drake that he sat at the edge of a cliff. A thin, black wire extended from the tree into the dark sky ahead.

"Oh, hell n—WHOA!" Drake yelled as the stool was kicked out from under him.

He shot forward, screaming above the storm as he suddenly dropped off the side of the cliff. Weightless in the freefall, his stomach lurched. Then, the harness tightened, catching him and smoothing his rapid descent to a less-harrowing angle.

"Talia!" he yelled behind him, though he suspected she was already out of earshot. "It's not that bad!" he shouted fruitlessly into the storm.

Ichiro's parting words echoed in his head. The world soared past as he shot like an arrow through the air. Exhilarated, he unhanded the single strand of rope connecting him to the wire above. Hands hovering beside the rope for a second longer, he gradually put his trust in the device. Slowly, he spread his arms until they were fully extended at his sides. Leaning back, he laughed despite himself, imagining this to be every bird's greatest joy.

As he flew lower to the earth, Drake began seeing the shadows of trees below. A panicked sense of dread returned as he realized he had no clue how this ride was supposed to end.

The line dipped into the trees, causing Drake to recover his tight grip on the rope and shrink himself into as narrow a line as he could manage. The wire ran parallel to the ground for some time, then began sloping back upward.

A vibration traveled through the rope as the metal device sliding along the wire bumped into something. A second later, he came to an abrupt stop, swinging forward as his momentum dissipated. His direction changed, and he slowly drifted backward until he hung from the lowest point of the cable.

He was alive.

He was alive and off that damned mountain.

Hopefully Ichiro would be able to coax Talia to take the flying crane as well. Drake's ungraceful departure was uninspiring at best, and he doubted her aversion to heights would inspire her to soar off the side of a mountain.

"Hello?" he called breathlessly to the forest. "The hell am I supposed to do now?"

"Siwa?" a woman's voice rose from the forest floor.

"Drake. Stuck in the trees," he returned tiredly.

A glowing light emerged from behind a trunk, then a hatted Taoxian woman carrying a lantern. "Siwa," she repeated, slower.

"Drake. Stuck. Tree," he answered, feeling like a pig on a spit roast.

Another woman emerged from the trees behind the first. "She's saying pull the orange color."

Drake inspected the rope above him, craning his neck to find the orange length. He found it on the back side. Managing to pull himself a little higher with his left hand, he tugged on the orange bit until the rope came loose.

Enter gravity.

Drake crashed to the ground, falling a couple feet before landing on his back. He heard a crunch from his bag and felt something sharp pressing against his spine.

"Why?" he moaned to Deus as he rolled onto his stomach. Forcing himself to his feet, he buried his face in his hands and yelling into his palms.

"Chu-guh," the first woman advised him, taking a step back.

"I'm done learning. I don't want to learn any more words. No appu," Drake shook his head.

"She says: move aside," the second woman translated helpfully.

A high-pitched buzzing reached him through the trees. He tilted his head toward the sound, trying to decipher what manner of creature it might be.

The buzzing evolved into an undulating scream.

Talia's rapidly approaching scream.

A blur broke through the trees from in front of him. He flung himself to the side as she barreled through, flying through the forest like a banshee.

Picking himself up out of the mud, he looked up and caught the eye of the small Taoxian woman who had tried to warn him. She shrugged innocently, then pointed a stick at the wire.

Talia swung back in front of him with a big smile on her face.

"That was kind of awesome," she said breathlessly.

"Awesome?" Drake repeated, shocked.

"I don't know why, but it was so much better than the box. Like the beginning sucked, but the rest of it I felt like a bird. Am I crazy?" Talia rabbled.

Drake concealed a smile and walked over to where she was dangling in the air. "There's an orange bit halfway up your rope. Pull on that?"

Talia craned her neck to inspect the rope. "This one?"

"Yeah," Drake confirmed.

She tugged on the rope, then yelped as she dropped to the ground. He extended his arms and caught her mid-fall, saving her from the muddy lesson he had learned the hard way.

"Woo. Thanks," she said, returning gracefully to her feet.

"Please. Allow me to show you to bed," said the second woman, giving a slight bow before lifting her lantern high and marching back into the trees.

Talia followed in her step, with Drake shortly behind.

As he walked past the first Taoxian woman, she placed two hands over her heart and tilted her head endearingly, a big grin on her face.

"That's enough out of you," Drake decided, wagging a disapproving finger in return.

Her smile grew wider as she chuckled to herself. Apparently enjoying the evening, she followed Drake through the trees, humming a soft, slow tune that made his eyelids quite heavy.

XXI. Consequences

Allen Lee

The heavy, imposing doors of Virgil's office loomed over Allen.

The dark wood appeared visibly aged in the indirect light. Cato rapped his meaty knuckles on the door twice, then took a respectful pace backward. They waited in uncomfortable silence for an answer from within.

An agonizing moment later, the door swung open. A familiar voice bid, "Thanks, chief," and exited into the hallway.

"Glasses," Ajax Sykes greeted Allen with a smirk, then proceeded down the hall without an escort.

"Master Virgil—if you have a moment, I have troubling news to report," Cato called inside.

"Enter."

A hand nudged Allen forward into the room. Cato slammed the door behind them, then addressed his teacher. "This curious cat was caught skulking in the forbidden section. His willful disobedience to posted signs is an insult to you and your noble Library. I propose we punish him accordingly."

A frown beset Virgil's face. "My dear Allen, I am troubled to hear that you would venture out of bounds without first seeking permission. Are you dissatisfied with the myriad of tomes available to you?"

"I'm sorry, Virgil," Allen apologized sincerely. "I was unsure whether the sign applied to disciples or pages."

Virgil leaned back in his chair behind the desk, rubbing his forehead with his hands. "Rules are rules, and one who endeavors to adhere to them should seek permission rather than forgiveness. Cato, your recommendation?"

"Were I judge, I would sentence him to death for this hubris," Cato said unflinchingly. "However, knowing your infinitely merciful temperament, I would instead recommend he be exiled from The Library. If he broke your rules once, he will surely be tempted to transgress again."

Virgil stroked his chin thoughtfully, studying Allen's nervous face. "Is this true, dear Allen? If I were to, in good faith, believe you erred simply due to a benign misinterpretation, would curiosity compel you to stray a second time?"

"Of—of course not," Allen stammered quickly. He took a moment to adjust his glasses. "I just didn't understand, that's all. I had never heard you or Meghana mention a forbidden section before—now that I know the gravity of the restriction, I promise I'll never go back again."

"Actions must have consequences," Cato asserted philosophically. "I would humbly implore you to ensure his transgression does not go unpunished, teacher. No lesson is learned from immaterial threats of consequences alone."

Virgil held up a hand to rein in his pupil, then turned to address Allen. "I believe you, Allen. I trust that you will respect the rules, having heard them expressly from me. Now, before I announce the consequences you will face, please ask the question lingering on your mind."

Allen glanced nervously at Cato, who glared loathingly back at him. Although he felt compelled to raise the concerns he overheard from Cornelius, a more pressing issue burdened his psyche.

"When I entered the stairwell under the library floor, I thought I heard screams from deeper in the mountain. What exactly is the forbidden section?"

"Bah!" Cato exclaimed, waving his hands in dismissive exasperation. "What utter nonsense."

Virgil nodded, folding his hands in front of him. "I suspect you did hear screaming, Allen. I take it you did not progress deeper belowground than the publication sanctum."

"Correct, teacher," confirmed Cato.

"Then you were fortunate indeed that Cato intercepted you in time. The restricted section has four zones. The bookshelves on the ground floor of the library contain pioneering and often unverified research. The publication sanctum is where most of our adepts coordinate and codify these innovative studies. East of the sanctum lies the halls of origination—an invaluable trove of history, containing priceless artifacts and dark secrets of the continent's past. In time, as you earn your place among the adepts, you will gain access to these."

Allen breathed a sigh of relief. Virgil had no intention of beheading or expelling him. He then realized the Mystic was waiting for the obvious question: "What's the fourth zone?"

The dark-eyed Mystic nodded gravely. "The fourth zone is one you may likely never enter, even as an adept. Under the library, we have built a hospital unlike any other. Here, patients from all over the world suffering rare ailments and deadly diseases are treated. We do our best to understand their afflictions and create effective cures. While we certainly want our innovative knowledge to spread, we do not want the same of these diseases. Our scientists follow strict sanitation protocols to ensure we do not transmit maladies to the rest of The Library. Given your group's apparent propensity for contracting native illnesses, I do not want you taking unnecessary risks of contamination."

A wave of reassurance washed over Allen. He was neither crazy, nor was Virgil harboring some nefarious secret. In light of this context, the screams from the hospital made Allen respect The Library's mission even more. Not only was this the cornerstone of the world's knowledge, but they even made a point of applying their medical sciences to the most challenging illnesses impacting the world beyond their own borders.

Just like Meghana.

Virgil rose from his chair and walked around the side of his desk to stand before his unexpected guests. "I trust you will keep your knowledge of the forbidden section a secret. You could imagine the visceral reaction our dear sheikh might have if he discovered we were sheltering patients carrying unknown, dangerous pathogens. Sometimes, although we wish it weren't so, we must conceal the extent of our dedication to truly help the world. This brings me to your punishment."

Allen swallowed thickly, preparing for the grueling task. He suspected something along the lines of latrine duty.

"Karim Al'Jaffar is departing to visit El Aria. He is gathering supplies for our hospital and delivering a curative substance we developed for theirs. If you feel confident on your new leg, I would like you to travel with him to learn more about our world and The Library's impact in it. I believe that would be the greatest lesson you could learn from this incident."

Seeing a mighty vein bulging on Cato's forehead as he battled his urge to explode, Allen hastily accepted the proposal. "My leg's been great since you last tuned it. I've still got a bit of a limp when I walk, but I'm beyond grateful for what you've done for me. Thank you. I'd love to accompany Karim."

"An excellent idea, teacher," Cato managed through gritted teeth. "I will task two guards to accompany them. The city can be dangerous, after all."

"No need," Virgil waved a hand. "I've already assigned two to Karim. However, there are other matters we should discuss. Allen, if there's nothing further, you are free to depart. Karim will be loading on the southern road."

"Thank you, Virgil. Actually, I did have one additional question," Allen shuffled his feet.

"The surest way to receive an answer is for you to ask," Virgil invited with a thin smile.

"I understand the enormity of the effort; I was just hoping... Do you know when the transporter will be ready?"

Virgil's eyebrow twitched. He clasped his hands in front of him and appeared lost in thought for a moment. "The science, dear Allen, was quite intuitive in hindsight. I have erected a factory in the desert to begin assembling the transporter, though my efforts to-date have been focused on developing the prerequisite technologies and materials. Even electricity was a radical invention to introduce here, done so with the express focus of enabling you to return to your home. I had dispatched a ship to retrieve as much of the wreckage from the original site as possible, but I'm afraid you are still a long way away from returning to your family. For that, dear Allen, I apologize."

"No—thank you, Virgil. It sounds like you've made incredible progress on an impossible task. If you do get a sense of how long you think it'll take—if that's days, weeks, months, or years—please let me know," requested Allen.

"Months or years, I suspect," ventured Virgil.

It made sense, but it was still disappointing. Especially with Meghana away from The Library, Allen longed for his family's company. The past two years had felt like an eternity, yet he would have to wait an eternity longer. "I see. Thanks again. Let me know if I can help in any way."

"Indeed," Virgil waved, signaling it was time for Allen to depart.

A black-robed page awaited Allen outside the office. The bulbous-nosed man stared at Allen for a long, awkward moment, then silently led him through the squirrel painting, down the stairs, and outside the library.

At the southern end of the plateau, Karim marked a checklist in his hand, then nodded to the brawny red-shoed soldier standing next to him. The soldier rounded the carriage and climbed onto the bench behind two chestnut horses, while Karim closed the rear doors on the carriage's trunk. He nodded as Allen hobbled over.

"Hey, Karim!" Allen waved. He could tell by the tenseness of Karim's shoulders that he was ready to get on the road.

"Allen. Always a pleasure to see you," Karim greeted unsmilingly.

Allen pointed at the carriage. "Virgil mentioned you were making a trip to El Aria and suggested I ride along to learn more about the city and our relationship with the world. May I join you?"

"Virgil," Karim raised his thick eyebrows in recognition. A surprised look dawned in his orange eyes. Running a hand through his untamed, black hair, he answered: "There is room. Come, come. Let us complete our trip while we have the sun."

"Terrific." Allen followed Karim through the side door and into the spacious carriage. The interior was nicer than he had expected, complete with upholstery and a small inventory of handheld fans for the added comfort of passengers. "How far of a drive is it?"

"Thirty, maybe forty minutes to the third ring."

"Third ring?"

"El Aria is not a circle today, but it was built in rings expanding from the sheikh's palace. The fourth and fifth rings are slums—we won't stop there. The inner and first rings are for the wealthy—we won't stop there today," Karim explained, picking at his lip.

"Ah. Cool," commented Allen.

"Hip," Karim moved his head side-to-side in a way that Allen received as empty enthusiasm. "You spend a lot of time with Meghana. How is she?"

"She's in the Lowlands. Helping cure a plague. Think it's going well, but I haven't heard from her in a little while."

"I see," nodded Karim. "And when will she return?"

"I don't know," shrugged Allen.

"I see," Karim nodded again.

A long silence followed, which Allen suspected was far more awkward for him than for the other passenger. "So, have a favorite book?"

"*Advanced Physics: Thermodynamics*—it is very informative," Karim restlessly tapped a finger on his leg.

"Terrific. Any books you read for pleasure?" Allen tried again.

"I find advanced physics highly pleasurable," Karim said woodenly.

"Right, learning is fun," agreed Allen. "But I meant more of a *pleasure* read. Something less serious, you know?"

"Ah," Karim leaned forward with a toothy smile and tapped his nose. He looked left and right as if concerned someone might overhear. "I have one *pleasure* read. The red novel: *Kiss Me in the Moonlight, You Saucy Vixen.*"

"Oh," Allen faltered, feeling his face turn beet red. "I—um. That's good to know. Thank you for sharing. Maybe, are there any good books you like for the story? Something culturally interesting, perhaps?"

"You really like books," Karim raised his bushy eyebrows and stroked his stubbly chin. "Culture story. You may like *The King's Rangers—Seven Sages of War*. It's mostly fluff, but the book is based on real warriors in Deuzos."

Sensing a topic with which he could engage Karim, Allen perked up. "What's the thesis?"

Karim leaned back against the wall and crossed the ankle of his right leg over his left knee. "In Deuzos, the land Meghana traveled to, rules a king named Gaius Godwin. Since his family first took the throne, a team of seven legendary warriors has protected them. Together, they are called *The King's Rangers.* Obviously, the original Rangers are long dead, but seven of their kingdom's best fighters still honor the name today."

"Intriguing. How do they choose who becomes a Ranger?"

"I imagine the difference between a good soldier and a legend should seem obvious. They are the seven sages—not the seven so-and-sos. They have to be the best," Karim emphasized the point by striking a fist in his open palm.

"Do you remember their names? Or what makes them so special?"

"They are special because they are legendary warriors," reiterated Karim. Circular logic. "Let's see if I can remember them all. There's Blaze Mustang, obviously, the Golden Knight. He's probably the most famous knight in the world. You have Miles Savage, the Bounty Hunter. Troy Havoc, the Valkyrie—he's one you never want to cross paths with. The girl—Deadeye Wynn Blackstone. Think they called her the Hornet. I forget the guy with the war hammer, but many people call him the Swine."

"That doesn't sound like a very respected name," commented Allen.

"It isn't. Landon O'Conor, that's his name—the Hungerer. He's a big, big man. Shorter than Blaze but probably twice as heavy. Maybe stronger. He was a hero in the Red War. Grew up poor in the Blasted Lands, so when Godwin invited him to join the Rangers, he ate up half of Highwind. Fat and stupid, but he can swing a hammer," Karim noted with indiscernible respect or prejudice.

"I'm counting five," Allen held out his fingers.

"Did I say Wynn Blackstone already?"

"You did."

"Hmm. Elias Hawkhauer?"

"That's six," Allen lifted another finger.

"Elias the Long Arm—of the law. Born noble, he rose to the top of the cavalry corps and stayed there until Gaius hand-selected him as a Ranger. He has the personality of a wet towel, but he's also the only Ranger who seems to work. 'Lias the Lance, they call him."

"Didn't you say the others were soldiers too?" Allen frowned.

"Were soldiers. Occasionally they lead army exercises, but most of the time, they stand around the castle as bodyguards. Elias is the one Godwin usually sends to do his business, unless the trip is a publicity stunt. Just like how each one has a unique weapon—it's all for marketing," speculated Karim.

"Marketing?" Allen repeated, not following.

"So they can increase sales. You know. Sell more weapons to unruly children. Hawk artwork to fat nobles who were dismissed from the cavalry. Those silly chair-riders. Imagine paying hundreds to idolize a portrait of a warrior who doesn't know you exist, as if you would become less of a rat-person from their painted gaze over your dinner table. It sickens me," Karim scowled.

"Wow," Allen remarked, appreciatively reflecting that this was now the longest conversation he had yet maintained with Karim. "And number seven?"

Karim swatted a hand through the air. "I don't remember the seventh. He doesn't matter. Read the book if you want to learn more."

"I think I will. Thanks," Allen said, unsure whether he would follow up on the commitment.

"I would ask you what your pleasure books are," Karim winced, "but I don't care. So I will not ask. Instead, I will tell you about the city of El Aria."

"That works," Allen accepted diplomatically, feeling only slightly insulted by Karim's candor.

"You feel how we are no longer travelling downhill?" Karim pointed to the carriage walls.

Allen nodded, taking a moment to sense their level path beneath the uneven wheels of the wagon.

"We should be entering the city now. Look outside—don't make eye contact, but look outside," instructed Karim.

Allen lifted the curtain to peek out the window. Outside, soldiers in familiar red and white uniforms lined the side of the road. Looking beyond these guards, he glimpsed into the crowded, chaotic life of El Aria's slums.

Long swaths of tattered cloth hung above decrepit shanties, covering the congested dirt roads from the oppressive sun. Every resident looked grimy and dusty, as if they had emerged from bauxite mines. The children ran around shirtless, jumping over decaying husks of impoverished men who littered the street corners. Clotheslines spanned the street in utter disregard for the notion of private space or any possibility the raggedy garments might be stolen.

Allen realized he couldn't see these rings from his picnic spot on the hill, where he had last marveled at the city's beauty with Meghana. Wondering if she had ever walked these streets before, he observed the starving and starless class of El Arians who dwelled in the shadow of the glistening white palace. It was hard to imagine having hope in a place like this.

"These are the scabs—the damaged residents of El Aria who will never heal. The second and third rings we serve are the inners; they benefit most from our gifts. We bring them health and science, and they build themselves stability. The scabs—they cannot. They are isolated from society. Forgotten. There is no hope for them to move to a higher ring. The wealthier El Arians want nothing to do with the lower rings. Four and five are places to be avoided, nothing more. There is no market for their dearth of knowledge and resources, nor opportunity to end their suffering, short of a swift death."

"That's horrible," Allen recoiled. "These people need the most help!"

"Noble thought, but unrealistic," Karim wagged a finger. "If the scabs get sick and we spend our limited resources helping them—what then? They return to their miserable lives. Days later, they starve and die. Or, because of their barbaric sanitation, they contract a new illness and die. Or a fire starts and burns down a quarter of the slums. They die. No—instead, we help the wealthy who can afford to sponsor our research. Their funding helps us help others. We then give aid to the second and third rings, who provide for their families and teach their children to carry on their self-sustaining ways of life, enriching each generation that follows. Society progresses from the top."

Allen's eyes lingered past the window, saddened by the grim realities of the fourth and fifth rings. "I'm assuming there's a reason you're telling me this?" he asked flatly, feeling like he was conversing with Cato.

His gaze landed on a living skeleton wasting away against one of the ramshackle buildings. The old man's skin had been scorched by the sun over many years. A tight, leathery wrapper covered his bones. Allen could count each rib above his impossibly thin stomach. A glassy expression ruled his eyes, seemingly lost in time and space.

The man's eyes flicked up to him, making Allen jump in his seat. A shiver ran down his spine as he let the curtain fall back into place, unable to look any longer. The animated corpse's harrowing gaze lived on in his mind.

"I told you not to make eye contact," admonished Karim. "The reason I am telling you this is to reset your understanding of the world. There is much good we can and do enact. You can accomplish none of it, however, if you refuse to leave your fantasy land of ideals. Today's trip will be short—we'll visit the souks and the hospital. While we are in the souks, I suggest you observe the people we meet. These are the people we help through our partnership with Sheikh Dohari and the city hospitals."

"Isn't recognizing injustice the first step to changing the world?" Allen challenged, his heart still with the people suffering in rings four and five.

"This city has people who can look around and decide to change the world we live in," mused Karim. "You are not one of them."

Allen shrunk back in his seat, ready for the ride to be over. He didn't much care whether Karim was right or not—he didn't want to hear it, especially in the gruff way the El Arian local spoke about his city.

The carriage soon came to a stop, and the door swung open. Karim climbed out first, calling over his shoulder: "Let me do the talking."

Allen followed Karim off the road and into the side streets. Far fewer soldiers patrolled the third ring, and none seemed to pay them attention as they walked into the souk.

Wooden stands and sandstone buildings lined the dirt roads, bustling with commerce. The awnings that protected these streets from the sun were vibrant and bright colored, matching the disposition of merchants selling food in the open air. Some fruit stands had little boys climbing precariously between the baskets to conduct aerial combat against flies and mosquitos looking to sample the wares. Elsewhere, mothers strolled the streets with their offspring in hand, bargaining with tailors for cuts of cloth to fashion into children's clothes.

A bug-eyed street urchin leaped out at Allen from around a corner, holding some strange, wooden trinket in his hand. "Tash'tari heda, nam?" he barked at Allen.

"No, thanks," Allen waved his hands, wondering if his translation app was broken.

With one hand on his hip, the hawker clicked his tongue against his teeth and gestured at Allen. "Maksura, ah?" he spat in his direction.

"What?" Allen looked to Karim for translation.

"He was speaking a local dialect," Karim explained.

"What's *Maksura* mean?" asked Allen.

"An unkind word," Karim answered shortly, quickening his pace.

Allen struggled to keep up with the heels of his colleague, hobbling as fast as he could through the alleyway of merchants. Looking behind him, Allen noticed one of the soldiers Virgil had assigned remained with the cart, while the other followed them dutifully through the ally. He wore a scowl, either a result of the sights and smells of the marketplace or to dissuade unsavory actors.

Finally, Karim ducked into one of the sandstone buildings, raising a hand in greeting to the proprietor. "Yalaskaar," Karim greeted him, which was answered in similar fashion.

Inside, Allen could tell they were in an apothecary's shop. Powders, elixirs, spices, and plants appeared in vials and jars lining shelves around the shop. Several instruments also hung from the walls, including scalpels, pestles, and scales.

Karim produced a slip of paper from his pocket and slapped it on the counter. "We ordered ahead."

The vendor made a *tsk* sound that Allen feared would precede another bout of spitting. The gruff man said, "What do you want me to do with this?"

"Read it," Karim suggested flatly.

"If I could read it, I'd be working in the second ring," grunted the apprentice. "Sara?"

A woman emerged from the back of the shop, coming to stand next to the vendor. "Can you read what this says?"

"I can try," she frowned, taking the slip of paper in her hands. "This says three ounces of fireweed, maybe *eight molars*, six pounds of tobacco..."

"It's for The Library," Karim explained in an effort to be helpful. "On Sheikh Dohari's account."

"Ah," Sara put the list back on the counter and retreated to the back of the shop, emerging a moment later with a large brown sack. "I prepared it this morning." She slid the bag toward Karim.

After taking a quick inventory, he gestured for the soldier to bear the load. "I'm grabbing a few more items we have need of. The sheikh will happily pay your full price," Karim strolled over to the side wall.

"Thank you. Praise be to Sheikh Dohari," Sara raised a hand before returning to the back of the shop. Allen wasn't sure why, but he did not get the impression she was happy with Karim's proposition.

Allen watched Karim add a few scalpels, a pestle, and some herbs to the bag. He pointed at a jar of yellow powder behind the counter, and the vendor retrieved it for him.

"Many thanks," Karim said, heading for the door. "Praise be unto Sheikh Dohari."

The proprietor repeated the phrase, raising his hand after them.

The overburdened soldier followed them into the streets.

"Guy Cornello," Karim said abruptly, turning down another alleyway.

"Excuse me?" asked Allen, bewildered.

"The seventh sage of war—Guy the Watcher. Always late to everything. Lazy as a donkey. Some call him *patient.* He is incredibly smart, a brilliant tactician, but I cannot respect him as a man."

"Ah," Allen voiced in answer, unsure of what else to say.

They entered a sizeable square dominated by a fountain featuring a giant scorpion. In front of the fountain, a small crowd was gathered around to watch a squad of six soldiers whip the bloodied back of a man tied to a post. His tortured screams rang thickly through the air.

Allen felt lightheaded. "What…"

"This way," Karim continued onward, circling around the far side of the fountain. "Prison space is limited in El Aria. Most crimes are rewarded with death or public discipline. He was probably a thief or a lecher."

Numbly following Karim's path, Allen felt dehydrated. His vision swam in and out of focus. He wanted to intervene and stop the barbaric punishment but suspected he would just be added to the display. If Khalifa's words were true, drawing attention to his metal leg could bring a whole lot more trouble.

"Here," Karim announced, knocking on the front door of one of the tallest buildings in the square. An emblem of snakes entangled around a rod watched over the street from the hospital.

A man wearing a patterned headscarf emerged from the hospital. The cloth was pulled back in a way that made him look like a cobra. Vaguely similar to the snakes above them.

"Yalaskaar, Karim Al'Jaffar. It is great to see you again," greeted the man, gripping Karim's right hand with both of his.

"Yalaskaar, Abbas Kotari," smiled Karim. "I would like you to meet Allen... Allen, a colleague of mine from The Library."

"Yalaskaar," Allen muttered uncertainly, extending a hand.

"Yalaskaar, Allen Al'Ain," greeted Abbas. "Please, come inside."

Allen followed Abbas, while Karim stopped at the door and instructed the soldier to stow their purchases and return with the hospital supplies.

Inside the cool building, Abbas led them into the first room on the left. It was a small office with a modest wooden table in the center.

"Please, sit. I prepared tea," he took the initiative to pour three cups.

Allen obeyed, taking a sip of one of the most flavorful teas he had ever sampled. Despite the scalding temperature, he immediately took a second sip.

"Allen Al'Ain," began Abbas.

"Allen is fine," he returned, waving away any perceived formalities.

"Allen," Abbas corrected himself. "I am sure you know, but we are forever grateful for your service at The Library. Thanks to you, less than half of our patients die. So many go on to live full lives, defying the cruel hand of fate. The mothers, the children—you save them through your research."

Allen nearly spat out his tea. In any other world, a hospital would have been ashamed to disclose a fifty-percent mortality rate. He reconsidered the statement and realized it had likely been far worse in the past.

"We are humbled by your praise," Karim answered on Allen's behalf. "We have brought with us a new cure to help with the recent rash of deadly fevers. Studies over the past few months conclude that many of your dying patients are not contagious but are being infected by parasites."

"Parasites!" echoed Abbas, astonished. "How can you be so sure?"

"On the distant continent of Baltos, they battled a parasitic infection called plasmodium. Mosquitos transmitted the infection to people, killing thousands. There, we also discovered a cure through the cinchona trees. Our servant has gone to retrieve two full vials of this powder, which you can mix as a solution for patients to ingest. Hot wine was used first, but I am confident tea or coffee would work."

"Karim, you always bring the most incredible news. This is why I love having you as an advisor to my humble hospital," Abbas beamed. "But tell me, if this is not contagious, how are so many falling ill? The mosquitos have gotten sick, you say?"

"How the local mosquitos have come to carry this disease, I do not know," Karim shook his head. "The recent numbers remain a surprise to me. Regardless, the parasite they carry causes the illness you are seeing. I have transcribed detailed notes on the matter in my upcoming publication."

"I will be sure to purchase a copy," Abbas took a loud sip of tea.

The soldier returned, carrying two large jars of white powder. Karim directed him to place them, carefully, on the floor by the doorway.

"Karim! You are a man of your word," Abbas commended gratefully.

"You see, Allen," Karim turned to him, "this is what we do. Mankind is better off because of our research at The Library. We find solutions to the world's gravest troubles and share our science. Today, we help Abbas cure his patients of their plasmodium. Similarly, our antiseptics have helped stave off infections during surgery, saving countless lives within this hospital."

"Oh yes—and will doubtlessly save many more in the coming years. With the military going on the march, that is," Abbas commented perceptively.

"The military is mobilizing? Against the other sheikhdoms?" inquired Karim.

"The Damari'is army is always on a warpath with El Aria, but I hear they're planning to march together—east, across the Khaliri," disclosed Abbas.

"What possible reason could Dohari..." Karim stopped midsentence, looking a little pale.

"Praised be his name," suggested Abbas.

"Praised be his name," agreed Karim, resting his teacup on the saucer.

"Well, now that we know the patients aren't contagious... Allen, would you like to meet one of the patients to whom The Library has given a second life?" Abbas invited, driving the conversation forward.

"I... Uh, yes," he answered sheepishly.

"Excellent," Abbas rose from his seat and poured a fourth cup of tea. Karim measured out a spoonful of powder, dissolved it in hot water, then handed the saucer and cup to Abbas, who smiled tearfully. "Come meet Priya."

Abbas exited into the hall, followed by Karim. Allen paused, then quickly turned back to the table to grab the handkerchief under his teacup. He coughed violently into the cloth, robbed of breath by his chest's contractions.

The El Arian soldier lowered his brow, fixing him with a stern gaze.

"Hot tea," Allen excused himself with watery eyes, tucking the bloody cloth into his robes. He fled the room in a hurry, jogging to catch up with Karim. Allen spotted him ascending a narrow staircase at the far end of the hall.

At the top of the stairs, they entered the first room on the left. Two beds were set close together with a nightstand dividing them. The one on the right was presently unoccupied, but a young girl lay under a frayed blanket on the left cot. Sweat beaded on her pained face.

Abbas rested the teacup on the bedside table and looked to Karim for confirmation, who nodded. The doctor slipped a hand behind the frail girl and helped her sit up. "Drink this, sweet Priya. You will feel better soon. Virgil's scholars traveled the whole world to make this for you."

Priya's foggy eyes cracked open, settling first on Allen. Through the pain and discomfort reflected on the young girl's weary face, Allen detected the slightest glint of hope and recognition in her eyes.

Priya opened her mouth as Abbas slowly tilted the cups for her. Mustering the last of her strength to swallow the medicine, she sputtered weakly as the drink went down. Her eyes drifted closed as her head slumped back against the pillow.

Abbas smiled triumphantly, tears welling in his eyes as he looked between the scholars who had allowed him to grant this patient the gift of life.

Karim rested a hand on Allen's shoulder. "Thanks to us—thanks to Meghana, Virgil, and all the adepts at The Library, this girl will see tomorrow."

XXII. Respite

Drake

Sunlight filtered through the green leaves, gently stirring Drake from his nap.

He sat up in his bedroll on the wooden floor of the open-walled shrine, lethargic, but nowhere near as groggy as usual. For a little while, he stared into the tranquil forest beyond the clearing, gold in the early sun. A breeze danced through the leaves, carrying an earthy scent that made him think of home.

The evocation lacked any details beyond the smell, as per usual, but he felt inexplicably at ease in this place. Although he had been on-edge the first few days of their hiatus at the shrine, he had grown to imagine this sanctuary in the woods was a secret haven. Just for them. To his surprise and relief, neither the soldiers nor the zealots had pursued him this far inland, and the monks harbored no nefarious intentions beneath their lives of stoic meditation.

Life here was almost uncomfortably peaceful.

In a strange way, he consoled himself with reminders that the future held many trials and tribulations still to come. A part of him held onto neurotic tendencies, scanning the bushes for movement and listening for predators on the prowl. Instead, he saw only squirrels scrambling from branch to branch. Heard only the chipper songs of the birds, accompanied by a gentle harp.

Drake rose to his feet, stretching out his back and neck. His bed was hardly a princely cot, but he had no complaints. Hikaru had urged him to rest until he felt recovered, and though it had taken a great deal of convincing from both her and Talia, he had finally decided to follow their advice. These midday naps were some of the most relaxing sleeps he could remember.

Following the harp's euphonic melody out of the three-walled shrine, he ventured around the side and found Aiko sitting on a simple wooden stool. The woman smiled toothily, continuing her piece without pause. Drake leaned against the outer wall of the shrine, listening appreciatively to her wordless tune.

He smiled as he thought of an earlier conversation with Hikaru. He had asked her why Aiko had a harp, as he thought the monks were supposed to absolve themselves of worldly possessions. Hikaru disclosed that most of the passengers on the vessel that brought them here were simple villagers and merchants, and while many of the men voluntarily became monks, most of the women settled for a quiet life in a village hidden in the shadow of the new monastery. They were connected communities, keeping the old traditions alive while making practical concessions to new ways of life.

One of these concessions came in the form of Aiko's harp. She had learned the instrument in her youth. Since arriving in Deuzos, Aiko regularly played tunes for the village at sunrise and sundown. Devoid of shopping and other old habits, many villagers began learning instruments themselves, carving clarinets and flutes from the forest and even trading for lutes and violins from the Freecity. Now, the whole village played music together as a study of the flow of the universe—*Kon'chai*. They would even perform with the monks during the blood moon demonstration later that evening.

Aiko concluded her piece in a climbing series of notes to the highest string. She gently brought the harp to rest against the ground, then placed her hands on her knees as she forced her weary bones to rise from the stool.

Drake smiled softly in approval. "I liked that one."

Aiko clasped her hands behind her back and bent forward slightly. With that same toothy smile, she lifted a small bag from next to her stool and extended it to him.

Drake reached out a hand to accept the food. Aiko pulled back at the last moment, pointing a finger at the shrine. He leaned forward to pluck the bag out of her hand, laughing as he said, "Fine! Okay. Let's go chat with Sato."

"Sato," she corrected, indistinguishable from his initial attempt.

Walking with her, he rounded the side and stepped up onto the slightly elevated floor of the open-faced shrine. A raindrop dripped from the roof onto his head, sending a shiver down his spine. He crossed the threshold and knelt before the stone statue of a fat, laughing man in ill-fitting robes.

Evidently, none of the merchants who had come aboard the ship were skilled sculptors. The statue's face was asymmetrical, and the eroded front of its belly looked fuzzy, almost as if resembling body hair. An upside-down crown rested at its feet, currently containing the remnants of burned incense.

Drake grabbed a fresh twig of incense from the pile by the cushions at Sato's feet. "Allow me," he said to Aiko as she reached to ignite the stick.

Holding the incense out toward the forest in case he overshot his effort, he puffed fire through the air, easily igniting the tip. A thin trail of white smoke rose from the stick as he turned back toward the statue.

He knelt on the pillow, followed by Aiko on his right side. Inclining his head to the fat effigy, he laid the incense in the bowl with the others and came up with his own makeshift prayer, making sure to throw in the old emperor's name every few lines: "Hey, Sato. Lovely weather we're having today. Have you been working out, Sato? 'Cause it shows. Good for you. Keep up the work."

Aiko cleared her throat and looked at him expectantly.

"Right," Holding a fist against his open palm, Drake bowed slightly to the homely statue. Aiko mirrored the movement. "Cheers, Sato, for what I'm guessing will be another bowl of rice in this bag. It's rice or bread, but I'm gonna go out on a limb and say it's rice. Also, looking forward to eating it for the next couple months, since Aiko and Hikaru have generously provided us with sacks of the stuff and, for some reason, each grain gets three times bigger when you cook it. Sato, *camoshi.*"

"*Sato camoshi,*" repeated Aiko, raising her eyebrows as if once again correcting his pronunciation.

"Pretty good today, right?" grunted Drake.

Aiko wagged a finger at him as he opened the bag to pull out a bowl of lukewarm rice.

"I know," he sighed helplessly, retrieving the two small sticks included in the bag. "I'm a rascal."

He proceeded to use the utensils as a shovel, scarfing down the rice in record time. There was a spice mixed in that made it taste like its own meal rather than an accompaniment to meat—which was good, since the only fresh meat he had enjoyed this past week came from a scrawny and luckless rabbit that had stumbled into his snare.

Finishing his lunch, he tapped the empty bowl with his two sticks and asked, "Any chance you brought seconds?"

In answer, Aiko poked his belly twice with a bony index finger, making a sound that suggested she would not be swayed to give him seconds.

"Lei lei," she beckoned, leading him back outside to the stool.

As Drake sat, Aiko knelt before him and took his right hand to inspect the wounds, unwrapping the natural bandages she had applied. Studying the healed skin carefully, she poked it a few times to gauge his reaction.

"I told you yesterday, it feels fine," he shrugged.

She took his other arm and unwrapped the compress. On the back of his left hand, a slightly darker patch of skin remained, running halfway down his forearm. It didn't hurt as she pressed, but the fact that his skin hadn't recovered from the burn was disconcerting.

The scar was a permanent warning left by his indiscretion. He knew now how precarious his use of Pyros' might could be. Only minor injuries came from his loss of control this time, but it could have been a lot worse.

It could have been a lot worse for Talia, too.

His mind turned to the recurring thought that never failed to make him uneasy. The obvious choice was to reject Pyros. To relegate his invocation to life-or-death situations only. Deep down, he knew he couldn't bring himself to honor that prudence. The Primal's boon was addictive. Its power, undeniable.

An initial illusion responsible behavior, Drake had reasoned that more frequent use of their connection might improve his control, making it safer for him and Talia whenever he truly needed the full extent of Pyros' strength. The truth was much simpler but far less satisfying: a fire was burning within him, and he couldn't put it out. He had to just hope for the best and trust his bond with Pyros would protect them. Like a raft in the raging ocean.

"Anyone home?"

"Over here," Drake answered the call.

Talia jogged around the corner, followed by Hikaru. She waved her hand excitedly, brandishing some kind of stick.

"Guess what?" she prompted.

"What?" he obliged. Squinting, he made out the weapon in her hand.

"Hikaru taught me how to knap," Talia reported proudly.

"I was napping myself, just a few minutes ago," Drake commented as she approached.

"Knapping, you goofball," Talia rolled her eyes. "It means to, like, make things."

Drake scratched his chin. "Well, why wouldn't you just say that?"

"Knap's a cool word," Talia said defensively. "Anyway, Hikaru taught me how to make arrows. Look, I knapped this from obsidian," she handed him the arrow.

Drake inspected the craftsmanship. It was obviously not the output of a professional blacksmith, but he respected the effort that went into it. The jagged arrow tip was sure enough cut from obsidian and affixed to the top of a long shaft. Three feathers were bound to the opposite end, held in place by some kind of reed or flexible bark. "Looks like a duck feather to me," he said dryly.

"That is a duck feather," Talia groaned impatiently. "Obviously, I'm talking about the arrowhead. Just be impressed for me."

"I'm very impressed," he said, sounding decidedly unimpressed.

"You're jealous because you don't know how to knap," Talia resolved matter-of-factly.

"One of your feathers is crooked," he identified, returning the arrow.

Talia huffed as she took the shaft. Closely inspecting the end for any deviances, she made a minor adjustment. "It was straight before you bent it."

"You know we can buy you some real arrows, right? I'm pretty sure they sell them in packs of twenty."

"Give a man a fish," Talia replied sagaciously, meticulously inspecting her arrow. Apparently deciding it met her heightened standards, she slipped it into the quiver on her back.

"Why would I do that? It's my fish," Drake demanded.

Talia shifted her eyes to him and let out a purposeful sigh. "Okay. Want to see something cool?"

"Show me."

Talia slung the bow off her shoulder and pulled out an arrow, nocking it onto the bowstring. "See that tree there? The one with the droopy branch?"

"I see it," Drake pointed to a tree thirty yards to his right.

"Check this out," she grinned, lifting the bow and pulling the drawstring back to her cheek. She released the arrow, firing the errant shot several yards to the right of the tree and into the forest.

"Damn it!" Talia stamped her foot.

"Told you the feather looked crooked," Drake contributed helpfully.

"You must be at peace with the wind. Find harmony in the movement of the world as your feet stand firmly in place," instructed Hikaru, moving her hands through the air in a slow, sweeping motion.

"Harmony," Talia retrieved another one of her six homemade arrows. "Harmony," she repeated to herself, drawing the string back to her cheek.

"Good luck," he interjected the second before he expected her release.

He saw her finger twitch, catch itself, then release.

The arrow spiraled perfectly into the trunk, lodging itself with an audible *thwack*.

Talia jumped in place with a broad smile, extending her bow toward the tree. "Boom! Can't be distracted. Harmony!" Talia gloated proudly.

"One for two. Not bad."

Talia rolled her eyes and drew another arrow. She nocked it quicky, held the tension for a moment, then released.

Thwack.

Another hit, just under the other successful arrow.

"Wow," Drake applauded dryly.

Talia drew a fourth arrow and fired it even faster than the first three. The projectile landed between the other two but broke along the shaft under the arrowhead. Shrapnel disappeared into the grass.

"That counts!" Talia declared, pointing a finger at Drake.

"Honestly, color me impressed," he relented. "Three for four ain't half bad. You're getting pretty good there, kid."

"I'm like the queen of archery," exaggerated Talia. "I'll bet I'm even better than you!"

"That ain't saying a whole lot. I'm half-decent with a crossbow but not much of a bowman," shrugged Drake. "Plus, it's one thing to hit a tree, but most trees don't move... and they definitely don't shoot back."

Talia opened her mouth to reply, then closed it again as she absorbed the information. "But it's still a good start, right?"

"It's a great start," Drake encouraged. "You keep practicing, you'll be the goddess of archery in no time."

"Now was that so hard to say?" she grinned, slinging the bow over her shoulder. "Mind helping me find that first arrow?"

"Sure." He followed her over to the tree. Behind them, Hikaru and Aiko exchanged words in another language.

"Wonder what ever happened to those men who were chasing us," Talia voiced.

"Deus knows about the fanatics. The soldiers are probably headed to the front. If they're holding Fort Banning, they might live a while. If they were heading to the Frontier, they're probably dead," speculated Drake.

"The one riding around in that gold suit of armor—what's his deal? I'm surprised his soldiers haven't just killed him and sold off his stuff."

"No clue."

"Just feels like you'd be able to give a ton of knights good swords and whatever for the same money they threw into that."

He grunted his agreement as they reached the tree. Talia removed the two arrows from the trunk, taking extra care not to break the heads.

"I think the first arrow's somewhere back there."

"Got it," Drake acknowledged, scanning the untrimmed grass. *There.* A brown shaft. Finding it was the arrow that had lost its head, he retrieved the damaged projectile and used it to rifle through the grass in search of the other.

The stick connected with something in the grass. Drake swatted the black coil again, instigating a sudden spur of motion as it slithered forward. He reflexively jumped back and flicked his arm up, sending the mid-sized snake sailing through the air and deeper into the forest. Inspecting the ground around him for others, he spat into the grass, feeling his heart racing. "Get out of here, you," he whispered sternly after the vanished reptile.

"Did you say something?" Talia called to him.

"No," he answered over his shoulder, continuing to cautiously comb through the grass with his stick.

He found the lost arrow and scooped it up with the help of the broken shaft. Exiting the woods decidedly faster than he had entered, he returned to the clearing to hand the recovered prize to Talia.

"Thanks," she tucked the projectile into the quiver with the others. "I like what you did with your hair, by the way. You look smart."

"Smart?" Drake recoiled.

"Like, dashing. Handsome. Don't worry, you don't look any brighter than usual," she clarified.

"Ah. That's a relief," he snorted. "Aiko cut it for me this morning after you left with Hikaru. Also trimmed my beard, which feels... smart."

"I hardly even recognized you without your caveman scruff."

"I don't know how you meant it, but I will take that as a compliment."

Talia opened her mouth to unleash another wisecrack but was interrupted by Hikaru. "You do not have to leave today, Drake. You and Talia may stay as long as you like."

"I appreciate that, Hikaru," he nodded graciously. "But I think it's time we get back on the road. Did you have a chance to ask Master Ichiro if we can get the horse to meet us west of the woods?"

Hikaru nodded, then told Drake the bad news. "It is not possible to bring the horse west of the forest in time to meet you. We would either have to bring it north and around the Emerald Hills or through the Duskwood parallel to us in the south. The trees here are too thick. If you would like to wait a few more weeks, I could ask Satoshi if he could find time to make the journey."

"No," Drake wavered, trying to decide which option would be better in the long run. He didn't know how treacherous the Cradle would be for a horse but suspected the animal's life expectancy would be lower in his company. He also recognized the Taoxians led a precarious existence in Godwin's kingdom and that Satoshi would face a dangerous two-way journey. He couldn't bring himself to impose like that on the people who had saved his life.

"No," he decided. "Thank Master Ichiro and Satoshi for their help. And thank you both, really. If that horse can be of use to you, all I ask is you give her a good life."

"She will live out her days in peace until she returns to the infinite cycle," Hikaru promised with a bow.

"I'll miss you, Hikaru," Talia bowed in turn. "Thanks for everything."

"It was an honor," the woman answered.

Talia exhaled deeply. "So, know where we're going?"

"West?" suggested Drake.

"Think it's worth asking for directions?" Talia prompted.

Drake grunted and brought Hikaru back into the conversation. "I've got a needle-in-a-haystack idea of where we are. Duskwood south, Highlands north—what's the best way to get to the Riverlands?"

"I am unsure." Drake shot a sidelong look at Talia, unhappy he had been forced to ask for directions only to be let down. Sensing the discomfort, Hikaru expanded on her statement. "I do not know the best way, but west of the forest, at the edge of the Foothills, a road travels north to the capital and south to the Basket. You may find your way on the main road there. If not, just keep going west—if you find yourself walking on sand, you have gone too far."

XXIII. Noble Intentions

Flynn Darke | Iko

Crisp evening air served as a reminder that winter was creeping upon the vale.

It never failed to amaze him how abruptly the temperature dropped at sundown. Hopefully, Lydia had managed to purchase some new quilts from the market today. Prices always surged after a cold snap, and Flynn suspected the first wall of true cold would arrive within a week. Much earlier than years prior.

As he strolled up the winding pass to his white manor on the hill, he felt revitalized. The frosty air innervated him, restoring focus to his exhausted mind. He was late to dinner, and Lydia would surely have some choice words for him upon his arrival. One had better enter a row with both eyes open.

He stopped outside his home to admire the six pearl-white columns on his portico. The ornate pillars had been handcrafted by a meticulous architect from the neighboring town, much to the dismay of Rudolphio, Barrington's homegrown pride and joy. Flynn had an eye for quality and was pleased with the work done by the Winter's Vale native. Every time he passed the pillars, he noticed a new detail engraved in the stone. Today, a carving of two lords eating in a deserted hall won his attention. Surprisingly, he had never noticed the scene before; located on the pillar opposite the two lords was his favorite image: a traitorous disciple murdering Deus incarnate at the Steppes of the Firstborn.

Barrington was an agreeable compromise between civilization and the northern cabin his family had temporarily occupied a few years back. Visitors were few and far between, and the population of retired nobles knew how to keep a connected community without overstepping personal boundaries. It was a village for those who wished to trade the world of politics and nation-building for two seasons and a safe bubble to enjoy personal and environmental wealth.

Drawing himself upright, Flynn opened the gothic-arched door and slipped off his white gloves. He discarded them into the bin and put on a fresh pair. The weighted door closed behind him. Not a second later, an audible throat-clearing emanated from the dining room.

Flynn hurried past the tasteful displays in the foyer, turning right into his well-lit dining room. Eight candles burned brightly from the chandelier, illuminating three diners seated at the long table along with one empty oak seat. Flynn took the open seat next to his youngest son, Cassius, directly across from Lydia and diagonal from his eldest, Lucian. Bread, mashed potatoes, and green vegetables awaited consumption on all four plates. Additionally, sizeable cuts of steak rested on every plate except Lydia's.

"Glad you could join us," she said icily. Something more than mild annoyance laced her crystal blue eyes. Even still, Flynn took a moment to admire how beautifully they contrasted with her inky hair and umber skin.

"Work ran late," he defended shortly. "Shall we eat?"

"Would you like to lead us in prayer?" his wife asked, commanding more than inviting.

"Sure," he clasped the hands of his neighbors. Sheepishly, he realized how little attention he had paid to her nightly incantations. "Thank you, Deus, for food... Thank you for the new quilts Lydia bought at the market today," he raised his tone in question.

Lydia raised her eyebrows, suggesting that he should continue.

Flynn cleared his throat. "And bless this family and my wonderful wife. May it be so," he ended.

"May it be so," his children repeated, eagerly diving into their suppers.

"May it be so," Lydia sighed before taking a small forkful of vegetables.

The dining room was quiet for a long minute. Even with the fifth chair gone, the table felt larger than it should. Emptier. Only the ravenous chewing of two hungry boys broke the silence.

"Chew with your mouth closed, Cassius," reprimanded his mother. He complied, chasing his last bite of steak with a swig of water.

Lydia looked over at Lucian. "*Chew* your food, Lucian."

Lucian shot Flynn a look as if to protest that he had, in fact, been chewing. Flynn wisely responded with a half shrug, dismissing the protest.

Lydia took a long sip of red wine, draining the remnants of her glass. She reached for the bottle in the center of the table, topped herself off, then returned the half-empty bottle to rest on the white tablecloth.

Flynn now realized he had only been assigned a water glass. "Is there another wine glass?" he asked, knowing the type of answer he would receive.

"In the kitchen, there is," Lydia answered flatly.

Flynn bit into a piece of lukewarm steak. It was seasoned excellently and, even cold, had great flavor.

"I was at the market today," Lydia said finally, cutting into the wall of tension that had manifested at the table.

"Did you find any nice quilts?" Flynn furthered the conversation.

"I did. Do you know what else I found there?" she asked dangerously.

Flynn felt the crux of whatever argument she had prepared against him precipitating. "What did you find?" he invited sportingly.

"An old friend." Lydia took a sip from her glass. "Lady Barrington. I asked how you and Winston were getting along. She told me she hasn't seen you at the castle in months," ended Lydia, demanding an explanation.

Flynn debated feigning surprise and answering *just because she hasn't seen me, doesn't mean I wasn't there,* but he was too smart to give that answer. He knew such an easily verifiable fabrication would be exposed within days. Instead, he opted to answer in partial truth: "I have a new employer."

"Who?" probed Lydia. Flynn could see the blend of emotion on her face despite her carefully practiced mask of neutrality. Distrust and suspicion, mixed with surprise and hurt that he had not told her sooner.

Flynn looked sidelong at Cassius, then back at Lydia, silently suggesting that they discuss the matter in private.

"Go on," said Lydia.

Flynn sighed heavily. "The king," he professed.

"The *king?*" his kids echoed in unison.

"I accepted a position as the head of the king's information network," he further explained to his wife. Halfway to a half-truth.

"Dad's a librarian?" asked Cassius, confused.

"Dad's a... spy," corrected Lydia, shocked and off-put. She scrutinized his face, struggling to decide whether she believed him. "How long have you been a spy?" she asked, fighting to keep her voice neutral.

"A long time," he said succinctly. The dazed look on his partner's face begged further comment. "Before we met in Alandria," he eventually admitted.

"But how could you have been a spy? Your father was Lord Darke of Hycrosse. You grew up a noble and came to settle down in Alandria when your brother inherited the family title. I remember meeting you as you rode into town on your white horse. When could you possibly have become a spy?"

"On my way down from Hycrosse, I was met by an envoy. Suspicions abounded that Lord Gareth of the Song Vale was a traitor. I had proven myself more than capable of acquiring key intelligence by thwarting three plots against my father's keep at Hycrosse, so I was sent to Alandria to verify these claims."

A housefly flew onto Flynn's goatee. Swatting it away, he felt the patchy beard developing under his chin. *I'll have to shave soon.* That under-the-chin scruff was a plague that refused to grow into a beard but nevertheless continued to return. The firm moustache and neat head of black hair was fine, otherwise.

"How come I never knew?" Lydia whispered, averting her eyes from him and snapping him out of his wayward thoughts.

"The more you know, the more danger you'll be in. I was trying to protect you and the kids," he explained truthfully.

"We're a team," she said hollowly, her lip beginning to quiver. "Aren't we?" she asked weakly.

As Flynn opened his mouth to offer her some form of reassurance, darkness passed over the table, briefly threatening to extinguish the flames of the overhead candles. A faint whisper accompanied the dark wind before light was restored to the room.

Heat fled his face, turning his cheeks ashen. They weren't supposed to know about this place. They weren't supposed to know about this life. He had never given any indication of where he went when he separated from the pack.

"I'm taking a walk," he abruptly rose to his feet, forsaking his plate.

"Now? Seriously?" Lydia asked, incredulous. Tears welled in her eyes.

"You clearly need time to digest this, and I need air," Flynn said flatly, tearing his eyes from hers.

He abandoned the dinner scene and entered the cold night air. A chill ran down his spine as a familiar, ominous presence bore down on him. Clad in Godwin's gaudiest golden armor, a wretched figure stepped out from behind a white pillar. *His favorite pillar.*

"What are you doing here?" Flynn demanded tersely. His initial fear was now giving way to anger. He regarded Axel's ugly face with disdain, loathing the pale visage and glowing red eyes. He wanted nothing more than to lop off the Cormack's pointy ears and wear them as a trophy around his neck.

"My, my... and I thought nobles were supposed to be hospitable!" Axel mocked with a grin.

The horrific beast of a Primal, Hadronox, flashed behind Axel. The deformed creature had no face—just a maw with a handful of spiked teeth. Two muscled claws and a pair of wispy tentacles supported its hunchbacked body. An irregular, broken-plated spine ran down the exterior of the creature's back.

"It's your turn, Iko. We've done our part," Axel gestured to a hooded figure behind the pillar with the two dining lords.

"Hello, Prism," Flynn greeted needlessly.

Her lips did not break their silence for him.

He still could not piece together the anomalous incident following their failed meeting with Lord Vayne. Flynn had briefly questioned her after they returned to the keep, and, for a minute, it was as if she were trying to answer of her own accord. Hadronox had joined them soon after, bringing the episode to a close and Prism back to her usual torpor.

"That was quick," Flynn remarked, turning back to Axel. They were ahead of schedule.

"As far as any doctor can tell, it was from natural causes. Prince Georg rides west, ready to soak his grief in bloodshed. We have a long twenty-four hours ahead of us," said Axel.

"Perhaps luck is on our side after all," mused Flynn.

"Destiny isn't luck. It's not divine providence. Destiny is a rogue wave. Either rise with it or get pulled under and drown."

A purple light enveloped his unannounced visitors. They vanished into the still night, whisked away by Prism, likely back to their unimpressive keep on Val'Kyros.

A regretful sigh, Flynn whispered, "Iko," stirring the Primal within. Shadows amassed around him, swallowing him in darkness. He closed his eyes and felt the cool comfort of their unseen corridors.

Lydia would inevitably stew in his absence, but she'd find a way to forgive him. She always did. He had to focus on his work.

Flynn opened his eyes and gazed upon the imposing stone walls of Fort Gerhart, home of Lord Gerhart Godwin and his adult son, Bastian.

Unlike his pleasant home in Barrington, the evening air was hot and sticky in the Lowlands. The bugs were far less abrasive here than in the swampy biome only a few days west of Linz, but an insatiable cluster of gnats were among the first to notice his intrusion.

Flynn moved his gloved hands to his sides, seeking the leather hilts of his foot-long blades. Unsheathing the dagger from his left hip, he scanned the nearest wall for an entry point. He could have replicated his onslaught at the garrison but decided it would be unnecessary. Perhaps even counterproductive to his goal of having the bodies discovered quickly. The only way news would reach the capital in a timely manner was if he left survivors to discover the scene in the morning.

That meant he had to be sloppier than usual. Leave enough evidence to incriminate the Crimson Hand. That would be easy enough to sell—all but the most casual observer knew Tallawyn's clandestine order of assassins had gone downhill in recent years. Not all knew that the timing had coincided with Flynn's departure from the Hand.

Bright braziers burned in each watchtower. Armed sentries walked the battlements with torches.

Fools, Flynn thought with a professional's disapproval. Torches were a bad idea for any sort of night patrol; they made for easier targets and ruined night vision. He understood it was only natural for men to cling to their light. The dark was terrifying for most to face—the notion of *that which lurks in the dark can see you, but you cannot see that which lurks in the dark.*

Through the shadows once more, Flynn appeared on the battlement behind an oblivious sentry. He spotted a vent from which smoke escaped the interior keep. Likely the kitchens. Flynn returned to the shadow walk, feeling his way through Iko's realm of dim lights in darkness. In a fraction of a second, he traveled through the vent and past the fire.

There. A pocket of dark beside a square of light. Opening his eyes, he materialized in an unlit room, standing on top of a large sack of grain. Light shone under the door, confirming he was off to the side of the kitchen.

Traveling through Iko's realm was difficult. He could easily conjure shadows and step through them if he had a visual line of sight to his terminus. He could traverse long distances if he was at all familiar with his destination. The guesswork came whenever he had to feel his way through the darkness. It was easy to get lost if he let himself wander too long. Thus, he preferred to do several smaller excursions into the shadows, rather than search immediately for his final objective.

The door to the grain storage swung open, admitting a young kitchen boy. He had not yet noticed Flynn standing stock-still in the darkness with a hood concealing his face.

The boy walked forward, stopping less than two feet away from Flynn. He stood on his toes to reach the top shelf. Succeeding in pulling down a bottle of red wine, he turned and exited through the door, leaving it slightly ajar.

"Where are the glasses? The lord will be sitting to eat in ten minutes!" cried a young voice outside.

Stepping out into the kitchen, Flynn saw the selected bottle of wine momentarily abandoned, now uncorked. There were three servants in the kitchen. One was chopping vegetables with his back turned to him, another was raiding the cupboards in search of glasses, and the third was roasting a whole pig on a spit. The latter seemed to be the oldest of the lot. Flynn guessed he was fifteen—nearly a man. He had a round belly atypical for serving boys.

"Why don't you find the damn glasses, then?" the pig-roaster suggested without turning around.

Flynn seized the opportunity and emptied the contents of a green vial—of which he carried three at any given time—into the wine. He shadow-stepped behind the cook and slid the emptied vial into the pack he wore on his hip.

Fleetly footed, Flynn stalked to the corner of the room and stepped back into the shadows, feeling his way out of the kitchen and into the hall. Corporeal again, he walked down the narrow corridor. The servant's wing was quiet, but he remained alert for any guards that might come around the corner.

In his most recent foray into the shadows, he felt a cavernous, dimly lit room he assumed to be the dining hall. He could have gone straight there, but he was being particularly cautious now. There was a plan in motion, and his target was on his way. No sense in jeopardizing the scapegoat. A lesser concern, there were likely also several foxholes throughout the keep Gerhart could slip through in the unlikely event alarms were raised.

So patience it was. He melded into the shadows, standing motionless between two far-apart torches that provided the only illumination in the hall.

His mind drifted to Lydia, at home with the boys. He hoped she would come around to his role as a spy. It sounded better than *radicalized assassin,* or *lieutenant to the god-king.* He could never explain the true nature of his role. She wouldn't understand. He could only do what he thought was best for them. Either serve the side that was destined to win and have a hand in carving the new world or stand aside and become a victim to the capricious whims of fate.

He could rise with the wave or get pulled under.

A pair of hurried footsteps came from the kitchen, sharpening Flynn's focus. The nervous boy he had encountered in the grain room came speeding down the hall with two goblets and a bottle of wine. He rounded the corner and muttered "'scuse me." Less than a minute later, he came back around the corner, traveling at his rapid pace.

Flynn crept to the end of the hallway, stopping short of the sharp left turn. "Iko," he whispered, extending a dark tendril around the corner. He felt the tendril glide along the floor, extending until it was under a large mass. He mentally guided the tendril upward until it reached what felt like the neck of a man. He constricted the tendril, listening intently for the sound of strangulation.

Several seconds of pressure failed to bring about any choked gasps. The sentry must have been wearing a full suit of armor. Flynn refocused Iko's tendrils into the gaps that allowed air into the helmet, then remotely fastened his grip around the man's neck. This time, faint gasps reached him around the corner as the knight struggled to draw breath. Redoubling his focus, Flynn tightened his grip around the man's throat and lifted him from the floor. After ten long seconds, the resistance folded. No more flailing limbs. Flynn let the shadows disperse, and the man sunk to the floor.

Breathing heavily, Flynn took a moment to compose himself. That task had been surprisingly strenuous for Iko. From dawn to dusk, it had been an exacting day with little time to rest. Hopefully, he would be able to wrap things up without requiring further assistance from his Primal.

Rounding the corner, Flynn saw the metallic mass of a four-hundred-pound knight crumpled on the floor. Odd that this hulking guard would be assigned to the servant's wing. Regardless, the man and his unimaginably heavy war hammer would be causing him no trouble this evening.

Flynn entered the grand dining room. Only two gormandizers were present, seated at opposite ends of the long dining table. To his satisfaction, he spotted a goblet of wine in front of either man.

"—because you're a Godwin!" the older man climactically pounded his fist in what must have been a heated argument. This muscular father—Gerhart— sat at the far end of the table. Now noticing the intruder, he demanded: "And who the devil are you?"

Flynn considered the older man. Gray spoiled his long hair and curly beard. Despite an ungraciously aged face, Gerhart was remarkably muscular. Certainly in better shape than his fit—yet not a little imposing—son at the nearer end of the table. The son, Bastian, turned to look at Flynn. He rose quickly, unsheathing his sword. Hardly a callus on his hand.

"Guards!" Bastian yelled, stepping sideways rather than toward Flynn.

"How was the wine?" Flynn asked nonchalantly.

A confused look flashed across Bastian's face. A moment later, the sword fell from his hand as he crumpled to the ground in convulsions. Foaming at the mouth, he seized and writhed on the floor like a forgotten hose.

"Bastian," his father muttered in disbelief. The look of horror on his face was replaced by defiance as it dawned on him that he would be next. You cowardly rogue," he lambasted Flynn. "Have to kill a man with poison, hmm? Won't let a man die with a sword in his hand? Where's your honor, cur?"

Flynn took the fork and knife from Bastian's plate and cut himself a piece of cured ham. Resplendent flavors. Warm center. Funny that an old war hawk like Gerhart enjoyed such comfortable living conditions. Flynn lifted the bottle from the center of the table as if to sample the wine but caught himself before he acted. "Whoops. Ha! *That* would have been quite embarrassing," Flynn remarked, returning the bottle to the table.

"You spineless knave! I've killed thousands of filthy vermin like you on the battlefield. You insignificant whelp!" roared Gerhart.

"We'll call it a thousand-to-one ratio, then," granted Flynn.

"If I had a blade, I swear by Godwins above, I'd spend my last breath gutting you like a fish," vowed the lord.

Flynn leaned over to pick up the well-crafted sword that lay in the hand of Gerhart's fallen son. "How's this one?" he asked, hefting it to test its weight. He tossed the sword underhand to Gerhart, who caught it by the hilt.

"Godless villain, you shall die!" he bellowed, rising from his chair and charging Flynn.

Flynn stood still until Gerhart was nearly upon him. As the Godwin thrusted at his chest, he stepped through the shadows and appeared behind his opponent. He pressed the flat of his blade against the front of Gerhart's neck, signaling victory. Having won the moment, he shadow-stepped several yards ahead of Gerhart—outside the man's range but back in his line of vision.

"Was that an honor?" Flynn taunted, returning his dagger to its sheath.

"So you're no man after all... Demon..." Gerhart acknowledged in defeat, breathing laboriously. Through great determination, he locked eyes with Flynn, visibly battling to keep them focused. "I am certain of only one thing," he declared in a steely voice, "if there is a hell, I will see you in it."

Lord Gerhart Godwin began frothing at the mouth. His eyes retained their ferocity even as he crumpled to his knees. The indomitable Gerhart—Bulwark of the Blasted Lands, Hand of the King and Defender of the Realm—

met the same gruesome fate as Bastian—nephew to the king and commander-to-be of Fort Gerhart's garrison.

There would be no talk of peace after tonight.

Following these heinous acts against each other's leadership, neither king would settle for an armistice. Only total, unconditional surrender would end the vengeful crusades that would follow—and Avalon would keep the scales balanced to prevent a decisive victory. Already, they had stoked the flames for an even bigger fire, adding kindling from the four corners of the world.

To better obfuscate the scene, Flynn stripped the family sword from Gerhart's hand and returned it to Bastian's sheath. He took the bottle of wine from the table and spilled a little on the carpet. When news reached the capital, this would likely be triangulated with the rest of the deaths in the long night, laying the groundwork for conspiracy. Someone would suggest these, and likely other, unintended tragedies, were all connected. And how rumors did love to run as soon as they sprouted legs.

Flynn returned to the hallway to leave bottled evidence on the floor by the fallen guard. Regardless of how the engineered truth was interpreted here, the next head to roll would not be the last. Acts in kind would be replicated in droves through the coming years. No hero or patron would be safe from the long knife of the night. Today, it was an early end to the long tale of a retired veteran who thought he had beaten the odds.

"Another one drowns in the wave," Flynn muttered as he returned to the shadows.

XXIV. Between Life And Death

Drake

Why doesn't Tallamar ever get weather like this?"

"Doesn't it?" Drake shrugged.

Talia rested her hands on her head and took a deep breath of crisp air. She unsuccessfully attempted to whistle a wandering tune, blowing short blasts of air through her teeth.

Drake tilted his head back to stare at the sky. Intermittent cloud cover hid the sun, inviting the cool breeze at his back. His brown jacket absorbed the sun's rays whenever it reemerged, perfectly balancing his temperature while savings him from breaking a sweat.

"Maybe some people just can't whistle," Drake offered as a resolution.

"Nah. Don't believe it." Talia turned to him and redoubled her efforts, breathing a puff of tuneless air into his face.

"I'll politely ask you to refrain from doing that."

"Oh yeah?" Talia repeated her noiseless whistle, no closer to acquiring a new skill. "And what are you going to do about it?"

"I'm warning you," he raised his eyebrows.

Talia abandoned her whistling effort entirely and blew two full cheeks of air at him.

"That's it," Drake announced, staring down at her over his nose. He took an exaggerated breath and whistled a line of one of his favorite folk tunes.

"No fair!" Talia complained, frustrated with her own progress.

"I warned you," cited Drake, raising a disciplinary finger. "Now, if you want to whistle, you do it nicely. Otherwise, leave the music to me."

"You still owe me guitar lessons," she retorted.

"If you find where I hid my guitar, we can start our lessons," he said sarcastically, gesturing to the woods on either side of the road.

Talia groaned in defeat. "Hey, Drake—if this whole *wandering outlaw* bit doesn't work out, you should be a comedian."

"Yeah? Maybe you could be my opening act—if you practice."

"Oh, as if you'd take another opening act!" she laughed, incredulous.

"I don't know. Could still be a solo act," he considered.

"Please," she rolled her eyes. "You'd be lost without me. We both know that I'd be the talent, and you'd be the... muscle?"

"Manager, at least," Drake countered. "And before you go bringing up the gaming house, I'd like to remind you that getting a few lucky rolls at dice doesn't make you a business magnate."

"Magnate," Talia raised her eyes and sputtered, exaggerating surprise. "Excuse me, *professor*. Now I see your brain is as big as that word."

"People say magnate all the time," he asserted defensively.

"Keep thinking that," Talia chuckled, returning her hands to rest on top of her head. "Signs."

"What?"

"Signs," she repeated, pointing south. "Wonder where everyone is."

Drake followed her gaze to a signpost farther down the road, then reflexively scanned the area around them. They had been traveling the road alone for most of the morning since exiting the forest. He had suspected that they were passing through less-traveled backroads, but the highway was wide and well-maintained as if used to heavier traffic.

"So, where are we, and where are we going?" Talia asked, staring at the boards with her hands on her hips.

"Let's see," Drake frowned as he inspected the city names carved into the boards. "All right. So back the way we came is Highwind. Styria and Saar are north, too. We're heading toward Tidestone and the Basket. The Aollean Forest is east, and there's a cluster of nearby towns to the west. Looks like Agrinthem and Gaixia are the closest two, probably under the protection of Fort Kagrash."

"That literally means nothing to me," Talia interjected with a frown.

"Yeah," nodded Drake, "Just getting my bearings. I don't see anything that says Riverlands on here, but if we keep heading southwest, I'm sure we'll get there."

"South and west it is!" Talia proclaimed, continuing down the road.

Drake followed in her energetic footsteps, sighing to himself. He knew it was unrealistic to ask of the Taoxians, but he wished they could have found a way to bring Shelby through the forest. Granted, they weren't in any particular rush, and he didn't mind the exercise, but a horse would have easily halved their travel time.

"Road branches here," Talia called out ahead.

He leaned forward and forced himself into a jog to catch up to her, uncomfortable with the lead she was creating. Reaching her side, he looked beyond the trees to his right and saw another highway merged with this road straight ahead.

"Still south?" Talia clarified.

"Still south," answered Drake, leading her down the fork in the road.

Not ten minutes later, he heard a disturbance upwind. He stopped and looked behind them, contemplating a dash into the woods. As the rhythmic beat traveled nearer, he realized the sound was that of thundering hooves. If the riders were bandits in pursuit of them, they would likely have numbers in the forest as well. He placed a hand on Talia's shoulder to bring her to a halt, then turned north, resting a hand on the hilt of his arming sword.

Riding on a midnight horse, a knight in black and gold armor appeared on the path. Sighting the pair of travelers, he doubled his speed and raced toward them.

"Stay behind me," Drake instructed under his breath, stepping forward to the challenger.

"Citizen, please move to the side of the road," the knight called from his horse, bringing his steed to a fast stop.

"What?" Drake shouted back, not fully registering the request.

"This way, please," the golden-haired knight nudged his horse's sides, sending the animal into a trot toward the west side of the road. "A large royal column is moving south to reinforce the Basket. Please move to the side of the road, so as not to delay their advance. We thank you for your cooperation."

Drake looked at Talia, who shrugged and obediently trailed the black horse off to the side of the road. Following on high alert, he hesitantly released his grip on the sword and moved to stand between her and the mounted knight.

"I thank you for your understanding," the knight said dutifully.

"Sure," Drake mumbled. He stared down the road to the north and saw another three horses traveling south in a loose formation. Likely a scouting party. The dark-haired rider split from the others, bouncing over to Drake and the golden-haired knight.

"Citizens," the newcomer smiled tiredly. "Claude, the wheel broke on the munitions carriage. Looks like it just hit some unlucky terrain. We'll have it back up soon, but I wanted to let you know the column has stopped for now."

"They say everything happens for a reason," Claude ran a gloved hand through his golden hair.

"Sure. Maybe Deus has a twisted sense of humor and wanted a laugh."

"Thank you for that, Pierce," Claude sighed, patting the mane of his black horse. He muttered under his breath, "There's always one of them."

"What brings you boys down from the city?" Drake asked between the two soldiers.

The pair exchanged troubled looks before Pierce finally answered: "Official business."

"Right," acknowledge Drake. "Guess you've got your hands full with the Tallawyns."

"I wish we were headed to the front," lamented Claude. "We've been dispatched to support the quarantine."

"The quarantine?" inquired Talia.

"You haven't heard?" Pierce asked in earnest surprise. "A horrible curse swept across the Basket. We received word from Tidestone over a month ago that the entire city was in danger. They tried sequestering the sick in their homes, but the plague kept spreading. We lost touch with the garrison, then all the other outposts in the province. Even Lord Rheinholm and the knights."

"A curse?" asked Talia, wide-eyed.

"Oh yes," confirmed Pierce, matter-of-factly.

"No," Claude interjected, failing to dissuade Pierce from telling his tale.

"The curse is so bad, Princess Ashe had to declare a quarantine on the whole province. I got a cousin out west, you know. Stationed at Seglin Lake. He saw it himself—ain't like anything you've ever seen. They had to hold the border against these... these walking corpses—husks of humans, bones and innards on display for the world to see. They'd lost their minds, screaming and charging the bunkers all crazy-like. Because they were already dead, they couldn't be felled by normal arrows. Only fire can keep them down for good," whispered Pierce darkly.

Talia shot Drake a terrified glance. "They were cursed into zombies?"

"Yes!" exclaimed Pierce, slamming a decisive fist in his palm.

"No," Claude rolled his eyes.

"Zombies!" Pierce repeated fiercely. "Probably cursed by a Mystic to roam this world evermore, stranded between life and death."

"Pierce, you're scaring the poor girl!" admonished the blond knight. "It's possible a Mystic was involved in this strange disease, but that's all it is—a disease. These people are sick. If we give them time and keep the sickness from spreading to the rest of the continent, it'll eventually take care of itself, just like every other plague does."

"What did he mean they were already dead?" Talia asked Claude.

"He meant his cousin's a notorious liar, and he wanted to try out a new ghost story," Claude shot his compatriot a warning look. "But I won't downplay the sickness—the southern border's closed for a reason, and it's going to stay that way for the foreseeable future."

"Or until Princess Ashe orders the purge," suggested Pierce.

"Pierce!" Claude scolded him. He looked at Talia and attempted to assuage the potentially traumatic experience. "There's no such thing as undead roaming the earth, all right? The sadder truth is there are a lot of starving and desperate people trying anything they can to get out. Unfortunately, it's our duty to the kingdom to keep them from spreading the illness. Deus knows we have enough of that already."

A horn sounded up the road to the north. Claude wheeled his horse around and raised a hand to bid farewell. "Safe travels."

Drake raised a hand in return.

Before Pierce rode away, he issued one final warning to Talia: "Look, kid. I don't know if there are undead or not, but what my cousin saw... they weren't people anymore. Bodies falling apart, riddled with sores and legions, frothing at the mouth, these howling terrors tore men's flesh from their bones with teeth and nails... even death rejected them. They were stuck in a perpetual state of dying, completely out of their minds, but no arrow to the neck or blade to the gut could kill the demons. Doesn't matter if it's a disease or a curse—you best stay away from the south."

The Godwin soldier rode away, leaving a cloud of dust in his wake. Drake glared at the back of his round head, seething with anger at the fear he had likely sowed in Talia.

"So, change of plans to avoid the zombies?" she suggested.

"There are no zombies," Drake growled, looking around the highway. He decided on northwest, in the direction of Gaixia. "Whenever people make up these wild stories, it's never firsthand sightings. It's always their cousin, or a friend, or a pet raccoon. Blondie had the right idea; the other guy's full of it."

"And the whole *rotting-skeleton-people-who-can't-die* thing?"

"If any of it is true, and that's a big if, they're probably just starving, desperate people willing to risk their lives to break out of the lockdown. Sounds like worse might be coming their way yet—can't blame them for doing their best to survive."

"You don't think it's possible at all? Not even if a Mystic's involved?"

"What, you think there's some kind of *Primal of Skeletons?*" Drake asked, heavy on the sarcasm.

Linthal, Primal of the After, Pyros supplied helpfully.

Did I ask you? Drake shot back irritably.

I do not believe Linthal was involved in this knight's tale, elucidated Pyros diplomatically.

"I guess not," laughed Talia. "He really had me going there."

"The real horror story's going to be crossing the Lowlands. I hear some parts are better than others, but last thing I want is to get stuck in a swamp," griped Drake.

"Doesn't look that swampy to me," Talia observed, looking at the forest to the west.

"We're not in the thick of it yet," Drake explained. "We still got a ways to go. Whatever the map says, we're basically still in the Foothills. You'll know the real Lowlands when we get there."

"You always know how to cheer me up," Talia grinned slyly.

In the following hours, Drake learned Agrinthem was not a city at all. Rather, it was a sprawling village with homesteads sporadically spaced out along a narrow dirt road. The path was eerily quiet, though certainly not abandoned. Unsmiling residents sat on their porches, resting pitchforks and bats against their rocking chairs. Some drank, some smoked, and others just stared as if looking into a world beyond.

Even the trees were subdued here, packed tightly behind the houses and kneeling at gloomy angles. Faded orange leaves littered the ground around their trunks. Throughout the woods on either side, patches of white broke up the black bark, as if the land itself was sick.

"This place is creepy," Talia judged out of the side of her mouth.

As she stared at a burly, shirtless man drinking moonshine from a jug, she stepped in a puddle, kicking up spatters of cold mud onto Drake's pants.

"Sorry."

"It's fine," Drake said through his teeth, feeling an unpleasant tingle run down his neck.

Ahead, the path sloped upward and made a sharp turn west. If not for the weathered sign at the beginning of the road, *Now Entering Agrinthem,* he wouldn't have so boldly ventured this way. It looked and felt like a pathway to nowhere, a detour into the forgotten fringe of society. He wondered if it had always been so stark and desolate. Maybe something had changed.

"Drake!" Talia whispered sharply.

Drake lifted his eyes, gazing ten yards ahead to the top of the slope. A pallid old man was shuffling his feet toward them, carefully picking his way down the slope. Sunspots marked the top of his balding head. Deep bags had accumulated beneath his sunken eyes. He crept forward with a stooped back, trembling as he inched down the path.

"We can squeeze by him on the left," Drake figured tactically.

The stranger teetered, losing his balance as his toe clipped a jagged rock. Unable to recover, the man spilled forward. His extended arms failed to stop his fall. Tumbling end over end, he crashed down the uneven path. His face splashed into a shallow puddle, and his withered body came to a stop.

Talia shrieked. "Are you okay?" she rushed forward to his aide.

"Talia, don't—" Drake ordered ineffectively, reaching a hand through the air where she once stood.

She knelt in front of the fallen man and placed her hands under his shoulders, lifting as well as she could. Grabbing onto her, he managed to return to his knees, his filthy face dripping with dirty water.

"Are you okay?" Talia asked, still supporting the shaken man.

He leaned forward, lips moving without forming any words. Suddenly, his eyes widened as a ragged cough conquered his body. The man toppled over sideways, shivering, but with his head out of water.

"Talia, leave him. One of his neighbors will come," ordered Drake.

She stood and turned, wiping a sleeve across her cheek and mouth. Drake noticed droplets of blood on her forehead and temple. Instinctively, he reached out to pull her closer. "What happened? Are you all right?" he asked, fretfully inspecting the wound.

She used her sleeve to wipe away the last of the blood. "I'm fine," she said stiffly. "It's not mine. Is he... is he dead?"

Drake studied the left side of her face carefully, still searching for a wound. As he began to register that she was all right, save for her quivering lip, he allowed his eyes to inspect the fallen man.

The wilted wanderer was shivering in the dirt. Drake gently nudged Talia forward, creating a pocket of space between her and the old man. He was alive, but his condition was not encouraging. "He'll live. We're not doctors, and these aren't our people—let one of them take it from here."

"I didn't mean to ignore you," Talia said wearily as she allowed Drake to lead her up the slope. "I know he could've been dangerous, and it could've been a trap—I didn't mean to ignore you. It's just... my body acted before I could think. I had to help him."

Risking a look over his shoulder at the motionless man, Drake sighed, finding the task of breaking through her compassionate disposition... difficult. "You're okay, so it's okay. What's done is done."

"Was it really the wrong thing to do?" Talia faltered.

"I think so," Drake answered heavily. "You said it yourself."

"It's so hard," Talia crossed her arms tightly across her chest. "Like, I get it. It's not our place to fix the world... but little stuff like that? I don't know. That just felt like what any decent person would do. Felt like what any person would do."

"Decent people don't tend to live long out here," Drake said grimly. "Being old doesn't make him decent. Taking care of ourselves doesn't make us bad people. It just makes us all survivors."

"Can't we be more than survivors?" Talia turned to Drake, a familiar glimmer of hope in her eyes. "We don't have to go out of our way to help everybody, but can't we try to be people? People who help old men up when they've fallen, who can talk to soldiers without killing them... you know?"

Drake gritted his teeth, bitter they had to revisit this topic and doubly bitter he needed to make a concession to rein in her impulsive altruism. "Talia, protecting you will always be my one and only concern. Promise to let me do that. Whenever you feel we need to take a risk out here, ask me. If you're going to keep charging in anyway, I'd rather you let me handle anything dangerous."

"Including helping up old men?" Talia joked facetiously.

"Especially helping up old men," Drake maintained firmly.

"I guess that's the best I'll get from you," acknowledged Talia. "All right. We have a deal. If I feel someone needs help, you'll help them unless they've obviously trying to kill us."

"I don't know if that's exactly the agreement we reached here," Drake raised his hands to slow her down. "But we'll give it a try. Don't let it go to your head—normal rules still apply. I'm trusting you."

"And I'll trust you," Talia smiled. They rounded the corner without any further discourse about the forgotten man.

Midway through the winding community, they passed a small hamlet with a couple dozen buildings. In the cul-de-sac between houses stood a thin, brown wagon with tall walls. A blanket was draped over the top, ineffectively shielding the cargo from a pestilence of flies.

Standing beside the cart, dressed in a black overcoat with matching hat and gloves, a grim watcher observed their westward journey through the village. The figure stood motionless, its face concealed by a strange, beaked mask. Its white nose hooked downward, resembling a bird and matching the tip of the cane that rested at its side. The bizarrely dressed local tilted its head, sizing Drake up through glass eyes.

Somewhere deep in the trees, a lone raven cawed to its foreboding lookalike. Drake faced the dark stranger, pausing expectantly for him to caw back to his flock.

Only silence answered the raven's grave call.

XXV. Star-Nosed Mole

Allen Lee

*E*qually surprising after all these years was the serenity of her temple.

While rumors of the sunken temple's existence are widely circulated and a not-insignificant number of pilgrims embark each year in search of her counsel, I encountered just seven others on their journeys to enlightenment, only two of whom reached their final destination. In the week I spent at the temple proper, I saw none but her and her disciples.

I postulate a myriad of factors keeps her storied seat hidden from the world, though I cannot fathom why the king does not exert his influence to control her boons of vision. A number of imposters and decoys in the north lead the simple astray, including the gaudy shop-and-shrine overlooking the Fourth Serpent. Farther down the river, far shabbier establishments sell trinkets and promise clairvoyance, but one would assume any pilgrims continuing this way should be capable of discerning fact from fiction.

To the south, beyond the imposing cliff, an impenetrable bulwark of vegetation divides the temple from the great sea. The western approach, though more challenging than the way from the north, appears to be the path least traveled. I encountered none who attempted those forgotten swamplands, but one remarkably unclean gentleman living in a shanty on the fringe informed me the zone was known as the 'Blackwater'.

The eastern approach, which my initial notes had erroneously labeled as the Blackwater, is a ghastly swamp. The insects were dreadful, gargantuan *apex predators roamed the murky waters, and the sparse islands of land in the mangroves threatened to submerge you under the earth while you slept.*

That I, a mere cartographer and explorer, have survived to record my experiences in this volume, should suffice evidence enough that the Lowlands are a legitimate, albeit hostile, realm for exploration. Having fully documented my encounters with the seer, I'll next set out to explore the Blackwater. Should I fail to produce a fourth volume by the next summer solstice, ninth of King Alarak's rule, I urge my devoted readers thus: boldly continue my foolhardy exploration, or burn down the Blackwater and name a gift shop in my honor.

Allen closed the book and inspected the titles on the shelf, moving his finger along the spines. He spotted volumes one and two by the same author, *D. Mantefour*, but the green-backed tomes appeared to have concluded with this third edition.

"Poor guy," commiserated Allen, tapping the cover of the book. He looked over his left shoulder, then his right. Spotting a poorly concealed black hood around a neighboring corner, he raised his hand, waved, and said in an outdoor voice: "Excuse me?"

Realizing he had been discovered, the lurking page rounded the corner and presented himself to Allen. He was a tall, lanky man with a crooked nose and remarkably pointy chin. "Yes?" he croaked.

"Do you know if there's a fourth volume?" Allen tapped the cover of the green book.

"Mantefour? No. He published three nonfictions and a compendium of maps. He also wrote a collection of youth fantasy books before he devoted himself to full-time exploration. Are you interested in reading those?" the page cocked a judgmental eyebrow.

"No, thanks," Allen returned the book to the shelf, appropriately slotting it in beside the second volume.

Since his last meeting with Virgil, any motivation to work had waned. He passed the days wandering the library aimlessly, stopping at random to skim books from the eclectic collection for hours at a time. Increasingly, he found himself drawn to the historical nonfiction and mythology sections of the library, finding a sort of catharsis in letting his mind roam far away from the present.

It might have been a figment of anxious imagination, but he felt the other students were giving him a wider berth than they had in the past. Despite their shared outing, Karim never seemed to be around or looking to converse either. His only conversations were book-related inquiries of the pages, one of whom always seemed to be lurking over his shoulder, keeping an eye on him.

His paranoia was well-founded in this last regard. He suspected Cato had commanded them to ensure he didn't return to the forbidden section. The dedicated chaperones felt superfluous, though, considering they now had a full-time watcher stationed at the front of the restricted area.

He had roamed past the section thrice. Each time, a black-robed sentry blocked the aisle, sat comfortably on a wooden stool. Twice, he had seen the same burly guard with a stature like Cato's; the other time, late in the night, a much shorter, wiry man occupied the stool. He wondered whether the guards were a consequence of his unauthorized expedition, or whether one had simply missed his watch leading up to the initial episode.

Sighing, Allen listlessly ambled down the aisle, no destination in mind.

Deflated, he stopped to lean against a bookshelf. *I wonder how she's doing.*

When Meghana had set off to the Lowlands, he knew she wouldn't be back by supper. Still, this time apart felt longer and longer with each passing day. In hindsight, he wished he would've lobbied harder to accompany her as an assistant. Despite the hoard of literature and entertainment at his fingertips, he couldn't bring himself to enjoy any of it.

The separation anxiety was crushing him, as was the pronounced loneliness. He had no one with whom he could share jokes or stories, discuss his prolific fears and concerns, or even admire a nice day's weather. Even a passing "hello" on her busier days had been enough to anchor him. Enough to abate his gnawing doubts and remind him that he wasn't alone in the void.

Now, with Meghana gone indefinitely, no way to message her, and no one else to turn to, The Library on El Aria no longer felt like a candidate for home. In turn, Allen withdrew into himself, avoiding lunches with the other disciples and shuttering himself away in library's deepest, quietest rows. He lived in the hollow memories of better times—alternating between two worlds, two fantasies, that couldn't be made real. In one, he was still an unremarkable starfish researcher. His beautiful wife, baby girl, older brother, and best friend were gathered around the dinner table for the holidays. In another, he accepted this stranded reality, but he had Meghana by his side to restore light to the darkest days.

Instead, he was alone.

Emotion stirred within his numbness. Allen condemned his lower lip for quivering. Adjusting his glasses, he raised a knuckle to the corner of his eye, wiped, and took a deep breath to bring him back to his stable ennui.

He meandered onward, scanning the bookshelves unmethodically for something to jump out at him. At the end of the dim aisle, a black-robed man rounded the corner and crashed into him, knocking him flat on his back.

"Ow!" voiced Allen, certain he had bruised his shoulder in the fall.

The cowled page extended a hand toward him. He met the hand and allowed the man to help him to his feet.

As the page rushed down the aisle to the left, Allen became aware of a dry material in his hand. Stepping around the corner in the opposite direction of the human whirlwind, Allen cautiously uncurled his fingers, revealing a slip of paper.

Zoology section. Treatise on Star-nosed Moles. 5 minutes.

Allen crumpled the piece of paper in his palm and subtly ejected the ball into a bookshelf. He paused at the intersection, waiting for his shadow. As the page came around the corner, Allen stepped forward to greet him, giving the lanky man quite the fright. "Can you lead me to the zoology section? I want to read about subterranean rodents."

"I... I would like you to know I was top of my class at the world's most prestigious university before coming here," the page straightened his shoulders importantly. He closed his eyes, huffed, then said, "Right this way."

After leading Allen through an impossible labyrinth of shelves, the page folded his arms across his chest and came to a halt. "This is the zoology section. This long aisle and the next six over to your right cover rodents. Everything from gophers to ground squirrels to prairie dogs—it all lives here."

"You know, not everyone knows prairie dogs are rodents. I can tell you were top of your class," Allen remarked cheerily, smiling to conceal the passive-aggressive dig.

The page exhaled a puff of air through his nose and leaned against the wooden corner of the bookshelf, arms crossed. He didn't dignify the comment with a response.

Allen started down the aisle, keeping an eye out for the star-nosed mole. He passed water voles, marmots, and beavers, but he couldn't find any rodents with a star nose.

At the next break in the shelves, he veered to the right, moving perpendicular to his initial path. He considered going row by row to look for the star-nosed mole, but the note's aggressive time constraint pushed him to understand the clue as a matter of positioning rather than atemporal content within a book.

Advancing to the seventh and final row of rodent erudition, he began his exploration of the deserted aisle, scanning the shelf to his left. Blind moles, coast moles, long-tailed moles, shrew moles... finally, he found the short section on star-nosed moles. At eye-level, in a massive encyclopedia five inches wide at the spine, he found the treatise.

Pulling the treatise free from the shelf, he uncovered a pair of nostrils intruding from the next aisle over. He almost stumbled backward as the nostrils lowered, revealing two peering eyes through the gap he had created.

"Pull yourself together, Doctor Lee!" a stern voice whispered through the books.

Allen looked over his shoulder and saw the gangly stalker round the distant corner, leaning against the shelves in preparation for several hours of silently watching another grown man read about rodents.

Composing himself, Allen turned away from the bored guardian and opened his encyclopedia, pretending to start from chapter one. He couldn't help but look through the hole as he whispered: "Samson?"

"Eyes on the book. Yes, it's me," instructed the voice in the shelf.

"Where have you been? What are you doing here?" Allen whispered back, turning his eyes to the page in front of him but reading nothing. His heart was racing. He didn't think he'd ever see the sergeant again.

"I've been sunbathing by the lake and developing a passion for origami. What do you think I've been doing?" hissed Samson.

"Really?" Allen asked despite himself.

"No, not really!" Exasperation loudened the soldier's voice. "I've been running over hell's half acre trying to figure out what's going on around here. Figured I'd try to stay alive while I'm at it."

"That's right—I remember hearing you disappeared from the barracks. It's been months since anyone's seen you; how did you survive all this time?"

"Set up a little camp in the desert. They've got jackrabbits and cactus galore out there. Also got these pink succulents that'll give you diarrhea so bad you could evacuate through a needle. Lesson of the day: always bring a second pair of trousers to extraterrestrial expeditions."

"I have so many questions," Allen disclosed, unsure where to start.

"The spare pair's in case you blow through the first," Samson sniffed. "You know, soiling yourself. In a hypothetical desert. Allegedly."

"That's... not exactly what I meant, but I'm honored that you feel comfortable enough to share that with me," Allen offered supportively.

"Save it for sensitivity training, Doctor Lee. This ain't a social outing. We got a lot of fat to chew and only your granny's dollar-store dentures for the job," snapped Samson.

"Sorry, sorry," Allen apologized. Having little idea of what that outburst was supposed to mean but a fair read of the tone, he added, "I've got some matters I'd like to discuss with you as well."

"First things first—who's still alive? Just you and Ajax Sykes, correct?" Samson triaged.

"Correct. Chip Hamal might be as well, but he's been taken to the infirmary," Allen noted.

"No Hamal in the infirmary," reported Samson. "So you and Sykes managed to live, and everyone else conveniently died."

"I—" Allen stuttered, aghast at the insinuation. "I'd never do anything to betray the team! I'd never hurt anyone!"

"I know," reassured Samson. "Fragile little bookworm like you, doc? Wouldn't have it in you. Sykes, on the other hand... He's about as crooked as a dog's hind leg."

"I saw him in the library the other day," Allen reflected. "Soldiers aren't supposed to be allowed inside, but he was upstairs meeting with Virgil. Hey, speaking of—how'd you get those robes? Are you all allowed in, now?"

"Never mind that," Samson laughed guiltily. "Poor sonny was shaking like a dog shitting peach pits."

"Pardon?" Allen asked, unsure whether he had heard that correctly.

"Nothing. I'd advise you don't ask Sykes to hold your rifle while you're taking a leak, is all. Speaking of, you got any pockets in that dress of yours?"

"My robe?" Allen subconsciously placed a hand against the cloth. "Sort of. On the inside. It's not great for holding things."

"I'm going to slide you my pistol. Sling the holster under your robe and over your shoulder when the coast is clear," Samson instructed.

Allen saw the barrel of a gun enter the slot and slither toward him. "What? No!" Allen stammered, raising his voice a little higher than intended. He put a hand against the slot, gently shoving the gun back in, worried it would go off into his hand. "I don't know how to use one of those things!"

"Point and click. Boom. Dead," Samson explained. "Preceding that, flip down the lever on the left side of the gun to disable safety. Then point, click... You get it."

"I don't need one of those!" exclaimed Allen, deliberately keeping his voice in check.

"Sure you do," persuaded Samson, persistently butting its barrel against his hand. "Everyone needs a gun."

"What would I even do with it?" Allen shook his head. "I'd never be able to use it on someone."

Sam relented and pulled the gun back through the slot. "I won't say I'm mad, but I am disappointed."

"I'm sorry," Allen apologized needlessly. "You said there was a lot to talk about. Did you get back in contact with Echo? Is it about the mission?"

"No word from Echo. I'm typically not one to give up on the mission, Allen, but it's time I admit the torch isn't ours to carry anymore."

"Sam?"

"Your subject friend there—Virgil—did he ever say anything about rebuilding the portal? What's the status on our return flight?"

"Yeah. He said he was building it out in the desert. He figured out the technology but hasn't been able to get all the materials together for it. I'm hopeful in the next few months or years we'll get to go back home," wished Allen, closing his eyes.

"Flip the page."

"What?"

"You've been staring at the same 'chapter one' page for five minutes. Flip the page so it looks like you're reading," suggested Samson.

"Oh," Allen obeyed, flipping to a hand-drawn sketch of the star-nosed mole. "I mean, but it's good news, right? Virgil has been trying to help us, and he's figured out the theoretical part. We just have to wait for him to scale up the technology, and we'll be home. You have people waiting for you too. Don't you?"

"Even better: I've got a fulfilling sense of patriotism and duty to country awaiting postcards from my vacation. Sooner we can find a mailbox, the better," quipped Samson. A strange note crept into his final words. "You said he was building it in the desert? That he told you he figured out how?"

"That's right," confirmed Allen.

"How long ago?" pressed Samson.

"I don't know—few days? A week, maybe?" Allen answered.

"I knew it," Samson muttered under his breath. "He's all hat and no cattle, Allen. I can't put my finger on why, but I'm damn sure we've paid the theme-park fare and been taken on a ride."

"What? That's impossible. I just told you about the great progress he led," defended Allen, taking the slight personally.

"I saw the facility—in the desert. I was there."

A chill ran down Allen's neck. He sensed Samson was about to tell him something he didn't want to hear. Something he *couldn't* hear. "And? What did it look like inside?"

"I never got inside," Allen could hear the concentrated frown in Sam's words. "But I staked it out, watched them coming and going from the outside. I thought it was off, them putting this huge warehouse in the middle of nowhere. One day, a big caravan rolls through, overflowing with chunks of metal. It was the bones of our transporter."

"So? Isn't that just proof he's a man of his word?"

"Negative. It's proof he's hiding something," asserted Samson. "Just over a week ago, the carts started going the other way. They tore down the facility—there's nothing left but sand."

"That's... I can't believe, it. Maybe they had to relocate it to keep it safe?" conceived Allen.

"Think, Allen. Is there anything he's done that made you wonder if he's really being strait-laced with us?"

"The restricted area," Allen mumbled to himself. "The forbidden section of the library."

"That sounds like the sort of thing you'd want to start a conversation with, in the future," speculated Samson.

Unfazed, Allen elaborated: "Deep in the library, there are some aisles I'm not allowed to enter. I snuck in once and found a hidden stairway. There were screams coming from deep below ground, but I got caught before I could investigate. Virgil said there's a hospital down there. They cure people of rare illnesses in secret so that the sheikh doesn't put a stop to their treatments."

"The hell have we gotten ourselves into..."

"Pardon?" entreated Allen.

"Let me get this straight. He said he's set up a full-scale hospital hidden inside a mountain, accessed via trap door, of course, and it's hidden because the sheikh doesn't like hospitals... and you're buying that?"

"His reasoning was more that the sheikh would be worried about accumulating exotic diseases within his borders," corrected Allen.

"All right, I'll bite. Riddle me this: if this hospital is such a well-kept secret, how do sick people from across the world know to come here? Where's the check-in desk, and how haven't any of the guards—"

Allen interrupted the questioning with a cough that threatened to burst his ribs through his chest. Blood splattered on the hand-drawn picture of the star-nosed mole, contributing a gruesome surprise for future readers. Dropping the book, he sunk to his knees and planted his palms into the carpet, coughing directly onto the dark floor. He attempted to bring his elbow to his mouth but couldn't muster the strength to keep upright without support.

The episode passed with one last hack, leaving Allen winded. He closed his eyes for a moment as a shudder flowed through his body.

"Great Caesar's Ghost! Finished your exorcism over there?" Samson asked with touching empathy.

"Just a little cough," Allen minimized, returning to his feet with the aid of the bookshelf's sturdy support. He retrieved the fallen black tome from the ground and flipped to a clean page in the middle of the book, fearing his flimsy ruse would soon be shattered.

"I have *just a little* problem with my credit," Samson said sarcastically. "Well, now that we've established you're alive and I'm financially sound, I'll state the obvious: we need to see what they're hiding underground."

"What could it possibly be, besides a hospital?" demanded Allen. "It's not like they're hiding a nuclear arsenal below. Besides, we're not allowed in the restricted section. I'm on thin ice, and if we get caught... I think that'd be the end of the mission. We'd never get another chance to go back home."

"As an enlisted sergeant, I tend to agree with you," conceded Samson. "However, as a God-fearing man who's seen more than his fair share of war... As a man with what might be one last chance to do something good for the meek and innocent among us, I have no choice but to insist we take a chance."

"What do you think is really down there?" Allen whispered, struck by his dutiful words.

"I hope I'm wrong," Samson offered in a non-answer, "but we have to know for sure. It's up to us. Now, I'm going to see this so-called hospital with my own eyes. Are you with me?"

Allen deflected, unable to say no, but uncomfortable with saying yes. "They assigned a guard to stand watch over the restricted section. We won't be able to walk in like last time."

"Does this guard have a pistol?" Samson questioned rhetorically. "Or a rifle? Years of perfectly-honed combat instinct and a side of raw masculinity—channeled into an unstoppable weapon of justice-serving ass-whoopery?"

"Well, no," Allen fumbled awkwardly, "but you can't just kill him. He's just an apprentice."

"They've only got one guard watching the restricted section? What, are these the same guys running security at self-checkouts?"

"I only saw one at a time on duty, but they have at least two rotating guards," Allen answered the first question directly. "The one guy's built like a mountain, but the night shift doesn't look so tough. I'm not sure about their relevant experience in retail sales."

"Never mind that. Listen, if we can't cut the mustard, we'll just have to lick the jar. Let me come up with a plan to get around the guard. On the night of the symposium, meet me at midnight in the modern symphony composition section—it's time for somebody around here to face the music."

XXVI. The Price Of Mercy

Drake

Hear that?" Talia asked, turning to him for confirmation.

"Yeah," he said, gazing above the trees to the dark clouds approaching overhead. Light flickered across the sky, followed a long moment later by a muffled grumble of thunder. The rain had not yet reached them, but he could feel the falling air pressure by the stiffness in his joints and the sweet, crisp air flowing into his nose.

"Gaixia," Talia gestured to a weathered sign. "Think they have an inn?"

"Worth a look."

The road was wider here than in Agrinthem, but no less chaotic and winding. Sparser tree cover lined the path. That meant more sweating under the sun, but less feeling like the jaws of the forest were closing around them. Wooden houses made a pretense of community—freestanding, but consistently within a stone's throw of their neighbors. A few chimneys coughed up smoke. Other gloomy homes showed no signs of inhabitance. The couple haggard residents Drake encountered gave him a wide berth, eyeing him warily as they circumvented the unfamiliar pair in off-road arcs.

"Is that town center?" Talia pointed at the forking path on their right.

"Perhaps," nodded Drake. The road widened at the top of the hill. "Doesn't look like much going on."

Ascending the gentle slope, they reached a cluster of twenty tightly packed houses around a cul-de-sac. No locals sat on the porches to receive them; in fact, there was no sign anyone still lived here at all. No light reached the street from indoors, no smoke rose from the buildings, and no children played in the yards. Among this collection of run-down shacks, like the hovels before, there were no placards to welcome weary travelers.

"Anything?" yawned Talia.

A raindrop hit Drake's neck, sending a shiver down his spine. Another landed on his head, then his arm, then his cheek.

"Well," he considered as isolated drops turned into a light drizzle. "No inn, but some of these houses look abandoned. I don't think anyone would mind if we squat here for one night."

Drake approached the third dingy house on the left, noting its state of disrepair as further evidence it was unoccupied. The wooden exterior was aged and warped. Planks showed uneven weathering. Moss grew on the tiles of the pitched roof, thriving in some patches and dying in others. Most windows were boarded up, but the nearer set of busted windowpanes was accessible. Carefully minding his step, he made his way over to peer inside.

Ambient twilight illuminated only a dusty floor beyond the window. "Anyone home?" Drake called into the gloom.

He respectfully waited an extra second for a response that didn't come.

"I'll try the door," offered Talia.

"Careful," Drake warned vigilantly. "Splinters and glass and all."

"I got it," Talia reassured him. She shouldered the door to no avail. "Locked."

"Hang on," Drake ordered, turning back to the window. He drew his knife and reversed his grip, using the hilt to punch out the remaining panes. With his free hand, he conjured an orb of fire in his palm for visibility. Holding the makeshift torch inside, he returned his knife to its sheath, climbed onto the window frame, and cautiously lowered his boots onto the pile of shattered glass. Holding the light in front of him, he willed the fiery orb to expand, spilling its unfocused glow onto the walls of the single-room cottage.

A broken bedframe rested in the corner of the room behind a simple, square table. The right third of the floor was sunken a foot lower than the rest and featured an inactive fireplace. Inside, a primitive tripod supported an iron pot, presumably once used for cooking. In the corner opposite him, a pile of burlap sacks rested in front of an old wardrobe.

"How's it look?" Talia called after him.

"Empty," he called back, turning to the door. "One sec—"

271

He disengaged the latch, then swung the door open. Talia flowed in with an air of faux excitement.

"Wow, Drake! I love what you've done with the place. This must have cost a fortune!"

"Make yourself at home." He shut the door and replaced the latch.

"Kind of cold," Talia shivered, dropping her backpack and detaching the bedroll.

"I'll get a fire going. Let me see if there are any blankets in the back," Drake proposed, crossing the bare floor to the wardrobe. He stopped midway across the room, hearing a faint rustle from the corner. "You hear that?"

"What is it?" Talia peered around his shoulder.

Drake drew his sword and advanced slowly. He stopped a foot away from the nearest sack and waited for the sound to repeat.

The bag behind the one closest to his foot twitched, making a *swish* sound as it settled. Crouching, Drake stroked his hand down the length of his blade, transferring the flame to his weapon. Palm extinguished, he reached out his left hand and flung the weighty sack forward as he retreated a step.

Soaring out of the bag, a gray blur shot toward him, baring long fangs below its black mask. He swung his burning sword through the air, missing his assailant but thwarting the attack.

The ring-tailed rodent made a cross chittering noise as it retreated from the light. Circling the room, the critter scurried over to the broken window and vaulted through, disappearing into the gathering rainstorm.

"Raccoon," Drake reported, defusing the alarm.

"Aw. It was kind of cute," chittered Talia, wrapping her arms around herself for warmth.

After a cursory look to ensure the raccoon didn't have any friends, Drake crossed the room to lay a log in the fireplace. He held the tip of his sword against the dry wood, willing the flame to crawl off the blade and onto the kindling. Sheathing his sword, he returned to the wardrobe once more.

Inside the wardrobe was an unremarkable collection of drab clothing. Frayed, old rope was coiled at the bottom. No blankets or other valuables remained, if any had once been there. The sacks contained an abundance of white flour. They were fortunate to have found dry shelter for the evening, but there was little else to salvage from this bare-bones home.

"Set your bed by the fire if you're still feeling cold," advised Drake.

Talia obediently dragged her bed a few feet over, then wrapped herself in its cocoon.

He knelt beside her and raised a hand to her forehead. It felt warm to the touch. Frowning, he retrieved her waterskin from the bag and placed it on her chest. "Keep hydrated. You might be coming down with something."

"I'm tired," Talia propped herself up to take a sip.

Drake returned to the cabinet to cut off a pantleg. Crossing the floor to the open window, he held the garment outside, allowing the cool rain to soak the linen. Finally, he returned to Talia's side, folded the wet cloth, and laid it on her forehead.

"That should help to keep your head cool. Get some rest. They say sleep's the best medicine."

"Kay," she said with a trusting smile, letting her eyes close.

Listening to the rain crash on the rattling roof of their temporary home, Drake scanned the room again to reassure himself that no additional intruders lurked in wait. He slowly walked over to the broken window and stared out into the turbulent night. A violent wind whipped the side of the house, punctuated by occasional flashes of light above the muted town.

Positioning himself with his back to the door, Drake slid to a seated position. Talia breathed deeply beside the crackling fire, perhaps already in the throes of sleep. After another long day on the march, she deserved some rest.

Leaning back his head, he closed his eyes and allowed the heavy rain from the raging storm outside to lull him to a dreamless sleep.

After what felt like only minutes later, a disconcerting noise roused him from his slumber. He bolted upright, eyes snapping open. Freezing in place, he attuned himself to his surroundings.

The ambient light filtering in from outside was still dim but heralded a coming sunrise. No rain hammered the roof or exterior walls, suggesting the storm had passed. Crackling no longer, the log in the fireplace had burned to cinders. Through the uncanny stillness, he listened carefully, trying to identify what had risen him from sleep.

A gargled sputter broke the silence, originating from near the fireplace.

Drake leaped to his feet and flew across the room, appearing at Talia's side in an instant. The resting embers burst to life as he raised a hand toward the fireplace, casting the room in a yellow glow.

Talia sputtered again, blood pooling in her mouth and overflowing onto the floorboards. He hastily rolled her onto her side, allowing the blood to spill out and flow free of her airway.

She gasped and gagged as she struggled to draw breath, invoking a wet cough that shook her clammy body.

"Talia! Hey, are you okay?" Drake stammered frantically, patting her back in an attempt to help her breathe. He placed a hand against her forehead and recoiled instinctively, then returned his hand to confirm his initial fear. She was burning up.

Talia moaned faintly, unable to form words through her agony. Her eyes did not open.

Drake squeezed her cold hand, desperately searching the room for an answer as the dying embers settled in the hearth. "Hang in there, kiddo. It's all going to be okay. Just a nasty little bug, that's all."

With Talia resting safely on her side, he retrieved the scrap of cloth that had fallen off in the night and doused it with water from his flask. Tossing his own aside, he grabbed her canteen and gently lifted her to a seated position, holding the water up to her lips. She managed three small sips and raised a hand to feebly swat away the drink before erupting into another coughing fit.

He laid her back down on her side and held the cold cloth against her forehead, feverishly searching the room for answers. The fading embers fed off his growing panic, glowing brighter as he felt his own temperature rising.

What should we do?

He ran a hand over her forehead. Fear and futility melded into an intolerable pit in his stomach. Closing his eyes, he racked his brain for ideas. Sickness was one enemy he couldn't battle in her stead, as much as he wished he could. Hopelessness weighed on him. He flipped the cloth over to its cooler side, sniffling as his worry swelled.

"Drake..." Talia murmured unintelligibly. "It's so... cold."

Beads of sweat ran down her nose. Her body shivered uncontrollably.

Anger mingling with dread, Drake repeated the question to Pyros, demanding an answer. *What should we do?*

This sickness is not one I know, rumbled Pyros gravely. *She battles for her life against a dire disease. This blood plague will likely overcome her.*

Not an option. How do we help her? Drake bit his lip in frustration, unaware of the blood he drew.

The dying man in Agrinthem—he, too, must have borne this pestilence. Perhaps the beak-masked doctor has answers. Without medicine, she will die.

Drake rose from his knees and added a fresh log to the fire. Doing what little he could to ensure Talia would be all right for the next couple hours, he slid the canteen under her hand and placed a bag behind her to prevent her from rolling onto her back.

"I'm going into town to look for medicine. Keep resting on your side. Drink water when you can. I'll be back soon—I promise," Drake said softly, unsure whether Talia heard his words.

He didn't want to leave her side, but he knew she was in no condition to travel. If Pyros was right, his only option was to find a doctor. Agrinthem was already too far away, but if a single soul in Gaixia studied medicine, he would do everything in his power to find them.

Drake climbed through the window into dawn's early light, nearly stumbling over an unexpected visitor as he landed on the grass outside.

The filthy boy tooling around in the mud raised his head, causing the long hair of his bowl cut to flop out of his face. "Hullo, mister," he greeted with a minor lisp.

"Kid," Drake muttered distractedly, feeling a kink in his neck.

The boy had a small, green bucket full of writhing worms. Sticking a finger in his mouth, he cocked his head sideways. "I'm not—I'm not s'posed to talk to strangers," the boy stuttered slowly. "What's your name?"

"Look, I don't have time to chat, all right? I need to find a doctor. Or an apothecary," he dismissed the child.

"I know where to find the doct-ler," the boy boasted in a singsong voice. "But I'm not s'posed to talk to strangers."

Drake raised an eyebrow, attempting to size up whether the kid was wasting his time. "Desmond." He had meant to give the boy a fake name but surprised himself when that particular one popped out of his mouth. The knot in his stomach tightened as he tried to keep his mind from tearing into itself.

"Hi Desmond," the boy grinned. "I'm Jack."

"Great. Show me where the doctor is, Jack?" Drake asked through gritted teeth in as friendly of a voice as he could muster.

"I'm digging worms. Do you see all the worms I found? See how—see how big they are?"

"The doctor, Jack," snapped Drake. "Worms can wait. Tell me where I can find the doctor."

"Um," frowning thoughtfully, Jack returned his finger to his mouth. "I don't rem'ber."

A malevolent fury awoke within Drake, but Pyros unexpectedly urged him to stay cool. He closed his eyes and exhaled a long breath out his nose, balling his hands into fists.

"But Adam knows. My brother knows everything."

"Let's go find your brother then, hmm?" prompted Drake.

"Okie," said Jack, reaching for his hand.

Drake swatted the little paw away and instead suggested: "Let's race. First one to find your brother wins!"

"Okay, Desmond! Ready? Set?"

The boy took off running down the hill, moving as fast as his little legs would take him but in no way a match for Drake's long strides. Down a winding road to the right, he followed Jack to a freestanding building with a forge and anvil under a stone roof outside. He passed by just three people along the way.

"I win!" declared Jack, turning to face Drake. He stumbled over his own feet and toppled to the soft ground, further soiling his britches in the mud.

A surprisingly young blacksmith, perhaps a few years older than Talia, looked up from the horseshoe he was working on at the anvil. He wore a protective glove on his left hand that matched his black apron. His hair was short and his arms stocky, which would have made him look rustic and mature for his age if not for his baby face. Acne scars riddled both of his red cheeks.

"Be careful now, Jack!" admonished the blacksmith, setting down his tools as he walked over to help up his little brother. He shot Drake a suspicious look. "Who are you?"

"That's Desmond," Jack said, freeing himself from the muck.

"You must be Adam," Drake guessed. The blacksmith folded his arms. "I ran into Jack while looking for a doctor. You see, I've got a kid who's come down with something fierce, and I'm hoping someone in town can sell us some medicine."

"You shouldn't've come through these parts, stranger," Adam shook his head. "Especially if youse are sick. Best you and your kid keep away from Jack; we don't need him catching it."

"I'm not sick," Drake countered tersely. "But I need medicine for the kid who is. Can you help me find the doctor or not?"

"Most doctors wouldn't have a clue what to do about this plague," Adam hawked a greenish black goo onto the ground. As Adam adjusted his mouth, Drake could tell that the spit was tinged by tobacco rather than blood. "One lady doctor came to town up on the west side a few days ago, mind. She's the only doctor not putting the sick on wagons."

"This doctor—she has medicine?" clarified Drake.

"Sure does. Ain't that right, Jedd?"

Another boy, leaner and taller with a thin mustache, emerged carrying a box of scrap from the building next to the forge. He set down the load and wiped his forehead. "What's that now?"

"That medicine lady. She fixed you up, ain't that right?"

Jedd raised his eyebrows at Drake to emphasize the understatement. "I thought I was a goner like ma and papa. That lady took me in her little healing hut, gave me some elixir, and two days later, I was right as rain. Made me stay a third day for an extra round, but I didn't mind none. She was real pretty. Wish I coulda stayed with her longer, but she said I got an auntie body now, and it was time I got back to my life. I said *shoot, you want to come with?*"

"You talk too much, Jedd," Adam warned sternly.

"Please, take me to her," Drake entreated between Jedd and Adam.

The boys exchanged looks. Jedd shrugged. "It's only a ten-minute ride with Rosie. Half-hour walk, tops, if you can't get her to motivate."

"What's in it for me?" Adam inclined his head toward Drake. "For all I know, you might be sick too. You want to walk west down that road, find it yourself, be my guest. You want me to take you there, tell me how you'll make it worth my while."

"Name a price," Drake pulled out his purse.

"We don't need your money," frowned Adam. "But food's been tough to find around here."

"Got a bag full of it," Drake answered noncommittally, "but I'm in a hurry. Now, money might not mean much to you, but it's still got value to me. How about I give you a bit to hold onto until we get the medicine. Then, you can take however much food you think is fair," proposed Drake.

Adam looked to Jedd, who shrugged again. "Fair's fair."

"All right," Adam held out a hand. Drake opened the bag to pull out a few pieces, but Adam shook his head. "Nuh-uh. I'm holding on to all of it; gotta make sure you live up to your end of the bargain."

Drake was about to protest but knew time was against him. He could always take the pouch back by force if necessary. Dropping the tied purse into Adam's hand, he added: "We might need some of that to pay the doctor."

"She don't take money, neither," Jedd piped in. "The medicine's free. She just wants to help people."

"All right," Adam tucked the pouch into an interior pocket of his shirt. "Jedd, you mind bringing Rosie around?"

"If she'll let me," Jedd hollered, jogging behind the building. He returned a moment later, leading a tawny horse by the reins. Its fur was shaggy and matted, but the saddle and horseshoes seemed of decent quality. The horse nickered as it came to a stop next to Adam.

"Climb on," Adam instructed, ascending first and slotting his feet into the stirrups.

Drake awkwardly mounted the back behind the saddle.

Adam clicked his tongue and spurred Rosie forward, accelerating into a quick trot. They traveled west down the road, passing many houses but few people. Adam raised a hand to greet one local on the road but otherwise kept quiet throughout the ride.

Eventually, the trail began to slope upward, reaching a treeless section of hill to the north. On the upper terrace overlooking the main road, a handful of people buzzed around one of the bigger houses.

"That's the hospital," identified Adam. "That's where she'll be."

"Let's see," said Drake, unwilling to let the blacksmith out of his sight before he got what he came for.

Rosie continued her trek up to the terrace, coming to a stop outside the house. One exotically dressed man, neither a Godwin nor a Tallawyn, was fetching water from the well. In front of the door, a shaggy-bearded local watched the foreigner carry out his work with crossed arms.

"Jeriah," Adam called out to the local.

"Adam," he nodded back.

"Is the doctor in?"

Jeriah shook his head. "Just missed her. She left about a minute ago, off to the Munson residence," he pointed behind them at a lone cottage on the opposite side of the northward road, thirty feet back from the street. "Maria's son woke up sick this morning. Heard her sobbing on my way to the hospital, so I went to check in on her. Poor woman won't leave the house."

"Still no room in the hospital?" Adam asked.

"For every one who gets cured, two more get sick," Jeriah raised his hands in defeat.

"Yeah, well," Adam shifted uncomfortably. "Not too many people left to get sick, I guess."

"Keep your chin up, sonny. Things look tough now, but it'll all get better soon. He has a plan."

"The doctor's in the house over there?" Drake asked Adam.

"Yeah. She'll probably be back in the next ten, twenty minutes, I'd guess," Adam said without any particular urgency.

"Let's go see her," Drake decided, sliding off the horse.

Adam wheeled the horse around to trot next to him. "Whoa, there. Not sure how they do it wherever you're from, but around these parts, it ain't polite to barge into someone's home uninvited."

"Tell me something," Drake began, not slowing his pace for a moment. "Sounds like the doctor's a busy woman, wouldn't you say?"

"I'd reckon," allowed Adam.

"Then what's the sense in making her waste time explaining things twice? She's probably giving Maria a rundown on this plague and the cure, and I'm gonna need to hear the same."

"Well," Adam breathed out a thoughtful huff as they crossed the road. "Guess that makes sense. You should still knock, at least."

"Noted," Drake acknowledged, quickening his pace.

He reached the front door of the standalone cottage and knocked twice before throwing the door open.

"Now, Missus Munson," addressed an accented voice. "It's important that you do not wrap Scott in a bundle of blankets when he's feverish."

"But he says he's got chills," protested the other woman in the room.

"I know," the first woman answered patiently. "However, wrapping him in blankets can cause the fever to rise and make the chills worse. Do you understand?"

"I can't lose my baby," cried Missus Munson. "I lost his daddy already. If I lost Scott, I don't know if I could go on. I should go check on him now."

"Missus Munson, your boy is fine. We just checked on him a minute ago. He's had some water, and the medicine will start helping soon. He just needs some rest. You do, too! Your newborn needs you to stay in good health. All right? We'll take care of all three of you."

"Is there a doctor in the house?" Drake interrupted, stepping inside.

"Apologies for the interruption, ma'am," Adam raised a hand from the doorway, remaining outside the threshold of the home.

"Who are you?" a brown-haired, puffy-eyed woman raised her head. She wore a simple, gray gown that canvased her gaunt, tired body. White mixed with her wiry black hair, but the dark circles and drooping lines under her eyes added decades to her appearance. Another woman sat across the table with her back to the door.

"I'm here to see the doctor," Drake said solemnly. Taking a cursory glance around the home from the entrance, he saw two additional doors which he assumed were bedrooms. The family room was in a state of disarray, sewn toys and clothes strewn carelessly across the furniture. A log was burning in the fireplace, crackling over the long-drawn silence that covered the room.

"Yes, I will be happy to help you," the woman facing away from him answered, rising from her seat. She turned and fixed her piercing green eyes on the new arrival. Her white robe accentuated the black bag tied around her waist. Some golden artifact decorated her hair. To the people of this sickness-ravaged land, she must have looked like an angel. The doctor offered a soft, kind smile. Her eyes looked tired, too. "Do you mind if I finish with Missus Munson? We still have a few items to go over for her son's recovery process."

"I still don't understand that," Maria pointed a contemplative finger at the three red vials on the table. "Why can't he take all of the medicine at once? Why does my boy have to suffer another two days?"

"Well, in addition to possible side effects, it wouldn't be as effective if you took them all at once. The body slowly works the medicine out of the bloodstream; it's important that the medicine is in there long enough to deal with all of the disease. It won't work faster just because you put more in. Three daily doses should be enough to cure Scott, but I like to give a fourth just to be safe," the doctor explained.

"Excuse me," Drake cut in, advancing deeper into the household. The doctor turned to face him, standing between him and the whimpering woman. "Doctor, does this medicine of yours stop the blood plague?"

"That's the intent," she nodded with sad eyes. "Why? Who's sick?"

"My," he swallowed the lump in his throat, blinking as he looked at the three red vials on the table. "My little girl. She's sick like nothing I've ever seen. I don't know what to do. Please, Doctor—can you help her?"

The green-eyed woman lowered her head and let out a long exhale. "It's far more widespread than anticipated." She met his eyes, though he could see it pained her to deliver the news. "I'm afraid I've run out of medicine. I'll make more as soon as possible, of course. I'm planning to teach some of the townspeople who have been helping as well. Unfortunately, my ship's stuck at the harbor, and the border's still closed."

"What are you saying?" Drake frowned, fearing he knew her answer.

"I'm sorry. I won't be able to produce any more medicine in time to help your girl," she simplified. "But I'll still do what I can to help. I can show you how to alleviate a fever, proper sanitation techniques to keep yourself from catching the disease..."

Drake felt lightheaded. He heard a faint ringing in his ear as he listened to the doctor. Failing to understand her words, he cut her off, asking directly: "And will all that cure her, Doctor? Is she going to be all right?"

He read the discomfort on the woman's face. "It's not unheard of for some to recover naturally from this plague. Especially when closely managing symptoms, it's possible she could pull through without any medicine."

"Give me a number?" asked Drake.

"I don't know," demurred the doctor.

"Take a guess," he insisted.

She carefully considered the question for a long, unbearable moment. "One in eight? One in seven, maybe?"

"Survive," clarified Drake. Her grave nod filled him with dread. "And people who get the cure? What are their odds?"

"You said almost everyone who's taken the medicine got better, right?" sniveled the widow on the other side of the table.

"Yes," the doctor answered her. Turning to Drake, she said simply: "Nine in ten."

Blood pumped in his ears as he digested the information. He felt like his spirit had slipped out of his body, unable to endure this grim reality—but Pyros wasn't taking over. It was still him, just in a hollower shell.

"Maria, was it?" Drake addressed the woman seated at the table.

"Yes?" she blinked through teary eyes.

"I'm sorry about your son. I truly hope he makes it," Drake stepped forward, passing the doctor. He approached the table and took her left hand in his right, giving it a gentle squeeze. "But that medicine's coming with me." He snatched the three vials before the woman could react.

"No!" she wailed in horror, clawing at his right arm.

He disengaged her, tearing his arm free and retreating a step from the table. She fell off the chair in pursuit of him, landing on her face and erupting in wrathful sobs.

"That medicine's for her son!" objected the doctor, barring his way to the exit. The blacksmith stood frozen in the doorway, torn between intervening and running to get help. The doctor reached into her robe and pulled out a short, narrow surgical blade. Holding it toward Drake, she tried to slow her breathing and reintroduce reason into the conversation. "I understand you want to help your girl, but she wouldn't want it—not like this. Please, give back the medicine, and I promise we'll do everything we can for her."

Drake tucked the vials into his jacket pocket. He couldn't risk them breaking. "This medicine's gone already," he drew his arming sword. "If you want to live, step aside and forget you ever met me."

"No!" An arm swiped at him from behind, hitting his left rib just below the medicine vials. He spun instinctively to protect them, surprising himself and the widow as the tip of his sword pierced her side. She howled in pain as the blade entered and fell heavily as it exited.

"You monster!"

Anticipating the lunge, Drake pivoted. His sword moved of its own accord, an extension of his unyielding experience. His blade caught the doctor under her collar bone, tearing through her muscle like paper.

Her scalpel clattered to the floor.

The doctor stumbled backward, grabbing onto the chair in a futile bid to support herself. Both crashed to the ground. She fruitlessly clutched a hand to her chest, attempting to stop the bleeding. Pain mixed with surprise in her green eyes, culminating in eternal fear.

He looked up from the body and caught a blur in the doorway. Racing after Adam, he burst through the door in time to see the horse galloping down and around the bend.

The blacksmith looked over his shoulder, meeting Drake's cold eyes before disappearing down the road east.

Drake chased after him, understanding the horrified look on the young man's face. When faced with imminent peril, some men freeze in fear, some accept their fate and make a late peace with their gods, and others scatter like roaches, desperate to hide themselves away to survive a minute longer.

A rare few stand against the danger, resolving to take retribution into their own hands.

XXVII. Hellfire

Drake

His heart hammered in his ears. Lungs threatened to explode.

Breathless, but unable to stop for even a second, Drake raced up the slope to the cul-de-sac. Spotting the abandoned house that he had sheltered in with Talia, he swallowed the lump in his throat and dashed forward, desperate to reach her side.

Cutting his hands on the jagged windowsill, he vaulted into the decrepit cottage with reckless abandon, falling over himself as he completed the final hurdle to his destination.

Looking up from the splintered floor, he saw a lone figure standing in the center of the small room, evidently both surprised at his entrance and expecting his arrival.

Adam.

Drake's stomach dropped. He rose to his feet, searching the room for any sign of her. Their packs were also missing from the floor by the fireplace. Only the blacksmith and the smoldering log knew where they had gone.

"If you want to see her again, you'll turn yourself in. Come quietly to stand trial in Saar," the blacksmith declared bravely, overcoming the tremor in his voice.

Drake took a slow pace forward, then another, feeling the muscles in his neck tighten with rage. Eyes brimming with fire, he closed in on the young man like a starved wolf after a cornered fawn. In a dangerously low voice, he growled: "You have no idea what hell's coming for you... but you will."

"What are you—stop!" squealed Adam, retreating as Drake advanced. His hand hovered over the hammer at his hip. "You will answer for the wicked you've done. You will face justice for your crimes. You will—"

The blacksmith drew his hammer and swung it heavily in an overhand arc. Predicting the clumsy attack, Drake stepped in swiftly to catch his wrist at the apex of the strike, stopping it preemptively. Driving his free hand into the blacksmith's stomach, he followed up with a knee to the A-frame and wrested the weapon from Adam's hand as he doubled over.

Moving without affording the young man any chance to recover, Drake swept the stocky blacksmith's legs out from under him, then pounced with a merciless thrust of the hammer head. A hair-raising crack came from Adam's chin as the metal made contact, leaving him stunned on the ground.

Drake crouched, taking a second to make sure the blacksmith stayed down. Adam's eyes rolled as his head lolled to the side. His hands lifted from the floorboards but quickly flopped back down, failing to muster the strength to move his body.

With his opponent soundly dazed, Drake strode to the cabinet and secured a length of rope. He passed Adam to retrieve a chair from the small kitchen, then returned to the fallen blacksmith. Dropping the hammer, he gripped Adam's apron with both hands. His biceps burned as he wrangled the weighty craftsman into the creaking chair.

To secure him in place, Drake tied Adam's hands behind the splat and bound his ankles to the chair legs. Drake returned to the kitchen to grab a second chair. Dragging it over on two legs, he faced it in front of Adam and sat.

"Now," he said slowly, calmly, despite the urgency burning inside him. "You're going to tell me exactly where she is."

Adam blinked as he refocused his eyes, finding the strength to hold his head up. He spat, landing a globule on Drake's pant leg. Though his words slurred as they came out, the result of a jaw that no longer worked properly, his meaning was clear: "Go to hell."

"Ah," Drake nodded, drawing the knife from its sheath on his calf. He slid his chair a little closer, then patted Adam twice on his right knee. Without warning, he drove the knife into Adam's leg, right above the kneecap, and violently tilted the hilt toward him. A sickly *pop* preceded the screams.

Leaving the knife in his leg, Drake gave the blacksmith two taps under the chin, making him lift his head. "I'm up here," Drake said, apathetic of the tears forming in the young man's eyes. "I asked you a question."

A tearful laugh escaped Adam's lips. His face twisted in vengeful anger. "I ain't saying shit. You hear me? I hope you both rot. Kill me and be done with it."

A dangerous smile crept onto Drake's face as he increased the pressure on the lodged knife. "You won't be getting off that easily." He yanked the blade free and wiped the blood on Adam's cheek. That rebellious spirit had to be cracked. To extract an answer, he had to exude control. Only one of them could drink from the chalice of dread.

"Do your worst," Adam shook his head, steeling himself. "Long as you never see her again, I'll die happy."

Staring out the window, Drake nodded slowly and returned the knife to its sheath. He circled behind Adam. With the ease of breaking fish bones, he snapped each callused finger on the craftsman's bound hands, one by one.

After eight cracks met by the most profane swearing a blacksmith could muster, Drake stood in front of him, bending forward to speak face-to-face.

"Is that all you got?" snarled Adam, his face wet from sweat and tears.

"What, that?" Drake coiled a small length of spare rope and looped it around his arm, then toppled the chair, knocking Adam onto his side. Moving to unlock the front door, he looked back at the impaired captive. "That's just to make sure you stick around for the main event."

Drake found what he was looking for underneath the bed of the house beside the forge. After a brief struggle, he returned to the cabin some five minutes later, sweating and dehydrated. He was acutely aware that Talia was being taken farther away from him with each wasted minute, suffering from that terrible blood plague.

She needed him.

Desperation poisoned his thoughts as he flung open the door to the cottage. His quarry was still squirming on the floor where he had left him.

"Adam!" squeaked Jack. His hands were securely tied behind his back.

"Jack...? Jack!" the blacksmith cried, wriggling futilely on the floor.

"Have a seat," Drake roughly steered the kid into the upright chair. He tied a loose cord around the splat, binding Jack's hands. The boy leaned side to side, shaking the chair in a desperate attempt to break the restraints. Drake placed a hand on the top rail of the chair, stabilizing the seat.

"I'm done asking, Adam. Tell me where she is," Drake demanded.

"Please," Adam begged, tears welling in his eyes. "Turn yourself in. Go to Saar. Let him go."

"Wrong answer," Drake snarled, dragging Jack's chair backward on its rear two legs.

The boy screamed and squirmed as he flew across the floor, moving farther and farther from his brother. Drake spun the chair around, leaning it forward above the hot, glowing embers in the fireplace. He held the back of the chair with one hand, suspending the boy's face over the thin cloud of white smoke rising from the faded fire, and looked back at Adam.

"Stop! Don't!" wailed the blacksmith.

"Where is she?" roared Drake.

Jack suddenly flailed, causing the back of the chair to slip away from his fingers. Grasping too slowly through empty air, Drake watched the chair tilt forward, pinning the boy in the fireplace.

A bloodcurdling screech ripped out of the boy as his face crashed into the hot embers. The piercing wail rang in Drake's ears as he leaned forward to pull the chair out of the fire.

"Jack!" Adam choked up.

The boy's howling pervaded the house, excruciating and unrestrained. The blacksmith responded in turn, breaking down into racking sobs.

"Last chance," Drake warned quietly, certain he had Adam's attention. He rested a hand on top of the warmed splat. From his position behind Jack, he could see just a sliver of the boy's cheek, white turned to red.

"Kagrash," choked out Adam. "Jedd took her to Fort Kagrash."

"If only we'd started with that," reflected Drake, leaving Jack's chair facing the fire. He walked quickly to the blacksmith's fallen chair and stooped to pull it upright.

"They'll be ready for you," Adam rasped with puffy eyes. "You should have turned yourself in. Justice will find you, monster."

Drake drew his knife, unmoved by the animus in the blacksmith's eyes. "Justice is blind." He buried his knife in the man's right eye. Ripping the blade free, he turned away, leaving the body behind without further ceremony.

Glancing at the fireplace, Drake paused and stared at the trimmed hair on the back of the wailing witness' head. An old soldier's adage echoed in his mind. *Mercy today, trouble tomorrow.*

Returning the knife to its sheath, he made for the exit, his destination clear. As he closed the door, he heard a watery voice squeak behind him.

"Adam?"

Stepping out into the sunlight, he glanced around the lifeless houses of the ghost town, then took off running.

He raced out of Gaixia to the east, returning to the last sign he had seen pointing to Fort Kagrash. Unflagging, he continued north despite burning legs and ragged lungs, stopping only once to drink from a rocky creek. At last, where the trees were cleared away and the road widened, he faced the high walls of the white fortress—and the garrison of soldiers defending it.

Archers manned the outer walls between Godwin banners, while four columns of armored soldiers formed ranks outside the open gate. From a distance, Drake spotted a broad-shouldered man with a feathered helmet under his arm. Standing beside him was the young man from Gaixia.

Bold to stand at the front of the formation. Also reckless.

Drake recognized they viewed him as a common murderer—perhaps a rare threat for them to police around these parts, but easily subdued.

They had no idea what he was capable of.

He quickened his pace with Jedd in sight, anxious to be reunited with Talia. She had been in no condition to travel when he left her that morning. Worry festered within him. In the hands of these careless statesmen, who knew how rapidly her health was declining?

Well within range of the walls, Drake noticed the soldiers unnecessarily readying their weapons. Jedd called out to him: "Where's Adam?"

"Not joining us. Where's the girl?" Drake answered evenly.

The hawk-nosed commander stepped forward. "Criminal, you have transgressed against the good people of Gaixia who are under Lord Jasper Korinz' oath of protection. As the designated commander of Fort Kagrash, it is my duty to see you apprehended. You will surrender at once."

Drake scowled. "Where's the girl?"

The commander made a dismissive hand gesture. "Somewhere on the journey between this world and the next. Her fate was sealed when the doctors determined she carries the blood plague. They'll perform a ritual to safely purge the pestilence from our stronghold... if she isn't dead already."

Fear and wrath flooded Drake's body, consuming him wholly. His eyes clouded as Pyros' fury roiled, hungry to be unleashed. His face contorted in rage as he pictured the beak-masked doctor decreeing that she be taken away from him.

"Fear not, murderer. I'm sure you'll be reunited—as soon as you meet the hangman," the commander taunted, signaling for his men to move in.

For just a moment, Drake felt his blood run cold. It dawned on him his worst fears had become reality. She had suffered in her final days, and he had been powerless to help. He couldn't bear the weight of his failure. His broken promise to protect her. When she needed him most, he had left her to face it alone. He couldn't imagine her fear as they dragged her off to this heartless place. Sentenced to die by an unholy raven.

First came the chilling, shattering realization.

Then came his burning wrath.

A whirlwind ignited around him, beginning as a low trail of flames. Maturing rapidly, the wild blaze climbed into the sky, evolving into a vortex of violently twisting flames around him. He couldn't see the faces of the horrified men beyond the all-consuming inferno, but their terror was audible even above the roaring conflagration.

Drake lurched forward as Pyros' unquenchable fury flowed through him like never before. This time, he did not hold the Primal back—he wanted the world to burn.

His vision darkened as his vengeance raged on. At first, he thought the skies had darkened with smoke and ash rising from the blaze. As his sight turned black, he hollowly realized that he had lost control.

For a short eternity, he stared into the vast darkness. No candle guided his way. No siren beaconed him through the great nothingness. Though he roamed the black plane, he found nothing. He felt nothing.

In the unexplored recesses of his mind, he distantly heard a woman's voice calling a name.

The darkness, he slowly realized, was a starless shoreline. His feet traveled lightly across the black sand, disturbing not even a single grain as he walked. As if the beach was merely a painted illusion. Silent water lapped onto the shore. Against the inky gray sky, the outline of unexplainable, chaotic rock formations jutted out of the water, twisting in every direction.

Farther down the shoreline, an immeasurable distance that looked only a few dozen paces away but felt like miles, rested a single, solitary boulder. On that rock sat a black-gowned figure, staring silently out to sea.

Drake urged his legs to hurry forward, but they could only muster a steady trot to bring him alongside the rock. The air felt charged around him, giving him the sense that the stranger recognized him. He reached his hands out to climb onto the boulder and saw that he, too, wore black robes.

Seated beside the stranger, a question left his mouth that he could not hear and immediately forgot upon uttering. The figure turned to him, and he saw her lips move to return an unheard answer.

As the moon appeared behind the cloudy horizon, a silver reflection danced across the water to reach them. He turned back to her, wishing he could make out what she was trying to tell him.

This time, the woman's lips did not move. Yet, somehow, a different woman's voice reached him through the darkness.

"Drake!"

He snapped back to his senses, disoriented as his brain tried to process the discordant shift to a vivid world. His eyesight returned first. He saw shapes and colors but couldn't yet interpret the world around him. Blue, gray, red, black. His hearing returned next, a crisp crackling that came from all around him. He could taste iron on his tongue, and a putrid smoke filled his nostrils.

The images gradually sharpened. A sky. Smoke. Buildings. There were little plots of farmland, armories, barracks, stables—some still standing, most reduced to piles of rubble and bare foundation. In every direction around him, in the flickering red and vanquished gray, was a world conquered by fire.

Drake sunk to his knees as his vision swayed. The raging inferno had given no quarter; what little hadn't been devoured entirely was scarred black with char and soot. As his head stopped spinning, he looked at the back of his hands and was surprised to find that they alone had come out unscathed.

A red pearl fell to the dirt below him.

Another red droplet spattered the ground, followed by another. Staring down the length of his nose, he realized the accumulating flow of blood was coming from his nostrils.

Tightness abruptly gripped his chest. The sensation grew to a feeling of suffocation in his throat, blocking his airway. He hacked a violent cough, leaning into his wrists for support as he spat up a thick, dark-red globule from within. It landed in the alarmingly expanding pool beneath him.

The ribs on his left side throbbed painfully as he attempted to move, forcing him to clutch his right hand across his chest. He coughed up another globule, this time feeling the dull pain extending through his back.

His fingers brushed the glass vials in his jacket pocket. In sudden panic, he gently tapped each of the three vials to ensure they hadn't shattered.

All still intact.

Despite the growing panic he felt at his staggering blood loss, relief washed over him. He didn't know what had happened to him, nor how much time he had left, but he remembered what brought him here.

Drake staggered to his feet, swaying as he surveyed his surroundings. He held his nose in a failed attempt to staunch the bleeding, resting his other hand against his sore ribs. Spitting another mouthful of blood into the dirt, he looked up to see the walls of the inner keep ahead of him. Whereas the other buildings were partially or wholly razed, including the ruinous front gate behind him, only the front turret of this stone structure had melted.

He lumbered up the hill toward the keep, encountering no resistance as he went. Aside from the crackling and sizzling fires, the fort was eerily quiet.

Out of the corner of his eye, a black mask caught his attention. He turned and immediately recognized the long beak as a feature of the unnerving plague doctors. Next to the sheltered mask lay a charred corpse of a man dressed in black. Another body lay on the seared cart beside him.

Likewise turned to ash.

"No," choked Drake, staggering to the cart in a daze. "Deus, no!"

He reached the wagon, battling an overwhelming rush of nausea as he studied the blackened remains of the patient. No features of the cremated body were recognizable.

Looking from head to toe, he shook his head, fighting back the tears that threatened to escape him. He couldn't believe it was her. He didn't believe it was her. "No... she wasn't that tall... You're not her!" Drake yelled deliriously at the corpse, stumbling backward.

His feet carried him away from the cart, back toward the damaged doors of the keep. He pushed the blackened wood out of his way, shambling inside without a clue where to look. He started down the hallway to the right, determined to scour every inch of this forsaken place before he would even consider letting himself die.

Throwing open the first door on his right, he stumbled into an empty bunkhouse. Cots lined all three walls, with a row of hammocks above them accessible by small ladders. He almost turned to leave, when he saw a flicker of movement in the corner.

Two pale soldiers cowered together under a cot. One buried his head in his hands, sobbing silently. The other accidentally met his eyes.

Drake pointed at him and rumbled: "Where... is she?"

"Who?" squeaked the soldier, voice trembling as much as his hands.

"Today... with the plague..." grunted Drake. He leaned against the wall for support but kept his eyes fixed on the cowardly warrior.

"The one from Gaixia? She's in confinement—downstairs!"

"Where?" Drake exhaled sharply.

"Straight down the hall, third door on the right! Please, spare us—we have families!" the man cried unashamedly.

"Never... again..." Drake pushed off the wall to stand upright.

"You'll never see us again, I swear! Please, just..." groveled the man before Drake had a chance to turn away.

Without another word, Drake exited the room. He struggled down the hall, using the walls for support. Some part of him dimly recognized he was leaving a trail of blood behind him, but it didn't matter now. Nothing would get in his way of protecting her—not now or ever again.

He reached the third door and swung it open, then delved into the unlit stairwell hidden behind. At the bottom of the stairs, another door defied him on the left. Hazily warning Pyros to be ready for any resistance inside, he flung it open.

Save for two jail cells and a torch on the wall between them, the room was empty. Relief was the first feeling to meet him, followed immediately by panic. He scanned the two cells again. His heart leaped from his chest when he saw a shadow stir on the left side.

"Drake...?" a small voice croaked from the darkness.

"Talia!" he cried, dashing over to the gate. He rattled the bars futilely before noticing a padlock secured the cell.

"The... wall..." she managed weakly.

Drake swiveled his attention immediately. He spotted the key ring below the sconce. With shaking hands, he took the keys and jingled one into the lock. Failing, he hastily tried the second key, which successfully disengaged the bolt.

Bursting into the cell, he fell to his knees beside the low bed and grasped her hand. "It's going to be all right, Talia. I'm here now."

"I know," a smile touched the corner of her mouth, but her eyes did not open.

He slipped a hand under her head and helped sit her up. "I brought medicine," he reached into his pocket and pulled out one of the vials. Flicking the stopper off the top, he brought the elixir to her lips.

"Thanks," she mumbled after downing its contents.

Drake pulled her into a hug. Two weak arms wrapped behind his back.

He couldn't stop the tears that were coming now. Guilt and fear and love tumbled off his tongue in an incomprehensible flurry of words.

"I was so worried. When I came back, and you weren't there... I don't know what I would've done if... I thought... I'm so sorry, kiddo," he sniveled into his sleeve, gently allowing Talia to lay back down.

"It's okay. I knew you'd come." Her eyes opened for just a moment, flickering as she studied his face in the dim light.

Between the blood and ash clinging to him, he had no idea what he looked like. Based on the reaction of the soldiers, it must have been horrifying.

"Thank you," she whispered with a faint smile.

Choking up, he wiped his eyes with the sleeve of his jacket. He didn't trust his quivering lip to keep its composure. Holding her small hand tightly, he nodded, at last allowing himself to take a breath.

She was going to be all right. Everything was going to be all right.

"I'm so sorry, Talia," Drake coughed, spitting on the floor of the jail cell. The words spilled out with his tears, unstoppable and incomprehensible. "I couldn't let them... You needed the medicine, but then they took you... I tried, but they wouldn't... I had to do it."

Talia rested a hand on his arm, interrupting his rambling apology. "It's okay, Drake. I love you, too."

Her eyes closed as she rested her head back on the hard bed. Her breathing was shallow and at times irregular, but her resilient lungs refused to give up. The medicine would help, but her fighting spirit was her own.

Though he was the one who had charged through the fire, he felt that she had saved him. He could never make his failure up to Desmond, but she had granted him more time. She had not abandoned him to wander this world alone with his mistakes. Her grace and love cleansed his soul of ash and blood. He was immensely grateful for the chance to love her better.

Drake stood by her side for a long while. He was sure their gear was stashed somewhere in the fort, and he suspected reinforcements would be summoned from the city to repair the damage, but everything else could wait.

Against the odds, he had found Talia—and she was going to be okay.

XXVIII. Infiltration

Allen Lee

Cavernous spaces like the library felt a lot eerier when empty.

Although he rarely socialized, Allen missed the quiet scuff of feet on carpeted floor. The rustle of a turning page. Lanterns dancing down the aisles.

Failing to conceal a longing glance in the direction of the library's exit, the lanky page thought it appropriate to restate his opinion. "Everyone else is going to the symposium. Don't you want to see what fascinating discoveries they present in the senate? The sheikh himself will be there."

"I don't like crowds," Allen shrugged in a half-truth. "Is there a section on symphony composition here?"

The black-cowled page sighed, patently unhappy with his station in life. "Of course. This is The Library on El Aria."

"Lead on," Allen invited with a swoosh of his white robes.

Growling an incomprehensible string of unkind words, the disgruntled page guided him deeper into the library and farther away from the biannual conference that every disciple had awaited eagerly since the eve of the last.

Allen's palms were sweating, though he couldn't pinpoint why. He was nervous about Samson's undisclosed scheme, but he was also disappointed he had to miss the festivities. Symposium was a night for the best and brightest of The Library on El Aria to come together and share pioneering insights with the outside world. Had he the same passion for science he knew as a younger man, he would have looked forward to any opportunity to learn or network his way onto exciting studies.

"Origins of symphony composition," announced the page.

Allen frowned, realizing he had never asked the man his name. Feeling it would be too awkward to raise the issue now, he just said, "Ah. I was actually looking for contemporary symphony composition."

"Of course you are." The man continued down the aisle, then made a right into the neighboring section. Three rows later, he paused and presented the aisle with a sweeping gesture. "May I inquire whether you intend to do something with these books, or is this simply pleasure reading?"

"Life's short, read what you enjoy!" Allen quipped brightly, feeling a heaviness in his chest as he spoke. The suspense of Sam's mysterious quest had crowded out much of the crippling loneliness, but intrusive thoughts besieged him with tormenting regularity, nevertheless.

He had taken an evening to collect his thoughts on paper, culminating in fourteen rambling pages written for Meghana. The letter expressed feelings ranging from unease about The Library, to excitement about the symposium, to thoughts of her. Pages six through ten described his loneliness and evolving emotions toward her, attempting to nuance the dissonance he felt in missing her while no less missing his family.

Meghana's absence somehow felt more real. Like a piece of him was missing that he had never truly understood or appreciated. He longed to see her warm smile. Hear the laugh that unfailingly dispelled his worries. She was like an elusive dream, an enchanted possibility made real only in the world beyond reality. When he woke from this uncanny slumber, he would be relieved to wake next to Alaina, to see Lyn once more—but the dream would fade to memory, forgotten as time forgets all, reconstructed only in fantasy.

Ultimately, Allen had given the courier only a single page to deliver. Three paragraphs about the slow goings-on at The Library and how he looked forward to her return. One sentence to wish her well and again congratulate her on the opportunity. A substantial omission of the labyrinth of emotions that plagued his every waking moment.

"Sound wisdom I'll be sure to keep in mind," the page folded his arms in bad temper and leaned against the bookshelf.

Entering the section, Allen thought he saw a black blur at the far end of the row. Pretending to skim the book titles concerning modern symphonies, he made his way down the aisle with an inconspicuous whistle.

"Hmm," Allen lifted a heavy book with musical notation as part of the cover graphic. "Cooper Orchovskidanea! He's one of the classics."

"She is," the page corrected flatly.

"Ah. Did she have a brother?" Allen inquired, awkwardly fumbling the book back onto the shelf.

"She did not," confirmed the unimpressed polymath.

"So many Orchovskidaneas to keep track of, these days," murmured Allen, quickening his pace down the aisle.

Reaching the intersection, he turned right and almost tumbled over the black-gowned sentry around the corner.

"Shh!" hissed Samson, lowering then immediately raising his hood to make himself known to Allen. "Run four rows back, left, the first left after that, first right. Wait for me there." Samson spun him around and shoved him into motion.

Allen reached the fourth row and banked left, glancing behind just in time to see his shadow round the corner. Like a varsity linebacker, Samson dropped his shoulder and laid the man out with a crunchy tackle.

Sometimes, *top of your class* just couldn't compete with two hundred pounds of brawn and athleticism. A side of raw masculinity, indeed.

Fixing his glasses, Allen ran down the aisle as fast as he could manage. He hobbled forward clumsily, bouncing between the ball of his right foot and the metallic extension on his left, attempting to move with as much stealth and grace as the prosthetic allowed. Reaching the first left, he stumbled around the corner, narrowly keeping his balance. Slowing to his regular limp, he arrived at the final turn shortly after.

Breathless from the thirty-second effort, he leaned against the shelf and stretched his arms above his head in an uphill battle to avoid cramping. He perceived a tightness in his right quadriceps but otherwise felt all right.

Suddenly, a sharp knot formed in his upper chest, denying him air. His eyes widened in fear as his throat tightened. Violent coughs brought him to his knees, racking his body with painful spasms. Rebellious lungs battered his ribs and expelled a fusillade of blood. He fell to his side, overcome by shivers down his arms and unseen daggers in his sternum.

The vile sensation passed, but Allen remained on the ground for a long minute after, eyes shut in resignation. When he finally dared to open his heavy eyelids, he discovered that he had not escaped the unending nightmare. He closed them again, letting his head rest on the floor.

Placing the back of his hand against his forehead, he found the skin to be warm. He couldn't truly tell if it was any worse than usual, but his otherwise deteriorating condition led him to assume the worst.

"Wake up, Doctor Lee."

Allen felt a sturdy nudge against his metal leg, registering only in his quadriceps. Opening his eyes, he found Samson hovering above him.

"No time for a nap, doctor. We've got work to do." Sam offered a hand and pulled him to his feet.

"I'm fine, thanks," Allen wiped his mouth.

"Got rid of beanpole back there. Now, onto phase two of the plan," Samson struck his fist in determination.

"Great. Excellent," Allen twiddled his fingers. "What's the plan?"

"Your mission, whether or not you accept it, is to find out what in Sam Hill is going on in that restricted section, and if necessary, put a stop to it."

"Put a stop to the hospital?" balked Allen.

"Donate platelets if it's that kind of party, but you'll know the Devil if you see him. Now, you said they have a sentry out front; I'll execute a tactical diversion to draw away the enemy. You will thereupon infiltrate the stronghold and find out exactly what kind of butter they're churning down there. We'll regroup at the extraction point in the restricted section."

"You swear you're not going to kill anyone?" Allen checked explicitly.

"Acceptable casualties: zero. If anything goes sideways, I'll handle the paperwork," vowed Sam.

"What if someone catches me?" Allen scratched his arm nervously.

"Turn around," instructed Sam.

"What?" Allen frowned. "I don't see how..."

"Damn it, Doctor Lee. Just turn around," Sam gestured with his finger.

Confused, Allen turned to face the bookshelf. He felt a black band wrap around his waist. It rotated, presenting a holster at his right hip.

"No, thank you!" Allen raised his hands away from the gun.

"Just a contingency plan," sighed Sam. "Safety is on. There's a lever on the left side you have to flick down for that to be useful. Red means dead—the other guy, that is."

"I can't point that at someone!" protested Allen, aghast.

Samson placed a strong hand on Allen's shoulder to reassure him. "Tell you what: if you wind up outside the gates of hell because of that thing, just tell them you're holding the table for me."

"Sam!"

"Doctor Lee, you wouldn't object to holding a pencil, would you? A scalpel? Everything and anything can be a weapon—especially a weapon, like that gun." Samson clapped his hands, startling Allen's already fraught nerves. "Now! I trust you'll use stopping force only in emergencies—remember to point the barrel away from you. Time to get this show on the road."

Allen clinked behind Samson as the sergeant led him deeper into the maze of bookshelves. He held his hands up at chest-height, unwilling to risk dropping his fingers near the live weapon. Feeling a nervous lump in his throat, he voiced his concern: "I don't think I can do this."

"Damn it, Allen! It's not like I'm asking you to eat a bushel of apples and shit a fruit salad. Be a man!"

"Sorry!" Allen recoiled. He took a few breaths to gather himself. "How do you do it? I mean, as a soldier. How do you walk around prepared to take someone's life?"

"If it comes down to it, better them than you," Sam fumbled around with his robe, eventually finding a cigarette. Unconcerned about endangering the centuries-old tomes around them, he ignited the smoke with a flick of his lighter. "But that's not the answer that works for you, is it?"

"If all human life is created equally, how could I ever play judge to decide who lives or dies?" Allen philosophized while subtly waving the smoke away from his face.

"It's easy." With an exhale of gray smoke, Sam Samson looked over his shoulder, motioning for Allen to walk beside him. "When you're fighting to protect someone you love, you don't care who's good or bad. What's right or wrong, who deserves to live or die—it doesn't matter."

"But," Allen frowned, attempting to see the world from Sam's eyes. "Who are you fighting to protect? Me?"

"Hell no," the soldier's shoulders shook as he laughed. "Well, you too, I guess. When I enlisted, I did want to protect the good guys. Be a hero for the people back home. But the minute you see war for the first time, that kind of thinking goes out the window. Did for me, at least. Watching good men die, holding your brother's guts in your hands as he leaves you behind to fight a hopeless war... you don't care to be the hero anymore. Don't give a rip about a shiny medal or ten percent off car insurance. None of it will bring your brother back from the grave.

"But I stayed and kept fighting because I saw hell with my own eyes—and I wasn't going to stand around and wait for it to come for my loved ones. My family, they're everything to me. My wife, Emily... Lord knows she could start an argument with an empty house. The boys, Bill and Levi. Our little terror, Terry the terrier, running around the farm. I pray one day I make it back home to see 'em again. Until then, I'll gladly go through hell every day so they don't have to."

"But you don't think we'll ever make it back home," Allen said heavily.

"I've been wrong before," Samson cracked his neck without further comment, inspiring little confidence in their chances. "Either way, the war's out of our hands. The people here, though... They have families just like us. If you won't stand up for the people back home, do it for the people who need you here. We all get just one ticket for the carousel of life; make your ride count."

Speechless, Allen considered Sam's unexpected words. Despite his simple manners, the soldier had a surprisingly emotive wellspring of honor. A humble brand of heroism that planted courage in those lucky to be beside him.

"Showtime," Sam said quietly, donning his hood. "Hide in the shadows by this shelf. I'll draw out the guard."

Cigarette still in mouth, Sam produced an empty bottle from his robes and stumbled forward. "Glug, glug," he hollered loudly, swaying down the row to the right. Scat singing, he teetered to a stop about halfway down the aisle.

A distinct watery stream hit the books.

"Hey!" called out a furious voice from the left. Thunderous footsteps preceded the sentry's appearance. He passed Allen without a second look. "What are you doing there? Cease at once!"

Rounding the corner, Allen risked a glance at Sam's distraction and nearly yelped. The soldier hummed his national anthem as he urinated on a collection of priceless physiology texts. Recovering his wits, Allen hurried down the aisle to the left, passing the sign marking the restricted section, the empty stool, and an abandoned lantern.

Undetected, he retraced the path in his mind's eye, exploring the dark shelves for the dead end. Reaching a familiar section of books, he stooped to the ground and searched for a frayed string. His fingers brushed a loose thread. Lifting with his back, he uncovered the trapdoor into the pitch-black stairwell.

Steeling himself with a deep breath, Allen lowered one foot onto the first step, then pivoted his mechanical leg to join him. He ventured another pace, lowering the trapdoor behind him to conceal his incursion. Relying on only his sense of touch to guide him deeper into the dark mountain, he moved prudently from one step to the next, reassuring himself that his abundance of caution would save him time in the long run by keeping him free from injury.

Finally, in the still, soundless passageway, Allen's hand reached the door at the bottom. He pushed it open, blinking as his eyes adjusted to the torchlight of the lower sanctum.

Stopping in the hallway, motionless but for his fluttering heart, he listened for any signs of activity in the offices. He heard none and likewise saw no shadows of authors working on their research. The antechamber of the hidden hospital had been abandoned, leaving only the irregular crackle of the watchful candles.

Allen lifted a torch from the nearest sconce and continued to the left. Entering the chamber of twenty-four white pillars, he instinctively flinched, half-expecting Cato to jump out and accost him for his repeated trespass. The halls remained silent, however, and he passed the beautiful pillars without incident.

The double doors failed to swing open on his initial attempt. He lowered his shoulder into the right door and heaved, slowly forcing the heavy frame to swing open. A short flight of marble steps led down to another set of identical doors, which proved equally heavy.

Allen paused in the empty antechamber beyond, reading the carved signs above the left, center, and right doors within. Respectively, they read:

Essence of the human condition
Biological engineering
Psychological fragility

Allen reread the runes titling the mysterious wards, unable to decipher what they could possibly mean in a modern world of medicine.

According to Virgil, the hospital was hidden for his protection and for the protection of its patients. Doubt crept into his mind as he considered the unintended ramifications his trespassing could cause; not only could he catch a terrible virus from the patients below, but he might spread his sickness to the immunocompromised, sealing their untimely fates. He wondered if they would be frightened to see him, panicked to know what it could mean for their health.

Looking back at the heavy doors behind him, he considered retreating up the stairs before anyone caught him. He could still join the symposium and perhaps apprentice on studies to help improve the state of medicine for local families. There was a lot of good to be done here. Plus, he could carry on his friendship with Virgil, and their hopes of building a portal to get back home would remain alive, however slim. Sam would be okay with that.

Reading the names of the three wards again, new doubts infected his thoughts. The pictures Sam had painted of both the hospital and the factory in the desert unnerved him, as did Cornelius' protests about Cato's unscrupulous activity. The truth was concealed somewhere in these stone halls, and if he left now, he might never have another chance to know.

Allen ventured his prosthetic leg forward, resolved to uncover whatever secrets were hidden behind the *Essence of the human condition.*

XXIX. Essence Of The Human Condition

Allen Lee

The air felt ten degrees cooler on the other side of the stone doors.

Stuffy and foreboding, the hallway stretched beyond the reddish-yellow glow of the lone torch on the wall. The darkness lurking on the fringe of the flame's authority taunted Allen, daring him to venture into its sinister mystery.

Lifting the torch from its bracket, Allen detected a neighboring ring of bronze keys, numbered as high as thirteen. He hung the key ring on a curved spike affixed halfway up the torch, freeing his left hand but inadvertently creating an idiophone that erased any pretense of subtlety. The lone beacon of light guided him down the gloomy hallway, jingling with his every uneven step.

Not twenty paces later, a wooden table blocked half the width of the hall. White quills, crumpled balls of paper, and loose parchment covered the long surface. Beneath the aged desk, an untitled journal rested beside a chair leg, forgotten in the dust.

Allen extended the torch in front of him, attempting to read one of the loose sheets. A series of numbers was recorded in a column labeled *Hours*, each lined up with another number ranging from one to ten. Checking the back of the parchment, Allen found no additional information about the tally.

A dry cough reached him from farther down the corridor, echoing off the stone walls.

Exposed under the torchlight, Allen froze. Heartbeat galloping like a thoroughbred. After an initial spell of dread, he realized no one was after him.

Torn between calling out to the unseen stranger and making a discreet exit, he found his feet slowly carrying him forward toward the sound.

Able to see only a few feet beyond the illuminant in front of his eyes, he detected a break where vertical, iron bars substituted for the stone wall. The cough repeated from within the cell, ending with an audible splatter of spit on the ground.

Lifting the torch between the bars, Allen craned his neck forward to make out the cell's hidden inhabitant. A huddled figure sat against the back wall. The stranger's face was obscured by shadows, but a tattered robe ended at his bare feet. The distinct aroma of urine wafted out of the cell.

"Hey," Allen called inside, tapping the iron bars. The stranger's feet twitched, then slipped under the brown robe as he hugged his knees to chest. "Don't worry, I'm not going to hurt you."

"You're not real," hissed the man on the other side.

Allen held the torch through the bars but still couldn't make out a face. Pulling the key ring off the handle, he asked, "Is it okay if I come in?"

"Annie? Is Annie there with you?" the voice asked feverishly, rising in volume and intensity.

"Annie's not here. Sorry," Allen answered, rifling through the keys. Raising key number one to the padlock, he hesitated, wondering whether the delirious patient was locked in for his own safety. The stranger mumbled her name over and over through ragged breaths.

Both defiant and pleading, a hoarse voice croaked a little farther down the hall: "He's unwell. Just leave him be."

Allen walked toward the voice, abandoning the cell for now. Reaching a new set of bars on the opposite wall, he held out his torch and illuminated the prone figure of a woman. She covered her eyes with her hands, attempting to block out the sudden light.

"What more do you want from me?" Her raspy voice was laced with resentment. "When will you just let me die?"

"I..." Allen was lost for words. He stared at the defeated husk lying before him, wanting to both console her and pry information. His right hand selected a key and tried the padlock, successfully disengaging the mechanism. The gate swung open, and the flame cast its light on the prisoner.

Resting the torch on the floor, careful to keep the light alive, he slowly moved to kneel beside the dark-haired woman. "What happened to you?"

Over the rim of her hand, green eyes scorched him with an accusatory glare. Her tawny nose scrunched as she frowned, straightening into an aquiline curve as loathing shifted to suspicion. "You're... with them, aren't you?"

Up close, he immediately recognized her long cheekbones and flat eyebrows. A fierce ambition burned behind the dust of the downtrodden in her eyes. Allen reached out in disbelief. "Meghana?"

She recoiled from his touch. Then, gingerly, her hand grasped the back of his. "Manali," she corrected, eyes searching for ill intent. "Meghana's sister."

"I don't understand. Meghana said you ran away?"

His head throbbed. Looking around the cramped cell, he rediscovered its confines anew. The lightless cell was barbaric, cold and devoid of color or other sensory stimulation. Decorated with only a thin floor mat and a chamber pot, the complex looked less and less like a hospital with each passing moment.

"No," she shook her head, hurt and abhorrence spreading on her face. "I told them I wouldn't help the sheikh carry out his twisted experiments on living people, so they arrested me and made me one of the subjects."

"What happened here?" Allen felt sick to his stomach.

"I... I'd rather not talk about it," Manali said quietly, wiping a rogue tear from the corner of her eye.

"Virgil told me this was a hospital," reflected Allen, crumbling inside.

"In all of Kyros, this place is the furthest thing from a hospital," Manali nearly laughed at the absurdity of the statement. "The Library was never meant to exist. For as long as this place has stood, its foundations have been built on the suffering of the meek. The unlearned and destitute across Ayrabos and beyond fueled lifetimes of human experimentation, and I once contributed to it—all in the name of our false prophet: knowledge."

"I don't understand," Allen held a hand to his head as the room spun. Another bloody coughing fit assailed him, but he experienced it as if outside of his own body.

It was all too much to comprehend. Part of him wanted to reject the claim. To argue with Meghana's missing sister and defend Virgil's kindness and warmth. The other part of him recognized Manali was telling the truth. Even faced with the evidence, he couldn't bring himself to believe the twisted reality evolving around him. He sat and buried his head between his knees.

"There's not a lot to understand," Manali said bitterly. "They decided long ago that their careers and curiosities were worth more than our lives, and nobody told them otherwise."

Had Sam known about this? There was no way—after all, Allen had first told the sergeant about the forbidden section. Yet despite all the time he had spent in the library, Sam's suspicions about this place had been sharper than his own. Even standing right outside those doors just weeks ago, he never once doubted that Virgil oversaw an altruistic bastion of knowledge.

And what about the others? Clearly, Cato, Felix, and the other adepts were in on the secret. In El Aria, when Karim was telling him about the greater good of their work... Had he known the whole time? Alevi must have, given her proximity to Felix.

Was it possible even Meghana knew?

A hand touched his cheek. Looking up, he saw the faded disfiguration on her forearm—likely scarring from chemical burns—then found the present in her eyes. She withdrew her hand, placing her palms against the floor as she staggered to her feet. "We can't stay here."

"How many of you are down here?" Allen rushed over to help her.

Manali nearly collapsed as her knee buckled on a shaky step forward. Allen caught her and supported her to the hallway, where she leaned against the wall to catch her breath, resting a hand over her ribs.

"Sorry," wheezed Manali, eyeing the ceiling as she caught her breath. "Haven't fully recovered since they took the lung. Give me a minute...?"

"Allen."

"Allen," she repeated in acknowledgement.

"Of course." Averting his eyes so as not to make her uncomfortable by seeming impatient, he busied himself by picking up the torch. He wanted to express sympathy about her surgery but couldn't find any appropriate words.

"Eight or so," she answered finally. "In this wing."

"Other prisoners?" Allen clarified.

She nodded. "Cassian is one over. Let him out. He'll free the rest."

"Will do."

After a short jog down the hall, he came to the next set of bars. Behind them, a mountain of a man stared back expectantly.

"It's about time," the mountain cracked his knuckles.

Trying to avoid eye contact, Allen hastily fumbled through the keys.

The prisoner was a head-and-a-half taller and three times as wide. He might have had difficulty squeezing through the doorway even without any bars. Perhaps that explained why he hadn't simply uprooted them with brute force. Veins crawled across his pale scalp. His bare chest flexed with anticipation as he cracked his burly hands. With thick hair on his knuckles, they looked like bear claws.

"The third key," Cassian suggested.

"Sorry," Allen gulped nervously, nearly dropping the ring as he spoke. Finding the right key, he asked: "What kind of experiments do they do here?"

Cassian folded his arms. "What haven't they done? Everyone gets their own personal hell, but I've been luckier than most—or unluckier, depending where you stand on living. After giving me three lifetimes in the torture block, they wanted to see what peak human condition looked like. How do I look?"

"Torture block?" Allen repeated, jamming a key into the lock. He twisted and failed. Reexamining the key, he discovered it was number two. A second attempt with the correct key sprung the lock.

"Psychological fragility. Whatever the hell they call it," Cassian cracked his neck to either side and stretched his arms wide, reveling in his newfound freedom. Upon closer inspection, Allen saw a plethora of cuts and scrapes across his chiseled body, including what appeared to be a collection of needle marks on his shoulders.

A metallic clank accompanied Cassian's step forward. "Damn. Almost forgot this," he turned back and scooped up a spherical stone almost two feet in diameter, impossibly shouldering the burden with one arm. The chain around his ankle clinked as he imposed on Allen's personal space. "Much obliged," he grinned, revealing a black-gummed mouth missing most of its teeth. "Keys?"

Allen extended the bundle to him, which he accepted in his free hand.

Cassian looped the ring around his thumb, then took the liberty of relieving Allen of the torch as well. "Walk with me, Glasses. Come and see the world you helped build."

Allen apprehensively followed the giant. As they approached the next cell, Cassian turned to face him, making him flinch.

"This cell is empty because you killed him yesterday," Cassian pointed to the empty chamber in disdain. "Amputated his arms and legs, made him lose his mind on hallucinogens, then tried to replace his heart with some poor bastard's from T-block. He screamed for fourteen minutes before they threw his bones down the chute."

"That's horrible," Allen shuddered, eyes lingering on the empty cell. He imagined a faceless ghost behind the bars, tearfully lamenting his untimely rescue. Guilt and sadness assailed him, while fear lived in the giant's shadow.

"Our next cell," announced Cassian, continuing down the hall, "Is also empty. You finished your sleep deprivation experiment after six or seven days—hard to say down here—and thought the T-block would help wake her back up. I heard the screams all the way from my cell—sounded like you were dissolving her in acid."

"How do you know all this?" asked Allen, revolted by the terrors he was hearing. "Were you once a disciple, too?"

"Nope. Just an unwanted convict," Cassian answered darkly. Below the tattooed mural on his back, patches of rent flesh added an unnerving third dimension to the picture. "Like I said, I've done my time here. Seen a lot of things you'd want to forget."

Allen tried to speak but was cut off by the larger man. "Giselle! Moira! We're breaking out," Cassian unlocked the next cell and stepped back to allow the captives egress.

After a stirless pause, Allen peered inside to find two girls, both little more than teenagers, huddled together in the back corner of the cell. One lay across the other's lap, staring motionlessly at the ceiling.

"She's still not herself," the one sitting up whimpered as she stroked the other's hair. She made no move for the door. Spotting Allen's white robes, she wept bitterly. "What was the point in all this? Why did you do this to her?"

"I'm sorry," Allen apologized reflexively, stepping forward with hands clasped in front of him. Unable to find strength to defend himself or encourage them to escape, he bowed his head shamefully. His eyes watered as he listened to the uneven sobs of the girl and the heartbreaking silence of her sister.

"Moira will be all right," Cassian promised from the doorway, starting toward the next cell. "But you might have to carry her out."

Up close, Allen could tell they were twins. The upright one, Giselle, looked unharmed. A little on the thin side. In stark contrast, Moira looked to be at death's door. The girl's chest rose and fell irregularly, stopping for long, worrying moments before slowly rising again. Her limp limbs were strewn on the floor. Her tiny pupils were similarly still. Cuts and burns scarred the pale face beneath patchy hair that appeared to have been torn out in clumps.

"I'm sorry," Allen repeated solemnly, retreating from the darkening cell into the hallway.

He caught up with Cassian, who shook his head as they passed another cell. "Body's still in that one," he noted. "Starved to death. Already a skeleton."

Allen stared into the dark cell, unable to see the cadaver. A nauseating smell struck him soon after, suggesting that Cassian spoke the truth.

"This is the lucky block. T-block is level two. You don't have the stomach to know what goes on downstairs. You get the picture yet?" Cassian eyed him up and down.

"Yes," Allen acknowledged grimly. "I... I just can't believe it. How could they? Against their own people! How could anyone justify this?"

"There are some bad, bad people in this world," Cassian opened the next cell. "Tonight, they're going to remember I'm one of them."

"Is it finally over?" A man emerged from the cell with an ivory tusk grafted in place of his left forearm. There was something unnatural about his ears as well, but Allen couldn't quite determine what.

"Jamori?" asked Cassian.

"Don't think so," the newcomer shook his head, flicking the long mop of black hair out of his eyes. "They took him downstairs. I heard them saying something about incubation."

"Deus take him," muttered Cassian. "Sorry to see you alive, Korvis. Have enough left in you to crack a few skulls?"

"Let's raise some hell," Korvis lifted his tusk-arm in support.

"Crack skulls?" Allen repeated nervously.

Korvis laughed, walking past him without further comment.

Cassian leaned close and advised: "Probably best you stay out the way. What, in those robes and all."

"You want to kill them?" balked Allen, trailing behind the giant. "But you're free—they're all distracted by the symposium. You can all sneak away. There's no need for more violence."

"Sneak? Take a good look at me," Cassian snorted a laugh, hoisting his ball and chain for show. "No. I've killed a lot of people in my time, for a lot of reasons—ain't never had a better reason than this. Gonna be a hell of a time to have Deus on my side, for once."

"What about Giselle and Moira? You can't just leave them behind!" Allen called after him.

"Giselle!" Cassian called into the sisters' cell in passing. "You coming?"

"I can't leave Moira," the girl refused, still inside the cell.

"That's that, then," Cassian decided.

"Wait!" Allen shouted, surprising both himself and the burly man with his conviction. "If you're just planning to leave them behind, leave the torch and keys with me."

"Suit yourself," Cassian dropped both at his feet and continued into the darkness, Korvis at his side.

Manali approached the edge of the fire's glow. Retrieving the torch and keys, she joined Allen outside the twins' cell.

"He's the only one I've seen come out of P.F. block with his sanity intact. There's no talking him out of what he's going to do. Cassian sees it as a command from Deus—the reason he survived everything he did."

"He should have stayed to help Giselle and Moira," Allen shook his head and entered the cell.

"What's going to happen to her?" Giselle asked him, trusting his white robes for an answer.

"I don't know," he answered truthfully, kneeling in front of the sisters. "She looks like she's been heavily narcotized. Usually, I'd expect the worst to have happened by now or for it to be wearing off. I'm not sure what we can do for her."

"I'm not leaving her," Giselle reminded him defiantly.

"I know," Allen nodded sympathetically, "but we can't leave you here."

"Here," Manali handed him the torch and keys. "I'll try to carry Moira. See if you can convince the man in cell one to join us—he can be a bit touchy."

Once Giselle and Manali were on their feet, Allen led them into the corridor, down the hall until they reached the first cell. "Can you hold this for a moment?" he asked, handing the torch to Giselle.

Manali rested for a spell, gently lowering Moira onto the floor before sitting herself. She gestured to the cell, signaling for Allen to continue.

Cycling through the weighty keys, he inserted one into the padlock and twisted, yielding a successful *click* from the bolt. Swinging the cell door open, he stepped inside with Giselle raising the torch behind him.

Inside the cell, he detected a scent of vomit mixed with urine. Carefully approaching the faceless brown robe and bare feet, he held a hand in front of him and said: "Hey, there. What's your name?"

"Go away!" the prisoner curled into a ball on his side. "Go away!" He might have groaned the name "Annie" between racking sobs.

"We can all go away, together," Allen encouraged the prisoner. Next to him, he noticed a wide glaze of dried blood on the floor around the stranger.

Giselle hovered uncertainly in the doorway. "What language was that?" She lifted her torch, casting light onto the disheveled man. "Is he Taoxian?"

"What?" Allen furrowed his brow, confused. Through the translation app installed in his glasses, he had heard the man's words as clearly as hers.

"Didn't sound like Taoxian to me," Manali opined from the hall. "Maybe he's from one of the tribes in Baltos?"

"Go away," the man ducked his head between his knees in avoidance of the light. "I feel it under my skin... How could you do this to me?"

"Hey—it's Annie," Allen lied, attempting to soothe the agitated subject.

"Annie?" Hope and confusion mixed on his dirty face. "No... Allen?"

"Yes?" he answered, taken aback. Studying the disheveled black hair that hung over sunken eyes, seeing the brown ring around enlarged pupils, it dawned on him. He gripped the prisoner's trembling hand, gritting his teeth as he watched his colleague's chest rise and fall fitfully.

"They got you too?" The prisoner asked through a new river of tears.

"No, Hamal," Allen fought back the tears in his own eyes. "You're free now. I've come to help you and the others."

Hamal recoiled. "I can't. How do I know this isn't a trick? Are you working with them? If they catch us trying to escape, I don't want to... I can't!"

"Hamal, it's okay," Allen promised, struggling to swallow his guilt. Despite his ignorance, he couldn't help but feel personally responsible for the engineer's condition. His complicity stung him deeply, as if he had physically swallowed a knot of barbed wire. "Sam Samson is upstairs. He's guarding the entrance. You're safe now. We're going to get out of here, together."

"I... I can't, Allen. Go on. Leave me behind."

"Allen, just for consideration: Cassian is likely causing quite the scene up there. We should keep moving while we can," suggested Manali.

"Please, Hamal?" urged Allen.

"I can't," he averted his eyes.

Allen stood and stepped back a pace. "I don't know what was taken from you, or how you must be feeling... but this doesn't have to be your ending. The world still needs Chip Hamal. Those two girls who suffered down here with you will need someone to look after them. If you won't live for yourself, find a way to live for someone else; I think Annie would want that for you."

Chip's jaw tensed. "I couldn't help them. My clock's ten to midnight, Allen, and I'm afraid we're all in the same time zone here. We should have died with the rest of them in New Phoenix."

"I can't force you to leave, Chip. If you want to stay here waiting for the disciples come back, I won't stop you."

Hamal pointed at the gun on Allen's hip. "There's another option."

"There isn't," Allen retreated another step, placing a protective hand over the weapon. "Besides, you said it yourself—the clock has another ten minutes. What if this wasn't all for nothing? What if God planned for you to be here so that you could help them?"

Hamal silently stared at the bloodstains on the floor around him.

"Nine minutes left," Allen turned his back and gently steered Giselle out of the cell. "Up to you if that means something."

In the hall, Manali lifted her head as Allen approached. "Ready to go?"

"There are still more people in the other two blocks, right?"

"Ten times as many," nodded Manali. "But we can't help them."

"What?" Allen recoiled, unable to hide his aghast expression.

"I'm not sure who, if anyone, is alive in P.F. block, but they wouldn't make it outside. Cassian was the exception to the rule; everyone else who lives there dies there. Some might survive *biological engineering*, but we can't risk them getting out into the world. The diseases they carry would kill thousands."

"There's got to be something we can do for them!" he protested.

"I don't like it either, Allen. I wish we could do more for them, but speaking from personal experience, I know they would be at peace if we could at least find a way to make sure that they were the last prisoners of The Library on El Aria—that there is no future for this place or the people who designed it."

"We still have eight minutes, right?" Hamal emerged from the cell behind him. He met Allen's eyes and gave him a subtle nod, then approached the semiconscious girl. Looking at her sister, he said: "I don't know if I can offer much, but I'd like to do what I can for you both. Lord knows you did nothing to deserve this."

Giselle shot Allen a confused look, who interpreted: "He wants to help take care of you and your sister—to be a family. Would you like that?"

Understanding dawned in her eyes. She paused for a moment, looking at Allen, then at Chip. Giselle stepped forward, wrapping her arms around him. She buried her head in his shoulder, nodding her agreement. "Teja."

"Thank you," translated Allen.

Hamal hugged her back slowly, as if afraid he might break her. He took a deep breath to calm his shaking hands. "Teja," he repeated softly.

XXX. A Way Back Home

Allen Lee

Demystified, the names of the three blocks oozed malevolence.

> *Essence of the human condition*
> > *Biological engineering*
> > > *Psychological fragility*

After seeing the *lucky* wing, he shuddered to think what was hidden behind the other two euphemisms for antihumanitarian experimentation. He wanted to rescue the other captives but wavered as he looked back at the group of four under his care. However unpalatable, there were kernels of good sense in Manali's words. He could come back to help the others, but his first duty was to evacuate those he had already gathered.

"This way," Allen instructed, hobbling past the antechamber door and into the ascending stairwell. Despite ample lighting in the stone hallways, he kept the torch ready, recalling the darkness in the long, narrow flight of stairs back up to the library floor.

"Where will we go when we get out?" wondered Giselle.

"Someplace safe," Allen gave a nonanswer.

The helicopter, still grounded at the far side of the mesa, would have been the ideal solution. They could have flown back to the ruins of New Phoenix and regrouped with Echo—assuming they were still there. But if Sam's report was accurate and the transporter's parts had been moved to the desert, there would be nothing to go back to, even if they had the means.

It was an issue that could wait a few more hours; their pressing directive was to get away from El Aria and The Library above it.

"What's that clanking sound?" asked Manali.

"That's my leg," Allen tapped his left thigh with his knuckles. "I lost it a year ago. It was wooden for a while, but Virgil made me this nice prosthetic."

"And yet, Korvis gets an elephant tusk for his arm," Manali observed with judgmental eyebrows.

Allen bowed his head in shame. "I didn't know of the tragedy behind the gift."

"But still, you use it." Manali held the door for everyone to exit the stairwell. As Allen stepped into the section with the twenty-four pillars, Manali marched past to resume her lead out in front of the group.

"It's been a great help. While its origins are tainted, I don't see any sense in rejecting it now. Logically, I would only be hurting myself to abandon the limb," reasoned Allen.

"You sound like him," she said with bitter disapproval.

Manali was visibly short on breath, but she stubbornly pushed herself forward. A discordant tension lingered between them, arising from the jarring duality of his identity and actions. She loathed his white robes and intellectual stoicism—reminders of his place among the disciples who had engineered her torment for countless unseen moons. His connection with her sister and, more pertinently, his decision to set her free endeared him to her. As a result, he could tell her heart wanted to both hate him and trust him—but her chaotic emotions unified in her desire to be rid of this place.

Hamal looked worse for wear but pressed on dutifully beside Giselle, Moira hoisted over his shoulder. Sweat drenched his robes, and he had twice succumbed to bloody coughing fits since leaving the cell, but his reignited determination did not falter. A thumbs up signaled that he was fine to continue.

Reaching the narrow stairwell up to the library, Allen took the lead and held the torch high for everyone to watch their steps. During the long, silent ascension, thoughts and emotions clashed wildly in his mind, hurting his heart.

The evidence was overwhelming, yet part of him still couldn't believe it. He was trapped in a terrible, twisted nightmare; a warped world of horror distorted reality around him, entrancing him in vile impossibilities. He could picture big, ruthless Cato as an architect of the horrific studies below, but he couldn't imagine the meek, unassuming man he had met in the New Phoenix lab—a deeply respected friend and mentor—was capable of such immortality.

The part of him that understood their vision—the part that sympathized with Karim and Virgil and Alevi and their earnest belief that they could do more for the greater good through hard sacrifices—absolutely terrified him. He was disgusted, regardless, but understood on some level that their ambition was to advance the healing of the world. At least, he hoped that was the rationale that compelled them to continue. That at the core of their heinous misdeeds was a shred of decency—a kernel of care for the world that erred on the wrong path. Even these nascent desires for a justification of the evil sickened him.

Allen couldn't believe so many people could see the injustice and stand complicit with, much less actively aid, these crimes against humanity.

At the top of the stairs, he lifted the trapdoor with one arm, careful not to burn his clothes with the torch in his other hand. He emerged into the dark aisles, immediately anxious about carrying an open flame over the carpet.

"Psst!"

Allen spotted an eyeball through the bookshelf behind the trapdoor. He stepped to the side, allowing Hamal to enter the aisle. "Samson?" he asked the eyeball.

"It's me. The hell happened down there? A six-hundred-pound gorilla came gallivanting out the aisle, swinging a boulder around like a—actually, hang on. I'll make my way around to the restricted section. See you at the entrance."

"Go on ahead," Manali encouraged Hamal, then waved Giselle on. "I need a moment with Allen."

"It's fairly linear to the entry," Allen said to Hamal, assuming Samson had removed the sentry. He made some directional gestures with his hand, instructing his colleague how to find the sign by the stool.

"Okay. You'll be right behind us?"

"Won't be long," promised Allen.

Hamal took off down the aisle with Giselle at his side and Moira in his arms. As he rounded the corner, Manali turned her eyes to Allen. "Allen..."

"I have to ask you something. I need to know," he interrupted.

She nodded. "Go on."

"Did Meghana know?" Allen swung his arm to point the torch at the trapdoor, accidentally showering embers onto the carpet. He urgently stamped out the red kernels. "Was she a part of all this?"

A sad look darkened Manali's face. "She should have been... but no. When Felix stole her life's work, he also stole her opportunity to join the inner circle. At first, I didn't know what I was doing through my studies. Now, I know I'll never find absolution. It's a wonder she never got caught up in it."

An inexplicable wave of relief washed over him. Meghana was pure. "She won glowing recognition from Virgil on her latest project. She's currently visiting Deuzos to cure a blood plague."

"Not bad, big sis," a ghost of a smile crept onto Manali's lips, failing to lighten her eyes. "We need to make sure she doesn't end up down there—on either side of the bars. It's our turn to help."

"I agree," Allen stroked his chin. "We need to find a way to prevent them from restarting the experiments with new victims. Perhaps, if we informed Sheikh Dohari..."

"Burn it." Manali's eyes reflected the torch's fire, glowing dangerously.

"Burn it?" Allen recoiled, unable to comprehend the thought. "But this library is Kyros' bastion of human knowledge. Countless lifetimes have been devoted to the unique works on these shelves—poetry, history, and... science. We can't just erase everything that's been built over hundreds of years. There must be a better way—one which also preserves this peerless collection."

Manali stepped close, placing a hand on his chest. "They'll just come crawling back like roaches if the warren stays intact. The only way we'll ensure this evil never happens again is if we erase this place and the people behind it."

Allen leaned away from her touch, shaking his head. "Not every author in this library was complicit. Many of these books are originals, single copies that people committed their lives to writing. These are the legacies of thousands of explorers, journalists, musicians, and mathematicians—their last breath. The echo of their days."

"Even after everything you've seen, you won't help stop them?" Gazing into his eyes, Manali gently rested her fingers on his torch-bearing hand.

"I can't," his eyes passed over the books on the nearest shelf. Their spines featured hundreds of unique contributors.

"I understand." Manali closed her eyes, then suddenly jerked his hand sideways toward the books.

The dry paper caught instantly. A wicked flame crawled from one shelf to the next, already beyond control. Retreating in horror, Allen dropped the torch. Fire traveled horizontally across the dark strip of carpet, separating Allen from Manali and the trap door.

"We have to get out of here, now!" Allen urged, transfixed in horror as the flames engulfed the ample supply of wood and paper. "Hurry, before the fire spreads!"

"Guess my clock's running ahead... It's midnight for me, Allen."

"What are you talking about? There's still time! We can both—"

"Like you said, we have to do something for the ones down below. If they can't walk free, at least I can free their spirits."

"Manali!" He retreated another step as the flames grew higher between them, scorching his eyebrows.

"Be brave, Allen. People are counting on you," she turned away. "Say goodbye to Meghana for me. Tell her I'm sorry... and that I'm proud of her." Without another word, she disappeared behind the wall of flames, delving back into the hell she had finally escaped after untold nights without hope.

Allen stood rooted in place, stunned as he stared at the open trapdoor. Watching the inferno's thick clouds of billowing smoke rise to the rafters, he finally turned and ran down the aisle, moving as fast as he could hobble.

The fire raged, climbing ambitiously to the ceiling, leaping hungrily from shelf to shelf. The ambient light guided his way as he clumsily hurried out of the restricted section. He sighted the small group gathered around the stool.

"Took you long enough!" Samson sniffed noisily. "Do I smell brisket?"

"We've got to go," Allen motioned breathlessly. "Fire. Big fire."

"Let's move!" Samson barked, swiftly comprehending the imminent danger. "Allen!"

Awkwardly limping ahead in a way that felt like he was perpetually falling forward, he passed Hamal and caught up with Sam, who jogged at the front of the pack with his rifle in hand. Words tumbled out of Allen's mouth, failing to convey his horror. "I can't believe... they were... on human beings!"

"Hamal filled me in," Samson interrupted. "Worse than I imagined, but I've been around the farm long enough to know one big pile of fly-swarmin' shit means you've got a horse nearby—and a horse nearby means..." his brow arched suggestively, allowing Allen to finish the esoteric metaphor.

The thick air burned Allen's lungs, stealing his breath and filling his chest with smoke. He coughed blood into the crook of his elbow, not daring to slow down with the heat rising on his back. Risking a glance behind him, he saw Hamal giving everything he had to bring the girls out to safety. Sweat drenched his clothes, dripping from his face and long hair as if he had just emerged from a pool. Allen recognized the pain and fear in Chip's eyes, mirroring his own.

His hard-set jaw and clenched teeth marked his determination, signaling to Allen that he had better not slow down.

Following Samson through a series of winding turns, Allen realized he was completely lost. He had to trust that Sam knew the way from here. At the rate the hungering blaze was devouring the labyrinth of dry tinder, they would be lucky to escape with their lives. Still, he couldn't shake a looming feeling of guilt. Running like a coward. "There are still people back there, Sam. Manali…"

"Damn it, Doctor Lee!" Samson growled, pausing at a fork in the aisle. He looked between the left and right paths, uttered a particularly creative curse, then chose left. "There's nothing but kindling back there. Unless you'd like to be part of it, keep your rear in gear!"

"What's the plan when we get out?" Allen panted, following Samson around another turn.

"Keep on not dying," Samson advised, stealing a nervous glance back toward Hamal and Giselle. Tapping his gun with an anxious finger, he looked at Allen's empty hands, then back at the liberated trio. "Save the elephants and cure world hunger tomorrow—first, let's get out of this forsaken place. Move!"

The fire was pulling ahead. The smoke layer descended rapidly over the cavernous room as flames raced down the long aisles. Several rows back, a resounding crash rocked the building as part of the roof collapsed, bringing the upper floor's shelves down into the inferno. A powerful blast wave emanated from the crash site, invigorated by the gust of new air.

"There's the exit!" Samson yelled above the roaring fire.

Despite the unfamiliar hellscape around them, Allen recognized the grand aisles approaching the exit. One hundred yards away.

"We're almost there!" Allen relayed the encouragement to Hamal, who looked dangerously close to passing out.

Whole body shuddering, Chip wheezed acknowledgement. His arms shook as they kept Moira balanced over his shoulder. Giselle looked in better condition, but the smoke stung her eyes red. Ash stained her cheeks black.

Ineffectively attempting to accelerate, Allen shuffled forward, one foot in front of the mechanical other. In his peripheral vision, he saw a crumpled set of robes on the floor. Without turning to look, he identified the fallen obstacle as one of the pages, either new or old in service to The Library. He suspected the unfortunate page had met Cassian and Korvis on their way out. In truth, the guardian of the books likely knew nothing of the despicable operations below.

"We're running out of time," Samson mumbled anxiously under his breath, taking stock of his four companions. He looked down the stretch of bookshelves still to go, then instructed Chip: "Hamal—let me take her."

"Agh!" Hamal slowed, panting heavily. Pain flashed on his face as he lowered Moira to be transferred, as if he thought he had let her down by giving up so close to the exit. Samson thrust his gun into Allen's hands, shooting him a look that conveyed it wasn't up for discussion. With his hands free, Samson accepted Moira onto his shoulder, turned, and dashed ahead.

Striving to be with her sister, Giselle took off in Sam's wake, easily passing Allen. Hamal jogged alongside him while he caught his breath. As the gap between them and Samson widened, Hamal nodded his encouragement, then willed his legs to carry him forward, leaving Allen in the rear.

The last fifty yards felt like a mile. The flames danced off the shelves, perilous and unpredictable as they twisted into his path. Gingerly cradling the foreign weapon in his hands, he made sure to keep the barrel pointed at the shelves. The rapidly encroaching fire should have been his only concern, but he shared equal aversion to the firearm. Light-headed from both the smoky air and his proximity with the automatic killing device, he stumbled onward.

Through terror and doubt, he reached deep within himself to draw strength from his family. Danny lent him the courage he lacked, helping him charge through the fire with rifle in hand. Lyn brought air into his depleted lungs, focusing him on his unfinished duty to Giselle and Moira. Alaina gave him the endurance he didn't think he had, renewed with an unyielding will to survive—to persevere so that he may one day return to her side.

He would give anything to get back home.

Hope whispered that it was possible. The way was just ahead.

Aided by their transcendent spirits, he broke past the burning towers of books and resolutely ascended the steps to the platform overlooking the library. The view that had once enchanted him now made him feel hollow. Despite the intense heat in the collapsing chamber, he stood for a moment and stared back at the colossal pyre.

Additional sections of the roof caved in, barely visible through the thick smoke over the crumbling bookshelves. Not a pocket of the blazing chamber had been spared the reach of the little flame he held in his hand only minutes ago. He felt Manali's retribution in the cackling flames, furious, yet incomplete. Despite his role in delivering this righteous fire, he felt only sadness to watch the millions of volumes burn. It was a funeral—for both the malevolent walls built upon dark secrets and the noble works that found shelter within them.

"Doctor Lee!" Samson shouted from the doorway. The others had apparently made their exit already. Sam ran over and relieved him of the rifle. "No man left behind. Time to go."

With a parting glance at the once glorious library, now forever lost, Allen turned his attention to the exit. Following Samson, he noticed a trail of blood curving from the doorway to an alcove on the left. "Is everyone okay?" he called to Sam, who continued outside without any indication that he had heard him.

Staring at the grand wooden doors just ten yards away, Allen stopped. His eyes followed the trail to the alcove. Smoke and embers cluttered the air, but the platform floor had yet to ignite. The directory of blue encyclopedias joined the casualty toll as the flames crept across the rafters and down the walls.

Determined to take a quick look, Allen staggered toward the alcove. He'd retreat to the exit if the trail ran too deep into the library. Rounding the corner, he found a familiar face—partially obscured by his long hair—slumped with his back against the wall. The man was bleeding from his abdomen. His right hand covered the wound, ineffectively attempting to staunch the blood flow. The reddened extension of his truncated left arm rested at his side.

Korvis looked up as Allen approached. "Is this hell? It's hotter than I was expecting."

"You're injured!"

"Ah. Thanks. Hadn't noticed," Korvis said calmly, seemingly at peace with his end.

"We've got to get you outside. This place is about to burn down," Allen offered a hand.

"Good," Korvis lifted his tusk meaningfully, making no effort to rise.

"Here," Allen grabbed the tusk and used it to tear a strip of cloth from the bottom of his robe. Doubling the cloth pad, he lifted Korvis' bloody hand to place the makeshift compress against the vertical wound.

"Still sort of feels like someone stabbed me," Korvis complained dryly.

"Come on," Allen awkwardly stooped to lift the injured man. Ducking his head between the tusk and body, Allen strained his shoulders and back to hoist Korvis to his feet. Thankfully, the man allowed himself to be moved, leaning on Allen for support. Together, they emerged from the alcove into a

thick cloud of floating ash, blown violently into the air as more of the structural support gave way.

"Damn it," Korvis flinched as hot embers landed on his chest. He struggled to match Allen's steady cadence toward the door. "I was ready to die!"

"Too bad."

Hacking a violent cough, Allen tried to tuck his mouth into his robes for cleaner air. Despite the impenetrable firestorm around them, he saw a clear path to the exit and focused his movement forward, blocking out the blazing roar of destruction that swallowed The Library on El Aria.

Fifteen yards away.

Korvis leaned heavily on his right shoulder. Allen's metal foot scraped the ground as he intermittently hobbled forward with his right.

Ten yards away.

Sam stuck his head through the doorway, visibly exasperated. "Allen! Move your bionic ass!"

Five yards away.

Allen heard a thunderous crack above him. Looking up, he saw a wide beam come loose from the rafters. The second before it crashed onto him, he flung the right side of his body forward, swinging Korvis ahead.

A wave of heat scorched his neck and back as he fell to the ground. Allen clawed at the floor, trying to escape the burning lumber, but he didn't have the strength to pull himself forward. Fragments of his shattered glasses cut his fingers. Blurrily, he looked at the flaming beam that had pinned his left leg to the ground. He was trapped.

"Cut it off!" Samson yelled, tossing him a knife. Then, distantly, "Crawl to the door!"

Allen could barely keep his eyes open against the scorching flames, inches away from his flesh. The fire was spreading. Holding the knife in his right hand, he swiveled his body to better access his left leg. Sam rushed over to pat down his burning robes, buying precious seconds. Allen cut the cloth above his leg to examine the metal mechanisms beneath. Hastily, he disengaged the lock and connectors that fastened the appendage to his socket.

The moment Allen freed himself, Samson's hands hooked under his armpits to drag him away from the fire. More sections of roof fell behind the first, spraying ash and soot onto his formerly white robes. Glancing down at the tattered sleeves, he could tell the skin underneath was charred as well.

"Hamal!" Samson cried out.

Allen's right leg dragged over the lip of the doorway as another beam fell from the rafters, sealing off the library behind them. He turned his head to the side, coughing thick globules of blood onto the steps as Sam dragged him away from the wooden structure and onto the well-lit grass.

The shapes to his right looked like bodies in the grass, though it was hard to tell with his abysmal eyesight. Red feet adorned the bottom of each corpse, ostensibly the El Arian moccasins. One particularly large body stood out; covered in dozens of small red marks, it lay next to a sizeable boulder.

Turning his head to the left, Allen discerned four other figures, three of whom appeared to be moving. He saw two with long hair, one sitting and one lying down, and assumed they were the twins. That suggested Hamal was tending to Korvis, whose tusk arm was recognizable even without glasses.

Though barely able to move, Allen assumed he was among the living.

"Everyone alive?" Samson straightened up as he cleared his throat.

"Been better," Hamal fell back on his rear.

"Thank you," Allen wiped his eyes. He could still feel the heat from the burning library but saw only violent plumes of red light consuming the dark shelter. Unable to make out any details beyond light and dark, he turned to look at the blur who was most likely Korvis. "Are you all right?"

Korvis' face turned toward him and made what looked like a frown. "Woa sochst du?"

"What..." Allen reached to adjust his glasses, but his finger ran through the hair above his ear instead. He turned to Sam. "Do you have a translator?"

"Never needed one. My HUD got night vision and range finder; yours got a dictionary. But that fries our pickle now, don't it?" sighed Sam. "Hamal?"

"They took mine," he answered bitterly.

"All right. Let me think. Our position will soon be compromised, as there's a zero-percent chance nobody notices the small-scale sun we made out of their library. So, moving: we're not a mobile group. The helicopter is behind the senate, where we believe most of the enemy are gathered. We don't know how to fly the helicopter and have no clear destination, but there are some extra supplies and ammunition inside."

"I feel the answer's not the helicopter," Allen thought aloud.

"Well, then speak up," invited Samson.

"I know Meghana and her sister, Manali, are from Ayrabos. I think the twins are, too. I'm not sure about Korvis, but he seemed to at least understand some of what was going on down there. If we can't converse, we'll need to settle into a place where they can at least interact with locals—and that's El Aria."

"Danger close to The Library. I expect they'll come looking for them," countered Sam.

"They don't know they escaped," Allen sat up, growing more confident in his idea. "I don't know if it's true, but I've heard the sheikh doesn't even know the lab existed. At least it's a well-kept secret. The only ones who know would be the adepts that ran it, and even they wouldn't necessarily suspect the fire was part of a breakout."

"Sounds to me like we need to thin out the white coats," Sam checked his ammunition.

"Chip, I feel you should lead these three to town and recover. Steal one of the carriages. Use this if you need," Allen wormed across the ground to offer him the knife.

"Are you two going to be okay?" Hamal accepted the weapon.

"Manali believed the experiments would never stop unless those who orchestrated them were removed. I can't go with you until I've had a chance to confront Virgil. I need answers," explained Allen.

"Don't worry, Hamal. We'll square things away here and be on the next cart after you," promised Samson. He walked over to the exterior banister and returned to Allen with a wooden stick. "Best I could find."

"Thank you," Allen said appreciatively, rising to his foot and gripping the makeshift cane in his left hand. It felt strange to be missing his leg again, but he found a shallow comfort in knowing he was more whole now.

"Godspeed, Hamal," Samson helped the engineer to his feet.

"Be safe," nodded Chip. He turned toward Allen. "Thank you both for getting us out of there. I'll do what I can to help them. We'll see you soon."

"Take care, Chip," Allen smiled in return, though he couldn't make out his colleague's face.

Hamal scooped Moira from the grass and gestured for the others to follow. Though neither Giselle nor Korvis understood his words, they got the meaning. Giselle bowed with her hands clasped together in thanks, while Korvis lifted his tusk in acknowledgment to Allen.

Samson led Allen toward the senate, a beacon of faded color glowing through stained-glass windows. "Not that I need your permission," Sam cracked his neck, "but I want us to be on the same page. I understand you're looking for closure from Virgil. You want answers. That said, I see the rest of his crew as war criminals. We might be short a jury, but the executioner's in town."

"Not all of them were part of this," Allen voiced with waned conviction. He wanted to argue for the preservation of human life, but Manali's words weighed on him. If Meghana did return, there was every likelihood she would get caught up in the same evil as Manali—forced to further the experimentation or be subjected to it. Not to mention the hundreds of scholars and victims yet to be ensnared by these atrocities. If he didn't act now, he'd be complicit.

"But enough were," Samson lit a cigarette. He took a deep breath of smoke, steadying his nerves before the confrontation.

Saying nothing, Allen stared at the stained colors escaping the senate. Shadows of the library's immolation danced on the shapeless expanse of grass.

A flurry of activity erupted out from the senate. A squad of eight white-robed scholars emerged, joined by six guards in red moccasins and another man in a red-and-gold robe. Allen assumed the royal-looking figure to be Sheikh Dohari himself.

"Freeze!" Samson aimed his rifle at the torch-bearing disciples.

Allen felt the condemning eyes of one man. Virgil walked ahead of the others, horrified by the inferno. "What have you done?"

An accented voice cried out in dismay for the library. Allen recognized the unintelligible words of despair as Cato's.

The sheikh barked an angry order in a foreign tongue. The guardsmen ran forward, swords raised and voices strained in patriotic ululation.

Sam dropped the charging soldiers with clinical accuracy, all center mass, then fired at the scattering disciples, felling several around Virgil.

"Leave Allen alive," Virgil commanded above the gunfire.

A muzzle flashed from the darkness behind the carnage.

Samson's gun fell silent as a burst of red exited the back of his head. The sergeant crumpled to the ground and stayed there, unmoving.

"Sam!" cried Allen. A horrible, mournful knot gripped his stomach as his blurry eyes traced the still edges of his fallen ally. Death was fast and firm. He lifted his eyes to the darkness, searching for the concealed shooter.

Stepping into the glow of the burning library, Ajax advanced with his rifle trained on him. "Don't do anything stupid, Glasses."

Allen raised his right hand in surrender, casting a long shadow over the ground between them. His left hand shakily squeezed the cane for support.

Advancing alongside Ajax, Virgil left his fallen adepts behind, dead or writhing in the grass. He shook his head in disbelief as he stared at his burning library. "How could you, Allen?" he asked with inconsolable disappointment.

Reaching Samson's fallen body, Ajax swiveled his gun away from Allen and fired a second bullet at point-blank range to confirm the kill. As he lifted his rifle, Ajax looked surprised to see the pistol in Allen's right hand, aimed at Virgil who stood just five yards away.

"You lied to me!" Allen accused his former friend. "This whole time, I thought you were a hero. I admired you. Your advancement of medicine was supposed to heal the world—but it was all a lie! You tortured people and called it science. You're not a philosopher; you're a monster."

"A thousand years, Allen," Virgil could not tear his eyes away from the burning library. "Your choices today have set the world back a thousand years. You have blindly ushered in a dark age devoid of science, history, logic, art, and medicine. Without the volumes of antidotes and remedies kept here, hundreds of thousands will die. Could you not see the reason for the continued existence of our Library? Did you not understand our purpose?"

"Your purpose was tainted, Virgil. You lied to yourself and everyone around you. If you were devoted to good, you never would have considered such twisted human experimentation."

"So you burned down the crowning achievement of world history to avenge the dregs of society? Ruthless killers, abandoned orphans, the incurably sick?" Virgil laughed mirthlessly, finally taking his eyes off the library. "How could you possibly judge their lives as more valuable than the thousands whom their suffering helps?"

"It's not your place to decide their suffering for them. No living being should be subjected to what you've done to those people," spat Allen.

"If anyone should understand, I thought it would be you," lamented Virgil. "At least I knew every subject by name. When it was you leading human experimentation, you knew me only as *Subject One*."

"That's... that was different. We had to save our home!" Allen nearly lost his balance as he thumped the ground with his cane.

"So bending the wills of proud, living beings to fuel your war machine is ethical, but gathering data to save lives is heinous," summarized Virgil.

"You grafted a tusk onto Korvis in place of his arm. What medical purpose did that serve?" demanded Allen.

"I suspect Felix's answer would concern the importance of anesthetics, sterile surgery, and finding low-cost-alternative prosthetics for the destitute in remote areas. There is a possibility it was simply a funded project to fuel our own war machines, but regrettably, we can no longer ask him for confirmation," Virgil gestured to the bodies in the grass behind him.

"And the transporter," Allen continued his accusation, unwilling to let Virgil into his head. "You lied about that too! You're not even working on it."

"I confess, I did mislead you about the transporter," Virgil raised a solemn hand. "However, I did not lie about my intent to return you to your home. I would have gladly done so, Allen. The technology was never an issue. I wished only for you to find happiness."

Allen squinted at Virgil's unfocused face. A purple apparition glowed behind like a nebulous cloud of smoke. Although he could not see it clearly, he sensed the shade was Logios, Primal of Knowledge. "Did you know?"

"Know what?" Virgil asked patiently, ostensibly unfazed by the foreign armament pointed at his head.

"Home," Allen croaked, trying to hold the gun steady. "About Alaina and Lyn..."

"Yes," Virgil admitted simply.

Allen swallowed the lump in his throat. He blinked rapidly. His cheeks were wet. "Were they..."

"Unfortunately, dear Allen, the portal can only transcend space. Not time." Virgil bowed his head, as if sincere in his empathy. "Regimes win wars. People lose battles. It's not too late for you to walk away from this, Allen."

"I don't believe you!" Allen tightened his grip on the pistol.

"Give up already!" Ajax stalked forward with Allen fixed in his sights. "It's over. We never stood a chance—and less after we lost the portal. There's nothing left for you in that world, Allen. It's all blown to hell."

"That's not true!" Allen screamed, finger trembling on the trigger.

The blurry shapes in front of his eyes began to fade. The world around him blended with the fantasies he kept alive. Those that kept him alive.

As the nightmare devoured itself, the dream seeped through the cracks.

He bit into his lip as he envisioned Alaina's loving face across the table. He heard Lyn's sweet laugh, hidden somewhere in the crackling fire behind him. They were waiting for him.

Meghana was smiling too, somewhere. She would be confused when she returned to find The Library purged from the hilltop, but she was the type to keep pursuing what she believed in. Perhaps she would open a school. Perhaps she would build a hospital in the city. Either way, he knew he'd see her again. They were lifelong friends, now.

He'd see them all in just a little while.

"Humans are unique creatures, Allen. We endure hardships, and we evolve. Our purpose is often metamorphic, but it should ceaselessly venture beyond survival," Virgil stepped forward, looking past the gun and into Allen's eyes. "You made a mistake—grievous, but not unforgiveable. Please: join me. Help me spread knowledge to the world. We can bring these people new hope. Together."

Allen's eyes stung from the smoke and tears. He smelled Alaina's chicken curry. It was slightly overcooked, but he'd enjoy it anyway. He loved her, and by extension, he'd love the extra-crispy chicken she made for them. The best part of his day was always spending time with his family.

"They're waiting for me," Allen smiled. He saw them clearly now. Mother and daughter, smiling at the table. They were happy to see him.

"Allen," Virgil's voice trembled for the first time. He reached out a placating hand toward him. "I am the last vessel of the irreplaceable sum of human knowledge you destroyed today. I alone can recreate all that was lost. It will take a lifetime, but we can preserve the hard-won advancements of the tens of thousands of scholars before us. Enlightenment does not need to be lost to this world. We can still bequeath Kyros a bright future."

He heard the phone ringing. That must be Danny.

"Allen—I alone can rewrite history. We can, together... but you must hand over the pen. Lower your gun, dear Allen. Don't—"

A resounding knock thundered at the door.

That must be Charles, early for dinner. Allen was excited to see him. It had been a few days, at least, since he'd seen his best friend. He was excited to hear all about the new job he had landed.

Allen's right hand fell to his side. The smoking pistol slid out of his hand. Ears ringing, he stared straight ahead at the dancing colors escaping the stained-glass rotunda. It would have been a cold night if not for the warmth of the roaring fireplace behind him.

A second knock thundered at the door.

Allen smiled as he fell.

It was time to see Charles again.

XXXI. The Time We Have

Drake

Take a deep breath. You've got this. I believe in you."

Drake folded his arms and leaned back against the tree, careful to make no sudden sounds. A lone ray of sun broke through the foliage, falling on his right eye. He squinted against the light, staring down the oblivious hare eating its lunch.

A short walk from the water's edge, the trees here were less densely packed than the dark forests of the Lowlands. A neighboring river flowed lazily, one of several that fed the meandering channel they had passed earlier that morning. On occasion, a daring fish would leap from the water as if taunting Drake to return with suitable fishing equipment. Instead, it was the land-based critter who had been selected for the afternoon's sustenance.

"But he's kind of cute," whined Talia, flexing the tension in her bow.

"Rabbits aren't the brightest animals," denounced Drake. "All they do is eat, sleep, shit, and die."

"And mate," Talia suggested.

"If they're lucky," Drake permitted.

"You sure you don't feel like more rice?" she attempted valiantly.

"Meat keeps you strong," Drake swatted a fly off his nose, causing the hare to halt its snacking and raise its ears. Once it returned its focus to the vegetation, he added: "And we need to keep reserves of food that won't spoil. Now, he's had his lunch; it's time for us to have ours."

"Sorry, bunny," Talia sighed, nocking an arrow on the bow. She drew the feather of the arrow against her right cheek, holding her breath as she focused her aim. At the last second, she slid her left hand a half-inch to the right, crunched a twig under her foot, then released the arrow.

The rabbit darted forward as the arrow flew, unwittingly moving into its path. Talia winced as the bolt connected, securing the kill and concluding their lesson in tracking.

"Nice shot," Drake commented with a raised eyebrow.

Talia exhaled her vexation, closing her eyes as she swung the bow over her shoulder. "I tried to help him," she confessed.

"I noticed." Drake stepped through the brush to collect their food for the afternoon. "Think you would've hit it if you were trying to?"

"Yeah," she said automatically, as if the answer should be obvious. "Well, probably."

"Moving targets are harder to hit." Drake pulled the arrow free and secured the pelt to his bag with a white string. He wiped the arrow clean against his pants, then returned it to Talia, who gingerly replaced it in her quiver.

"I know."

"If you catch them by surprise when they're bored or distracted, makes it a lot easier," he advised. "There's also a sweet spot in range. If they're too far away, you've got to account for wind and their movement and the like; if they're too close, you might lose your nerve if they charge you. Half the battle's getting a good position before the battle starts."

"We still talking about rabbits?" Talia frowned.

"Life lessons." Drake took a deep breath of the sweet forest air. He looked through the trees to the west, parallel to the water. "Come on."

"Think we shoulda stayed on the road?" She swatted a bug on her arm.

"A little nature's good for you," insisted Drake. "Besides, the roads out here aren't any better than a forest trail. At least we get some peace."

"I'm sure if we walk far enough in any direction, we'll hit another road eventually," Talia mused philosophically. "Didn't you say Long Fan told you about a town out in the Riverlands? What was the name—Crossroads?"

"That's right."

"Who were Long Fan's friends he said to look for? John and Luke?"

"Mercenaries. Not friends," Drake corrected meaningfully. "And that sounds close. Luc for sure. I forget the other one—Jack, or Tom, or Kyle..."

"Kyle sounds right," decided Talia. "Aren't they around here too?"

"Could be," he shrugged. "No telling if they're still here on contract or if we'll run into them. Hey, look at this!" Drake knelt in the soft dirt and placed a hand next to hoof imprints leading south. He studied the trajectory of the tracks, noting the trodden grass and disturbed leaves that marked a path. "See these tracks?"

"Oh yeah," she smiled, kneeling to place a hand over one of the prints. "Neat. What kind of animal do you think it was?"

"Why don't we take a look?"

Talia scratched her head. "We have time?"

"Sure." He led the way south, scanning through the trees as he walked the faded path. Looking back to check that Talia was following, he spotted a toothy grin on her face. He turned forward, trying to conceal one of his own.

"Aha," Drake stopped at the top of a small mound, pointing to further evidence on the other side. "Look, fresh tracks."

Talia followed him over the mound. Upon sighting the *evidence*, she recoiled in disgust. "Ew, Drake! Why are you making me look at bear crap?"

"It's *scat*," he insisted defensively. "And bear scat don't look like this. See the oval pellets? That's an herbivore. You can tell by the firmness it eats a lot of twigs, leaves, bark..."

"That's so gross, Drake," Talia shook her head.

He tested one of the pellets' tactile properties in his gloved hand. "You can see it's shiny, right—and it's still cooling."

"Why are you touching deer poo?" Talia feigned a gag.

"Scat," Drake corrected with as much dignity as he could muster. "I'll have you know, touching this deer *scat* tells us our friend was here less than an hour ago."

"I don't believe it," Talia huffed at the absurdity of the analysis.

Unabashed, Drake wiped his glove on the grass and continued onward through the woods. Passing through the thicket, he lost track of the deer at the short grass of the sloping hill. Undeterred, he pressed forward, picking through the maze of low-hanging branches until he reached a clearing.

"Come here," he whispered, beckoning Talia over.

"I don't want to see anymore deer poo," she asserted willfully.

"Just come here," he insisted, pulling down a branch to give them a better sightline.

Her eyes widened as she peered through the brush and sighted the beautiful creature. "Wow," she said simply, stunned by the animal's brilliance.

In the center of the clearing, a pristine white elk grazed on a bed of orchids. Its wide antlers branched into eight points each side, totaling sixteen unbroken tines. A thick, white coat wrapped its neck, streaked with hints of gold. Its broad face supported small, docile eyes and floppy, attentive ears. Nearby, a little fawn grazed under her father's watchful gaze, flower petals stuck on her tan coat, between speckles of white. The majestic elk did not rear its head at the onlookers, though Drake suspected it knew they were there.

Talia's smile faded abruptly, and she glanced at the bow slung over her shoulder. Meeting her eyes, Drake shook his head and reached out a soothing hand. "We have all the food we need today. Just watch."

A thankful grin brightened her face as she slipped the bag off her back and settled in to marvel at the beautiful animals.

The fawn stumbled around the clearing on its young legs, drunkenly leaping and skipping from one bed of flowers to the next. Chasing a butterfly through the field, she inadvertently tottered closer to the bushes. The butterfly ascended out of reach, leaving the fawn to stare blankly ahead into the forest. Curious brown eyes studied Talia from less than five feet away.

The bull's eyes turned toward the thicket as its child played, finding Drake among the trees. It munched the orchids warily, having spotted the potential threat but not yet concerned enough to leave its banquet behind. As its offspring wandered back into the clearing, the bull seemed to relax a little.

"I could watch them for hours," fawned Talia.

An almost indistinguishable rustle sounded from the bushes to the north of the clearing. The elk raised its head, ears perked up on high alert. A second twig snapped in the brush, frightening the animal. It let loose a throaty bleat, instructing its youngling to follow. The pair galloped out the opposite side of the clearing, leaving a trail of dislodged orchids in their wake.

"No," Talia whispered sadly, stretching a hand after the fleeing animals. "Come back!"

"Those white ones are rare. One in a million," Drake claimed, though he suspected that he was likely inflating the rarity.

"I can't believe how lucky we were," Talia smiled wistfully. "That was amazing. I just wish they would have stayed a few more minutes."

"Nothing lasts forever," Drake sighed, rising to his feet despite protest from his locked knees, "but that's what makes these moments so special. We can't ask for more time, but we can make the most of the time we have."

XXXII. All Cooped Up

Drake

Talia insisted they cross the river.

"I know it's wide, but it doesn't look too fast or deep. There would be people at the mill, right? We can ask them for directions."

"I don't like people," Drake grumbled, continuing south along the water's edge. "And I don't need directions. We just keep going west."

"Which is across the river, as it were," she remarked smartly.

"A bridge or something will come up soon. You can never really tell how deep water is from shore," he dismissed, eyeing the waterwheel affixed to the side of a weathered barn across the water.

"A little swim won't hurt you," Talia rolled her eyes. Walking between him and the gentle vale, she gazed at the glinting water and added: "When I was a kid, we would sometimes go to the lake outside of town."

"You're still a kid," Drake reminded her offhandedly.

Her eyes admonished him, but she chose to ignore the jest. "Baron loved to swim—he always knew when we were getting close. As soon as he heard the lake, he'd go charging off. Always trying to drink the water as he paddled around. Silly dog."

Drake still felt a little lost for words whenever discussing her past life. Sometimes, it felt worlds away. "Oh yeah? Was he a good swimmer?"

"As good as I was," she chuckled. "I was a handful to teach. I had this fear that a big fish would eat me if I went too far in the water."

"I don't think there are many people-eating fish," Drake considered.

"I know," Talia assured him.

"Sharks, of course. I don't know if crocodiles count as fish, but they're still nasty little snappers."

"Thank you, Drake. I've already gotten over my fear of big fish."

"Mind you, I think the small ones are just as bad. You've got leeches, jellyfish, poisonous urchins..."

"I said thank you, Drake," Talia swatted his arm. "Looks like you got your wish—no swimming today." She pointed out a series of large stones that formed a path across the river. The white water coursed past the impediments, washing over some and around others.

"I don't know," he waffled.

"It's a bridge," she insisted. "Get over it."

"Well, we're still too far downstream to bother going back to the mill," Drake negotiated.

"Fine," Talia ran forward, willing to be the first to cross. "Where there's a mill, there's a way. We'll find other people nearby. Right?"

"Careful on the rocks," Drake warned as she stepped onto the first stone. "Any underwater or covered in moss are slippy. Take your time."

"I've got it," she called over her shoulder, stretching her arms out for balance as she hopped from one boulder to the next.

Drake planted a boot on the first stone to test it, rocking the loose boulder in-place. With a resigned exhale, he trusted his weight to the rock, hurriedly bringing his second foot under him. Feeling a bit like a perched mountain goat, he outstretched his leg again, daring to cross to the second rock.

"Whoa—careful on this one!" cautioned Talia, a third of the way across the river.

"Got it," Drake acknowledged. Unsure which stone she was referring to, he slowed his measured pace, choosing to distrust all of them.

"How far do you think we are?" Talia teetered to the side but caught her balance before skipping to the next rock.

"From what?" Drake advanced another step.

"The Oracle," she clarified.

"Closer than we were yesterday," he estimated.

"Isn't the Cradle of Life in the Riverlands?" Talia stooped to peer into the water. "Oh, a fish!"

"It is," Drake answered without taking his eyes off the path. "We'll be there soon."

Pyros hovered at the edge of his mind. *What?* Drake demanded, carefully stepping onto a mossy stone.

Those rocks look precarious, the Primal warned importantly.

"I am well aware," snapped Drake.

"What?" hollered Talia.

"Nothing," growled Drake. He lifted his back foot and felt his balance shift as his standing foot slipped forward. Flailing his arms in a wild struggle to right himself, he overcorrected and suffered gravity's irresistible pull in a new direction. Pitching left, he fell off the path and into the cool river.

A fin brushed against his leg. He violently kicked through the water, protruding his head above the surface. Letting the current take him a few feet downstream of the rapids, he planted his feet on the river floor and stood, water dripping from his arms and chest.

"How's the water?" Talia inquired innocently, scooping a handful from her dry spot on the rocks.

"Refreshing," Drake said flatly, running his hands through his sopping hair. He ruefully carried on, moving across the remainder of the valley in a half-swim, half-wading movement that was neither quick nor dignifying.

"I told you to be careful," she reminded him as he approached the shoreline.

"That rock had it out for me," griped Drake. Water seeped from his drenched clothes as he crawled onto the riverbank.

"At least the sun's out," Talia noted optimistically. She attempted to conceal a smile, appearing all the more pleased for the effort. "I'm sure you'll dry off quickly.

Drake took the pack off his shoulders and squeezed the bottom of the bag to hasten the draining process. *Care to help, Pyros?*

The sun is out, echoed the Primal lazily. *And I told you to be careful.*

Following the dirt road west, ignoring the northbound offshoot to the mill, they soon reached a farmstead. Inside the gated perimeter, a bungalow stood at the end of the raked path that splintered off the main road. A motley assembly of farm animals loitered around the neighboring barn.

"Bet whoever lives here could tell us where we are," suggested Talia.

"I'd hate to impose," Drake shook his head. "The road continues west. We can find an inn or something."

"But the gate's open," Talia noted, wandering onto the property. "They wouldn't leave it open if they didn't want visitors, right?"

"I don't think that's an invitation to trespass," Drake disagreed, hovering uncomfortably at the boundary.

"I'll do the talking," Talia started toward the farmstead. "Besides, what if we passed the Cradle already?"

"The road," Drake groaned his dissent but reluctantly followed her fearless footsteps. "A town or inn, maybe."

"Look," Talia turned, walking backward as she explained herself. "We don't exactly have a great track record with small-town inns, right? Well, maybe these farmers will be more open to giving directions to two lost travelers on a nice day. Farming folk are friendly folk, they say."

"Who's *they?*" Drake scoffed. "Nobody says that."

"You know," Talia waved her hands nebulously. "They."

She reached the front porch steps and ascended to knock on the blue door. The paint was peeling, but muddy footprints provided evidence that the farmstead was still inhabited. Several windows offered views into and out of the house, though Drake made an effort to respect the homeowner's privacy.

Receiving no answer, Talia knocked again. She leaned her ear to the door, then returned down the porch steps to announce her findings. "Nobody home. Maybe they're in the barn?"

"We came this far," Drake sighed, gesturing for her to lead on. He followed with crossed arms, on the lookout for potential threats. Aside from a few cows grazing behind the barn, all appeared to be peaceful. For now.

"What's that little shack on the side of the barn?" Talia inquired, gesturing to the wooden structure closest to them.

"I'd guess it's either a tool shed or a chicken coop," postulated Drake.

"Ah, I've got one! Why did the chicken cross the road?"

"I don't want to hear it," he declined immediately.

"Come on!" she protested. "Please?"

"Nope. No chicken-road jokes. You're better than this."

"But it's a really good one!"

"Now you're setting my expectations too high," he said, unmovable.

"Please?" she persisted. "Why did the chicken cross the road?"

Drake sighed. "Why?"

Talia grinned. "No one knows—but the road sure was pissed."

"All right. You won me back," he nodded appreciatively. "I don't know if I'd call it *egg*-cellent, but it was pretty good."

"That was... Yikes. I mean, way to lower the bar, Drake. I almost regret starting this."

"I declare fowl play," he retorted. "You know... fowl. Like foul."

"I get it," Talia sighed. "Let's just focus on finding the farmer."

She knocked on the door, then swung it open inward. "Hello—oh."

"Uh..." A bewildered voice replied from inside.

"Hi," Talia recovered, clearing her throat.

"Hello?" the voice answered. That of a young man.

Drake hovered behind Talia in the doorway. He followed her gaze and spotted a surprised Val'Kyran dressed in overalls and a flannel shirt, who was distributing chicken feed to the clucking swarm around his ankles. The grain slipped out of his gloved hand as he sized up the newcomers, inciting the red-headed hens to frantically flap their wings to batter away their competition.

"Afternoon," Drake greeted from the doorway, meeting the eyes of a chicken that looked suspiciously like Bruce.

"Sorry to intrude," Talia began nervously, twiddling her fingers. "We're a little lost and were hoping you could give some directions."

"Afraid I can't be much help. Could try asking Mrs. Miller," the young man suggested, spreading another round of seed for the chickens.

"Ah," Talia nodded. "Do you know where we might find her?"

"Around here someplace," the farmhand rolled the bag of feed closed. Cautiously stepping over the unflappable fowl in his path, he rested the sack against the wall. He paused awkwardly after finishing his task, staring through the doorway. His eyes lingered on the sword at Drake's hip.

"Long shot, here," Drake leaned against the door frame, blocking the shed's exit. "Would you happen to know a Luc or Kyle?"

"Doesn't ring a bell," the Val'Kyran scratched his head. "Why?"

An annoyed voice approached the shed from outside. "Luc, I thought you were coming to help stack hay!"

"No way. What are the odds?" Talia attempted a whistle.

A taller Val'Kyran man rounded the corner. He paused upon sighting Drake, then moved one hand to the hilt of his broadsword and the other to the brim of his straw hat. "We're not expecting any visitors. You're trespassing on private property, friend."

"Easy now," Drake defused, folding his arms. "We just stopped by for directions, but I think we might have an acquaintance in common."

"You all right, Luc?" the older man called out. He looked a few years younger than Drake.

"Fine," called back the chicken feeder.

"Long Fan," Drake cut to the chase, prepared for a range of reactions, "mentioned two brothers, Luc and Kyle, were out here on a hunting contract."

The man looked unimpressed. "What's your business with them?"

"Assuming you're Kyle, I'm hoping you could help us find a temple."

"Giles," corrected the Val'Kyran. He pulled the straw hat off his head, wiped off the accumulated sweat with his sleeve, then donned the cap once more. "And there are plenty of temples. What do you need us for?"

"Why don't we all step out into the sunlight and talk it over," suggested Drake, aware of the tension in the air. He stepped out from the doorway with Talia in tow. Luc emerged from the shed and shrugged at his older brother, who patted him on the head.

"If you wanted to open a contract, you should've asked Long Fan for someone who can help you," said Giles. "We don't have time."

"Giles?" A gaunt woman approached from the side of the barn. She gauged Drake with a confused, disapproving look. "Who's this?"

"They're lost," Luc answered.

"And were just leaving," Giles added meaningfully.

"Apologies for the intrusion, ma'am," Drake raised a hand in greeting. "Name's Drake. We were just passing through these parts and needed a little direction. Turns out Giles and I have a mutual friend."

"Well, whatever you do, stay off the road to the north," Mrs. Miller warned emphatically.

"Why's that?" asked Talia.

"Thugs," the woman denounced venomously. Her wrinkles deepened as she frowned, adding years beyond her graying hair.

"The Crossroads have a bandit problem. Can't get an egg to Elmbrook without them *taxing* half of it," clarified Giles.

"Godwin hasn't sent anyone to help?" Talia asked between them.

Mrs. Miller scoffed. "They're taking the help if anything. All the good men were drafted to the frontlines with my husband. Now, it's just thugs and criminals left... and they're dragging the boys into it, too."

"Sorry to hear that," Drake offered his condolences. "We're looking for the Oracle. We've heard she lives in the Cradle of Life, somewhere in the Riverlands. Can you help us?"

"I only know the world as far as my fence posts," smiled the crone.

"I've heard of it," Giles frowned. "Somewhere out west of Elmbrook. If you follow the main river all the way down, you should get close."

"Thanks," Drake nodded. "If you've finished the hunting contract, we'd be interested in hiring your help to get there."

"We gave up on the contract," Giles folded his arms.

"That alligator's mean as hell," Luc commented, earning a backhanded smack from Giles. "Mean as heck. Damn!" Luc bobbed his head, dodging the second strike of censorship.

Giles huffed. "The money wasn't worth it. Besides, we met a lot of good people in Crossroads who needed our help. With all that's going on, we couldn't just leave them to suffer."

"Deus himself sent these two angels to me," Mrs. Miller pinched Giles' cheek. "I don't know what I would've done without these strapping young men around the farm. Everyone appreciates them. Dan the barman, Larry the half-blind butcher, the O'Conors—the whole town gets by with their help."

"Dang. How much are they paying you?" Talia inquired.

"It's not about the money," Giles rested his hands on his hips. "These people are barely getting by. Especially with Steele's gang shaking people down at the bridge, they can't trade with Elmbrook like they used to. We can't just abandon them."

"I offer what I can, but they won't accept more than a roof to sleep under and some food from the garden," Mrs. Miller shook her head.

"What if we solved your bandit problem?" Talia offered, earning a wary eyebrow from Drake.

"There's more than two dozen of them," Giles shook his head. "No offense, but if we couldn't clear them out, I doubt you two can."

"Two dozen?" Drake suppressed a laugh. "All right, hot shot. How about a wager? If we clear out the bandits, you'll take us to the Cradle."

"I don't know," Giles cracked his neck. "We're talking a two-week trip each way. I don't think Mrs. Miller could do without us that long."

The elderly woman slapped the Val'Kyran's arm with a turnip. "I'm not just some lumpy old bag of bones, you know! I've been on this farm for forty years. Besides, on the off chance this deluded vagrant can get the roads open, I could hire extra hands to help with the harvest. No offense, dearie."

"I've been called worse," waved Drake. "So, merc—we have a deal?"

"I'll show you where the bandits are, but it's on you to deal with them. I'm not putting Luc in danger for nothing," Giles wrapped an arm around his brother.

Drake glanced at Talia, who nodded encouragingly. "Works for us."

Giles reached out a callused hand. "Then we have a deal."

XXXIII. No Camping

Drake

Gravel crunched under his boots.

He marched on, ushering an air of purpose forward with him. Giles shadowed him several steps behind, followed by Luc and Talia, who were engrossed in curious and inconsequential conversation.

"That's it. You're making this up now," Talia accused flatly.

"It's true, I swear! Giles?" Luc looked to his brother for confirmation.

"It's true," Giles answered over his shoulder without much enthusiasm.

"Two?" Talia clarified incredulously.

"Deus take me if I'm lying," Luc raised his hand to the sky, welcoming divine judgement.

"You believe it, Drake?" Talia scoffed.

"Sure," he shrugged without slowing to join the conversation. "He caught two fish. Happens every day."

"But with his bare hands?" she objected.

"Why not?" Drake squinted against the sun as he scouted the gentle valley to his left. The grass swayed idyllically in the breeze, but no creature stirred on the sloping hills around the waterway.

"I guess Rivas blessed me," laughed Luc.

"Fine. I can shoot a hare from eighty yards," Talia countered proudly.

"It was more like forty," corrected Drake.

"Well, that one was," muttered Talia. She resiliently maintained her bluster. "But I could do it from eighty!"

"All right. That's pretty cool," Luc admitted fairly. "Giles never taught me how to shoot."

"You don't even have a bow. Why would you need to know how to shoot?" Giles reasoned with his brother.

"So I don't get shown up trying to impress a cute girl?" ventured the cheeky teenager.

Drake's eyebrow sprang up involuntarily.

"Slow your roll, friend," Talia let him down easy. "It takes a lot more than eighty yards to impress me."

"Should have told her it was three fish," Giles teased in good humor.

Luc opened his mouth, closed it contemplatively, then turned to Talia. "Did I mention it was three fish?" he reattempted.

"This is good," she commended supportively. "If you keep practicing, you might actually have a shot with the next cute girl that walks by."

"Damn," Giles unsuccessfully tried to stifle a laugh, cackling twice as hard when it finally broke through. He recomposed himself and tapped a hand on Drake's shoulder. "What about you—what's your story?"

"I don't have a story," Drake eluded gruffly, accelerating his pace to prevent further uninvited contact. "I'm sure you could find a minstrel or a poet someplace around here if you need one."

"Scaly," decided Giles. "Well, you know all about us. Two orphans without a home in Tallamar or Deuzos or Val'Kyros, taken up with Long's mercenaries. Wouldn't it be fair to give a hint where you're from?"

Drake said nothing. Trying not to dwell on the gaping hole in his memory, he watched his growing shadow instead. An hour or more until dusk.

"He's not exactly an open book," Talia answered on his behalf.

"But you could tell us where he's from, right?" Luc whispered loudly.

"Honestly, I really don't know," she replied quietly. "Somewhere on Kyros. Probably Destos?"

"Well, where'd you meet him?" tried Luc.

"Tallamar," Talia revealed, earning a stern grunt of disapproval from Drake. "Don't tell anyone, though. That's a secret."

"Long way from Tallamar," Giles noted.

"About as long as from Arillia," Drake answered evenly. "Hopefully, a short way from the Cradle."

"We'll cross that bridge when we come to it," Giles deferred. "But I see a closer bridge you can cross."

Drake squinted at the long, narrow structure farther down the road. A triangular, red roof covered the bridge, forming an open-sided tunnel about forty yards in length. Water flowed lazily under the landmark, casting blinding reflections along its westward journey. "Bandits on the bridge?" he rolled his shoulders in preparation for combat.

"A couple of them should be," Giles confirmed.

"Or on the other side," Luc contributed.

"You'll have to get them to take you to their camp. It's somewhere past the trees, but I haven't seen it myself." Giles saluted in farewell.

"Stick around. This won't take long," promised Drake.

"If you say so," Luc scratched his nose. "Hey, uh, in case I don't see you again..."

"You heard him," Talia interrupted, walking backward to Drake's side. "This won't take long."

"Good luck!" offered Giles. He received no acknowledgement.

Drake spotted movement in his peripheral vision. In the green to the right of the road. Some distance before the bridge. Focusing his gaze, he identified the figure as a diminutive old woman in a straw hat. Reviewing his full field of vision once more, he detected no others lurking in wait. Warily, he watched the woman harvest tomatoes from the vine. Possibly not an ambush.

"So, what's the plan?" Talia inquired enthusiastically.

"You want to know my plan?" Drake cocked an eyebrow, suggesting that she did not.

"The usual," Talia sighed in realization.

"Could be dangerous with all those bandits. Might be best if—"

"I'll be fine by your side," she dismissed preemptively. "I know you'll take care of me. Just try not to go overboard, okay?"

"I always try," he declared in his own defense.

"I know you do," she shook her head in abiding acceptance.

Drake's eyes darted back to the huddled crone as she approached them, basket in hand. His palm rested on the hilt of his arming sword.

"Yoo-hoo!" squawked the old bird, waving a ratty, red rag. "A minute to help a little old lady?"

"No thank you," Drake answered curtly, prepared to draw his blade at a moment's notice.

"We could at least hear her out," Talia suggested nobly.

Drake generated a guttural groan of disapproval without opening his mouth. "Speak," he invited benevolently.

"My darling grandson didn't bring any lunch with him this morning," cooed the crone. She shakily raised her wicker basket. "I've picked some fresh vegetables. Could you please bring Bo and his friends this lunch? He should be just over there, watching the bridge."

Drake frowned, but Talia spoke first. "Hang on—is your grandson one of the bandits that have been terrorizing these roads?"

"He's such a sweet little boy," the wrinkled woman asserted from under her bonnet. "He wouldn't harm a fly. It's that devil, Ransom!" She lifted a shaky fist, then lowered her voice as if worried she might be overheard. "He's making all the nice young boys of the village join his band of thugs. But my dear Bo and his friends are good children—you mustn't hurt them! It's not their fault they're mixed up in this bad business!"

"Look, lady," Drake opened frankly. He saw Talia bury her head in her hand, already predicting the tone of his response. "I've got a job to clear out the bandits in these parts. I'm not taking his lunch to him, but I'll take his head if he's all in with that lot."

"No!" the old woman weakly thrashed his arm with her basket. "Bo's a darling little boy!" She swung at him again, jostling his bicep with the vegetable carrier. "Don't hurt him or his nice friends! They're good boys!"

"Ma'am," interjected Talia, attuned to the rising irritation on Drake's face. "If Bo cooperates with us, he'll be fine. We're only interested in putting an end to the highwaymen who are robbing the traders from Elmbrook."

"So you'll bring little Bo his lunch?" the woman pleaded hopefully.

"We will not," Talia declined firmly, patting Drake on the back to send him into motion. He continued forward, drawing a deep breath to expel the tiresome crone from his conscience.

"Diplomacy," Talia proclaimed in self-congratulation after establishing a comfortable distance from the woman.

"I'm sour that I wasted time listening to her prattle," scowled Drake.

"Patience is a virtue," Talia said brightly.

Drake spat off to the side before planting a boot on the first wooden plank of the bridge. "Not one of mine."

As he crossed the creaking walkway, he kept a vigilant eye out for any traps or nooks that might hide a bandit. No brigands vaulted the side railings of the bridge, nor did any crawl through panels in the roof or floor. Passing the halfway point, he identified the likeliest place for a stickup would be at the end of the bridge—a brief stretch of shadows enclosed on all sides.

"Stay behind me," Drake placed a protective hand on Talia's shoulder and took the lead. Drawing his sword, he advanced into the shade at the end of the bridge. Planting his left boot ahead, he paused, prepared for the ambush.

Two assailants rounded the corner onto the bridge. Each held a knife and wore scraps of armor made from leather. One was outfitted with a brown breastplate and a lone pauldron affixed to his sword arm. The other wore what appeared to be a fur kilt under his jerkin. The taller, lanky boy had a long face with sallow cheeks. Zits that looked like he had picked a fight with a hornet's nest and lost. Stray whiskers on his chin. Looks that could curdle milk. A mop of blond hair hung in front of his face, requiring constant intervention to keep out of his eyes.

The other boy, a head-and-a-half shorter, had chubby cheeks and a naturally red complexion that pocked his pale skin vindictively and at random. An unfortunate wart plagued the end of his boxy nose. His chin doubled as he issued a threat: "Give us all your money, and no one gets hurt!"

Drake stared at the pair, unsure how to react. He was puzzled, amused, indignant, and bored by the affront at the same time.

"What are you, deaf?" the taller boy asked in a voice far too shrill for his body. "Give us what you've got, and we'll let you live!"

Drake looked between the two of them, unsmiling. "My listening's not great," he toyed with them, picking at his ear with his pinky. He examined his own sword with sudden surprise, as if noticing it for the first time. *Deus Chaeri.* A wolfish grin crept onto his face. He lowered his voice. "Give you what I've got? Did I hear that right?"

"Y-your money!" stammered the pudgy boy, extending his little knife as menacingly as he could muster. "Or else!"

"Right," said Drake, making no move to produce his wallet. "Well, this was fun. Tell you what: take me to the hideout, and I might let one of you live."

"This is your last chance! We'll stab you; I mean it!" the taller bandit warned before shrinking under Drake's cold gaze.

"Joke's over. Take me to Ransom—before someone gets hurt."

"He doesn't like to repeat himself," advised Talia. "I'd think carefully about your next few words. Your lives really don't mean anything to him."

The porky boy swallowed his fear and puffed out his sizeable chest. "If you don't give us your loot right now, I'll kill her!" he pointed his knife at Talia.

Drake's forgiving demeanor vanished at once. Malice burned in his eyes as he stalked forward. The knock-kneed adolescents retreated a step, looking between themselves for reassurance. He singled out the fat boy on the left. "What did you say, you little shit?"

"I—" the boy stumbled over himself as he backed up. His knife fell to the ground as he scrambled with both hands to regain his footing.

"Should not have said that," Talia grimaced on their behalf. "You really should not have said that."

Drake grabbed the boy by his thick neck and slammed him against the wall. In his peripheral vision, he saw the lankier bandit swaying, contemplating whether to rush to the defense of his ally. Drake held the tip of his sword up to the captive's belly. "Drop the knife or I'll cut out his intestines and ram them down your throat like a link of sausages."

Sensing a hint of hesitation, Drake drove the tip of his blade an inch into the restrained bandit, yielding an unworldly howl of pain. The other boy threw down his knife and raised his hands in surrender. "All right, all right! Stop hurting him!"

"Hurting him?" Drake echoed. "That's not hurting him. *This* is hurting him." He slammed the porky bandit's head into the thin wall, stunning him and causing him to lose his footing. As the boy fell forward onto the wooden planks, he knelt over him, drew his knife, and stuck the boy through the thickest part of his plump ass.

The enfeebled highwayman yowled in agony. Drake whispered into his right ear. "You didn't answer me. Before I flense you for lantern oil, I want you to tell me what you said."

"Bo!" the lanky bandit cried out in horror.

"I'm sorry!" bawled the battered bandit. "I'm sorry, please!" his throaty cries emulated the pulsating vocalizations of a weighty cetacean in great distress.

"Move, you pathetic swine!" Drake ordered the wailing boy, issuing him an inspiring kick in the rear. "Where's Ransom?"

"He'll kill us if we bring you to the hideout!" protested the lanky boy who had thus far escaped injury.

"I'll kill you if you don't," resolved Drake.

"Just do it, Marsh!" sobbed Bo, once more continuing his communion with any nearby aquatic mammals.

"You're coming too," Drake decided mercilessly, returning his knife to its sheath. He used his free hand to heave the heavy boy off the ground, allowing Bo to clumsily return to his feet. Drake spurred him forward with a sharp prick from his sword. "Oink for me, little piggy."

"Oink!" sniveled the portly boy, following his concerned friend off the path and into the trees.

"Louder!" he jabbed the unlucky bandit again.

"Oink!" Bo wept remorsefully.

"And you, Musk!" Drake hollered at the boy out in front.

"Marsh?" the inept bandit asked in confusion.

"Musk!" Drake reasserted, daring him to try a second correction. "If I sniff wind of either of you trying to pull something smart..."

"Sausage links," gulped Marsh. "Wouldn't dream of doing anything smart, sir!"

"I want Ransom," Drake reminded him.

"It's not far this way," Marsh gestured through the thin woods.

As Drake allowed Bo to advance a few steps ahead, Talia returned to his side. He slid his sword back into its sheath, suspecting the two bandits would be in no hurry to provoke him further.

"I think you made Bo wet himself," commented Talia.

Drake raised his voice just enough for Bo to hear. "You think he'd make good bait, or do gators prefer lean meat?"

The boy's body shuddered as his defeated whimpers spilled out onto the forest floor.

"Stop it," Talia rolled her eyes at him.

"He got off lucky," Drake whispered back. "If they looked halfway like real bandits, I wouldn't have left two alive."

"The camp's up ahead," Marsh stopped, dread gripping his features. "What are you going to do with us?"

"That all depends on you, Musk," Drake answered reasonably. "Get a move on. I want you to point out Ransom for me."

Drake heard the rowdy bandits before he saw them. Beyond the trees, a camp of over a dozen brigands carelessly caroused as they drank from a pilfered keg. Brigands sat on stolen crates and barrels, laughing and shouting into the twilight. Two of the younger bandits wrestled while a small crowd of jubilant watchers egged them on.

"That's Ransom," Marsh pointed out a long-haired man. He was facing the fire with his back to Drake.

Bo fell to his knees and crawled desperately toward the gathering. "Help!" he screamed. "Help us!"

The hive of bandits slowly noticed Drake and Talia at the edge of the woods. A few additional short swords emerged from the small cave nestled in the local hill, eyeing the intruders with surprise and suspicion.

"Ransom!" Drake called out the bandit leader.

As the long-haired man by the fire turned to see who dared wander into his camp, Drake felt Pyros' bloodlust awaken within him. Barely managing to contain the Primal's boiling hunger, a thin trail of smoke vented from his nose as he exhaled. He met the gaze of the impenitent outlaw.

Beneath his wild mane of brown hair, Ransom wore gaudy strands of pilfered jewels, a fur cape, and a heavy knife with a curved blade. He drew the weapon with his left hand, taking a hearty swig from the bottle of brandy in his right. A strong forehead and prominent nose gave him an imposing scowl, bettered by the rugged beard that swept across the lower half of his face. Staggering forward cockily, he pointed the knife at Drake. "You stumbled into the wrong wolf's den today, brother."

Drake looked around the gathering. Most faces showed amusement or uncertainty. Few showed fear, but that would soon change. "I'll give everyone one chance to lay down your blades, return what you've stolen, and give up robbing for good."

"Yeah? Or what?" snarled Ransom. He tossed his shoulders back in an arrogant laugh, which contagiously spread throughout the camp.

"There's twenty of us and only one of you!" added one arithmetically gifted bandit.

Drake held up a finger. "I will give this chance to everyone except for Ransom," he angled his sword toward the bandit leader. "Your time is up."

"Did he just threaten Ransom Steele?" one of the older boys gawked in disbelief.

"What an idiot!" laughed another.

"You'll regret this!"

Ransom smiled, glowing in the deference of his men. "I'm gonna make you suffer. Then, I'm—"

Drake lifted his hand and released the spiritual levee restraining Pyros. Their combined wrath manifested in a pillar of fire, swallowing the haughty bandit leader in an unforgiving blaze. Ransom's anguished screams carried far into the forest beyond the camp. A wave of dread washed over the witnesses as his fiery torment drove him to the ground. His unbearable suffering ended with a final, ragged gasp. An eerie silence hung over the camp, broken only by the starving flames that crackled over his charred remains.

Gagging on the smell, Talia burrowed her nose in her elbow. "Ack! Drake!" She eyed him sideways, silently communicating her wish for mercy.

"One chance," Drake announced to the stunned raiders who were now rapt with attention. "Drop your weapons, go serve your home, and never look back... or you can join him."

The drunken group by the keg dropped their knives and dispersed into the trees beyond the camp, running away as fast as they could.

"He's a demon!"

"He's a fire caller?"

"It's a Primal!" the third voice identified, terror and awe in his words.

"Run! We'll regroup later!" shouted a bald bandit near the fire.

Drake swatted his hand at the firepit, causing the flames to leap from the campfire into a vortex around the devious highwayman. Pyros bolstered his voice as he roared over the terrified screams. "You cannot escape my gaze. I am in every fire. Eternal. Deceive me, and I will hunt you down."

A bawling mass crawled across the ground in front of him, heading for the trees behind him. Drake identified the pitiful lump as Bo.

Only two bandits remained in the clearing, defiantly clenching their swords. As the sentient fire danced behind them, their long shadows twisted and writhed ominously.

Talia stepped forward to help them resolve their minds. "You both have a lot of good to do, if you don't want to end up like him," she tilted her head toward the charred husk of the bandit leader, then lowered her voice to a whisper. "They say the souls of those he kills burn forever. If you listen closely, you can still hear the screams, drowning in eternal hellfire."

In the distance, somewhere deep in the woods behind Drake, Bo's mournful wail haunted the night.

The bandits fell to their knees and threw down their weapons. "Please! Spare us! We'll do anything!"

Pyros materialized behind Drake to watch the pathetic worms squirm in the dirt. He exhaled a deep ring of smoke from his bullish nose, then spoke in unison with his Mystic: "I never want to see you rats again."

"Y—yes, of course!" stammered the balding man, laying his head and hands on the ground in submission. "We'll do good, I swear! I swear!"

"Be gone!" Drake bellowed, sending the pair scattering into the woods.

Then, they stood alone in the clearing. Talia held a sleeve over her nose. "What a mess," she stared at the smoldering remains of the bandit leader.

"It was the only way I could think of to save the rest," Drake explained in what might have been considered an apology.

"You did the best you could," Talia commended him understandingly. "I mean it."

"Where'd all that come from?" Drake nudged her. "Didn't know you were carrying so much yarn."

"Came up with it on the spot. Pretty good, right?"

"I'll say," he smiled. Turning his back to the abandoned campsite, he placed a guiding hand on her back and led them into the trees. "One hell of a knack for telling ghost stories. You're gonna go far, kid."

"Diplomacy," Talia corrected importantly. "And yes—I will."

XXXIV. Lost In The Dark

Drake

What, you don't agree?"

"Huh?" Yawning, Drake returned his attention to Talia. Rubbing his eyes with his knuckles somehow resulted in an afterimage in his left eye. He blinked repeatedly, shifting his gaze from the shimmering water that spanned the wide valley to the sloping hills that guided its flow. A black patch in the center of his vision followed doggedly, an echo of the afternoon sun.

"You're not hearing anything I'm saying, are you?"

"Sorry," he lifted a hand in apology. "I'm listening. A little tired, is all."

Sighing, Talia followed his gaze to the golden reflection on the river. "We've been at it pretty much nonstop," she reflected quietly.

"Had a nice break with the Taoxians," Drake countered optimistically.

"Aside from you almost burning your hands off and that gold-plated knight nearly killing us—yeah. Had a few relaxing days with some monks in a strange forest," Talia recounted flatly.

"Point taken." He subconsciously touched his scarred hands, running his fingers over old scabs and calluses. His burns had largely faded, save for one stubborn patch of discoloration on his left hand. "Well, can't be much farther."

"I know," Talia preempted. "I wouldn't let you turn back now if you begged me. We're seeing this through," she swung a hand through the air in front of her, grasping for the balance of her thoughts. "It's just... It'd be nice to settle in somewhere after this. Just for a little while. Don't you think?"

"What, you miss Lyon?"

"No," denied Talia. "Well, kind of. It's complicated," she huffed.

"Go for it," Drake encouraged softly.

"Like," she blew air out of her mouth, visibly frustrated at her jumbled thoughts. "I do miss Lyon, but I mostly just miss the way things used to be. With Amma and Baron and... you know, everyone before."

"Right," Drake acknowledged.

"But I wouldn't want to go back now. There's nothing left for me."

"Might still be a wanted poster or two for *Talosa Blaine*," he quipped.

"Ha," she rolled her eyes. "All I'm saying is, it'd be fun to have somewhere to call *home* again."

"City or countryside?"

"I don't know," she shrugged. "I feel like I've done the whole *city* thing, but there's always something exciting happening with so many people around. Something a little quieter could be cool for a while."

"Like Laval?"

"Not Laval," she held her arm, shrinking into herself uncomfortably. "I don't think I'd feel right waking up around Desmond's family every day."

"So not Laval," accepted Drake. "But something like it?"

"Maybe a little bigger," suggested Talia. "It could be cool to have some people around. Try to make some friends my own age."

"You wouldn't like people your own age," Drake grinned knowingly.

"What's that supposed to mean?" she elbowed him in the side.

"Ow," he laughed. "I'm just saying, you've experienced a lot more than other people your age. Most kids don't know a life outside the farm. Or they're spoiled brats who go looking for trouble 'cause they've never had any of their own. You've seen more of the world than you realize."

"There's gotta be some *young adults* who are all right," Talia reasoned. "What about Luc? He seems cool."

"Maybe," Drake eyed the two brothers who were enthralled in their own conversation ten yards ahead. Though still wary of their new companions, he felt a natural trust arising from the fact that they were likewise alone out here, disconnected from kings and clans with nefarious intentions. "Kid seems to have his head on straight."

"Can you believe he's never ridden a horse before?" Talia shook her head in disbelief.

"Not everyone's had all your experiences," Drake said philosophically.

The brothers halted their advance and turned to face them. Drake stopped as well, resting his hands on his hips.

Giles pointed across the river ahead of them. "That's the hanging garden," he announced meaningfully. Drake followed his finger to the peculiar landmark on the far side of the wide river. A concave stone wall emerged from the still water below. The precarious ledge at the top supported a cluster of untamed foliage. Vines and green overgrowth spilled forth from beyond the crooked trees, dangling almost ten feet down from the grassy floor above. Two small waterfalls broke through the vines and tumbled to the water below—one an irregular drizzle, the other a steady stream.

"Neat," Talia approved, unsure of its significance.

"It means we're going the right way," Giles declared with confidence. "If we follow the valley southwest, it should bring us through the thinnest part of the Blackwater. The Cradle should be close on the other side, I think."

"*Blackwater* doesn't sound particularly inviting," speculated Drake.

"You should hear some of the monster stories," Luc grinned devilishly. "Legend says, under the black water swims a thirty-foot long snake with thick, impenetrable scales and rows of sharp teeth the size of your head. One can bite a bison clean in two, but they always hunt in packs."

"You're telling me there's a bunch of bison wandering around the swampland?" Talia raised her eyebrows skeptically.

"Maybe," Luc maintained, folding his arms.

"Didn't you say you were hunting an alligator?" checked Drake.

"Yeah. The Crossroads don't see a lot of them out this way, which is why they sent a contract all the way to Arillia," said Giles.

"Sounds like that might be your thirty-foot snake," Drake guessed.

"Could be," Giles shrugged, earning a dismissive reaction from Luc. "Never been to the Blackwater. Guess we'll see what's what soon enough."

"What the hell?" Luc gawked, staring past his brother.

"Damn it, Luc!" Giles readied a hand to swat his brother's foul mouth, then cringed as he caught himself in the act. "Language!"

"Look, Giles!" Luc pointed toward the water.

The water at the widest part of the river stood eerily still. Impossibly, the river continued to flow before and after the plane halted in time, as if skipping the twenty-yard gap between. Defying nature itself, two strangers in hooded robes stood on the glassy surface of the water as if it were solid rock.

"It's them," Talia identified as Drake raised a hand to block the sun.

He squinted at the pair on the river. Unflinchingly, they stared back. "How did they find us here?"

"Friends of yours?" Giles asked suspiciously.

"Not friends," Drake said tersely. "You and the boy better hide here. Stay low. I'll deal with the Mystics."

"I'm coming with you," Talia decided.

Drake gritted his teeth. "Maybe it'd be safer if you stay back with them. I don't want you getting caught in the crossfire."

"Isn't that the woman who teleports wherever she wants?" challenged Talia. "Don't you think I'd be safer next to you?"

Drake took a step toward the duo and faltered. Fear crowded out any better alternatives. He saw a brief shimmer of purple light reflect on the water's surface, preceding the appearance of a rapier in the slenderer figure's hand. "Maybe they're just here to talk. Either way, I think it's better you wait up here. Between Pyros and me, we should be fine." He looked over his shoulder and nodded to Talia before addressing their guides. "Giles, keep an eye on her?"

"Not sure what bad business you've got with those Mystics, but we'll watch over her. Stay safe down there."

Drake started down the grassy hill, mindful to slow his acceleration as he progressed toward the water. *Any chance you have a plan?*

He felt Pyros' warm presence within him, crackling like a familiar hearth. *Burn them.*

I meant about the river, Drake took his eyes off his feet to survey the battlefield.

Water is difficult to ignite, the Primal pondered thoughtfully.

Drake grunted at the frustrating advice. He suspected the one with the rapier was *Prism,* and he assumed her companion was the Val'Kyran, Iko. The Cormack they had encountered before the Twins was another possibility, but he couldn't guess how they were balancing on top of the water. Although ready for a fight, he was hopeful he'd find a way to avoid one.

His toe crunched against a stray rock, stealing his balance and sending him tumbling. "Damn it!" he cried out as he tucked his head, bracing his arms to help him roll onto his shoulder. His eyes closed before he hit the ground.

A jolt in his stomach made his head spin with nausea.

Tensed for impact, Drake lay still for a long moment. A cool sensation brushed his hands. He opened his eyes. Rising slowly, disoriented, he realized he was neither falling nor standing on the hill. Instead, the motionless river inexplicably supported his weight.

Leaning forward from a crouched position, he jabbed his straightened hand through the unseen barrier. His fingers connected with the gentle current under the surface, cleansed by a cool, unyielding flow of water.

"You say you don't want to be found, and yet you make it so easy," a harsh voice laughed in front of him.

Drake rose to face the black-robed duo, now fifteen feet ahead. The broad-shouldered one lifted a black-gloved hand to remove his cowl, revealing demonic red eyes and flowing blond hair. The woman stayed unmoving, eyes maintaining a faint purple glow beneath her hood.

"Unfortunately for you, we're back in the prime kingdom of Deuzos. That meddlesome Iko won't be here to save you," the Cormack sneered.

"Save your breath," Drake drew his sword. He ran a hand down the length of the blade, igniting the artifact. "Get out of my way or die."

"So testy!" Hadronox clucked disapprovingly. "But I see you've finally found your flame. Perhaps you'll be a useful pet to me, after all."

"You know, there's one thing that's been bugging me since last I saw your ugly mug," Drake confessed with a frown.

"Oh yeah?" the Cormack smirked playfully.

"She can bend space, which clearly has its uses. The Val'Kyran can move through shadows, and even though I kicked his ass last time, I can see where he'd be helpful. But you?" Drake pointed his sword at the Cormack and shook his head. "You're nothing but a yappy purse dog in need of a stiff boot under the table. Sure, you make the sky a little darker, but so do clouds. Why the hell does Avalon need you?"

The Cormack laughed coldly. "Such hubris. You remind me of myself in earlier days. You do not understand darkness, but you will."

Drake launched a salvo of arcing fireballs through the air. The woman showed her palm, and the fiery orbs instantly vanished from flight. An array of lights flashed in the water below before fizzling into nothingness.

"I will break you to my will," snarled Hadronox. The vile, disfigured abomination of a Primal appeared above the Cormack's head.

Drake loaded his weight to dash forward, but his step was stopped by an inescapable gravity. He willed his feet to move, but his screaming legs were immobilized.

Color faded from his surroundings. The water, vines, and hills turned varied shades of gray. His eyelids felt heavy as he glared at Hadronox, who smiled and strolled toward him slowly.

The Cormack's creepy voice soured the air, tinged by an echo both shrill and gravelly. "Oh, my! Haven't you been a naughty boy?" The man's laugh made Drake's hair stand on end. "I sense it all. Your fears, your regrets, your wrath... Poor girl. She would never have come all this way with you if she knew what a *monster* you truly are..."

Drake grunted, unable to unclench his jaw. His eyelids grew heavier. Though he fought to keep them open, that persistent afterimage returned to his eye. Its black-burned shadow expanded, blinding his left eye completely before creeping into his right. He blinked furiously, unable to restore his sight. His limbs went numb. No longer responded to his commands.

All he saw was darkness.

A raspy voice in the dark convicted him. "You vile, irredeemable soul. How many have died by your hand?"

"Damn... you," Drake managed. He stared into the black miasma, unable to sense his body.

"Men, women, children... but none of them mattered to you, did they? You don't care how many lives you've stolen. You only regret not taking more. Isn't that right, you twisted murderer?"

"That's not... true," panted Drake.

"But it must be. Fort Kagrash was just the latest on your long list. The orphan boys from Gaixia, bandits, soldiers, farmers, lawmen, lords... You have no code. No reason. You even killed that poor Mystic boy."

"I didn't kill Desmond!" shouted Drake.

"Liar! You knew the boy would die when you refused our sanctuary at Haven. You led him to death. You could have protected him, but instead you watched him sacrifice himself to save you—*his protector*. Does the little girl know you'll do the same to her?"

"I didn't... I'd never..." A hot tear stung his cheek. "I'll..."

"You'll what?" snarled the darkness. "*Protect her?* Don't make me laugh. You destroy everything around you. That is who you are."

"No!" cried Drake.

"Your single purpose is to burn the world to ashes. You know you can't control the blazing ire within you. Even she sees you for the monster you are. She's disgusted by you. She'd run far, far away from you—if only she had anywhere else to go."

"I'll kill you!" Drake challenged furiously.

The voice laughed, suddenly familiar. "Of course you will. I am you."

Shutting his eyes, Drake called on Pyros to dispel the gloom. Coldness filled his chest; the Primal was far, far away.

Alone in the darkness.

Abandoned.

He let his eyes close for good, resigned to expire in the cold embrace of this vast emptiness. His scattered thoughts jumbled hopelessly in the back of his mind, refusing to coalesce into sentience. Only the dull ache of despair reached through the oblivion, reminding him that he was unfortunately alive.

A tired wave lapped onto the shore.

At first, he thought he had only imagined it. Gradually adjusting to the dim twilight, his eyes began to perceive the shadowy form of a beach. Every ten seconds, a quiet wave crept onto the shore only to fade back into the dark sea.

His boots trudged across the black sand, leaving a shallow footprint behind with every step. His hands appeared at his side, at last responsive to his commands, though his mind remained empty.

At peace.

He took in the beach as he walked the shoreline, trying to make sense of the twisting shapes that rose from the shallow water. They were smooth like bones, bending and splintering off in chaotic directions. None of the trees, creatures, or natural formations he knew left behind such uncanny sculptures— an artificial cage that made no true effort to prevent him from leaving.

Farther ahead, the dull light of a tired moon hung among the clouds, just above the horizon. Its pale glow lived on in scattered echoes on the water's surface. Broken reflections of its muted radiance. Against the moonlight, he could make out the silhouette of a lone boulder in the sand. Someone sat on that distant rock, staring off into the quiet ocean.

His feet traveled slowly across the soft sand. No urgency polluted this twilit realm. He attempted to glance inland, but there was only darkness away from the sea. Behind him, his footsteps in the sand had already faded, though no winds blew, and no waves dared travel so far onto land. Strange. The fleeting thought passed as a meaningless observation, and he carried onward.

Fixated on the depressed moon floating on distant waves, the silent watcher on the rock paid him no greeting as he approached. She did not turn her head as he looked up, nor did she answer his question immediately.

"What is this place?"

Drake stared at the moon in silence. After a while, he abruptly realized he had been overlooking a rowboat at the shore's edge the whole time. He spotted two oars fixed inside the oarlocks, paddles dug into the sand to prevent the boat from slipping away. Walking toward the boat, he stared into the dark waters surrounding the island.

A bizarre texture painted the water. Like eyeless faces trapped in tar, disturbing abstractions bubbled up from beneath the surface. Whenever he tried to focus his vision on any one spot, he saw only the blanketed stillness of the dark ocean.

Finally, she answered. "Nowhere."

Drake turned to face the watcher. Resting her hands behind her on the rock, she lowered her gaze from the moon to the water. She wore familiar black robes. The hood hid her face, though small patches of skin were visible on her chin and neck. Her pigment appeared gray in the lighting.

"Who are you?" Drake stepped closer to the rock.

"No one," she said tonelessly.

"You must be someone," he reasoned, climbing onto the boulder. He sat next to her, facing the moon and the rowboat.

"I suppose I must, mustn't I?" she considered.

"Don't you know who you are?" pried Drake, surprised but without judgement or anger.

"No," she answered hollowly. "Do you?"

"Of course," he scoffed. "I'm..." He thought about it for a while, then kicked his heel against the boulder in deflated realization. "No. I guess I don't."

"I see."

"So, what are we supposed to do now?"

"There's nowhere to go but the sea," she stretched her foot out toward the moon.

"What's out there?" Drake asked, nervous, but finding a will to explore within him.

"I don't know," she said, puzzled. "I went out there, but it seems to go on forever. I can't remember if I drowned or if I'm still searching."

"How's that possible? You're sitting here next to me," reasoned Drake.

She looked down at her legs. "Oh," she said with surprise, as if noticing for the first time. "I suppose I am."

"I think I'm looking for someone," Drake confessed suddenly.

"Are they out there?" she stared at him from under her hood.

"I don't know," he murmured. "I want them to be. I guess I won't know until I look."

She nodded, then turned to stare at the moon again. "I hope you find them," she wished pleasantly.

"Thanks," Drake slid off the boulder. He took two steps toward the rowboat before turning back toward the rock. "You know, you could come with me, if you'd like," he offered.

"But I'm already out there," she said. He could see she was frowning as she tried to make sense of that fact.

"Well, would you like to go out again with me?" Drake rephrased.

Her frown deepened. "I would, but I can't. I think I'm looking for someone, too."

"I see," Drake nodded. He walked over to the rowboat and gently slid the hull into the shallow water. "Well, then I hope you find them, too."

He planted a foot in the boat, preparing to cast off.

"Drake!" called a faint voice behind him.

"Pardon?" he turned, looking back to the rock.

The boulder stood alone on the beach, dimly visible in the moonlight. The mysterious woman had vanished.

Drake cocked his head, scanning for footprints or other clues about the voice that had called out the name—his name—but found none. "Better get going," he said to himself, turning back toward the rowboat.

The boat, too, had vanished. He stood ankle-deep in the water where it had been only moments ago, staring at the broken reflections that stretched to the moon across the sea. Wave after wave traveled the ocean to brush against his shins. Perhaps he could swim there.

"Drake!" the voice erupted in his ear, ripping him from his nightmare.

A chill ran through his body. His eyes snapped open. Sputtering as his lungs purged the liquid, he lifted his face from the water. Gasping for air, he rolled onto his back and saw a face looming over him. A hand reached around his neck to support his head as he sat up.

"Damn it, Drake!" Talia slapped his cheek. His eyes focused on her as he coughed up another mouthful of water.

Breathe, feeble human! Pyros demanded from within.

"What—" A violent cough overtook him. Turning to prop himself up on his knees, he realized, impossibly, he was lying on top of the water. Raising his eyes, he saw a furious blond man climbing out of the river, pulling himself up onto the same invisible platform that supported Drake.

The Cormack was drenched from head to toe. Beside him, the black-robed woman clutched her head in apparent agony.

"I almost hit him!" Talia announced proudly.

"What are you talking about?" Drake winced. Gradually, his senses returned to him. He remembered he had been poised to fight the Cormack when something had come over him, ostensibly causing him to faint.

"With my bow," she indicated the weapon over her shoulder. "It was like *this* close to his head. I think I grazed his face. Are you all right?"

He sized up his opponents. Right below the cheekbone, a thin gash had been added to the Cormack's ugly face. The woman seemed distracted, perhaps finally strained by the effort of suspending the river. "I'll take it from here," Drake vowed quietly, readying his sword.

"You were mine!" hissed Hadronox. "Tell me, how did you escape?"

"What the hell are you talking about?" Drake scowled.

"No matter. I'll break your will once more," the Cormack resolved, raising a soaked hand.

Drake charged across the water. Vermillion flames ran down his blade.

"What are you doing?" the Cormack scolded his partner. "Stop him!"

Drake leaped through the air and swung his sword in a downward arc. His arm abruptly halted its movement above the Cormack, though sparks showered down from his blade, singeing Hadronox's boxy face.

The Cormack screamed in pain. Wiping hot embers from his nose, he yelled, "Kill him, damn you! Gut him!"

Prism lowered her finger, returning Drake's control of his sword arm. "He is not my enemy," she said groggily.

"I command you to kill him!" hissed Hadronox, scrambling to his feet. "Do as I say!"

She turned her head toward Drake. A purple glow spilled from her brown eyes. Every word was a battle; she grasped the side of her head in pain as she managed: "You... are not my enemy."

"Insubordinate!" Hadronox's eyes flashed crimson. He lifted a hand toward his comrade, and the world began to lose its color once again. "You will suffer for your disobedience. You are *mine!*"

The purple-eyed Mystic shrieked in pain. Gripping her head with both hands, Prism collapsed sideways. The water swallowed her like quicksand, slowly dragging her under as she writhed.

Drake charged forward, spurred by her agonized howls. He slashed at Hadronox, who leaped backward out of reach. Hadronox raised his other hand against Drake but failed to slow the assault.

Drake's mind raged with bloodlust and madness, though he resiliently focused his attacks on the cold-blooded Cormack. He felt his sword connect over and over, yet no scars appeared on his opponent's flesh; no blood spilled from his sundered veins.

"Die!" Drake roared, slashing wildly ahead of him. He fell forward into a shadowy ripple.

Cold shocked his body. Then he reemerged on the grassy shoreline. Talia appeared at his side a moment later. Shuddering, she looked up to him for an answer. He stared back over the water, observing the two black hoods.

"Iko, you coward!" snarled Hadronox. "Where are you hiding?"

Prism lifted her head as the Cormack's focus broke. Gasping for air, she slapped a palm against the water. The air warped around her, then she disappeared.

Hadronox fell into the river. Thrashing and sputtering, he struggled to stay afloat. Against his protests, a shadowy mist formed on the water. Faster and faster, the shadows circled. Slowly, then all at once, they converged and spirited him away.

Panting like a shaggy mutt in summer, Drake stared at the water for a long moment. Adrenaline coursed through him, causing his temples to pulsate rapidly. He anticipated the enemy was regrouping. They would reappear at any minute to resume combat. The spell of peace grew longer and longer, and he gradually began to realize they would not soon return.

"Hey, are you all right?" Talia shook his shoulder. Concern dripped from her face. Her eyes searched his for an answer.

A pang of guilt moved him to pull her in closer. "Sorry, kid," he whispered earnestly.

"I think the words you're looking for are *thank you*," she returned.

He swallowed thickly.

"You're welcome," she said magnanimously. "I'm glad you're okay."

Drake heard footsteps approach from uphill. He gripped the hilt of his sword and turned, ready to face the aggressors.

Giles held his hands up in surrender. "Whoa, easy there. Just checking you were both all right."

Luc doubled over and rested his hands on his knees. Cocking his head sideways, he looked at Drake, squinted in disbelief, then shook his head. "Man! What the hell?"

"Hey!" Giles lifted a reprimanding finger toward his brother, but he couldn't take his eyes off Drake. "I mean... Damn! What the hell, man?"

XXXV. Second Chances

Flynn Darke

She could have gone anywhere in the world.

But he had a feeling she'd gone to the one place she now knew better than anywhere else.

The familiar cool of shadows wrapped him. He appeared at the fringe of the torchlight and opened his eyes to the inornate stonework of the fortress basement. Noting the layer of dust on crates and barrels stored down there, he shook his head in disapproval, reminiscing about the finer castles he had enjoyed in a past life. In any respectable house, a servant would be flogged for leaving such careless coatings of filth. A greater horror still, two floors above his present position in the squat fortification, dust clung to the windowsills and frame of Avalon's makeshift throne.

The lack of attention to detail irked Flynn. It was as if he was the only one who cared to keep the grounds in a presentable state. The fanatic cult of townsfolk at the base of the island certainly would have kept the premises spick and span if requested, but Avalon had decreed a firm boundary halfway up the mountain. An unusually gaudy shrine featuring a sculpture of the god-king oversaw the border, staring out at the world with an eternal glare of contempt.

A muffled groan from the nearest cell ripped him from his frivolous brooding. He composed himself and advanced around the corner, passing the place between the iron bars where a door once stood. He rested a hand on his hip as he considered the party across from him, who shuddered as if suffering withdrawal.

"Prism," he addressed her flatly, warily awaiting her nonresponse.

Ever since their foray to the most disagreeable Lord Vayne's parlor, he had begun to suspect something was amiss. Her inexplicable disobedience in combat with Pyros had vexed him, not by her overt misbehavior alone, but rather due to the implications that underlay her inaction. He had suspected then, as he did now, that somehow Hadronox's hold on her was slipping.

She let out another short cry of agony. Burying her head into her palm, she pulled her knees close to her chest, curling into a rather sad-looking ball.

He considered her carefully, stroking his mustache to his orderly beard in one fluid motion with his thumb and index finger. Since the incident at Lord Vayne's, she had shown no further signs of rebellion. They had carried out their tasks in the north without delay, and she had continued to ferry Haven's governing members wherever they needed to go. With overflowing pride, Hadronox had even boasted at length of their last bloody adventure and how efficiently she had executed their quarry. Was this convulsion merely a side effect of the dark Primal's ebbing and flowing control?

No.

His hand fell from his face to rest on the hilt of his dagger. Something felt different about this outburst. From the shadows of the reeds, he had watched her openly defy Hadronox. If only for a moment, she had broken his chains and found the means to free herself from recapture. That is, after all, why he had intervened to banish Hadronox.

Arms shaking, Prism began to push herself off the floor. She planted both palms on the tan stones and lifted her head, challenging his calculating eyes with an unflinching gaze. Behind a purple haze, her brown eyes looked undeniably awake. Alive. Although her olive skin appeared pale in the low light, she seemed to be gaining more of herself back with every ragged breath of the dungeon's musty air.

"If you're going to do it, do it," she spat coldly.

Flynn looked over his shoulder, as if expecting to find Avalon and Hadronox standing behind him. He suspected the golden-eyed god-king was either ruminating in his throne room or walking the grounds. Nothing short of the royal orchestra would be loud enough to reach him from the basement. Hadronox would be of no immediate threat; Iko had marooned him at the one place Axel knew only too well. Trapped again at the Dark Horizon.

Axel would surely be vindictive when he returned, but Flynn couldn't predict how Avalon would react to this betrayal. Poorly, he imagined. Especially if coupled with Prism's death or disappearance. The only mitigating factor would be his utility as the last remaining Mystic capable of fast travel.

Flynn let his hand fall from the hilt of his dagger. "I'm not going to kill you," he spoke softer than intended.

She pushed herself to one knee. Brown hair fell in front of her left eye as she leaned forward, gritting against the pain. "I can't... I won't go back."

"Are you... yourself?" he marveled.

"No," she swallowed thickly. Her eyes glowed with fiery retribution. "But I'm not your or anyone else's pet."

How is this possible? Flynn's mouth opened, but no words came out. Until now, he had thought Hadronox's dark hex to be inescapable. Though he had always wondered whether fragments of the broken might be left behind, he never would have imagined that a soul could be fully restored once taken.

She believes you are allied with Hadronox. Let her know you mean no harm, Iko advised perceptively.

"I am not your enemy," Flynn managed.

"No? Then why did you stand idly by for years while I suffered?" she demanded evenly.

"What could I have done?" Flynn spread his hands in an appeal for clemency, bearing the weight of the undeniable charge against him. "I cannot kill him. Even if I wanted to, I harbor too much darkness in my heart to strike him down. He would only feed off my hate."

"So that's it," she tilted back her head to examine the ceiling.

"I am sorry," he said in earnest, stepping closer. "If I could have done something sooner, I would have. I assure you, I took no pleasure in watching you suffer so indignantly." He extended a hand to her. "I am not your enemy. That's why I stepped in to help you against Hadronox, though I fear my actions may yet have grave consequences for me."

Her contempt scorched him a moment longer. With a slow exhale, she dropped her eyes and accepted his hand. Still weak from her mental battle, she swayed as she stood.

Flynn gently guided her to a neighboring crate and helped her sit. "But you... How did you escape his hold? I assume he did not release you willingly."

She shook her head. "I don't know. It's all one big mess. I can't quite separate what was real from the endless nightmares. The agony I endured—that I inflicted—it's without measure."

"What was it like?"

Eyes closed, she pointed to a spot in the air and spoke as if watching the memories play out on the inside of her eyelids. "I'm standing in a place without time. A Dark Horizon. Behind me, a beach of black sand. Ahead of me, the midnight ink of a vast ocean. The shore is quiet, but I cannot stay long. The sea calls, and I must answer. On the water, bubbles rise to the surface. I reach out to some, and when I am close enough, I see visions. Memories of things I have done, or maybe, things I will yet do. I am the reflection in the bubbles. You and Hadronox are, too." She shuddered at the mental image and opened her eyes. "We did things to people. Awful things. I need to know—were those visions real? Was that really me?"

Confronted with her revelation, Flynn felt the only honorable answer was the truth. He stiffened his chest and straightened his head. "Though your memories are darker than mine, they are likely founded in the same reality. We've killed countless people together, Prism."

She shook her head in disbelief, swallowing thickly. "That's not who I am. Don't call me that."

"My apologies," he nodded shortly. "What name would you prefer?"

"I..." The purple glow faded from her eyes. She wiped away a tear before it could fall, and then the purple haze was back. "Don't call me anything. We aren't on the same side."

"It's hard to gauge the sides of a sphere," Flynn crossed his arms and leaned against the iron bars. "I have chosen my path, but you are still free to choose your future. Whether they were your actions or only Hadronox acting through you, the past is the past. No sense torturing yourself about it. If you forgive yourself, perhaps you could find your way in this life once more."

"My way in this life..." a scowl darkened her face. Her hand balled into a fist at her side. "All I can think about is killing him. I want him to feel what I felt, then I want him to suffer the deaths the others died."

"No!" Flynn warned sternly. "Look at you. You're in no condition to go picking a fight with Hadronox. Besides, you wouldn't win. He feeds off your hatred and grows stronger. If that is truly how you feel, you would only be running back to let his darkness control you again."

"But—"

"Hear reason, Prism!" He tensed, disappointed in himself for having raised his voice. "I'm sorry. I did not mean to call you that. Please, do not let hatred consume you now. You've been granted a second chance that I did not believe was possible. Think back through the visions—before you arrived here with Avalon."

Flynn allowed her a moment to reflect. Her brown eyes widened as she digested the information, apparently working back through the horde of painful memories to find a time before her imprisonment. He saw understanding in her tired eyes and hoped she now remembered life before darkness. Even if they were recollections of hatred, a reawakening of unresolved vengeance to take on Avalon, perhaps they could anchor her to other pieces of her past.

"There must have been something beyond hatred and retribution. What had life promised? What have you lost?" As he asked the question, he subconsciously attempted to answer it himself. He felt something missing, buried in a blind spot he had long ignored, but that seed of yearning had not yet sprouted into conscious thought. "You didn't break free just to fall back into darkness again. Why did your soul awaken? Who's out there that you weren't ready to leave behind?"

The questions dragged her through a field of torment. She clutched her head, covering her left eye as she wrestled with the past. Bravely, she pieced together her broken memories in an attempt to separate who she was from what she had done.

"After everything... Do I deserve to be happy? Can I really just walk away from all this?"

"Second chances don't come around often." His burdensome guilt swelled as he looked into her downcast eyes. Offering her a hand, he willed Iko to wrap them both in shadows. "I think you deserve to try."

XXXVI. The Cradle Of Life

Drake

T old you we're lost."

Groaning, Talia reached forward to extract Luc from the deceptively deep puddle he had stepped into.

Giles grabbed the boy's other arm and hoisted his muddy brother free from the hole. "If you have a better guess, you're free to lead. I told you—this is new territory for us."

Drake cautiously circumnavigated the puddle, advancing ahead of the entangled trio. A resilient coating of dust and mud covered his own hands and trousers, but he had been lucky to avoid the myriad of traps in the Blackwater.

Except for the python. That vile, slithering serpent was reason enough to blacklist the swamp from consideration as a future excursion.

Frowning, Drake tuned out the ensuing exchange of teasing quips and sarcastic rebuttals, focusing instead on his surroundings. Through the dark and listing trees, he gazed over small strips of soft mud that formed interconnected islands above dark pools of tarlike water. An omnipresent chorus of insects and birds flitted through the air from places unseen, providing an idyllic cloak for deadlier hunters lurking in the mire. A quiet hum distinct from the rhythm of their song lured him deeper into the marsh, west toward the afternoon sun.

"Where's he going?" demanded Luc.

"Drake!" Talia called after him, louder than necessary.

"Picnic's over," Drake said over his shoulder. "Let's keep this caravan moving."

Luc pouted. "We're never getting out of here."

"Is complaining going to help any?" challenged Giles.

"Is it going to hurt any?" countered Luc.

Drake heard the faint rhythm grow louder as he made his way across a chain of spongy islands. Studying the dark waters around him, he noticed a buoyant twig riding a slow current deeper into the hazy swamp. Leaping from island to island, he followed the twig on its lazy course.

"You know, it's possible there's nothing here but swamp, swamp, and more swamp," Luc considered pessimistically. "I mean, have you ever actually met someone who's seen this place?"

"You are free to walk back any time," Giles invited airily.

"First off, I know you don't mean that. You're bluffing," guessed Luc. "Second, you know I'm not about to start swimming past alligators alone."

"Then quit moping and put one foot in front of the other," Giles said groggily.

Luc wiped his soaked pants and flung a clump of mud at his brother.

"What's the thought process here?" frowned Giles. "I'm already muddy. We're in a swamp. That was just disrespectful."

"Well, you're being ugly," criticized Luc. "I just want to feel heard."

"Hey," Drake called behind to the rest of the pack, gesturing toward the stick. The current had picked up speed. The twig drifted under a cross made by two fallen trees and escaped his line of sight.

"Wait," Talia stared beyond the cross. "I think I hear something."

"Yeah. Up ahead." Scoping out a path forward, Drake traveled a long arc across connecting islands, not daring to step into the treacherous water. As he approached the crossed trees from the other side, he took added care in planning each step, aware that Talia was following close on his heels.

Light pierced through the dark trees ahead. A faint hiss called to him, urging him forward. He paused for a second, turning to see Talia jump the gap to his island. "You hear that?" A cautiously optimistic smile formed on his lips.

"Is that... a waterfall?" Talia squinted as she searched for the source of the sound.

Drake pressed on, counting the islands between him and the break in the trees as he went. From four to three to two and finally one, the light guided him across the chain, pulling him to the edge of the morass. Rounding the trunk of the last tree, he rested his eyes on the impossible treasure nestled deep in the heart of this inhospitable backwater.

Standing at the edge of the precipice, he stared in awe at the three-hundred-foot walls that sheltered the lush forest below. Uncannily symmetrical, the crater stretched over one thousand yards across to the sheer rock face on the opposite side of the bowl.

"Whoa," Talia whispered, marveling at the natural beauty of the basin.

"What do you see?" Giles quickened his step to come alongside them. "My, my..." He whistled at the splendor and laughed freely in relief. "That's it, right? That has to be it!"

"The Cradle of Life," Drake folded his arms. Squinting, he tried to survey the crater for a temple. Though he couldn't spot any structures down below, he noticed a conspicuous absence of foliage near the center of the ring.

"Cool," Luc clapped his hands together. "Really great. Now, how are we supposed to get down there?"

Talia looked down over the edge and immediately fell backward onto the damp safety of solid ground. "Deus," she gasped with caught breath.

"Luc's got a point," Giles gestured around the perimeter of the crater. "I don't see a path down. Might be something on the northern slope there, but I can't get a good view."

Luc bravely ventured to the edge of the crag, swiveling his head from side to side as he inspected their options. "Unless you can fly, I don't think we're getting down there." He turned to cock an eyebrow at Giles, then Drake. "Well? Can you fl—"

Mortal fear flashed on Luc's face as the ground beneath him cracked. Luc swung a hand toward his brother, but Giles couldn't move fast enough to catch the extended arm. A shriek of terror ripped through the air as Luc disappeared over the edge.

Drake rushed forward beside Giles and dropped to one knee at the brink. Miraculously, Luc had the sense to lean into the cliff as he slid, avoiding an outright tumble off the rockface. A trail of pale dust chased after him, like his spirit had been left at the top and was desperately racing back to its body. About halfway down the escarpment, the slope curved outward enough for him to slow his descent to a halt.

"Luc! Are you okay?" shouted Giles.

"I could've died!" Luc's high-pitched voice bounded up the wall.

"Are you all right?" Giles repeated with an edge in his voice.

"Yeah," Luc rested his head against the wall, shaken by the experience. "Yeah, I'm good."

"I gotta get down there."

Before anyone could interject, Giles dropped off the side, planting his gloved hands against the rock wall to help control his slide down to his brother. Drake couldn't hear the exchange but watched Giles wrap a steadying arm around his younger brother and gesture farther below. Luc hugged the wall tighter, then Giles started sliding again. Luc reluctantly joined him. Somehow, both reached the bottom without incident.

Drake looked back to Talia. She laughed, shaking her head from a seated position. "Come on. You can't be serious, right?"

"We can take it slow," Drake reasoned calmly. "I don't see a better way down. Plus, it's really not as steep as it looks. I just watched Giles slide all the way down, and it looked like he was in control the whole time."

"First off, if you don't see a better way down, how do you know there's a way back up?" challenged Talia.

"There has to be a way back up," Drake answered without providing further evidence.

"Did you spot a single person down there? I didn't," Talia retorted. "Also, you realize we could die if we hit one bad bump going off this cliff, right? Like, literally die."

"That's not going to happen," Drake tried to sound confident. "Look, here's what we'll do. I'll go ahead so I can catch you if you start to fall. Just put your weight against the cliff. And, here," he knelt beside her and opened his pack to retrieve the roll of bandages. Taking her hands, he prepared a thick wrap to protect her palms against friction burn.

"I hate this idea," Talia breathed deeply, attempting to psych herself up. Like wind-whipped waves crashing on the shore, her chest rose and fell in a furious rhythm. "I hate that you're making me do this. I hate geology and the natural formation of rocks. Deus can join the club, too."

"You've got this," he encouraged her. With his pack secured, he pulled her to her feet, then continued over to the edge. He turned to let himself down feet first, straining his forearms as he dug his boots into the wall. "Ready?"

"We could have just been farmers," lamented Talia. "I like sheep. Cows are cool."

"Maybe you'll see one down there," Drake said dryly. Talia did not look impressed. He tried a smile instead. "I'm here for you. This one's easy."

"If I die, I'm going to haunt you forever," Talia pledged wrathfully. "My ghost won't let you hear the end of it."

"Someone's being a little dramatic."

"Yes, I'm being dramatic about hurling ourselves off a cliff. Sue me."

Seeing she was at least moving toward the edge, Drake readied himself. "Remember, don't look down. Just face the wall and slide," he said, looking down as he prepared to slide. He let go of the ledge, and gravity took charge.

The initial stretch was a dizzying blur. Then, as the wall took a gentler angle, he dug in his toes and slowed himself to a stop thirty yards down.

He looked up and saw Talia deliberately force herself over the edge, one foot at a time. Shakily breathing with her whole frame, she held herself up by her hands while she worked to improve her footing. She stared at the rock wall two inches from her nose, not daring to look anywhere else.

"I've got you—go!" hollered Drake.

Talia peeled one hand off the ledge and planted it on the wall. As soon as she released the other, she lurched downward, shrieking in surprise.

Drake was ready for her when she came sliding down. He held a hand up to catch her, but her momentum dislodged him from his stationary position. He regained his balance and dug into the cliff, slowing both their descents.

"Don't stop," breathed Talia.

"What?" Drake yelled louder than he meant to.

"Let's get it over with," she sucked in a deep breath of air, preparing to begin the slide again.

Drake recognized her waning determination and pushed himself to start down the remainder of the escarpment. Focused as he was on his balance, he was doubly focused on staying ahead of Talia so he could catch her if she began to fall.

Reaching the gentle ledge halfway down, Drake kicked his feet over, ready to finish the last leg of the harrowing descent. "Keep going!" he called up, inspiring Talia to follow his lead after a five-second delay.

At last, the wall curved outward, and his descent slowed to a stop. Talia reached his side a few seconds later. After determining that she looked to be in one piece, he began to lead the way down the rocky pile at the bottom of the cliff. "Not so bad, right?" he tried supportively.

"You're on thin ice, mister," Talia wheezed, keeping her eyes on her feet as she followed his path.

"I'm proud of you," praised Drake.

"Sticks and stones," Talia shook her head ruefully.

Luc and Giles sat waiting for them under the shade of a thick-branched tree with orange fruit growing on its limbs. As they approached, Luc stood and planted his hands on his hips. "You're welcome," he said expectantly.

"You're lucky," Drake answered evenly, turning his attention to Giles. "Think I saw something in the middle of the crater. Unless you've got any better ideas..."

"Middle of the crater sounds good," Giles stretched his shoulder.

Talia silently took the lead, still visibly shaken from the descent. Drake followed close behind, tailed by Giles and Luc.

Unlike the miserable swamp they had traversed over the past few days, this crater was teeming with life—and predominantly not the kind intent on killing them. Trees as thick as cattle wore skirts of moss with dense packets of leaves adorning their sturdy limbs. In the ample space between the wooden guardians, emerald grass blanketed the forest floor. Blue and gold butterflies fluttered aimlessly through the warm air, just beyond the reach of sly foxes and squirrels that chased them around the grove. Though his hand rested on his sword, Drake felt a deep-rooted tranquility in this place. A slumbering land that knew only peace.

Two blue-jacketed, white-bellied birds observed Drake from a low tree limb, tilting their heads in suspicion as the strange biped approached. Soon, he crossed a line the birds deemed dangerous. They took flight on long-feathered wings, escaping to the sky and fleeing toward the center of the Cradle.

"It's kind of beautiful, isn't it?" Talia smiled softly. "You know, even if we are going to be stuck here the rest of our lives because there's no way out."

"There will be a way out," Drake smiled despite himself. "But you're right. It's a wonder Godwin never put a summer palace here."

"The Oracle's somewhere 'round here?" Luc frowned. "Do Oracles just sit in trees all day, waiting for someone to show up?"

"Obviously not," Talia rolled her eyes. "Oracles sit in temples all day. We're looking for a temple here."

"All right. So, we all get our fortunes read or whatever... then what?" Luc addressed this question to Giles.

"Then we're square with them. I guess if the Crossroads don't need us anymore, we can go wherever we like."

"Somewhere with money," urged Luc. "I'm tired of being broke."

"We're not broke," corrected Giles. "We're frugal. Besides, you need to learn to appreciate an honest day's work. You'll never know the value of a kroner if it's just given to you."

"One kroner's always worth one kroner," groaned Luc. "That's the point of money. It stays worth whatever it's worth. Otherwise, we'd all be running around trading cows for things."

"Arillia's always got work," suggested Drake.

"Not all of it's honest," Giles cracked his neck loudly. "I'm not typically a big city guy, but I'm thinking maybe Highwind next. Got to be the richest city on Kyros."

"Always plenty going on there," shrugged Drake. He couldn't think of a worse place to settle down than a crowded capital, but there was no sense in pissing on someone else's parade. Not like it concerned him at all.

"Think it's true? What they say about this place?" Talia whispered to Drake as her eyes fixated on a small creature resembling a sloth.

"What do they say?" asked Drake.

"That everything that ever was started here—that this was the birthplace of life."

"Maybe," Drake scratched his head. "I mean, that'd be Deus, right?"

Pyros burned at the edge of Drake's thoughts. He let the Primal flow through him, and in an instant, the flaming form of the fire soul was hovering dangerously close to the rich forest floor. *This is where the triumvirate forged the world. Ordos bestowed Deus the hammer to create all things to come, then gave the reaping scythe to Karax so Deus would never tire of his forge. Thus, all that begins in your realm must end—and all that will be began here.*

"So says legend," Giles challenged tacitly.

So says legend, agreed Pyros, fading from view.

"That's creepy," Luc shivered. "I didn't like that at all. Don't do that."

Talia took the lead and pointed up ahead. "Looks like a path?"

After another twenty yards, Drake spotted the dirt road. They emerged from the woods and started down the groomed path, heading south toward the gray outline of unfathomably ancient ruins.

Drake walked in stunned silence toward the primeval temple. The dirt road ended eighty yards ahead, sloping down to a stone bridge that bisected the square lake around the structure. The walkway, stamped by large rune carvings at regular intervals, was submerged in about an inch of water.

Purple lilies floated on the serene surface of the lake, drifting above the only bridge to the step-pyramidal temple. The base of the pyramid was visible through the clear water, extending perhaps fifteen feet below the surface. Four pillars marking the corners of the drowned ruins were similarly half-submerged; they would have otherwise stood three-quarters as tall as the central feature.

Warring waves of relief and anticipation met within Drake, bringing him to a full stop before the stone walkway. He quietly reflected on the journey that had brought him here. After traveling to the ends of the earth to find this fabled temple—after beating the odds time and time again, somehow surviving to gaze upon the lost site of origination as old as the world itself—he couldn't help but feel humbled by his luck.

"Looks like we made it," he said finally. A part of him felt the struggle couldn't truly be over—that this was either a mirage or another one of fate's traps plotted vindictively against his life. After all he had endured to get here, it felt inconceivable that he could suddenly be rewarded with the promised prize he fought for. He wrestled to come to terms with the fact that there was more than the battle; there was also the victory.

"Are you ready?" asked Talia, placing a bandaged hand on his arm.

Across the stone walkway, a barefoot woman dressed in the white robes of a priestess drew water from the quiet lake. She stood and balanced the urn on her head, then ascended the steps to the entryway in the upper third of the pyramid, ten feet above the waterline.

"I guess this should be the easy part, right?" Drake looked to Talia for reassurance.

"We've come this far," she patted his back with a smile, then ventured a foot onto the submerged walkway. "Might as well see what's waiting on the other side."

XXXVII. The Oracle?

Drake

"If I was a god, my temple would be made of gold."

Luc's critique of the stonework was accompanied by the sloshing of his feet through the shallow water underfoot.

"You're not a god, and this isn't a temple for one. That's the Oracle's home," corrected Giles, bending to inspect the purple lily by his shin.

"Man, why'd we come all this way to see a *poor* oracle? If they were any good, wouldn't they be stinking rich?" Luc rolled his eyes.

"There are more riches in life than money," Giles answered wisely, leaving the blooming flower behind.

"That's what broke people say when they're broke," sighed Luc.

"He's right," Talia interjected to Luc. "Money can't buy happiness, right? Well, it can't buy friends, or love, or meaning, either. How many of those frilly-shirted nobles in Highwind have ever seen a place like this?"

"Well said," Drake nodded his approval. Talia grinned at the praise.

His thoughts were torn between curiosity and caution. Having finally arrived at what must be the home of the Oracle, he could hardly stand another second's delay—he had to know if she could restore the missing pieces. At the same time, his guard was up, knowing there were strangers around.

If this well-hidden temple was merely a masterful ruse designed to prey on travelers, somebody would answer for it. He had not come this far to leave empty-handed.

"I bet you that oracle is at least a hundred years old," Luc speculated in a deliberate change of subject.

"I'll take the under on that," Talia cocked an eyebrow.

"Ditto," Giles chimed in. "Drake?"

"I don't gamble," he answered coolly.

"Good!" Talia praised with a mischievous grin, assuring him that his shortcomings in Dunloy had not been forgotten. "At least he's learning."

"Watch your step," Drake advised on the perfectly level stairs, hoping to cut off any related conversation.

A woman's sonorous voice greeted them from the top of the stairway, stealing the party's attention. "Welcome."

Drake looked up to see a fair-skinned woman in lavender robes. Her hair was concealed by a matching veil, though her sparkling blue eyes paired with a gentle smile. She clasped her hands in front of her and bowed slightly.

A brief look of confusion flashed on her face as she inspected the new arrivals, but she recovered swiftly. "You must have traveled far," she sucked in a short breath, seemingly anxious about offending the visitors. She spoke her next words slowly and articulately: "Can you understand me? Or shall I return with our Val'Kyran sister?"

"We understand you," Giles said in a voice neither hostile nor friendly.

"Oh. Good," she exhaled in visible relief. "You must be here to see the Oracle, I presume?"

"What, popular tourist stop?" Luc jested.

"Yes," Drake said over him. "Will you take us to her?"

"Of course," she half bowed again. "My name is Miriame. Please, follow me."

Drake fell into step behind her as she led them through the narrow passage into the temple, followed by Talia and the mercenaries. Beams of bright daylight entered through gaps in the stone, while a series of regularly spaced sconces provided the balance of the interior illumination. Beyond the entry corridor, the temple opened into a sparse, square chamber. A fountain featuring a small sculpture of a bronze woman acted as the humble centerpiece, complete with a pitcher and several bronze cups ordered neatly to the side.

Another priestess sat on the edge of the fountain, sipping from one of the cups. She lowered her drink and stood, tucking a strand of red hair into her veil. She retrieved a thin bell from a pouch on her hip, rang it four times, then greeted the arrivals with a familiar half bow and smile.

Drake nodded his acknowledgement, uneased by the clear signal to hidden parties but not immediately threatened by her diminutive, unarmed figure. He scanned the room and counted three discreet passages that delved deeper into the stone walls. The smallest was in the back-left corner, only five feet tall and two feet wide.

Miriame gestured to the right side of the room where two white sheets hung below wooden signs. "I sense your journey has not been an easy one. Behind these doors, you will find heated baths. You may cleanse yourselves and meditate on what you would desire to ask the Oracle, while we wash your soiled garments. The men's bath is on the left; the women's is on the right."

Drake exchanged a look with Talia and instinctively lifted a hand to object. "Now hold on just a minute. I'm none too keen on you splitting us up and leaving me buck as the day I was born. I'm fine to see the Oracle as I am."

Miriame tried to smile, but Drake saw the frustration in her shoulders. "I strongly believe the experience would be more pleasant for both you and the Oracle if you took the opportunity to purify yourself."

"I'll be fine, Drake." Talia prodded the sleeve of his brown jacket, dislodging a patch of dried mud onto the stone floor. She eyed the fallen filth, then added softly, "I do think you could use a bath."

Frowning, Drake lowered his nose to the shoulder of his jacket. A light whiff carried the many scents of the swamplands—an odious mix of sweat, dust, mud, and worse. Glancing at his trousers, he saw the coating of grime was thick and rigid like plated armor.

"I can wait out here with Luc until you're both done, if it helps put you at ease," offered Giles.

Talia sized up the two petite priestesses, then shrugged at Drake. "On the off chance I get into any trouble, I could yell for them to come help," she suggested. "Cool?"

Drake gritted his teeth. Equally unsure about that proposal, Miriame added: "We do have separate bathing facilities for men and women and would ask you all to respect that privacy. Of course, no harm will come to this young lady. The temple is a place of sanctuary and rejuvenation for all."

Drake moved to rub his eyes but stopped short, having spotted the layers of filth on his hand. "Fine," he ceded. "Thank you, Giles."

"On the racks inside, you'll find fresh robes you may wear following your baths. We'll retrieve you once the Oracle is ready to meet you. Please, do try to relax and enjoy the healing waters."

Drake gestured for Talia to enter first. "Check it out, let me know if anything looks off?"

"Sure." Talia disappeared behind the sheet on the right. "It's a bath," she reported dryly. A faint splash. "Water's warm. I'm fine!"

"Holler if you need anything," Drake reminded her, rather loudly.

"Will do," she called back.

The red-headed priestess appeared under his left arm, nearly suffering the brunt of his elbow as he turned. She stepped back and made an apologetic half bow. Absentmindedly picking at her eyebrow, she looked up at him with a nervous smile forming under her wavy nose. Her shimmering blue eyes had a somewhat tranquilizing effect as she spoke. "My name is Grace. I will be taking care of your gear while you meet with the Oracle. Please slide your clothes, bag, and sword under the curtain once you've disrobed inside."

Cocking an eyebrow, Drake removed the scabbard from his waist and handed the sword to Giles. "No offense, ma'am. Just that I don't know you," he countered, dropping his pack at his feet.

Drake lifted the sheet to the men's bath. Peering inside, he scanned the walls for secondary entrances but failed to uncover any. Against the side wall, a wooden bench held eight sets of folded robes. The garments came in white and light-blue options, striking him as an odd choice within Godwin's borders. He stepped inside, letting the curtain fall behind him. A smoky, almost eggy odor filled the room, though it was hard to tell whether it came from the bath itself or through slits in the ceiling that reached the outer world.

He kicked off his boots, folded his jacket, and stripped his stained undershirt. Sitting on the wooden bench, he pulled off his socks, then inspected a pair of white robes. *What do you think?* he asked within, entreating Pyros to either calm his nerves or stoke his suspicions.

It looks like a bath, the Primal rumbled indifferently.

With a relenting sigh, Drake finished disrobing and slid the pile under the curtain. His hand hovered over the dagger on his calf.

No—he preferred to keep that one on hand. *Just in case.*

Drake unstrapped the sheath and laid his weapon on the floor beside the bath, then cautiously lowered a foot onto the first submerged step. The water was on the higher side of warm but not quite uncomfortably hot. He dipped in a second foot, then continued forward until the water reached his hips. With a deep breath, he closed his eyes and dunked his head. Resurfacing, he wiped the hair out of his eyes and stood facing the door for a long moment, subconsciously expecting an assailant. When none came, he let the tension out of his neck and drifted over to the far corner of the bath, sitting where he could comfortably see the door, the bench, and the back wall in his field of view.

The warm water was soothing on both body and spirit. Resting his eyes for a brief minute, he considered that he may have greeted the priestesses too harshly. Then again, they must be used to tense customers; any traveler who made it through the Blackwater would surely be a little rough around the edges.

Do you know what you will ask her? probed Pyros.

"I think so," Drake reflected, picking a spot on the wall opposite him and fixing his eyes as he sorted through his thoughts. "She either knows or she doesn't—*who am I?*"

Who were you, Pyros amended carefully.

Though he felt provoked by the correction, he exhaled the feeling and consciously tried to relax his shoulders. "Perhaps," he allowed. He could hear Giles and Luc exchanging directionless banter beyond the doorway but couldn't discern the conversation. Closing his eyes, he sat with his thoughts for a time.

To Pyros' point, there was another risk he had never considered. He would hardly call himself perfect as he was now, but he felt sure in his ways. If he opened this door to the past, he might discover something he'd have sooner forgotten. A looming feeling in his subconscious warned him of guilt, rage, and dread lurking in the sealed passageways of his mind. If he opened that door and didn't like what he found, there would be no going back.

"Sir?" an uncertain voice called from behind the curtain, interrupting his brooding. "Please robe yourself. The Oracle is ready to see you."

Steeling himself to meet destiny, Drake climbed out of the bath. He dried himself with the white robe he had tossed on the ground, then slipped on one of the light-blue ones. The garment was comfortable, but he yearned for the familiar weight of his gear. Looping the cotton belt around his waist, he took a deep breath, then threw the curtain aside and entered the antechamber.

Grace was waiting patiently outside, standing next to Giles and Luc. Now that Drake was clean, the mud-caked brothers looked twice as dirty as before. Giles gestured to the room behind the curtain. "Good bath?"

"Not bad," shrugged Drake. He scanned the room and spotted Talia in a white robe, filling a cup of water from the central fountain. "Hey, kiddo."

"Oh, wow!" she suppressed a smile as she turned to face him. "I didn't know someone was under all that mud. Nice to see you, Drake."

"Funny," he commented flatly. "Ready to see this Oracle?"

"Oh," Talia scratched her head sheepishly. "I already met her. Just got back. Luc was right, by the way—always bet the over."

"What did she say?" Drake was relieved to see that Talia was fine, but it unnerved him to hear they'd been shuffling her around the temple without his knowing.

"Not a whole lot." A rogue strand of hair fell in front of her eye. She blew a puff of air at it. "Said she knew I traveled all over, didn't have a place to call home... that although I've had my troubles in life, I'll get to have a happy future and settle down somewhere quiet. Pretty basic fortune-teller stuff," she summarized, sounding disappointed. "Oh, she also said a rich and powerful admirer will fall in love with me in the next three years. So, there's that."

"What a load of shit," Luc rolled his eyes.

Giles readied the back of his hand to discipline the comment, but a solid *crack* sounded through the air before he could. He raised his eyebrows in shock at Miriame.

"My apologies," she breathed sharply, bowing her head. "That manner of language is not permitted in this temple. Please refrain from speaking such obscenities about the Oracle."

Giles pursed his lips and nodded in approval at her decisive form. "You're good."

"For what it's worth, I agree with Luc," Drake commented to Talia. "Sorry to hear it."

"Ah well," Talia shrugged. "We didn't come here for me. We came for you—so, go see if she has what you're looking for!"

"I'll be back soon," Drake promised. He smiled once for Talia, then followed Grace across the chamber. The priestess led him into the narrowest of the neighboring passageways, where he was forced to do an awkward sidestep shuffle to advance.

The tight corridor curved right and deposited him in what looked like a small throne room. Two torches hung on the side walls, spaced just enough to throw flickering shadows in the middle of the room. A contrived manufacturing of mysterious aura. The other surfaces were covered by colorful tapestries and cloths, many overlapping each other. Raised on a small pile of cushions atop the two-step stage, a wrinkled face looked inexplicably surprised to see him.

"You have come!" she gasped in some grand realization of purpose, spreading her hands in wonder. "Please, O Destined One—sit and let us speak your fate!"

Drake eyed the worn, round cushion at the bottom of the steps in front of her. The Val'Kyran attendant off to the side of the room gestured a sweeping hand toward the pillow, inviting him to take a seat. He lowered himself onto the cushion apprehensively, crossing his legs as he examined the colorful Oracle.

Her outfit was a hideous abstraction of post-impressionist art. Without any discernable patterns of size or placement, green swirls resembling clouds were embroidered on her indigo robes. Pointy yellow clogs peeked out from under her dress. Above her painted face, she wore a peculiar square headpiece, complete with strands of dangling beads hanging off the front and back. No two colors were a match.

The Val'Kyran stepped forward to offer Drake a wide bowl of water. "Please cleanse your hands in the holy waters of purification, then be connected with the Oracle."

Drake eyed the rather normal-looking bowl of water. "I thought y'all were supposed to introduce yourselves before you make us do chores."

"My name is Oshun," she provided succinctly.

Drake gingerly dipped his fingers in the bowl. "Long way to come to serve in a sunken temple, Oshun."

"A long way for us all," she reflected thoughtfully, returning to her place by the wall.

"And you, Oracle? Do you have a name?" Drake asked irreverently.

"She is the famed Oracle Lak'Sha," Oshun said on her behalf. "She has served the wanderers of our world for nearly a century, indiscriminately offering guidance and peace to all who seek her."

"Well, Lak'Sha, I take it you know why I'm here," Drake probed.

"Of course," the Oracle nodded seriously, causing the beads in front of her face to jingle against one another. "You've come seeking answers, and I will help you find them. Come, give me your hands."

Doing little to hide his skepticism, Drake outstretched both arms and was received by the Oracle's leathery fingers. She closed her eyes and began mumbling an incantation of nonsense, punctuated by startling single-syllabic outbursts. "Mah!" she barked, tossing her head to the side. "Choo! Choo! Chi!" The bizarre performance continued for the better part of a minute. It was a miracle the old hag didn't snap her neck with all the thrashing about. Finally, her eyes rolled to the back of her head, then focused on Drake with a new air of gravity.

"You," she slowly pointed a bony finger at his forehead. "You come from humble roots and have the hands of a warrior. You're not one for creature comforts, and you never shy away from hard work. You have seen many horrors in your life—battles that would end a lesser man, acts against Deus that would leave a priest cold in the streets—but still you go on. Perhaps you have lost much along the way, but you have found new reasons to live; the girl has saved you, and you have saved the girl."

She took a long, ostensibly thoughtful breath. "Your future is cloudy, young man. If you turn to a holier life, one filled with gratitude and kindness, you may yet find joy in this life. Happiness is attainable! But, if you cannot let go of your vices and short temper, you will meet great sorrow. Lastly, do not be afraid of your feelings—our hearts remind us that we're all human."

Unimpressed, Drake snatched his hands away with an impatient frown. "You didn't actually say much."

"You haven't actually asked much," she returned evenly, playing with one of the beads on her hat.

"You were supposed to help me fix the holes in my memory," growled Drake. He felt the rage of newborn hopelessness flare in his chest, burning his ears as he fought to keep a semblance of composure. "I traveled halfway across the continent for answers—show them to me!"

"The answers are within you!" exclaimed the charlatan. "Let's discuss your uncertainties, and we may find your peace together. Inner peace!"

"Tell me who I am, damn it!" Drake slammed his fist against the pillow beneath him. He heard a quiet bell ring behind Oshun. The attendant avoided his accusatory eyes.

"You are whoever you want to be!" emphasized the Oracle, as if her conviction would make the statement any less absurd. She rested a thoughtful finger on her lips. "Who do you want to be?"

"What the hell is going on here?" Drake demanded, rising to his feet.

The bell rang again, a little more frantically this time.

The Oracle spread her hands and tried to placate his rage, speaking in a calm voice. "A little mindful meditation would do you well. Try taking deep breaths and picturing yourself in a happy meadow of smiling grass."

Footsteps echoed down the corridor behind him. Drake wheeled around to find two unfamiliar priestesses in the entryway, both tan and athletic in physique. The one with the bulbous nose and half-shaved eyebrow reached into a tawny pouch on her hip.

Drake pulled the left lapel of his robe aside to reveal his birthmark. "I wouldn't try it," he snapped his fingers, summoning a ball of flames in his right hand. "I've been through hell and back trying to find this musty shithole. Now, either one of you is going to tell me what the hell happened to the real Oracle, or all of you are going to—"

"Enough!"

A fifth woman had emerged from a concealed passageway behind one of the tapestries on the wall. She raised a hand to the priestesses by the main entrance in a signal to deescalate the situation.

Drake stared at the newcomer in stunned silence, letting the flame die in his hand. She wore sleeveless, silky white robes that swept the temple floor. Silver bracelets lined her golden arms, and a purple amethyst hung from her neck on an ivory chain. Intricate wooden beads were suspended between her neck and her lower back by her braided black hair. Dark eyes, accented by shadows of blue paint, studied him intently.

In that one look, he felt the secrets of his heart were laid bare. They had never met before, but she knew him better than he knew himself.

"Somehow, I knew you would find your way to my temple, Pyros."

XXXVIII. The Oracle

Drake

*V*anya.

The name reverberated through Drake's head. He narrowed his eyes at the newest priestess. Pyros crackled expectantly at the edge of his thoughts. "Vanya?" he repeated.

She smiled knowingly. "Come with me. We have much to talk about."

"But—Oracle! He readily set his heart on killing us!" protested the taller of the two women by the door.

"Peace, Sibi. No one is killing anyone. It was only a misunderstanding."

"Your will be done," the pair of guardians bowed. Despite the lingering concern evident on their faces, they obediently exited through the main door.

Drake followed the younger Oracle to a hidden passage in the wall, eyeing the imposter as he went. With an unabashed shrug, the old woman took a fan from her mountain of cushions and went about airing herself.

Another narrow passage. The stone stairway descended to a dim room below. Only two torches illuminated this second chamber, though the reflective floors did well to disperse light. The simple room featured an orderly collection of crystals, spices, and containers on the wall, vaguely reminding Drake of an Apothecary. Two round throw pillows, both in significantly better condition than the one he had tried above, rested in the middle of the floor.

The woman, surprisingly short for a legendary Oracle, took his hand and led him to sit on a cushion. She sat on the second one, facing him. "I know you must have many questions, Drake," she began understandingly.

"How do you know my name?" he frowned suspiciously.

A spectral, yellow being shimmered behind her. Of course the Oracle was a Mystic. Her Primal had a pin-shaped head and a body encased by four symmetrical arced plates, each separated from the next by a few inches. A lone eye studied Drake from the center of its head. An unblinking observer.

Drake felt Pyros appear behind him without invitation. Though he normally would have scolded his Primal for such an impulsive act, he somehow sensed the two had history between them.

"I am Zara. Some know me as the Oracle. Through Vanya, I see all in this world and beyond."

"If you saw me coming, you'll know why I'm here," challenged Drake.

Zara smiled sadly. "I can see everything, and yet I am blind to what's not in front of me. In my dreams, I look through the kaleidoscope of destiny and catch glimpses of the millions of souls tethered to this world. I cannot act on these visions, however, and often find myself overwhelmed in the mornings. I don't know where or when my dreams take place, nor what futures might evolve if I dared to intervene."

She drew a steadying breath and gazed through the windows of his eyes. "That's why I don't tap into the third eye when I'm awake. It helps to know there's a world grounded in reality. One where I can be present with my surroundings. But with you here in front of me, I can be present in you. I can see what you see—now and forever."

Drake held up a hand to pause the rapidly progressing conversation. "Ignoring that last comment which sounded both deeply uncomfortable and intrusive—why make me go through that whole circus with the screwy lady upstairs? What was the point in that?"

Zara laughed brightly, nodding her understanding. "Lak'Sha has been a part of this temple since my predecessor's earliest days. She cares more deeply about our traditions than I do. Twenty years ago, the late Oracle prophesied to one of the Godwins. Though they came for truth, it was not what they wanted to hear. Months later, one of their assassins returned to silence her. Lak'Sha blames herself for Amelia's death. Now, she insists it's her penance to play the part of the Oracle and shield me from any who would wish me harm. Though she means well, I often wonder if I'm failing my legacy by allowing her to speak in the name of the Oracle. I always listen in on her... predictions... and on the rare occasion the traveler is one from my dreams, I like to meet them."

"You saw me in your dreams?" inferred Drake, rapt in her sincerity. Though he had dismissed that woman upstairs as a loon, he felt compelled to believe Zara. At the very least, Vanya had Pyros' quiet approval.

"I did," Zara wiped a tear from her eye. "You've gone through much. Or... you will go through much. It's hard for me to tell," she frowned.

"The man who told me to find you said you could reawaken the part of me that slumbers. I have these holes in my memory... I can feel something on the other side, but it hurts when I try to break through the fog. I need to know who I am."

"So, you've met Eamon," Zara bit her lip and nodded to herself as if mentally rearranging the pieces of a puzzle. "Oh. Yes, of course. Even now, I see the splintered fragments of your soul. Each shard is perfectly intact, right next to one another, but it's as if someone severed the cord connecting them."

"Can you fix me?" He felt his heart hammering in his chest. He urged himself to breathe, but the anticipation was unbearable.

"Yes," she took his hands. A gentle comfort flowed through her touch. "I can bridge our dreams to show you all I see. If you wish to crack open the forgotten sepulcher of your soul, I will help you. But," she leaned forward, lowering her voice as she delivered the warning, "know that I can't take away the truth once it's yours. If you have attained peace in this life, I would urge you to reconsider whether you truly want to carry the burden of the past. There is a hardship to remembering—a curse of visions. The present mind is often not forgiving of yesterday's sins."

"I know," Drake exhaled deeply, "but I have to know. I came all this way because I feel something missing inside. I can still feel the pain and anger behind the veil—I have to know why."

"I believed you would say that," Zara flicked a strand of rebellious hair away from her eyes. "Of course, I had to give you the choice. That's the tricky thing about seeing the future of souls—there's always a choice."

"Hey, whatever pays the rent, right?" he shrugged.

Zara grinned at this, but a darker shade of lament soon enveloped her eyes. She reached out a hand to touch the back of his. "You really need to take better care of yourself."

"I'm fit as a fiddle," Drake pulled back his scarred hand.

Zara rolled her eyes. "Not here," she smacked his bicep. "Here," she tapped a gentle finger against his birthmark, slipping past the fold of his robes.

"I did what I had to," Drake averted his eyes.

"I only see, Drake. It's not for me to judge," Slowing her breathing, Zara closed her eyes and pressed her cool palm against his skin. "You must try to take care in the future. Already, I sense irreparable damage within you. Time does not heal all wounds, I'm afraid."

"What are you talking about? I feel fine," he frowned.

She smiled wistfully. "The thread that sews your destiny together with Pyros' is like a candle wick. Each time you ignite the candle, you place yourself in mortal danger. If your flame burns too long or too hot, you may consume your thread entirely, ending your existence on Kyros."

"That doesn't sound right," Drake shook his head. "I've never had a problem before."

"I suspect you may have," she returned gently, artfully avoiding direct confrontation. "At least, I suspect you've seen this truth in others. The pirate captain, the blond boy I see in your memories..."

"Desmond." Drake closed his eyes and recalled the scarring scene at the Twins. He winced as he visualized the boy unravelling into nothingness.

"The boy's thread burned too hot," Zara explained apologetically. "He consumed his life in summoning that comet. He was neither spiritually nor physically ready for such an effort."

"Which is why Kika—" Drake's eyes widened with realization.

"Yes. The pirate captain has honed her body into a powerful conduit for Hydraxia," nodded Zara. "She, too, pushes beyond her limits. Like you, she has been damaged beyond repair, and her condition is only worsened each time she strains her thread."

"That can't be," Drake pushed the Oracle's hand away from his chest. He felt his anger flare inward, directed at the unusually silent Pyros. "How the hell does that make any sense? What's the point in having a Primal if it's just going to kill you?"

"It's the balance of life, Drake," Zara closed her eyes, summoning the spectral form of Vanya behind her. "We're not gods; we're merely the Primals' link to this world. With time and practice, you can learn to burn the candle slowly—chipping away only a little at a time, limiting risk to your life thread. But you must know that every action you take to bring them into this world brings you closer to theirs. At Fort Kagrash, you nearly crossed the point of no return. Those scars are yours for life."

"What, these?" Drake inspected the faded burn marks on the backs of his hands. Now that the pain was gone, the minor discoloration hardly bothered him at all.

"Your organs were damaged a lot worse than your skin," she diagnosed bluntly. "There's little you can do about it now, but at the very least, you should stop drinking. A shot of whisky might as well be rat poison to you now."

"Any chance I can get another Oracle to give me a second opinion?"

"I'm serious, Drake. There are people who need you in this world. Do it for them."

Drake scratched his head, then nodded acquiescence. "Yeah, all right. I can live with that." Though naturally still a little skeptical, he was willing to heed her advice. For now. "So what did you mean, *we'll dream together?*"

Zara silently rose from the cushion. Moving to the cluttered table, she busied herself with an assortment of tools. After pulverizing a purple plant in a bowl with her pestle, she added two handfuls of spices from a jar and mixed them together with an odd fork. She carried the bowl with her over to the wall and explained, "I've prepared a blend that will allow you to see visions. Your mind will naturally explore the dreams; I'll help guide you toward the lonely memories that have been forgotten, and you'll reconnect them with the rest."

She lifted a torch from its sconce, lit the blended herbs, then replaced the torch on the wall. Thin, purple vapors rose from the dark ceramic.

Drake gestured to the bowl as Zara returned to her cushion. "I'll admit I'm new to this whole *spiritual journey* thing, but I'm pretty sure you're trying to drug me."

Zara smiled playfully. "I promise it won't be like that time you and your brother broke into the abandoned mill."

"I have... a brother?" He felt dizzy. The spices didn't help.

"Be warned: these visions are intense. You might realize you're in a dream, but you'll still feel everything around you just as you did then. When you awaken, you'll feel the unrestricted weight of your memories crashing like a tidal wave. The visions can often be disorienting or painful for those who gaze into the future or think on loved ones lost, but yours will be overwhelming."

Drake was embarrassed to find his right leg was shaking with anxiety. "I'm ready," he steeled himself, forcing his mind and body to be still.

Zara added a pinch of some other herb from her pocket, turning the light-purple vapors into a thick haze of dark smoke. She made a wafting motion above the bowl, then handed it to him.

The purple tendrils leaned and swayed before his eyes, a seductive dance of promise and danger. Finding reassurance in Zara's smile, Drake held the bowl up to his face and took a deep breath of the sweet vapors.

Lowering the bowl, Drake reeled as the room started to sway. The torchlight raced in and out from the walls, washing over him as if the sun had become one with the tides. Zara's hair stood on end, rearing like a cobra before sinking back down. Though his fingertips were numb, he could keenly taste the sweet smoke lingering on his tongue. The evasive flavor was beyond imagining.

"One more breath," Zara's sonorous voice encouraged him softly. She helped him lift the bowl.

He took another deep breath of the vapor, then dropped the bowl. Though he was certain he saw the ceramic shatter, it made no sound. He heard only the muted tinkle of the priestesses' bells.

Vanya appeared behind Zara, glowing in a brilliant yellow. Brighter than a thousand suns. Its lone eye scanned the room behind Drake, making him feel warm and protected. The wandering gaze finally landed on his eyes, and he was wholly, irreversibly mesmerized. He lost sight of the room but saw with perfect clarity the lost visions of his past.

XXXIX. First Impressions

Drake

The memories shelled his mind like a column of trebuchets laying siege.

A bombardment of cataclysmic lightning, echoes of the past flashed by faster than he could focus on any individual scene. He felt as if he were caught in a turbidity current, drowning in an incomprehensible flood of his existence—both rendered immediately in front of him and simultaneously restored within the forgotten recesses of his mind. The old joined the new seamlessly, like an atoll lagoon reclaimed by the ocean.

The recollections that captured the attention of his adrift mind played out without a discernible pattern, varying wildly in chronology and significance. As the days of his life unfolded before him, he began to merge consciousnesses with his dream-walking avatar, transitioning from a state of passive observation to living through the eyes of his past self.

The collage of memories was a nauseating cocktail of emotions—an overpowering drink of nostalgia, pride, happiness, fear, and remorse. Each scene shifted to the next before he could fully grasp its significance, leaving him disoriented and confused as he adapted to the new, unrelated sequence.

In one scene, Drake saw a bearded man with a blocky head crouch in tall grass, holding a finger to his lips. His woolen shirt and scratchy pair of leather trousers were damp with sweat. The man, his adoptive father, beckoned to his brother and pointed at a quiver of arrows. Wyatt handed an arrow to his father, who nocked it on his longbow. The seasoned hunter removed the black hat from his head, wiped a forearm over his gray-speckled hair, then eyed the pronghorn at the river's edge.

Another scene. Crisp autumn air. He sat in the back of a wagon, staring out at golden-amber hills. A child's hand, his hand, blocked out the glare of the sun. Birdsong filled the valley. Aside from the rattling wagon, he had felt a deep tranquility in this place. Warmth in nature's care. He remembered its peace, but it didn't feel quite the same. It was a little sadder. Nostalgic. Though the memory hadn't changed, he now knew he'd never see those serene hills again.

The pervasive stench of smoked cigarettes struck him before his eyes had a chance to adjust to the dim light. Smelled just like home. His adult-sized hands lifted a pot of coffee and poured the black liquid into a tarnished tin cup. He looked up at his older brother, trying not to get distracted by his black ponytail. "They're going to catch you one of these days, Wyatt." Drake realized the words had come from his mouth.

"Haven't caught me yet," Wyatt laughed arrogantly. "Oh, hey! Meant to tell you, kid—you got a letter."

"*The* letter?" Drake noticed his voice sounded higher. More vibrant, somehow. He leaped up from his worn-out chair, accidentally spilling the pot of coffee over the table.

"I'll clean that," Wyatt swatted a hand through the air to stop him, then produced a sealed message from his shirt. "See what they want from you."

Drake accepted the note. After admiring the blue seal on the front of the envelope, the royal crest of Tallawyn right below his name, he thumbed open the letter and hastily skimmed its brief contents. He stared at his brother in a transcendent daze. "They chose me," he tapped the letter in disbelief. "I'm going to be an apprentice to the Great Plains' Guardsmen."

Zara's voice drew him into an ethereal, white mist. "Follow me," she instructed. He felt someone grab his hand and pull him in deeper. The fog turned a deep purple. Then, he was back in the two-bedroom cottage outside the city, sitting in the same old chair where he had received his invitation almost a decade ago.

Drake lifted a cup of cold coffee to his mouth, took a long sip, then returned the vessel to the table. "They're going to catch you if you keep doing that," he chastised his older brother.

"How many years have you been saying that now?" dismissed Wyatt. "Unless you plan on turning me in, I've got nothing to worry about."

"How is it that I still seem to be the only one paying for anything?" Drake groaned as he rose from the chair. He bent to grab his helmet from the floor beside the table. The blue feather on top always made him smile.

"Investments," Wyatt declared shrewdly. "It takes money to make money. But I'm telling you, one of these days, it's all going to pay off. Don't worry, little brother. I'll take good care of you when it does."

"Is that how that's pronounced? I always thought it was *indictment,*" remarked Drake.

"You're a funny guy," Wyatt pointed meaningfully. "You know, if this guardsman gig doesn't pan out, you could always be a circus clown."

"Depending how this new assignment goes, I just might." Drake slid on his helmet and did a once-over to ensure his uniform was presentable.

"Oh yeah, that's right. You're the sap they picked to babysit that lord's daughter, ain't ya?"

"She's a lady in her own right," Drake set the record straight. "Don't forget, her father commands the largest navy in the world. You don't want to be on the Marquess's bad side."

Wyatt rolled his eyes. "Firstly, the High Commander runs the navy. Her dad's just a stuffed shirt like the rest of them. Secondly, what're they going to do? Sail their boats across the Great Plains and strap me to the figurehead?"

"Disparaging a noble is a crime," Drake warned, mostly joking.

"Best get going before you wind up an accomplice," Wyatt countered, flicking wax out of his ear.

"For once, I think you're right." Drake crossed the floor of their small cottage to head outside. His white horse was right where he had left her, tied to the hitching post out front. He gently stroked her forehead. "Might be a week or two till you're home again, girl. Say bye to your squirrel friends." He slid one foot into the stirrups and climbed up.

Wyatt leaned against the doorframe. Loosely held, an unlabeled jug of spirits dangled from the hand that lacked a cigar. "If she takes a fancy to you, we'll have a drink when you're back. If she don't, we'll drink just the same."

"My duty is to protect the Lady until Prince Georg returns from Mines. Don't make me throw you in a jail cell until then."

"At least they have free food," Wyatt took an unflinching swig of his hard drink.

"You have free food here," Drake said pointedly, spurring his horse into motion to avoid prolonging the conversation.

Riding down the highway to Cairnes, he couldn't help but admire the beautiful summer morning. The sun showered glory over fields of gold, freely sharing its radiant warmth, asking nothing in return. A good omen for the day.

Though he was an early riser, he knew the harvesters had been in the fields for hours already. One gray-haired farmer along the roadside saluted as he rode past. Drake returned the motion, raising a gloved hand to his feathered hat. He felt only a little self-conscious about the flowing blue cape on his back.

The uniform's just another responsibility. Comes with the title, Drake justified to himself.

Riding up to the gates of Cairnes, he passed the disorderly queue of merchants and hailed the guardsmen on duty.

"Officer Lone," one of the halberdiers greeted neutrally, stepping aside to make room for the horse.

"Soldier," Drake nodded in return, riding through without delay.

As his horse trotted down the bustling city streets leading to the keep, Drake reflected on his blessings. He had worked his way up from the bottom, earning his spot as one of the few non-noble officers in the GPG. Though he doubted he would ever ascend the ranks to Commander, he still held ambitions to one day earn the title of Captain. At the very least, the Knight Commander had personally recognized him for his valor in dismantling the Long Tooth highwaymen, and he had the honor of meeting Prince Georg following a strong performance in the exhibition rounds of the annual tournament. If he stayed focused and put in the effort, a bright future was sure to be his.

Though some of his fellow officers had mocked his appointment as bodyguard to Lady Alivia of Dominion, making predictable, derisive comments about chaperoning the marquess's daughter, he suspected they were simply envious that he was given the opportunity. It was a simple duty, but it had the potential to be a high-visibility assignment. He would likely encounter Prince Georg when he returned, and he was confident he would be duly rewarded for keeping the Tallawyn's bride-to-be safe in his absence.

Crossing into the grand courtyard through the outer gate, Drake gazed up at the pearl walls of the palace. Although nowhere near as fantastical as the royal castle in Talos, the estate was kept in immaculate repair as Prince Georg's summer retreat and the ancestral home of the Tallawyns.

Artemis, his reliable steed, knew where to go from here. She pranced proudly across the stone courtyard to her tidy stall in the private stable. Drake dismounted, gathered his equipment, and fed Artemis a parting apple before allowing the squire boy to lead his horse away for grooming.

Anxious to meet Lady Alivia Fiore, he half walked, half jogged to the servant's entrance connecting the stables to the palace. Hopefully, she wouldn't cause him too much trouble in the coming weeks. He knew plenty of horror stories and had personally witnessed the foulest personalities nobles could possess. On the two ends of the spectrum were the brats who constantly snuck out to *see how the other side lives* and the snooty, upturned noses that seemed incapable of anything aside from barking orders. Born of high nobility as she was, Lady Alivia manifested in his imagination as a powdered face set in a permanent frown, squeezed into a dress that barely fit through a doorframe.

If he was lucky, she'd think too lowly of him to give direct commands.

Sucking in a deep breath ahead of the big day, Drake ascended the last two flights of stairs and emerged in the long hall that led to the throne room. Already, a line of evenly spaced knights flanked either side of the corridor, dressed in formal regalia and insignias. He started toward the throne room, figuring that's where he would find the commander and further instructions.

"Drake!" hissed one of the guards to his right. Drake paused to search for the source of the voice. "I mean *Officer Lone,*" the soldier rolled his eyes. It was Micky.

"Good morning, Micky," greeted Drake. They weren't close friends. In fact, he didn't particularly like the man. Micky was a slacker. Worse, he openly shared his dissatisfaction with being in the GPG. Still, he was one of the first people Drake had met as an apprentice, and consequently, they shared some history. They could be work friends.

"You're late!" warned Micky.

"The Lady isn't supposed to get here until noon," Drake said coolly. "We've got plenty of time."

"The Lady and her entourage arrived ten minutes ago," Micky raised his eyebrows.

Drake mirrored his high brows, waiting to see if the junior guardsman was pulling an ill-timed joke. When Micky didn't break character, Drake felt his stomach drop. "Aw, hell."

He tore off down the carpeted hall, passing dozens of knights as he ran. Many of those who recognized him laughed at his distress, calling out "Officer Lone!" in passing.

His clanking greaves came to a halt in front of the double doors at the end of the hallway. The sentry posted outside the throne room just shook his helmeted head.

Stepping forward, Drake flung the door open a little harder than he had intended. The heavy wood thumped against the wall inside, rebounding loudly to announce his presence.

Several heads turned to witness his unceremonious entry into the throne room. Among them were most of the GPG stationed against the walls, half of the nine white-clad soldiers from Dominion, and the Commander of Cairnes' Armed Forces.

The commander's steely eyes shifted to Drake. Though he maintained composure, his tired face conveyed a sigh. "... with the utmost professionalism and chivalry," he finished saying to the lady. "I bid you a restful stay at Cairnes Palace. Allow me to introduce you to your assigned protector. Officer Lone," the commander testily summoned him over with a snap of his fingers.

"Reporting, sir!" Drake hurried past the confused Dominion soldiers, stopping to salute his superior at the front of the room.

Drawing a breath of patience, the commander forced a smile onto his face. "Officer Lone will take care of all your needs at the palace. He is sworn to your protection and will most happily die for you if the occasion demands it."

Lady Alivia Fiore turned to meet Drake's eyes. Her empathetic smile made him feel seen. Told him that she recognized him as a person, not just another pawn at her disposal. Thin, soft lips spoke appreciation: "Thank you, Officer Lone."

Drake awkwardly nodded and waved in return. As he stared into her mesmerizingly deep eyes, almond irises that danced with life like a thousand kaleidoscopes reflecting diamonds in the sun, he was paralyzed with unbound admiration. Chestnut hair tumbled onto the shoulders of her white gown, which was sparsely decorated with the blue and silver stars of the Strand. In every detail—her olive skin, pronounced cheekbones, lightly-freckled nose—she was perfection.

His dizziness suddenly intensified, threatening to steal his balance. In a spell of desynchronization, he saw her white dress morph into a black robe, her brown eyes glowing purple. The staggering vision passed as quickly as it came, leaving him alone with the most beautiful woman he had ever encountered, and very possibly, to have ever existed. In an instant, he knew if she ever asked him, he would gladly bring her the moon and stars.

The commander's gruff voice ripped him from his smitten fantasies, reminding him that they were not alone in the room. "Captain Orgast, thank you for delivering Prince Georg's bride to the Great Plains. Please feel welcome as guests in our city—we have room for you at the palace, and Cairnes has much to offer."

"I couldn't possibly," declined the foremost soldier in white. He wore a pretentious milky naval hat, complete with a thin blue ribbon that signified he was technically part of Tallawyn's kingdom. The tenured captain eyed Drake up and down. "Assuming Lady Alivia is now in... capable hands... our duty is complete. She now belongs to the Prince, and we must return to conduct joint military exercises with Port Eastwind. I bid you good day, Commander." The man clicked his heels, then addressed Lady Alivia Fiore: "Lady Tallawyn."

The nine white-clad soldiers exited the room in single file, marching with uncanny precision. Drake knew Dominion's naval forces underwent the most grueling training across the kingdom and were often recruited directly into the Royal Guard. Port Eastwind's naval infantry were no joke, but he suspected the joint exercises would be tough training for them.

"Officer Lone, why don't you show Lady Alivia to her chambers?" suggested the commander. "The envoy from Dansk is expected to arrive this morning. I have many preparations to oversee."

"Yes, sir!" Drake lifted the luggage left behind by Captain Orgast, then smiled at Lady Alivia. "Please, this way."

He led her into the corridor. Wisely opting for the alternate route to avoid Micky and any other jeering knights, he guided the noble fiancée down the long hall to the room Prince Georg stayed in whenever he visited. It was all going swimmingly until he tried the handle of the heavy wooden door. *Locked.* Sheepishly, he realized he didn't have the key.

"Well, this is your room. It's pretty early in the day, though. Might I interest you in a tour of the grounds?" Drake offered in an attempt to buy time.

"You don't have the key?" guessed Lady Alivia.

"I don't have the key," he admitted. "Also, I'm not sure who would have the key," he let his candor run free.

"I could see where that would make opening the door a challenge," Lady Alivia remarked in good humor.

"The suite next door was originally designed for the Countess, but she decided she preferred her chamber on the ground floor," suggested Drake.

"I'm sure I'll survive," she reassured him. "As long as you have the key for that one."

"I don't," he scratched his head. "But I know where it is."

"That's a good start," smiled Lady Alivia Fiore.

Drake led her to a similar wooden door a short walk down the hall. Reaching above the doorframe, he ran his fingers along the header until they connected with a heavy brass key. He disengaged the lock and swung the door inward, following inside to ensure the room was presentable. Artwork hung prominently on the teal-painted walls. Sunlight shone through billowing curtains onto the canopy bed. The silver tea table looked rather inviting on the carpeted floor. Fit for a princess.

Holding the door, Drake made a sweeping bow to invite her inside.

"Pah!" she spat, wincing and swatting her hand as he looked up.

"Oh. You don't like it?"

"The room's fine," Lady Alivia clarified. "You just jabbed your feather into my mouth."

His face flushed. Mortified, he stammered an immediate apology. "I am so, so sorry."

"Take off your helmet," instructed Lady Alivia.

"Pardon?"

"Helmet off!" she repeated. "We'll have no more feather mishaps. Besides, I couldn't possibly take you seriously in that thing. You look like a peacock."

"Oh," Drake cleared his throat. He removed his helmet and tucked it under his arm. Free from his hand, the heavy door slammed shut with a loud bang. "Sorry. Again."

"You can place my bag at the foot of the bed," she invited.

"Yes, of course," he moved with purpose, gently laying the bag down as instructed. "Can I get you some water, perhaps?"

"Tea would be great." Lady Alivia explored the room, inspecting the paintings intently. She ran her hand through the fluttering curtains and took a deep, pensive breath in her new abode.

He exited the room, then scanned the hall for a subordinate to make a run to the kitchen for him. A young man rounded the corner, holding a tray with two tea pots and two glasses. "Louis!" Drake exclaimed with relief.

"Officer Lone," he greeted. "Commander asked me to bring these to Lady Alivia Fiore. He knows she likes tea but wasn't sure if she felt like black or green."

"I'll take it from here," Drake lifted the tray from his hands. "Thank you, Louis. Dismissed."

"I—yes, sir," the junior knight accepted reluctantly.

Drake reentered Lady Alivia's chambers.

"That was fast," she remarked.

"Sorry it took so long," he set the tray on the table. "I didn't know if you wanted black or green tea."

"Black," she took a seat before he could pull out a chair for her, "but why don't you try the green and let me know how it is?"

Drake finished pouring the two cups and set the black tea in front of her. "It's hot," he warned in passing.

"Tea often is," Lady Alivia mused smartly, lifting the cup to try a sip. "Oh. That's quite good."

Standing next to the table, Drake sampled a sip of his own tea. It was, indeed, quite good.

"Have a seat," invited Lady Alivia. "I promise I don't bite."

"Oh. Of course," Drake rested his helmet on the floor and took a seat at the table.

"So, *Officer Lone*," she began between sips of tea. Her nose wrinkled as if a bitter taste in her drink had taken her by surprise. "I spend far too much of my day bound by all this dreadful formality. Do you have another name I could call you by?"

"Drake Lone," he said, pleased with how it sounded. "Well, that's what they call me around here, anyway."

"Strong name," she lauded thoughtfully. "What's your real one?"

"Ilya," he confessed, studying her receptive eyes. "Ilya Drake Lone."

"Ilya... like the poet?" she clarified.

"Like the poet," he confirmed.

"It's a pretty name," she smiled.

"Men aren't supposed to have pretty names," he felt like an arrow had pierced his heart. "They're supposed to be hard, you know? Like—*I'd love to have a beer with Drake. That Drake's real good with a sword. Hey pal, Drake will kick your ass if you ask him to write you a poem again.*"

Lady Alivia snorted a laugh, inelegantly spraying tea onto the table. Eyes bulging, she leaned forward and tried to avoid making a mess of her white dress as she struggled to swallow the mouthful of tea. She started coughing, choking on the liquid that traveled down the wrong pipe.

"Drink water," Drake advised with great concern, offering more tea.

"I'm choking on water," she sputtered, placing a hand against her chest as she worked through it. After a prolonged recovery, she wagged a chastising finger at Drake. "Don't make me laugh when I've got a mouthful of tea!"

"Would you believe me if I said this was my first day as a bodyguard?" Drake grinned sheepishly.

"And here I was thinking you treated every lady who walked through your door like this."

"I'll top you off," Drake offered, reaching for the tea pot.

"I've got it," she countered, reaching as well.

Their hands collided as they both grasped the handle. Drake nervously released the pot, bashful of any improper contact with Lady Alivia. The lady had a similar reaction, causing the silver container to freefall away from their hands and off the side of the table.

"Ahh!" Drake braced for the tea to splash all over the carpet and walls.

The teapot froze in midair. Escaped droplets drifted through the spout back into the container. The pot hovered uncertainly for a surreal moment.

Drake looked at Lady Alivia. Her eyes glowed a faint purple.

She stared back. Her cheeks burned red with embarrassment as she muttered, "Shit."

The teapot crashed to the floor, spilling all over the fine carpet. Drake paid the costly blunder little mind; his eyes were fixed on her. "Your eyes," he marveled at their complex beauty even as the purple glow faded. He saw now the kaleidoscopic shapes in her irises seemed to form a pattern of indiscernible runes and glyphs. "Are you..."

"You can't tell anyone what you saw!" she silenced him, her face ashen.

"I won't," he swore at once. "I just... Wow."

"How could I be so careless," she withdrew into herself, burying her face in her hands.

"Hey, it's all right," Drake reassured her. "I'm just a normal guy who's named after a stuffy poet. You can trust me. I promise."

"You don't understand," she shook her head. "I've been so careful to keep that a secret, ever since our vizier... You don't know what people would do if they found out what I was."

"Nobody's going to find out. Nothing even happened. I knocked over some tea—that's it."

"There are people who would kill me if they knew, Ilya," Lady Alivia whispered seriously.

"I'm sure there are people who would worship you, too. Luckily, neither of them will ever know." He saw the unmitigated horror in her eyes and quickly continued speaking, desperate to put her at ease. "Look, my word means something. I may not be the brightest around, sure as hell ain't the richest, but you can trust me. Okay? I'm an open book. yours to read—ask away. I'll keep no secrets from you."

"How can I know you won't tell your commander the second you walk out the door?" she pressed. "If I didn't know better, I'd worry you fit the type of knight who'd off his own brother for a promotion."

"Funny you should mention that—I do have a brother, who sometimes does things that others might call *slightly criminal.* But, hey, never turned him in," Drake counted the statement as a credit to his side, holding up a finger to keep track. "Plus, I sure as hell ain't noble. A knight? You should see the shack I call home outside the city—it's a dump. I mean a real a dump. I share it with my part-time criminal brother. Would I like a promotion? Sure, who wouldn't. But I sure as hell wouldn't ever backstab or cheat my own to get there."

"You do sound a lot more... country than before. Hard to imagine you growing up that way in any noble house. I'm almost inclined to believe you."

Drake laughed despite himself. "Darling, I'm about as civilized as the hogs and horses out back in the stables—only difference is they're better at keeping appearances."

"How did you possibly become an officer?" marveled the lady.

Drake shrugged. "Guess I've been trying all my life to be more than I was. Had a shit childhood—whoops. I know I'm not supposed to swear in front of a lady..."

"Who gives a shit," she grinned back. Reservation lingered in her eyes, but she seemed to be warming up to him. "Our little secret. Go on."

"Long story short, got my shot at becoming something when I turned sixteen. Started out as an apprentice for the guardsmen. Kept my nose on the grindstone and did my best to do things the right way. Still, always had to put up with those damn knights having their laughs. Everyone knew I didn't come from a house with a family crest. But I did good work. I was always there when the captain needed someone to step up, and eventually I caught a break and earned a spot as an officer."

"Why?" pressed Lady Alivia.

"What do you mean, *why*?" Drake laughed. "So I can make something of myself. So I can be more than just some no-name guy with a rake in the fields. If I work my way up, I'll have money and respect... maybe then I'll find a wife, have a family of my own, and my kids won't have to start off on the same bottom rung I did, way down in the mud."

"Speaking as someone who's had access to more wealth than any one person could use, I'll let you in on a secret—it's not better at the top. It's just *different.*"

"That's a load of horse crap, ma'am," Drake refused. "No offense, of course, but look at you. I'll bet you've never had to do a day's work in your life. You had servants bring you whatever you wanted, whenever you wanted it—hell, you're marrying a prince, for Deus' sake."

"True," she nodded solemnly. "I've had servants and tutors and every delicacy in the kingdom. I've never gone to bed hungry. I had an unparalleled education. There's a lot that money can buy—but there's a lot more it can't."

"Like what?" he scoffed.

"Happiness, for one. Hell, how much do you really need to be happy? Food to eat, a place to sleep, water to drink—everything else can come and go. It won't buy you love or more life. Sure, I've had pretty dresses, but I've never had freedom. Even now, I'm shackled to a future written by the powerful men around me. *Sit up. Look pretty. Don't speak when the men are talking—marry the Tallawyn and be a good wife so that our kingdom may prosper.*"

"Well," Drake frowned, instinctively wanting to argue, but recognizing her argument had some merit to it. "Can't you tell them to piss off?"

Lady Alivia couldn't help but laugh. "You have no idea how many times I've thought that. Unfortunately, my life is bigger than me. It belongs to my family, my name, the citizens who rely on unity and prosperity between our houses... If I were to back out now, I can't imagine the tension it would cause between the capital and our kingdom's most heavily armed province."

"What? I figured it was every girl's dream to marry a prince," Drake leaned back in his chair, studying his conversation partner intently. "But it's not what you want, is it?"

"I don't even know the man, really," she spread her hands in defeat. "I've met him twice for all of five minutes, and we never got past formalities. I mean, I feel like I know you better in half an hour than I know him after years of arranged courtship. Everything I think I know is all second-hand based on his reputation; *he's patient, smart, and fair*—which is ten times better than his older brother, at least. But he seems so stiff and cold—kind of like how you were when I first met you."

"Guy sounds like a tool," Drake murmured to himself gruffly.

"Pretty sure a guardsman isn't supposed to talk about the Prince like that," Lady Alivia teased dangerously.

"I meant me—the earlier me you met," Drake clarified hastily. "The me that thinks he's supposed to become a noble someday."

"It's overrated," she dismissed. "I think you're better as you are."

Drake topped off their cups with the second teapot, hoping the green tea wouldn't mix poorly with the black. He hadn't experimented much in the tea world before, but he figured it would be all right.

"I suppose I have a couple more weeks to warm up to the idea," sighed Lady Alivia. "I heard Prince Georg is tied up in Mines, putting down some kind of labor strike. I'm sure Alwin would have been done with it by now—hopefully, that just means Georg is taking a more diplomatic approach."

"That's the spirit," Drake encouraged, betraying his budding feelings. "Plus, think of all the time you've got to spend with a new friend... even if his table manners leave a lot to be desired."

She hesitated before answering, immersed in her own thoughts. A delayed smile spread over her face as she registered his last sentence. "I have a feeling we're going to be good friends, Ilya."

"Still time for that tour of the grounds," Drake suggested, rising to his feet. He offered her a hand. "Care to see the horses, Lady Alivia?"

"Please, call me Alivia," she invited warmly, taking his hand. "And yes, I hope yours is a beautiful white horse to match my pretty dress."

XXXX. Promises

Ilya 'Drake' Lone

Damn it, Wyatt.

Leaning against the bedpost, he reopened the letter he had discovered on the table of his cottage home the night before. It was a short note, written in his brother's almost-indecipherable handwriting. A sense of loss and frustration plagued him as he scanned the tattered page, silently moving his mouth as he read each word.

Drake—they finally caught on to me. Searching for gold out west—W.

He sighed, shaking his head as he scratched the parchment with his thumb. Despite his frequent warnings to Wyatt, part of him was truly surprised the law had tracked him down. His older brother was the epitome of cunning, always finding a forgotten hole to evade the iron hand of justice. Even now that the jig was up, he had performed a final vanishing act, disappearing into the dark of night.

"Looks like quite the crowd," Alivia commented as she stared through the window, one hand holding back the expensive curtains.

Drake folded the letter in his hands and looked up from his spot by the bed. Though he was unable to see out the window from his position, he recalled the obscured vantage point saw neither the courtyard nor the stables very well. Every knight and half the common folk in Cairnes must have joined the crowd—it was a hero's return, after all. A celebration fit for a prince.

Alivia looked over her shoulder and spotted the letter in his hand. Stepping away from the window, she asked, "Is that the cloud that's been over your head all morning?"

"I think there are a few of them up there," Drake answered vaguely, gesturing out the window.

Alivia returned an amused grin, then swiped her hand through the air, whisking the letter out of his grasp from afar. Since the teapot incident, she no longer bothered to hide her Mystic nature when they were alone. Alivia started to unfold the note but stopped short of opening it. "May I?" she asked in a voice that assured Drake she would duly respect his privacy if he wished.

"'Course," he nodded shortly. "No secrets between us."

Her eyes lingered on him for a second longer, waiting for any potential reservations that might follow. When none came, she flipped the parchment open and read the single line Wyatt had penned for his younger brother.

"Searching for gold out west," she considered aloud, returning the note into his hand with a tap of the page. "You think he's riding for Deuzos?"

"I never told you he took my horse," Drake frowned. He was a little taken aback that she had deduced Wyatt's plans so efficiently—of course the clue referred to Deuzos, but he had spent the morning thinking his brother was riding northwest to join the gold expedition in Mines.

"You mentioned you were late this morning because you couldn't take Artemis," she countered shrewdly.

"He's insane, right?" Drake shook his head in disbelief. "It's not like you can just waltz into Deuzos unannounced and start a new life there. He's been a Tallawyn his whole life."

"Georg has been a Tallawyn his whole life," Alivia countered, moving to sit on the edge of the bed beside him. "Wyatt's just been living in Tallamar. There's a difference."

"You think Godwin's border patrol will care for that distinction?"

"Who knows," she shrugged, letting the stifling air hang in silence for a moment. "What'd they get him for?"

"Smuggling, likely," Drake crossed his arms. "Though they could have written him up for any number of things. Thieving, breaking and entering, conspiring against the state..."

"What was he smuggling?"

"A bit of everything," Drake sighed. "He was involved with some shady folks in the past. Drug rings and all... but lately, it's been mostly crops. He's just connecting farmers with buyers outside the Great Plains and moving the stock outside of taxable channels—or so he says."

"Doesn't sound so bad," she mused, resting a finger on her lip. "Then again, anything to do with the taxman carries a long sentence."

"Which is going to be doubled when they charge him with desertion."

"Or he'll avoid hard time entirely if he makes it across the border," she countered. "Sounds like even odds for a smuggler to take."

"If he does make it, I wonder if he'll actually take the chance to start over... he'll probably just find a new warren to do business out of."

"It's funny, you two sound like polar opposites," Alivia inspected him as if contemplating whether he would make a capable smuggler.

"Sometimes, I think that, too." Drake sat with her on the edge of the bed, staring at the wall of paintings across from him. "Sometimes, I think we've got more in common than I expected."

Quick to console him, she rubbed his arm tenderly. "Regardless, I get that he's the only family you had left here. I'm sorry to hear him go like this."

Drake closed his eyes and exhaled a slow breath. He reopened them and stared at the painting of a woman who held a pink parasol on a tightrope. Despite the subject's predicament, the artist had given her a look of wide-eyed curiosity, transfixed by some unseen object across the chasm. Perhaps he, too, needed to look ahead to the other side.

"Hey, we've got about another hour before they get here. Five minutes, best painting wins?"

Alivia rose from the bed with a laugh and walked across the floor to the tea table. Out of thin air, two blank pieces of parchment appeared across from one another on the table. Seven bottles of colored paint appeared shortly after, along with two brushes. "Winner keeps both pieces from our first duel?"

Drake pointed at the two pictures on top of the cabinet, which they had framed with a short length of fabric cut from the bedspread. "I'm keeping my fish no matter what."

In their initial attempt at painting, they had sat in silence for two hours, each carefully constructing a work of art. Alivia had completed a beautiful and remarkably realistic image of a lone tree on a hill, surrounded by the oranges and reds of autumn leaves. With eight efficient strokes of his brush, Drake had drawn the minimalist outline of a fish—which, to his credit, included three wavy pieces of seaweed sprouting from the implied ocean floor.

"I refuse to part ways without that curio," she maintained adamantly.

"Better try a little harder than the first time, then," Drake teased, taking his seat at the table.

"On your mark. Get set," she grinned.

Drake grabbed the brown and yellow paint bottles, dumped a little of each into the palm of his other hand, and blended the colors with his fingers.

"Hey!" Alivia objected with a bright laugh.

"Go!" he announced, beginning to paint tan lines with his fingers.

"We have two brushes," she suggested, shaking her head as she picked up the finer-tipped one.

"My creativity won't be stifled," he answered proudly, earning another giddy round of laughter.

After the first minute, she glanced over at his paper, squinting to try to decipher what he was working toward. "No peeking!" he chided her, wrapping his left forearm around the top of the page to shield his work from prying eyes.

"I wasn't peeking!" she objected with a broad grin, reaching her brush for the yellow paint at the same time his finger moved to the bottle. "Oop!"

"Go ahead," he waved his multicolored hand toward the bottle.

"No, you were there first," she held her brush in the air.

"I insist."

"A true gentleman," she dipped her brush in the yellow paint. Drake's eyes followed the brush to her paper, which looked to be turning into a brilliant sunset over a shadowy foreground. She wrapped her arm around the front of the page to mirror his position and reprimanded him, "No peeking!"

"I wasn't!" he claimed, scooping some yellow paint for himself. "I was just looking for inspiration. From your page. In the things you were doing."

"I won't hear a word of it," she bit her lip as she focused on blending the horizon from yellow to orange.

Drake dabbed his yellow fingerprint on the page, then studied Alivia's face. Her brow furrowed in concentration as she applied short, delicate strokes to the page. She looked up and caught him staring. "What?"

"Nothing," he said with a bashful smile, returning to his own painting.

"What!?" she demanded.

"No, it's nothing," he said. "Yours is just starting to look kind of similar to mine, that's all, but it's nothing."

"One minute remaining," she declared arbitrarily, ignoring the jab.

"Imitation," Drake commented with sagely concentration. "Something, something, flattery."

"It's not a long phrase, Ilya!" Alivia giggled in exasperation.

"Wait!" he gasped in horrified realization, studying his near-complete artwork. "I have to sign this masterpiece. I need a pen!"

Alivia rolled her eyes and swiped a finger through the air. The gaudy blue feather from Drake's helmet appeared in his hand. "Thank you." He dipped the quill into the black inkwell, then scrawled his name across the bottom-right corner.

"Time!" Alivia announced, lifting her page off the table and holding it close to her chest so that he couldn't see it.

Drake mirrored her move, feigning a tear in his eye as he examined the majesty of his masterpiece. "Ladies first," he invited.

"As you wish." She laid her page on the table and turned the picture around to face him.

"What is it?" he squinted as if the impeccably drawn sunset wasn't self-explanatory. Rocky and grassy textures came to life in the darkened foreground below the falling sky. She had added more purples to the highest layer since he had last seen the page, making the beautiful scene a little darker.

"It's the mountain from when you were a kid," she said incredulously, taking him at his word that he couldn't make sense of the page. "It's the sunset you described to me."

"Oh!" Drake let out a long-drawn sound of realization. "I can kind of see it now. That's not half bad, Miss Fiore. You might have a future in the art world if you practice a little harder."

"All right, Singani," Alivia teased, referencing a renowned sculptor of the sixth century. She folded her arms and leaned forward, ready to see his page. "Let's see how many strands of seaweed you worked up to this time."

Drake buried his head in his palm. "Agh! I knew I forgot something. The seaweed!"

She chortled at his goofiness, tossing her head forward and covering her mouth with her hand. After fixing her hair, she clasped her hands patiently in front of her. "And how long do you plan to keep a lady waiting?"

"All right," Drake took a deep breath, then laid the page on the table, spinning it to face her. "Isn't that a piece of fine art?"

"It's a piece of something," she snickered. "It's... what is it?" she asked with a confused smile, surprised to see a non-aquatic illustration from him.

"It's you," he said of the brown-haired stick figure with a big smile.

"Who's that?" she pointed at the other stick figure on the page. She leaned closer, staring at the yellow orb in his hand. "And what's he holding?"

"It's me," Drake tilted his head to view the page from her perspective. "I'm giving you a mango."

"A mango!" Alivia exclaimed in realization. She dipped her brush in green paint, then drew three thin lines stemming from the top of the painted fruit. "There's a type of fruit that grows in the trees near our winter home. It's shaped like a yellow star," she laid down the brush, a wistful look forming on her face. "Legend says if you share it with the one you love, your souls will always be connected with each other, intertwined in this life and the next."

Drake was quiet for a long moment, unable to find the right words to express himself. Beneath the joy they had shared these past two weeks was an unspoken, despairing awareness that their time would soon come to a sudden, irreversible end. "Sounds better than a mango," he said finally.

For a long minute, they both stared in silence at the simplistic drawing on the table, whose figures were blessed with unfading smiles that transcended their encroaching melancholy. Finally, Drake discovered an available supply of words, though they were not the ones he was looking to share. "So, Alivia Tallawyn," he tested the name and found it bitter on his tongue. "Your prince must be close now. How are you feeling?"

It was a subject they had spent little time discussing since the early days of their acquaintanceship. As their bond had grown stronger and stronger, they had silently agreed to let the outside world wait for a while. They had lived a blissful fantasy, enjoying each other's company as if they were two ordinary strangers, destined to be a part of each other's world.

"I don't know," she shifted in her chair and searched longingly out the distant window. "I guess nothing's changed. I'm still intended for him, as he is for me. It's possible I'll grow to love him, given some time."

Drake leaned back in his chair, reading the unspoken words in her eyes. "But...?"

"You know," she said softly, holding his gaze. "It's not like I haven't thought about it, but we're in two completely separate worlds." Her eyes fell to the page in front of her. She slid her sunset forward, handing the impossible dream over to him. "Besides, it's bigger than me."

"What if it wasn't?" tested Drake. "What if your feelings were just as important as the rest of 'em?"

"What if isn't a smart game to play," Alivia sighed, standing slowly. She walked over to the cabinet and slid it open to take out a silver necklace. "My father, the Fiore name, the kingdom—not to mention Prince Georg, who's been led to believe for the past year that I was excited to be his bride."

Drake wanted to argue with her, to help her find her voice and reason, but instead felt compelled to accept the hard reality of their shared situation. "I guess it wouldn't really work. I don't imagine the Tallawyns would be too keen on rejection, and it's my duty to keep you safe until Prince Georg returns. I guess... I guess I'm just lucky I got to meet you."

Alivia offered him a sad smile. She turned away, moved her long hair in front of her shoulder and held the necklace clasps around her neck. "Could you help me with this?"

"'Course." He walked the floor to take the two delicate silver clasps in his hand. A faint scent of lavender struck him as he leaned in to fumble with the intricate string.

She was watching his focused eyes in the mirror as he joined the loops and looked up to meet her reflection. She turned in place, bringing their faces tantalizingly close together. He looked down at her thin lips, only inches away from his own, then found himself lost in her kaleidoscopic almond eyes. She rested a hand on his chest and stared back, gazing between his eyes, his lips, and his eyes again. He saw the uncertainty suspended in her gaze, a whirlwind collision of desire, nervousness, hope, and wistfulness.

Her courage wilted in his hesitation. She swallowed the moment and slowly leaned forward, burying her head in his shoulder. Her arms wrapped around his waist, and he pulled her in closer, reaching the small of her back over her shoulders. He felt her body shudder as she let out a long, wistful breath, sealing away the unresolved eternity between them.

He closed his eyes and exhaled, knowing he had missed his moment.

They disentangled themselves, Alivia to slide on a white corsage, Drake to stand in front of the painted woman with the pink parasol. Although his tongue felt like lead in his mouth, he attempted to fill the air with conversation, painfully aware that there was no longer anything left to say. "So, what comes next for a princess?"

"Technically, Prince Alwin's bride becomes a princess," she corrected. "I'll merely be Lady Alivia Tallawyn instead of Lady Alivia Fiore." Needlessly, she returned to the mirror to ensure she looked presentable. "Well, I suppose tomorrow brings the official wedding in Cairnes. Once formalities are taken care of here, I assume we'll return to Talos for a ceremonial wedding in the cathedral. Then come the litany of hosting balls, meeting dignitaries, and being an unproblematic wife for Prince Georg." She patted down her dress with a sigh. "Maybe Wyatt had the right idea after all."

A knock came at the door, signaling that time had no intention of waiting any longer. "Lady Alivia, the Prince has arrived. Please come to meet him at once."

"I suppose this is farewell," she clasped her hands and stood in place across the room, making no move toward either Drake or the door.

"If you're ever back in my neck of the woods," Drake offered hollowly, retrieving his featherless helmet from the floor. He took one last look at the beautiful brown eyes that had ensnared his heart, bowed formally, and exited the chamber without a second glance.

In the hall, he encountered a group of four men wearing the Tallawyn crest on their pauldrons. He recognized them instantly as part of the Royal Guard, sent to escort the prince on his journey from Talos. He knew Georg was likely already in the courtyard outside, if not enjoying an extended parade through his ancestral city. The cheering masses would be proud to claim they met their prince in person.

With a hollow feeling in his chest, Drake navigated the stairwell down to the side door that led outside—the servant's entrance. The throng of people gathered in the courtyard was dense and unwieldly, restrained from the direct path of the prince's procession by two walls of soldiers assigned to maintain order.

"Officer Lone!" a shield-bearing soldier beckoned to him. He butted his shield against an uppity commoner who was getting a little too close to the guards' line, sending a clear message that peasants should express adoration for the Tallawyns in a strictly orderly fashion. "Officer Lone!" repeated the man.

With considerable effort, Drake pushed through the dense crowd. He reached the guardsman and recognized the eyes and cheeks behind the visor. "You doing all right, Micky?"

"Fine, sir!" reported the foot soldier. "The other insignias are gathered in front of the castle. I heard you're all going to get to meet Prince Georg when he rides through!"

Drake glanced over at the huddle of important military officials, which included other officers, captains, and the commander. In no mood to meet the prince, he folded his arms and frowned. "I think I'll hang back here with y'all."

"You feeling all right, sir?" Micky asked, turning his head as he took a break from battering the front-most members of the crowd.

"I'm fine," Drake growled, staring out through the courtyard's gate. A vanguard of flag twirlers was making its way inside, accompanied by the fanfare of drums and horns.

"You sure?" checked Micky. "You sound like you took a bad slip on the moonshine."

"Mind your tone, soldier," Drake's back grew rigid. "You're speaking to a superior officer."

"Sorry I asked," Micky kicked an eager blacksmith vying for a spot at the front, unleashing an unnecessary strain of obscenities to complement the strike. "Sir."

A white steed flanked by standard bearers entered view, met with a roar of approval from the assembled crowd. Drake's eyes darted from the gallant horse to the front of the palace, from which Alivia Fiore had just emerged. For a brief second, her eyes searched the far side of the crowd, passing first over the nearby huddle of officers, then to the wild throngs behind the flank of soldiers. The commander reached her side and gestured to the prince, snapping her attention back to the parade.

Trumpeters and minstrels heralded his arrival, psyching up the already-frenzied crowd, much to the chagrin of the foot soldiers attempting to restrain the masses back to the permitted areas. Against the late sun, Drake squinted his eyes to see the prince atop his steed. Despite the artificial height advantage of a massive horse, the highborn man was shorter than he remembered. Even considering his coronet and billowing royal blue cape, Drake decided that the prince looked remarkably unimpressive.

At the halfway mark of the courtyard, Prince Georg dismounted and continued on foot, giving Drake an even greater appreciation of the height of that white horse. The prince first shook the hand of the commander, who bent his knees in a ridiculous bid to appear shorter than Prince Georg. One by one, the officers grasped the royal's small hands and basked in their momentary sense of importance.

Then, Prince Georg reached Alivia.

Despite his thick-soled boots vying to give him the edge, the prince was still an inch shorter than her. He grabbed her hand and planted an exaggerated kiss, then exchanged a round of inaudible words.

"Whoa," Drake heard over his shoulder. It was Micky. "Lucky prince."

Stepping closer, Prince Georg raised a hand and gently stroked her cheek, tucking a loose strand of hair behind her ear. Drake's chest tightened as the prince slid his fingers under her chin. Prince Georg leaned in, and jealousy thrust a cold knife through Drake's heart.

He looked away, deaf to the enamored crowd. They were electrified to see their hero's triumph at the end of his journey west; Drake stared numbly at the insatiable masses. Long after the procession had entered the palace, after most of the crowd had dispersed, he remained behind in the streets like a stray.

As the soldiers ushered the stragglers out of the courtyard, Micky's words reached him through the haze of defeat. "Get out of here, you sewer rats! It's your damn fault I can't be out on the town tonight. Unbelievable!"

"You're not drinking with the rest of them?" Drake asked hollowly.

"Obviously, I'd love to drink with the rest of GPG, hear a few stories from the Royal Guard—but I got the short straw," cursed Micky. "I'm stuck on gate duty all night—a romantic little rendezvous with Buck-Tooth Larry... Sir."

"You know what, Micky? Go have fun tonight. I'll cover your post."

"Now I know you're not all right," guffawed Micky. "But if you're sure, I won't fight you over it. Thanks for covering, Officer Lone."

"Drake's fine," he sighed, turning toward the stables.

As he walked away, he heard Micky mumble behind him, "Whatever, man. Thanks."

To the great surprise of the stable boys, Drake spent the rest of the afternoon filling hay feeders, mucking out stalls, and talking to the animals. One by one, the boys finished their chores and took off to join the festivities in town. The first were hesitant to leave while an officer did their duties, but the last to go hardly spared him a glance on their way out. Before long, he was alone.

As the sun fell below the horizon, lively orchestral music spilled out of the palace, traveling a long way from the great hall. Resting against a shaggy brown horse that belonged to one of the GPG who had traveled with the prince to Mines, Drake hummed along to the infectious waltz that cursed the air.

The band fell silent a couple hours later. A gaggle of drunken chatter flowed out from the pristine palace walls and poured into the streets, heading into town. He patted his equestrian companion's stomach and stood, emerging from the stables and moving through the lonely shadows of the outer wall to take his post at the gate.

In the watchtower to the left of the open gate, he approached the other unfortunate soldier relegated to missing a jubilant night of drunken revelry.

Buck-Tooth Larry heard him coming and hastily tried to play off the fact that he had been picking his nose by scratching its tip instead.

"That Micky?" Larry asked in that grating, atonal voice of his.

"It's Officer Drake Lone."

"Officer!" Larry turned around and revealed the terrible overbite that inspired his nickname. "What are you doing here? I thought I was posted with Micky tonight."

"You boys have been working hard," Drake put a hand on the junior soldier's shoulder. "I decided to take your shifts and watch the gate myself—let you loose on the town for a night. As your ranking officer, I order you to go have fun down there."

"But Commander specifically picked me to watch the gate… I wouldn't want to disappoint him if anything happened," demurred the despicable grunt.

"Who's going to attack the palace in the middle of the night? Besides, there are plenty of Royal Guards inside. You don't think anyone's getting past those guys, do you? Or me, for that matter?"

Larry sized him up, as if considering whether a common hoodlum could best him. "Well…"

"Get out of here," Drake slapped him on the back. "If Commander asks, I'll tell him it was my idea. You've got nothing to worry about."

"Why are you being so nice?" Larry squinted suspiciously, unsure if he was being set up.

Drake sighed in frustration. His niceness was nearing its limit. "Look, are you going to go have fun, or do I have to put a boot up your ass to get you off my damn watchtower?"

"That's all I needed to hear," Larry decided, heading toward the stairs. He looked back once to check he hadn't failed some sort of test, then hurried down to join the rest of the soldiers flooding into town.

Once the courtyard was still—silent save for the rowdy celebration on the wind from town—Drake stepped away from the wall. He stalked down the staircase, eyeing the enormity of the palace. Evidently, every lord, soldier, and servant who had attended the evening ball had agreed the night must go on in the pubs and taverns that littered Cairnes. Most likely, a small retainer of disciplined Royal Guards would be inside, but even the skeleton crew of GPG soldiers he hadn't relieved from their posts were gone.

The only sign of life in Castle Cairnes came from the flickering glow of a candle in a third-floor window. Judging by the window's position between the stables and the courtyard, he was certain it was Lady Alivia's.

Careful to remain undetected, he skirted the courtyard in the shadows of the walls and slipped into the private stable like a ghost. Orienting himself mostly by smell and the occasional shaft of moonlight that illuminated his progress, he crept through the barn. Luckily, it was just him and the animals.

A sound at the end of the walkway corrected his assumption. Scurrying into the nearest stall, he found himself face to face with a pig. The gentle swine snorted softly, earning a light *boop* on the snout from Drake.

Faintly exposed by a distant torch, a shadow stood in the doorway between the stable and the palace. The shape of his armor set the man apart as one of Prince Georg's personal guards.

Drake recognized his skulking through the barn would raise questions, doubled by the fact that he had failed to report to the commander earlier that evening. Clenching his jaw, he crawled through the muddy hatch and emerged into the pig pen outside. He climbed from the fence onto the roof of the stables, then crept along until he reached the palace wall.

Acutely aware that an elite guard was directly below the last section of roof, Drake moved as quietly as a field mouse. He looked up at the trellis that supported the wall's blue-flowered vines and gripped the wooden structure with his hand. It withstood his initial pull, encouraging him to test a little weight.

The moment of truth. He trusted his full weight to the wooden trellis. Miraculously, it didn't collapse on him. Balancing speed and caution, he scaled the wall to the third floor, forcing himself to keep quiet as the hanging plants scratched his face. He side-stepped across the wooden support beams until he reached the end of the wall. Sucking in a deep breath, he made the perilous transition around the corner, switching his feet to the front-facing wall.

"Yes!" he whispered to himself, successfully snaking his way past the flowers that brushed his cheek. "Damn it!" he amended as his boot knocked loose a crosspiece, sending the wooden block tumbling to the ground.

It echoed quietly in the empty square.

Drake gritted his teeth. If anyone caught him now, he would certainly be turned over to the military police. Sacrificing stealth for speed, he crawled across the wall as fast as he dared.

Reaching the glowing window, he planted his hands on the windowsill and pulled himself up to see curtains blocking his view inside. Resting a palm against the window, he tried to slide the pane sideways but found it locked.

"Damn it!" Pain shot through his tensed fingers. He desperately tapped on the window, attempting to strike a balance between alerting anyone inside and waking the entire city.

He heard footsteps approaching the window. The curtains flew back, the lock disengaged, and a silhouette of a woman's long hair and puzzled face appeared. "Ilya?"

"Howdy. I'm starting to lose my grip here. Mind if I come in?" Drake said hurriedly.

She stepped back from the window. He pulled himself up over the ledge and gracelessly landed on the carpeted floor.

"What are you doing?" Alivia demanded worriedly, dropping to a knee to help him up.

Drake found his feet, and although he was still searching for the wind that got knocked out of him, he confessed, "I couldn't leave it like that."

"Ilya..."

"Alivia," he countered, reuniting his hands with hers. "I've lived more in the last two weeks than in the last twenty years of my life. I know I've found something special in you, and I don't ever want to let it go. There's no other woman like you in this world or any other, and I don't believe some damn prince knows that half as well as I do." He got down on one knee, with neither a ring nor a kingdom to offer, knowing his only hope of gaining eternity was to ask. "Alivia, if you'd have me, I'd like to spend the rest of my life with you."

"Oh, Ilya..." She dropped to her knees with him, holding their clasped hands to her chest. "Where would we go? What would we do? The wedding's tomorrow, and... he's a Tallawyn."

"We'd be together," Drake answered with more certainty than he had ever known before. "We'll steal away in the night, take a horse, and ride west. He might be a Tallawyn, but he's not a Godwin."

"You're serious about this," she realized.

"Aren't you?" He searched her eyes, hoping that behind the fear, he could connect with the love they had fostered over these short few days.

A tear welled in her eye as she grappled between the life destiny had chosen for her and the one she knew her heart desired. "Okay," she nodded with growing conviction, wiping away the tear. She exhaled to compose herself, letting him know she spoke with unclouded sincerity. "Yes. I'm yours, Ilya."

His heart soared in his chest, unbearable anxiety swiftly replaced by rapturous hope. He cupped the nape of her neck in his hand and met her lips, sharing a timeless moment of passion unchained—a euphoric release of the trapped love that had blossomed so intensely between them. With bliss on his tongue, he withdrew to look his love in the eyes once more.

She saw him through his enamored eyes, briefly looked at the lips that encouraged her to defy destiny, and placed a tender hand on his cheek. The corner of her mouth twitched upward as she slowly realized she could truly, uncompromisingly hope for what might lie ahead. A future of their own.

Before leaning in for a long kiss, she whispered the most effortless wish Drake could ever have the pleasure of granting.

"Promise me that this moment will last forever."

XXXXI. Paradise Undone

Ilya 'Drake' Lone

The end of one dream, the beginning of another.

An errant beam of light refracted through the square window and cut across his cheek, stirring him from a deep slumber. A short gurgle escaped his throat as he adjusted his neck on the pillow. He blinked himself awake, taking notice of the small dust particles dancing across his vision below the oak ceiling.

Turning his head, he saw a sleepy brown eye open, its counterpart shut tight against the pillow in hopes of a few more minutes of rest.

"Good morning," she croaked groggily.

"That time already?" he moaned in return, stretching his back without rising from the bed. He smiled softly as she closed her eyes and slid her hand beneath the pillow to hold his. Sunlight filtered through the window to glow on her olive back, illuminating her brown hair with added shades of radiance. Her knee stuck out of the twisted sheets that were half draped over her.

He swiveled onto his right shoulder and rested his left hand between her shoulder blades. She scooted in closer as he gently stroked her back, nestling her head in the space under his chin. "You snored," she mumbled the complaint into his chest. "You snorer."

"Sorry, darlin'. Had to practice my bear impression."

"That's barely acceptable."

"Hmm," he grunted in return, an amused smile on his lips.

He suffered a light jab to the belly. "You would've laughed if you made that joke."

"I know," he clenched his teeth as he grinned, forcing himself not to laugh at his own thoughts. "That's because I've mastered comedic timing. It's an art form, you know."

"Like your beautiful self-portraits?" she ribbed.

"You mean paw-traits?" he bounced his eyebrows. Comedic timing.

"Wow," she exclaimed, incredulous.

"Jokes that good should be against the claw." She pulled her head back to fix him with a deadpan expression. "Against the claw," he repeated with great emphasis.

"Wow!" she echoed in a long-drawn syllable, turning away from him.

"I hate to be the bear of bad news," he cleared his throat meaningfully. "But I do think it's time I stop hibernating. Would you like a cub of tea?"

Her groan may have woken the neighboring village. "Go," she playfully pushed herself away from his chest. "Depart. Immediately."

"Hey," Drake couldn't help but let a little chuckle slip. "Alivia, hey."

"You're at four already," she warned. Early in their relationship, they had reached a hard-fought compromise that he would be allowed no more than five puns per day. Upon breaching the agreement later that same day, he was forced to recommit to the pact under the signed witness of the village chief, Harrison Craft. "Is this one worth it?"

Drake contemplated his position carefully and let his carefully honed instincts take over. "It is."

"Proceed," she braced herself.

"How," he began his philosophical rumination, "do you know when a bear is moving houses?"

She tilted her head slightly, as if trying to work out an answer before he could tell her.

Sensing she was nearing the right neighborhood of thought, he rushed to the punchline. "He puts up a *fur sale* sign."

Alivia buried her head under the pillow. "I regret starting this."

Laughing in her stead, Drake tried to coax her out from under the pillow. "Hey," he tapped her shoulder.

"What?" she surfaced her head, revealing a head of mussed hair.

"I love you." He looked into her eyes and felt the warmth that coursed through his body run into his lips, forcing them into a hexed smile yet again.

She smiled back warmly. "I love you, too." A quick kiss, then she laid her head back down on the pillow.

Drake leaped out of bed with newfound energy. "You know what today is?" he prompted, pulling on a clean shirt.

"Saturday?" she guessed hopefully.

"The twenty-seventh," he checked over his outfit to make sure he was presentable to the outside world.

"Woohoo," she cheered groggily.

"I'll be back in twenty—you'll have a feast fit for a marchioness."

"You don't have to go through all that trouble," she sat up in bed.

"Oh, but I do," he countered. "I've got it all worked out. All you've got to do is rest in bed a little while longer."

"Not too much longer," she reminded him. "I told Craft I'd walk him through the plans for the fish farm at noon."

"I'm sure that'll go swimmingly!" he slipped his boots on.

"Six," she groaned as he escaped through the front door.

A blur of desynchronization struck Drake as he stepped onto his front porch to survey the village he had forgotten. He was at once both in the sunken temple and here, staring at the concentric ring of houses inside the humble wooden palisade. An unseen force pulled him toward the village commons, a central gathering place commonly used for town meetings that consisted of a bonfire pit, a well, and four rows of benches.

The disorientation passed as his feet moved down the three steps of his front porch, treading along the dirt road to the bakery. Among the fifty or so dwellings in Daheim, the bakery was the only one with a green roof, making it an easy-to-find destination for the hungover and the still-drunk. On the west end, the wide barn that occasionally housed animals in the winter was another standout property, as was the log house on the north end—Daheim's oldest building and home to the village chief. Otherwise, each home was a simple frame of nailed-together wood, existing in a state of varying disrepair.

Although the baker was a former naval officer in Godwin's army, he had lost his pride in an accident, along with half his face and the mobility in his left arm. Bernard was a quiet man, but his elderly mother was a beacon of kindness in Daheim, loved by all. She worked day in and day out in the 'galley', often helping by kneading the dough and collecting eggs from the coop out back. Even Drake had begun to view her as the village's mother, and he was consequently a little more open with her than with the other villagers.

A bell rang above the door as Drake entered the bakery. Bernard's son, Jonah, raised his head from behind the counter. "Hi, Drake!"

"Jonah," Drake nodded cordially. "Resting up that ankle?"

"Yes, sir," the boy answered proudly.

"Good," Drake folded his arms. "Keeping out of trouble? Staying busy helping Dad and Grandma run the place?"

"Yep!" Jonah grinned. He was newly missing several baby teeth.

"If Jonah were any busier, he'd be doing his job," croaked a woman from the back kitchen. Angela ambled to the front section of the bakery and swatted her grandson with a used towel. "Your father needs a hand cleaning up a spill."

"Yes, Grandma," the boy groaned, throwing his head back in dismay. "Bye, Drake!"

"Be good, kid," Drake shook his head.

Smiling broadly, Angela came around the counter doing a little jig that mostly involved her bouncing her arms and shoulders up and down. Her short, gray hair bobbed with her. "It's a big day!" she reminded him needlessly.

"I know," he laughed, accepting her enthusiastic hug. He wrapped his arms around her gently, concerned he might damage her brittle frame. When the moment passed without injury, he added, "Thanks again for helping me out. How much do I owe you?"

"Oh!" she scoffed. A frown of disbelief doubled the wrinkles on her forehead. "If I've told you once, I've told you a thousand times! Your money's no good here, Drake."

"I'm not sure if that's the best way to run a business," he countered lightheartedly.

"This isn't a business; this is a family," she said in earnest, brushing aside his joke. "It wouldn't be right to take money from family. Besides, it's not like you ask for money every time you take little Jonah out to learn the woods."

"True, but he did fall out of a tree and twist his ankle on my watch. I feel like I owe you something."

"Boys fall out of trees," she said dismissively. "If it weren't meant to happen, Deus would've given them a little more sense."

"I can't believe how fast he's growing," Drake remarked.

"He's looking more and more like the spitting image of his mother," she shook her head sadly. "Poor thing."

"Well, if you won't take my money, can I at least help in the kitchen?" offered Drake.

"Not a chance, sonny," Angela refused. "I've been up since the crack of dawn getting ready for your big day. I cooked the eggs; you slept in late, and they got cold. So I cooked up some more just now."

"Well, let it be known that I appreciate you," he accepted defeat.

"It is known," she confirmed. "Jonah? Be a dear and bring Grandma Drake's breakfast?"

"I'm helping Dad clean!" the boy shouted back.

"Jonah?" she repeated.

There was a brief pause, perhaps just long enough to fit a sigh. "Fine."

"Do you have it on you?" Angela whispered.

"Have what?" Drake played dumb.

"The rock," she raised her eyebrows meaningfully.

"Of course," he grinned bashfully, reaching into his pocket.

"Well? Let's see it," she snapped her fingers eagerly.

He produced a small pouch and loosened the drawstring to retrieve the prize inside. The golden ring spilled onto his palm—a simple, smooth band with a short engraving on the inside.

Angela handled the ring delicately, lifting it up to better read the capital letters carved into the band. "My... moaning... star?" she raised her eyebrows in question.

"My morning star," he corrected, double checking the engraving to confirm the lettering. Seeing her confused but excited look, he explained himself as he returned the ring to the bag. "It's an Ilya Astaire poem. *Bow not to kings, pray not for riches; no mortal gain can answer my wishes. I care not for bright sunshine, nor glinting gold from afar; I'll follow my love—she is my morning star.*"

"That's beautiful, Drake," Angela cooed, clutching her heart in a rush of vicarious romance.

"Thanks," Drake put away the pouch, then wrung his hands together uncertainly. "Do you think she's going to like it? I mean, I wasn't sure because she grew up with all these nice things, and maybe she had always dreamed of getting one with a bunch of expensive jewels on it, and the guy I got to do the engraving—he's in the city, the engraver—he had a bit of a shaky hand..."

"She's going to love it," Angela reassured him with the unshakeable confidence of a grandmother.

"Thanks," Drake nodded, self-conscious about his nervous rambling.

Jonah appeared from behind the counter carrying a tray with two plates on it. Each plate was loaded with eggs, two kinds of sausage, plum tomatoes, sliced cucumbers, and a piece of Angela's famous fluffy milk bread. Two empty glasses were balanced on the tray with a bottle of fresh pear juice between them.

Drake gratefully accepted the gift with both hands, careful not to spill anything. "You're an angel, Angela. Can't thank you enough!"

"I made the eggs!" blurted Jonah.

"The chickens made the eggs," Angela corrected wisely. "Jonah helped me cook them."

"Thanks, Jonah. Thanks, chickens," Drake gave Angela another nod of appreciation before slipping outside.

With a bubbling mix of excitement to get home and caution to keep the loaded tray from tipping, Drake hurried past the dormant bonfire, feeling the tension in his hips as he went. He had nearly made his way home when a voice called out to him from beneath the porch of the house two doors down from his. "Is the coast clear?"

"Kurt?" Drake tilted his head. "The hell you doing down there?"

"Shh!" Kurt shushed him, shimmying out from under the woodwork. Checking over his shoulder, he dusted off his checkered long-sleeve shirt. "Oh, meant to give you this last night," he briefly disappeared back under the porch, then reemerged with a mason jar full of brown liquid.

"Hands full," Drake bent his head toward his tray.

Frowning, Kurt searched for a spot to place his home-brewed whiskey. He slowly reached for the bottle of pear juice and started lifting it from the tray, raising his brows for confirmation. Drake held his gaze with a stony expression, suggesting that he did, in fact, want the pear juice. Pursing his lips, Kurt slowly returned the bottle to the tray. Struck by a sudden epiphany, he nodded to himself. "If daylight's burning, so can the whiskey." He opened the bottle and tipped a hefty pour into a glass.

"Whoa!" Drake objected without moving the tray.

"And that's before you got a mouthful!" Kurt commented knowingly, topping off the second glass. "The taste of this one will have hints of apple, the oak cask it was aged in..."

"And whiskey?" guessed Drake.

"Mostly whiskey," Kurt conceded, scratching his thin, black mustache. "But, hey—a couple shots of this bad boy, and you'll be three sheets to the wind by sunup."

Drake knew better than to point out that the sun had already risen; Kurt would doubtlessly use the fact as evidence that they were behind schedule. "Why are we hiding from Maria today?" he diverted.

"Shh! Not so loud," Kurt checked over his shoulder as if his wife might appear from the floorboards. He turned to Drake and confided, "She wants me to wash my shirt."

"Sounds like a reasonable request," Drake took a half step backward, not overly keen on smelling the offending garment.

"Well, she was nagging me that she always has to clean my clothes, so I told her not to clean anything. I said I'd never wash my clothes again, and I'd be happier for it."

"I'm not sure I'm tracking your logic," confessed Drake. "There comes a time every shirt needs to be washed... or thrown out. Hell, wash it yourself if it's that big a deal."

"That's what she wants!" Kurt grasped the air in frustration. "If I wash my own shirt, she wins. I'll sooner be buried before—"

He cut himself off midsentence as the doorhandle rattled. Before the door opened, Kurt glanced behind him, decided he didn't have enough time to dive under the porch, and instead planted one foot on the wooden support beam to vault onto the roof.

Maria stepped outside with a well-earned scowl on her face. She planted her right hand on her hip, gripping the shaft of a worn broom in her left. Her discerning gaze swept across the quiet village grounds. Spotting Drake, she held up a hand, instructing him to stay put.

"Run!" Kurt whispered urgently through his teeth.

Drake looked at his friend on the roof, then back at Maria. Standing fixed in place, he was quite certain he wanted to risk no sudden movements with the tray of food in hand.

"Drake!" Maria confronted him. "Have you seen my weasel husband?"

"I, uh... no, ma'am?" He made a pedestrian effort at acting naturally.

Maria leaned forward and scrutinized him, peering into his soul with an unsettlingly perceptive gaze. "Uh-huh," she gripped her broom handle with two hands, alerting him that the situation was about to deteriorate for somebody. "Well, I'm sure you've smelled him! Isn't that right, Kurt?"

She spun on her heels and began thrusting the brush of her broom into her poorly hidden husband. "You stupid man! Give me that damn shirt!"

"No!" he covered his head with his arms, suffering the not particularly forceful but likely still unpleasant thrusts of the bristles. "I will not! I shall not!"

"You filthy little piggy! The whole town is going to think I let you live like a slob! Is that what you want?" chastised Maria.

"I am a *man*!" Kurt defended himself, voice rising on the last word of his proclamation. His pitch vaulted even higher. "A man!"

"A stupid, stupid man!" Maria berated him, successfully pulling on his pant leg and swinging his legs off the side of the roof.

Kurt clung desperately to the rooftop, clawing for a better grip like a cat that had narrowly misjudged a leap to the sofa.

"See you, Kurt!" Drake called behind him, fleeing the scene lest the broom be turned on him.

Approaching the front steps of his home, he saw that Alivia was already outside, seated in one of the rocking chairs beside the small wooden table. She wore a beige cardigan that doubled as a blanket for her knees. "Kurt and Maria are awake," she observed wryly.

"She wants him to wash his shirt," Drake explained, laying the tray on the table.

"Ah," she accepted with a cocked eyebrow, understanding without fully understanding.

"I'll do a load of our dirty stuff tomorrow," volunteered Drake.

"Guess I won't have to borrow her broom," Alivia grinned.

"I don't reckon it'll be free any time soon," he sat in the second chair, letting out a small grunt as it rocked backward.

It was a lazy morning in the village, accentuated by the carefree chirps of unseen birds. The farmers were already out working the fields; others were moseying around without anywhere in particular to be. A steady breeze rolled in from the west, carrying only a trace of salt from the distant lake.

"Looks delicious. Thank you, Ilya," Alivia lifted the nearest plate onto her lap. She dipped a fork into the egg, then ripped off a piece of bread to soak up the running yolk. An appreciative moan accompanied her first bite. "I'll never get over Angela's bread."

Drake reached into his pocket to reassure himself that the pouch was still there. Feeling the soft bag, he shifted in his seat, wondering if now was the right time. He had practiced many iterations of what he wanted to say, but in that moment, they all felt stilted and disconnected from how deeply he loved her. He wanted to tell her that she was everything he wanted from this life, that he'd promise forever and reaffirm that promise every day until his final breath. Instead, he only managed, "I wonder how she gets it so fluffy."

"Right? I have to learn her recipe one day," Alivia reflected through mouthfuls of food. "I wonder if she learned it from someone or discovered it herself."

"Speaking of recipes," Drake gestured to the tray.

"That was my next question," Alivia pointed her fork at him, then gestured to the glass of whiskey. "Kurt?"

"Kurt," he confirmed.

Alivia set down her fork and pursed her lips in thought. She tentatively lifted the cup and held it under her nose. After briefly swirling the liquid and seemingly looking for something on the glass, she took a brave swig. "Actually, it's not bad," she reported.

Drake tried a sip and was pleasantly surprised by the smoky flavor.

"Spicy. Bitter. Maybe oak barrel?" surmised Alivia.

"Yep," Drake nodded, swirling his glass. "Any apples?"

Alivia contemplated for a moment following another sip, then shook her head with a laugh. "Tastes like whiskey."

"I'm sure that's in there," laughed Drake, appreciating another sip.

Two energetic village boys, Zac and Hayden, came running from the north side of town, pretend-sparring with thin twigs. The eight-year-olds cut a path through the center of town past the bonfire, loudly playing their game.

"I killed your arm! You can't use that arm!" Zac asserted emphatically.

"Nuh-uh! My arm grew back," Hayden claimed in flagrant disregard for the rules, running as fast as his little legs could carry him toward the gate.

"Aw," Alivia smiled at the carefree boys. Resting a hand under her chin, she turned to Drake. "How do you feel about us starting a family?"

His heart skipped a beat. Every word in his vocabulary raced to fly from his mouth at once, causing him to stutter a short sound of nonsense. "I would love that," he amended succinctly after a quick recovery. "That would be perfect. How many are you thinking?"

"Hmm," she reflected thoughtfully. "I'm thinking two. That way, they'll never outnumber us."

"Two sounds nice." Drake nearly choked on his last sip of whiskey.

"You good?" Alivia asked, lighthearted but waiting for a serious answer.

He sputtered a bit more before recovering. "Just getting a little choked up about it, is all."

"Stop dying or I'll report you to the chief," she threatened playfully.

"Sorry," Drake apologized, pulling himself together. "Just figured, you know, in case those were my last words..."

"Right," Alivia laughed at the absurdity. "I'm sure that's exactly what you'd want on your headstone. *Here lies Ilya, a little choked up.*"

"Continue," invited Drake, sorry for the interruption. "Boys? Girls?"

"Assuming we could choose," she reasoned.

"Assuming we could choose," he granted.

"I want to say two boys?"

"Really?"

"Yeah? I don't know. What about you?"

"I'd want a boy and a girl," Drake answered. "Our boy, maybe a bit of a rock-head like me. Our girl, maybe more graceful, intelligent like you."

"Don't forget beautiful and modest," she bantered.

"Oh, your kids? Goes without saying." He swirled his drink in his hand, fumbling for the words to say. Taking a breath, he decided to start with the easy ones. "Happy anniversary," he raised his glass to meet hers in the air.

"And many more to come," she smiled, taking a short sip of the half-drunk whiskey. "I think this is starting to catch up to me," she confessed.

"Plants look thirsty." Drake joined her in jettisoning the strong drink.

As Alivia quickly rinsed out and then topped the glasses off with pear juice, he reached into his pocket again. He didn't know how he was going to start the conversation, but he knew how he felt. He wanted to tell her she made him smile like nobody else could, that she made the tough days bearable and the good days better. She was his morning star, and he would rise tirelessly each day to pursue her.

All he had to do was start with one sentence, and the rest would come.

"I, uh..." Drake stared off into the town square. His hand searched for the bag as his heart looked for the courage to pull it out. He squeezed the surprise in his palm.

Hailing from the south gate, Hayden came running clumsily across the grounds, waving his stick in the air.

"I've been meaning to say..." Drake turned his head to Alivia.

"Drake!" Hayden's shrill cry was somewhat muffled by the breeze.

Ignoring the boy, Drake shifted forward in his seat, holding the unseen bag between his hands. "Alivia, I love you more than anything, but not as much as I'm going to love you tomorrow and every day, ever after for the rest of—"

"Drake!" Hayden squealed again, this time unignorable at the bottom of the porch steps.

"Damn it," Drake muttered, bowing his head in frustration. He glared down at Hayden. "Come on, kiddo. Why don't you go play with Zac?"

"Frankie needs you right away," the boy reported breathlessly.

"Frankie?" Drake frowned. He was one of the six young men under Drake that formed the town's watch. Frankie, Lachlan, and Sean rotated shifts at the front gate; it must have been his turn to stand guard.

"Hurry!" cried Hayden.

"All right," Drake's anger ballooned at the untimely disruption. He had planned the morning so thoughtfully and had nearly made good on his big moment. Someone had better be dying to constitute such an urgent emergency.

"Need me to come too?" asked Alivia.

"Umm," Hayden stuck a finger in his mouth and thought about it. "Just the captain—but Frankie needs you right away!" he urged Drake.

"All right, I'm coming!" Drake stood from his chair and accidentally tripped over its jutting leg. Tumbling awkwardly, he tried to break his fall with his hands as he landed on his side.

"You okay?" Alivia asked, rising from her seat.

"I'm fine," Drake lied, picking himself up. He addressed Hayden: "Go tell Craft too, okay?"

"Okay!" The boy nodded his understanding, then began his wild run to the chief's log house.

Drake raised his left hand and found it scraped red. He gingerly picked out a splinter, then stumbled over to the door of their home.

"Here," offered Alivia, discreetly warping his sword onto his hip.

"Thanks," Drake mumbled, turning back toward the town center.

"You sure you don't need me to come?" checked Alivia.

"I'm sure it's nothing," he dismissed. "Enjoy breakfast. I'll go clear up whatever this is."

"Okay. I'll save some juice for you," she said, returning to her seat.

Drake stormed down the porch steps and hustled across the village, determined to make this as short of an interruption as possible. He reached the tall wooden gate, swung open from a single hinge on the left side. It was halfway closed for some reason, blocking his view of the outside world.

He slipped past the barrier to step out onto the main road. Frankie was outside, his back turned to Drake. He faced two unsettling, unfamiliar men. One of the strangers was gripping the back of Zac's shirt, holding him in place.

"What's going on here?" Drake demanded gruffly, stepping forward with one hand on the hilt of his sword.

"These two showed up out of the blue, trying to force their way inside. I told them to leave, but they won't piss off."

"My patience wears thin," the nearer of the two strangers disclosed. He wore silky black pants and a sleeveless gray shirt that matched the tone of his frown. Judging by his erratic silver hair and pointed moccasins, Drake could tell he was not one of Godwin's delegates on official business. A strange symbol was engraved on the back of his left hand—a faded silver color that didn't quite match the man's aureate wristlets, gilded belt, or piercing, golden eyes.

The man restraining Zac was twice as wide, twice as thick, and another head taller. He wore no shirt, revealing red skin with the texture of tanned leather. An intricate tattoo covered his sizeable belly, a chaotic flow of little pockmarks that appeared to surge and break through the enclosing ring in three locations. His bald, rectangular head suited the rest of his frame, and his earthy voice matched. "Shall I kill this one?" the stranger gripped the boy's head in his massive left paw.

"Let him go!" Frankie drew his sword and held it in front of him with both hands.

"Why are you here?" Drake growled, sizing up the golden-eyed one. "Is it money? We don't have much, but..." he rifled through his pockets but found them empty. Completely empty.

"I've heard you have a Mystic in this town. She will be leaving with us."

Drake gritted his teeth. He hoped his face didn't betray his surprise. His fear. "The hell are you talking about? This village is so small, we don't even make it on the map. We don't have any Mystics here."

The black-eyed Mystic addressed his partner. "Reasoning with these beasts is futile, Avalon. Let us take what we came for and be on our way."

The golden-eyed one took a step toward Drake, evidently unconcerned by the armed gatekeeper now within striking distance. "You fail to understand. There is no need for deceit, nor attempts at resistance. You and your village are of no consequence to me. I will spare you if you obey, or I will erase you if you do not. The end result is the same—the Mystic will join my Haven."

Drake froze, paralyzed with inaction. His first priority was getting Zac away from the leathery beast of a man, but he couldn't risk putting Alivia in harm's way. He had to do what he could to repel these men without disclosing her presence. He had to figure this out on his own.

"I wonder if I could crush the boy's skull with my bare hands," the black-eyed one wondered aloud.

"Xeno," Avalon warned in a stern tone that suggested toying with the villagers was unbecoming.

"I could just melt it."

"Get away from him!" Frankie roared, dashing forward.

Xeno threw Zac into Frankie. The collision knocked them both off balance, sending them to the ground. Frankie's sword clattered to the side as he used both hands to catch and hold the boy. The gargantuan Mystic slapped his palms against the ground, roaring as the symbol on his stomach glowed red.

In an instant, the ground beneath the toppled pair blackened, broken by glowing red fissures. Drake averted his eyes as a molten burst exploded from the earth, an earsplitting blast, but not loud enough to drown out the terrible screams. A wave of heat flared in front of him. He attempted to shield his face, but hot ash bypassed his guard, stinging his ears and cheek.

"Xeno," Avalon's commanding voice cut through the rumble. "Do not bury this village yet. I want her alive."

When the heat wave passed, Drake dared to look at the murderous wayfarers. His eyes passed from the red belly to the golden eyes to the empty space where Frankie and Zac had stood only moments ago. Finally, his brain deciphered the horror he had witnessed.

Two flaming skeletons floated atop a bed of settled lava, still cradling each other in death. Behind the ashen corpses, Xeno sneered proudly, as if enjoying Drake's mortified expression. "Where's the girl?" he asked pointedly.

"You... monster!" Drake snarled, unsheathing his sword. He didn't know how he was going to beat them, but he wanted to cleave them in two. Had they been wanton killers without a cause, he might have rushed in to meet the same fate as Frankie. What stayed his blade, and likely saved his life, was knowing that they wouldn't stop at his dead body. They'd keep looking for her.

In that hesitation, against the rushing blood in his ears, he formed a plan. Judging by Alivia's abilities, he guessed all Mystics had some form of indomitable power at their fingertips. Evidently, the red-bellied monster could summon magma from the depths of the earth. However, the golden-eyed one had yet to reveal his hand. Even if Drake could kill one, he doubted he could stop them both. But then, perhaps, Alivia would be able to manage a single opponent. She had always beaten him in their practice duels.

"Drake?" a call came from behind him. It was Lachlan, standing next to Harrison Craft.

"Close the gate!" Drake shouted back. "Now!"

The junior watchman ushered the chief inside, swinging the gate shut behind them. The heavy latch locked into place, sealing the village away.

Avalon stared into Drake's eyes, as if attempting to decide whether sentience was truly home or whether he was just another mindless animal acting on instinct. With miniscule effort, he raised his left hand, the strange mark glowed a silvery-golden hue, and an ethereal silhouette of gold flashed behind him. Without warning, a devastating ray struck from the heavens, vaporizing the entirety of the front gate, leaving a smoking crater in its place. The earth shook and the air rumbled, but Drake stood his ground.

Avalon looked beyond him, searching the faces of the gathering crowd for his target. "Come peacefully, and no more will die today."

"Wait!" Drake exclaimed, down to his last hope. If he was going to throw himself onto the pyre, he had to make sure it was worth something. He refused to abandon her in this world without a final act of service.

Deafened by his hammering heart, Drake carefully inverted his sword and sliced through his tunic, cutting away from his body. He pulled the severed cloth away from his chest, revealing the faded birthmark that Alivia had once incorrectly identified as branding him a Mystic.

If he couldn't fight for her, he could at least take her place.

"I'm the one you want!" he yelled. "Leave these people alone!"

Xeno cocked his head sideways. "Doesn't look like a woman."

Stepping forward, Avalon examined him with those cold, golden eyes. The ethereal creature hovered behind him, conical with broad shoulders and strange masses like tentacles escaping the back of its head. "If you are as you say," the man and the monster said in unison, "reveal yourself, Pyros."

"Can't you see the damn birthmark?" Drake growled in helpless anger. "Take me!"

"Pathetic," ruled Xeno, slapping the earth once more.

For a fleeting instant, Drake felt hell open up beneath him. The soles of his boots burned away, and his feet were immediately blistered by the heat. Before he could even cry out, a cool, nauseating sensation filled him, and he was suddenly standing at the front of the assembled crowd, twenty feet back.

"Prism is here," Avalon advanced carelessly over the molten ground.

Alivia warped herself in front of the villagers. "I'm sorry, everyone," she bowed her head in heart-wrenching apology. "I don't know who these people are or how they found me, but I won't let them hurt you."

"Where's Zac?" Hayden's voice cried above the crowd.

"Why are you here?" Alivia spat at the strangers.

"To take you to Haven. These human-infested warrens are no place for us. I will give you a better life where our kind may thrive in peace—where our world may flourish free of man, as it was always intended."

"I don't care about your Haven. I'm happy where I am."

"In time, you will appreciate my grander vision," Avalon patronized her. "Your ignorance will give way to thanks, your hostility to gratitude."

Alivia's inherited rapier appeared in her hand. "I will not go with you."

Xeno smirked. "Too bad that's not up to you."

As he bent to strike the ground, Alivia replicated herself into seven mirror images. The duplicates teleported forward, piercing Xeno's thick skin with a volley of one hundred thrusts. As he fell to his knees, the clones rejoined with the original, hovering in the air between the intruders and the villagers.

Avalon waved his left hand and the punctures covering Xeno's body closed. Xeno rose to his knees, unperturbed by the near-fatal wounds. Tilting his head to the side, he soon recalled his original intention.

He planted his palms on the ground and pressed into the earth. A short spout opened in front of him, launching a geyser of magma through the rock surface and into the air over the assembled villagers.

Alivia moved her hands through the air, redirecting the molten lava toward Xeno. Seeking his skin as if drawn by a magnetic force, the lava covered his body from head to toe. The runes on his red belly glowed through the hot slag washing over his body. He laughed and flung a handful to the ground as easily as if he had emerged from a mud bath.

Prism's purple form glowed behind Alivia. *Her second soul.*

A sudden deluge of water—a liquid ceiling a foot-and-a-half deep—fell from the sky. It warped to encircle Xeno, cooling the lava that covered him.

As the sulfuric rock hardened around his partner's body, trapping him inside, Avalon just stared. His face was marked by an almost unreadable look of surprise, perhaps tinged by shades of amusement and annoyance. Whatever he was thinking, the eerie sculpture was allowed to solidify undisturbed—a solid monolith of obsidian, twelve feet tall and eight feet wide. An obelisk of strife.

"You suffocated him," Avalon noted in a toneless voice.

"You're next!" Alivia encircled her golden-eyed foe with a small army of mirror images.

"This farce ends here." Avalon raised his left hand. A pulse of energy rippled through the air, throwing the onlookers from their feet and dispersing the clones. As Alivia struggled to pick herself up, Avalon closed in on her.

"Alivia!" Drake screamed, pushing to his feet. He grabbed the sword in the dirt beside him and charged, howling as he rushed forward.

"Ilya!" Alivia shouted, reacting too slowly to stop him.

Drake raced past Alivia and swung his sword in an overhand arc.

Without turning his head, Avalon lifted his right hand, caught the blade mid-swing, and squeezed. The steel shattered into dust like crushed chalk.

Drake's shock and fear dissipated as soon as they manifested, replaced by unrelenting zeal. He swung his left fist in an ill-intentioned hook.

He never got close to his mark.

The second most painful sensation he had ever experienced exploded across his body. Pure, undiluted agony. It was as if Deus had smitten him with divine hellfire, transcending the threshold of what nerves could physically bear.

All sensory processing fried, he lay face down in the dirt, unable to comprehend the world around him. He heard Alivia's voice, what sounded like her crying, but he could scarcely remember where he was.

After what felt like an eternity between this world and the next, he inched his head up from the dirt. The blurred images before him didn't quite register in his brain. He saw a black lump. A blue background. Strange shapes moving away from him into a shadowy pool.

Then, an instant after it was far too late to change the hand of destiny, Drake experienced the single most painful sensation he had ever known.

His soul shattered, his world imploded, as he saw the last strands of Alivia's hair disappear into the darkness, stolen away to worlds unknown by the monster with the golden eyes.

XXXXII. Reignited

He lay there for hours.

Face down in the dirt.

Unable to make sense of the world around him.

Numb.

This couldn't be reality. It was incomprehensible. Impossible.

Yet not even a nightmare could be as outlandishly cruel as this. This misery was beyond even his imagination. He knew of no drug strong enough to orchestrate such anguish. The only explanation he could muster was that he had already died a long time ago—that this incarnation of tragedy was the device of his eternal tormentors.

But not even the guardians of hell could be so devoid of compassion.

Broken.

Eventually, one of the villagers stirred him as they prepared to lay him in a grave. Finding him alive, they reacted with shock and relief and a flurry of other emotions beyond his grasp, but he was not present to hear them.

They must have moved him from the mud at some point. He survived, but he didn't eat. Whether he slept out of exhaustion or not, he was unsure. Rest was out of the question. He existed in a continuum of fluctuating light and darkness before his eyes, but it was always dark.

One rainy afternoon, for the darkness had not yet replaced the light outside, he heard a voice.

"I wonder where they took her..."

Drake's eyes sharpened their focus. He saw the cloudy sky beyond the roof of his front porch. His arms rested by his sides in the rocking chair. The breakfast tray had been removed, but the table remained alongside its memory.

For the first time, he saw Kurt sitting in the chair beside him, staring into the village center.

"What?" Drake's voice croaked, hoarse from lack of use or water.

Kurt's eyebrows shot up, evidently surprised to elicit a reaction. "Just, you know, they must've gone somewhere. The world's a small place. I wonder where they took her."

Understanding gradually dawned on Drake. His hands balled into fists so tight that his knuckles nearly snapped under their own force. A distant flash of lightning cut through the sky, but it made no sound—no more sound than the hollow rain, anyway.

He closed his eyes and saw that chilling, golden gaze.

Vengeful.

As he stood from the rocking chair, memories raced through his mind's eye, clashing and colliding in a disoriented flurry. He was briefly in the sunken temple, then he was back in the world reborn from wrath.

The recollections flowed logically at first. He recalled his wayfaring journey away from home. His failure to enlist the Godwins' help in returning her or finding her captor. Rejection by the rulers of Ayr, Graz, and Leeds, all the same. Imprisonment in Highwind for his unruly demands. How the traitors and rebels he supported failed to support him. The bandits he hired stole from him, cheated him, and left him to die.

But he rose again.

He traveled the countryside in search of the man with golden eyes, meeting false lead after blank stare. He gave in to sanctified vengeance, a lone crusader with unstoppable retribution.

Finally, he reached Arillia. Offering everything he had and more, well beyond his reach of begging and stealing, he pled his case directly to the master of mercenaries himself. Mercer MacLeod. Before long, Mercer sold him to those strange slavers from Baltos. They ran their experiments, they damaged his body and stole his memories, but they could never steal his wrath.

The visions continued without any semblance of order, whipping past before he could make sense of them.

He saw himself lying in the snow. No, not him. A baby in the snow.

His hands were hot as he scaled the edge of a volcano. Alternatively, the volcano was hot because of his hands. Perhaps Lukewarm.

A wolf den: the wolves ostensibly surprised to see him but otherwise abiding.

Smugglers took his money. They didn't take him. Commerce? Profit?

He ascended a mountain, a small army in blue and white chasing him. There was a second peak.

He prepared for battle, proudly wearing his blue Tallawyn colors as he surveyed golden fields.

He prepared for battle, wearing his gold, black, and red colors as he surveyed scorched fields. Death tended the garden.

He sat in a dark, stone room. Alone.

He sat in a dim, stone room, sitting across from a rather short woman. She was the Oracle.

He sat in a dim, stone room, sitting across from a rather short woman. She was Zara the Oracle.

XXXXIII. Missing Pieces

Drake

The whirlwind blew from his eyes to his soul.

Once the room finally ceased its violent spin, he slowly lifted his head and at last noticed the flask of clear liquid Zara held under his nose.

"Drink," she commanded.

Still nauseous from the ordeal of the purple smoke, Drake gingerly accepted the bottle. He sniffed the contents, suspicious of the elixir. Pouring a few drops onto his tongue, he felt a tingly sensation in his mouth and frowned.

"I like to put a little lemon in my water," Zara said with a patient smile.

The citrusy flavor now identified, Drake sucked back half the bottle in two great gulps, sputtering a little as he choked down the second mouthful. He returned the water to Zara, who lowered the flask onto the floor beside her.

"How do you feel?" she asked softly, resting a hand on the back of his.

Drake frowned, still in the process of working that out for himself.

How do I feel, he reflected inward, inviting Pyros into his reflection.

Wrathful, decided the Primal intuitively.

His frown deepened as he considered just how close he had come to Avalon during his imprisonment. He could have struck him down then and there. Could have buried those golden eyes in the cold, metal tomb beneath Baltos. Instead, Avalon remained free to roam the world without fear—while his lieutenants toyed with Drake, he sat wholly unbothered in his self-constructed haven, untouchable.

Drake's body brimmed with ire. Zara retracted her hand from his, wincing as she did so. He could not rest until his vengeance was delivered. He would know no peace until Avalon suffered as he had. If he had to expose every shadow, overturn every rock, raze every thicket to find those golden eyes, wrath would capably carry his flickering flame until his candle burned down.

Pyros stirred within him, conveying a surprised—if not reverent—tone. *Perhaps, also, hopeful.*

Sifting through the overwhelming flood of memories and emotions, he slowly unclenched his fists. There was more than just anger and sadness left behind. Despite all he had lost, there was hope.

He had seen her face beneath the black hood, and she had seen his. Though neither had known it as they stood on opposing sides, her blade resting on his cheek, their bodies had surely remembered their other half. For the first time, replacing the confusion, bitterness, and loss within him, he had hope.

A new urgency burned within him. He staggered to his feet, speaking before registering his own words: "I've got to find her."

"Whoa," Zara caught him as he lost his balance. "I understand, but you need to take it slow for another minute while you regain your senses."

"Where do you think I should start looking?" Drake brushed her off and staggered toward the door. A few steps in, he lost his balance and stumbled sideways into a wall of paraphernalia. Oddly shaped wooden equipment fell to the floor, but that was someone else's problem.

He had to find her.

"Easy," Zara slipped under his shoulder to support him. "Take one more sip of water for me, and I'm going to help you up the stairs, all right? It's all going to work out, Drake. You will find her."

Drake begrudgingly swallowed another mouthful of the liquid, then started again toward the stairs. Zara grunted as she struggled to keep his large frame upright, but eventually found a workable position slightly in front of him.

"She's out there waiting for me," he began to sweat.

"It's okay, Drake," she tried to calm him. "Tell me about the village."

"The village?" he repeated, unsure what she was looking for.

"Yes. Are you going to go back to the village once you find her?"

"Oh," Drake mumbled. He hadn't thought that far ahead. "I suppose we could. The village... I had a house there. Where else would we go?"

"The village looked lovely in your memories," Zara grunted as she helped him up the last step, back into the well-carpeted room. "Daheim, right? Perhaps you could once again spend your days there. Together."

"Yeah," Drake smiled fancifully. "It can all go back to the way it was. Just like before."

"Oof," Zara slipped out from under his arm. Stretching her shoulder, she considered him wistfully. "No man steps in the same river twice, for it is not the same river, and he is not the same man."

"I wasn't talking about rivers," Drake blinked in confusion. "I meant we'll go back to the village."

"Of course," deferred Zara, aware of his agitated state. She continued helping him down the hallway. "Tell me about the others you came here with."

"I came here with?" pondered Drake. "Well, the two brothers—Luc and Giles, I think. They're mercenaries. Then there's Talia, of course. She's not a mercenary. We've been traveling together for quite some time now."

"Ah," Zara sounded. "And what of Talia? Will you take her back to the village as well?"

"Well, sure," Drake nodded, finding the question odd. "She hasn't got any place else to go. Of course she'll come with us. The village might even have some kids her age. I think she'd really like it." Drake turned the corner and took a few more steps in pensive silence. "She said she'd like to live in a small town for a while. Can't think of too many towns smaller than mine."

"That sounds wonderful," Zara smiled supportively. She stopped him just short of the antechamber. "Drake, you may feel strange at times in the coming few days. You're still processing a lot, and your subconscious has vastly expanded its network of associations. Before I let you go, I want to make sure you're fully present. Are you with me, Drake?"

"Of course." Drake looked around the dim hallway in confusion. Could this still be a dream? He closed his eyes for a long moment, considering the tapestry of memories he had seen. Unless this moment of remembrance and thought was itself a memory, he must be living in reality once again.

He squeezed his thumbs against the tips of his fingers, assessing his sensory functions by digging his nails into his thumb pads. He tested his ability to freely recall the past, thinking back on his days with Alivia in the village, then his time in the Nordos mountains, and finally his escape through the sewers beneath Lyon. Although his mind wandered freely, he remained firmly rooted within the stone walls of the sunken temple, fixed in time and place.

"Yeah," he composed himself. The euphoria of new discoveries faded into ambience. "I'm here. Thank you, Zara. For everything."

"I would hardly be worth the mantle of *Oracle* if I turned you away," she bowed modestly.

He nodded his appreciation. As she turned back down the hallway, he reached out to stop her. "Hey, wait a minute. You said every time we call on our Primal, we shorten the wick of our candle."

"This is true," she clasped her hands patiently.

"How much of your life did helping me cost you?" Drake inquired with a pang of guilt.

She smiled. "Only as much as it was meant to. Our destinies crossed, colliding in a luminous spark for but an instant, bound to drift their separate ways. You have played your role by finding me, and I by aiding you."

"We'll meet again," he promised in open defiance of her prophecy.

"Not in this lifetime." Her voice was calm as always, though sadness tinged her eyes. "Go on, Ilya. Love awaits you within and without the temple."

His mind still swimming, Drake crossed into the antechamber of the temple. He immediately spotted Talia and the two mercenary brothers standing around the central fountain. As he crossed the floor, Talia leaped to her feet and dashed over to wrap him in a hug.

"Drake!" she chirped happily as she squeezed him.

"Hey, kiddo," he hugged her back. "What's got you all riled up?"

"You were gone a while," Talia noted worriedly. "I was starting to think that the old bird did you in. Figured she hauled you off in one of her carpets."

"Old bird?" Drake frowned. He remembered the unpleasant woman who had falsely presided over the Oracle's seat and fed him a load of hog-slop fortunes. "Oh, the old hag."

Miriame's eyebrow shot up from the corner of the room. She began marching purposefully toward him.

"I mean, the old bag," Drake hastily corrected himself as she neared. "I mean... aw, hell. Just give it to me, Miss."

A shockingly biting smack reddened his ear. As the priestess held up a finger to scold him, he took the initiative. "I know, I know. My bad."

Talia attempted to conceal her amusement, but her eyes kept drifting to his ear. "So, I take it no luck?" she asked, fearing the worst.

"Nothing too eventful. I'll tell you all about it some other time," Drake said, conscious of the others listening in. He let a small grin touch the corner of his mouth, signaling to Talia that their arduous journey hadn't been for nothing.

She smiled in return, not fully understanding his need for secrecy but glad to see him in a good mood. "Well, what now?"

"I could go for another bath," Luc shrugged.

Drake ignored the boy. "I think it's time we head home," he nodded to Giles. "Thanks for taking us this far."

"A deal's a deal," the older brother reached out to shake his hand. "If you're ever in Highwind, look us up."

"Settling down for a while?" Drake asked.

"Yeah," Giles stretched his back. "The whole mercenary thing's a little too unpredictable. You start off chasing a gator, do a little farmhand stuff on the side, and wind up tailing a Mystic through a swamp." He looked sideways at Miriame, unsure if he had disclosed too much. "Am I allowed to say that?" he turned and pointed a warning finger at the priestess. "Don't say a word!"

"All the best in Highwind," Drake bid, turning toward the exit.

"We'll meet again," Talia waved farewell to Luc, following Drake out of the temple.

"Aren't we going that way, too?" Luc asked his brother quietly.

"Yeah, but now we've already said goodbye. We have to wait a minute. Otherwise, it'll just be awkward, walking down the same road in silence," Giles explained as he filled a cup of water for himself.

"I like those two," Talia disclosed as they emerged into the twilight.

"They're not so bad," agreed Drake, eyeing the submerged road that led away from the temple.

"Hey, is that..." Talia gestured to the lone black-clad figure standing on the water bridge.

Carefully navigating the weathered steps, Drake squinted to better see the stranger. The silhouette stood between the purple lilies, an ornate rapier at her side. The brim of her hood wavered in the breeze, but otherwise she stood motionless, her head angled toward the sunken temple.

"Hang back here for a minute," Drake whispered to Talia, descending alone to the submerged path. His feet splashed in the shallow water, passing between the floating lilies. Stopping two yards short of the cloaked figure, he waited in the wind, staring at the purple glow that shone through the shadows.

A lump caught in his throat. After all the lost time between them, he didn't know if he could find the words to say. He remembered his broken promises, the anguish they felt in losing each other, and the unyielding love that carried him to the ends of the earth. He thought of their more recent, tainted battles, how they had unknowingly clashed time and time again. In a sense, she had betrayed him by serving their enemy; in a sense, he had betrayed her by letting her face it alone.

He swallowed thickly. It was possible she didn't even recognize him—that her purpose here was a malevolent one—but it didn't matter. He would rather die a foolish dreamer than live a loveless survivor. Their blind skirmishes were in the past. Whatever wounds he had suffered were of no consequence. After years of almost hopeless searching, he had to look no further than right in front of him.

He had finally found her.

Her hood whipped off in the breeze, revealing a face he could never forget. Her brown hair flowed over her shoulder, dancing freely under the endless sky locked between day and night. The rapier vanished, leaving behind a shower of falling sparks in its place. At last, the purple glow abated, her feet splashed into the shallow water, and her runic, almond eyes found him.

"Alivia, it's me," Drake managed, stepping closer. Her lips trembled as she stared into his eyes as if truly seeing him for the first time. He took another step forward, venturing into arm's reach. His heart was suspended on a string of hope, not yet allowed to crest into jubilance, for the fear of failure was still too real to ignore. "Is it... Is it you?"

She stepped forward to meet him halfway. As his arms gently found her waist, she rested a palm on his chest, her other hand reticently reaching toward his face. She hesitated, as if he might disappear once her touch landed. At last, her fingertips grazed his beard and caressed his cheek, rediscovering the man she had once thought lost to the world.

A tear reached her eye, followed by a forgotten smile on her lips. She held him tighter, unwilling to let him go now that she had finally found him. His name on her tongue alone was enough to let him know they would find a way. Together, they could find a fit for their broken pieces.

"Ilya..."

Perhaps, if he only let it, this moment could last forever.

Justin James

was born in a small European town and moved to a suburb of Toronto at a young age. An avid reader, Justin discovered a passion for storytelling at 14. A year later, he released his first young adult fantasy novel, *The Conquest of Night,* beginning his journey as an author. By 18, Justin completed the trilogy with *The Citadel of Night* and *Rise of the Ancients.*

In 2020, he wrote *Primal,* the first book of his fantasy fiction series by the same name. Its sequel, *Visions,* followed in 2021, and *Promise* concluded the trilogy in 2023.

In addition to writing, Justin's other enduring passion is travel. With an insatiable curiosity about different cultures and the stories of their people, Justin draws inspiration from his global adventures. Having visited over 50 countries so far, he currently calls Austin, Texas home. To reach Justin and learn more about his novels, visit JustinJamesBooks.com

www.ingramcontent.com/pod-product-compliance
Lightning Source LLC
Chambersburg PA
CBHW022203030726
47494CB00019B/155

* 9 7 8 0 9 8 8 1 0 0 6 4 0 *